THE UNAUTHORIZED GUIDE TO DOCTOR WHO

2007

SERIES 3

TAT WOOD & DOROTHY AIL

Also available from Mad Norwegian Press...

AHistory: An Unauthorized History of the Doctor Who Universe [4th Edition forthcoming]
by Lance Parkin and Lars Pearson

Unhistory: Apocryphal Stories Too Strange for even AHistory: An Unauthorised History of the Doctor Who Universe (ebook-only supplement) by Lance Parkin and Lars Pearson

Running Through Corridors: Rob and Toby's Marathon Watch of Doctor Who (Vol. 1: The 60s, Vol. 2: The 70s) by Robert Shearman and Toby Hadoke

Space Helmet for a Cow: An Unlikely 50-Year History of Doctor Who
by Paul Kirkley (Vol. 1: 1963-1989, Vol. 2: 1990-2013)

Wanting to Believe: A Critical Guide to The X-Files, Millennium and the Lone Gunmen
by Robert Shearman

The About Time Series by Tat Wood and Lawrence Miles

- *About Time 1: The Unauthorized Guide to Doctor Who* (Seasons 1 to 3)
- *About Time 2: The Unauthorized Guide to Doctor Who* (Seasons 4 to 6)
- *About Time 3: The Unauthorized Guide to Doctor Who* (Seasons 7 to 11) [2nd Ed]
- *About Time 4: The Unauthorized Guide to Doctor Who* (Seasons 12 to 17)
- *About Time 5: The Unauthorized Guide to Doctor Who* (Seasons 18 to 21)
- *About Time 6: The Unauthorized Guide to Doctor Who* (Seasons 22 to 26)
- *About Time 7: The Unauthorized Guide to Doctor Who* (Series 1 to 2)
- *About Time 8: The Unauthorized Guide to Doctor Who* (Series 3)
- *About Time 9: The Unauthorized Guide to Doctor Who* (Series 4, the 2009 Specials)

Essay Collections

- *Chicks Dig Comics: A Celebration of Comic Books by the Women Who Love Them*
- *Chicks Dig Gaming: A Celebration of All Things Gaming by the Women Who Love It*
- *Chicks Dig Time Lords: A Celebration of Doctor Who by the Women Who Love It*, 2011 Hugo Award Winner, Best Related Work
- *Chicks Unravel Time: Women Journey Through Every Season of Doctor Who*
- *Companion Piece: Women Celebrate the Humans, Aliens and Tin Dogs of Doctor Who*
- *Queers Dig Time Lords: A Celebration of Doctor Who by the LGBTQ Fans Who Love It*
- *Whedonistas: A Celebration of the Worlds of Joss Whedon by the Women Who Love Them*

Guidebooks

- *I, Who: The Unauthorized Guide to the Doctor Who Novels and Audios* by Lars Pearson (vols. 1-3, ebooks only)
- *Dusted: The Unauthorized Guide to Buffy the Vampire Slayer* by Lawrence Miles, Pearson and Christa Dickson (ebook only)
- *Redeemed: The Unauthorized Guide to Angel* by Pearson and Christa Dickson

Published by Mad Norwegian Press (www.madnorwegian.com).

Content Editor: Lars Pearson.
Cover art: Jim Calafiore. Cover colors: Richard Martinez.
Jacket & interior design: Christa Dickson.
ISBN: 978-1935234166. Printed in Illinois. First Edition: October 2017

table of contents

how does this book work?

About Time prides itself on being the most comprehensive, wide-ranging and at times almost *unnervingly* detailed handbook to *Doctor Who* that you might ever conceivably need, so great pains have been taken to make sure there's a place for everything and everything's in its place. Here are the "rules"...

Every *Doctor Who* story (or, since 2005's relaunch, episode) gets its own entry, and every entry is divided up into four major sections. The first, which includes the headings **Which One is This?**, **Firsts and Lasts** and **Watch Out For...**, is designed to provide an overview of the story for newcomers to the series or relatively "lightweight" fans who aren't too clued-up on a particular era of the programme's history. We might like to *pretend* that all *Doctor Who* viewers know all parts of the series equally well, but there are an awful lot of people who - for example - know the 70s episodes by heart and don't have a clue about the 80s or 60s. This section also acts as an overall Spotters' Guide to the series, pointing out most of the memorable bits.

After that comes the **Continuity** section, which is where you'll find all the pedantic detail. Here there are notes on the Doctor (personality, props and cryptic mentions of his past), the supporting cast, the TARDIS and any major characters who might happen to wander into the story. Following these are **The Non-Humans**, which can best be described as "high geekery"... we're old enough to remember the *Doctor Who Monster Book*, but not too old to want a more grown-up version of our own, so expect full-length monster profiles.

Next is **History**, for stories set on Earth, and **Planet Notes** otherwise - or sometimes vice versa if it's a messed-up Earth or a planet we've seen before. Within these, *Dating* is our best-guess on available data for when a story happens. Also, given its prominence in the new series, we've added a section on *The Time War.*

To help us with the *Dating*, we may have recourse to **Additional Sources**: facts and factoids not in broadcast *Doctor Who* but nonetheless reliable, such as the DVD commentaries, *The Sarah Jane Adventures, Torchwood* or cut scenes.

Of crucial importance: note that throughout the **Continuity** section, *everything* you read is "true" - i.e. based on what's said or seen on-screen - except for sentences in square brackets [like this], where we cross-reference the data to other stories and make some suggestions as to how all of this is supposed to fit together. You can trust us absolutely on the non-bracketed material, but the bracketed sentences are often just speculation. (Another thing to notice here: anything written in single inverted commas - 'like this' - is a word-for-word quote from the script or something printed on screen, whereas anything in double-quote marks "like this" isn't.)

The third main section is **Analysis**, which comprises anything you might need to know to watch the episode the same way that anyone on the first night, sat in front of BBC1 on a Saturday teatime (or whenever), would have; the assumed background knowledge. Some of this is current issues or concerns - part of the "plucked from today's headlines" appeal of *Doctor Who* right from the power-politics over new technology in the very first story (1.1, "An Unearthly Child") - some of it is more nuanced. Overseas or younger viewers might not be aware of the significance of details that don't get flagged up overtly as worth knowing, such as the track-record of a particular performer and what that brings to the episode, or what a mention of a specific district of London would mean to UK viewers. These are your crib-notes.

The Big Picture handles the politics, social issues and suchlike occupying the minds of the authors. Many *Doctor Who* fans know that 15.4, "The Sun Makers" was supposed to be satirical, but even an apparently throwaway piece of fluff such as 17.1, "Destiny of the Daleks" has a weight of real-world concerns behind it. New for this volume, **English Lessons** (and sometimes **Welsh Lessons**) tackles the allusions and vocabulary that BBC1 viewers all have at their fingertips and all the nuances underlying apparently innocent remarks. More than ever before, the **Oh, Isn't That...?** listing will tell you why what might seem an innocuous piece of casting means more to us first-nighters than to anyone else.

Up next is **Things That Don't Make Sense**, which in this volume continues to cover plot-

logic, anachronisms, science-idiocy, characters' apparent amnesia about earlier stories or incidents and other stupid lapses, but rarely the production flaws or the naff effects and sets for which the series was hitherto notorious. Finally, for this section, **Critique** is as fair-minded a review as we can muster; when necessary, this has required a bipartisan approach with *Prosecution* and *Defence*.

The final section, **The Facts**, covers cast, transmission dates and ratings, overseas translations, edits and what we've now taken to calling **Production**: the behind-the-scenes details that are often so well-known by hardened fans as to have the status of family history. We try to include at least one detail never before made public, although these days finding anything nobody's said to any of the dozens of interviewers hanging around Cardiff is increasingly hard, unless you get into outright gossip or somehow manage to crack BBC Wales' occasionally impenetrable news-management arrangements.

A lot of "issues" relating to the series are so big that they need forums all to themselves, which is why most story entries are followed by mini-essays. Here we've tried to answer all the questions that seem to demand answers, although the logic of these essays changes from case to case. Some of them are actually trying to find *definitive* answers, unravelling what's said in the TV stories and making sense of what the programme-makers had in mind. Some have more to do with the real world than the *Doctor Who* universe, and aim to explain why certain things about the series were so important at the time. Some are purely speculative, some delve into scientific theory and some are just whims, but they're *good* whims and they all seem to have a place here. Occasionally we've included endnotes on the names and events we've cited, for those who aren't old enough or British enough to follow all the references.

We should also mention the idea of "canon" here. Anybody who knows *Doctor Who* well, who's been exposed to the TV series, the novels, the comic-strips, the audio adventures and the trading-cards you used to get with Sky Ray ice-lollies will know that there's always been some doubt about how much of *Doctor Who* counts as "real", as if the TV stories are in some way less made-up than the books or the short stories. We devoted a thumping great chunk of Volume 6 to this topic, but for now it's enough to say that *About Time* has its own specific rules about what's canonical and what isn't. In this book, we accept everything that's shown in the TV series to be the "truth" about the *Doctor Who* universe (although obviously we have to gloss over the parts where the actors fluff their lines). Those non-TV stories which have made a serious attempt to become part of the canon, from Virgin Publishing's New Adventures to the audio adventures from Big Finish, aren't considered to be 100 percent "true", but do count as supporting evidence. Here they're treated as what historians call "secondary sources", not definitive enough to make us change our whole view of the way the *Doctor Who* universe works, but helpful pointers if we're trying to solve any particularly fiddly continuity problems.

It's worth remembering that unlike (say) the stories written for the old *Dalek* annuals, the early Virgin novels were an honest attempt to carry on the *Doctor Who* tradition in the absence of the TV series, so it seems fair to use them to fill the gaps in the programme's folklore even if they're not exactly - so to speak - "fact".

You'll also notice that we've divided up *About Time* according to "era", not according to Doctor. Since we're trying to tell the *story* of the series, both on- and off-screen, this makes sense. The actor playing the Main Man might be the only thing we care about when we're too young to know better, but anyone who's watched the episodes with hindsight will know that there's a vastly bigger stylistic leap between "The Horns of Nimon" and "The Leisure Hive" than there is between "Logopolis" and "Castrovalva". Volume 4 covers the producerships of Philip Hinchcliffe and Graham Williams, two very distinct stories in themselves, and everything changes again - when Williams leaves the series, not when Tom Baker does - at the start of the 1980s. With Volume 7, the amount of material has necessitated that the remainder of the Russell T Davies era will be covered in Volumes 8 and 9.

There's a kind of logic here, just as there's a kind of logic to everything in this book. There's so much to *Doctor Who*, so much material to cover and so many ways to approach it, that there's a risk of our methods irritating our audience even if all the information's in the right places. So we need to be consistent, and we have been. As a

result, we're confident that this is as solid a reference guide / critical study / monster book as you'll ever find. In the end, we hope you'll agree that the only realistic criticism is: "Haven't you told us *too* much here?"

X3.0: "The Runaway Bride"

(25th December, 2006)

Which One is This? The Rise and Fall of Donna Noble and the Spiders from "Mars".

Firsts and Lasts The habit of pilfering titles from old films for Specials starts here... *Runaway Bride* was a film with Richard Gere and Julia Roberts. (It's entirely possible that there was a plot beyond the title, but hardly anyone remembers it and even that title was borrowed from an earlier film.)

Anyone with foreknowledge of future seasons will see this as the first full appearance of Donna Noble – the sort of companion many people had been waiting for since they first watched the resurgent series – following her brief and shocking cameo at the end of "Doomsday" (X2.13). Notwithstanding the trial run with Peter Kay (who was cast between drafts so X2.10, "Love & Monsters" contorted around his screen persona), this is the first time that a character has been made to work as an extension of a guest-star's shtick (but see also 25.4, "The Greatest Show in the Galaxy"; the diptych of X5.11, "The Lodger" and X6.12, "Closing Time" and – albeit not in the broadcast episode – X7.0, "The Doctor, The Widow and the Wardrobe").

In fact, it's much more the model for Davies's "specials" format than the previous Christmas incident: a guest star serving as pseudo-companion; David Tennant being moody about the fate of everyone who travels with him; more-or-less festive subject-matter; London/ Britain/ the Universe in dire peril and a snide remark or two about the series' clichés. And in one of those deliberately-throwaway-non-throwaway lines Davies liked to stick in – often before he had any real idea what he would use it for – we hear about "Mr Saxon" for almost the first time. (Technically, there were written hints – including Victor Kennedy's *Daily Telegraph* in X2.10, "Love & Monsters" and the "Vote Saxon" posters were in *Torchwood* Series 1.)

In production terms, this is the first episode made at the new, swanky studios at the Upper Boat complex. And this was also the first Christmas Special to get the "Adventure Calendar" treatment on the souped-up, more corporate BBC *Doctor Who* website.

Series 3 Cast/Crew

- David Tennant (the Doctor)
- Freema Agyeman (Martha Jones)

- Russell T Davies (Executive Producer)

We get a brace of Season Five one-off freak incidents brought back into the regular repertoire of TARDIS tricks. Most obviously, the Doctor here gets to steer the Ship in the atmosphere to take part in a low-speed taxi chase (see 5.6, "Fury From the Deep" and associated essay). It's also the first time since "The Enemy of the World" (5.4) that we see the TARDIS doors opening into empty space – this version lacks the whole air-rushing-out-of-a-sideways-on-TARDIS element and just has the companion looking out and marvelling while the Doctor looks on smugly. Writers seem to enjoy doing characterisation during these "open door" scenes, and the next showrunner, Steven Moffat, kept the tradition going. (See also 17.5, "The Horns of Nimon", which elaborates on this feature of the Ship; X7.2, "Dinosaurs on a Spaceship"; and X5.2, "The Beast Below" for an abuse of this bordering on the ludicrous. Oh, and X3.11, "Utopia" and X7.16, "The Time of the Doctor" for instances of people clinging to the TARDIS exterior in transit.)

The Doctor also hits the Slitheen surfboard (X1.11, "Boom Town") to skip an alien tractor-beam (as in 5.5, "The Web of Fear") and displays another weird facility of his remarkable vessel by making it snow. You might think that trivial but there are many instances where such a feature could have materially affected the outcome of an adventure. (See, for instance, 1.4, "Marco Polo"; 15.1, "Horror of Fang Rock"; 2.1, "Planet of Giants" and especially 6.5, "The Seeds of Death". Making it *not* snow could have been handy too – X7.6, "The Snowmen", for example.)

It's the first time the Doctor uses the phrase "Molto bene" (Italian for "very good"), which will thankfully not be used quite so often as "Allons-y". (This was tried out in the cut scene in "The Christmas Invasion" as a possible replacement for "Fantastic".)

And, most noticeably, this is the episode where the Doctor "reveals" the name of his home planet.

Hardly a big secret – some of us have known since 1973 – but actually hearing the name "Gallifrey" spoken by David Tennant is right and proper and Murray Gold makes a big thing of it.

Watch Out For...

• It's *Chri-i-i-i-stma-a-a-as*! Of course it is. Noddy Holder says so, in that record you also heard this time last year (and all through December every year since 1973, if you're from around here).[1] All that blue sky, strong shadow and greenery is a freak meteorological effect. The Mill tries to damp down the sky's colour in post-production, to no avail. As you will recall from Volume 7, the week this began filming – the week after "Army of Ghosts" (X2.12) – was an unprecedented heat-wave, with London hotter than Arizona and Cardiff not much more comfortable. Pity the extras in thick jumpers and woolly hats and, especially, the Robot Santas.

• We also get the almost-traditional specially-written song for the festive episode. This time, Neil Hannon belts out "Love Don't Roam", a ditty with a more-than-passing resemblance to Northern Soul classic "The Snake" by Al Jackson and lyrics about a wanderer missing someone. Just in case we don't take the hint, we even get a (scripted) flashback to a moment the Doctor shared with Rose. (Well, sort of – the shot selected is actually of Cassandra in Rose's body; see X2.1, "New Earth".) The whole episode makes a big thing of the Doctor "needing someone" having just "lost" someone, and the last line of the episode is him telling Donna "her name was Rose'. Suddenly, the abrupt, brusque companion-departures of "Warriors' Gate" (18.5) and "The War Machines" (3.10) seem a lot more palatable.

• Director Euros Lyn has retained his usual cinematographer, Rory Taylor, so the TARDIS interior is honeyed and cheerful, rather than the usual greenish lighting Ernie Vincze gives it. So, for continuity purposes, the entire pre-credit row between the Doctor and Donna had to be reshot to match (as close as possible) the previous version made three months earlier.

• Last Christmas, the TARDIS landed out of the sky. This year, it not only flies away at the end like a rocket, but there is a whole sequence of chasing a taxi around what may look like the Chiswick flyover to anyone not wondering why there are signposts towards London. Better than that, though, are the children avidly watching Donna's getaway on the motorway, who enthusiastically punch the air when the TARDIS zooms off into the distance.

• In a quieter moment, we see the Doctor cheering up an uncharacteristically deflated Donna with the creation of the Earth. Kid-friendly astrophysics, The Mill doing what it does best and a conclusion that could only appear in *Doctor Who*. (And another joke about the Isle of Wight – see X1.8, "Father's Day" and 9.3, "The Sea Devils".)

• Murray Gold has decided that, this being a comedy episode with a one-off companion, it's time for another whimsical tango. This works, especially in the sequence where the usual running up and down corridors is replaced by Segways down our old friend the Millennium Stadium basement (see X1.6, "Dalek"; X2.0, "The Christmas Invasion" and dozens more), and Donna finally realises that she's having a good time saving the world by absurd means. It's less successful later, as (SPOILER ALERT) they decide to bring Donna back full time and – as a twenty-first century companion – she gets lots of bawling-the-eyes-out material with wistful reworkings of her comedy-style tune.

The Continuity

The Doctor He's literally just stopped talking to Rose after the events of "Doomsday". Donna's abrupt appearance bewilders him, and he starts getting snappy after she's harangued him for a few minutes. It isn't until he's rescued her from a life-threatening situation that they start getting along.

One of his talents is those ear-splitting whistles so beloved in sheepdog trials or for hailing taxis [or, according to Donna, Fulham FC matches – X4.6, "The Doctor's Daughter"]. He's surprised that Donna doesn't have a mobile on her. [Possibly Rose's influence at work there.]

Discussing the aliens at the battle of Canary Wharf ["Army of Ghosts"/ "Doomsday"] doesn't bother him as such, so presumably he thinks that Britain's got the hang of aliens now. [Remember, for him this may only have been hours ago, depending on how long it took to find a supernova so he could chat with Rose.]

The working relationship between Donna's fiancé Lance and the Racnoss Empress warrants his scorn. [Intriguingly, Lance's actions are motivated by the usual sorts of things the Doctor looks

Why Weren't We Bovvered?

Try as we might, one of the hardest cross-cultural translations is that *frisson* that UK viewers enjoy when they get something that transgresses the local norms: one-time emotional shocks that derive their power entirely from upending the viewers' expectations.

You can explain the context after the fact, yes, but simulating the sense of surprise is another problem altogether. In other words: Catherine Tate abruptly appearing in the TARDIS mere seconds after the Doctor's tearful farewell in "Doomsday" (X2.13) wasn't just unexpected, it was the most dramatic change of pace imaginable for the intended British audience – but explaining *why* that's the case is a bit of a trick. So we're going to tackle the problem from another angle, and talk about all the ways that it makes perfect sense for the star and co-writer of a BBC sketch-show to suddenly materialise on *Doctor Who*. Because it does.

We keep coming back to the same point in every *About Time* volume: anyone who tries to judge *Doctor Who* solely by the standards of *Star Trek, Battlestar Galactica, The X Files* et al is making something of a category error. It is a bit like assuming that any band from Georgia must be Country and Western, and then listening to the B-52s. The PBS networks in America and Channel 9 in Australia would frequently bracket the reruns with BBC sitcoms, historical dramas and *Danger Mouse* (although *Doctor Who* was also sometimes bundled into "Sci-Fi Nights" alongside *Red Dwarf* and *Blakes 7*). Apart from that strained period in the 1980s, and the subsequent half-life of the series (see **What's All This Stuff About Anoraks?** under 24.1, "Time and the Rani"), *Doctor Who* was often considered to be closer to comedy than to anything else that might have had a spaceship in it. Note, "closer to", to "interchangeable with": it's more about how an audience engages with the story being told than about content (and here we point you towards **Is This Really an SF Series?** in Volume 4).

We are, after all, discussing a show whose original lead had enjoyed his television break in one of ITV's first sitcoms (*The Army Game,* written by Barry Took and Marty Feldman, who would later give the world *Round the Horne* – and that's a book in itself), and as a result appeared in the first *Carry On* film. William Hartnell had got into acting after seeing Charlie Chaplin on screen, and spent his pre-war career as a comic actor before moving into straight roles postwar with greater success. *Carry On Sergeant* (1958) is notable for many things, but mainly that Hartnell doesn't get a funny line – he's the threat against whom all the other characters respond. Nonetheless, his timing and ability to keep his dignity in the increasingly silly situations requires a lot of experience doing comedy, which is the main thread of this essay. The curious parallels between these films and *Doctor Who* is an essay in itself (one we wrote for Volume 1 and might one day use). What we'll find is that comedy writers and performers best known for comic roles are the staple diet of *Doctor Who*, not the freakish aberrations some commentators from abroad seem to think.

When launching *Doctor Who*, story-editor David Whitaker's first thought was to get in touch with Associated London Scripts. This seems perverse until you recall three things: first, the agency was set up by and for writers, and especially a group of idealistic comedy writers who thought they were more than just gags-for-hire. The founders were Johnny Speight (of whom more later), Ray Galton and Alan Simpson (of whom more in a moment), Spike Milligan (of whom more elsewhere in these books and a mention soon) and Eric Sykes. Sykes was star and author of a sitcom with an agenda – it's not to get easy laughs by belittling anyone. He never made a big statement, unlike the early 80s Alternative Comedy movement whose unwritten but strictly-adhered-to manifesto was basically Sykes's practices applied to political satire and stand-up. It was better that he simply found other ways to get laughs than commenting on his co-stars' attributes (his twin sister was played by Hattie Jacques, who was a lot plumper than him, and his next-door neighbour, Mr Brown, was Richard Wattis, who with hindsight is astonishingly obviously gay).

Everyone in the episodes treated the increasingly ridiculous situations with utter seriousness. This is noteworthy, because Sykes was, in the 50s when his TV show first ran (it was revived in the early 70s to even greater success), also helping rationalise Milligan's scripts for the radio... err... "comedy show" is too mild a term for *The Goon Show*, the same way "box office hit" doesn't really describe *Star Wars* or "pop group" sum up the Beatles. Sometimes, listening to these now, it's hard to tell if it's Milligan having a breakdown or him trying to stay coherent and the world going mad. Sykes found an internal logic for each epi-

continued on Page 11...

for in a potential companion and – after his similarly harsh treatment of the disappointing Adam (X1.7, "The Long Game") and what might be seen as rejection of Captain Jack (X1.13, "The Parting of the Ways"; X3.11, "Utopia") – there seems to be more on the Doctor's mind than just missing Rose.] Donna turning down the chance to travel with the Doctor evidently wrongfoots him [he's used the time travel ace-card already; see X1.1, "Rose"].

Sylvia Noble comments that the Doctor seems to enjoy a crisis that only began when he arrived. [Others will make a similar point (X4.7, "The Unicorn and the Wasp").]

• *Background.* He seems less concerned by a legendary foe from his people's past than one might expect [although, after his earlier encounters with mad spider-women caused him an especially traumatic regeneration (11.5, "Planet of the Spiders"), perhaps he's being doubly brave]. He's cautious about revealing his origins to the Empress, saying that he's "homeless" at first. Very unsurprisingly, he's sensitive to the Empress's comments on being the last of her kind [contrasting that, see X5.8, "The Hungry Earth"].

For some reason, he objects to Donna talking about dinosaurs at the centre of the Earth when they're being threatened by a giant spider and he's deducing things. [She's alluding to *At The Earth's Core* (1976), so maybe Peter Cushing is just a touchy topic – see the end of Volume 6 if this isn't instantly comprehensible.] He knows that the robot Santas' brass instruments are weapons [so Rose or Mickey obviously told him about that; "The Christmas Invasion"].

Oh, and it appears that he's from somewhere called 'Gallifrey' [11.1, "The Time Warrior" and several hundred mentions thereafter].

• *Ethics.* The Doctor gleefully destroys several robots. [As per well-established conventions of family television, blowing up robots "doesn't count", unless it's a Tom Baker story.] He hacks the cash machine the same way he did in "The Long Game" (X1.7), and makes it spew fivers for the general public to enjoy when he needs a quick getaway distraction.

In line with his statements in "The Christmas Invasion", the Doctor gives the Empress one chance for mercy and then – when it's rebuked – deals with her ruthlessly, killing the Racnoss children in the spaceship. When she teleports back to her ship, he doesn't seem concerned about her ultimate fate. He continues the assault even after he has manifestly won, and only breaks off when Donna – scared both by the explosions and what he's capable of doing – begs him to and points out that they will also be killed if they stick around. [See X4.11, "Turn Left" for more on this. There's a school of thought that he and Donna cheer about the spaceship blowing up, although in context it's more that they have survived the something-like six potential ways they could have died.]

Donna tells him he needs someone to tell him when to stop.

• *Inventory: Sonic Screwdriver.* It appears to have an "auto-hack" app; when applied to a smart phone, the screwdriver pulls up the true owner of H. C. Clements almost instantly, after rummaging through dozens of sites [including the British Rocket Group's from last Christmas] in a second. When pointed at a sound system, it can create a high-pitched feedback that discomforts humans but blows apart robot Santas. [This seems to be some kind of beat-frequency effect, which was our conjecture for what the original sonic screwdriver did when it just undid screws with sound (see **How Might the Sonic Screwdriver Work?** under 15.6, "The Invasion of Time"). The screwdriver creates a sound that the mic picks up and plays through the PA (made by Magpie, apparently; see X2.7, "The Idiot's Lantern") to be picked up by the mic again and so on. This could conceivably do more damage to the wet-slushy brains inside hard bony skulls than any machinery, but the Doctor seems to control what is essentially a Chaotic reiteration.]

• *Inventory: Extrapolator.* Somehow, the Doctor has the transdimensional surfboard bequeathed by Margaret Slitheen, back from Satellite Five. ["Boom Town", "The Parting of the Ways". And it's interesting that he uses it to over-ride the Empress's transduction of the TARDIS in exactly the same way that a custom-made gadget did this to evade the Great Intelligence ("The Web of Fear"), despite there not being a space-time shockwave to "surf".]

• *Inventory: Other.* Finally, it's confirmed on screen: the Doctor's clothes have dimensionally-transcendental pockets, as proven when he pulls the Roboform control unit and killer tree-baubles from them. He also has a biodamper in the form of a metallic wedding-sized ring [there's time for him to have retrieved it from the TARDIS, so he might not have been carrying it]. A pannier-like cloth container on one of the TARDIS balconies

Why Weren't We Bovvered?

continued from Page 9...

sode he worked on, and made it at least *seem* to hang together while being performed. (We've mentioned Spike Milligan and the inspiration he provided to an entire generation of British comics, including *Monty Python's Flying Circus*. See **Did Sergeant Pepper Know the Doctor**? under 5.1, "Tomb of the Cybermen" and keep this apostolic succession in mind for later.)

What's significant here – the second of those three things – is that Milligan and Sykes took on a young unknown from Cardiff and that this lad, Terry Nation, applied the techniques Sykes used to adapting science-fiction stories for television in the anthology series *Out of This World*, produced by the commercial Manchester-based ABC company under the auspices of Sydney Newman. (One of these was the short story "Imposter", making Terry Nation the first person to adapt a Philip K Dick story and about the last one to get it on screen during Dick's lifetime). He also took over from Galton and Simpson as script-writer for the volatile comedian Tony Hancock. (See also **Who *Really* Created the Daleks?** under 1.2, "The Daleks".)

Here is where our story really begins, as Hancock's career until this point was a sort of Dogme 95 approach to comedy, moving away from implausible situations and catch-phrases, silly voices and a stock company of performers towards some notion of "truth". As he and his series became more successful, he divested himself of everything that wasn't under his control, first the minor characters (usually played by Kenneth Williams), then the entourage (Hattie Jacques, Bill Kerr – 5.4, "The Enemy of the World" – and, crucially, Sid James), then Galton and Simpson, and finally his agent, Beryl Vertue.

Galton and Simpson applied what they had learned to a new project: a sitcom about generational conflict, social mobility and aspirations called *Steptoe and Son*. For this, they got actors with integrity who approached it as though it were Ibsen or Chekhov, but could still get big laughs and keep straight faces when the studio audience were reacting. The Steptoes were rag-and-bone men, junk-collectors. One of the things Beryl Vertue made a career from was taking formats such as this, or Speight's *Till Death Us Do Part* (about a ranting East End bigot and his family, including the "randy scouse git" son-in-law[2]) and retooling them to work in America. *Sanford and Son* and *All in the Family* began as BBC shows. Comparison between these and the originals reveals a lot about what both countries expect sitcoms to do. Galton and Simpson were essentially writing 30-minute Harold Pinter plays, with jokes and occasional slapstick (later episodes increased the latter until it became another series with the credit "Action by Havoc"). They are emphatically not aspirational or escapist. And that's the third thing: comedy wasn't a genre so much as a tendency.

The generic boundaries for what television could do were more fluid in the late 50s and early 60s. As an example – not directly connected to *Who* but significant in how programme-makers and the public saw things – let's look at what Arthur Lowe, now best known for *Dad's Army*, did shortly beforehand. (And we could do a whole book about what *that* sitcom says about us, not to mention the similarities to 70s UNIT stories.) He had become famous for playing Leonard Swindley, a fussy, punctilious character in *Coronation Street* in its first few years (it began in 1960 and is still running, produced by Phil Collinson until recently). Then Swindley got a spin-off sitcom, with a studio audience. *Pardon the Expression* ran for three years, and then Swindley and colleague Walter Hunt were sacked in the last episode, leading to Lowe and Robert Dorning (who played Hunt) setting up as ghost-hunters in a "straight" spin-off-from-the-spin-off *Turn Out the Lights*. It's like Harold from *Neighbours* joining Torchwood. (An American equivalent is harder to find, but Lou Grant showing up in *The X Files* is roughly right. Not Ed Asner, who really did appear in the series, but the character Lou Grant from the sitcom *The Mary Tyler Moore Show* and spin-off drama *Lou Grant*.) Nobody questioned this.

Similarly, the early years of *The Avengers* had a semi-regular character, Venus Smith (Julie Stevens, later a *Play School* presenter) who sang in clubs and mysteriously got gigs in places John Steed was investigating. They stopped the plot for four minutes at a time for a song. Thus, the series kept the option of being more of a variety-show than the relatively straightforward crime/ espionage series it had been, or the fantasy franchise it started becoming after Cathy Gale had become the regular foil for Steed. Such genre-creep seems weird to viewers now, but *Doctor Who* was intend-

continued on Page 13...

contains various bits and bobs, including an ophthalmoscope that he uses to test Donna. There's a fire-extinguisher near the door and a lot of sisal and string handy for bodging up a steering system for the TARDIS controls. Later, for the first of many occasions in this lifetime, he pulls a stethoscope from his pocket [perhaps the one Jackie used in "The Christmas Invasion"].

The TARDIS The Doctor seems slightly befuddled when flying the TARDIS in atmosphere; he jury-rigs a pulley system for the relatively simple task of maintaining a constant speed in a straight line down a highway. [Nonetheless, it's odd that a powered, directed flight of the Ship is not only possible but the first thing the Doctor thinks of to do. To summarise **How Can the TARDIS Fly?** from "Fury From the Deep", this seems to be a perpetual materialisation and dematerialisation just before gravity affects the Ship significantly, a few feet along each time. There was a "Hover Mode" introduced in 18.5, "Warriors' Gate", although named in 18.2, "Meglos", and this seems to be related to the other incomplete materialisation glitch we saw – or rather, didn't – in 6.3, "The Invasion" and X6.1, "The Impossible Astronaut".]

The Doctor describes the TARDIS as having a 'Chronon Shell' with an 'interior matrix'. After Donna's appearance and a noticeably strained landing, the Doctor becomes rather worried about his Ship and wonders what she's 'digesting'. [We'd rather not remind you of 27.0, "The TV Movie", but this isn't the only time that Davies seems to be drawing on it for information about the Ship.] The force-field [or whatever] that protects console room-inhabitants from the vacuum of space seems to kick in automatically; the Doctor seems surprised by this [see 17.5, "The Horns of Nimon" and X7.15, "The Time of the Doctor"]. After the flying rescue of Donna from the taxi, the Ship needs at least an hour to recuperate. It also needs a fire-extinguisher to cope with the various console room explosions.

An ancient waveform [alternatively known as Huon particles and Huon energy, as is consistent with the nature of light] is found in a 'remnant' in the heart of the TARDIS. This allows both for Donna's initial escape into spacetime and materialisation inside the console room, and for the Ship to home in on her and surround her (and the Doctor) when summoned with more of these particles. This doesn't happen like a conventional materialisation, but is instead like a swarm of bees smothering them and forming a police-box-like vortex. [The whole "materialising around something which then fades into being inside the console room" trick has been tried before, since 18.7, "Logopolis", but this unmanned remote control "rescue" is unprecedented. Something similar happened successfully in X1.13, "The Parting of the Ways", with a more conventional materialisation, but the Doctor was piloting the Ship then. Ditto, give or take, the twelfth Doctor's rescue in "The Return of Doctor Mysterio" (X11.0), while Nardole is driving. Using the sonic screwdriver as a Stattenheim Remote Control – see Season Twenty-Two – is here only possible because of Donna's peculiar state.]

The Doctor can imagine an alarming number of possibilities for a human involuntarily transporting into the TARDIS, including a subatomic connection, something in the temporal field, something pulling Donna into alignment with the Chronon shell and something macro-mining her DNA within the interior matrix. [See X6.4, "The Doctor's Wife". All of this, in addition to the two ways we've actually seen it done: tremendous psychic force in 13.3, "Pyramids of Mars" and "The Greatest Show in the Galaxy" and formidably powerful time-energy in 22.5, "Timelash".]

The lamp on top can create 'atmospheric excitation' rather like a soft white firework to induce snow. [Snow-that-isn't-quite-right is a running gag in the Davies specials. Despite all the stereotypes about white Christmases, London hasn't seen one in over a century.]

The Supporting Cast

• *Donna Noble.* It appears that she's a fairly lowly temp who has been attached to H. C. Clements for about six months[3]. [This seems to allow her time off for holidays abroad and enough money for her wedding – but note how we later see Sylvia and Wilf cutting out money-off coupons. In reality, if Donna really is 100 words-per-minute, she could probably afford this and more and would not have been set to work in libraries ("The Doctor's Daughter"). Even an outfit as dodgy as HCC should have given her a more senior post.] A dull spell at a double-glazing firm came before this.

The church that she's abducted from is St. Mary's on Hayden Road in Chiswick. [We'll later learn that she also lives in Chiswick and was born

Why Weren't We Bovvered?

continued from Page 11...

ed right from the start to do that as a matter of routine, with only the four regular cast-members and the TARDIS in common between a seven-week phase when it was a drama-documentary about life in Imperial China (1.4,"Marco Polo") or a three (or four)-part series about how our houses would seem if we were one inch tall (2.1,"Planet of Giants").

Here we pause for a look across media: while the moments of comic "business" were ways of undercutting the tension, there was never really any idea of a character being included purely for comic relief. A few jokes that the viewers at home might have made under similar circumstances make Ian or Vicki broadly sympathetic, while the Doctor being a slightly childish empiricist can be amusing when the stakes are so high that most of us would simply run away or yell for help. That's not the same thing as what Roy Castle or Bernard Cribbins did in the 1960s feature film adaptations of the first two Dalek stories. Both had been type-cast as comedy actors, despite Castle always giving the vague impression that he was just temping until his jazz trumpeting career resumed. They did similar things in other films with Peter Cushing, and both played approximately the romantic lead in early *Carry On* films.

Televised *Doctor Who* never had such characters; Harry Sullivan (12.1, "Robot" et. Seq.), Mickey Smith (X1.1,"Rose" and onward) and Rory Williams (X5.1, "The Eleventh Hour") were characters planned from the outset to progress from slightly out-of-their-depth outsiders to competent action-heroes. The nearest to a comic-relief companion we've had is Wilf Mott, played, conveniently for our thesis, by Cribbins – but that character was a brief cameo (X4.0, "Voyage of the Damned") who later absorbed Geoff Noble's plot functions, and got more to do as the production team and public wanted to see more of him. (An argument could be made for Nardole to be an attempt at comic-relief – Missy even calls him that in X10.11, "World Enough and Time" – but his development into a full-time regular came with the change in his function toward being the Doctor's conscience. A lot of episodes relied on the fact that it was Matt Lucas saying the lines to make them amusing, but he was more usually the Doctor's straight-man.)

Cribbins, even more conveniently, plays the obvious author-surrogate for Dennis Spooner, *Doctor Who*'s second story-editor, in an episode of *The Avengers* in which Music-Hall turns become assassins. Spooner had worked in comics (not Marvel/ DC, but the peculiarly British papers we've tried to explain before; see **Why Did We All Countdown to TV Action?** under 8.2, "The Mind of Evil" and **Are All the Comic-Strip Adventures Fair Game?** under X4.7, "The Unicorn and the Wasp"), and created ITC action series (*The Champions, Department S, Randall and Hopkirk (Deceased)*) as well as writing for all the others being made. Just as writers with an aptitude for one style could resist being confined to it, so could actors.

Indeed, it's a measure of *Doctor Who*'s promiscuity – the programme's willingness and need to mix up styles, genres, approaches and moods within any given episode and across any transmission-year – that writers and actors associated with so many disciplines met on equal terms and worked towards making a scene, a story or a made-up world function. Or not. Often, a moment or whole story will fall apart when a director decides "let's make this funny". Often a situation is inherently comic *until* someone does a silly voice or pratfall, or an oversize gesture. Novice writers for the series so often think they are the first to notice the potential absurdity of the basic *donnée*, and many times a known comedy-writer in charge of scripts will have to housebreak a plot-synopsis, removing the obvious gags and set-ups so that the writer just tells a story.

Dennis Spooner had to de-joke synopses to reveal the logic. "The Space Museum" (2.7) was written as a comedy and made more cohesive (yes, really), but solemn. He had learned his lesson after a well-crafted but mistimed experiment of his own, 2.4, "The Romans" (and the bad luck of trying to run a humorous episode right after Churchill's funeral). Donald Cotton's scripts (3.3, "The Myth Makers" and 3.8, "The Gunfighters") were outright comedies, until the last episode when the stakes got so high that people were slaughtered through the same misunderstandings that had been amusing before. Apart from "Prison in Space", mercifully nixed in pre-production in Season Six, the next comedy writers to work on the series were Douglas Adams and Andrew Smith (and a lot of comedy writers and wannabes who all submitted scripts to Adams; see **What *Else* Wasn't Made?** under 17.6, "Shada").

continued on Page 15...

there; X4.3, "Planet of the Ood".] Given the circumstances, she quickly guesses that the Doctor's alien, and calls him 'Martian' as shorthand. By the time they've been at this a few hours, she's giggling with the Doctor about the fun of riding Segways through secret passages in order to go save the world.

She's been to Spain and arranged a flight to Morocco for a honeymoon [which doesn't really fit with Lance saying she couldn't find Germany on a map]. It seems she fell for Lance because he was considerate enough to make her coffee, and show her a little attention in a large and perplexing company. Her description of her engagement bears little resemblance to the flashbacks shown on screen.

At first she's outraged that all of her friends and family went ahead and enjoyed a party without her. Then, when confronted with a room full of angry and confused reception guests, she ostentatiously cries on Lance's shoulder until public sympathy is restored; she winks at the Doctor to indicate that it's an act. Her first guess about the "abduction", that her friend Nerys 'got her back' for something-or-other by arranging it, seems slightly justified by how good a time Nerys is having with Lance. [Sour comments about Nerys continue right up until Donna's more successful wedding in X4.18, "The End of Time Part Two" but there's a weird sidelight in X4.6, "The Doctor's Daughter".]

Lance claims that Donna's interests are boringly mundane, saying that she's only concerned about her appearance and celebrities. ([Though the examples he cites are oddly cheerful human interest stories rather than, say, juicy tabloid scandals. Given this, the lack of pop-culture references in any of her dialogue becomes more noticeable; in fact, the only such comment is a slightly garbled reference to *At the Earth's Core*.]

After Donna's fiancé gloats that he's been dosing her with deadly particles and is cohabitating with a giant spider woman, her response is to look stricken and she says that she loves him. Once his manipulation is confirmed, she explicitly switches her concerns to the Doctor and insists that she's willing to die for him instead. It's against this background of emotional betrayal that she turns down the chance to travel with the Doctor, though she's astute enough to tell him to find a companion.

A line of dialogue indicates that she once kept a dog, which she offered to give up so she could move in with Lance. [Either way, like Dr Watson's bull-pup, it will never be mentioned again.]

As a child, Donna was sent home for biting on her first day at school. She isn't hugely fond of people retelling this anecdote.

• *Sylvia Noble*. Her main trait here is an inability to treat her already-mature daughter as an adult. [This is going to get worse. After Jackie Tyler and Francine Jones, Sylvia is the latest in a string of mothers, all devised by Russell T Davies, who seem to chiefly exist to emotionally grind their daughters down to the bone.] Sylvia's husband barely gets a word in. His name's 'Geoff' [and we hear more about him *in absentia* in Series 4 than when he's present here].

• *Torchwood*. They bought out H. C. Clements's company 23 years ago, and have a secret lab underneath the Thames Flood Barrier... including a honking big sign on the door declaring it to be Torchwood property. Oh, and a laser-drilled tunnel to the centre of the Earth. Somehow, this hole penetrates all the way down without releasing Dr Evil-scale outpourings of magma, or even raising the temperature of the room.

The Non-Humans

• *The Racnoss*. [On the Racnoss conflict with the Time Lords, see **History**.]

They're omnivores with a fondness for meat and may have a matriarchal structure. [If the Empress is anything to go by. Her power and her ability to lay thousands of eggs seem connected, as is traditional with insect-like aliens in space-opera.] The Racnoss ship monitors Earth's culture, with multiple screens amid the Empress's literal web-site. It is an asymmetric star-shaped vessel, capable of firing electrical bolts at the ground and hovering above ground in order to strafe individual Londoners.

• *The Empress of the Racnoss*. Yer bog-standard alien queen, really. The basic look is big red spider with human woman body, in a centaur configuration. The head has several black glassy eyes, many of them compound, allowing almost 360 vision. Her two front arms end in claws rather like the mandibles of a more orthodox insect. With these, she can operate buttons on a console, but may not be too dextrous. [We have no idea what her other appendages might be capable of, so it's possible she can manipulate Earth technology without Lance's help.]

Why Weren't We Bovvered?

continued from Page 13...

Their own scripts were driven by internal logic and such jokes as there were came out of the situation (and Smith's 18.3, "Full Circle" was relentlessly pruned of wit by the humourphobic Christopher H Bidmead).

And, again, we have to bring into the spotlight a usually-unexamined assumption: these days, it's possible to see *Doctor Who* in the context of various American-made shows with spaceships and monsters in and judge it on those terms. In 1963, it was a strange drama series. As potential rivals emerged, the writers tended to subvert the glossier imports by pointing out how people, especially British people, would *really* react. America gives us futuristic Manifest Destiny in *Star Trek*, we reply with jaded recent-history-mapped-onto-Space-Opera (9.4, "The Mutants"; "The Space Museum"; 16.1, "The Ribos Operation" and many others – see also **Is This Any Way to Run a Galactic Empire?** under "The Mutants" and **Is This the *Star Trek* Universe?** under X4.6, "The Doctor's Daughter"). *Star Wars* offers limitless, easy travel in space-U-hauls, *Doctor Who* has package-holidays with all the tedium, bureaucracy and being treated as luggage (17.4, "Nightmare of Eden", but see also 10.2, "Carnival of Monsters" and 6.6, "The Space Pirates"). Even the most *Trek*-like moments in 10.3, "Frontier in Space" are undercut by the Master impersonating Dixon of Dock Green, busting the Doctor for speeding and asking if he is the owner of the vehicle, or by there being a prison-camp for anyone not as gung-ho as the people with the uniforms with decals on the chest.

The point is that this was all a consequence of taking the premise *more* seriously than the stunted, restricted world-view where only the things that matter to the heroes of space-opera TV shows ever happen[4]. The writers of these supposedly "silly" accounts were taking all the possible consequences of the basic idea into consideration, rather than limiting the incidents and responses in the story to what a small child or a zealot would think to mention. Bidmead may have bridled at Adams being "silly", but one could argue that his "Logopolis" (18.7) is the most ludicrous story of all, not least when it tried to be "realistic"; it had Tom Georgeson trying to arrest the Doctor for possession of Barbie Dolls and a scene where we discover that the Master-code for the cosmos is preserved on an eight-bit bubble-memory.

The Adams/ Bidmead schism is crucial for understanding where Russell T Davies and Steven Moffat have based their conceptions of *Doctor Who*. Within the hardcore of old-series fandom, the regime-change of 1980 caused ructions unlike anything in other television support-groups. As we've covered elsewhere, *Doctor Who* fans had ambitions to write, act or direct and saw the series-makers as the people to beat (and indeed, many of them are now making the BBC Wales version). Many other fan-groups treated the broadcast *ur*-text as something finished and complete, allowing for studio interference, so criticism characteristically took the form of fan-fic rewrites rather than detailed analyses of authorial intent and institutional pressures.

That difference is less pronounced now, but still underlies a lot of the reception of the new episodes. *Doctor Who* criticism is heated in a way familiar to anyone who has looked at comedy websites (which are especially vitriolic, for reasons too complex to go into here). *Doctor Who* fans came to understand how television happens far more intensively than fans of any other series who weren't in contact with *Who* fans. As we keep saying, the 1980s was the point at which *Doctor Who* fans became noticeably different from just the British viewing public. Davies, when push comes to shove, belongs in the pre-1980 camp. Moffat, although originally a comedy writer and once using techniques demonstrated by Galton and Simpson, John Sullivan and others (notably the "seeding" of a plot development within a scene that is a joke in and of itself, as well as an info-dump for later), is instinctively pro-JN-T and consciously followed his lead.

Douglas Adams, with his Cambridge degree in Literature disguising a third-generation photocopy of Robert Sheckley and Alfred Bester as originality, was treated as some kind of expert on how Science Fiction and Comedy differ. The *actual* difference is how much specialist writers in each field get paid and how much kudos they get from the Sunday papers. Adams was keen to downplay his SF-ness (hence his disavowal of his manifest ripping-off of Sheckley, see 17.1, "Destiny of the Daleks" for a recycled idea he claimed was Asimov's). He was, he said, an adherent of Kurt Vonnegut (who was fashionable, so that was all right) and an associate member of the *Monty Python* team. An appearance by at least one of the

continued on Page 17...

Her vocabulary and idiolect are laced with contemporary Earth references. [She's clearly been monitoring the planet for some time, although it's delivered in a playful, sing-song sort of way, as with the Toclafane in X3.12, "The Sound of Drums".] It's strongly hinted that the Empress and her WebStar ship have been active and hovering in extragalactic space since the Dawn Times. So she has picked up enough about English culture to make a number of culturally-specific gags (Christmas dinner, wedding rituals, what doctors do...). When the Doctor slips in disguised as a robot, she notices and tells him off for it. Despite the fact that her entire plan rests on using Donna as an involuntary catalytic key to invade the planet, she seems offended by Lance's contemptuous view of his fiancé and kills him.

• *Roboforms.* [Back again from Christmas last year, which speaks well of their ability to escape notice of both UNIT and Torchwood.] This time, they are employed by the Empress rather than the 'Pilot Fish' [whoever they were] and it takes a lot more than waving a screwdriver at them to stop their advance – although it's still sound that destroys them, amplified through a wedding-disco PA. Once again, they've adopted the Robot Santas disguise, and they're sophisticated enough now to be looking for Donna by cab, as well as drive on the left, use a gear-stick and evade pursuit in heavy traffic. They can sneak up on people and abduct them without a sound.

Planet Notes

• *Earth.* It turns out that if you drill a hole to the centre of the Earth, there's a spaceship at the exact middle of it. This was the initial gravitational point that started attracting the particles that became the planet. [Who'd have guessed? See **What's Wrong With the Centre of the Earth?** under 7.4, "Inferno".]

History

• *Dating.* The Doctor and Donna witness the creation of Earth, and definitively date it to 4.6 billion years ago.

For Donna and company, it's 'Christmas Eve', 2007. [It's after the Battle of Canary Wharf in "Doomsday"; the Doctor both encountered the Roboforms and had Christmas dinner with Rose's family 'last year' in "The Christmas Invasion". That story was set at Christmas 2006, following Rose returning home late in X1.4, "Aliens of London", which pushed the "modern day" episodes to a year ahead of broadcast.] If Donna is anything to go by, there's still some disbelief among the public concerning the existence of extraterrestrials even after the Battle of Canary Wharf, the destruction of Ten Downing Street and 1/3 of the population of Earth standing around on rooftops as a giant stone spaceship hovered over London then went and got zapped from various locations around the city ["Doomsday", "Aliens of London" and "The Christmas Invasion"].

According to the Doctor, the Racnoss date back to the Dark Times, fought a war with the fledgling Empires of the day and were all killed. [This obviously has to have happened before the Earth's formation, and probably a lot longer before that.] The Empress recognizes the name 'Gallifrey' and says they murdered the Racnoss. [If we combine the two accounts, it's possible that there was a pre-time travel Gallifreyan war over natural resources: the Huon particles that were eventually incorporated into timeships. Unlike just about every other time that this Doctor mentions Gallifrey, no one refers to Time Lords (in fact, the Doctor's very cagy about his Ship's time travel capacity this story), and it's just possible that the Empress wouldn't recognize the term. Given this all happened at least 4.6 billion years before now, this could well reflect ancient Gallifrey's pre-Time Lord past, if such a concept pertains. We'll revisit this concept in X3.2, "The Shakespeare Code".]

The Analysis

The Big Picture As we'll see in **The Lore**, "The Runaway Bride" is mainly built around set-pieces planned for two other stories, and needed an hour-long episode to justify the elaborate logistics. The plan to have the core of this story as the sixth episode of Series 2 was dropped very early, once it became obvious that there would be a Christmas episode every year.

It's worth taking a moment to consider that in more depth. As we discussed in "The Christmas Invasion", the main thing that can be done in a Special of this kind is to suspend the usual rules of a series. In this instance, the TARDIS does many unusual things, including three we'll never see in any other story. The nature of the story, and the assumption that audiences would be less critical of such things under the circumstances, allow more leeway. This also extends to the level

Why Weren't We Bovvered?

continued from Page 15...

Pythons (17.2,"City of Death") is almost as obvious a gag as John Cleese making an unannounced cameo in *Ripping Yarns*. Adams had written sketches for the spin-off albums (notably *Monty Python and the Holy Grail* – the "Logic" sketch and the interview with the producer using dead film stars were his with Graham Chapman).

But there are more fruitful places to look for similarities in show dynamics between *Who* and *Python*, one of them an entirely different project: Eric Idle's *Rutland Weekend Television* (1975-7). Entertainment on a budget that made even the *Doctor Who* monies appear munificent by comparison, it was an exercise in doing very clever things with very limited resources. (The BBC gave more money to Light Entertainment than Comedy, so Neil Innes did a song every week so they could afford costumes. Bear this rule in mind when we get to *The Young Ones*.) The show's entire motif – straight actors doing ridiculous things while taking them with perfect seriousness – was taken to an extreme but familiar trend in British humour.

The cast has three performers who'd been in *Doctor Who*: most obviously Henry Woolf, who played a monster almost without make-up in 15.4, "The Sun Makers", but in the previous story Wanda Ventham had been covered in gold (15.3, "Image of the Fendahl"), while Terence Bayler was in both 3.6, "The Ark" and 6.7, "The War Games". Most clearly *Who*-like, though, was its completion of the project Idle had been following in the two previous series he'd worked on, *Python* and *Do Not Adjust Your Set*, of taking the formats and formulae of different television genres and replacing the content with wildly "wrong" material, to see how TV companies would handle it. Using television against itself was at the heart of both the pseudo-documentary approach of many of his sketches and the Yeti-in-a-Loo approach to alien invasion kerfuffle of the early 70s.

But if we're talking about a true 70s BBC comedy institution, there's only one place to look. (Well, two, but *Monty Python's Flying Circus* co-exists almost exactly with the Jon Pertwee years.) Usually when we're talking about *Doctor Who*'s sister show, we're referring to *Top of the Pops* or *Blue Peter*, but in this case it's more instructive to look at *The Goodies*: a programme that was almost universally beloved in its day, but since then has been far more rigorously ignored than *Doctor Who* ever was.

A one-line summary for anyone unfamiliar with this show would be: *Monty Python*'s kid brother. The product of Cambridge Footlights alumni Graeme Garden, Tim Brooke-Taylor and Bill Oddie (i.e. from the same talent-pool that gave us *Python* and *The Two Ronnies*), *The Goodies* (sort of a post-modern sitcom) featured three mismatched graduates who ran an agency with the slogan "We Do Anything, Any Time". Their adventures were broadly themed around trying to make life better for someone (well, for the first five years, at least). It had the same remit of family entertainment as *ToTP* or *Doctor Who*, though aired well after tea and allowed to get away with slightly more. We've talked about 1973 being *Doctor Who*'s annus mirabilis in an earlier essay; it's worth knowing that some rather clever scheduling had the episode "Invasion of the Moon Creatures" air a mere week before Season Eleven started with "The Time Warrior". Tim and Bill wave at a police box in the process of driving a spaceship to the moon and Patrick Moore – see "The Eleventh Hour" – appears as himself.)

The show's aesthetic – knowingly cheap and absurd-looking, and coupled to content that has to be taken terribly seriously to be funny – has a very familiar resonance. It goes deeper: as it was made for the minority BBC2 and only later repeated on BBC1, it had a head start in using colour sets and costumes, lighting and film. Thus, it was the first BBC series to really play with the potential of CSO. When "Doctor Who and the Silurians" (7.2) was made, it was in a state of desperate scrabbling to get it done on time and in-budget, so it was only later that Barry Letts made that promotional clip on the possibilities of the new technique. When The Goodies were making their show, they had blue-screen jokes every five minutes or so. In the second episode, broadcast in November 1970 but recorded 29th October (around the time that recording 8.1, "Terror of the Autons" was giving Letts ample opportunity to show all the things CSO couldn't *quite* do yet), there's a long opening sequence where they show off all the potential of the Colour Separation Overlay in amongst more obvious prop gags and ridiculous costume-changes. This had obvious costume and set-design implications, and it's worth noting how many BBC staffers graduated from this to *Doctor Who* (most noticeably designer Roger Murray-

continued on Page 19...

of self-criticism, self-parody and reflexive humour in the dialogue. For one night only, the Christmas episode is given permission (by the viewers as much as anyone else) to reconfigure *Doctor Who*.

Thus we have an episode comprised largely of Scenes We Would Like To See, including the car-chase with a helicopter-like TARDIS, the giant spider-woman and more lethal Christmas decorations. These coincide because the chosen genre for this year's festive offering is the 30s-style Screwball Comedy. Note the "30s-style" part of that: the classics of the subcategory were made then, yes, but subsequent generations of film-makers have sought to recapture the mood and carefree approach to farce-plotting.

While hard-and-fast definitions are difficult to make stick, the key difference between a Screwball Comedy and your standard rom-com or farce is the sense of escalation, as an accretion of white lies and small deceptions trap the protagonists in a situation that only they comprehend. This, rather than attraction, is the basis of what usually lands up as a marriage. The majority of the core films everyone agrees belong in any list feature Katherine Hepburn, Cary Grant or Clark Gable. What happens is often at the limit of what the Hays Code would have permitted to be shown on screen, and generally uses characters who have both been married (often to each other, hence their acrimony and shared understanding of things others don't get) to ensure that everyone involved knows the score.

Doctor Who has always had this sub-genre in its armoury. Any adventure where two characters who – like the audience but unlike everyone else in the story – are aware of the true nature of the situation will have a lot in common with *It Happened One Night* (1934). Much of any such story involves the Doctor and his companion trying to avoid complicated and potentially-dangerous revelations that they are time travelling visitors from another planet. (Once this idea takes hold, it is hard to watch 9.2, "The Curse of Peladon" without expecting the Venusian Lullaby used to pacify Aggedor to become "I Can't Give You Anything But Love" as per *Bringing Up Baby*).

Ultimately, the films mutated into other kinds of story, meaning the true heir to Frank Capra's crown was Alfred Hitchcock (who may well have made two of the best unofficial specimens of the 30s type in *The 39 Steps* and *The Lady Vanishes,* but was definitely tapping into it when he cast Cary Grant and James Stewart[5] in so many 50s thrillers – his non-thriller film, *Mr. & Mrs. Smith*, was definitely in this category). Like the 30s films, Hitchcock's 50s and early 60s movies have many set-pieces where the protagonist and the villains are the only people in a crowded room or social situation who really know what's going on, and many authority figures fail to get the point of their eccentric behaviour. The characters are forced into extreme – and physically risky situations – to get out of trouble. Now consider the number of vehicles used in this episode (even without the cut scenes of Donna's tiny pink car and the bus-ride with Mrs Croop). Then consider that the last of these, the Segway chase, is the point at which Donna finally realises that she's enjoying the crisis.

Two other characteristic features of the genre are pertinent here: a strong female lead should take control of otherwise relatively straightforward situations and, for her own ends, mess things up with half-truths and misunderstandings. One of the protagonists will almost invariably have some normal, dull wedding planned; the arrival of the other creates disarray, and reveals it to be fundamentally unsatisfying. Check and check. But purists would argue that the closure required to make this fit the classic form is Donna recognising that she belongs with the Doctor and jilting Lance – or being jilted by phone while in jail or something halfway through. If we take "Partners in Crime" (X4.1) as the second half of this story, we have a slam-dunk, although nobody (least of all the production-team) knew that this was on the cards. Nonetheless, Donna's insistence that the Doctor needs someone to stop him is close enough to the recognition scene where the protagonists admit that their previous lives were a sham to warrant counting this, even on its own terms.

The other side of the equation is the Huon Particles plot. It was an axiom of the Virgin Books *New Adventures* series, of which Davies had been a part, that a phase of the Time Lords' past had entailed their engaging in complicated warfare to determine the very nature of reality. This idea will develop as the rest of this volume unfolds, but it's worth recalling a notion idea Ben Aaronovitch threw into the pot: that the Time Lords had grown Earth around a Nexial Point of some kind, hence all the bizarre phenomena and invasions. Nonetheless, the main upshot of this thread was that whenever an author wanted something freak-

Why Weren't We Bovvered?

continued from Page 17...

Leach) or did shift on both (Special Effects designers, the Radiophonic Workshop and various stunt-arrangers).

Doctor Who differed from these series in degree rather than kind. There wasn't a studio audience (just as well when we get to the most *Goodies*-like stories, such as 9.5, "The Time Monster" or 11.5, "Planet of the Spiders"), nor was there any attempt at internal continuity in the comedy series, to the extent that the world ended in two separate episodes. Many episodes were, as with the *Rutland Weekend* sketches, small observations blown up through relentless logic into vast threats, much as the Yeti-in-the-Loo stories that formed the spine of the Pertwee era were. (Pertwee was a guest-villain in *The Goodies*, as were Patrick Troughton, Philip Madoc, Frank Windsor, Beryl Reid, George Baker and many others you may have seen in *Doctor Who*. Indeed, Troughton's episode, "The Baddies", has more convincing android duplicate mayhem than 13.4, "The Android Invasion", made three years later.)

A more fundamental similarity lies behind the scripts of 1970s *Doctor Who* and *The Goodies* and the post-*Python* series: they assume an audience who know a cliché when they see one. These can be incidents, such as time-bombs, threats to physically punish underlings or opponents and so on. (16.2, "The Pirate Planet" was written so that the Captain was knowingly playing the part of a stereotypical space-villain so nobody would suspect his true intentions; ditto the Three Who Rule in 18.4, "State of Decay") or generic set-pieces and requirements. Here, another post-*Python* series is a handy yardstick: *Ripping Yarns* began as a one-off spoof of *Tom Brown's Schooldays* (see X3.8, "Human Nature") and was partly made in a conventional studio, but later episodes (another eight were made) were all on film and look like the sorts of adventures they parody.

Sometimes, the parody is too exact to be genuinely laugh-out-loud funny but they were all about examining and exaggerating the unspoken assumptions of pre-war British life as exemplified in its popular fiction. The writers, Michael Palin and Terry Jones, went on to make documentaries of varying degrees of seriousness. Palin usually played at least two roles in any given episode of *Ripping Yarns*, and the one thing that strikes anyone coming to these films today is that it's obviously as big an influence on the writer/ performers of *The League of Gentlemen* as *The Goodies* was on *The Mighty Boosh*, and this is where the links to the BBC Wales *Doctor Who* start to become inescapable.

If you've been following the **Oh, Isn't That...?** listings assiduously, it can't have escaped your notice that several of the same programmes keep coming up. In one version of this essay, we tried a variant of the Pete Frame/ John Tobler *Rock Family Trees* for the half-dozen or so most common cross-over shows, but it required a sheet of paper the size of a garage, folded into a Mobius Strip and using three colours. To summarise, there are a few clusters of performers and writers, including some individuals who do both, that have established themselves as latter-day Associated London-style networks. In the essay about the relaunch pre-launch (**Why Now? Why Wales?** under X1.1, "Rose"), we noted that Charlie Higson's reboot of *Randall and Hopkirk (Deceased)* had employed Mark Gatiss and Gareth Roberts as writers. It goes deeper than that, though, as Gatiss and *League of Gentlemen* colleague Steve Pemberton (X4.8, "Silence in the Library") play semi-regular roles as policemen, and the first episode has David Tennant as the murderer (well, one of them), with Jessica Stevenson (as she was then, "Human Nature") as the Polish housemaid.

But pay attention: Higson's main claim to fame up to then was as writer-performer of *The Fast Show*, in a clique including Arabella Weir (X7.0, "The Doctor, the Widow and the Wardrobe" – earlier David Tennant's landlady), Mark Williams (X7.2, "Dinosaurs on a Spaceship"; X7.4, "The Power of Three") and Paul Whitehouse. Whitehouse had been successfully working as Harry Enfield's wingman when Higson was just writing material (and the Enfield gang included Martin Clunes, 20.2, "Snakedance"; and Caroline John from Season Seven – and Sean Pertwee) and had drifted into performing when working with Vic Reeves and Bob Mortimer, which links us to David Walliams (X6.11, "The God Complex") via Matt Lucas (now finally in *Doctor Who*, starting with X9.13, "The Husbands of River Song"), who'd been in *Casanova*, knew Russell T Davies socially and had become famous on the Reeves/ Mortimer dadaist gameshow *Shooting Stars*. *Randall and Hopkirk (Deceased)*, as revived by Higson, featured a character called Wyvern which was specifically written

continued on Page 21...

ishly beyond the laws of knows physics, they would invoke the Dark Times. Hence the related *Missing Adventures* book *Goth Opera*, in which garlic bread causes complex quantum effects that stop descendants of the Great Vampire (18.4, "State of Decay").

Specific to "The Runaway Bride" is the idea that Huon Particles can be bred inside a woman about to get married. Is this daft? The model at work here seems to involve hydrogen fusion taking seawater and filtering out the minute amounts of deuterium, then fusing them with tritium to generate energy. Deuterium oxide, so-called "heavy water", is not radioactive, but has the potential to produce vast amounts of energy (and has been used in nuclear reactors since the 1950s, mainly for moderating other nuclear reactions). This is not only possible but happens, yet only at very high temperatures so far. There was a long period when people chased the dream of "cold fusion", creating the right conditions for this to happen at normal temperatures, and much of what Lance and the Racnoss Empress have cooked up in the lab looks like the notorious Fleischmann-Pons procedure that got a lot of people excited in 1989. There's another, older version of cold fusion, not using bubbles or ultrasonics, called "Muon-catalysed fusion". This is practical as and when anyone can find a way to generate Muons (sort of like big electrons) without using more energy than you'd get out of the reaction. Huons... Muons... well, Muons were originally called "Mu mesons", but they were found not to be actual mesons at all: the "mu" bit is from the Greek letter. There isn't a Greek letter "Hu", so either there was (or will be) a Chinese physicist or the author's playing around with the programme's title again.

A base under the Thames Barrier was chosen, it seems, mainly because of the water needed to filter out these exotic particles. This barrier was constructed in the early 1980s to prevent flooding of low-lying areas in London. The river is tidal up as far as Teddington, some ten miles from the Barrier, but the Estuary narrows just before the docks, making the stretch between Greenwich and Silvertown the most practical place to have put it. Fear of freak floods, such as that in 1928, had grown in the 1970s (hence the lyrics of The Clash's hit *London Calling*), and the ten-year programme to construct a moveable dam ended in 1984, just as redevelopment of Docklands began in earnest (see 21.4, "Resurrection of the Daleks"; X2.5, "Rise of the Cybermen"; and X2.12, "Army of Ghosts"). This was almost the last significant act of the Greater London Council. The Barrier was intended to be used in extreme high tides or potential floods due to excessive rainfall, and that it would be shut maybe once a year. In 2003, due to global warming, it had to be closed 19 times. The average over the last 30 years has been five per annum.

In case you missed it as the Doctor and Donna rolled by on them, the launch of the Segway personal transporter was supposed to be the single-most significant development in transport since the internal combustion engine. The pre-launch hype, and secrecy, led people to expect hovercars or something, but a gyroscopically-powered one-person buggy is actually pretty handy for some things. The BBC has used them, in conjunction with SteadiCams, to do "guerrilla" shoots where the time and effort of laying tracks for a camera-dolly would impede the hit-and-run spontaneity of a shot.

Just at a very basic level, this story is an exaggeration of the traditional 60s sitcom scenario with a woman screaming because there's a spider in the sink, and the husband flushing it down the drainpipe. Davies had his windows open a lot in that heatwave we were discussing earlier. Oh, and if you missed it, Donna's discovery that the driver who's taking her away from her destination is a robot in a mask is almost identical to the second cliffhanger from 8.1, "Terror of the Autons".

Additional Sources There are, as we will detail later, a few cut scenes, but one of note is Lance's rationale for his villainy: after the Canary Wharf incident and the two recent spaceships to visit London, Earth seems so insignificant. This doesn't entirely explain how he has managed to put this scheme together, but if the Racnoss was looking for a recruit, it's apparently going to be easier after those events than before. (See "The Invasion" for the nearest we've had to this hitherto.)

English Lessons

- Chiswick (n.) It's a commuter district in North West London. It's next to Shepherd's Bush, the area where Television Centre was, so it's BBC shorthand for "normal and boring", just as Acton is "normal, boring and a bit squalid" and Perivale is "so boring even people from Acton sneer at it" (see Volume 6). In fact, all of these districts are

Why Weren't We Bovvered?

continued from Page 19...

for Tom Baker – if he'd said no, the subplots and character would have been ditched.

Let's pull on another thread... news satire *The Day Today* was the first significant television work by Christopher Morris and Armando Iannucci, and featured soon-to-be-famous performers who, by and large, haven't bothered with *Doctor Who*. But on the writing side were two ex-music journalists, Graham Linehan and Arthur Mathews, who got a sitcom that nobody watched, called *Paris* soon after. It was a vehicle for Alexei Sayle (22.6, "Revelation of the Daleks"). Undaunted, they launched a second series called *Father Ted*, and that was a hit. They also worked with Sayle on a sketch-show, which was less funny than his previous one, but had a lot of recognisable cult TV references. (Notably a *Time Tunnel* spoof called "Drunk in Time" with Jenny Agutter and Peter Capaldi. The one about Hadrian's Wall is very like X10.10, "The Eaters of Light".) Once *Father Ted* ended (and see X3.3, "Gridlock" for a Catherine Tate-scale piece of surprise casting), they did a sketch-show called *Big Train* featuring Simon Pegg and Tamsin Grieg (X1.7, "The Long Game"), Tracy-Ann Oberman (X2.12, "Army of Ghosts") and Tate, as well as omnipresent performers Mark Heap and Kevin Eldon. Grieg went to work on Linehan's next solo project, *Black Books*, with Bill Bailey ("The Doctor, the Widow and the Wardrobe") while Pegg – aside from a one-episode part in that show – was next seen in Mathews's *Hippies* (but only by about 14 people). Also in these series were a lot of the same faces (Sally Phillips, Julian Rhind-Tutt, Johnny Vegas, Gatiss, Eldon and Peter Serafinowicz – although he was just a voice in *Hippies* or X9.4, "Before the Flood"). Many of these people turn up in various other related series (check out *Green Wing* for Michelle Gomez joining this gang), and we've only picked the obvious ones from a long list.

Let's concentrate on the mother-lode: *Spaced*, written by Stevenson and Pegg, with Heap, Bailey and Serafinowicz in regular roles. That was the first sitcom to be written from within a cult TV sensibility (if Kevin Smith had known about *Bagpuss* and Billie Piper and had written a *Mallrats*-ish sitcom about people in North London in 1999, it might have turned out similar). Viewers were assailed by references coming from all directions. In one episode, Eldon and Gatiss play Men in Black (heavily inflected by Agent Smith from *The Matrix*) chasing Simm. That episode begins as a pastiche of Woody Allen's *Manhattan* with a side-swipe at *Apocalypse Now*, but also has Pegg's character burning his *Star Wars* merchandising (in the manner of the pyre in *Return of the Jedi*) after the horror of seeing *The Phantom Menace*.

Meanwhile Gatiss, Pemberton, Reece Shearsmith (X9.9, "Sleep No More") and Jeremy Dyson took this approach in a different direction with *The League of Gentlemen*, appropriating situations and characters from British-made horror films, *Coronation Street* and miserable small-town life and conveying a sense of a community that followed its own rules, but with the three performers playing 90% of the speaking-parts. In both *Spaced* and *League*, there was a world-view informed by what was on their televisions circa 1978 and what had subsequently gained a cult following – and the experience of being a fan of such widely-ridiculed material. Unashamedly fannish allusions to *Doctor Who* came on and off screen (see X1.3, "The Unquiet Dead" for the anecdote about Gatiss telling Eccleston he looked like the Doctor).

You're getting the picture... there's a generation of actor-writers who came to television around the time Tom Baker was the Doctor, who have embraced the whole of popular culture and were, by 1999, unashamed of their affection for unfashionable old stuff. Inevitably, when *Doctor Who* came back, they were keen to be involved. More to the point, they were big enough and well-connected enough to be assets any series would want to have. The surprise isn't that Gatiss acted in and wrote for the BBC Wales series, but that neither Pegg nor Higson wrote episodes. We could almost as easily have followed the Linehan-Morris-Iannucci line and got a list of actors who've been in the new version of *Doctor Who* (by way of *The IT Crowd* and *The Mighty Boosh*, and then we have to extend our vast Mobius-strip family tree to include subloops of Judd Apatow and *Garth Merengi's Darkplace*[6] – to say nothing of Series 9).

But let's wind back and look at one established writer who never wrote for anyone else's projects (with one obvious exception), Steven Moffat. He's not as isolated as that: apart from his series having launched a lot of careers, he connects both to the start of our story via his mother-in-law (Beryl Vertue, as we hope you remembered from last

continued on Page 23...

now fairly upmarket and Chiswick has a few award-winning restaurants. At the time of this episode, it was home to the Ballet Rambert. It's bisected by the M4, the Motorway heading west and into Wales, so Russell T Davies and anyone else making post-2005 *Doctor Who* will have been literally looking down on it from the flyover that's supposedly where the TARDIS chases the taxi. (That scene was not all filmed in London, as you'll have guessed – incidentally, the real Chiswick flyover was opened by Jayne Mansfield.).

However, as is clear from the emails in *The Writer's* Tale, Davies (and apparently director Euros Lyn) believed that it was in the east, hence the weirdness about Donna running to Greenwich in X4.11, "Turn Left" and some anomalies in this episode. It's an old enough place for the spelling to differ from pronunciation – as per "Greenwich", "Keswick" and "Norwich', we skip the W.

• "You've Been Framed" (n): like *America's Funniest Home Videos*, but slightly less inane. Currently narrated by Harry Hill (we refer you to earlier volumes), with a peculiar stream-of-consciousness commentary occasionally connected to what's on screen.

• Double Glazing (n.) There's a strong connotation of dodgy door-to-door salesmen that goes along with the phrase. They are also the people most likely to make unsolicited phone calls during prime time.

• Blinking Flip (interj.): As with a lot of Donna's vocabulary, this mild euphemism is what someone who was a child in the 1960s might just recall being used un-ironically when children were listening (fast forward to Series 4 for more *Grange Hill*-style U-certificate swearing).

• 4H (adj): UK pencils come in various categories, depending on the proportion of graphite and clay. H denotes hard, more clay than graphite, B the other way around (blackness, with the extreme being just charcoal). Most pencils are 2HB, so a 4H is, as they say in these parts, well 'ard.

• CV (n): Curriculum Vitae. In Britain, it's what Americans call a resume. What Americans generally call a CV is more of a scattershot approach rather than tailored to the specific job for which you are applying.

• Posh (n.): Normally an adjective. Lance, however, is referring to Victoria Beckham, *nee* Adams, one of the Spice Girls. You may have heard of them. She's also married to David Beckham, the one football player of whom even Americans had heard of before 2014.

• WH Smiths (n): As Donna uses it to indicate normality, you will have guessed that it's a familiar sight. This was the first newsagent/ bookseller to get concessions in the new railway stations in the 1850s. A town without one can be considered to be the back end of beyond.

Oh, Isn't That...?

• *Jacqueline King* (playing Sylvia Noble, Donna's mother). Well, she's been in things like *Doctors* and *Casualty*, and was Georgina Hodge on *55 Degrees North*. This is precisely the kind of "Oh, isn't that...?" familiar face that used to get this kind of part rather than big names from soaps, so we're almost proud she's not a soap-star.

• *Howard Attfield* (Geoff Noble, Donna's father). A jobbing actor if ever there was one, he'd been in almost all the usual long-running ITV comedy-dramas of the 90s (and *Chucklevision*) as well as a couple of things one might not have expected (*Lexx* and the peculiar film version of *Brothers of the Head*). When Donna was brought back, it was intended that he would do more than gape as Sylvia ranted, but he died during rehearsals for "Partners in Crime" and some of his plot-functions went to Wilf Mott ("Voyage of the Damned").

• *Rhodri Meilir* (a wedding recorder named "Rhodri", there's lovely) had, days earlier, been Bilius the God of Hangovers in the much-hyped Sky One TV adaptation of Terry Pratchett's *Hogfather*.

• *Don Gilet* (Lance Bennett) later became an *EastEnders* stalwart, but he had also been in the hairdresser drama *Cutting It* (see Volume 7 for all the other people who commuted between Manchester and Cardiff to be in this and *Doctor Who*). He was also in *55 Degrees North* and a lot of those bread-and-butter BBC dramas (*Casualty, Doctors* and so on). Two days after this episode aired, he was in the Phillip Pullman adaptation *Ruby in the Smoke*, Billie Piper's first post-*Who* starring vehicle, which also gave the world Matt Smith. Latterly, he's playing Freema Agyeman's dad in *Old Jack's Boat* on CBBC (the Christmas episode of this later RTD project also had someone marrying on Christmas Day).

• *Sarah Parish* (the Racnoss Empress) had just been the female lead in *Blackpool*, in which she was married to a slightly dodgy entrepreneur (David Morrissey; X4.14, "The Next Doctor") but sleeping with the detective investigating him

Why Weren't We Bovvered?

continued from Page 21...

volume) and to the comedy mainstream. In his first year as executive producer, he elicited scripts from Simon Nye and Richard Curtis. Curtis is, apart from his long history of sketches and sitcoms before inflicting his films on us, one of the mainstays of the charity telethon *Comic Relief*. The last two broadcasts have included sketches by Moffat set in the TARDIS with the regulars – and included on the DVDs as canonical episodes. The 2007 extravaganza had Tate and Tennant reunited in one of a series of sketches using Tate's regular characters (in this she was Lauren Cooper, with Tennant as a supply teacher who turned out to be equipped with a sonic screwdriver[7]; Tate wrote this). Simon Nye's big hit was *Men Behaving Badly*, also the first major hit for Hartswood Films (run by Beryl Vertue, although her attempt at a US reworking was as abortive as Moffat's *Coupling*), which really launched Clunes and gave Enfield an acting gig instead of impressions and sketches.

The obvious impression to get from this is that the period when *Doctor Who* appeared to be taking itself grimly seriously, from "The Leisure Hive" (18.1) to roughly "Revelation of the Daleks", was the aberration. If, as many have suggested, the problem with this period is the over-influential Big Name Fans telling the production team that the massively popular previous style was "silly", we have then to retort that the last phase of the series had a star known for knockabout humour, and some of the most deliberately odd design decisions in the series' long history. Never mind that Sylvester McCoy had worked with the Royal Shakespeare Company, nor that the writers were attempting to toughen up the series – it's here that the accusation was flying around that the producer who had removed all trace of amusement from the series when he took over wasn't taking it sufficiently seriously. It may well be that he wasn't taking those pompous fans seriously, but had realised that the scripts needed some sense of what it would look like to the average viewer. Not all of the directors quite got this. The uneven tone and awkward lurches of Colin Baker's stories was a difficult transition back from the earnestness and stilted dialogue of Peter Davison's tenure. Davison, an actor mainly known for light comedy, struggled to make long dull technobabble speeches sing. He could, on occasion, adroitly move between this and humour, but Nathan-Turner vetoed the majority of his efforts to do so.

This sort of thing reaches its natural extreme with Sylvester McCoy's stint. McCoy had begun in theatrical farce, and had his television break doing comedic stunts on children's television shows such as *Vision On* and *Tiswas* – so when given a lot of hurried slapstick constructed in the gap between script editors, he pulls it off vigorously. McCoy's credentials were no more inappropriate than Jon Pertwee's, the main difference being that Pertwee resented the assumption that he would provide comic relief in his own show. He kept doing funny voices on *The Navy Lark* all through his term as the Doctor, whereas McCoy did fringe theatre work, some of it very grim and unsuitable for children. The connection between them, and the majority of the other Doctors, is the ability to flip between moods in a heartbeat.

This is one of the main ways in which *Doctor Who* would always beat US imports rife with one-note performances. Once we switch over to the sort of story that Andrew Cartmel (script-editor in the last three years) would rather have been telling, we have comedic moments underscoring the general seriousness of (say) 25.1, "Remembrance of the Daleks" without missing a beat. One of the writers who Cartmel had approved of enough to invite back was Stephen Wyatt, another Footlights Revue alumnus who had originally scored himself a slot by sending Cartmel and Nathan-Turner the script of a comedy he'd just finished for BBC1. "Greatest Show in the Galaxy" (25.4) – particularly the Doctor's variety show in episode four – is perhaps the most characteristic story of the lot, in that both the story and actor shift from broad comedy to melodramatic seriousness and back again. That turn-on-a-sixpence ability is now becoming standard in American "cult" shows, but in the 1980s only *Doctor Who* was attempting it.

Similarly, the casting of the Doctor was generally a process of alternating between an actor formerly noted for serious roles lightening up (Troughton, both Bakers, McGann and most spectacularly Eccleston), and actors generally thought of as comic showing their range (Pertwee and McCoy in particular, but also Hartnell reminding people of his earlier career and Davison making Season Nineteen and a sitcom simultaneously). Indeed, looking at the various actors considered – or reportedly considered – for the role, it's significant that what we got and who else the pro-

continued on Page 25...

(David Tennant). And they all burst into song every so often. No, really. She'd also played Tennant's wife in *Recovery*, a drama about head trauma. And you will barely be surprised that she was in *Cutting It* too. She's also one of many now-prominent actresses to have got her break in bizarre 90s adverts for Boddington's beer, but you'll have to investigate those for yourselves, since you'd not believe anything we told you. More recently, she was Queen Pasiphae in *Atlantis* (see the essay with X4.10, "Midnight"). And, as many of you will know, she was in the third and final series of Chris Chibnall's *Broadchurch*.

• *Catherine Tate* (Donna Noble). Didn't we do all this last story? If you missed that, just accept that after years on other people's sketch-shows, she got one all her own and became a household name – with greetings-cards containing sound-chips of her catch-phrases – so the cliffhanger to "Doomsday" was sort of like if they'd ended *CSI: Miami* with Horatio finding Tina Fey sat at his desk and claiming to be the new Chief of Police. Except even more incongruous than that. (See this story's essay.)

• *Neil Hannon*. Yes, the frontman of the Divine Comedy recorded one of the songs for the reception. Murray Gold wrote him a special ballad (and there was an attempt to get it to No. 1; see **The Lore**.)

Things That Don't Make Sense When we first hear the Empress, as she caresses the Doctor's image on a screen in a cliffhanger-to-episode-one-of-a-Tom-Baker-story sort of way, have a look at the other screens. For some reason, she's watching footage of the funeral of Diana, Princess of Wales. Several times over. Another screen shows Concorde.

There's a pre-emptive attempt to have the Doctor ask why *anyone* gets married at Christmas, but this is just the start of the weirdness. (If there's Asian Flu doing the rounds, affecting Wilf – see X4.4, "The Sontaran Stratagem" – there are even more reasons not to have it on this particular day or get on a plane for the honeymoon). It's Christmas Eve and, as with last year, it's a lot easier to get a taxi in London than anyone who's ever tried it might expect. It's also a lot easier to get a church mere hours before the biggest night of their year and to get a venue for a reception, never mind the catering staff and DJ – or for the guests to get to either venue. The wedding's off to a bad start anyway, with the organist playing the Mendelssohn piece used for *leaving* the church as Donna walks down the aisle (traditionally, they use the Wagner wedding march for that).

Oh, and the roads out of London aren't normally good for high-speed chases, especially not the one that leads to Heathrow Airport. (Best to not ask how we know this.)

So, Lance or the Empress hired Roboforms to dress up as Santa and learn to drive taxis. Why? It seems improbable that either of them expected that a TARDIS would be around, or that Donna would vanish in a puff of orange sparkly pixy-dust and land up anywhere other than H. C. Clements's basement. Moreover, what purpose is served by whisking Donna from Central London to wherever they're taking her (Wales? Heathrow? Stonehenge?) once they've found her again? If the Roboforms are indeed the same ones from last year, it's theoretically possible that Torchwood collected them up and the Empress reprogrammed them, perhaps to harvest food for the hatchling Racnoss babies... but why is one milling about in a taxi?

[And this Santa-cab is unoccupied despite being in central London on Christmas Eve – fat chance of that! Even if the robo-cabbie left the FOR HIRE sign unlit until seeing Donna, how did they obtain a TX1 Hansom Cab? They either mugged a real Hackney Carriage driver on the busiest and most lucrative day of the year – nonetheless, with the time allotted this is most likely – or they realised that Donna had gone missing and very quickly got on eBay or Gumtree and stumped up three grand. Then learned to drive a diesel with complicated gearing in a built-up area. However, maybe that's what they've been doing since last Christmas and there's a whole unseen story of androids doing the Knowledge to pass the London cab exam and get licences (getting loans from the Alien Invasion Start-Up Fund who bankrolled Chameleon Tours, Bubbleshock, Adipose Industries and the third Nestene assault). Or maybe this is just more evidence that Uber was genuinely invented by evil aliens rather than just seeming like it.]

It's understandable that when you're first attempting to use ancient particles that can only be activated through a living catalyst, you might take a few months to get the dosage right. It even makes sense that once you know what the precise dosage *is*, you can repeat that amount with some-

Why Weren't We Bovvered?

continued from Page 23...

ducers (allegedly) considered are so similar in track-record. Pertwee was asked at the same time as Ron Moody, while the reports we have of Dame Judi Dench being the first choice for the abortive relaunch in 2000 and of David Thewlis being in line for Doctors nine and ten in rapid succession have never been denied. Likewise, Paterson Joseph's career prior to not-being the eleventh Doctor after all includes fantasy and comedy, as well as grim dramas.

For these reports to have struck so many observers as plausible suggests that the parameters were agreed by people fairly high up in BBC drama. Anyone can "leak" a random actor, but the proximity of these names to who we got is suggestive. Conversely, McGann stands out from the names the TV Movie's production team were looking at for, primarily, a lack of prior comedy roles. Compared to Tony Slattery or Hugh Laurie (who is still considered a comedian here after 20 years of being posh for a living and getting hit or insulted by Stephen Fry), he's a wild-card choice but an obvious contrast to the "dark and mysterious" seventh Doctor played by that bloke from *Tiswas*.

So at the end of "Doomsday", Catherine Tate shows up like a punchline. It was a surprise, because she was known to be so busy and because almost everything she did was newsworthy then. It was a shock, because it compounded the knowledge that Rose wasn't coming back – even though before the first episode, the idea of a former pop-star aboard the TARDIS was treated as ridiculous. Then there was the shock of recognition, much as we'd had with John Cleese admiring the TARDIS or Andrew Marr commenting on Slitheen (X1.4, "Aliens of London"). But for anyone who'd seen Tate's work prior to the all-conquering sketch-show, it was the most natural thing imaginable.

one else and not necessarily wait all that time. Waterboarding someone with the stuff, however, lacks finesse. The whole point is to get him to swallow most of the water. Spider-woman can do this because she's gauged the precise levels using the data from Donna's dosing. But that was done over six months, during which Donna left the country for a holiday, without Lance. Wouldn't this have affected the measurements? In fact, given how little regard Lance has for Donna and how well he gets on with Nerys, why not just slip Nerys the mickey finns instead?

Donna scuba-diving, apart from possibly setting up some space-suit shenanigans later that never came, covers her not knowing about the Battle of Canary Wharf. Why someone saving up for a wedding and honeymoon (and a church wedding and reception on Christmas Eve, even more costly) ducks out and goes to Spain for a week or more – without her fiancé – is more baffling than anything else here. It obviously wasn't her parents who paid for the wedding, as next time we see Sylvia she's cutting out coupons. In America back then, maybe Geoff's medical expenses could have eaten into their savings – but this is Chiswick. It's not impossible that the Nobles planned to bankrupt themselves for their daughter's big day, just uncharacteristically altruistic of Sylvia.

Huon energy/ particles/ waves are affected by emotional states. We can live with this, as so much of our conjecture about Artron Energy requires some kind of quantum-level influence by consciousness (see X3.10, "Blink" et seq, **How Does the TARDIS Work?** under 1.3, "The Edge of Destruction" and **What *is* the Blinovitch Limitation Effect?** under 20.3, "Mawdryn Undead"). Trace elements of this stuff in water can be made to generate more of it, along the model of deuterium or a fast-breeder reactor. The ideal particle-accelerator isn't a giant underground magnetic doughnut the size of Switzerland, or even CERN (see X10.6, "Extremis"), but a stroppy temp about to get married. It's Christmas, so we'll let them off with that one too. Where it starts to go wrong is that whereas the Doctor insists in one scene that huon particles are merely hypothetical and rumoured, he can A) identify them on a wedding video (which wasn't affected by the magnetic flux that one might expect), B) can tell them apart from all the other identical orange-sparkly-pixy-dust that happens in RTD era *Doctor Who*, and C) suddenly becomes an authority on this substance.

All right, at first sight he seems to be bluffing: the Doctor insists that the particles are inert, but also deadly, but also that Donna will be just fine after all. Yet his every guess about how the particles and the stroppy ginger producing them will react under different stimuli proves to be spot-on... how does that work? And, let's not forget, there's some aboard the TARDIS and the Doctor knows this. So it can't be as obscure as all that. He also tells Donna that 4.6 billion BC is as far back as he's ever been, but we know better (17.1, "Destiny of the Daleks", for starters; definitely 19.1, "Castrovalva" and probably 1.3, "Edge of Destruction").

Either it's much easier to put somebody into a TARDIS than take them out again, or the author's forgotten his setup in "Bad Wolf" (X1.12), in which it appears nothing short of Dalek technology would be capable of snatching people out. It's not so much Donna herself as the sheer variety of ways that the Doctor envisions to teleport someone into his supposedly impenetrable Ship. If so, why don't the baddies do that more often?

A tank drives past Henrik's department store... with Cardiff Castle clearly visible behind it. And a "To Let" sign with a Cardiff phone number. The Doctor's reaction to finding a giant hole in the ground (*so big and sorta round it was*), is to exclaim "*very* Torchwood!" (as if he'd even heard of them six hours earlier). And he should consider that when talking a damp woman in a wet, sleeveless satin dress in December after dark, it's probably best not to A) keep her talking on a street-corner for ten minutes, and B) make it snow.

# # #

Pull out your bus-maps of London and brace yourselves, it's time for the timetables discussion...

The first we see of the Racnoss ship is when the sun's setting in France (so about 2.00pm GMT, although given The Mill's muddled track-record for this sort of thing, let's not put too much faith in that). The WebStar arrives at dusk (say, around a quarter to four, this being London in late December). Working back from that, and with the location of the office roof fairly obviously in the City of London (somewhere near Liverpool Street) and H. C. Clements being close to the Thames Barrier, we have two long journeys across London to factor in. On a good day, such as a normal Sunday, Liverpool Street to Chiswick would be about an hour. (The cut scene says they took a bus, but the Tube might be quicker – Donna's dress might get people to give up seats or let them queue-jump but the Piccadilly Line would still be rammed. Sadly, this journey takes at least two buses.) Ditto driving all the way out to Greenwich, the other side of the Thames and right across London, in Lance's car. Christmas Eve is not a good day.

Before all that, there's the Chiswick flyover incident, in which Donna finally notices the taxi's taking her away from the church after a long-ish drive from Henrik's (which, as we established in Volume 7 is probably on Regent's Street, although a nearby street with a Police Box in it was curiously devoid of shoppers). As a Chiswick resident, Donna would know that the turn-off for the M4 via the Hammersmith Flyover ("flyover" being a noun, meaning a road that goes over residential areas, in this case Chiswick) is a lot earlier, more or less from Hyde Park, and that to get from Regent's Street to Chiswick you turn left and go down Kensington High Street. Even if this shopping precinct was also impassable (because: Christmas Eve) there's a more practical route you can take from Cromwell Road, just after the Albert Hall, but after that you can't get off the flyover until you've pretty much passed residential Chiswick and have to turn back to Hogarth Lane. She would have raised the matter with the driver long before she does. Even if she was that angry, she'd expect a cabby to take her via various other routes (e.g. the Hanger Lane Gyratory) unless there was a good explanation (like traffic) which the driver would have mentioned and asked if this was all right, as it would cost a lot more. In the mood she was in, an argument with a taxi-driver trying to fleece her by going a weird route would have started within a few hundred yards, when "he" took a left down Brompton Road.

Add to this all the pratting about with Segways and wedding disco malarkey, and it's looking as if Donna flew away from the wedding at around 11.30am. (In a church, on a Sunday.) That's at the very latest. Donna's watch, in the rooftop, says 3.30 and yet it's still light when they get to H. C. Clements. So everyone was there on time, on a day when London's almost *impossible* to traverse, yet nobody's eating at the reception. Nor are they giving statements to the police. (The script, for what it's worth, states that the wedding was at 15.00 hrs and that the Doctor, Donna and Lance got to H. C. Clements at 17.20. Even allowing for amazingly fast crosstown transit, the sun should have set long before this and the flurry of tenners would have taken place at night. Just to remind US readers, London is 51.5 degrees N, further north than Calgary or Montreal, and this is a week after the Winter Solstice, so there's only six hours of full daylight.) Compared to this, the idea that Sylvia would have come from the wedding to make a full Christmas dinner on Christmas Eve is almost normal.

# # #

The remainder of this section will be devoted to our in-house pedant, Dr Science, trying to work through this extended business of drilling to the centre of the Earth and chucking things down the hole...

Just to cut to the chase, it's a 2900 km drop, and a human body falling through still air reaches terminal velocity of 195 km per hour, so Lance won't hit the Racnoss ship until about 7.00am on Boxing Day. The water, however, would disperse and fall in smaller droplets, which will evaporate even if they've somehow managed to cool the magma and core sufficiently for this gaping maw not to blast infernal heat at all times. We rather hope the heat and toxic gases are still there, otherwise Lance will be alive and conscious for the 15 hours it takes to fall before he splatters into the side of a spaceship.

Back-of-envelope calculations indicate that the amount of material removed from the Earth is about 910 million cubic metres (assuming a straight ten-metre cylindrical hole, as it appears here, without it opening out as it goes down). That much straightforward rock and clay would be hard enough to shift, but we're talking super-dense iron-nickel core, magma and suchlike. Even if they magically evaporate it without anyone noticing, there's going to be a slight wobble in the Earth's rotation, enough to affect satellites and thus satnavs (maybe this was how ATMOS got popular – "The Sontaran Stratagem") even without the magnetic field disruptions causing possible bald-patches in our protection against solar radiation. But we're talking about magic Torchwood alien theft, so this needn't disturb us as much as what almost ten billion litres of air being sucked away down a hole under London might do to the weather, or how much seawater ought to have burst through the Thames Barrier once nothing was on the other side as a counterweight, and where all that ocean would go.

Yes, *ocean.* The shot where Donna claims they've drained the Thames is from Woolwich, east of the Thames Barrier (the Dome, now the O2 Arena, and Canary Wharf are clearly visible *behind* the Barrier), so the Doctor has actually tipped the entire North Sea and possibly the English Channel and Atlantic Ocean down the plug'ole. The loopy flood-the-console-room scene in "Logopolis" now seems as sensible as rice pudding by comparison. Old Father Thames is still a going concern in every subsequent story, so one option is that there's an enhanced outer barrier (rather like the small one near Barking) which, in this version of London, has enough force and speed-of-use that it shuts off a small stretch, perhaps half a mile from the main barrier, like the lock in a canal. Maybe it was installed as a precaution after the Skarasen paid Parliament a visit (13.1, "Terror of the Zygons"). Another, bearing in mind a similar flaw in "Rise of the Cybermen" and various episodes of *The Sarah Jane Adventures*, is that the *Doctor Who* universe has a Millennium Dome in Lewisham instead of Greenwich. That doesn't really chime with the whole "Greenwich Meridian" theme of the Millennium celebrations and, anyway, it's back in its usual place in the pre-credit sequence of X5.1,"The Eleventh Hour". A third is that Torchwood were uncharacteristically sensible and took precautions when someone theorised that drilling a big hole right under the Thames might, at a pinch, result in some secrecy-compromising ocean-disappearance.

If, on the other hand, enough water sluiced down to fill that hole and it all got down a ten-metre diameter tube, we still have problems. Ten billion litres of water (about three billion gallons), rather more than the Great Lakes contain, ought to have been enough to flush out the Racnoss even allowing for the evaporation due to friction with the air we mentioned earlier, but then we still have the heat to excuse. Even without the subterranean rock-melting temperatures we usually associate with holes to the Centre of the Earth, that much water rubbing against that much air would have made enough steam to satisfy Professor Zaroff (4.5, "The Underwater Menace").

And let's take time to consider *how* they did this. If they had drilling techniques more advanced than, say Project Inferno (er, "Inferno") then Torchwood, staunch advocates of giving the British Empire all the technological advances to keep the UK as Top Nation, ought really to have offered their support for this limitless fuel-source and potential bio-weapon. Considering how difficult Zaroff found drilling a few thousand feet through a crustal bald-patch and the alarming consequences of this plan (splitting the Earth in half, "Beng! Beng! Beng! Nossing in ze Vorld ken schtopp me now!" etcetera), the alien tech in

Canary Wharf must have included a lot of force-fields to keep the fizzing hot magma from lowering property values in Greenwich. With a tremendous hole virtually beneath the Thames; the water table will ooze in and collapse it. And there's a Tube line right there.

Really, there are many more stable parts of the world in which to conduct such an experiment. *Something* must have made it a good idea for Torchwood to buy out a locksmith's company in Greenwich and drill from there rather than, say, a British-run isolated part of Antarctica or a remote town in Scotland. It's not a good idea to have your main base of operations almost literally a stone's-throw from the highly dangerous laser-powered drill to a volcano and beyond, but with Canary Wharf so close to the Thames Barrier, it's as if they were hoping that all their appropriated alien goodies would protect them if anything went wrong. But we've seen where that kind of thinking got them.

In both iterations of the Dalek plan to drill that deep (2.2, "The Dalek Invasion of Earth"; A2, "Dalek Invasion Earth 2150 AD"), the canny pepper pots chose a nice stable and relatively remote bit of the Home Counties *not* on top of the Jubilee Line. (We can imagine Donna's grandad advising them: "Don't dig there, dig it elsewhere". Of course, what with Britain's underground being full of green goo that turns people into rampaging monsters, intelligent reptiles who regard all humans as rampaging vermin, leftover nuclear bunkers and the like, it's possible that Torchwood just couldn't find anywhere else to dig the hole.) This is an agency that has a Tube line from Canary Wharf to Cardiff, so they must have evaluated the risk of lava pouring in to either of their bases. The only sensible conclusion is, therefore, the force-field we posited earlier. Fine, but *if* Torchwood can produce an energy-field capable of holding back that much lava and extending 29,000 km, why is London so defenceless every other time some alien chancer pops in for a quick invade? And why would the Doctor go to such absurd ends to flush out the baby spiders, when that force-field must have had an off switch? (Magma suddenly not under compression would kill them a lot quicker and more cleanly, and restore Earth to its proper proportions. Whatever the case, the hole must have been plugged some time between 2007 and 2157, or else the Daleks would have used it for their own bonkers scheme.)

All right, so we might, at a stretch, conjecture that the Racnoss nest-ship is generating the force-field to keep the walls cool and non-oozy and stop all London's air from rushing down it in a perpetual hurricane. So how does the water (and Lance) get close to the hatchlings? How can the Doctor be so sure that the Racnoss spaceship is defenceless at the end? Yes, the Racnoss Empress has been using energy left right and centre, but that's an awfully big assumption. All of this requires the Racnoss to have hired, or at least collaborated with, the agency set up by Queen Victoria to keep aliens *out*. Yet nothing else makes as much sense.

The alternative is that a Torchwood scheme was abandoned and left in useable order after the Cybermen and Daleks usurped the organisation as their bridgehead, and that an alien empress and a wide-boy somehow joined forces to capitalise upon it. Lance certainly gives every impression that it's been a rogue operation on his own initiative since Torchwood left, as he's both handling Donna and interacting with the Empress. But trying to figure out how Lance got involved in all of this in the first place is baffling. A first draft of this book involved our trying to lay out how/ what he must have known about Torchwood, the Doctor et al, and giving ourselves an aneurysm for our trouble – was Lance a lowly pen-pusher for H. C. Clements beforehand, as a Torchwood plant or just because? If the latter, he's an amazingly gifted technician and con-man, which makes his ultimate death all the more puzzling. Then again, if the technology's so old it's become folklore even for the Doctor, perhaps the Racnoss told Lance how to use it... fair enough, but the more you ponder how that alliance came about, the more baffling it becomes. Do ancient alien spider-women get in touch with HR types at a moderately-successful locksmith's office via small ads on Gumtree?

Critique It's hard now to recapture what a risk this episode was at the time. After a fairly conservative second year, during which the nation was swept along on sheer momentum despite a couple of dodgy episodes, they were replacing Rose with... well, Donna begins as a frumpier, older Lauren Cooper, and that's what we saw at the end of "Doomsday". She develops into a sort of Jackie Tyler surrogate as the episode progresses, unimpressed by the Doctor's antics and just wanting to get back to normal (however remote this prospect becomes). We knew, then, that Donna wouldn't be back so this was a gimmick, an easy lead-in to a post-Rose series. It paid off. However, it's in the nature of innovations that the ones that work become standard and almost invisible, while the ones that don't are glaringly obvious. Anyone coming to this episode after discovering *Doctor Who* in the Pond era will have to take on trust that many of the things that characterised the series later began here and looked a little odd.

Considering how often marriage was used to write out companions, it's strange that we've only had one wedding-themed story before now. That was swashbuckling doppelganger farce "The Androids of Tara" (16.4), a story in which even its sternest critics will concede nothing goes disastrously wrong. It seems obvious with hindsight that a wedding – a traditional soap ratings gambit and a high-stakes day in any family's life – ought to have been a good hook for a *Doctor Who* episode. The idea of starting a story with a wedding rather than ending with one was taken at the time, by some, as a sign that this iteration of *Who* was too soap-like – as if Barry Letts had never tried soaping-up the series. If anything, weddings were as close as most people got to the basic material of the series, an interruption of everyday life by something out of a film or a fairy-tale (in theory, and people spend a lot of money trying to achieve exactly this effect). The clever switch on the soap formula here is that the betrayal isn't – as with *EastEnders* or *Coronation Street* – someone failing to live up to the standards the fantasy of wedded life requires, but is Lance living up to the current *Doctor Who* version of everyday life and Donna, out of the loop, behaving like someone from everyday life in our world. The tension between the two world-views is still just about negotiable at this stage, and creates a lot of the best jokes, but the rest of this volume will see this reach breaking-point.

With this in mind, it's notable how many concessions are made for anyone just joining – all the episodes that keen viewers would expect to be mentioned can be alluded to via Donna's ignorance. She's the butt of jokes for it, but Donna is the casual viewer who might not even have seen the last Christmas episode. Over half the people slumped in front of the telly on Christmas Day will have been actively looking forward to the episode, but a fair few would be new to all this. The *real* audience-identification characters, however, are the kids in the back of the car, not least because the TARDIS performs feats even the Doctor didn't know She could do.

We are already well into the trend towards ending an episode six times in succession, but normally this services the ongoing storylines. In this story, apart from a throwaway line, we have none of that and the last of the tag-scenes is notable for the Doctor's emphatic use of the past tense about Rose. However, Russell T Davies can't resist the urge to bitter-coat a sugar pill with some kind of I-am-writing-proper-DRAMA set-piece about how the Doctor is all scary and dangerous unless a human acts as his moral compass. This time it seems gratuitous, as if added out of obligation. Producer Julie Gardner insisted that they reshoot the climax to include a supposedly iconic close-up of the Doctor realising he'd gone too far, but it just looks as if David Tennant's thinking *I'd better stock up on Night Nurse*. Earlier changes of pace advanced the plot and gave texture to Donna, but this one intrudes on the episode. Even knowing with hindsight how often this shot will be re-used doesn't justify it being dwelt on.

That aside, we get just enough rest for the otherwise relentless *brio* to work for an hour. They don't ram the Christmas-ness of it all down our throats; it's there just enough to remind us that this episode works by Christmas Special Rules, but it's not as grotesquely shoehorned-in as we're going to get later. Such a Special has to be brisk, spectacular, self-contained and funny, all of which this one makes look easy. However, with one direct precedent, it's still possible to ring the changes and get everything needed in. The obligatory paper snow is there as a joke at the end, the obligatory new song is in the background at a wedding disco after the obligatory Slade. Once this becomes a ritual event, the desperation to make it unique and still Christmassy leads to the kind of "this'll do" triteness we got from Perry Como in the 70s. Donna is refreshingly honest about not liking Christmas, which helps sell the episode to anyone not watching it on that one day in late 2006 on BBC1.

Outside the context of a Christmas Day premiere, the main flaw is the Racnoss Empress. Not that Sarah Parish is actively bad, but the dialogue and the physicality of the prop rely on an indulgent audience. After the last two years of increasingly assured computer wizardry and deft prosthetics, this was worth a try and made a nice change – but their lack of faith in it almost invites the viewer to look for flaws. Which is to say: the fast-edited close-ups of bits of her look suspiciously like they're trying to hide a bad monster-suit. Once we see it in full, they at least resist the temptation to swamp it in dry-ice fog. It doesn't help that this creature is given some whimsical fairy-tale lines, but Parish gives us a hint of a being who has learned Earth customs imperfectly from watching bad television. That's less noted than it should be; we've mentioned before (and will again) how often Davies characters talk like Davies, but each major part here has a separate verbal idiom. Rose would *never* have said "Will I blinking flip jump!", but Lance makes jokes that sound like someone on a DVD commentary glad to get a word in. The Doctor isn't quite so generically anti-generically written (i.e. deliberately not like Jon Pertwee, but interchangeably with Eccleston as early on in Series 2).

It's also clear, watching this a decade or more later, that the outrageous stunt-casting of Catherine Tate was as sure-footed a move as getting Billie Piper. With the recent precedent of Peter Kay not having pleased everyone ("Love & Monsters"), this was another gamble. With later writers either giving Donna lines written for Penny (see "Partners in Crime") or dialogue written after seeing this episode, it's hard to imagine the part was made without her in mind, but it wasn't. Hindsight also gives undue prominence to Jacqueline King and Howard Attfield as Donna's parents, but they are as good as needed in relatively small roles. What hindsight *also* gives us is the way Don Gilet (as Lance) looks at first out of his depth, but is, in fact, guiding events his way. Previous depictions of humans making Faustian pacts with aliens have been quasi-Bond Villains with minions, but Lance is a wide-boy whose reaction to the revelation of extra-terrestrial life is plausible and hitherto under-explored. He's almost, but not quite, companion material himself, wanting more than mortgages and TV dinners. His methodology rules him out and, this being an RTD episode, means he's "earned" a nasty death. We can see how that was heading towards becoming a cliché that needed undoing, but it simply looks like a form of punctuation in this instance. He's done all he needs to, so they write him out.

As a counterweight to all this hindsight, imagine showing this to a BBC viewer around the time "The Androids of Tara" was first broadcast. They'd recognise most of it: the cinematic look and quality of the effects might be slightly alarming; the youth of the Doctor and his fake Cockney accent a bit estranging; you'd need to explain what that cutaway of the blonde girl falling over was and why any composer would want to deliberately pastiche early 60s easy listening. (Murray Gold has his film-score emulator switched to "Elfman" rather than "Zimmer" or "Morricone".) Even so, this is clearly in the same trajectory the series had been taking since 1973. Then show it to someone recovering from Colin Baker's first year. The fact that *Doctor Who* can do things like this would have made people angry that it wasn't even trying. Neither of these hypothetical viewers would have believed that BBC Wales, known in those days mainly for Max Boyce sing-along stage-shows, was capable of being so ambitious.

The Lore

Written by Russell T Davies. Directed by Euros Lyn. Viewing figures: (BBC1) 9.4 million (and an 84% AI), (BBC3 repeats) 0.6 and 0.2 million.

Repeats and Overseas Promotion The episode was shown once on BBC3 in the first week, and received a late-night broadcast with in-vision signing for hard-of-hearing viewers (something often done for documentaries, but rare for dramas other than genteel crime shows). After this critical seven days, during which the final ratings were assessed, it was repeated on BBC3 twice more that year, and has shown up every time they do a countdown to the new Christmas episode by showing all the others in a row.

As with "The Christmas Invasion", the hour-long episode (without ads) was unwieldy for inclusion in the usual runs for many networks and saved for a special occasion, or dropped. In France, as *La Bride de Noel*, it was shown out-of-sequence after Series 3 had premiered. (It appears that getting a French Catherine Tate was a hurdle, since Donna's surprise arrival at the end of "Doomsday" was left with her undubbed and mute as le Docteur repeated "Quoi?") BBC America cuts out the Segway chase, the wedding reception carrying on as Donna arrives, Donna's failed attempts to get a lift, "her name was Rose", "blinkin' flip jump" and almost everything else that made it worth watching. Disney XD, as usual, fades the word "hell", which in this case makes everyone seem to be a lot more foul-mouthed than they were on BBC1. In Germany, it was called *Die Aufgelöste Braut*, a literal translation.

Production

Once Lorraine Heggessy, BBC1 Controller, had decided that there would be a Christmas Special for 2005, Russell T Davies made provision for it being an annual tradition. A story idea he had pencilled in for Series 2, wherein a bride materialises aboard the TARDIS, was removed and what became X2.2, "Tooth and Claw" was brewed up (see also **Was Series 2 Supposed to be Like This?** under X2.11, "Fear Her"). Similarly, an image he'd had for decades – of a bored kid in the back of a car seeing the TARDIS flying past – was the starting-point for what became "School Reunion" (X2.3) before the idea of a military base or school being infiltrated had started to gel. Having already had the conversation with the effects teams, he could write this in with a degree of confidence. After a blind-alley about basing the story in Salisbury to have the Racnoss Empress use Stonehenge as her base (we had to wait until X5.12, "The Pandorica Opens" for something like that, but note the taxi's peculiar route here), the story was based in London on Christmas Eve.

• Davies's script was sprinkled with suggested music-cues (not all of which were followed), and made a point of suggesting constant travel, in as many vehicles as could be afforded. The long-shots of London were specified as being far enough away to avoid matting in Christmas decorations in the streets. Not all of the finished storyline was complete when the shock ending on "Doomsday" was shot, but the script was in the works as the later episodes of Series 2 were shown. In the meantime, David Tennant was making other dramas, notably the harrowing *Recovery* in which Sarah Parish played his wife (they'd worked together before; see **Oh, Isn't That...?**). By now, Tennant's personal life was newsworthy – his relationship with Sophia Myles (X2.4, "The Girl in the Fireplace") made the papers, including the holiday in Sardinia where he read the script for this episode.

• The third series was, as usual, divided into blocks. After all the trouble they had with Series 2's over-runs, and damage-limitation after the weather afflicted both "The Christmas Invasion" and "New Earth" (X2.1), this special was given a block to itself. (For future reference, the rest are: X3.1, "Smith and Jones" and X3.2, "The Shakespeare Code" as Block Two; X3.3, "Gridlock" and X3.6, "The Lazarus Experiment" were Block Three; the Dalek two-parter, X3.4 and X3.5, Block Four; the one-off, double-banked episode X3.10, "Blink" was Block Five and made concurrently with Block Six, which was X3.8, "Human Nature" and X3.9, "The Family of Blood"; Block Seven was X3.7, "42" and X3.11, "Utopia"; and the finale, X3.12, "The Sound of Drums" and X3.13, "Last of the Time Lords" was Block Eight. So that's done now.) After his bravura double-stint last year, Euros Lyn only directed this one episode. That was enough of a challenge, not least because they were moving to a completely different studio.

• To recap: the production team wrapped on X2.8-2.9, "The Impossible Planet"/ "The Satan Pit" and all subsequent shots for the series were done in various locations but, unbeknownst to all but a select few, one brief scene was shot in the TARDIS set of the Doctor reacting to the appearance of a woman in a wedding-dress. The team had smuggled Catherine Tate, at this stage just about the busiest and most recognisable performer in Britain, to Cardiff for an evening. Louise Page, the head of costumes, had secretly obtained measurements from her to get a wedding dress ready (to be stored under her legal name, "Catherine Ford"). In fact, they needed six identical dresses, in various states of repair for different parts of the story, and these had to be sourced in a hurry, in secret.

This brief scene was shot in just over half an hour on 29th March, the day before the production team left the Q2 studio complex for good. Davies was revising the initial proposed story as an hour-long piece in between launching two spin-off series, *Torchwood* and *The Sarah Jane Adventures*. He wrote the pilot for the former and co-wrote the latter's first story with Gareth Roberts (see "The Shakespeare Code"). Lyn received the script in two halves, with a cliffhanger just as the Empress appears. His biggest worry was staging the taxi-TARDIS chase, and he worked out the logistics with model cars he'd brought to the Tone Meeting.

The big surprise of the Bride (as she was identified in the end credits of "Doomsday") being Tate was maintained by elaborate subterfuges and through logistical necessities working to everyone's advantage. Tate was phenomenally busy that year, with three films and a slew of TV appearances, so was unavailable for the read-through on

29th June. Sophia Myles read Donna's lines. Helpfully, there was another bit of companion news to feed the press, as Freema Agyeman was announced as Martha shortly after we saw her as the doomed Torchwood member Adeola in "Army of Ghosts". This took two photo-shoots, as Tennant's holiday beard was thought unsuitable for young audiences or something.

• Shooting began with the long-shots of the real Thames Barrier, seen from the south bank of the Thames Estuary at Charlton. That was on Tuesday, 4th July. The following day had the taxis and cars seen from above on the real junction between the A4 and the M4, in real Chiswick. The bulk of the chase would be shot in Wales ten days later. The near-collision at the start of the sequence was executed as if for real, without the road being blocked. There had been an offer to use a part of the M4 leading off the flyover, in the small hours, but the timetable was too tight (the dates offered were ten days before the first day the team could shoot), so the remainder of the shots were done at the other end of the M4 in Cardiff.

The first location shots with Tate, on the rooftop looking towards St Paul's Cathedral, St Bride's Church and the Gherkin, were conducted on a helipad on Shoe Lane, in a working day (Thursday, 6th July, just before "Doomsday" was broadcast). Office-workers could easily identify the TARDIS and Tennant, but not the woman in the wedding-dress (one eye-witness authoritatively stated it to be Elisabeth Sladen). Tracie Simpson, the production manager, was smuggled out of the building with a coat over her head, to draw off any onlookers seeking a glimpse of the un-named performer in the title role. It took a bit of negotiation to get the TARDIS prop erected there, and some effort to secure it with the wind (real and generated by big fans) which also required a lot of overdubbing.

Tate and Tennant spent the next two days at the spanking new Upper Boat complex, paradoxically trying to make sure nobody saw any difference between what they were doing in the remount of the opening scene (about to be shown that Saturday) and the differently-lit original take with Ernie Vincze as director of photography. In between this and the other TARDIS scenes, the two stars tried to master the Segways the production had been loaned. A company representative was on hand to tutor (and sell) these gizmos. Tennant claims he was tempted, if only he had somewhere to use such a device. One shot that was dropped (it entailed a special effect not budgeted for) was the Doctor hurling Rose's top out of the door in a fit of pique at Donna's interrogation.

Tennant then got two days off, but Tate was back on the Tuesday, on location at the Atradius building in Cardiff Bay chasing Don Gilet down a stairwell in the flashbacks. They also made some memories (so to speak) at a pub (the Waterguard) and a nearby street (Riverside St). The next two days were spent at the Baverstock Hotel (rather an ironic name – see Volume 1) in exotic Merthyr Tidfil, which became the "Manchester Suite" (see X1.2, "The End of the World"), the function room for the reception. Tate bore with good grace the various children following her shouting "Am I bovvered?" Friday the 14th was their day at the church. This was St John the Baptist's on Trinity Street.

• Cardiff City Council had allocated two four-hour periods when the A4232 Ely Link Road, an orbital around the city, could be closed for filming over the weekend. The scenes of Tate were scripted to have Donna remove her veil (because there was green-screenery afoot in the next few shots and thereafter). The sun came up at around 4.30, meaning a 3.00am start. One of the cars, the green Saab on which the TARDIS bounces, is the one Gwen Cooper has in *Torchwood*. Another vehicle is a flatbed lorry, on which there was a crane. A location shot of Tennant looking from the TARDIS to the taxi were done by strapping Tennant to a plank on the back of the lorry. This was legal, because they had a police escort. For most of this day, the Welsh constabulary arranged a rolling road-block; their own cars created a clear space around the various vehicles without closing the road completely.

• Location filming on the 24th, in Cardiff city centre, fell on the first weekend of the school holidays. St Mary's Street, now familiar as the fake London street with Henrik's, was mobbed. Fortunately, Tate's involvement and the Robot Santas had become known to the public, so filming in front of an excited crowd was less of a problem than it could have been.

• Stop us if you've heard this one before: the bank notes that flew everywhere when the Doctor breaks open the cashpoint were mockups with pictures of David Tennant (bearing the legend "No Second Chances" and a promise to pay the bearer ten satsumas; see "The Christmas Invasion") and Phil Collinson (plus a garbled version of a line from 12.1, "Robot" about being childish). These are now, inevitably, collector's items. They were necessary because faking UK currency, for any reason, is a felony.

• The crowds who had come for the sunshine and spectacle were less in evidence the following night, when the WebStar shot at last-minute shoppers and an unseen Mr Saxon ordered a tank to shoot it down. (In fact, the line about "Mr Saxon" was dubbed later, once the idea had occurred to Davies.) The tank had been announced well in advance, but *apparently* one tourist missed the announcement and was woken in her hotel: after a spell in a middle-eastern war-zone, she wasn't expecting this in Cardiff. (That was the story in the press, anyway, however *ben trovato* it seems.) Earlier that day, the TARDIS had landed in Churchill Way, just off the main streets, for Donna to exit, freak out and run away. (The phone box she uses to call Sylvia was in fact in Upper Boat some time later.)

• It had been decided early on that the Empress would be a prosthetic rather than computer-generated. Cost was a consideration, but also a desire to resist doing the obvious. After all, this was a Christmas episode, so a physical – almost theatrical – villain was appropriate here if not elsewhere. An early design, picking up on the episode's title, had a Miss Havisham-style wedding-dress made of cobwebs. Four people moved the practical prop body around, swinging the torso and head sinuously, like the masthead of a ship.

Sarah Parish had, as Tennant relates it, spent almost the whole of the last year bending his ear about how much she'd love to play a monster in *Doctor Who*. She is reported to have endured the discomfort this entailed through showbiz bravado and painkillers. Spending three hours a day in make-up, using contact-lenses for the first time and having to drink carefully with her "Dick Emery" teeth, then being forced to kneel for hours plumbed into a giant see-saw that put all her weight (and that of the headpiece she wore and the prosthetic claws on her wrists) onto her lower back was therefore not something she had grounds to complain about.

Indeed, as it was only for three days, it didn't get routine enough for her *to* complain. Millennium Effects had taken a full-body cast of her, as well as a head-casting. The only CG element, as with the Slitheen, was the blinking eyes. She required two sets of contact lenses, one inside the other, to make her own eyes (almost) match those of the prosthesis. Another non-CG effect had been decided upon – the flooding of the Flood Chamber required a replica of the Millennium Stadium basement, since computer-generated water still looks fake. A company called Lucas FX got this task.

• In a scene that was cut, we had a brief return of Mrs Croop ("Love & Monsters"), which would have been on the bus to the reception, and the first time the Doctor and Donna were mistaken for a couple. Unlike all subsequent similar scenes, Donna plays up to expectations and whispers "just go with it" to the Doctor, later telling him not to get any ideas. Other cuts include: a conversation about Lance being unable to drive because he'd been drinking (in which Tennant's parents, sister-in-law and nieces were in the background); the next scene of them crammed into Donna's tiny car and the Doctor being hurt as they go over speed-bumps (two versions of this, as Julie Gardner hated Donna's pink car and they got another one in a different colour, with doubles inside to save time); arriving at the church to be told it's too late and the next couple to be married that day have arrived.

• Murray Gold now had the full resources of the BBC Orchestra of Wales at his disposal, and had a notion to make a score like those of Nino Rota. (Note *La Strada*, especially that wistful song; *81/2; The Godfather*; and the Zeffirelli *Romeo and Juliet*, although for people in Britain that's slightly tainted[8]. The music he uses for Martha Jones has a passing resemblance to some of these.) Gold's music was by now being released on a soundtrack CD. In the process, he re-recorded "Song For Ten" ("The Christmas Invasion") with Neil Hannon on vocals and a new last verse.

At the same time, they recorded the new song "Love Don't Roam", which replaced the scripted "jaunty" "Song For Ten" in the wedding reception scene. This was put on the CD as a teaser for the Christmas Special. The rigging of downloaded single charts was a brief fad when these were included in the main charts earlier that year – there had been a bid to get Billie Piper's "Honey to the Bee" back to No. 1 – and some fans attempted to game the figures to get "Love Don't Roam" to topple whatever product Simon Cowell had engineered to get the lucrative Christmas No. 1. This didn't work, mainly because only tracks released as singles count (see X3.7, "42"). Gold performed in a big *Doctor Who* concert for *Comic Relief* in November 2006, and, as part of this event, he conducted the orchestra in a live performance of the taxi-chase music, with the scene shown for the first time on a big screen. This was the launch of a big push for "The Runaway Bride", as the concert was used to promote both the Red Button facility on digital television and the series's relaunched website.

• Whereas the previous Christmas had been marked by promotion for the new Doctor's debut and the concept of a Christmas Special *per se*, this time around there wasn't the embarrassing problem of a now-departed Doctor's face on the toys, annuals and games. Over the course of the previous year, the merchandising had been dripped in episode by episode and, as we saw in "Rise of the Cybermen" and **Has All the Puff *Totally* Changed Things?**, the BBC had sanctioned a number of publications and spin-off programmes. The summer had been a bumper one for shops selling such stuff, and the release of (as they're called) the "Classic Series" DVDs had included some genuinely desirable items (including "The Invasion", with animated versions of the missing episodes one and four; and "Inferno"), and this momentum was maintained with the CD and birthday cards, Gary Russell's making-of book, audio recordings of old stories, audio recordings of the BBC books and those books themselves.

• Tate had, in the interim, made more films and had therefore been on the chat-show circuit promoting these and the episode, while Tennant was heard on Christmas Eve co-hosting a show on Radio One, the BBC's pop music station, with self-proclaimed fan Jo Whiley. BBC1 featured the Special, still something of a novelty, as a key part of its curious trailers (using "Christmas with the Devil" by Spinal Tap, despite nobody in Britain really being that familiar with "Carol of the Bells", the source of the chimes at the start that formed the opening to the trailers). On Boxing Day, the notion of a whole family watching the episode together provided a partial truce in a long-running storyline in *The Archers*, and the next week also saw the broadcast of the last episode of *Torchwood* Series 1 and the pilot of *The Sarah Jane Adventures*. It seemed that *Doctor Who* was inescapable.

X3.1: "Smith and Jones"

(31st March, 2007)

Which One is This? "Judoon platoon upon the moon." Martha Jones shows up and the Doctor becomes a patient.

Firsts and Lasts We see the first "Vote Saxon" poster (other than the ones in *Torchwood*) and the Doctor's got a new suit (it's blue, but exactly like the other one). It's Martha Jones's intro story, though Freema Agyeman's second. This means we're introduced to the whole Jones family here as well (her mother Francine; her father Clive and his girlfriend, Annalise; her sister Tish and her brother Leo); they'll be back later in the season, but not all at once. Martha gets a slow, lush waltz – less piano-ish than the one for Rose (but with a more-than-passing resemblance to the song from the old adverts for Cadbury's Flake that anecdotally steered British teenage boys towards manhood). It's the first story directed by Charles Palmer, who'd worked with many of the team on other projects (including, inevitably, *Linda Green*). He'll be in this book a lot and then back for Peter Capaldi's last year a decade later.

This is also the first time we see the *2000 AD*-esque Judoon, space police for hire. And a rather tricky bit of setup for "The End of Time Part Two" (X4.18) happens here, when the Doctor first establishes that he has the capacity to soak up tremendous amounts of radiation.

In this episode, someone (Martha) says "bloody" for the first time. The Doctor gets to use the term "fetish" for the first time, though. And this is the first episode since "Rose" (X1.1) not to have a pre-credits sequence.

Watch Out For...

• There's a scene in *Queer As Folk* when Russell T Davies made four people calling Vince at once (while he was on his first date in years) do the dramatic work of six episodes of a conventional soap *and* make it funny. Similarly, the opening scene here introduces Martha via her attempts to juggle all of her family calling while she's on her way to work (thus introducing them as well, and sketching in their opinion of each other and hers of all of them), and then drops in the punch-line of a joke that won't be set up for another 40 minutes as the Doctor comes up to her in the street...

Why Does Everyone Forget about the Aliens?

You'd think that a small matter such as whether or not the public have caught on to the existence of aliens would be absolutely, definitively, settled in scripts *by the same author in a three year period*.

Not if that author's Russell T Davies.

Barry Letts (in concert with Robert Sloman) can destroy Atlantis in two mutually-exclusive ways (8.5, "The Daemons"; 9.5, "The Time Monster") but he's clear on who's in the loop (Jo Grant and, apparently, her uncle, plus Mr Chinn from 8.3, "The Claws of Axos") and who isn't (the Royal Navy in 9.3, "The Sea Devils", Cambridge University in "The Time Monster" and Devesham Space Centre (!) in 13.4, "The Android Invasion", directed and partially rewritten by Letts). Steven Moffat can seemingly forget a story he himself wrote that went out on BBC1 weeks earlier (so many to choose from but let's just mention Orson Pink and have done with it: X8.4, "Listen"; X8.11, "Dark Water"). Yet even he did what he could to tidy up after each alien incursion (e.g. X10.8, "The Lie of the Land", despite many other contradictions between this and X10.6, "Extremis" and all sorts of reasons why six months with a dirty great pyramid on top of the Bank of England, Lloyd's of London and Liverpool Street Station might leave memorable and practical consequences beyond the reach of an amnesia field).

The obvious inference is that Davies wants us to consider the anomaly as part of a bigger picture. Like many television professionals, he has a low opinion of the public-as-a-whole, while the willingness of individuals to go with the herd for the sake of a quiet life is the basis for much of his writing. Sometimes compliance stems from moral cowardice, sometimes it's the price of compromising to protect loved ones, but it's frequent enough in his work for the similarities to show. People get to make long speeches about it in *Queer as Folk*, whilst *The Second Coming* develops the theme through incidents. *Bob and Rose* examines peer pressure from almost the last perspective one might have expected – the problems of a gay man falling in love with a woman and having to resist self-stereotyping as much as anything else. Mickey Smith's initial refusal to board the TARDIS is more-or-less typical of how Davies's characters react to extraordinary situations. The most characteristic moment of Davies's early *Who* scripts is Jackie phoning the authorities to tell them about the Doctor (X1.4, "Aliens of London"), and one of the few times this world-view returned full-strength was the mob-xenophobia in X4.10, "Midnight". What's remarkable in Davies's work for *Doctor Who* is the way in which he takes such strong feelings and downplays them, using this topic almost exclusively as the source for comedy. It's amusing that the public see aliens arrive, shrug, then get on with their lives.

Therefore, the general public's reluctance to accept that aliens exist and have been messing things up a lot lately has to be part of the same pattern. But, as with all manifestations of the dreaded Yeti-in-the-Loo syndrome (see **Is Yeti-in-the-Loo the Worst Idea Ever?** under 5.5, "The Web of Fear"), the problem comes when such incidents occur in rapid succession. In any one incident, it might just about be possible for the public to Simply Forget. Any *one* episode might be the first a specific viewer had seen, so it would be plausible. Another problem comes when you have three in the space of a calendar year for the characters and within 13 weeks for the audience. Plus as many again in each of the two spin-off dramas. Plus flashbacks to earlier unmentioned assaults from space, when it turns out that this incident wasn't in the present-day or near-future, but shortly before one or two of the others (X5.1, "The Eleventh Hour" is especially guilty on this score). After all the effort put into plausible characterisation, the basic idiocy of the characters' reactions if seen in the wider context is an unfortunate obstacle. Is this deliberate too?

Once it became clear that all (or most) of the previous series' invasions were still in play as historical events in the twenty-first century *Doctor Who* Britain, the public's ignorance or amnesia became glaringly obvious. Rose clearly had no idea about anything Sarah Jane Smith was telling her (X2.3, "School Reunion") despite Mickey's now-obsessive Doctorological researches. What's interesting is that, by this point, the new series had generated enough invasions and general weirdness for the basic joke of X2.10, "Love & Monsters" to be how anyone could *not* be aware of all this. Throwing all the 1970s allusions into the mix was a premeditated act, and one with inherent risks. There had only been one outright continuity reference to the previous iteration of *Doctor Who* – the Doctor plucking the name "Jamie McCrimmon" from out of the air (X2.2, "Tooth and Claw"). Hitherto, all the references to the Doctor's presence in our history were new-fangled things like the cheesy Deeley Plaza still (X1.1, "Rose"), in an episode that re-worked a previous mass panic

continued on Page 37...

and *then* we see her get to work at a hospital, register some strange men in black leather (the Slabs) and put on her white coat. The elapsed screen time from the end of the titles to Martha getting a static shock: exactly two minutes, by which time we know her as well as we ever got to know Tegan or Vicki.

• The Doctor's encounter with the Stig... sorry, the Slab in the X-ray room ends with a peculiar little scene when we find that Time Lords can channel radiation into their socks to be discarded. Apart from the obvious question of why he doesn't do this after visits to Metebelis III (11.5, "Planet of the Spiders") or the Naismith ranch ("The End of Time Part Two"), it's worth noting that he gets his shoes and socks back when running up and down corridors later.

• Try to count the Mr. Saxon references, including a gratuitous one about his opinion on the existence of alien life. The most intriguing is in a bonus scene, added long after the shoot had officially ended for this episode, where the intern Morgenstern claims credit for saving the Hospital. This is usually interpreted as being a bit rich, as he blustered and caved in to the Judoon, but he probably *did* save a lot of lives by not resisting overtly, setting the tone before anyone unwisely stood up to the invading space-rhinos.

• There's a moment just before the Doctor emerges in his new suit when Martha gets into the idea of being in space. There's a story we could have had – a medical student saving the world solo – which might be interesting in another series, just as Martha's supervisor, Mr Stoker, had potential to have been a more substantial character under different circumstances.

The Continuity

The Doctor Apparently he just happened to notice some suspicious plasma coils at the hospital and checked himself in a few days ago, claiming severe abdominal pains as a cover [possibly faking Haemochromatosis to make his heart abnormality appear symptomatic]. The Date of Birth on his wrist-band as 'John Smith' reads 18/7/81 [ten years younger than Tennant, which makes the following Doctor's comments about this life's 'vanity issues' (X7.16, "The Time of the Doctor" *re* X4.13, "Journey's End") seem valid]. He again demonstrates a bewildering fondness for the tacky little gift shops attached to large institutions [X2.1, "New Earth"].

Rose's disappearance profoundly bothers him; he pointedly insists that Martha will not be a replacement and warns her that she'll only be getting the one trip, as a reward for saving his life. [If that's what he's truly intending, it doesn't fit with the rest of the episode where he seems to be sizing up her potential and generally testing her.] Her rational deductions [or simply not being a nervous sobbing wreck like everyone else in sight] attract his attention.

The fake biography he improvises: he's a happily married postman who likes cake and banana milkshakes. [So he's not thinking at all about fanciful domestic bliss then; keep this in mind for one very unusual coping stratagem we'll see half a dozen episodes from now.] Somehow, he absorbs and concentrates a massive x-ray burst [50 times the normal dose] into his left plimsoll.

Having his blood drained kills him, but he gets better with the aid of Martha doing CPR on both his hearts. His skeleton appears human.

• *Background.* He's familiar with Judoon and isn't overly impressed, referring to them as 'space police' before correcting it to 'thugs' for hire. [There's no opportunity to explore whether the Doctor would have handed over Florence, the deadly Plasmavore present, to the Judoon or not; see also X1.11, "Boom Town".] Mr. Stoker's grey, drained corpse is a clue that a Plasmavore is at large.

The Doctor says he doesn't have a brother 'any more' [the tie-in books and audios suggest this is Irving Braxiatel of the Braxiatel Collection (17.2, "City of Death"), but a lot else about them has been contradicted]. In Gallifreyan nurseries [as Time Tots, maybe], playing with 'Roentgen blocks' was perfectly normal behaviour.

At some point, he assisted 'Ben' Franklin with the famous electricity-and-kite-flying experiments, and got electrocuted into the bargain. Somewhere along the line, he owned a laser spanner which 'cheeky' Emmeline Pankhurst nicked. [Some notes from the tie-in works: the novel *The Many Hands* by Dale Smith and the Big Finish audio *The Founding Fathers* have the Doctor meeting Franklin; the book *Casualties of War* by Steve Emmerson has the eighth Doctor claiming he met Pankhurst.]

• *Ethics.* Crossing his own timeline is acceptable if it's strictly for 'cheap tricks': here he slips back, approaches Martha's slightly younger self and

Why Does Everyone Forget about the Aliens?

continued from Page 35...

from an earlier story emphatically not referred to (7.1, "Spearhead from Space"). The Doctor's track-record is mumbled about in X1.4, "Aliens of London", but this is clearly intended to be a First Contact scenario gone wrong. The end of that story (X1.5, "World War Three") has Mickey incredulous that the public buys such a flimsy cover-story instead of the evidence of their own eyes – but it's significant that he isn't enthusiastic about the Doctor's offer of a virus to remove all trace of past Doctor-activity from the public record. Instead, he takes over Clive's website for a while (at least on the BBC site) and flags up previous Doctor incidents. If Mickey could find this stuff, so could anyone else (and some do: "Love & Monsters" and Donna's life before X4.1, "Partners in Crime"). As we'll see, this changes shortly afterwards, but a window of opportunity exists for anyone suspicious about how they've been made to disregard something as flagrantly real as a smashed major London monument to do a bit of cyber-fossicking.

And it's not as if they would have needed to dig too deep or too hard. Despite Torchwood's well-documented ineptitude (see **All Right, Where Were Torchwood?** under "The Sea Devils"), most of these incidents happened in public and were fairly noticeable. UNIT, after all, are an internationally-renowned global body given many high-profile tasks and with practiced PR skills. No, really – apart from two odd incidents when a flustered Brigadier Lethbridge-Stewart claims that he's in charge of something so secret that nobody has ever heard of it, the simplest fact to glean from the old episodes is that UNIT are about as prominent as the International Red Cross (also based in Geneva, oddly enough). The obvious place to start is the remarkably frequent appearances of Lethbridge-Stewart on telly. We are left to assume that Harold Chorley ("The Web of Fear") interviewed Colonel Lethbridge-Stewart (as he was then) after the Doctor softly and suddenly vanished away. Chorley seems to have been rather prominent (a hybrid of David Frost and Alan Whicker, both regularly on our screens in 1968). By the time the strange "Man from Space" is reported to be at Ashbridge Cottage Hospital ("Spearhead from Space"), a huddle of reporters can identify the Brig in a flash and he's perfectly willing to do a press conference, with film crew and stills photographers. He's also on a live broadcast of the link-up between Recovery Seven and Mars Probe Seven (7.3, "The Ambassadors of Death") and the global link-up arranged by General Carrington ends with UNIT arresting the would-be saviour of humanity.

Admittedly, when BBC3 covers the dig at Devil's End ("The Daemons"), Sgt Benton has to explain who UNIT are to the BBC (although they seem to have hired the Brigadier to do a spot of continuity-announcing), but the very next story had UNIT handling the security for the World Peace Conference at Auderley House (9.1 "Day of the Daleks"), and once again the cameras aren't prevented from having the head of this supposedly hush-hush organisation in full view on the BBC news. Similar ambiguity happens in 8.2, "The Mind of Evil", which has the prison's Governor ask what UNIT is (for new-viewers-start-here purposes as much as anything), but ends with the Brigadier raiding that prison and making an announcement that assumes that hard-cases who've been banged up for years know who he is and what UNIT does. "The Time Monster" has UNIT well-enough known that Stuart Hyde can recognise their logo from a very long way away and be unsurprised that official scrutiny of the TOMTIT machine includes them. The first time anyone says anything about UNIT being secret is the Brigadier castigating Dr Tyler, in the notorious "Liberty Hall" gag in "The Three Doctors" (10.1). Moments later, we see *a dirty great sign outside UNIT HQ* proclaiming that the site is run by Brigadier Lethbridge Stewart but owned by the Ministry of Defence, bafflingly, and no unauthorised personnel are admitted. It's not exactly Men In Black. Other than that, a confused Brigadier reiterates UNIT's official non-existence to the Doctor, notably in 20.3, "Mawdryn Undead", and that's yer lot.

Off-screen, the UNIT pages on the BBC's website claimed that there was a low-key admission after the Sycorax incident, but that they had no idea how the ship blew up (because this was being written while the whole Torchwood storyline was unfolding). Within the halo of off-screen material about the television episodes, there was the curious detail that Mickey – the main source for anyone looking to find out more about the aliens after the episode ended – left our dimension and the series shortly after the Deffry Vale incident ("School Reunion"). The in-universe account seems to have been that he'd finally decided to use the disc the Doctor gave him at the end of "World War

continued on Page 39...

undoes his tie, then pops forward with the loose tie so she knows that he does actually have a time machine. He apologises before full-on snogging Martha – a means of transferring a bit of his genetic material as a ruse – instead of just asking permission. Even so, he seems largely oblivious to the idea that she might interpret it as anything more than a convenient way to save the day.

• *Inventory: Sonic Screwdriver.* It speeds up the process of hacking a hospital mainframe to look at patient records. It blows up when the Doctor plugs it into an X-ray machine to help fry a Slab with radiation.

The Doctor has another screwdriver at the end of the story that needs 'roadtesting'. [We might take this as the first example of what X5.1, "The Eleventh Hour" proves, that the Ship grows them for him. However, in X7.15, "The Day of the Doctor", we get a whole sequence about how the device each iteration of the Doctor carries is the same one with a different case. The implication is that, once again, we can use the mobile phone analogy and consider the basic core of the machine to be like a SIM card.]

• *Inventory: Other.* He's hung on to the dressing gown from X2.0, "The Christmas Invasion", the one with the Satsuma in the pocket. Ditto the pyjamas. [Later on, he pops out of his hospital bed fully dressed, so he must have had his new suit and stuff on hand somewhere. He changes back into the old suit to pick Martha up later that night – where's he been in the meantime? Perhaps it takes longer to obtain a replacement screwdriver than it appears. Or perhaps he just skipped to the evening.]

The TARDIS Has a number of familiar technobabble control devices the Doctor demonstrates during dematerialisation: the gravitic anomaliser (you close it down), the helmic regulator (that's fired up), and the hand brake. [These all appeared in earlier stories: 17.5, "The Horns of Nimon" and 12.2, "The Ark in Space" for the first two, and the Eccleston stories showed us a hand-brake but never referred to it until now.] The Doctor doesn't correct Martha's statement that the Ship is made of wood. [The number of times that circumstances keep pushing this suggestion at us, in spite of what we know about Police Box design and Time Lord tech, is getting worrying.]

The Supporting Cast

• *Martha Jones.* A medical student at the Royal Hope Hospital. [That's reason enough for her to be tetchy about usage of an unearned title. Technically, despite what Francine thinks, she can already put 'Doctor' on her passport and driving licence.] She's in her final year. [So she must be about 25. The script says 23, which is bordering on Doogie Howser territory, but also claims that Tish is two years older.]

She's the social glue upon whom everyone in her family calls to negotiate with the others. This includes a sister, Tish [abbreviated from 'Letitia']; a brother, Leo; a mum named Francine... and a dad named Clive who's dating a young, leggy blond named Annalise (of whom the others don't approve). Whether or not it's because Martha is in shock after her day on the Moon, Leo's 21st birthday party descends into utter chaos and they all start screaming at each other.

They're not much more affluent than the average companion's family, despite Clive buying himself a flashy sports car as part of his mid-life crisis. [NB: The cost of training doctors is mainly borne by the National Health Service once certain criteria have been met, so Martha becoming one is no indication of the Jones family's wealth. Tish complaining about her 'inheritance' isn't to be taken at face-value, though, as they are clearly not in such an exalted income-bracket as all that. Especially if two of the three children have been through university recently and the third's just become a dad, and a divorce is in the offing. Tish is grasping at anything with which to berate Clive, avoiding the real issue of his dating a woman about the same age as her.] Martha strives to be diplomatic, but hatches a fiendish plan with Tish to disincline Annalise from attending Leo's 21st.

She's heard about the most high-profile alien interventions in the last few years, including the battle at Canary Wharf which claimed her cousin Adeola [X2.12, "Army of Ghosts"]. Nevertheless, she doesn't initially believe the Doctor's claim that he's non-human. It takes a platoon of charging Judoon shouting the same thing and running a scan on him to convince her.

As befits a doctor, she demonstrates presence of mind when confronted with an unexpected situation, such as working out that hospital windows aren't air-tight. She despairs for a moment when the Doctor's apparently dead, then sets about CPR in a perfectly professional fashion, with correction

Why Does Everyone Forget about the Aliens?

continued from Page 37...

Three" and wipe his and Clive's files and all other online evidence of the Doctor. (This seems to be the Bad Wolf virus that made LINDA have to work harder in "Love & Monsters".)

Add to this two separate evacuations of London ("The Web of Fear" and 11.2, "Invasion of the Dinosaurs"), Nessie in the Thames (13.1, "Terror of the Zygons") after a mass radio blackout that must have annoyed viewers, everyone dozing off unexpectedly (6.3, "The Invasion"), Concorde going missing over the Atlantic (19.7, "Time-Flight") and a fairly serious health-scare starting with a Whitehall official (7.2, "Doctor Who and the Silurians") and it's no wonder that everyone seems to have heard of UNIT... except when no-one has. Moreover, the Doctor has appeared on screens on a number of occasions, often with UNIT nearby but not always ("The Daemons", for example). By the time he's being photographed arriving at 10 Downing Street ("Aliens of London"), it's pretty clear that he knows better than to draw attention to himself by Obviously Not Wanting to be Seen.

So how can anyone *not* know about aliens even before the Slitheen scam? Temporal jiggery-pokery is one possibility, but here the migraines begin. It's *just* about feasible, for instance, that one of the biggest on-screen incidents we see is from a timeline that's somehow been removed (see **Was There a Martian Time-Slip?** under X4.16, "The Waters of Mars" for the argument that "The Ambassadors of Death" has un-happened and what complications this causes). Similarly, one could argue that "Dalek" (X1.6) takes place in Harriet Jones's erased Golden Age, as it occurs in a 2012 when nobody knows anything about Daleks, or Cybermen, or the Doctor, or Torchwood, where the Toclafane never killed the US President (X3.12, "The Sound of Drums") and where Adam can think he's a bit of a rebel for believing that aliens have visited Earth. The Daleks removing Earth, flying down to zap random pedestrians and making Paul O'Grady do a gag about it seems to have been one of those awkward moments of continuity that fell down the crack in Amy's wall (X4.12, "The Stolen Earth" et seq, X5.3, "Victory of the Daleks").

We could, at a pinch, include "Invasion of the Dinosaurs" in this list, as it seems to end with the Timescoop shoving part of the story into a limbo dimension that only those people who've been in a TARDIS can recall (see **He Remembers This *How*?** under "World War Three" and **Is Arthur the Horse a Companion?** under X2.4, "The Girl in the Fireplace"). Sadly, the rewritten event's not the part of the story that has London evacuated when Dinosaurs Rule the Mall. Nevertheless, you'd think it would come up in the endless revisions of 70s British History that get trotted out, along with the supposedly much more significant week or so when rubbish wasn't collected and the allegedly world-shattering appearance of the Sex Pistols on a local news show watched by about 15 people, most of whom were warming up the telly for *Crossroads* and probably on the toilet or making tea when it happened. The ways in which public memory can be manipulated will be investigated further later on.

Personal memory, however, is another matter. There is only so much an official cover-story can conceal. Incidents in anyone's life are possible to bury if they have no consequences but the loss of a relative, or having to move house, or even simple matters such as working on something that is abandoned (think of all the construction workers who must have been hired for the various Big Scientific Bases in Season Seven) will be there in the family's story, glaringly at odds with the orthodox received opinion. These days, such things get memorialised online so, even if only a few people ask questions or bring up inconvenient facts, the cumulative effect will be there for anyone to find...

...*should they wish to*. This is, ultimately, the most damning thing Davies has to say about the public: that they don't question enough. It's evidently possible that anyone who holds a minority opinion about the activities of various governments might be right once in a while – there are so many people fulminating online, even if 1% of them are onto something (rather than just on something), it could be explosive. But even if Clive Finch is exactly right, who would know in amongst the green-inkers and tinfoil hat-wearers, Moon Landing Deniers, hoaxers and Katie Hopkins? The Slitheen cunningly made their plan so like David Icke's deranged theories (see 18.1, "The Leisure Hive"), or those dumb Hollywood blockbusters where aliens attack London's tourist spots and leave the infrastructure alone, as to be unbelievable until it had happened. Nonetheless, the process of asking questions is not invalidated because these assorted loons online believe they have

continued on Page 41...

for the extra heart. She seems less than sure of her medical expertise when her instructor puts her on the spot, as is traditional, and she's sufficiently muddled concerning the patient's bicardial system. When told to operate the X-ray machinery in a siege crisis, she starts the instruction manual at page one, proceeds for a few seconds and then abandons this for just hoping she's hit the right button.

Until the Doctor gives her a full-on snog, Martha doesn't show any signs of romantic interest – but she's clearly bowled over by the 'genetic transfer' and spends half of her intro TARDIS scene trying to tease the Doctor into showing some interest. When this fails, she temporarily eases off an increasingly awkward conversation and tells the Doctor that she "only goes for humans". As with Rose, Martha initially demurs on the offer of travel in a spaceship, but perks up after learning it's a time machine [though she'll not show any special interest in history except as a tourist location].

• *Tish.* Flighty and apparently more concerned about money than Martha, Tish spends most of the day trying to get her sister to magically repair all the family problems. She's suitably concerned when the entire hospital vanishes, but promptly returns to normal when Martha shows up again in one piece, if noticeably the worse for wear.

We don't hear Tish say anything about impending employment – despite her getting two high-profile jobs in the space of four days later this series – or indeed the election [although with Saxon getting such a majority, it might not make for very interesting news]. She's the only family member who's planning to have lunch with Martha [depending on one's interpretation, this is considerate, clingy, or a simple coincidence stemming from her having the day off (somehow)]. Cheap presents offend her sensibilities, and seem to confirm her opinion of Annalise as a gold-digger. [We'll see in X3.6, "The Lazarus Experiment" that "soap" is her all-purpose put-down.]

The Non-Humans

• *Judoon.* Large stocky humanoids with rhino heads. The head is exactly like a terrestrial rhinoceros, to the extent of having two horns in line along the nose [most Skiffy approximations just have the obvious one]. They wear black leather-looking spacesuits with large metal helmets, and small skirts made from strips of leather. They have reinforced boots with platform soles. [The net effect made a glimpse of them in a trailer convince older fans that the Sontarans were coming back (see next year and Volumes 3, 4 and 6).]

As space police, they seem to conform to their own legal codes [see X4.12, "The Stolen Earth" for the probable source of these] and have no interest in anyone else's notions of morality. They have some sense of responsibility, paying Martha compensation of some kind for a lengthy scan. When threatened, they perform an instantaneous judgement and kill the offender. They are pedantic, officious and entirely governed by the rules [literally hide-bound, in fact]. They're not terribly bright – when the Doctor hacks the system to identify the patient they seek, they delete the entire database instead of looking at it themselves. As he calculates, they don't bother to re-check a floor they've already been through, unless prompted by a chance discovery of alien genetic transfer.

The Judoon use a technology reliant on water and static electricity to teleport the hospital to the lunar surface, out of Earth's planetary embargo and thus within their jurisdiction. [Mention of "static" and teleports seems to indicate repurposed Dalek tech; we later see, in "The Stolen Earth", that the Judoon work for the Shadow Proclamation, and thus may have been part of how the Higher Races put things back together after the Time War. See **Things That Don't Make Sense** for the water aspect.]

Biologically, they require air, but have lung reserves great enough to keep them functioning in an airless location for the length of this mission. Their language seems to consist of gruff monosyllabic words rhyming with "door", so a typical sentence might be "Tor! Dor! Mor! Gor! Lor! Nor!" [In the script, helpfully posted on the BBC's *Writer's Room* site, it's written as 'Bo! Sco! Fo! Do! No!' and so on, but Nick Briggs's delivery is more like what we said.] The spaceships they use are cylindrical and resemble office-blocks with small landing-struts ["small" in the sense of "only the size of a lamp-post"].

• *Slab.* An animated hunk of leather, used as heavy muscle by other species. They prefer to travel in pairs. At least for Earth purposes, they look like motorbike courtiers in reflective helmets. We don't hear them talk at any point.

• *'Florence Finnegan'.* The Plasmavore posing as a little old lady presents symptoms consistent

Why Does Everyone Forget about the Aliens?

continued from Page 39...

found The Answers, any more than their refusal to listen to any doubt makes doubt a bad thing.

However, the characteristic of twenty-first century threats to London (and the rest of the world, mentioned in passing) is that we get to see the ordinary families get affected, children menaced by Cybermen in their living-rooms, and wives blubbing as husbands stand on rooftops – as opposed to just having "ordinary bloke" characters who info-dump and then die, leaving the city in the more experienced hands of Sgt Benton, Mike Yates and assorted cannon-fodder. Many, if not most, of the members of the public who witness these remarkable, if increasingly frequent, incidents live to tell the tale. The biggest incident of the lot, the day everyone became the Master (X4.17-4.18, "The End of Time"), must have been recorded on CCTV and have seeped into folklore as the Christmas everyone had the same nightmares, but can't remember what they were doing for a few hours. This *can't* have unhappened, because the Doctor regenerated as part of it (and the incident is referred back to in *The Sarah Jane Adventures*, by a Doctor who's sealed the Crack but, as we've seen, this isn't conclusive on its own). Other than this, there are Ghosts all around the world (X2.12, "Army of Ghosts") who become Cybermen, a world-wide eco-disaster (X4.4, "The Sontaran Stratagem") and umpteen others we'll list shortly, but most obviously of the ones we can't brush under the carpet, a third of the population of Earth spent Christmas morning standing on high ledges ("The Christmas Invasion") and thus in the middle of a global crisis, the British Prime Minister takes over the airwaves to ask the Doctor for help. By name. Nonetheless, we are expected to believe that LINDA are the only people to have been curious about this man, even though they themselves never mention this incident.

People can live with their personal memory not matching the consensus version. As we saw in Volume 3, the general impression of Britain in the 1970s has been worked on by the media and politicians to confirm a simple, self-consistent impression, regardless of how many incongruous details or bits of family history don't fit the story. For example, it suits the Conservative Party for everyone to forget that it was Ted Heath who caused the power-cuts, not Labour. Social psychologists have investigated this phenomenon thoroughly and it's clear from countless experiments that confabulation – inventing ways to make actual sense-data conform to a pre-agreed narrative (or "schema") – is something that happens to individuals and societies alike. (For the curious reader, begin by looking up Bartlett's *War of the Ghosts* and then Allport and Postman, Loftus on Eye-Witness reliability and then get into the vexed subject of Provoked Confabulation.)

The various drugs and gadgets used to inhibit the production of memory-traces (notably the Torchwood get-out Retcon pills and the still-inadequately-explained behaviour of the Silence in Series 6) are almost surplus to requirements. Memories lose their rough edges and get worn smooth by constant handling, becoming more clichéd, more conventional (as in, following narrative conventions) and more consonant with everyone else's. Every so often an anomaly might get noticed, commented upon and then left, but soon the story reverts to normal. The folk-memory version of events gets governments elected. What makes the accumulation of anomalies overflow into a new normal is a big subject, one documentary-makers would love to have an answer for to make their jobs easier. (Or not, if they make a living from towing the party line and calling anyone who points out inconvenient facts "revisionists". These are the media-friendly historians who get television series and recycle the same four or five clips from the archives to "prove" their point, or just assume it to be self-evident and trot out daft theories.) Similarly, the efforts of various agencies to "remind" everyone of things that aren't true are obvious in contemporary politics, so the supposedly advanced technology of the Monks in Series 10 are surplus to requirements (luckily, as they can't even get their story straight on how big the Pyramid on top on Liverpool Street Station is and rather draw attention to themselves by driving around in vans with MEMORY POLICE on the side in dirty great letters).

Nonetheless, sooner or later, the scales fall from people's eyes. Each new generation asks itself how the one before it could live with something staring them in the face that they refused to acknowledge. The most damning thing about "Planet of the Ood" (X4.3) is not that people in the forty-second century are as callous about owning slaves as that loveable Caecilius family (X4.2, "The Fires of

continued on Page 43...

with a salt deficiency, as her metabolism rapidly assimilates the blood of other species. [It's unclear from the script whether she actively feeds on blood, or is merely uses it as a temporary genetic camouflage. She seems to enjoy playing the part of a gourmet when taunting Mr Stoker.] Within an hour of ingesting Stoker's blood, she needs a boost to register as human on a Level Two scan.

She prefers to infiltrate hospitals, both to loot their blood banks and have their equipment handy as a fallback plan... she can reconfigure an MRI scanner to generate a 'monomagnetic' pulse of 50,000 Tesla, to fry the brainstems of every chordate organism in a 250,000 mile radius [she uses both SI units and miles, for viewer-convenience] except her, within the scanner-room's shielding [c.f. the Doctor's plan in X1.13, "The Parting of the Ways"].

She killed the Child-Princess of Padrivole Regency Nine, mainly because the kid was blonde and pink-cheeked and simpered [so she and Martha have at least one thing in common].

Planet Notes

• *Earth*. [The *Doctor Who* universe version of St. Thomas' Hospital is called the Royal Hope, but sits on the same location on the Embankment.]

Intergalactic law determines that while Judoon aren't permitted on Earth proper, the Moon is neutral territory and therefore fair game. [This chimes with the Level Five designation we hear about in X3.13, "Last of the Time Lords", and various other mentions of Earth being under cultural sanction until we develop a few steps more ("The Eleventh Hour" and 16.1, "The Ribos Operation" have more to say on this topic).

[It's worth noting that the Doctor-less X4.11, "Turn Left" has Sarah Jane Smith intervening in the Royal Hope situation, which makes it worth asking why neither she nor any of *The Sarah Jane Adventures* regulars can be seen anywhere this time around. Parking the TARDIS well away from all the action has some awkward consequences for the script – but if it was a calling card, Sarah might have dropped by and known not to worry.]

History

• *Dating*. Martha's expecting exams relatively soon, which may help settle this in semester terms. [We've got two essays about the timing problems that come when accounting for the UK political system, but let's assume that this is a Monday, Tish's job for Prof Lazarus ended on the Wednesday, the Election was (as usual) on Thursday and so on. If "Smith and Jones" is after "The Runaway Bride" chronologically, then it's a Monday in 2008. That cuts it down to a mere fifty-two possible dates. The lack of Christmas decorations whittles out five of those.]

English Lessons

• *Mister* (honorific): As we mentioned with "Spearhead from Space" (7.1), senior surgeons in the UK aren't just doctors, the tradition is that they get to be called "Mister". A mere doctor read it all in books, but a chirurgeon (the original spelling, that's how old the custom is) has experience, innate skill and training and, if you're lucky, surviving former patients to burnish his reputation. Medicine's moved on since the seventeenth century, but we stick with the status-inversion for consultants.

• *Letitia*: Not that uncommon a name, especially after 1985 when Letitia Dean played one of the original teenagers in *EastEnders* (and kept coming back over the next 30 years). Certainly a more plausible name for a Londoner of her imputed age and backround than 'Martha'.

• *Ronald Biggs*: One of the gang who carried out the Great Train Robbery in 1963; he escaped from prison by ridiculously easy means and became a sort of folk hero for evading capture. He spent most of his time in Brazil, away from extradition, but nipped back into London to make a record with the Sex Pistols. He returned to the UK to serve the rest of his sentence in return for treatment for cancer and reconciliation with his family.

• *Zovirax* (n.): A cold-sore remedy, more properly called Acyclovir, for which someone got the Nobel Prize for Medicine. It has a number of other uses but, as a commercial product, it was sold in Europe as a specific topical cream for mouths. It was relaunched in 2000 with a TV ad about a female motorbike courier whose coldsores embarrassed her so much, she kept her helmet on when swimming or in the gym. That she drives a powerful bike around Italy while wearing high heels detracts from the whole leather = protection motif.

• *Quizmania* (n.): An allegedly interactive late-night TV quiz show, originally on Sky (the digital network) then ITV1. The idea was that the questions were so easy, the show paid for itself with everyone phoning in on premium rates with the

Why Does Everyone Forget about the Aliens?

continued from Page 41...

Pompeii"), but that after the Doctor asks Donna to consider where her low-cost supermarket clothes come from, the matter is dropped. Twenty years from now, this might be as unacceptable to anyone watching a rerun as the casting of John Bennett as Li Hsen Chang (14.6, "The Talons of Weng-Chiang") is to some viewers these days. We know this to be prosaically true; explaining Segregation to anyone not in America in those years, or conveying the seeming normality of the IRA's mainland bombing of Britain over 20 years, is hard because the daily experience that seemed so prosaic at the time is, once you think about it afresh, shockingly wrong.

It could be that something more than a simple assumption of gullibility and collective amnesia is at work here. We know that by the time Martha Jones is whisked off to the bloody Moon, there has been a concerted campaign, over at least a year, to make everyone not-really-think-about a lot of related topics. In the space of a few minutes, we're introduced to the ideas of the subliminal suggestions put out via the Archangel satellite network and the shiny new *deus ex machina* of the Perception Filter. We've had casual mentions of this before, mostly connected to the Chameleon Arch and the watches containing Time Lord Essence in orange sparkly pixie-dust form (X3.8, "Human Nature"; X3.11, "Utopia"), but now a lot of effort is put in to making the two ideas chime ("The Sound of Drums"). The Doctor's version is a Glamour, a method of making people not take in what's right in front of them. His plan is to use this on the Master to counter-act the Archangel signal and, somehow, make everyone see him for what he is.

We've been working on the assumption that, after the end of this story (X3.13, "Last of the Time Lords"), Captain Jack or the Doctor jury-rigged Archangel to make everyone blasé about the US President being destroyed on live TV in front of, well, everyone, by aliens working for the now-vanished British Prime Minister. It seems to fit, yet nowhere in any of the three series is this ever stated or alluded to even in passing. The subsequent stories assume that everyone's fine with Winters being zapped and yet another power-vacuum in the UK after the most popular Prime Minister ever disappears into oblivion. As we have seen (in **How Long is Harriet in Number 10?** under "The Christmas Invasion"), this is not long before the *Titanic* almost hits Buckingham Palace in a near-deserted London, so the public are beginning to get the hint – and yet the Doctor, who was Britain's Most Wanted along with Martha and the head of Torchwood (who went back to being secret soon after) could wander around unspotted. Evidently, *something* has been done to the public.

Look at what's *not* said, though. The Perception Filter scam works by everyone failing to properly register something – its use in subsequent stories (e.g. X5.4, "The Time of Angels") means that it could just as plausibly be called a "Stupidity Ray". If something disrupts this cloud of unknowing, then all of this is undone. Every time a new alien menace appears in the skies, the bubble would burst and all the other ones would spring back into everyone's recollection with the additional question of what could have made everyone forget. And if they all forget *again*, the next one will have that additional outrageous mass-deception to add to the anger. After a while, this would fail to work. We saw in "Frontier in Space" (10.3) that when a small external interruption is introduced (in that case, a high-frequency pulse that triggered the brain's fear-response), memory and perception altered themselves to fit the subject's stimulated prejudices, but the key point there was that once people knew that this was what was happening, it failed to work. The most important part of the spell is its own invisibility.[9]

That would make life easier if people didn't still act as if nothing like (say) the Sontarans had ever happened before, even after the Saxon scam. The Perception Filter theory doesn't cope. Admittedly, the deaths caused by the Adipose (X4.1, "Partners in Crime") make the headlines, rather than the small army of cute glutinous sacks and the spaceship landing in West London; admittedly, we know that Mr Smith is running interference, and that Sarah Jane operates a side-line in creating more plausible cover-stories than the government/s have managed, but the cracks are showing.

It's a running gag in *Torchwood* Series 2 that the police and random old ladies in Cardiff sort-of know about them. "Sort-of-knowing" is the stage between outright denial and simple acceptance. In Britain, we're used to hearing stories about racial segregation in 50s America or 70s South Africa and wondering why nobody did anything.

continued on Page 45...

answer. In practice, the fun was seeing people getting very basic questions very wrong, since anyone with any glimmer of intelligence recognised it as a scam and stayed well away from entering. It went off the air around the time this episode was shown.

The Analysis

The Big Picture As usual, we'll start with the bleedin' obvious. From some pop-science book or other, Russell T Davies has picked up the factoid about kissing being an exchange of pheromones and enzymes, reinforcing a chemical bond between partners. As a method of setting up the whole unrequited love plotline, it's a quick and easy fix (although apparently only if the recipient is young and female – and see **Things That Don't Make Sense** for the first of many quibbles this year about the inability of anyone involved to look up what "DNA" or "genetic" mean).

The second most obvious thing to point out is that shortly after Series 1, there was a Disney-funded film version of *The Hitchhiker's Guide to the Galaxy* (2005). This had a lot going for it, not least some new jokes at last (after the 1978 radio series had been done as a book, a record, *two* stage-plays, a dodgy TV series and itself repeated about once every two years), and in particular refined the roles of the Vogons. These space-monsters were, in the Radio 4 version, exaggerated versions of the jobsworth demolition men trying to knock down Arthur Dent's house (and their leader was played by Bill Wallace in both cases), but this got lost in various reiterations and they became all-purpose spoof *Doctor Who* monsters. The film not only reactivated their blinkered, bureaucratic, by-the-book approach, but gave them a look not a million miles away from how the Judoon appeared – and spoke. As the voice-artistes were the League of Gentlemen (see last volume and most of this one), with singing by Neil Hannon (see last story) and narration by Stephen Fry (see X2.11, "Fear Her"), we have a lot of grounds to make a claim that this is what Davies had in mind.

Just to seal the deal, the book and record describe the Vogon Constructor Fleet's arrival with a memorable phase about the ships looking like office-blocks that hang in mid-air in "much the way bricks don't". The animatronics on both species were by the same company. This episode's gags about receipts and compensation claims are part of the general sense that police-work has become bound up in the insurance/ redress culture that has followed deregulation of the legal profession, and that most of policing now is paperwork. Although we are still nowhere near as litigious as the US, the last 20 years has seen a ballooning of the first-resort use of lawyers and daytime television is stuffed with ads for ambulance-chasing solicitors. Aliens who look like Earth animals stomping around the Moon in space-suits was also a feature of Gareth Roberts's *DWM* strip "The Lunar Invaders", but this time they were cows. This was, of course, derided as "silly" by people who, 12 years later, had no problem with rhino-men.

The Slabs have an obvious referent in couriers and, as stated by Martha, the Zovirax advert, but also the blank visors of astronauts (Steven Moffat will play off that *a lot*, but it was done pretty much as well as possible in 7.3, "The Ambassadors of Death"), the Stig, a supposedly anonymous driver from the bafflingly popular reboot-before-last of *Top Gear* and, most overtly in the dialogue, the Leathermen from *Barbarella*.

On to obvious bleeding: in a story about a 'Plasmavore' (because 'Haemovore' has already been taken – 26.3, "The Curse of Fenric"), it's sort of assumed that you'll wink at Bram Stoker somehow. "Horror of Fang Rock" (15.1) alluded to the vampire story it had replaced by having a character called "Harker", but here they make it plain by having a senior consultant called 'Stoker'. This was also the name of a character in the children's ITV series *Children's Ward* created by Paul Abbott, for which Davies and Paul Cornell, among others, wrote. Stoker is, of course, patronising and brisk when leading a gaggle of junior doctors around to observe patients as though they were only in hospital to serve as visual aids. This approach to medical training is still vestigially around, but belongs in a 1950s/ 1960s British comedy film.

Trust us on this – the Rank studios churned out so many that there were two based on the same stage-play in three years (*Twice Round the Daffodils* and *Carry On Nurse*), but the *real* benchmark for this sort of scene is James Robertson Justice as Sir Lancelot Spratt in the umpteen film adaptations of Richard Gordon's *Doctor* books (see 25.1, "Remembrance of the Daleks" for our Doctor reading the first book). There were seven films, (and then a TV series that went into seven iterations) and a radio version, and that's without the

Why Does Everyone Forget about the Aliens?

continued from Page 43...

The most sensible answer is that any one person who *did* was squashed like a bug, and any group of people would have been met by force from the institutions or a similarly-motivated group of citizens who favoured the status quo. Nobody wants to be the first. (This is also true of confronting elderly racists on public transport, or – until recently – complaining about outright lies in newspaper headlines.) Taking a stand isn't considered cool so, once again, while making waves on any alien planets they visit might be possible, the Doctor and his chums try not to do anything that might change present-day Britain. In *The Sarah Jane Adventures*, the whole "cool" issue has been defused, and the one character who constantly swallows the official explanation of what she's just seen is Chrissie, Maria's mum. We know from her last appearance that she's been fully aware of what was going on, but settled for a simpler life – one that made sense within her usual frame of reference.

Anyone seeking to inhibit the widespread public acceptance of aliens doesn't have to nudge too hard. A Stupidity Ray might handle any one incident, as might a flimsy cover-story, but making anyone who says "hang on..." seem like anything other than a lone nutter takes more effort by more people. It requires generations of habits-of-thought to be unpicked.

Thus, when the Royal Hope Hospital pops off to the Moon, there's a ludicrous story about mind-altering substances in the air which – apart from not explaining why the plumbing and electricity of the hospital building would need to be reconnected – is manifestly not working on anyone smarter than Annalise. (Which is everyone, really.) Perhaps such a transparently implausible story is part of Saxon's campaign. The long-term cover-up of aliens is something he wishes to expose and end, as part of his image as the man with the truth about Earth's destiny. Once again, on its own this makes sense. The trouble is that *next* time the aliens mess with us, everyone's not only forgotten Saxon's antics but all the things he made such a fuss about making sense of at last.

Davies's view of the public is not a generous one. He shows the ease with which the most popular Prime Minister in living memory can be toppled with six words in the right ear ("The Christmas Invasion"), has people duped by consumer technology and money-off vouchers ("Rise of the Cybermen", "The Sontaran Stratagem" and of course "The Sound of Drums") and assuming that anything unusual is the work of some tabloid bogey-man (X4.11, "Turn Left" and "The Sontaran Stratagem" again). Add to this his take on Sunny Delight's bizarrely successful UK launch and abrupt fall (*SJA*: "Invasion of the Bane") and the repeated message is "you are all sheep". Let's be generous and assume that he's trying to goad people into being less compliant.[10] Yet within the world of this apparent allegory, we need to find some analogue to the mass-manipulators who would routinely be blamed for such maleficent machinations. Which is to say: within the *Doctor Who* version of current society, who stands to gain from such hoodwinkery?

There are several bodies who might want the public to not know about the existence of aliens – or at least not yet. We are constantly being told, not least in *Torchwood*'s title-sequence, that things are about to change and the world has to be prepared for it. The aliens themselves (or at least those not planning an invasion, who obviously have their own reasons for not wanting anyone here to suspect their nature and intent) seem to have a cultural embargo on Earth until it is ready. We have a separate essay on the apparent anomalies between the three – *three* – official bodies who seem to be policing this (**What Happened in 1972?** under "Dreamland"), but it might well be that some more orthodox agencies have a lot to lose if the public stops thinking of Earth as the be-all and end-all. The advent of an intelligent, advanced race is bad news for most of the NASDAQ companies and a large selection of the FTSE 100. A consortium of car manufacturers, defence contractors, computer hardware developers and similar soon-to-be-vanquished companies might well want to delay the public's decision to not bother with anything locally-made. We have seen how powerful industrial and economic organisations intervene – through advertising, paying for slanted news coverage or other more devious means – to stop the public changing from a set of profitable (for the companies) habits to one that is more sensible. Consider how long it took to get anyone to listen to health warnings about smoking when the tobacco lobby held sway over TV and sponsored politicians, or the amount of money that's gone into making fears

continued on Page 47...

various *Carry On* films (and almost-*Carry On* farces such as *Nurse on Wheels*) that trod the same ground. And they all had Joan Sims in (23.1, "The Mysterious Planet"). If you were watching telly in 70s Britain, you would have seen literally hundreds of versions of that scene. (We will return to this in the next story.)

Something so obvious, we almost forgot it is the number of medical-based series on telly when this was first aired. The main one is, of course, *Casualty* (sort of the sister-show to *Doctor Who* when it began in the late 80s) and its spin-off *Holby City* (in which Freema Agyeman had first worked with Hugh Quarshie – see X3.4, "Daleks in Manhattan"). These are made in industrial quantities. The only way ITV could compete was by setting their medical dramas in picturesque rural areas (notably *Peak Practice*) the past (e.g. *Breathless*) or both (*Heartbeat* and its spin-off *The Royal*). The private lives of doctors made *Cardiac Arrest* (1994) the obvious comparison for critics when the US *Casualty* (which is how *ER* seemed at first) began.

Ten years later Jed Mercurion, that show's creator, followed it with *Bodies*. Then we got nurse-drama *No Angels* (an obvious riff on the 70s/ 80s BBC *Angels* – see Volume 5) created by Toby Whithouse (for whom see last Volume and the 2010s) who would re-use the setting in *Being Human* a bit after all this. This is ignoring all the nurses and doctors in soaps – every setting had at least one character who works in the NHS (it being Britain's biggest single employer) and the daytime *Doctors* (apparently being kept in production mainly to road-test new writers). That was the other pet project of Mal Young, whose role in getting the 2005 *Doctor Who* off the ground is often neglected (we had a go in **Why Now? Why Wales?** under X1.1, "Rose"). If you're creating a character who's a career-woman with no time for a love-life but a desperate need for some balance to her stressful job, a junior doctor is the first-thought option (followed by secondary school teacher – see Series 8 and 9).

But yes, vampire semiology requires a Full Moon (regardless of logic: **Things That Don't Make Sense** has that covered), thunderstorms that start in fixed locations from otherwise clear skies, invisible signs that a trained hunter can detect (such as the Judoon hand-scanner – note they use a crucifix mark to denote "clean") and people coming back from the dead. Setting such a story inside a modern, well-equipped hospital isn't entirely original either – vampires and blood-banks have a long association in pop culture even before *Buffy the Vampire Slayer*. Even on *Doctor Who,* it's only a year since they did a zombie story in an analogue of current medical practice ("New Earth").

An aspect of the early twenty-first century cultural matrix of the UK that will have baffled or been lost on most overseas viewers – or, to be fair, any future generations reading this – is the suspicion of most people here towards Caucasian people with too much fake tan (or a real tan gained either in an overpriced salon or an expensive holiday). The general contempt for anyone "orange" comes partly from knowing what they will look like in a few years' time (unless melanoma claims them first), but mainly for their vacuity and conspicuous consumption. (Inevitably, this has come back to haunt us, as mentioned in X10.7, "The Pyramid at the End of the World".) Game show hosts, wannabe Californians (especially those resident in nouveau-riche districts such as where Essex borders on outer London) and bimbos of both sexes are included in this category. (American readers may be getting an idea of this stereotype via *Jersey Shore,* but, as you may recall from Volume 7, the Essex Man/ Essex Girl caricature has a long history here.)

In this specific instance, anyone in Britain at the time would have been aware, if only dimly, of Annalise Hartman: a character in Australian soap *Neighbours* who exemplified many of these traits. What's odd is that Martha's father Clive sort of acquires a tandoori-tanned bottle-blonde called Annalise along with the red open-top sports-car, as if trying to do a by-the-book version of the classic American-style Mid-Life Crisis. Men in Britain, even if they have that kind of income, don't really do that sort of thing – except in soaps.

At heart, though, this story is one that begins, as a number will this year, by thinking about what they haven't done yet or would do differently this time. There have been alien invasions, but not a mass abduction; the advent of space-creatures has been greeted with curiosity, sarcasm and wonder, but not blind panic (this is, as much as anything, a strategic move to make Martha stand out for her level-headed approach). The public weren't in any position to comment on the last one, as most of them were more worried about everyone with A Positive blood standing on top of a nearby tall

Why Does Everyone Forget about the Aliens?

continued from Page 45...

about global warming seem like a lunatic fringe belief based on dodgy science, despite the acceleration of "once-in-a-century" events happening almost annually.

Theocracies, or nations where religious groups hold sway over decision-makers without any official mandate, might well prevail on their governments to dispute the existence of extraterrestrial intelligences. Since the seventeenth century, theologians have pondered what the presence of a civilisation on another world would mean to their livelihoods. After all, Christianity would have to come to terms with either a race that has no conception of God or Jesus, or that the aliens were also redeemed at the Crucifixion. Or maybe they'd find that each species had its own Saviour, and the humans weren't as uniquely "chosen" as advertised. Or worse, the churches might fear that the aliens had proof that religion as a whole was a parochial tradition. We've had 1500 years of religious wars, inquisitions and attempted genocides between just those three faith-groups, and they all worship the same deity and claim descent from Abraham. Imagine how they'd react to a proven threat to their beliefs. Within *Doctor Who*, we have had examples of the act of belief works as a psychic barrier, regardless of what is being believed ("The Daemons"; 26.3, "The Curse of Fenric"; X2.8, "The Impossible Planet"; X6.11, "The God Complex"), and yet the Vatican, the General Synod, the Knesset or the Caliphs don't seem to know about these events or this facility.

Governments, too, might wish to keep the people from taking their eyes off the various smaller-scale issues that have provided the politicians with a power-base. Where voters are given the chance to choose, the tendency has been to exaggerate the slim differences between the parties, much as two brands of detergent manufactured by Proctor and Gamble might be advertised as rivals. Many large institutions fund more than one party, just in case. If something genuinely different showed up, this convergence would become apparent. In America, the race to the White House is so frequently between a range of bored, telegenic millionaires; in Britain, we have few people in Parliament who didn't go from studying Politics at university to working for their party until they got a safe seat. (Sometimes, with a small detour into a law firm to give the illusion of real-world experience – David Cameron's one job was doing PR for the not-very-good local ITV company Carlton.) Anything requiring the public to consider the big picture, beyond a four or five year cycle of elections, is genuinely unsettling to them.

Which brings us back to Donna Noble. Whilst her insularity and inability to see the writing on the wall was played for laughs, the joke was on *us* for not resisting all the ways the public are encouraged in this view. In other works, Davies is scathing – if sympathetic – on the subject of people going along with something they know to be wrong for the sake of a quiet life. Yet, for drama to happen, there has to be a point at which this becomes untenable. What then? In different side-lights on main *Doctor Who* narrative, he offers different versions of where people draw the line. His one solo *Sarah Jane Adventures* script, "Death of the Doctor", has the former viewer-identification figure Jo Grant (see Volume 3) transformed into a globe-trotting activist constantly throwing herself into danger to protect the world from what she opposes, and somehow managing to square the circle of child-raising and political-engagement (which in *SJA* and elsewhere has been presented as an either-or for most characters). Davies tends to have no middle-ground between the domestic and the cosmic. The version of Donna who never met the Doctor ("Turn Left") screams at the soldiers taking the non-native families away to "work programmes", but in the next scene is thinking about joining the army simply to feed her family.

Even *Torchwood: Children of Earth*, which showed what happens when a government cover-up from 1965 is exposed, has everyone act as if this alien incursion is unprecedented despite several previous potentially world-shattering events in *Torchwood* that didn't really go anywhere either, *plus* the similarly apocalyptic incidents in *Doctor Who* that weren't removed from history or memory soon afterwards, *plus* the various times Sarah Jane and her Famous Five managed to prevent impacts from meteors, *plus* the Sun going out or the Moon crashing into Earth in defiance of the Roche Limit.

By following the traditional *Doctor Who* habit of making every alien invasion the first one anyone in the story (other than the Doctor's cohort) have experienced, the BBC Wales series has had an opportunity to comment on the public's inertia in a way that hits home. Alien invasions are fads, like

continued on Page 49...

building ("The Christmas Invasion"), so this is the first time we are privy to a First Contact situation without the military or politicians in the way.

Those viewers of 70s British telly would also recall an American import, not entirely dissimilar to *Butch Cassidy and the Sundance Kid*, in which Kid Curry and Hannibal Hayes went straight and adopted new names – hence the title *Alias Smith and Jones*. In the 80s, a *Not the Nine O'Clock News* spin-off starred Mel Smith and Griff Rhys-Jones and was called *Alas, Smith and Jones*. These are proverbially the two most common surnames in the UK, and statistically they are still in the top two spots closely followed by "Williams" (see "The Eleventh Hour" et seq.). The Welsh spelling of "Davies" is sixth. There are half as many Joneses as Smiths, though, and just in London everything's different.

And in between programmes in the mid-70s, you could have seen adverts placed by Unigate dairies in which sneaky beings called "Humpreys" stole milk with the aid of long, stripey, slightly bendy straws (this was all we saw of these entities). Muhammed Ali did one of these adverts. Davies stipulated "A Humphrey straw" for Florence.

Oh yes... a Judoun is a sort of Arabic guitar.

Additional Sources The BBC's website had an alien "fact file", narrated by Captain Jack Harkness, detailing all the things that could get you in trouble with the Judoon – the most interesting thing is that they were banned from Earth a hundred years ago after "The Balmoral Incident". Apparently, even not having a television licence is bad news.

The first of the "quick reads" BBC books, *Made of Steel* by Terrance Dicks, has Martha meeting Cybermen and enlarges on the idea that she knows some of what happened to her cousin Adeola and the Doctor's role in it.

Oh, Isn't That...?

• *Anne Reid* ("Florence Finnegan"). To readers of these books, she was Nurse Crane in 26.3, "The Curse of Fenric", but she's done quite a bit more than that. She was Daniel Craig's love interest in *The Mother,* but had earlier been half of a double-act in Victoria Wood's sitcom *dinnerladies* (sic) with Thelma Barlow (X3.6, "The Lazarus Experiment"). She'd been in *Linda Green*, so the production team knew her (she was Mrs Mott in the episode Russell T Davies wrote). She'd been in *Life Begins*, directed by Charles Parker. She was the voice of Wendolene in *Wallace and Gromit: A Close Shave*. But more, much more than this, she was Ken Barlow's first wife in 70s episodes of *Coronation Street*. Basically, she and Roy Marsden are television royalty. Speaking of whom...

• *Roy Marsden* (Dr Stoker) has a long line of cops under his belt – notably Adam Dalgliesh in the PD James adaptations – but had earlier been something of an action-hero. His stand-out role was as Neil Burnside, in the remorselessly realistic espionage series *Sandbaggers* (calling it a spy show is massively misleading). Then came a more dashing role in the Sunday night series *Airline*, in which he co-starred with a Douglas DC3 (which he learned to fly for the series) and his real wife. He had been in the peculiar post-apocalyptic play *Stargazey and Zummerdown* in the 70s and has about half a century of television work under his belt. He's now concentrating on theatre directing.

• *Adjoa Andoh* (Francine Jones) had been one of the cat-nuns last year, but is mainly a theatre performer (and an occasional lay-preacher). She played Condoleeza Rice in a play at the National Theatre. Her telly credits are nonetheless extensive, especially playing mums (such as the rebooted *The Tomorrow People*, see X2.12, "Army of Ghosts"), doctors, lawyers, senior cops – and the head of MI9 in kid's show *MI High*. Her main feature film role is in *Invictus*.

• *Reggie Yates* (Leo Jones). Popular and busy DJ, then presenting Radio 1's live Top Forty countdown every Sunday. He'd been one of the last good things about *Top of the Pops* as the BBC moved it around the schedules, put increasingly incongruous guest-stars as host and changed channels – all in an attempt to make it lose ratings so they could cancel it. (Sound familiar? See Volume 6 if not.) His unavailability for parts would cause some logistical kerfuffles for the production team. More recently he's presented BBC3 documentaries and has become a respected current-affairs presenter. However, his biggest claim to TV immortality is as the voice of Rastamouse.

• *Trevor Laird* (Clive Jones). Aside from a bit part in "Mindwarp" (23.2), he's known for a moderate-size role in *Quadrophenia*, another in *The Long Good Friday*, a regular role when *The Lenny Henry Show* went from sketches to a sitcom for a couple of years, parts in practically every long-running drama and a lot of theatre work,

Why Does Everyone Forget about the Aliens?

continued from Page 47...

"Gagnam Style" or Rick-rolling. The Davies era ended with a phase when everyone now knew that it was true and got on with their lives with subtly different emphases, although Steven Moffat pressed the reset button and then had the Silence – who were walking, talking reset buttons – allowing Davies to retool *Torchwood* for American TV by having yet *another* world-shattering incident that nobody talks about anywhere else.

Right back at the start of the programme's development, in early 1963, the template for the series and its compact with the viewers was set. The whole point of all the Adventures in History, visits to other worlds and trips "sideways" in time was to have been a set of strongly-made hints about our world, especially Britain in the 1960s. The one "sideways" story that was made, eventually, manifested as "Planet of Giants" (2.1). It was the first idea anyone suggested for the series, even before it had a name or writers (see **Where Does *All* of This Come From?** under 1.1, "An Unearthly Child"). The object of that exercise, even in the transmitted version, was to alert the viewers to how much of their everyday life they ignore or pass over without really considering. *Doctor Who* was a series about curiosity. Part of the process of making the world fresh and strange is to comment on the ways in which we are encouraged *not* to do this by so much of quotidian life; school, popular culture, work, mortgages and so on. Thus, the repeated comment on how the public react (or fail to) in later stories, both UNIT-era Yeti-in-the-Loo stuff and BBC Wales multi-series cross-continuity, is a motif picking up on something in the programme's grain since before Day One.

(See also: **What Happened to UNIT?** under X4.5, "The Poisoned Sky", and **How Long is Harriet in No.10?** under X2.0, "The Christmas Invasion".)

mainly with the National Theatre. He's in the original London cast of *One Man, Two Guvnors*, for example.

• *Gugu Mbatha-Raw* (Tish Jones) went from this year's episodes to the notorious *Bonekickers* (see X6.3, "The Curse of the Black Spot" and the essay with X4.10, "Midnight"), some US television work and the lead in *Belle*, the film about the Mansfield adjudication. In summer 2017, she received an MBE.

• *Vineeta Rishi* (Julia Swales, medical student) had been a regular in *The Last Detective*, opposite Peter Davison.

Things That Don't Make Sense The Doctor's taking something of a risk hanging about a hospital – certainly, one where the interns check your heart rate with a stethoscope every morning. Lucky, Martha keeps putting hers on back-to-front.

Martha's a final-year medical student. Ergo, she's at least 25 years old and has been in a hectic, full-time course of training and practical hospital experience for about seven years. She can already put "Doctor" on her driving licence and passport. The hospital shifts alone would have caused her to be incommunicado for weeks at a time. Francine's had a lot of time to adjust to her elder daughter not being a kid. She would also know that after all of this training, it's very nearly impossible for Martha not to complete her stint on the wards and that by this stage it's more a matter of what she will specialise in next rather than whether she will ever be a 'real' doctor.

Wouldn't Tish getting a job with a hugely famous scientist that comes to fruition the following night – and wasn't even on the cards that morning – be something else to discuss over dinner? Professor Lazarus mentions an interview panel, so she can't have just waltzed in like a Temp the morning of the press-launch. Francine hits the roof about the elder sister hanging out with someone not approved by the family, so this highly dubious recruitment of the younger girl at such short notice would have set off alarm bells and got the parents to sing from the same hymn-sheet instead of bickering. And if Martha's at work at 12.30, in a hospital in London, has she got time for a long lunch with Tish, as seems to be the plan? Tish is going to be busy that day, the day before the launch of the Lazarus project, and isn't really dressed for the job we're supposed to think she's got. (As the first line of dialogue is Martha telling Tish "You're up early", the evidence points to her not having got the Lazarus gig yet. That's going to make less sense five episodes from now.)

What's the one thing everyone knows about the Moon? It's not got its own air. What's the one thing everyone *forgets* about the moon when making films or TV shows? It has 1/6th Earth's gravity. So why is everyone in the hospital walking around nonchalantly and not colliding with things as they miscalculate their momentum? Running (and stopping) would be especially hard. Running *barefoot* might be slightly easier, but the Doctor magically regains his shoes and socks in some long-shots after binning them when irradiated. He also manages to take off plimsolls without unlacing them first. (Fine, let's assume that if the Judoon can teleport the hotel to the Moon, they have other tech, including a gravity compensator. That said, while emergency generators are well and good, there's other considerations beyond just running out of air – plumbing, electricity and computers all work, and the place can be sutured back into London with no problems. Quite why the air in the hospital would stop being breathable the very second that the oxygen tanks all simultaneously run out is puzzling, though. It's not physically escaping from the force-field, or else everyone would burst open. Air that's been breathed isn't lacking in oxygen, it's just got added CO_2. Adding oxygen to this extends its utility for a few hours, making the cut-off point for breathability harder to predict. See X10.5, "Oxygen" for a similar mistake.)

What's the thing The Mill always forget about the Moon and the Earth? Different bits get lit by the sun at different times. If you can only see half of the Earth from the Moon's surface, it's because that bit of the Earth is pointed at the sun. Since the same bit of the lunar surface always points at Earth, anyone looking from Earth would see a half-moon. So if a half-Earth's right in front of you, the bit of the Moon you're on must be around where the sunlight is about to end (the terminator, in other words). So, seen from Earth, it's a half-moon. Yet later that day, when Martha's family are having a row, it's a full moon.

Just this once, as the landing Judoon ships make the ground shake and thus vibrate the air within the force-field, it's all right for the camera to shake and a spaceship to make a noise. However, the ships fire their engines when flying right on top of the hospital, with no scorching of the ground around the edge of that force-field, nor even a slight ripple of plasma.

An "H_2O scoop" and rain going up are effective images in the context of what's on screen. However, we're forced to admit that the Doctor's avoided explaining a phenomenon by describing it. The big problem here is that it's a dry day, despite the Judoon making it rain upwards, and... the hospital's right next to the Thames. How is the hospital more of a target than a bloody great river? How Tish can see that it's raining upwards from about half a mile away is a smaller problem. (We *say* half a mile, but the Principality Building Society sign indicates that she's in Swansea staring at the South Bank of the Thames.) With the benefit of hindsight, we wonder why if the Royal Hope's so close to Parliament, and has been there so long, Astro-Piggy got taken to the Albion Hospital, supposedly "nearest" – despite it being out in Limehouse (X1.4, "Aliens of London"; X1.9, "The Empty Child")?

The Judoon aren't massively bright, but their plan to scan everyone present and mark those "clear" with a magic marker does rather require no-one in the hospital to have another marker handy.

Let's take it as read that the Doctor thinks he get away with snogging Martha as part of a 'genetic transfer' without emotional consequences, even if most of Martha's character-arc is spent proving this assumption massively wrong. Fine, but the practical consequences of this technique are alarming. Imagine how simply (and less stupidly) the Doctor could have resolved X3.5, "Evolution of the Daleks" by this method (or something similar, like the hug-in at the end of X2.1, "New Earth"). If this is a *real* genetic transfer (and X4.17, "The End of Time Part One" needs it to have been, unless Lucy Saxon's not washed or eaten anything in two years), he's presumably spliced his DNA to Martha's in a way that would make her a prime target for the Silence and Madame Kovarian (X6.7, "A Good Man Goes to War"), unless the swabbing for the Master's 'biometrical signature' is looking for something else entirely that's transferred by a Time Lord kissing a human. (In which case, how can the Judoon detect it with their scanners set to 'non-human phenotype', rather than something more specific?) Why didn't the Family of Blood spot this with their hyper-sensitive Time Lord Detector Van? Seriously, that's a whole two episodes *later the same year* that don't work if this happens the way they tell us it does (X3.8-3.9, "Human Nature"/ "The Family of Blood"), even if the effect is transient and won't lead to her having quarter-Time Lord children.

If she's got a little straw and everything, you'd think that Florence can tell the difference in taste between species, especially as she's developed a sense of how a consultant's diet will make *his* blood different from other humans. Moreover, how does Martha's CPR, even when done on both hearts, cure the Doctor of not having any blood left?

Why is Leo's 21st birthday party happening in a pub when he has a partner and a small baby daughter? Surely, everyone would rather spend time with little Jonesy? (A few episodes from now, or tomorrow night in story time, Leo will be out on another social event in a rented tux with his sisters and mum, at which he gets concussion, then two days after that he'll abruptly announce that they're off to Brighton to see his mate Boxer. His un-named wife/ girlfriend must be amazingly tolerant.) Clive is grumbling that he paid for half of this event, but even if they've got the downstairs room in their local entirely to themselves, it's a hundred quid for the night, tops. With a car like that, he's easily paying more than fifty nicker a week on petrol, washes, insurance…

Truly nit-picking now, but there's a slight anomaly on the DVD sound-edit whereby the crashing of tea-things when the hospital's stolen is just the same three sounds over and over again.

Critique After the relatively carefree go-for-broke Christmas Special, we're back with the production team leaving nothing to chance. It would have been unfair on the new co-star to have done anything else. Instead, we're shown the Doctor being first an interruption to Martha's complicated everyday life and then an alternative to it. The routine saving-the-world-from-aliens biz ends ten minutes before the episode does. Apart from the (at first) strange business with the Doctor showing Martha his tie, his arrival in her life is well into the episode.

There's a precedent for this in "The Rescue" (2.3), when the idea of replacing a TARDIS crewmember was tried for the first time. For the majority of people watching "Smith and Jones" on first broadcast, *this* was the first time. The notion that the Doctor had travelled with anyone but Rose was a disturbing novelty in "School Reunion" (X2.3). The solution was, once again, to make it look like a series about the new main character and then drip-feed *Doctor Who* into it as the episode progresses. In a lot of ways, everything up until we find that Martha's got a white coat is like *Linda Green* recast with black Londoners. They did this well enough, showed us everything Martha would be leaving behind and why the Doctor invited her along, but we went into the episode knowing she would. This makes it as much an exercise in housekeeping as an episode in its own right, and the story seems slightly perfunctory.

The Judoon in particular seem like a parody of the BBC Wales episodes. The use of Earth animal-heads on spacesuits or boilersuits was already as by-the-numbers as the putty noses or mottled foreheads of 90s *Star Trek* franchises, but this borders on taking the piss. There's a big difference between being "child-friendly" and being "for kids". However well-executed the animatronics, let's concede that the Judoon are for kids. If anything, their re-use in *The Sarah Jane Adventures* was less infantile than this. Their "alien" language is less like Klingon (see "The Christmas Invasion" for an attempt at that) and more akin to "Flobadob" from *The Flower Pot Men* (another of Peter Hawkins's contributions to how 60s kids think all aliens ought to talk – see Volumes 1 and 2, plus X2.13, "Doomsday").

Florence the Vampire is just slightly overdone. Anne Reid's performance is fun, yes, but the part's written to allow – even encourage – mugging. In most essentials, the internal shape-changer who adopts elements of whoever she's just eaten is the Abzorbalof Mk II (2.10, "Love & Monsters"), right down to the Lancashire accent. The idea was probably to hide the alien menace in plain sight, but she and the Doctor seem to be the only patients Martha has ever treated. Even if you don't recognise one of the most familiar faces in Britain, it barely exercises the leetle grey cells. (Still, at least she seems to be enjoying herself.) As the *Being Human* pilot proved shortly thereafter, a hospital is a good location for a lot of creepiness – with ordinary humans forced into extreme situations there anyway, you can go a bit further into the abnormal than in any other workplace setting. A couple of Pond-era stories used Rory's day-job in passing, but there's still mileage. At the time, it seemed as if they'd ticked it off a to-do list without really making the most of it.

On top of this, we have two new longer-term storylines to get under way: the Saxon stuff isn't obtrusive yet, but the crush subplot is begun in the most publicity-seeking way possible and never really gels. The pretext for the Doctor and Martha snogging is silly (and if it had been Morgenstern instead of Martha, they might have gone ahead with it anyway but you can bet some plausible alternative would have been found in case the BBC bosses objected). It's pretty much a done deal that she was going to be at least invited along for the ride, but the terms of that – the Doctor's constant refusal to admit she's a fixture and the messy attempt to suggest a romance – are going to grate. Even after stepping so confidently into a post-Rose phase in the Christmas episode, the constant effort to make Martha's presence on the TARDIS seem contingent and temporary makes the Doctor look like a bit of a git. The episode goes to great lengths to show her being the one person in a hospital able to cope with a crisis (err... you what?) and admiring the view while everyone else (except the Doctor and Florence) is running around like a headless chicken. Even someone who'd avoided all the pre-publicity and never seen the series before would have worked out she was going to be one of the main characters – if she'd been a one-off, there would have been a "why not bring Martha back?" campaign.

So with every effort being made to avoid putting a foot wrong in case Freema Agyeman got blamed for a perceived falling-off, we have a story that's tasteful but flavourless. She's all right, with a bit of a spark when needed, but possibly too girl-next-door to be a convincing final year med-student (next episode's comment about A&E is harder to sell, after seeing her fumble getting a stethoscope on here). It holds the episode back from being as zingy as it could have been; they go to the bloody Moon, but never leave the building.

So job done, but not a lot else. Next, please.

The Lore

Written by Russell T Davies. Directed by Charles Palmer. Viewing figures: (BBC1) 8.7 million (and an 84% AI), (BBC3 repeats) 1.0 and 0.4 million. The BBC3 showings were the following day and the next Friday. BBC1 first night AI's were 88%, but for the first repeat, on a channel where hardly any casual viewers would be tuned, they were 90% and it was the most-watched programme that evening.

Repeats and Overseas Promotion Disney XD, as usual, excises the word "hell", making many lines seem ruder than they were. The line "Someone's got one hell of a fetish" ends with "one", making no sense at all, and Florence dies shouting 'Burn with me", which is curious with hindsight.

On France 4, it's *Le Loi des Judon*, i.e. The Law of the Judoon. The word "Judon" reverts to the English spelling in the end credits. The stellar plods say words ending with "-on", e.g. *Ton Don Ron Fon Lon*.

Einmal Mond und Zurück (to the Moon and back) is Germany's name for it.

Production

In seeking to make the new companion more than just Not-Rose, Russell T Davies opted to make the new girl's life more complicated and harder to leave behind. She would be older, and with a career that had already demanded some sacrifices and dedication. He also decided to revisit ideas explored in *Queer as Folk* about unrequited love being more honest, enduring and plausible. Furthermore, at some point it was decided that the best way to sidestep Rose's popularity was to have this character feeling second-best, until proving herself in the season finale, and then deciding to go back to her responsibilities once a crisis redefined her relationship with her family.

Most of these decisions had been taken by the time shooting began on Block Four of Series 2 (X2.5-2.6, "Rise of the Cybermen"/ "The Age of Steel"; X2.12-13, "Army of Ghosts"/ "Doomsday"). During the auditions for these, Phil Collinson had spotted potential in Freema Agyeman, who was playing a Torchwood staffer, Adeola, in "Army of Ghosts". An elaborate masquerade began – Agyeman was told she was auditioning for a lead in the recently announced *Torchwood*, and given Eve Myles's lines to read in a screen-test. Eventually, she was told the truth but asked to keep mum for a while; this gave her time to bone up on the programme's past (*Star Trek* was more her thing – photos circulated of her in costume at a convention) while keeping a roof over her head with a stint at Blockbuster Video. Unlike Billie Piper, whose native Swindon accent sporadically poked through the generally-convincing London vowels, Agyeman was a real Londoner, born in Finsbury Park (the bit just under Tottenham, near where Arsenal FC's ground had been until lately).

• As Adeola's episode was screened, news of Piper's departure had broken. As we saw at the end of the last volume, the public interest was such that not even the World Cup or a record-breaking heatwave could dent the ratings for the finale, nor the interest in everything going on backstage. Days before the viewers had to get their heads around Catherine Tate being in the Christmas episode, the press were called in to a photo-shoot of the other newcomer. Actually, this happened twice, as Tennant was stubbly from his much-publicised holiday with Sophia Myles. BBC Wales wanted him looking more Doctor-ish (despite a spectacularly lurid shirt). A nation started learning to pronounce "Agyeman" (soft G, emphasis on the first syllable), and less-experienced fans struggled to comprehend how *anyone* who'd played another *Doctor Who* character beforehand could be cast as the companion (see, of course, 2.8, "The Chase"; 3.4, "The Daleks' Master Plan"; 10.2, "Carnival of Monsters"; 16.6, "The Armageddon Factor" and look ahead to X4.2, "The Fires of Pompeii").

• Work on "The Runaway Bride" began the day after the second photo-shoot, on 4th July; just over two weeks later, the first scripts of Martha's debut episode – as yet untitled – were released. By now, Davies had thought to throw in a small hint that Adeola's relatives only vaguely understood her disappearance at Canary Wharf. The "Mr Saxon" idea was seeded here and retrospectively dubbed onto the final edit of "The Runaway Bride"; the last few episodes of *Torchwood* Series 1 had some of the pro-Saxon posters we see in "Smith and Jones" as well. Davies had thought of the name "Harold Saxon" for a malignant character in another project, and opted to use this rather than an obvious anagram of a foreign word for "Master". (This didn't deter fans, who naturally rearranged "Mister Saxon" to come up with "Master No. Six".) Note that there are a couple of Saxons in Davies's *The Second Coming*, along with an anti-Christ called "Tyler".

• There was a story doing the rounds that Davies added the line about "Judoon platoon upon the Moon" to tease Tennant about his occasional lapses into a Scottish accent when doing "oo" sounds (admittedly, his pronunciation is naturally closer to something like "Jidnnn"). This anecdote is a version of the interview Tennant had with Radio 1 DJ Chris Moyles two days after broadcast, but it's not clear if there's any more to it than that. One idea Davies confirms *was* in an early draft was the Doctor and Martha escaping from the Judoon with a window-cleaning cradle, a prototype of the scene in "Partners in Crime" (X4.1).

• One idea for the opening was that a junior doctor would get in to work and find a patient – the Doctor – unconscious on a stretcher. This didn't seem to work, as the viewers would know more about the situation than the new identification-figure. Instead, we would follow her on a seemingly-ordinary day and watch it go crazy and her cope with it. (That said, the scene of Martha seeing a stranger take off his tie, even as she coped with a family meltdown, was considered for a pre-credit teaser, but looked stupid out of context.) In early versions, the action was based on the Judoon trying to confiscate the TARDIS, which was secreted in the hospital's cellar. Once it was decided that the Ship was parked outside, the rest of the story became clearer, although this entailed the Judoon translating everything into English and the lengthy exposition scene as Martha finally sees the blue box at the end of the episode. The business with the oxygen tanks was a late addition to tell the story visually – even though there is no actual correlation between gas in the tanks running out and the air in the hospital becoming unbreathable.

• If you've read Volume 7, you will be unsurprised to find that incoming director Charles Palmer was a veteran of *Linda Green*. There's something about him no guide can avoid mentioning, but we'll try to resist for now (see X4.0, "Voyage of the Damned"). He had worked with Anne Reid before, as had Davies.

• Peter McKinstry made a concerted effort to make the Judoon technology consistent-looking. To this end it was, where possible, red and cylindrical. The hand-scanner had been built for Jake to use on Mickey and Ricky ("Rise of the Cybermen"), but that scene was cut, so it was available. In the Tone Meetings, the two main features discussed were the patients' attitude towards being abducted (genuine panic rather than the curiosity or stoicism we'd seen so far) and the degree to which the Doctor's look should change. Louise Page rejected ideas that the Tennant Doctor's silhouette should change beyond recognition, while Tennant thought more variety would A) establish time elapsing since Donna, and B) that the Doctor is not wearing a uniform, as had been the tendency in the 80s. One option was a suit and T-shirt, rather as the not-quite-Doctor would look in X4.13, "Journey's End". The Slabs were intended as a relatively inexpensive but identifiable costume, but there are few leather motorbike suits not festooned with logos. Page had to source some from abroad.

• Oddly enough, after using the Cardiff Royal

Infirmary for locations – and it doubling as a wartime hospital, a military base and Alexandra Palace – the crew opted not to use it for this story. Instead, Martha's workplace was a composite of three locations and one of the non-studio parts of the Upper Boat complex. The first day of shooting was 8th August, and began with the location work at the School of Sciences at the University of Glamorgan, a teaching hospital closed for summer recess. On the 11th, they filmed the TARDIS scene – Tennant improvised the Doctor mouthing "It's bigger on the inside..." in the last take.

• Next morning, it was back to the University of Glamorgan complex. Anne Reid had planned to play Florence with a Germanic accent, but Davies persuaded her that this would tip the wink of her bloodsucking ways a little too early. She and Tennant corpsed continuously when she had to drink the Doctor's blood. The next three days were also spent there, for assorted crowd scenes and the running up and down corridors – something Davies had decided was worth doing definitively in the new series. In one scene, when the Judoon leader (Paul Kasey, of course) scans Morgenstern inside his radio-controlled rhino-head, he couldn't see and shone the blue light up Ben Righton's nose before apparently scanning his hair and a nearby wall. When the scene with the Doctor carrying the unconscious Martha was rehearsed, Agyeman became concerned at the way that Tennant was carrying the dummy they used – he kept bumping the head against doorways and benches.

• On Saturday 19th, the production moved to the Singleton Hospital, Swansea. Later, the hospital's library doubled for the Royal Hope's foyer (with a little shop). Six Judoon costumes were made, only one with a working head beneath the helmet. The boots were a commercially-available design (Nu Rock, a company based in Spain). To multiply the six Judoon into a platoon, the crew did multiple takes from locked-off camera positions. There was supposed to have been a scene shot here using the staff kitchens, but the over-run meant that they did this the next day in the canteen of Upper Boat itself, during shooting for the next episode. Indeed, the director was too busy to remount the X-Ray machine scene, so James Strong handled this on 25th while working on the *Torchwood* episode "Cyberwoman".

• On 2nd October, they remounted the scene at the Market Tavern, Pontypridd, and Martha seeing the TARDIS just off Market Street. Earlier that day, we'd had the "Meet the Joneses" scenes of Tish, Leo, Clive and Annalise and Francine, as well as scenes of Shakespeare in his room for the following episode. Recording for "The Lazarus Experiment" (X3.6) began the following day, so most of the cast were on hand. On Friday 13th, the sequence of Tish on the phone was added, and a foot-double splashed into a puddle reflecting a full moon.

And it *still* wasn't quite done; an under-running episode could stand a bit of expansion, so the scene of Martha preparing to go out and hearing Morgenstern claiming credit and talking about Mr Saxon was shot on the 19th. Then on 7th November, the resuscitation scene was reshot and a few more inserts committed to tape; all were shot at the same location used for the lab in "Evolution of the Daleks" (X3.5). The edit was almost complete when the BBC's licencing manager, Ed Russell, spotted that the Doctor was using the sonic screwdriver on the lock after he'd wrecked his tool in the X-Ray. Palmer came back on 17th January to redo the shots, with the Doctor securing the door with a cheeky flip of a latch.

• By this time, Davies had decided not to call the episode "Martha", as it was too much like "Rose", but instead had hit on the teamwork implicit in the two surnames. Episode titles were generally withheld for longer this year, partly because of late changes of mind, but mainly to keep the suspense going.

• The aerial shots of the bit of riverside with the Royal Hope Hospital absent were processed from leftover footage shot for "Aliens of London" (X1.4). In their effects mix, The Mill added a manic blue glow to Florence's eyes as the MRI scanner went into overload. Palmer dubbed on Arrested Development's recent album-track "Sunshine" from an album released in 2006 – it hadn't been released as a single and indeed never was in the US. There was much debate over whether the camera should shake as the Judoon arrived, with the lack of air being a reason not to but, oddly, not a reason to omit any engine-noise. Palmer was of the opinion that if you have noise you can have shake but Davies – who had prevailed over noise – thought the shake was excessive and "unrealistic".

• New season trailers were made, this time emphasising the flirtatious side of Martha's interest in the Doctor, and ending with a slightly creepy split-screen shot with Tennant and Agyeman's faces forming a composite.

X3.2: "The Shakespeare Code"

(7th April, 2007)

Which One is This? *Love's Labour's Lost Confidential.* The Doctor meets Shakespeare (for the first time, honest) and three witches show up to tell his future.

Firsts and Lasts To disentangle the whole story from various tie-in works and three previous broadcast stories, it's simplest to say that this is the first time Shakespeare has met the Doctor, rather than the other way around. (We'll elaborate later.)

This is the first televised script for the series by Gareth Roberts, who did the interactive game *Attack of the Graske* and many of the TARDISodes last year. He was also co-author of *The Sarah Jane Adventures* pilot and had done an awful lot of other stuff, either *Who*-related, soap-ish or with members of the current BBC Wales regime, over the last decade. (We'll elaborate on that later, too.)

It's also the first time there something familiar from the 1960s *TV Comic* strip has cropped up in broadcast episodes. We'll have another later this year, and one next time Roberts writes an episode, X4.7, "The Unicorn and the Wasp". (We'll do a whole essay to elaborate on that.)

Discounting 15.1, "Horror of Fang Rock" (made in Birmingham, entirely in the studio), we have the first location shoot in Warwickshire, what with there being so few decent Tudor streets in Cardiff.

Watch Out For...

• Yes, that's the *real* Globe Theatre... or rather the modern duplicate that was built to approximate the best-guess of where it had been and what it was like. (They may have got it slightly off-site and only half the capacity, but the construction materials and relative cost of seats and standing-area tickets are about right.) They amend history a bit by staging the play at night, despite the whole candles/ wooden building/ straw roof business that's the main reason the original wasn't available for filming. On top of all that, there's genuine period locations in Coventry and Warwick, close enough to Cardiff to be practical (and to have escaped redevelopment, bombing raids or significant pollution from diesel fumes).

• Fanwank in-jokes? We gottem! Before his exalted post, Senior Fellow at the Shakespeare Institute at Stratford-upon-Avon, Dr Martin (J) Wiggins used to write for fanzines such as *Skaro* and *The Frame* – he once wrote a magisterial riposte to young master Roberts's accusation that he wasn't smart enough to see the virtues of Season Twenty-Three. Media journalist David Bailey (known to his intimates as "Dolly") wrote for *Doctor Who Magazine* back in ye day and was in Roberts's circle. Characters called "Wiggins" and "Dolly Bailey" meet unpleasant ends here.

• Shakespeare jokes? You betcha! As the episode unfolds, they might as well have done a little quote-counter in the corner of the screen. If that kind of thing's your idea of fun, just wait until they do Agatha Christie ("The Unicorn and the Wasp").

• Generations of scholars have debated whether the present-day Warwickshire accent is close to how Shakespeare would have sounded (imagine Noddy Holder or Ozzy Osbourne reciting the Sonnets). We know that the current Southern English vowels were only just coming in when James I was on the throne, but did any of the actors at the Globe sound like that? *Doctor Who* dodges the issue by making Shakespeare Mancunian, and Dean Lennox Kelly plays him as Liam Gallagher with a brain. Unlike many rock-stars, he makes leather trousers seem almost cool.

Then again, he affects a very posh tone when (finally!) managing to make the words "Hey nonny nonny" seem natural and appropriate. Anyone familiar with the career of Leslie Phillips (see Volume 3) will recognise the precise inflection, such as his use of "Ding Dong" in the *Doctor* films (see X3.1, "Smith and Jones" and X7.16, "The Time of the Doctor").

We also get another reference back to the Eternals (20.5, "Enlightenment"; X2.12, "Army of Ghosts"). And, an arrow that embeds itself into the TARDIS's woodwork and stays until the next time the Ship lands (as per 25.3, "Silver Nemesis"). Plus, a line from "The Crusade" (2.6) crops up as part of the alleged script for *Love's Labour's Won*. And we haven't even got to the stuff from *TV Comic* yet...

• "Fifty-seven academics just punched the air!" No sooner does *Doctor Who* provide a novel answer to the question of who the "Dark Lady" to whom Shakespeare wrote the Sonnets might be then the whole issue of half of them seeming to be love-poems to a young man gets a name-check. The script, like the Bard, seems to be having it both ways.

The Continuity

The Doctor He's a complete fanboy for Shakespeare, though not to the extent of encouraging an unsubtle come-on. Between this and Martha's own curiosity about the fate of *Love Labour's Won*, he's easily persuaded to stick around for more than "one play and that's it". The potential temporal paradoxes of his mentioning lines that will be written in later plays don't seem to bother him, even if he does stop short of allowing the Bard to nick a Dylan Thomas quote ('Rage, rage against the dying of the light'). He rolls his eyes when Shakespeare claims to be improvising Sonnet XVIII for Martha. (It's one he was commissioned to write for a blond boy, maybe five years before, but he's proclaiming her his 'Dark Lady'.)

The Carrionite attack stops one of his hearts, and Martha has to restart it – again [see last episode]. He's not impressed by the Carrionite Lilith's apparent attempt at seduction, telling her: 'Now, that's one form of magic that's *definitely* not going to work on me.' He doesn't believe in magic and believes that the source of the Carrionites' power ought to be scientifically explicable. With this in mind, he has no trouble playing along with the form of their methods, urging Shakespeare to do a bit of improv that turns their system against them. Pure witchcraft he decries as impossible.

It doesn't faze him to share a bed with the girl who was just teasing him about dating; nor does it seem occur to him that she might view it as anything other than platonic. (A line along the lines of "We're quite lucky really – for an inn this century, there might easily be two more complete strangers with us in a bed this big" would have done wonders for both Martha's peace of mind and period authenticity.) Rose still haunts him; as soon as a puzzle turns up, he starts bemoaning Martha's novice status and says to her face – while they're lounging about in bed! – that his old companion would be saying something useful right now. When Lilith tries using Rose's name to attack him, he snarls that it keeps him fighting.

The Carrionites' "naming" attack has no effect on him [as his true name remains hidden; see X4.9, "Forest of the Dead" and X7.14, "The Name of the Doctor"].

• *Background.* The Time Lords had a driving test for the TARDIS – the Doctor failed. He passes himself off as 'Sir Doctor of Tardis', since he's been given royal permission to call himself that [albeit centuries after this; see X2.2, "Tooth and Claw"].

[A cut scene referred to the Doctor's previous claims to have met the Bard. On screen, we know of at least two – one when Shakespeare was a boy who didn't say much, and later when he dictated *Hamlet* to the Doctor (both 17.2, "City of Death"). "Planet of Evil" (13.2) referenced Shakespeare being a 'terrible actor', possibly the latter occasion again. The Doctor watched Shakespeare on a Time and Space Visualiser in 2.8, "The Chase", where the writer looked more like the usual image of "The Bard" – the Doctor warns the young Shakespeare at the end of "The Shakespeare Code" not to rub his head because 'you'll go bald'. Martha's comment that the author doesn't much resemble his portraits perhaps inspires the present of the massive Elizabethan neck-brace ruff (which still doesn't resemble any of the ones in the portraits, so perhaps Shakespeare discreetly disposes of it later on).]

When attempting to explain why leaving in the middle of a crisis doesn't work, the Doctor brings up Marty McFly in *Back to the Future* [instead of showing Martha a devastated 1980 as per 13.3, "Pyramids of Mars"]. He borrows the name Freedonia when telling Shakespeare about Martha's upbringing [so he's seen the Marx Brothers' film *Duck Soup*]. He tells Martha he cried over the seventh *Harry Potter* book [unpublished when this was shown], and is apparently fond of Rowling generally. [In fact, although the idea of Harry getting middle-aged, marrying and ending his adventures might alarm the Doctor – see X2.8, "The Impossible Planet" and X3.8, "Human Nature" – it's not really such an emotional ending compared to, say, *As You Like It*. Even though the turning-point of the rather protracted duel between Harry and Voldemort really is the use of *Expelliarmus*.]

At some prior point, this incarnation has so offended Queen Elizabeth that she calls him her sworn enemy and orders the guards to shoot him. The Doctor has no idea what he's done to warrant such attention and is rather curious to find out. [This will be picked up in X4.17, "The End of Time Part One" and X7.15, "The Day of the Doctor".]

Why Does Britain's History Look So Different These Days?

So often, when Trekkies want to score points over *Doctor Who* fans, they bring up television's first inter-racial kiss happening on *Star Trek*. The sad fact is, though, that's just *American* TV – in Britain, there had been one in 1964 on an ITV soap. Moreover, *Emergency Ward 10* had it as the fulcrum of a storyline about a doctor-nurse relationship, whereas Kirk and Uhura were under the mental influence of evil aliens dressed as Greek gods so it seemed a bit of a technicality anyway. (Although, it being prime-time American television in 1968, it was a brave move all the same.) In fact, that soap opera event was two years after a recently rediscovered play shown on British television in 1962, although fewer people saw that. Moreover, exactly a month after *Star Trek* started in America, therefore two years before that eventful snog, *Doctor Who* was doing something more interesting.

Rather than just making a big thing of a character coming from Africa and being allowed to answer the phones on a starship, in "The Tenth Planet" (4.2), the minor character of Williams – written as Welsh – was cast so that Earl Cameron could go into space as part of a vision of 1980s life where race was irrelevant. That his co-pilot was an Australian called "Bluey" (all Australian characters who weren't called "Digger" or "Bruce" have that name) and where an Italian character is introduced singing *La Donna i Mobile* and shouting "Mama Mia! Bellissima!" on sighting Polly's legs in the Antarctic blizzard need not detain us. The script has its lazy stereotypes, as is usual in anything Kit Pedler wrote, an attempt to limn a future where scientists are an international fellowhood.

But director Derek Martinus nonchalantly complicated the Welsh stereotype through one of the BBC's first positive examples of colourblind casting, on prime time in October 1966. (It helped, and may have been the original reason, that Cameron's Bermudian accent was more transatlantic – because a Welsh-accented astronaut would have been mildly ridiculous back then. Given the trouble they had casting General Cutler and his son to sound similar, this is plausible.) There were a few wonky ones too, but these days it's part of how the BBC does things as a matter of course, which can cause problems when you're trying to do stories set in the past. Especially British history.

The thing is – to state the obvious – Britain isn't like America. There have been non-white Americans since before there was an America. Once that whole United States thing got started, it was with a population whose parents or grandparents had come from somewhere else – some of them voluntarily. America's self-image relies on the idea of immigration equating to opportunity, although how much this is encouraged changes from decade to decade. To base status on how long one's family has been in the U.S.A. ought to make the majority of African American households more well-established than the majority of the billionaires running Hollywood and Silicon Valley.

In Britain, it's a lot more complicated. In some ways, we've been doing this far longer; in most ways, UK race relations are a generational conflict. Percentages and numbers have fluctuated wildly over the last five centuries. Attempts to map the American experience onto our tangled racial relations only make things more confused. *Doctor Who* has been broadcast during the half-century when things have changed more rapidly than at any time since the Romans showed up with an army drawn from East Europe, North Africa and the whole Mediterranean. It's been a perpetually changing aspect of British life, especially in port cities, so it's hard to generalise. Late Victorian and early twentieth-century Britain (especially London) was odd in being so white that it was plausible that this had always been the case, so generations grew up thinking that it had. Anyone born before 1970 has seen parts of the nation, mainly metropolitan but not exclusively, abruptly get a lot more diverse. A lot of people born before 1950 wonder what happened.

What *did* happen? Well, three things. One was the advent of international jet travel, making it a lot easier to physically get from place to place; another was the shift from Empire to Commonwealth, making it possible for most people born in a former British holding to acquire the relevant passport; third and most interesting was that the Government actually invited eligible people to Britain as part of the post-war rebuilding programme. The most notable instance of this was the recruitment of staff for the fledgling NHS, a process overseen by junior Health Minister Enoch Powell. You can google him if you don't appreciate the irony, but the quest for easily-teachable land marks has made the arrival in 1947 of the SS *Empire Windrush* in London from Jamaica a fact as well-known as Trafalgar or Agincourt. We'll return to this in a few paragraphs, as we try to sketch in what overseas *Doctor Who* viewers aren't seeing

continued on Page 59...

• *Ethics.* He uses the Vulcan Mind Meld again [X2.4, "The Girl in the Fireplace"] to ascertain what's happened to the institutionalised Peter Streete, going straight to the point without attempting to gain consent. [Whether or not someone this damaged can even *give* consent is a question for a medical ethics board, although Mr Stoker's now unable to advise.]

The prospect of trapping the Carrionites in the TARDIS forever doesn't trouble him. [Is this more or less merciful than the very similar situation last season, when he decided to kill the Wire instead? Though at least this time, he's not giggling over the situation.]

• *Inventory.* The Doctor's casual attempt to fake credentials at the inn fools Martha, who's not seen his psychic paper before. Shakespeare can tell that it's blank, and the Doctor remarks on this as evidence of genius. [See **Are All Famous Dead People Psychic?** under X5.10, "Vincent and the Doctor" and, tangentially, X8.9, "Flatline".] The Doctor also has a spare toothbrush with Venusian spearmint [if you're not already familiar with the Venusian gag from the Pertwee era, try Volume 3].

The TARDIS [If we're right about the relative proximity of Martha and Tish's work-places – X3.6, "The Lazarus Experiment" has a lab right next to Southwark Cathedral, and Tish was walking to work when she saw Martha's hospital removed from St Thomas' location – and the pub they chose for Leo's birthday was around the corner from the Jones house and Martha's flat, then this one quick trip is a move of 409 years and a few yards. Since it keeps happening, we'll return to the question of why the Ship makes such a palavah about a purely temporal relocation, compared to how things go when they move planets or galaxies.]

One of Queen Elizabeth's guards shoots an arrow into the TARDIS door, where it stays put [more on this in the next story]. The Doctor plans to keep the Carrionite orb in an attic in the TARDIS. [We later see it in a trunk in the console room, under the grille floor, filed under C; "The Unicorn and the Wasp".]

The Supporting Cast

• *Martha.* She's not up enough on her Shakespearian scholarship to have been familiar with *Love's Labour's Lost* and his son Hamnet, or on the era's terminology (the Doctor: 'an imbalance of the Humours'), though she paid enough attention to history to pick up 'Tongues will wag'. On the other hand, her knowledge of basic time travel is up to scratch [the butterfly story she mentions was Ray Bradbury's "A Sound of Thunder", not the only time Bill in Series 10 seems to share Martha's cultural referents] and she knows the score well enough to bring up the grandfather paradox, plus correct her own when/ where grammar without prompting.

It's in this context that she asks about recording and flogging a genuine Elizabethan performance, and she's quick enough to take the point when the Doctor simply says 'no'. [The most remarkable thing is that after all this talk of altering history and respecting local customs, Martha has no compunction about practicing medicine in a crowded street despite being obviously female, black and dressed oddly. Letting a patient die simply won't do, even in history where, for all she knows, that person was always "supposed" to have died.]

She's concerned about the racial differences in an entirely different time period, but accepts the Doctor's casual reassurances that it'll be all right. The sight of Bedlam sets off all her nearly-qualifying-as-a-Doctor instincts.

With the time-traveller she's just met scruffing his hair and saying that the Carrionites seem to be using witchcraft, asking whether witchcraft does exist strikes her as a reasonable question. [It doesn't sound like something she'd normally take seriously.] Martha turns up her nose at a bedroom that looks absurdly clean given the time period [odder still that she's not surprised by the mucky streets].

Shakespeare offers her a kiss that she turns down, on the grounds he's got bad breath. [Earlier she expressed concern about flirting with a man she knew had a wife. Whether she's genuinely uncomfortable engaging in this sort of behaviour, or is so besotted with the Doctor that even the greatest writer in the English language comes off a pale second – or she just doesn't want to kiss anyone before the invention of the toothbrush – is probably not something Martha herself can figure out at this stage. Given that for her it's only hours since Annalise embarrassed the whole family, we'll go with the first of these.]

At the theatre, she's the sort of person who shouts 'Author! Author!'. She's apparently a fan of Peter Kay [X2.10, "Love & Monsters"] and uses his 'you're Bard' gag on Shakespeare, to no avail.

Why Does Britain's History Look So Different These Days?

continued from Page 57...

and what the series-makers – past and, more worryingly, present – have got right and howlingly wrong.

Also in 1947, the botched transition from British rule of India to East and West Pakistan, Ceylon and India as separate states with different religious and ethnic groups in charge has to be noted. It was traumatic and bloody, tainting relations between the five countries for generations. East Pakistan became Bangladesh in 1971, Ceylon is now Sri Lanka. This official end of British rule in the subcontinent left about a billion people with very mixed feelings about their former colonial... well, "rulers" is only part of it. The Raj had created an educated stratum of society who thought of a country they'd probably never seen as "home": the source of the values with which they were raised. They weren't ashamed of being Indian, or Pakistani, or Bangladeshi or Sri Lankan, and in most cases there's a sneaking sense that they think they helped civilise the English. If you speak to someone from an older generation – Desi or British – they have more in common with each other than with their own grandchildren. ("Desi" is one term used for people from these backgrounds, but in Britain they are mainly identified as "Asian", there being proportionately far fewer people from other bits of Asia.) The British, as we have seen in earlier books, adopted many Indian customs over the two centuries of the Raj, to the extent that whether the evening meal is called "tea" or "dinner" is indicative of class-status.

Yet underlying this, especially after the catastrophic Partition, was resentment for the activities of the Raj as an institution – regardless of whether any one British officer or administrator had been fair or sympathetic or any specific Indian had been a willing participant. Many of the soldiers sent to India resented it too. (Although some married local girls, or consorted with them out of wedlock – one day soon, it will be possible to find out how many of today's loudest Pakistani critics of Britain have Celtic DNA.) As soon as World War II was out of the way, the Empire was wrapped up and a less centralised Commonwealth set up, still with the monarch as titular head, but intended to be bottom-up rather than top-down.

The four nations of the Indian subcontinent have spent the last 70 years in conflict with each other, but Westminster has no more legal right to tell them to stop, or send in troops, than have America or China. There is, however, more clout from a British Prime Minister suggesting a ceasefire than any other head of state would have. Centuries of shared history can't go away in two generations. Many of the leaders and ministers of these nations in the first forty years attended Oxford, Cambridge or Sandhurst. Thus, despite the many horrifying things done in the two centuries before Partition, people from these four nations believed that, if they wanted a new, better life outside their native land, it was more sensible to come to the UK than risk America. Jet travel accelerated the process.

Yet in many ways, this wasn't unprecedented. The scale may have stepped up, but there was a non-white presence in British life for at least 300 years before this. What was different was that this time, these newcomers married each other a lot more than they married locals. Hitherto, small nooks near ports had been the focal points for intermarriage for generations. Often, these areas were fairly deprived, and thus affordable, and near workplaces where having multiple languages was an asset. One of these was Limehouse, in London – the site of the original Chinatown, and the source of a lot of prurient lore about opium dens and white slavers. Sadly for fans of Victorian melodrama (if no-one else), the evidence seems to indicate that it was a few, massively-publicised incidents rather than an endemic criminality. (For that, you needed the deprived white kids half a mile north in Bethnal Green – see 14.6, "The Talons of Weng-Chiang" for the background to this, but we'll be back in that story's purlieu later.) It was one of those regions where the East Asian community could be called a "community" rather than a few – or a lot of – single men, and thus local businesses began to cater for them and, later, were run by families of Chinese or Malay origin.

Another area with a long history of this is Cardiff. The part of the city where *Doctor Who* is made is now called "Bute Town", but for about 150 years before the gentrification it was Tiger Bay, and was the sort of place Welsh Presbyterian ministers would warn the flock away from. BBC Wales, shockingly, doesn't include this in its publicity material. Neither does the Earl of Bute's membership of the naughty Hellfire Club warrant a mention. Occasionally, Dame Shirley Bassey's upbringing in that district is acknowledged in other BBC

continued on Page 61...

At work, she's done the late night shift in A&E. She drops the odd U-certificate swear-word every so often [though the Doctor doesn't reprimand her for it like he will Wilf or Clara]. As with last episode, she gets the Doctor's hearts going again with a solid thump.

She's read *Harry Potter* as well.

The Non-Humans

• *Carrionites.* A species that relies on word-play to pull off the same tricks that most species handle with computers. Rhymes are their main method of setting actions in motion. The three we see adopt female forms. [We have no way of knowing if that's "normal" for them, or they've adopted the closest parallel suitable for the local colour.] Lilith can appear human, young and ginger, dressed as if wealthy. She suggests that the other two Carrionites with her – Doomfinger and Burbage – are her 'parents', even though they're both female, and that her species regards men as 'puppets'. Their society is definitely matriarchal.

The Carrionites possessed an empire at the start of the universe, but the Eternals ["Enlightenment"] banished them to 'deep darkness' so effectively, even the Doctor wasn't sure if they were real. [As we will see in other things Gareth Roberts writes (especially *SJA:* "The Secrets of the Stars"), pre-existing Universes before the natural laws of our cosmos solidified are a way to "excuse" outright magic within *Doctor Who*, and the language-based version of Block Transfer Computation (18.7, "Logopolis") is self-consistent within this story's rules. (See also **How Does 'Evil' Work?** under "The Mind of Evil").] Shakespeare's genius, combined with his grief at the death of his son, served to free these three Carrionites from the darkness; now, they plan to use a carefully designed theatre and a play by Earth's greatest playwright to release the rest of their compatriots. To that end, they have visited Peter Streete in his dreams and seeded his mind with the idea of a 14-sided building, to match the number of suns their lost world had.

The Carrionites kill the Master of the Revels, Lynley, by adding a lock of hair [not the follicle?] to their DNA replication module – a doll-like mannequin – then plunging it into water, which causes him to drown on dry land. [Lynley's avatar is held underwater in a rain butt, so the drowning may be simple teleportation of water from the doll to its original. It's enough like the bizarre hydrogenic virus in "The Waters of Mars" (X4.16), to be suggestive, even though it also fits with the "Evil-as-a-substance" motif of "The Mind of Evil".] However the Carrionites' DNA replication module works, it's effective on Time Lords.

The attempted Carrionite spell of "naming" Martha fails to kill her, just renders her unconscious for a few minutes; Lilith claims the lack of potency owes to Martha being 'out of her time'. [There are any number of other explanations why this might not have worked, but we might as well go with the given one.] "Naming" the Carrionites themselves will banish them away from a locale, but only works once.

Planet Notes

• *Earth.* Humans do have psychic energy. It can even be channelled, it would just take a generator the size of Taunton [cf. 16.2, "The Pirate Planet"; 11.5, "Planet of the Spiders"; 8.5, "The Daemons"].

History The crowd at the Globe Theatre writes off an entire attempted alien invasion as special effects [presumably why it never makes it into the history books]. The final *Harry Potter* book ended with a tearjerker, apparently.

• *Dating.* The Doctor says '1599'. [It must be after early July, because that's when the Globe opened and Shakespeare moved to Southwark from Silver Street. His precise whereabouts are unclear, but the script's suggestion that he was lodging now at the Elephant Inn (a notorious bawdy house, mentioned in *Twelfth Night*, just around the corner from the Globe) is definitely plausible. It can't be much later than early August, as London isn't acting like a city under siege. (There was a rumoured Spanish invasion; possibly a ploy to warn the Earl of Essex off attempting an armed insurrection via Ireland, a perceived threat mentioned in *Henry V*, the first big new play we know to have been performed at the new venue. The military emplacements and call-up of men from the field, just as the harvest was due, caused ructions and price-rises.) Shakespeare returned to Stratford-upon-Avon in early September on family business.]

In our story, Shakespeare has (belatedly) finished the sequel to an earlier play from 1597, resolving the cliffhanger ending of *Love's Labour's Lost*. [With only the final scene to go, this play would probably have been ready to go relatively soon regardless. Presumably there's some astronomical phenomenon that the Carrionites are

Why Does Britain's History Look So Different These Days?

continued from Page 59...

publicity material. If you met anyone who looked mixed-race before 1970, the odds were that person would have a Welsh, Cockney or Scouse accent. (Or Brummie, but Birmingham isn't a port – it's just got lots of canals and, back then, heavy industry. As they used to say, "you can always tell a Brummie by the shamrock in his turban"). It wasn't an especially rosy picture of living together on a piano keyboard, but it happened – despite attempts to airbrush it from the official record.

(Don't worry, this history lesson is going to have a point soon...)

The differences between the UK experience of race and the American one can cause confusion on both sides of the pond. In Britain, attempting to graft US policies and approaches onto our needs can make life difficult. For example, schools in England and Wales have adopted October as "Black History Month" – but much of Britain's experience of race was to do with India, and many teachers from Pakistani families find themselves negotiating a tricky path. Most of the cheery or ghastly stories being taught have the same basic plot: an individual struggled against prejudice, then was almost forgotten so another individual 50 years later had the same problem. In America (and to some extent Australia), the country's history *is* Black History. In Britain, the practice is, inadvertently, creating a sort of temporal ghetto.

Some teachers struggle against a notion that there's "real" English History (the stuff that the Conservative Party thinks ought to be the bedrock – Wellington, Henry VIII, Churchill) that you teach for 11 months and then time out just before Hallowe'en – with a week off for Half Term – for the stuff they are obliged to mention for sake of "balance", but which is almost always a string of homilies. In rural schools, where the minority population is vanishingly small, this seems spectacularly irrelevant. In schools in deprived urban areas, with practically no white pupils, the idea that Britain was ever *not* like their experience is hard to get across. Racial diversity is geographically concentrated into a few areas even in twenty-first century Britain.

This is simply because when anyone arrives in a new country, they tend to want to be near other people who – literally and figuratively – speak their language. It's not just a racial thing; the concentration of Australians in Earl's Court was a national joke in the early 70s, likewise Irish residents of Kilburn or Digbeth. When the first large numbers of men from the West Indies came to London, many of them were housed in a former air-raid shelter under Clapham Common. When they went to register for work and National Insurance, they did so at the nearest major office, in Brixton. That's where they all settled, and brought their wives and kids. So the next lot came to stay with auntie and uncle in Brixton, and they all moved to houses around the corner... by the mid-1970s, Brixton was home to one of the biggest Afro-Caribbean communities on the planet. (And that, for all the MTV viewers now in their 40s who wondered, is the location of Electric Avenue, as mentioned by Eddy Grant. Brixton's conveniently close to the Oval cricket ground, too.) We could tell similar stories about Greeks and Greek Cypriots in Wood Green, just north of Alexandra Palace, or Italians in Bedford and Glasgow.

Women from India had skills that the garment industry needed. The main centre for socks and trousers was Leicester. Thus a Roman encampment, named after King Lear, became the first city in Britain where the white residents were no longer a majority. It's still the only one. Similarly, all those cotton-mills in Lancashire and Yorkshire became focal points for Indian and Pakistani immigration in the 70s. And in London we have the traditional first-stops for immigrants – in East London's garment district and along the main travel routes at what was the first cheap bit, plus Hounslow, right next to Heathrow airport. So while a criticism of "Closing Time" (X6.12) – that the two non-white speaking characters are the two who get killed – has merit, the fact that they opted to cast two characters out of three non-returning speaking roles with minority actors is more remarkable, especially for anyone who's visited Colchester. (The number of children in this episode is similarly unrealistic, but that can keep until we write it up.)

A side-effect of importing Black History Month has been finding traces of Britain's previous engagement with the issues in the canon on Eng Lit. There was a fad for assuming that Heathcliffe in *Wuthering Heights* must, by virtues of dark, curly hair, a pout, flashing eyes and being a foundling from Liverpool (one of the centres of the slave trade) be of mixed origin. It's available for that interpretation, but the debate over whether Emily

continued on Page 63...

trying to cash in on, although the big one would have been the supernova of 1572 that caused scholars to finally abandon Aristotle and reconsider the Ptolemaic model. That's probably what Shakespeare was talking about in *Hamlet* I:i.

[The dates for Shakespeare's plays are fairly well-established and, as he's not talking about any plan to do *Julius Caesar*, it must be well before the 21st September opening of that play. Bethlem Royal Hospital is now used almost exclusively as an insane asylum and visitors can pay to watch the inmates – this definitely puts this story after 1598, when this decision was taken by the new management, although laughing at the freaks was not a popular day out until a bit later. Sadly, the clearest written record of *Love's Labour's Wonne* is also from 1598.]

The Doctor here seems to deliberately and knowingly seed the name 'Sycorax' into the playwright's mind, a quarter-century before he uses it for Caliban's mother in *The Tempest* [see X2.0, "The Christmas Invasion"].

English Lessons

• *Sectioned* (v.) Committal for people with possible mental health problems. It requires a qualified professional to invoke Sections Two or Three of the Mental Health Act (Section 2 is for observation, Section 3 if the patient is considered to be at risk, or to be liable to put others at risk). This isn't the technical term, however, and Martha, as a healthcare professional, is being a bit cavalier over something which, under normal circumstances, would constitute a civil rights violation if anyone not officially qualified did it to someone.

• *Taunton* (n.): A small town in the West of England, best known for making strong cider and having a picturesque cricket ground. It's due south of Cardiff, across the Bristol Channel (see Volume 3 for discussion of "Mummerset"). As county-town of Somerset, it would have been known to Shakespeare by reputation but it hasn't significantly grown since, so as a handy benchmark for size it works for him or Martha. In Roberts's debut novel, *The Highest Science*, the Doctor claims to have run the town for two weeks in the eighteenth century "... and I've never been so bored". Nothing much has happened there since Judge Jeffreys.

• *You're Barred*: What pub landlords say to undesirables.

• *A&E* (n.): Accident and Emergency. Late shift includes a higher percentage of injuries caused by violence.

• *Political Correctness Gone Mad*: What in America is termed "political correctness" is here more commonly thought of as just good manners. However, the more rabid tabloid editors, and the people who write fulminating letters and emails to them, used to use the formula to refer to anything they didn't like (not just same-sex marriages and votes for women, but regulations to prevent industrial accidents or even entirely spurious reports that the European Union was planning to ban bent bananas). Eventually, it became a running gag on satirical puppet-show *Spitting Image* that barking mad blue-rinsed matrons would yelp something like "forcing people to take tests before they can drive? It's Political Correctness gone *ma-a-a-ad!*"

The Analysis

The Big Picture We'll start with the one that most long-term *Doctor Who* fans would have spotted right off. As we discussed in Volume 3B (**Why Did We Countdown to TV Action?** under 8.3, "The Claws of Axos"), there had been a downright bonkers *Doctor Who* comic strip in *TV Comic* from 1964 to 1971. In between the Doctor meeting Father Christmas and the Pied Piper, managing pop groups and fending off Mondas-model Cybermen in their bids to drill under the Atlantic, the Doctor came across a number of peculiar one-off foes – two of which we'll come across, slightly altered, in this very book. This topic has thus enough mileage for a whole essay later on (**Are All the Comic-Strip Adventures Fair Game?** under X4.7, "The Unicorn and the Wasp"), and we'll run into one in six episodes from now (X3.8, "Human Nature"). When the Troughton Doctor and his comic-strip grandchildren John and Gillian were confronted with Witches ("The Witches", *TV Comic* #837-841; and later "Return of the Witches", *TV Comic Holiday Special 1968*), it was pretty much par for the course and had fewer innuendo-adjacent lines.

Seeing them again in the more sensible BBC Wales series, almost exactly as they had appeared in 1967, was... well, imagine if the miserably earnest Christopher Nolan *Batman* films had included Bat-Mite. Only Gareth Roberts would have dared, or even bothered, to throw in a reference to this specific embarrassment. That's perhaps the

Why Does Britain's History Look So Different These Days?

continued from Page 61...

Bronte intended it – or the historical validity of someone like that moving to rural Yorkshire and not being noticed – is more illuminating than what this would bring to the book. Race relations show up in that "real" English History we were told was all-white, too. Not just the prospect of at least two (allegedly) mixed-race Princesses of Wales, but the decision-making processes re the Crimean War, Napoleon's campaigns in Egypt and treatment of Toussaint L'Overture and even lurking in Jane Austen and World War I.

Most importantly, and a worrying precedent for today's attempts at inclusivity, the one time we can definitely speak of Britain having a substantial black community prior to 1950 was the late eighteenth century, with up to 15,000 persons around the country who would have been made to sit at the back of the bus in Mississippi a generation back. Some were nobility, some were the privileged servants of the aristocracy (and in themselves a significant capital investment, so shown off by their employers/ owners), some were freed slaves who made good – with or without sponsorship from a white family – some joined the armed forces (Nelson's fleet was more racially mixed than some parts of Britain are now), but the majority were slaves or escapees who hid in the grotty bits of the port towns.

This underlines another problem here – namely, that race and class get muddled up in knotty ways. These days, the acceptance of mixed-race grandchildren has been the biggest factor in alleviating the traditional racism of Working Class White English people over 50. It's numerically a significant proportion of families defined as Working Class, moreso than the supposedly more liberal Middle Class (those terms don't really work over here the way Americans use them, so be careful). In the Regency era, the major cities had posh bits built on money made in the slave trade and less-posh bits with beggars, many more of whom were black than at any time before or since. The proportion of non-white beggars in London escalated after those ex-slaves from America who were offered money and land if they fought for the redcoats in the American War of Independence expected the losing British side to keep to the deal. Begging in London was marginally better than being shot or re-enslaved in the Thirteen Colonies, so over a thousand ex-servicemen came across the Atlantic. Between those two periods, though, there is a phase when the only visible ethnic minorities were fugitive Jews from Eastern Europe and isolated concentrations of Indians in ports. Of course, if you were at the elite schools or universities, you had a higher chance of meeting the son of a Maharajah or an African prince than meeting a shopkeeper's son. Another legacy of Imperial rule was that the best and brightest had more chance of meritocratic advancement if they were from a British-run territory than if they were from Britain.

A small aside here about X10.3, "Thin Ice": Bill says, in 1814 London, that "slavery is still totally a thing". Yes and no. After 1807, you couldn't be a slave in Britain, but you could still own slaves overseas and trade in them, which is how the sugar industry worked in the West Indies. There had been a famous legal precedent that a slave from Boston, Massachusetts who'd been brought to Britain was no longer a slave: this was the popular interpretation of the so-called "Mansfield Decision" of 1772 (which led to, it's been argued, both the Declaration of Independence and the name of Jane Austen's *Mansfield Park* about a family whose money is from Antigua, but which allows a poor – white, probably – cousin to flourish once she leaves her restrictive background). Slavery was abolished outright in 1833, but laws about intermarriage never got anywhere; third-generation "black" Britons identified as white and, unlike the Deep South in the twentieth century, nobody questioned this or kept records. We don't know how many Victorians would have been caught by America's "One Drop" rules. (Immigration restrictions were imposed in 1905, but that was to stem an expected "influx" of Eastern Europeans fleeing the pogroms. There had already been quite a few: Brick Lane had bagel shops long before New York.)

You're getting the picture, we hope. Rather than a smooth, linear chronology of progress towards today, we have a set of situations where things have been different. We have no guarantee that the conditions in Britain today will last, any more than the situation of the 1780s proved to be permanent. You can make binary oppositions of rural/ metropolitan, old/ young, affluent/ deprived for the population of Britain and their attitudes towards most things, but you can't make a simple black/ white split, nor even a white/ non-white one. And, to be clear on this, whilst the term "black"

continued on Page 65...

most significant consideration here: that the senior fans were now able to embrace the whole of *Doctor Who*'s past, however silly, well-thought-of or credible any part of it might be. Next episode, we'll have a visit from the Macra, after that we get the same basic set-up as "The Chase" (2.8), and shortly after that a Virgin Books *New Adventures* reworked for broadcast.

Another comic adventure for the Doctor was one written by Roberts himself, "A Groatsworth of Wit" (*DWM* #363-364), which was sort of *Amadeus* in tights, with Robert Greene as Salieri. Greene had written the first known bad review of Shakespeare, and had put on earlier plays based on the same stories Shakespeare had adapted more durably and successfully at the time. He may also have partially inspired Falstaff. Roberts's story has aliens homing in on the psychic force of Greene's resentment at being outshone by a Brummie with no University background, pitched against the Eccleston Doctor – who, in his last *DWM* strip adventure, reassures Shakespeare that he would not be forgotten.

Meanwhile, the interest in William Shakespeare's biographical details had been given a big boost by a slew of thoroughly-researched works all coming to fruition at around the same time. The London years of the playwright were marked by a number of financial transactions, dodging bills, suing people for money he was owed and paying fairly substantial sums to buy land back in his home town to restore the family's status. His father had been an Alderman, and had been able to send his eldest son to one of the new Grammar Schools, but it had all gone horribly wrong, somehow. William Shakespeare got the prestige of his family name back up to the point where he and they warranted their own family crest, which he was able to pay for after incrementally enlarging the holdings of land in small parcels each year. The paper-trail for this and his other activities is, contrary to the previous orthodoxy, substantial. William Shakespeare's existence and employment is easier to trace than the life of almost any other non-aristocratic Londoner of the era.

Roberts made a point of not reading James Shapiro's *1599*, which came out at around the time he was writing this. However, Michael Wood, who usually visited ruins in South America or talked about Anglo-Saxon remains, had done a series for BBC2 shown at prime-time on Saturdays which had followed many of the same leads, and come to more headline-grabbing conclusions about the Dark Lady's true identity. This series, shown at around the time the Eccleston series ended, had the BBC camera-crews visiting places where Shakespeare had lived and some others that look like them – some of the locations for this episode were those West Midlands streets. The consensus among these and the other books coming out at roughly the same time (we could cite *Will in the World* by Stephen Greenblatt and Frank Kermode's final addition to his life's work) was that 1599 was the year Shakespeare's craft and ambition moved up the crucial final notch. From being a gifted and popular writer he "became" Shakespeare, after years of competing with nearly-equally-gifted authors who died, fled or retired.

The teaching of Shakespeare's plays in British schools was, and usually is, highly politically-charged. Education ministers and Opposition figures, especially towards the right, tend to use "Shakespeare" as a brand-name for various supposedly-unique British virtues, and as a counter to whatever nasty modern things they want to berate. The problem there is that actually studying Shakespeare shows that he was closer to the "modern" attitudes and styles – indeed more extreme in some ways – and can be recruited just as readily by advocates of completely different, cosmopolitan, liberal values, or of more restrictive, Draconian policies. However, the use of the plays as a means to keep a mixed-ability class – with pupils of differing standards of English – all passive and engaged is increasingly frowned-upon. Shakespeare is "good for you" and thus imposed upon, and resented by, teachers and pupils alike. To help with the basic problem that 1590s English and Iambic Pentameter aren't something anyone under 30 knows about, there have always been ways to try to make Shakespeare "fun". The grim nature of this "fun" can be imagined.

One method used, with more effect than some, is to establish that "The Bard" is an obstacle to understanding and enjoying what were written as plays for the public; it gives Shakespeare a "story" as a young lad who made good through talent, in the face of snobbery and a repressive regime. This is the *Shakespeare in Love* approach. Various groups have made a claim to recruit him for their cause: he was a closet Catholic, tutoring the children of recusants before going to London; he was an adherent of the School of Night and a follower

Why Does Britain's History Look So Different These Days?

continued from Page 63...

has been occasionally appropriated for people of South Asian descent, by themselves or others, it's less loaded here than in the US. "African American" may be the least controversial term in America, but no phrase for anyone in the UK really works that way. We have a high proportion of Afro-Caribbean residents from Africa, especially Uganda, Kenya, Zimbabwe and Somalia, who have arrived more recently than the grandparents of most of the West Indies-derived citizens. There are tensions between these two groups; this is yet another odd thing with Martha's family background as represented on screen. Moreover, the biggest single group of "Asians" are from families whose ancestors were moved from India to Uganda in the nineteenth century; they came here in the 70s after they were expelled by Idi Amin and taken in by the UK (as was their right as passport-holders). Skin-colour has, to date, been the preferred source of self-identification for most British citizens of Afro-Caribbean descent.

So now (finally!) we can return to representations of race in British television since 1963 and the specific problems of *Doctor Who*. It deserves a whole book, but we'll try to cover everything – or at least remove the underbrush for anyone wanting to tackle this at length...

The most simple one is the idea of progress. Compare the London of 25.1, "Remembrance of the Daleks" (or indeed 1.1, "An Unearthly Child" or 3.10, "The War Machines") with that of X1.1, "Rose", and you'll notice the difference. Quite simply, we have a series about time travel where Earth's past and future show up. The Future (with a capital F) is characterised as a melting-pot, with ease of travel making everyone who's good enough eligible for top jobs (consider 6.5, "The Seeds of Death" having a posh girl called "Gia Kelly" in what is obviously London). Just as the ITC adventure series of the 60s used ethnic minority actors to represent cosmopolitanism, especially America, so *Doctor Who* in that period tried to suggest not-like-us-ness through nonchalant use of non-white extras. Few of them got speaking lines (beyond the occasional *aaargh!* as monsters killed them), but the most positive aspect of this was that the "us and them" dynamic was humans vs aliens in most cases.

In *most* cases... but we have to consider what exactly everyone involved in "The Tomb of the Cybermen" (5.1) thought they were doing. In between all the English actors doing ropey American accents (see **What are the Dodgiest Accents in the Series?** under 4.1, "The Smugglers"), we have: the producer's wife, Shirley Cooklin, made up to look like a member of an undefined ethnic group and given the peculiar name "Kaftan"; Roy Stewart as a muscular chap whose job is to A) stand around being muscular and menacing, B) grunting occasionally and C) dying just after he says a whole sentence; George Pastell as exactly the kind of character who's always played by George Pastell. (In any "Mummy's Curse" film made in England between 1950 and 1980, there Pastell would be, turban, fez or shaven headed, plotting against the good guys.) Stewart, a body-builder, is there to be statuesque and black. Kaftan, the exotic eastern woman in a party of middle-aged men, is using him as an attack-dog. (In all honesty, this production is almost as patronising to the English – Cyril Shaps gets to play the paranoid, effete wimp against all the butch *faux* Americans – and the Welsh party-leader, Parry, who is a dupe and a second-rate archaeologist. Nobody comes out of this well except the Doctor and the alleged yanks.) In essence, the equation of "foreign" with "evil" works if you pretend that the space-rocket crew are from England, but have picked up weird mid-Atlantic accents somehow. But the equation of non-white with malicious is manifest, even if one of the non-whites is a Caucasian woman in make-up. Or *especially* if.

What's significant about this in the context of British television in 1967 is that it's so old-fashioned. For most viewers at that time, black = cool, especially if it's American and black. Toberman is initially noticeable for being dressed in the sharpest sports-casual gear in the entire story, and that includes a lot of Ben Shearman shirts (see **What are the Most Mod Stories?** under 2.7, "The Space Museum"), and the 1930s nature of the basic storyline is obscured by the *Top of the Pops* visual style. In any other TV show of that year, especially ones watched by Britain's under-10s, blackness is aligned with internationalism, cosmopolitanism, youth, style and excitement, set against stodgy, white, pedestrian everyday life.[11]

Now let's jump forward ten years and look at "The Robots of Death" (14.5). Here, the class issue is denoted by the ambitious Sandminer commander, Uvanov, who has a Russian-sounding

continued on Page 67...

of Giordano Bruno; he was gay; he was a womaniser.

Over the last few decades, the idea of "Shakespeare, Our Contemporary" has adjusted to fit whatever "contemporary" means. Thus in the 70s, John Mortimer's TV series had Tim Curry play him as a struggling author buffeted by attempts to constrain artistic and cultural permissiveness (as Mortimer himself was doing in his other career as a barrister), while Anthony Burgess wrote an account where he was giddy with the possibilities of new words (much like, say, Anthony Burgess). Tom Stoppard wrote the screenplay to the film *Shakespeare in Love* and depicted the writer as a dashing, hard-up author adjusting awkwardly but brilliantly to changes in what theatregoers wanted, and slipping in commentaries on the way writers are victimised in authoritarian regimes. You know, like Sir Tom Stoppard, the Human Rights activist who's been writing plays for half a century. The film's most famous moment is a last-minute reprieve following a cameo by Dame Judi Dench as Good Queen Bess. As with the Mortimer/ Curry version and "The Shakespeare Code", we see a young, hairy, foxy Will living on his wits in a new kind of city, one closer to our age than to anything anyone had experienced since Rome fell to the Goths. (See **Are We Touring Theme-Park History?** under X2.7, "The Idiot's Lantern", for the pitfalls of contriving ways to make a place or time in the past too familiar.)

The existence of a play that was – at least at one point – called *Love's Labour's Won* (or variant spelling) is a given. It's one of maybe half a dozen plays we know to have been attributed to Shakespeare and performed in his lifetime that we can't find now. (With collaborations where his input has been watered down over the centuries, such as the borderline-canonical *Cardenio* and the accepted 51% works *Pericles* and *Two Noble Kinsmen*, there's even more doubt about where "written by William Shakespeare" begins and ends than has been allowed by the "Bad" quartos.) Some have claimed that it's an alternate title to another play we already know – maybe *The Taming of the Shrew, Much Ado About Nothing* or *All's Well That Ends Well*. However, *Loves Labour's Lost* doesn't so much end as just stop, with the expected betrothals delayed by a year because of a bereavement and with some of the self-deluding scholars apparently not having learned the error of their ways. One of the characters just approaches the audience after a song-and-dance routine and tells them to go home. ("The words of Mercury are harsh after the songs of Apollo. You that way, we this way.")

The play's pretty confusing as it is, being apparently amalgamated from two versions, one played at the Curtain theatre for the paying public, the other a revised edition played at court. In the second act, Berowne either goes way out of character or gets another character's lines after that character was excised but the amusing scene retained. The play's stuffed with what seem to be topical allusions to cliques within the court. (It's a motherlode for theorists wanting to find occult, Neoplatonic or subversive subtexts – see 18.6, "The Keeper of Traken" for the accretion of ideas about his works and those of his contemporaries.)

The text we have inherited may well have been what was performed, but what it meant to theatregoers who'd shown up because the bear-baiting was sold out is anyone's guess. The one fact on which most people agree is that, with the seat-prices at the Globe lower than at many other venues, they had to have a full house every night to break even. Which, with a capacity of about 2000 people in a city of almost a million, meant a rapid turnover of new plays, ideally by the "name-brand" Shakespeare.

With the building of the replica Globe, interest in finding traces of the other theatres from the era has grown. Since the 1970s, Sam Wanamaker had been trying to get a suitable facsimile built and, with the late 80s discovery of some plausible ruins in a good match for the location shown in the engravings, the momentum built. Wanamaker died shortly thereafter, which made it almost a done deal. The new Globe was opened in 1997. It is pretty certain that the "authentic" Globe is on the wrong site, but nobody can agree on the right one, and it's probably on something that cannot be demolished because it is itself historic and precious, or occupied by a big multinational. The original Globe was built in very short order from the timbers of the previous base for Burbage's company, imaginatively called "The Theatre", after their landlord raised the rent. These were smuggled to the South Bank at night in December 1598. (Theatres were not permitted within the city limits, so the earliest were just outside the old Roman walls, all those bits of what's now central London with "Gate" at the end of the name mark

Why Does Britain's History Look So Different These Days?

continued from Page 65...

name and an occasional Brummie accent (a Scottish actor doing it), resenting the way the descendants of the first Twenty Families get all the top jobs and band together. Zilda, who is played by a black actress, represents those families. It's commonplace to think of the robots as a metaphor for class struggle, but if we think of them as an *ethnic* group (and Taron Capel's rants support this interpretation), then the decision by the "very mad scientist" to use make-up to join his "brothers" is significant. It's like growing dreadlocks (with all that that entails in Britain – it's not a fashion-statement any more than a hijab would be). In this light, the plot's dependence on characters who have been in service so long, they are invisible, is interesting and the fact that the undercover agent D84 has a jet-black metal covering – and is the one robot we come to care about as a character – fascinating. (Hollywood's had a lot of fun making such an equation between robots and Civil Rights over the years, from the curious ending of the deplorable *Short Circuit II* to the way we're 20 minutes into *I, Robot* before we see anyone important who isn't black or a machine, and he's the murder victim.)

Once we look at this, the decision to cast Tariq Yunus as Cass is remarkable. He appears to be there *just* to be non-white, much as Rick James was in 9.4, "The Mutants". (Contrary to the impression this story gives, Yunus can act, really. The jury's still out on James.) His is the only non-English accent in the story. There is little attempt to denote class or status through voice – the robots sound more posh than Chub or Uvanov, as do Poul, Toos and Zilda. The plot is, essentially, that a group of beings ignored by those in charge are a threat to those in charge, and only the outside visitors (the Doctor and Leela) can see this because they've not been raised to overlook them. The same plot is used in the next story ("The Talons of Weng-Chiang"), but, as it's set in England in the nineteenth century, there are problems. There's one big one – the casting of John Bennett as Li Hsen Chang – and a lot of smaller but no less knotty ones. We'll come to these presently, but just one more thing about Poul and the gang first...

The way in which *Doctor Who* has allegorised race is with people resembling the BBC audience put into the position of inferiority by more powerful opponents. Beginning with arch-xenophobes the Daleks, carrying on with Mighty Kublai Khan and the Imperialist slave-owners of Rome (1.2, "The Daleks"; 1.4, "Marco Polo"; 2.4, "The Romans") and culminating with the most complex and intractable example of rubber-suited actors calling white actors "puny humans" (7.2, "Doctor Who and the Silurians"), the series has routinely inverted the "us and them" dynamic to remind us that we're "them" to someone. If we go with the racial reading of "The Robots of Death", the notion that it takes a disaffected, mentally-ill human to rouse the brothers into revolt is uncomfortable – but in a way that's familiar from some white southern politicians' reaction to the Civil Rights movement.

Compared to something that's a slam-dunk allegory about race, "The Mutants", the idea that the racial mix of the oppressors has to be more-than-usually varied to make the point clearer seems to be one BBC directors have gone with even when the writers weren't planning it. Three stories earlier (14.2, "The Hand of Fear"), there had been an Indian actor, Renu Satna, playing a doctor who treated the Doctor because that was a common sight in the NHS of the 1970s. We were now living in the future we'd expected in the 60s, so at last we get a non-white speaking part in a present-day story.[12] That character didn't absolutely need to be Indian, but the scene worked slightly better because a skilled comic actor defused the medic's slight self-absorption and made the brief scene work as "the Doctor being frustrated by delays" rather than "incompetent junior doctor annoys Time Lord". Cass didn't need to be Indian either, but Yunus didn't bring much to the part.

What there is, though, is a sense of the world of the Sandminer being different from ours in a number of subtle ways beyond just being an alien planet with robots and face-painting. It's either a far-off humanoid race or, on the strength of the synth renderings of nineteenth-century light music, a far future colony from Earth. In "the Future", racial problems will be resolved among humans, it seems, and our prejudices and exploitation will be inflicted on robots (see also X4.3, "Planet of the Ood"). In stories set in Earth's future, therefore, there's no reason to assume that non-white means non-English. Now that we really *are* in the twenty-first century, this is prosaically true. Representations of present-day Britain can be as racially mixed as representations of twenty-first century life in 60s *Doctor Who* tried to be, but now

continued on Page 69...

the boundaries, alongside burial-grounds, hospitals, plague-pits and brothels.). Bethlem Royal Hospital, "Bedlam", was originally just around the corner from Shakespeare's previous base, Silver Street, as was the Theatre and several early venues. The move to Southwark's hitherto boggy wasteland wasn't as silly as it might seem – the main method of transport then was by boat. Once Burbage's posse had established itself, there a lot of other companies moved to the district.

The "O" Level History syllabus of the 1970s included an optional course on the History of Medicine, which was popular with teachers who thought it would help with other courses, so the Four Humours and their relevance to interpreting Shakespeare's jokes used to be a given, just as knowledge of Joseph Lister had been [4.6, "The Moonbase"; X2.2, "Tooth and Claw"]. Once again, the changes in the syllabus have been the subject of political name-calling.

This episode's script is dotted with paraphrases and pilfering's from Roberts's favourite places. There are lines from *Blakes 7* ['Co-radiating crystals'], *The Tomorrow People* ['Rexel IV'], a line from "The Crusade" ['The eye should find contentment where it rests', spoken by Jean Marsh in episode three], the Milton Subotsky film *The Monsters' Club* [whence "Shadmock"], Roberts's own Virgin novel *Zamper* [the Arrionites], and, inevitably, Pertwee-era *Doctor Who* ['Venusian spearmint' and Lynley's death]. 'Dravidians' were mentioned in 13.5, "The Brain of Morbius".

Earlier drafts had more overt references to Shakespeare's status within the programme's lore, in "The Chase" and "City of Death" amongst others. There are also, as noted, fannish in-jokes in the names of characters. Within the tie-in works, Shakespeare has been invoked in two different Virgin novels: *The Empire of Glass* by Andy Lane and... oh, look, *The Plotters* by Gareth Roberts. This was a note-perfect pastiche of a Hartnell Historical about Guy Fawkes (who dies before history dictated, it turns out) and had the Doctor participating in the committee-meetings for the King James Bible. Both authors had fun with the combination of the Globe Theatre and "Billy Fluffs" (see Volume 1).

In similar vein, one of the 80s audio plays made by semi-pro fans had a notional Doctor (played by Nicholas Briggs, of monster-voice fame) unable to escape Bedlam in the Regency era. *Minuet in Hell* was later reworked as a Big Finish audio set in the near-future and with descendants of the naughty Hellfire Club instead of the real thing (the Doctor this time was Paul McGann, but Briggs was in it as someone who was so mad, he thought he was the Doctor – see, and you probably guessed this in advance, X4.14, "The Next Doctor"). We also can't ignore the resemblance between the premise of this story and that of "The Masque of Mandragora" (14.1), especially after Roberts wrote another closely-analogous story for *The Sarah Jane Adventures* ("Secrets of the Stars").

And there'd been a book a few years earlier called *The Da Vinci Code*, which riffed on the sort of loopy ideas Henry Lincoln had been peddling since stopping work on "The Laird of McCrimmon" (see Volume 2).[13]

Oh, Isn't That...?

• *Dean Lennox Kelly* (William Shakespeare). Began as a stand-up comedian, but Paul Abbott's *Shameless* was his big break. You may also have seen him in the cheesy-but-endearing *Frequently Asked Questions About Time Travel*. Shortly before this episode, he had played a variant on Puck in the BBC's *Shakespeare Retold* series of present-day dramas using situations from the plays.

• *Christina Cole* (Lilith). When Sky One decided to make a teen-drama about supernatural high school kids, *Hex*, it wasn't quite in the *Buffy/Charmed* mould. Cole played Cassie in early episodes, in a series that also gave the world Michael Fassbinder and Colin Salmon (X4.8, "Silence in the Library").

• *Stephen Marcus* (Jailer) is probably best known as Nick the Greek in *Lock Stock and 2 Smoking Barrels*, but had been in films since Stephen Frears's *My Beautiful Laundrette*.

• *Matt King* (Peter Streete) was a regular in *Peep Show*, which had a huge cult following on Channel Four (see X7.2, "Dinosaurs on a Spaceship").

• *Andree Bernard* (Dolly Bailey) is often cast as a barmaid, notably in *Only Fools and Horses*, but had a semi-regular part in various *Hollyoaks* spin-offs as Liz Taylor-Burton (no, not that one).

• *Angela Pleasence* (Queen Elizabeth). She'd had a go at the 1500s as Catherine Howard in *The Six Wives of Henry VIII*. Shortly before *Doctor Who* returned, Charles Palmer had directed her as one Miss Hartnell in ITV1's purist-irking quasi-adaptation *Agatha Christie's Marple*. Amid all the expected cop-shows and long-running series, she's barely been off our screens or radios since the 60s

Why Does Britain's History Look So Different These Days?

continued from Page 67...

we have a vast pool of actors who don't need to be made up to look "ethnic" and are known to be capable of saying their lines. Directors weren't always so confident.

So racial difference in Earth's future has been "solved" by ignoring it and diverting antipathy to non-humans. Hooray! The past consists of a lot of countries where the TARDIS crew are outsiders, and many of those countries, back in the, um, black and white era of the series, had non-white majorities. This was a problem when the directors didn't know many non-white actors – but, back then, nobody was *that* worried about the idea of white actors being given heavy make-up to play other races. Today, it seems weird that the majority of the cast of "The Crusade" (2.6) who were playing non-white characters were white and blacked-up, just as it seems perverse that future *EastEnders* regular Oscar James is relegated to a non-speaking role as one of El Akir's grunts, alongside Roy Stewart. What's *really* hard to comprehend now is that the production team, all fairly enlightened and progressive, seriously thought that Susan's replacement ought to be an Indian girl played by the manifestly non-Indian Pamela Franklin.

Blacking up to play a role from another culture was thought no more wrong than wearing a wig or contact lenses. Sometimes, it was simply the lack of anyone who looked right being able to do the lines, which might make the key question "Why did they do a story about Aztecs, when there weren't any Mexican actors in London?" (1.6, "The Aztecs"), but in some ways that's like asking why the whole script was in English. There were any number of possible actors who could have been hired, but whether audiences could always follow what they were saying was a concern. That's a problem from an era when the Leader of the Opposition, Edward Heath, could claim – plausibly – that he couldn't understand what the Beatles were saying, and they could reply in the same way. As late as 1971, Andy Ho's diction got him replaced by Kristopher Kum as Fu Peng in "The Mind of Evil" (8.2), with consequent changes to the script. When writing *Gangsters*, Philip Martin (22.2, "Vengeance on Varos"; 23.2, "Mindwarp") made the scripts more comic-strip to get around the achingly slow delivery of some of the performers. By the late 1970s, this wasn't a problem and all but one of the Chinese characters in "Talons of Weng-Chiang" were played by Anglo-Chinese actors.

The odd one out was, of course, John Bennett as Chang, and this raises another problem about presenting race in history – commenting on it accurately means having otherwise likeable characters being horrifyingly racist. Just as self-styled parents' groups are now coercing librarians and banning *To Kill A Mockingbird* for its unflinching reporting of racism and unabashed use of the n-word, so "Talons" is now routinely described as *being* racist, rather than being *about* racists. The single most significant fact about Chang is that he doesn't look especially Chinese to anyone who's looking carefully, yet this is ignored by everyone in London except the Doctor and Leela. As with the Sandminer robots, it takes people not brainwashed into ignoring the very existence of a whole class of intelligent beings to spot the potential threat. That threat is manifested in someone whose DNA has been buggered about with by Greel using fifty-first-century technology to the point where only a bigot would fail to notice. The Doctor is the only non-bigoted male Caucasian-looking character here. His verbal fencing with Chang culminates with the line "I understand we all look the same" and, to everyone except the Doctor, Leela and us, they do.

Of course, there is a *big* difference between this story and "The Robots of Death" in that robots are a made-up category whereas real people were, and are, ethnically Chinese. The attitude of the people making the story is hard to define, as so many individuals were involved in the decisions made. It could be argued that nobody in 1977 made a distinction between make-up and accents to turn English actors into approximations of Chinese characters and the peculiar strangulated vowels of American actors trying to sound English. Many people in England are simultaneously amused and appalled by Dick Van Dyke, Keanu Reeves, Anne Hathaway and many others as they talk like people recovering from strokes to match what Americans think is a "Briddish" accent. In both cases, it's a third or fourth-generation copy of something that really existed – but which they haven't experienced at first hand, so seem to think is just made-up. The case could be made that the various white actors in countless Hollywood films who've tried to sound "Oriental" differ from Bert the Chimney-Sweep in degree rather than kind. Acting is, after all, just pretending.

continued on Page 71...

– you can see her in Swinging Sixties romp *Here We Go Round the Mulberry Bush* or hear her in the *Foundation Trilogy* (the BBC Radio version from 1973 with charcoal-burning monophonic synths – she's Bayta Darrell in that).

Things That Don't Make Sense We could talk about how odd it is for Shakespeare to be complaining about the Queen's lack of interest in his plays, given that the first recorded production of *Love's Labour's Lost* was held at court. He'd naturally recognise the line from *Henry V*, because that was the one playing shortly after the Globe was built, and was a hit both in box-office and sales of the script. Courtiers were quoting it. We can forgive the play being anachronistically played at night, because that was the only time that the *Doctor Who* team was allowed into the Globe for filming (see **The Lore** for more).

We could discuss why everyone has such rotten teeth long before the importation of sugar from the West Indies. We could comment on whether the character "Kempe" is supposed to be Will Kemp, who'd stormed off in a huff in January 1599, apparently refusing to work with Shakespeare or Burbage again, and danced to Norwich about a year later. We could even bring up the odds of the Queen just hopping into a boat, crossing the Thames, risking being seen in public (when she'd forbidden any comment on how old she looked now), and walking through the streets to burst into the Globe without anyone outside making any kind of hubbub – but let's leave aside narrative conventions of Elizabethan-set stories and just get on with the logical glitches...

Lynley's death tries to patch over the otherwise bewildering question of how a play that hadn't been passed by the Master of the Revels could have been performed (aside from letting the play go forward at the Carrionite timetable, it prevents anyone with authority from having a look at a play that goes very strange in the epilogue). What it doesn't allow is how the Doctor can claim never to have seen a death like it, when it's what killed Professor Kettering in "The Mind of Evil".

The Doctor can identify the 14 planets of the Rexel planetary configuration, and the instigator as a Carrionite, even though later on he's almost surprised to find out they aren't fairy tales after all. And there's certainly no convincing reason for them to want to wipe out the whole human race before starting out on their vendetta of blood magic, especially as they plan to erase the planet anyway. If they need blood, why not have it a bit fresher?

Lilith's oddly vague about how she and her mothers escaped; they refer to Shakespeare's grief and passion about his son's death allowing them a loophole through the mind of a genius. All right, but their tech doesn't work off emotions *per se*, and this version of Shakespeare is the one who's so broken up by his son's death that he writes *Hamlet* in response... two years later, *after* this story's supposed date. By any reasonable ordering of events, you'd think they'd have shown up for *those* words; as it is, we can't even tell which play's words they might have used to escape. If the pseudo-mathematical ordering of verbal tokens is the key that unlocks their dimension, then the Sonnets might have done the trick, but other writers of the time were doing much more complex and heartfelt geometrical patterns of imagery, allusion and metre – why isn't this "The Donne Code" or "The Herbert Cypher?" Elizabeth's Thought-Police had rounded up and tortured Thomas Kyd, so he would be a more likely conduit instead of an absentee father who barely bothered to see his son growing up.

[It's *ju-u-u-ust* possible to see this as some sort of awkward temporal loop that they tried to tack onto an event that was already happened, even if no one ever says anything to the effect. Still, if we go with that explanation, we could even think they might have borrowed something from *Macbeth*. Under the circumstances, it's hard not to think that someone is borrowing from someone, but in what order is still tricky.

[Alternatively, it's quite tempting to think that Lilith's lying to protect their verbal supply-line, and that they slipped in a decade ago when a fresh young playwright wrote his gore-fest, *Titus Andronicus*. Needing to delay until the Globe was constructed would account for the period of waiting, and Lilith's suitor at the start indicates they've been in London quite some time already. Nonetheless, it's Peter Street – or 'Streete' as he is here – who'd be the focus of their plans, and they kill him. Once Shakespeare has let three of them escape their dimensional incarceration, he's not the only source of patterned words and deeply-felt torment in London that summer. This story's ending seems to need raw emotion, which isn't what we were told the Carrionites need to escape, and

Why Does Britain's History Look So Different These Days?

continued from Page 69...

The key difference is in intent. The extent to which you characterise the American cockernee accents as "ignorance", "ineptitude" or "innocence" varies from case to case but nobody – not even Don Cheadle in *Ocean's Eleven* – meant to cause offence to British audiences (assuming they thought anyone in Britain would be watching, or cared). They simply couldn't do it properly. They were basing it on other Americans in earlier films, until the voice-style they were doing took on a life of its own, like "English muffins" or, for an example from here, the way "Morris Dancing" (see 8.5, "The Daemons") came from supposedly third-hand reports of "Moorish Dancing" taught to people who'd never left their village.

That's dumb, and occasionally grimly amusing when the execution falls far short of the aspiration, but there is no malice.[14] While many Londoners, of all races, think of Dick van Dyke as being on the same moral plane as Groundskeeper Willie rather than Al Jolson, it is universally acknowledged that Mel Gibson hates us, will lie about us in film after film and belongs in a padded cell. We give marks for effort.

Was "Talons" maliciously conceived? Whereas "The Crusade" sets out to portray the Saracens in a more favourable light than some of the Crusaders (who were actually, despite being held up as paragons of Englishness for centuries, more French than English) and redress the tendency in a lot of textbooks and dramas, there are no positive depictions of *anyone* in "Talons". Litefoot seems to think that the Opium Wars were valid and just, Jago is a bigot and the other Londoners are caricatures. We know that the Tongs exist, and that there were a few opium dens in Limehouse, but the depiction of the Chinese characters – whose point-of-view is barely acknowledged – seems more pejorative. Perhaps this is simply because the other types of Victorian clichés have been complicated by the number of BBC dramas about them. We accept Jago as a character, not as emblematic of all the things a white English Victorian can be in a story like this. The only Chinese-ish character to say anything other than "Yes Master" or "No Master" is Chang, whose purple repertoire is "permitted" by his having been changed by Greel (and cast as a white guy with make-up – they probably expected Bert Kwouk to be available). The production doesn't seem to indicate that anyone involved knows any different, that Robert Holmes, David Maloney (director), Philip Hinchcliffe (producer) and the cast have ever thought to ask anyone whether this is in any way insulting.

What's perhaps most surprising is the lack of complaint from the Anglo-Chinese population, who either accepted this story as a step up from *One of Our Dinosaurs is Missing* and endless spy shows, or simply didn't watch. These days, some people feel obliged to be retroactively offended *on behalf of* the British Chinese community, but that community itself seem to have enjoyed it, or shrugged. Chang's casting was, anecdotally, thought of in the same way that David Carradine in *Kung Fu* was – finally a vaguely interesting and cool character who was at least supposed to be like them. (Although Mr Sin was the real hit. He was played by an Anglo-Indian actor now best known as the Oompa-Loompas in the Tim Burton *Willy Wonka*.) That local station in Toronto that refused to broadcast the story presumably thought that the comedy cockernees, drunken Irishmen and avaricious impresario were documentary-realism.

The sad fact is, the part was written for an actor who could be Tom Baker's match and could show Chang adopting the "me velly solly" accent to make people underestimate him. If Bert Kwouk, David Yip or whoever had played the part, people would still have problems with the use of the "Yellow Peril" motif of Victorian penny-dreadfuls, but the debate would be on how far Robert Holmes was subverting those clichés rather than just cut-and-pasting Sax Rohmer et al. Bennett's performance is now a distraction. The real problem is that fandom as a whole has decided that the main exponents of the unacceptable attitudes – Jago and Litefoot – are "loveable", since they resemble characters from other cosy Victorian fictions and were played by actors who made them better than their lines.

There was racism in the past. We can't ignore this, although BBC Wales is giving it a good try. They've amended history so that Victorian schoolchildren had Teddy Bears named after President Theodore Roosevelt and therefore twentieth century – instead of Golliwogs (X4.7, "The Unicorn and the Wasp"; X7.6, "The Snowmen"). "Talons" is at least honest in the description of attitudes from the period in which it's set. "The Shakespeare

continued on Page 73...

a baffled audience hearing gobbledegook from *Blakes 7* isn't going to feed emotionovores the way *Henry V* did, or the more rabble-rousing Marlowe could have done for them.]

So how does the Carrionite tech actually work? It's described as being analogous to Block Transfer Computation ("Logopolis" and 19.1, "Castrovalva"), but using words instead of numbers. Numbers are unambiguous, they have the same value in any language. Words, as Shakespeare spent his career proving, allow a lot of leeway. Unless, in a bizarre backhanded gesture towards Robert Holmes, the Carrionites actually speak Elizabethan English – and did so in the time before the laws of the universe gelled – this is a bit haphazard. For example, if we follow the hint from X4.2, "The Fires of Pompeii", then saying something Latinate, to people who speak Latin, would sound Welsh.

One specific way this affects the story is the climax. Although Rowling spells *Expelliarmus* – a nonsense-word supposedly to disarm someone – with an R, Martha's pronunciation makes it seem to sound like *Expeliamus*. That word might literally translate from the Latin as "we are going", or "allons y" – like most words ending "amus", it has the sense of "we are doing something", probably expelling. (So Shakespeare might have heard Martha say *Rydym yn troi allan*.) In context, a spell designed by a late-twentieth-century author to make people drop their weapons isn't actually going to have the effect on the Carrionites that we see here, since they *are* the weapons. Moreover, the sphere, which might be the weapon in this case, doesn't fly into the Doctor's hand as it would in a Potter adventure, so it's not Martha's intentions that save the day. Therefore, it's not the meaning of the word Martha intended that worked, but the meaning the Carrionites and Shakespeare – and those of his audience who'd been to school – *thought* she said. So perhaps Martha's Norf Laandun accent saved the world.

Most of Martha's culture shock about the era is fairly comprehensible, arguably underplayed, but for a medical student in London not to be aware of Bedlam is peculiar. As a London resident, she'd know that the final site for the Bethlem Royal Hospital was where the Imperial War Museum is now, just around the corner from the supposed site of the Royal Hope Hospital where she's worked for five years. (It's a popular pub quiz question, so see X3.7, "42" for why it's almost inevitable she'd know it.) Also, with only 20 people at the hospital at the turn of the seventeenth century, the freak show aspect is slightly anachronistic.

... and so are the three other non-white theatregoers. (This is a hotly-contested subject, but the Elizabethan attitudes to colour aren't easily mapped on to our contemporary notions. There's obvious racism, mixed with colossal ignorance, but also some hard-to-recover notions derived from antiquity. The simplest way to put this is that even if Martha's under some kind of protective perception-filter spell from the Doctor, and can walk around as if she owns the place, the people who really *do* own the place would be aware of her. Moreover, this aura, unmentioned in the dialogue, wouldn't cover every single person of colour in London. There were some, and not all were diplomats or trading delegations, but few of them would have been anything less than nobility – so the odds of a black man being in the groundlings, the cheap standing-room-only stage front tickets, are minuscule. He certainly wouldn't have been just accepted as part of the furniture, as happens in those scenes. See the accompanying essay.)

Martha, moreover, is wearing men's clothing, but is manifestly not even pretending to be male in the manner of the female protagonists of so many Shakespeare plays. (This is doubly odd, as Roberts can't have not thought of this: Vicki, in *The Plotters*, goes undercover in 1605. See **The Lore** for more.) London in 1599 was virtually a police-state, expecting another Spanish invasion or a coup. The Lord Chamberlain would have busted her, if he'd lived, but so would any of the mysteriously absent militia.

We'd never spotted it before, but the panel on the TARDIS door that doesn't open, the "Free For Use of Public" thing, now says that *officers and car* (singular) *respond to calls*. As they'd say in *Allo Allo*, "what a mistake-a to make-a."

[And it would seem that in 1599 the Doctor is Elizabeth I's mortal enemy. But in "The Day of the Doctor", there's a letter for him in the UNIT archive with a confirmation of its authenticity by means of a Gallifreyan painting. If she's outraged enough at the Globe to want him dead on sight, why doesn't she tear up this letter afterward? Does it just slip her mind? Either way, we *still* don't know what caused their falling-out between 1563 and 1599, except that she's now got her hands on

Why Does Britain's History Look So Different These Days?

continued from Page 71...

Code" makes token gestures towards the potential problem, then adds it to a catalogue of lame jokes about 1599 being "just like us". It's of a piece with the way everyone in 200,000 got their clothes from Top Shop (X1.7, "The Long Game") or that Caecillius and his family are affluent Romans with no visible slaves (X4.2, "The Fires of Pompeii" – one employee, "Rhombus" (sic), status unspecified, is fried by the Pyroviles before he says anything on the subject).

Rather than celebrate the strides towards equality and tolerance that have been made in the last generation, these are ignored and – sometimes – vindicated by being presented as always having been unnecessary. The struggles made by minority groups (except gay men and lesbians) didn't happen, because they didn't *need* to happen, because the conditions that made those struggles have to happen didn't exist in a past that was just like today. It seems to be part of the long-term project of Welsh *Who* to project contemporary attitudes onto the past and future and make any comment on the changes to society that technology might bring the preserve of "nerds". They don't exhibit the same faith in the viewers' intelligence or wider background awareness of the world as writers of the original series had. It's all cut-and-pasted from other things, mainly 70s *Doctor Who*, rather than thought out from first principles or basic real-world knowledge. Grumbling about historical inaccuracy – of any kind – is as "sad" as complaining that the science is embarrassingly stupid and ill-researched. Inability to create new and different worlds is only to be expected when the writers and crew can barely get present-day London right.

To be absolutely clear, *Doctor Who* isn't alone in this. The "me-too" BBC franchises *Merlin* and *Robin Hood* were set in a weirdly modern-looking Middle Ages; the Corporation's higher echelons were anticipating a directive to make the casting racially-inclusive, in defiance of all probability. Diversity, at least in front of the camera, is now an imperative. Rightly so, although it needs thought rather than just box-ticking. Projecting our attitudes (where "us" is twenty-first century London or indeed American TV-normal, as per *Buffy*) onto the past in such a self-congratulatory way not only assumes that our "normal" is perfection, but that it wasn't *achieved* but simply *occurred*. It removes agency from those people who made a stand, since current attitudes were so self-evidently right that they just happen spontaneously the moment everyone realises what year it is. While trying to show a Britain that is recognisably the one most viewers know, and in the case of these three series that Britain is mainly under 30, the BBC Drama heads have made a point to be up-to-date. Hooray! But making that normality hold good for all times and places is just as arrogant and ignorant as having an all-white speaking cast for "The Crusade" or "The Abominable Snowmen" (5.2). One-size-fits-all thinking is as troublesome now as it was in the 1950s when film and television assumed that everyone in all of the past had white skin, 50s haircuts and Received Pronunciation. The working-class Indian woman in the crown at Tyburn (X9.6, "The Woman Who Lived") was more bizarrely improbable than – and probably had a more interesting story than – the fire-breathing lion-man.

As we saw in **Are We Touring Theme-Park History?** under "The Idiot's Lantern" (X2.7), the former distinction we could make between "Adventures in History" derived from popular fiction, and "Historical Adventures" geared towards discussing the processes of historical change, no longer works now that the latter format has been discarded as too hard for viewers to comprehend. That distinction was never as clear-cut as some commentators made out, even to the writers, but is a useful heuristic, a tool we can use as a way into the topic. Because the TARDIS will always get the companion home safely these days, there's no prospect of having to live in any past setting for any length of time. This, as much as anything, encourages a certain homogeneity about all the places and times visited. "The Shakespeare Code" does better than most in at least showing the crude toilet facilities and having Shakespeare's breath smell (even if that might not be accurate), but in most cases the visual display is all we get now.

Hiring extras and putting them in funny hats is part of that display. They are literally window-dressing in the scenes in the Globe. Applying a colour-bar when hiring extras, on the grounds of historical authenticity, is complicated since – as we've seen – the all-white nature of English history isn't as clear-cut as previous generations of historians and broadcasters made out. On the other

continued on Page 75...

some formidable alien tech and a fez (cf. 25.3, "Silver Nemesis").]

The big one, though... you've decided to show your twenty-first century med-student a Shakespeare play as it was performed at the time. Of the 37 known plays you could have picked, you start her off with the one that's two hours of topical allusions, half of which the general public didn't get in 1597, and which doesn't even end properly. Even if we go with the usual idea when long-term fans are writing new series episodes, that the TARDIS misses its intended date (because it *always* did when they were watching Tom Baker), how can Martha possibly be that enthusiastic about *Love's Labour's Lost*? It's a parody of bad courtly poets, followed by a spoof of a kind of play nobody's done since 1620, followed by a clodhopping, overlong pageant-cum-Morris Dancing routine after the plot runs out. Anyone who gets any of the jokes earns a PhD for explaining it.[14] And there's the small detail of the play's sequel having been publicised – and thus probably performed – before the Globe opened.

Moreover, Shakespeare was often in his own plays (and those of other Globe writers), so the 'Author!' scene's even more unlikely – he would have been in any revival of *Love's Labour's Lost*, probably as one of the old men, his preferred kind of role according to some reports. This probably applies to any sequel he might have written with the same characters, as the only death in the original is an off-stage report of a king's passing in another country.

In fact, what did the paying customers actually *see*? The majority of the action is invisible from within the theatre, and the fires and flying objects over the South Bank would have been cause for the city's defences to go into an even higher alert and launch cannon-fire at the Globe. What the Groundlings would have seen is silhouettes of women in mid-air against a fiery orange glow and three people on stage shouting nonsense.

And it might just be a peculiar alien name, but isn't it odd that a species named 'Carrionites' like their meat fresh?

Critique If we *have* to have the Doctor acting like a galactic autograph-hunter, buttonholing any famous author he fancies meeting, then this is the way to do it. The existence of so many good locations gives this the edge over any American series, and the cast also have the home advantage. It looks extraordinary, more grimily real than *Shakespeare in Love*, but more enticing than many alleged marvels in later series. Crucially, the production isn't relying on spectacle and set-pieces but is, so to speak, allowing them. It's hard to go wrong with Tudor buildings and *Raiders*-style spectral forms (and they'd done almost the same thing in X1.3, "The Unquiet Dead"), but this surpassed expectations.

The storyline is fundamentally "The Masque of Mandragora", with the enigmatic energy-helix replaced by comic-book witches. Of all the possible stories to tell about the Doctor in Shakespeare's London, this is perhaps the one with the highest risk of cheesiness, but also perhaps the one with fewest far-flung locations. It's hard to over-act a witch of this kind, so that allows the ripeness of much of the dialogue to be set against the deliberately un-period conversations elsewhere. The Carrionite performances are exactly as one would expect, although Lilith-as-human is a more demanding part and done well. Everyone else does as required, but the episode is stolen by Dean Lennox Kelly. His rock-star Bard is fully aware of how good he is and what it cost him, but what makes him shine is that he-knows-that-we-know-that he-knows-that-we-know game of Will, the lad from Warwickshire, being 'Shakespeare" when in public. He comments on the Doctor's constant performance, and lets Martha know that he's seen through their cover-story, but can't risk letting his own guard down.

The most refreshing aspect of this, looked at again today, is that comment about Martha looking at the Doctor in disbelief that he exists. This is a more interesting line to have taken than the whole unrequited crush subplot, but doesn't rule it out. Being in Elizabethan London is just part of being near the Doctor, and Freema Agyeman gives a solid account of someone who knew how the world worked *that morning* and is now figuring everything out from scratch. It's only when you look at later episodes that this timidity clearly shows up as an acting decision rather than a slightly under-powered performance. Agyeman's vocal delivery never changes much, but compare her stance and eyes here to when she's preparing to use the Osterhagen Key (X4.13, "Journey's End") and it's more obvious. They play up her newness to all of this but have to keep banging on about Rose. Otherwise, it's a good first trip, a fact underscored by the way that the rest of the story

Why Does Britain's History Look So Different These Days?

continued from Page 73...

hand, if they had gone for authenticity, or if no extras from minority background had applied, someone – probably an American online commentator – would accuse the BBC of racism in whitewashing the past. The thing is, there are five separate non-white extras in the episode, and only one is dressed well enough to be a visiting emissary. All five are simply ignored, not stared at, openly mocked or made way for. (Of course, having non-white extras in a scene set in a castle in 1138 – X9.1, "The Magician's Apprentice" – is only the smallest potential anachronism in a sequence deliberately stuffed with them, but mixed-race Kaleds does seem to be missing the point a bit.) When setting a story in twentieth-century New York (X3.4-35, "Daleks in Manhattan"/ "Evolution of the Daleks") the writers feel obliged to explain, if not dwell on, the lack of segregation even in this most cosmopolitan of cities, but xenophobic Tudor London has everyone simply accepting Martha and the unspeaking black Londoners. In 1995, maybe, but not 1599, not even 1959.[15]

Because *Doctor Who* is now made to as breakneck-paced 45 minute story-episodes, instead of unfolding in serials that allowed time for reflection and discussion – and thereby following the series' original remit to explore other cultures and ways of life rather than just show pictures of explosions happening in exotic locales – we never get to ask any of these people how they feel about being black in Elizabethan London, or ask any of the other Londoners what they think about it.[16] The Globe isn't alone in this – a hanging in Tyburn in 1651 has a mix of Caucasian, Indian and Afro-Caribbean Londoners alongside anachronisms such as cocktails, all within a story that could have been set a century later with no changes and fewer glaring errors. (But then it would have been even *more* like that episode of *Blackadder the Third* with the squirrels.) Where and when it's set and who was around in this milieu is irrelevant, as it's all just a backdrop for the same kind of story as before. This is the exact opposite of what the people who invented the series had in mind.

(See also **Martha: What Went Wrong?** under X3.13, "Last of the Time Lords".)

looks as if it'll end with Shakespeare joining her and the Doctor in New New York or wherever.

The matter of what made Shakespeare unique is ducked; he's "a genius" (one of many anachronistic terms we can just about accept, coming as they do from the man who added more commonly-used words to English than anyone else) but this manifests as his resisting the Psychic Paper and working out that Martha's from the twenty-first century – even though the idea of the past or future being different isn't anywhere in his plays (except maybe *Cymbeline*, written when he was much older and had lived through more turmoil). Recognising lines from his plays is a game for viewers but ultimately he's special because the Doctor keeps telling us he is. We get what purport to be explanations of where he got all his ideas but not why he was already so popular. That's almost beside the point, though, as this Shakespeare is less a character than an Event – a piece of walking, talking landscape to be visited. The one time he does what we know him for, alien puppeteers are pulling his strings. We get an example of him freestyling verse to seal up the rift but, amid the sound effects and music, it's hard to work out what he's even saying.

The dead giveaway is that they feel obliged to begin with a caption saying "London 1599", as if they don't trust the audience. Everything here seems to work on the assumption that they have to "sell" Shakespeare, even though the story hinges on everyone having heard of him and his ability being more potent than any entity in the whole of history, on any planet. In contrast to the *Horrible Histories* approach that was so successful at the time (especially for the target audience of BBC-watching pre-teens), this story avoids any hint that the past was weird or especially different – except where the plot demands a trip to Bedlam, although this is more a feature of a later century. Roberts's main conceit about this era is that everyone's on the pull all the time; this is a legitimate extrapolation from Shakespeare's torrent of innuendoes in even solemn historical dramas, but it's also the world-view of *Hollyoaks*. Casual viewers are eased into this world rather than dropped in to the full strangeness of it (as a Hartnell-era story would have handled such a tale). It works as a taster and yet this fascinating and crucial era has only been revisited in a tie-in computer game about Guy Fawkes and as a backdrop for Zygons and Doctor-on-Doctor kvetching. We've seen more of the rather dreary forty-second century than the late sixteenth or early seventeenth.

Now that they've proved that they can do it, we needed at least one more story set around this time, to explore the strangeness of a genuinely alien world that is within reach of us geographically and historically. X9.6, "The Woman Who Lived" wasn't it (nobody involved seemed to know that 1651 and 1751 were any different from each other, let alone from now). That hypothetical story seems far off, though, as the subsequent production team has somehow made the likes of Vikings, pirates and cowboys boring – but one day, one hopes, Gareth Roberts can stop languishing in Colchester-set Yeti-in-a-loo filler episodes and be given the chance to Defenestrate.

The Lore

Written by Gareth Roberts. Directed by Charles Palmer. Viewing figures: (BBC1) 7.2 million (and an 84% AI, but lower for BBC3), (BBC3 repeats) 1.0 and 0.5 million. This episode, and X3.7, "42", were alone in having audience-share of 37%, while most managed 40 or 41%. This is still impressive even before the 2012 digital switchover moved the available number of channels from a minimum of five (one slightly patchy with regard to reception) to 40 or more.

Repeats and Overseas Promotion *Pienes D'Amour Gagnées, Der Shakespeare Code.*

Production

Gareth Roberts has a track-record as long as your arm for *Doctor Who*-related activity. He attended his first convention as a child, but was on the periphery of organised fandom until the early 1990s. He had submitted a novel for the Virgin *New Adventures* series, *The Highest Science* (1993), which bucked the trend for grim third-generation photocopies of William Gibson in favour of a sly, bittersweet lark involving quadruped cyborg tortoises, a stranded train and dairy products (see **Wot? No Chelonians?** under X5.12, "The Pandorica Opens" for the problems with mentioning these aliens in the dialogue). This was rapidly followed by *Tragedy Day* (1994), a more obvious satire, and then a string of hits for the *Missing Adventures* range (*The Romance of Crime*, *The English Way of Death* and *The Well-Mannered War* – all later adopted for audio by Big Finish) in which he managed the almost impossible feat of getting Season Seventeen pastiches to work on the page.

He also, as the joke (his own?) at the time had it, went through fandom backwards, from novels to the Fitzroy Tavern to a fanzine (*Cottage Under Siege* co-run by Neil Corry) and re-joining the convention crowd. And he wrote strips for *Doctor Who Magazine*, again resisting the rather adolescent solemnity that was usual in the format for something equally serious, but less ashamed of fun and invention. His debut in that format was "The Lunar Strangers" (*DWM* #215-217; see X3.1, "Smith and Jones") in 1994. He also did Big Finish audios, often co-writing with *DWM* editor Clayton Hickman, including *The One Doctor* and *Bang-Bang-a-Boom!*. When the rights for the books reverted to the BBC (to put it tactfully), he made fun of the process by ending the last Virgin book, *The Well-Mannered War*, with a strong hint that everything from 18.1, "The Leisure Hive" onwards involved a non-real Doctor (see 6.2, "The Mind Robber" for the rationale).

Meanwhile, he was working undercover for television soaps. Apart from getting Thelma Barlow to use the words "Cartmel Masterplan" on air (see Volume 6) in *Coronation Street* and a sequence in a *Brookside* episode where the nation heard "... that Gary Russell's weird", he played with a straight bat. When a group of former Virgin Books staff staged a coup and took over *Emmerdale*, he was one of the storyliners slipping in allusions to *Doctor Who* and *Blakes 7*. When Paul Abbott and Russell T Davies created an apocalyptic Magic Realist soap, *Springhill*, Roberts and Paul Cornell took over as script-editors for the second series. On top of all this, he was writing for sketch-shows and collaborating with Charlie Higson (see **Why Now? Why Wales?** under X1.1, "Rose") on *Fast Show* spin-off *Swiss Tony* and the second series of *Randall and Hopkirk (Deceased)*. In the latter, he appeared in one of his episodes in a giant babygro and managed to get Sir Derek Jacobi to give pathos and gravitas to a line plundered from 17.4, "Nightmare of Eden" ("He died." "How did he die?" "He... died"). His being approached to write for the new *Doctor Who* seems almost like a fait accompli now but, to begin with, he was a bit tied up as lead writer on *The Sarah Jane Adventures* and the Series 2 *TARDISodes*.

• Freema Agyeman had already been cast but not announced when Roberts was finally offered the spot, giving the author scope to make Martha more mature. Roberts, after a tip-off from Script Editor Simon Winstone, was sent a text from Russell T Davies just saying "Shakespeare". (Roberts has suggested that this came even before the commission for "A Groatsworth of Wit".) Davies was discussing story ideas with Roberts when the notion of the lost Shakespeare play came up; as a hook for a story, it seemed ready-made.

Other ideas were kicked around, including auditions parodying *X Factor* (Martha going undercover to join Burbage's troupe); Susannah, Shakespeare's elder daughter, disguised as a boy to find her dad; and allusions to the Doctor having met Shakespeare before this. There was never a notion that aliens or Sir Francis Bacon would have authored Shakespeare's plays, nor that the Doctor made the young Will turn into a playwright – although malign faeries were an option briefly considered before settling on witches.

One of Roberts's Big Finish stories, *The One Doctor*, had a tag scene where the Doctor and Mel have Christmas dinner and follow it with the Queen's Speech – via the Time-Space Visualiser – but get the wrong Queen Elizabeth. Davies proposed they work something similar into the end of the episode. Lilith, Bloodtide and Doomfinger were sisters, in early goes. Later drafts of the script included Bloodtide and Doomfinger pulling Streete down into the earth (see 21.3, "Frontios" for what Roberts probably had in mind). It was decided early on to aim for a time-neutral dialogue style – skipping the "verily" and "videlicit" stuff, but not contorting the speech into something overtly modern and likely to date. The episode was called "Love's Labour's Won" until very late on.

• As the script developed, it became obvious that the story would extend across a lot of London. This required a search for suitable Elizabethan locations, and it became clear that the majority of the story would take place at night. Davies was keen to get a cross-promotional tie-in with the Shakespeare's Globe theatre, despite the slight discrepancy in the dates. This later caused problems when there was a dispute over contracts. Plans were made for relocating the story to one of the temporary sites the Lord Chamberlain's Men had used while the Globe was being built, thus setting the story a few months earlier. As it was, the use of the Globe for a TV drama – a first – was a fiddly negotiation for the theatre and BBC Wales, not least because the available dates were in summer, while the theatre was in use for live performances in the afternoon and evening. There were fewer hours of darkness, and night shooting wasn't exactly authentic. (Then, and to some extent with the rebuilt Globe now, the theatre relies on daylight. The modern version stretches a point for summer evenings and very discreet illunination.) It did offer the prospect of more spectacular effects at the end, and a line was dropped in (but was later cut) of the Master of the Revels permitting a nocturnal performance.

It is also an odd space acoustically, designed for everyone on stage to be audible but not the "groundlings" or other audience-members, using technology not designed to drown out lorries and jets. BBC4 had broadcast a live performance by the in-house company a few years earlier, so the technical aspects weren't entirely unfamiliar – but this had been with a paying audience, rather than extras, so one of the tasks ahead was making 50 costumed atmosphere artistes look like a thousand. As time in the theatre was limited, the cast rehearsed all the crucial shots in the venue ahead of time, and mock-ups of small sections were used for anything they could get away with remounting in Cardiff.

• In between these, Tennant and Christina Cole (Lilith) had to learn a complex sword-fight. Regular stunt-double Gordon Seed and Maxine Whittaker worked out the moves, which were shot against green-screen and shown to Tennant and Cole before they shot it for real.

• The Carrionites' chamber was a studio set, to accommodate a lot of flying-harness work. (You will be seeing it again, as both Sarah Jane's attic for *The Sarah Jane Adventures* Series 5 and Adelaide's childhood bedroom in X4.16, "The Waters of Mars"). Some more work on the swordfight took place later in the day – Peter McKinstry had built a broom-like sword for Lilith. As she needed to wear a wig with the prosthetic witch-face anyway, Cole was given a red wig as Lilith in both her forms – confirming the anti-ginger prejudice which Elizabeth I had faced. The other two Carrionites found that wearing all-over masks in record-breaking heat was a bad move, and had little vents cut in the latex so that they could let off steam between takes.

By the 24th, Charles Palmer's scheme for the swordfight was becoming impractical (Seed had been rushed to the hospital after Whittaker had accidentally poked him in the eye) and a new scene, of Lilith failing to seduce the Doctor, was hastily written and shot, retaining her flight through the window at the end. It was on the following day that the negotiations with the Shakespeare's Globe company had a wobble, and the plan to use a country house near Cardiff was looked into. This was Friday. The "Grand Tour" of period locations was due to begin on Monday.

• The plan was to go to Coventry, Warwick and then the Globe in a ten-day swoop beginning on August Bank Holiday and ending on 3rd September. These would all be night shoots; the two Midlands cities complicated matters, as the period buildings were all in residential and commercial areas. Coventry, formerly the centre of UK car manufacture, had realised that its locations were an asset and had set up a specific agency. Despite the devastation wrought by Nazi bombing on one night in 1941, there were isolated pockets of Tudor and Mediaeval buildings in the city centre. While the cast rehearsed in a nearby church, residents at Ford's Hospital (originally a "hospital" in the old sense of alms-house or way-station, but now an old people's home) were taken for a night in a hotel so that the courtyard could be used for the Allhallow's Street and a couple of other shots. Other views of the same scenes were shot around the corner at nearby Cheylesmore Manor, which was also the route to Bedlam.

• The song performed by Wiggins in the pre-credit sequence was written by Roberts and Murray Gold, and pre-recorded for Sam Marks to lip-synch to and approximate playing a lute. On the following night, the even-more complicated shoot in Warwick took place on the miraculously well-preserved High Street. Lord Leyster's Hospital is now the local tourist and heritage centre, as well as a home for retired soldiers, and is near many local businesses. There is a balcony and a courtyard virtually unchanged since the seventeenth century – the same agency administered all of these, so only one set of negotiations was needed. This is the street where the TARDIS lands and leaves, so a trained longbowman was on hand along with three camera teams. One of these made full use of the extras by grabbing green-screen shots to be put into the vista of London Martha sees. (If you look closely, the effects shot of the Globe in the pre-season trailer at the end of "The Runaway Bride" is rather different. It was decided that the theatre was too close to the street-corner.)

Next night, they returned to record Lynley's death. Chris Larkin had a thin pipe concealed in the luxuriant beard, coming out at his bottom lip to jet out water. The shot of his mouth full of water was troublesome – he choked on it as Agyeman moved his head for Martha's examination. As the next day dawned and time ran out, Tennant got the giggles and ad-libbed.

• That night was the start of the Globe shoot, now that the legal hassle was resolved. The resulting deal ruled out food or drink on site, and strictly limited the hours when the BBC could be there. Palmer made the maximum use of the six hours per night allocated by grabbing long-shots, wide shots and stage scenes. For the daylight scene of the Doctor surveying the empty theatre and deciding to visit Streete, and the Queen's unexpected interruption, reflective blimps were lit to simulate daylight. On the second night, they recorded the one and only performance of *Love's Labour's Won* by Gareth Roberts and William Shakespeare (additional material by David Whitaker). Roberts had been asked to supply dialogue for Kempe and Dick to perform (and for the graphics department to write in what could be Shakespeare's handwriting) but – to his fake annoyance – only the line from "The Crusade" is clearly audible. This was the first time since *Doctor Who*'s revival that rain had significantly affected a location shoot, ten minutes before the end of the day.

• Tuesday saw the team back in Cardiff, for the Elephant tavern scenes. There was a line of Martha commenting on the unconvincing pub-sign, and the Doctor pointing out that nobody's seen a real elephant. In one version, Lilith was to have crawled up the wall of the Elephant in a manner like the 1922 *Nosferatu,* but this was lost in the interests of time and practicality. On Thursday, the basement of Newport Indoor Market became the cellars of Bedlam, although the meat-market's huge fridges necessitated redubbing all of the dialogue. The public cottoned on to what was happening, so Tennant snuck out under benches to avoid being mobbed by teenage girls.

• The Globe Theatre enthusiastically participated in the promotion and offered the episode on sale in its shop. Roberts, in *Doctor Who Magazine*, promoted the episode by claiming that the controversial "Celebrity Historicals" were the way forward, because nobody wanted to see a story about the Defenestration of Prague. This irked many people, not least those who would rather have liked a story with Transylvanian emissaries in 1612 hunted down by townsfolk with pitchforks and surviving a fall from a third-floor window. Roberts later claimed that he simply wanted to get the word "Defenestration" into print.

X3.3: "Gridlock"

(14th April, 2007)

Which One is This? The Macra Tourer.

And in between the brief cameos by (almost) everyone's favourite not-very-good Troughton-era monsters, we get a world of resolutely oddball drivers and their vehicles stuck in a ring-road, until the Face of Boe saves the world and the Doctor pulls a few levers.

Firsts and Lasts This is the last appearance of the Face of Boe (discounting a flashback and a dubious, laboured reference later on), and it's the final part of the New Earth trilogy (1.2, "The End of the World"; 2.1, "New Earth"). And yes, this is the first story the Macra have been in for (almost to the month) four decades, in 1967's "The Macra Terror" (4.7). Aren't you thrilled?

If you're quick, the first naked woman in *Doctor Who* is here. (Unless someone finds any wiped episodes to prove otherwise. We very much doubt that nudity features in any lost Hartnell or Troughton stories, but saying this might intensify the search. The first known naked man was Jon Pertwee.) We also have our first (acknowledged) same-sex married couple.

Watch Out For...

• *Doctor Who Confidential* had it right for this one; the effort the production team went to in making their one-car set convincingly double for half-a-dozen different environments is impressive. Several of the drivers are sight-gags – including one couple killed in the pre-credit sequence who look like Grant Wood's iconic painting *American Gothic* (one of two connections to Iowa in this episode; keep reading).

• Whereas earlier versions of *Doctor Who* accepted that religion of almost all kinds was a mug's game, the new version hedges its bets for overseas sales. Thus, while the hymns are a cheap trick pulled by the long-dead authorities to keep everyone optimistic and community-minded, the scene where the survivors all belt out "The Old Rugged Cross" (written by an Iowa pastor) is genuinely affecting. However, the really odd *Songs of Praise* moment is at the end, when the Doctor's description of his obliterated home is drowned out by "Abide With Me" (see also 19.3, "Kinda").

• There's another unexpectedly emotional scene when the Face of Boe dies, finally out of his fish tank after at least 400,799,947 years (given that X1.7, "The Long Game" was in 200,000 and we're now in Five Billion and Fifty-Three AD).

• A tiny, throwaway shot that probably cost more time and money than the entire effects for, say, "The Daleks' Master Plan" (3.4), has a kitten saying "Mama". The cat-people from "New Earth" and the red, white and blue-skinned people are back, and the most voluble of these is a cat-man dressed as Biggles.[17] This is all perfectly fine until he opens his mouth and – depending on your experience – you hear either a generic Irishman or Father Dougal Maguire.

• And his wife has a jumper knitted from cat-fur. She looks familiar.

• Although we've now mentioned it twice in this entry, the appearance of big crab-like claws was, on first broadcast, a tantalising moment of "they wouldn't dare – would they?" They dared. It's effective on its own terms, but for veteran fans who'd paid their dues and watched reconstructions or – in some cases – saw the now-lost Troughton adventure with something similar, the Doctor's announcement that these are indeed the Macra was the single weirdest thing of the year. What other second-string aliens would they be bringing back? Bandrils? Mandrels? Castellan Spandrel? (See, of course, **Wot? No Chelonians?** under X5.12, "The Pandorica Opens".) We await, apparently in vain, for a series where the "Big Bad" is Yartek, Leader of the Alien Voord.

The Continuity

The Doctor Finds kittens adorable and likes a bit of rain. He's quite chummy with the Face of Boe, calling him 'old friend'. [To judge by Boe's last two appearances, exactly how that came about is unclear. Given that the Doctor knows that the Face will impart his secret on their next meeting, the decision to come to this world at this time is interesting. Why he waits until he has a companion is unclear, as is whether he thinks that visiting New Earth necessarily means saying boo to Boe.] Predictably, he's hopeful about the Face's chances to live and is depressed by his death [being the last of one's kind is motivation to keep going despite the cost and pain]. Considering the Face of Boe's prophecy, the Doctor gently, but definitively, rejects Martha's suggestion that she might be what keeps him from being alone.

It takes a while for him to identify Novice Hame 30 years on [interesting, since he's always been good at recognising humans when they are much older or younger than when he saw them last]. He hugs her, then remembers that she was a genocidal monster.

He continues his strange reluctance to confirm Martha's status as full-blown companion, and yet keeps stretching the definition of 'one trip'. That said, when he offers her an extension, it appears that he's already set the controls before bringing up the subject [which may mean an unseen message from the Face of Boe, or a desire to try out this exciting city to see if he has better luck than when he took Rose]. He acts as if that wasn't his first visit to the Undercity.

The hymn service leaves him looking bored and impatient, but he's respectful enough to not actually start invading people's cars until after it's concluded. He's very attached to his coat, but purple isn't his colour. His respiratory system enables him to get down to the bottom of the car system without an oxygen mask, though he's coughing quite a bit by the end. As usual, he complains about other people's teleports.

• *Background.* He confirms that all his family and friends are really most sincerely dead.

Gallifrey's sky is burnt orange and the forest is silver [shamelessly nicked from Susan's description in X1.7, "The Sensorites", so she would appear to be Gallifreyan after all]. Its second sun comes up from the South. [This suggests that either the rotational and magnetic poles are at right angles, or that this other sun isn't the one that Gallifrey and the other six worlds orbit (see **The Obvious Question – How Old is He?** under 16.5, "The Power of Kroll"), but is a fair distance away and thus relatively constant in the night sky. If there's a bit of obliquity, like Earth being tilted 26 degrees and having seasons, there could be a sort of midnight-sun effect making this apparently impossible event happen. See also the essay with X4.3, "Planet of the Ood".] The citadel is encased in a glass sphere [as seen in X3.12, "The Sound of Drums", et seq]. When the wind comes through the leaves, it sounds like music.

The Doctor's brown coat was a present from Janis Joplin. [See **What Actually Happens in a Regeneration?** under 11.5, "Planet of the Spiders" for the inherent absurdities here.]

• *Ethics.* It distresses him to see a woman who uses a Forget patch to stop thinking about a personal loss right in front of him, regardless of societal norms and the person's own voluntary choice. [It's probably having more painful reverberations for him than normal.]

He essentially lies by omission to Martha, telling her about his home planet, but leaving out the fact that it was destroyed [and he never mentions that he was the one responsible], as he 'liked' pretending that it was still around. It takes the Face of Boe letting the cat out of the bag (so to speak) and Martha going on strike before he finally settles down and concedes that his homeworld is gone. It's ambiguous whether he has any idea what Martha means by 'ever heard the word "rebound"?'

The Macra's fate after the toxic fume environment they've been living on vanishes doesn't worry anyone in the story, including him.

• *Inventory: Sonic Screwdriver.* Is very good at opening car panels and opening doors. [A few quick flicks allow the Doctor to get a driving report on a blank screen; the rest of New Earth technology might work the same way.]

• *Inventory: Other.* He acquires a paisley bandanna, to mask the smog, from two *kawaii* girls. He leaves it in the car driven by "Mr Benn" when Novice Hame abducts him.

The TARDIS Somehow, the arrow that Queen Elizabeth's soldiers shot at the Ship in the last story remains embedded during a trip in the Time Vortex. [That's odd on a number of counts. Generally, objects don't manage to even stick to the Block Transfer Computation, let alone endure a trip in the Time Vortex. The end of X9.12, "Hell Bent" confirms this. Then again, see 25.3, "Silver Nemesis". Perhaps the Doctor has got a setting to disable this if he's curious, or wants to give someone a good lesson in graffiti scrubbing.]

The Supporting Cast

• *Martha.* She associates rain with Wednesdays. The poor weather douses a lot of her excitement about her first alien planet, especially when the Doctor confirms that he's already been here with Rose (she works that much out for herself). She's seen enough submarine films to know when to cut the engines. [Anyone growing up in Britain

Must They All be Old-Fashioned Cats?

Brannigan's amused perplexity at the marital status of the Cassini "sisters" seems odd for a catman married to a human woman and with a mess of talking kittens. However, what's noticeable about the ideas of future family in "Gridlock" is how much more conservative it is than it pretends to be. The visuals make the exotic and colourful occupants of the various cars seem diverse and eccentric, but it's almost entirely single people or monogamous couples. There's one set-up with a female Goth cat and two female humanoids with Victorian nighties, but they get killed once their info-dump purpose is served, so we never find out what's going on there.

The nuclear family is presented as one of those universal facts – along with a money system of some kind and gravitational pull exactly like Earth's wherever they go – that never gets shown as arbitrary or local. For a series so keen to avoid being heteronormative, this is peculiar. They can announce a story with the title "The Husbands of River Song" knowing full well that this will raise eyebrows (X9.13). Even in our own time, on this planet, alternatives to this common set-up are present, if kept under the radar in mainstream culture. The Kibbutz system was only the tip of the iceberg, but even this has vanished from documentary series since the peak of interest in the 70s.

So, no gay couples with kids (unless you count a throwaway mention in *The Sarah Jane Adventures* and a laboured misunderstanding in X6.12, "Closing Time"), no species where three or more parents are needed to make babies, no parthenogenesis (apart from perhaps the Daleks, and their reproductive systems have become increasingly indistinguishable from cheesy horror films – we'll return to the Sontarans in a mo) and not even an on-screen mixed-race human couple with children (Clara's charges in Series 7 might have counted, if they'd even mentioned mum). When one compares this to *Doctor Who*'s original run, it gets weirder still.

As with a lot of 50's monster movies, the main concern with a lot of the Yeti-in-the-Loo and Base-Under-Siege stories of yore was preventing the non-human thingies from spawning. Even in a phase where the writers couldn't assume that the core audience knew where babies came from, the number of times a hatchery or spore-producer was ultimately blown up is remarkable. For most purposes, a mad computer hypnotising the world's population to create more pollution would have kept UNIT busy, but "The Green Death" (10.5) has the giant maggots about to pupate and start flying around the world laying eggs. Even the Cybermen were available in ovoid form (5.7, "The Wheel in Space"). The Cybermen are an interesting example of the way the series blurred the distinction between reproduction and recruitment, as they used both physical alteration and hypnosis to convert humans to their cause. This gets even weirder with the Wirrn (12.2, "The Ark in Space"), who lay eggs in people (apparently) and leave slime that gives humans a thorough-enough makeover for the afflicted human to lay eggs himself. However, the emphasis here, as in "The Seeds of Doom" (13.6), is on what it feels like to be eaten alive and subsumed by a non-human consciousness. Reproduction has been radically separated from sex.

That is one tradition that the BBC Wales version has maintained. People get into all sorts of relationships, but baby-making is another matter entirely. Now that we no longer have companions who were found under mulberry bushes (and we'll pick up on that too), everyone has a family and that family is always Trouble. The shift of focus towards soap-like relationship drama (because Russell T Davies believed that there was a thing called drama over *here* and a thing called science fiction over *here*) made every story have to be about families, and nuclear ones to the exclusion of all other possibilities. It was a feature of his term as Executive Producer that fathers were the source of all evil. People commented as much online, but the peculiar bit is that there was never any option to do without fathers. In many stories, the narrative thrust was towards "healing" a family, and that means having all the members together at any cost. Rose Tyler appears to have indirectly caused a massacre at Canary Wharf by combining her epic-scale neediness with the power of the space-time vortex (see **Bad Wolf: What, Why and How?** under X1.13, "The Parting of the Ways") to put someone who's a bit like her dad together with her mum.

More perniciously, the impact of "The Idiot's Lantern" (X2.7) is muffled by Rose (and the Doctor) virtually ordering Tommy to go to his abusive father and offer an olive branch after Eddie is finally kicked out of his mother-in-law's house. A family that tries to get along without the paterfamilias is, in Davies-era stories, more doomed than

continued on Page 83...

will have seen a lot of these on afternoons, and someone Martha's age will most likely have seen then on Channel 4 in school holidays, things like *We Dive at Dawn* or *Above Us, The Waves* where someone, usually Bryan Forbes, goes nuts.] Recreational drugs disgust her – when she's told Cheen is pregnant, she actually rips the patch off her neck. [The reaction suggests that her instincts were right in this case; the couple looks shifty as a modern couple might if one of them was smoking.]

She's starting to doubt that the Doctor might return her adoration someday, and she's cognizant that she's gone on a joyride through space-time with someone she barely knows, and that her family would never know her fate if she died now [a concern she repeats in X3.7, "42"]. She now knows when the Doctor is ducking a conversation, and stops him cold by refusing to go back to the TARDIS until he tells her the truth about his people.

She briefly tries a bluff her way out of a kidnap with a gun lying conveniently next to her. The commuters all singing "The Old Rugged Cross" first bores her, then brings her to tears. [Oh, and her "I've got faith in the Doctor" speech to Milo and Cheen looks like a test drive for the season finale; in two minutes, she convinces a couple who's never heard of the Doctor to buck up and stay hopeful. The religious component of the hymns is indirectly compared to her own faith in the Doctor, even as she realises she's only just met him.]

• *Face of Boe.* After countless millennia [going by X1.7, "The Long Game" et seq], he dies. His message for the Doctor is a simple four-word hint: *you are not alone* [see, inevitably, X3.11, "Utopia"].

Boe's death finally comes from sacrificing his life-energy to power up the shutters containing the smoggy ring-road, and allowing the survivors to get into daylight and fresh air. For the last quarter-century, he has been wired into the grid to replace the city's mains. His 'smoke' [whatever it is] shielded himself and Novice Hame from the virus. [If Boe contacted the Doctor off-screen, either by Psychic Paper as last time or another means – make your own Facebook joke – this must be at the limit of his oddly-extended lifespan. If not, then the Doctor is arguably responsible for the long delay in rescuing the motorists, because Boe held on to life to give his message.]

• *Novice Hame* is still a Novice [the rest of her order seem to have died, so there's nobody to invest her]. Her penance for her role in the hospital scandal ["New Earth"] is to tend to the Face of Boe. When the plague wipes out the Upper City, she helps Boe to preserve the motorists, awaiting the Doctor's return and the opportunity to relieve Boe of the burden. The idea of the ancient jar-bound alien dying seems inconceivable.

The Non-Humans

• *Macra.* According to the Doctor, they built up 'a small empire' 'billions' of years ago by using enslaved humans to mine their food source: toxic gas. The Doctor insists that the Macra were the scourge of the galaxy at one point [going by "The Macra Terror", this has to have occurred off-screen], but that they've devolved since then. The scale of their claws to their spindly legs makes them look like they'll topple over at any moment. They still thrive on pollution, but seem far less intelligent. They now feed off passing cars, attacking them directly rather than sneaking about and manipulating the minds of people above-ground. [See **Things That Don't Make Sense** for how giant crabs could invade the bottom of a city that's uninhabitable for them until the traffic-jam starts.]

Planet Notes

• *New Earth.* The requirements of the automatic quarantine [see **History**] have sealed off New Earth for an expected hundred years. Someone's been running holograms to maintain the illusion of civic services, including police who are always on hold and a driving report. The latter, presented by 'Sally Calypso' (who also conducts the prayer-meetings) has a stylised Statue of Liberty graphic behind her. The odd convention of number/ random word combinations that we've seen in the last two Boe stories continues, with Car Four Six Five Diamond Six.

There's a variety of easy-use pharmaceuticals for what seems to be very low prices, including Sleep, Happy-Happy, Mellow, Forget and [oddly] Honesty. They come in varying strengths, marked by numbers, and work like nicotine patches, absorbed through the skin on the upper arm. The lettering is in a typeface like the *New Yorker* masthead. One of the most popular, Bliss, carried a lethal virus and so was responsible for the Overcity's destruction. All the patches have the green hospital crescent on them. [As per "New Earth", but hardly fits the way they're treated as

Must They All be Old-Fashioned Cats?

continued from Page 81...

one with a toxic dad. Jackie Tyler is depicted as "hilariously" trying to get a boyfriend once her daughter's old enough to move out, but she's legitimately a widow, despite the scripts depicting her as a cliché soap-single-mum-on-the-pull. Martha's dad isn't given any credit for trying to get out of what's clearly a doomed marriage, and the whole of Series 3's botched story-arc is given over to getting this messed-up family back together. The set-up in "Fear Her" (X2.11) is even more alarming, as the death of a father who was the single scariest thing Chloe had ever encountered is presented as the start of her psychiatric/ alien-playmate reign of terror rather than a transition.

In the Moffat era, this has been reversed to make dads comically ineffectual – but the best way to show how things have changed, and yet stayed pretty much the same, is by comparing "Fear Her" to "Night Terrors" (X6.9) by Mark Gatiss, a story apparently intended as a repair-job on the former. Here, we have a more flagrantly John Wyndham-esque set-up even than the vaguely *Chocky*-like Isolus, wherein an alien impregnates someone and the resultant child's psychic force threatens the putative father and thus the whole world. In Gatiss's version, the resolution comes from embracing the boy as his own and healing the psychic trauma of possible rejection. In both stories, moreover, the threat to the child's world-view comes from the Doctor explaining the extra-terrestrial origin of the family secret and he is removed to a fantasy-land of either drawings or a doll's house. Woe betide anyone who dares to say that a nuclear family, however screwed-up, isn't "right". In "Night Terrors", the Doctor sticks around until George's mum returns from work – but in "Fear Her", he and Rose have cakes and fireworks rather than talk to Chloe and Trish about what they'll do next.

Dads got a better press once one took over the series and, in many ways, the most characteristic story of the Moffat phase was the two-part Silurian story (X5.8-5.9, "The Hungry Earth"/"Cold Blood", in which father-son bonding and mother-son protectiveness are what make humans dangerous and worth defending. Except... there's a lot that fails to add up about that family's dynamic and with the odd androgynous names, it's possible that Mo and Ambrose got swapped and sex-changed somewhere in the rewrites – an angry mum apparently being more plausibly psychotic and murderous than an angry dad. The intended contrast with the reptilian warriors is undercut by the cost-cutting use of the same actor for two of them, making them have to be sisters with a closeness we're usually told is uniquely mammalian (not least by zoologists). Another of the family (at least, the same performer and mask) is now part of the aforementioned Paternoster Gang, but doesn't get genocidal when confronted with mammalian kinship bonds. In fact, she's in one herself. After many coy references to being married to Jenny, Madame Zastra engaged in on-screen lip-contact with her – but with the "justification" of trying to replenish her wife's air supply. Even with this (forgive the phrase) mealy-mouthed approach, the tabloids hit the roof when this went to air (X8.1, "Deep Breath" – even the title made the excuse clear).

The biggest change is with the audience-identification figures. Looking at one-story companion-surrogate and narrator Elton Pope (X2.10, "Love & Monsters"), the big revelation is that the Doctor was with him when his mother died. No mention is made of a father. Elton's just *there*, with his elective family, LINDA. Elective families were the big trend in current TV when *Doctor Who* was being resuscitated; from *Friends* to *Neighbours* to *Spaced* to *Buffy the Vampire Slayer*, the biological families were less important than the people "inside" the protagonist's world. However, with female TARDIS crew, the story was about choosing between these. Hitherto, the majority of companions had been de facto orphans, if not literal ones. Adults may have had jobs to get back to, but there was no mention of their folks (except for Ben, but they created a whole backstory for him that never made it to screen), unless seeing them die was what made them have to leave for Adventures in Space and Time.

Think about this: the first companion to have had two parents we hear about was Victoria, and their deaths are both significant to the plot (4.7, "The Evil of the Daleks"). Jo's off-screen uncle and Sarah's Aunt Lavinia aside, the next relative we meet was Leela's father, very briefly. The remainder of the series' run was so family-free that Tegan's domestic arrangements (see **Who Attended Aunt Vanessa's Funeral?** under 21.2, "The Awakening") and Ace's problems with her mum

continued on Page 85...

standard commodities.] Medical services can ascertain the sex of a baby by scanning.

A good many location names are borrowed from the old New York – there's a New Fifth Avenue, New Times Square, and even a New New Jersey [for Heaven knows what reason], but Fire Island, Battery Park, and Brooklyn don't get the "new" appellation. [The body of water outside the city presumably connects up to the New Atlantic.] They use imperial measurements for distance, but Celsius for temperature. One of the mood-pushers has a Glasgow accent. The metropolis is described as a 'City-State' [reinforcing the suggestion of autonomy].

The cat-people are inter-fertile with "Time Lord"-looking humans, with Brannigan and Valerie's two-month-old offspring resembling an ordinary basket of kittens. The motorway has a slang vocabulary that matches twentieth-century language; people hitchhike onto cars or get taken by carjackers, and hope that they don't encounter pirates. Access to the fast lane requires three adults per car [supposedly a fuel-economy directive – see **Things That Don't Make Sense**] and there's even the odd monster urban legend. [Quite who's survived the monsters and come back to tell the tale is, as with so many urban legends, left as an exercise for the reader.] There are communication systems set up between cars, rather like CB rigs, with social media settings available so you can exclude anyone you've not "friended". All the cars are, of course, right-hand drive.

Guns are fairly rare [but must be enough in supply for a threat with a mock-up to be taken seriously]. Houses made of wood are terribly exciting [as with several other Davies scripts]. Some Undercity inhabitants hope to get jobs at foundries and laundries when they get out of the city. [The Doctor's exclamation that they're all ignoring the possibility that the motorway never ends doesn't seem quite as simple as that, even if the M25 is underlying a lot of this story's assumptions.] Each day at a specified time, there's a communal hymn sing consisting of old Earth classics. [We never discover whose idea this is – maybe the Face of Boe started the tradition, as the duration of the travellers' stay became apparent. It's not something the Senate would think to do in the last seven minutes of their lives, nor something a piece of software would necessarily conceive of as important.]

People swear by Jehovah, although 'God' gets one mention. Gay couples are worthy of comment [or at least mild teasing by old-fashioned cats], but that's about it. Nudists and Goth cats aren't considered remarkable. [The various cars that the Doctor runs through demonstrate an amazing number of people with varyingly odd kinks. One imagines that with years of nothing in particular to do in tiny enclosed spaces, it would be a fairly popular form of entertainment. Nevertheless, several cars are apparently inhabited by only one person each.]

New Earth is '50,000' light years from Earth. [That puts it firmly within our own galaxy, rather than M87 as previously stated – *that* galaxy is 53 million light years off, and moving Earth was enough of a hassle when the Time Lords did it in 23.1, "The Mysterious Planet". So maybe the Doctor mis-spoke to a factor of a thousand. That said, our galaxy and Andromeda are going to have merged by Five Billion AD, so maybe M87's moved significantly closer too.]

History

• *Dating.* It's the year Five Billion and Fifty-Three, or 30 years after the Doctor's last visit ["New Earth"]. Twenty-four years ago, a mutated virus-plague became airborne and wiped out the Senate and everyone in the Overcity. The Face of Boe's smoke protected him as well as Novice Hame; everyone else died in seven minutes, with just enough time to close down the Undercity and have the Senate of New York declare a quarantine. Since then, the city power has gone down as well; the Face of Boe has been powering the system with his own life-force, else it would all have fallen into the sea. He and the Doctor here reopen the city so that everyone in the motorway can emerge to the Overcity.

The Doctor rather suspects that Novice Hame will be the new leader. [Given she's the only person on the planet who actually knows what happened 24 years ago, this is either quite likely – *or* she's facing another prison charge from anyone alive with sufficient authority. We don't even know if there's other people or cities on this planet, though Hame's dialogue suggests that New New York is the only settlement.]

English Lessons

• "Abide With Me" is traditionally sung at the start of the FA Cup Final, which used to be the climax of the football season, in May. Now, there

Must They All be Old-Fashioned Cats?

continued from Page 83...

(and assumption that baby Audrey was born out of wedlock – 26.3, "The Curse of Fenric") were perceived at the time of broadcast as comparatively realistic and refreshing.

In the twenty-first century, we have a situation where Amelia Pond's lack of any immediate family is the first clue that something is amiss with the spacetime continuum (X5.1, "The Eleventh Hour"), even though said missing parents are only wheeled on at the end of that series and with stupid Roald Dahl-style names. (See also X7.2, "Dinosaurs on a Spaceship" for the way Amy and Rory's wedding was even odder than it seemed on first broadcast.) Clara Oswald's storyline was a shambles: she had a dead mother, an annoying stepmother straight out of Davies, a comedy gran, a clueless dad, a cute story about the Doctor's role in her parents' meeting and a peculiar domestic set-up involving her being a Victorian-style governess to what may (or may not) be a set of mixed-race parents. (We've only seen the kids – much as we might wish not to have encountered them – and a five-second glimpse of dad.)

In another life, she was also a *genuine* Victorian governess for a different widowed dad's children who was, for some reason, moonlighting as a barmaid and (therefore) part-time hooker. (Let's not even think about Danny Pink's backstory.) Clara's Christmases were miserable, either with her revised nuclear family (X7.16, "The Time of the Doctor") or alone (X9.0, "Last Christmas") and when she died, there was no effort to contact her dad or her gran – just a bit of graffiti-art on the TARDIS as a memorial. Bill's adoptive mum, Moira, is more like a landlady and the daydream version of her birth-mother never gets to say anything, just be a fond wish (one which, if X10.8, "The Lie of the Land" is taken at face value, everyone else on the planet also had, so it's not that special any more).[18]

And while Amy and Rory's marriage was the hinge-point of the cosmos, their own parents were oddly insignificant. The one time we saw Amy's olds, she was amazed that they even existed (X5.13, "Big Bang"), but at least they showed up to the wedding. Rory's dad apparently missed a police box arriving on the dance-floor and someone called the Doctor, looking like a young Douglas Wilmer, stepping out in evening dress from the 1930s. Nobody even showed him photos, it seems. When we did finally meet Brian Williams, he was a comic-relief inept dad, but there was no mention of a mum ever having existed.

Nonetheless, the trend of each companion's storyline has been from having the Doctor disrupting the family dynamic towards him becoming part of it – and this is entirely in keeping with how things were panning out in *Queer as Folk* (until two lesbians decided to have a baby). The ideal towards which Davies-scripted families aspire is to be a "proper" family *and* have all the benefits of the excitingly carefree "other" world available on the mum's terms. This is the underlying storyline of *The Sarah Jane Adventures*, but is more interesting where it runs athwart the other soap-like tendency of making Doctor-companion relationships look like mundane boy-meets-girl romances.

What's interesting is that under Davies, the over-protective mother who can't quite believe her daughter's old enough to do her own shoelaces up was borderline-plausible when it was Rose, who was aged either 18 or 19 (depending on which D.O.B. you go for) and already in a long-term relationship. When it's Francine's relationship with her elder daughter Martha, the 25-year-old med student, or worse yet Sylvia Noble, mother of an already-married and obviously mature Donna, credulity is stretched like mozzarella on a pizza until it pings. The single worst thing about the end of "Journey's End" (X4.13) is that Donna is denied the opportunity to tell her mum where to get off. This is, in some ways, more realistic, but the story's pretence at narrative closure comes undone in its refusal to let Donna confront Sylvia.

As has been noted, the skewed critical tradition we've inherited means that conflict between fathers and sons is the very substance of the Great American Novel, while mother-daughter conflict is for soaps. The characteristic of soaps is that they don't end anything (unless the ratings are suffering), whereas novels have to have climaxes and a "shape". Donna's fate is to have an enormous reset button pressed so that she reverts to her factory settings, rather than have a novelistic transformation. In many ways, this is precisely what is needed – Donna was intended as a comic character, therefore one who reverts to type in the most inappropriate of circumstances. So when Donna comes back (X4.17-18, "The End of Time"), she is exactly as she was, but Sylvia has adapted to circumstances

continued on Page 87...

are lots of international trophies and matches all year. Quite why such a funereal hymn, a plea for help, is associated with Wembley Stadium is unclear. (The other hymn, "The Old Rugged Cross", is mainly associated with Scotland here, the one part of the UK to take Country and Western seriously. It occasionally turned up on ITV's mawkish *Stars on Sunday,* but isn't widely used in churches in Britain. If we are to trust Wikipedia, the main British referent for the hymn is Dennis Potter's *Pennies from Heaven*, broadcast in 1978, and a single in the lower end of the Top 50 in 1974, but not much since then.)

• *Carspotter* (n.): It's a play on the term "trainspotter". Given that the cars are all exactly the same design and can't even be seen properly for more than ten feet in any direction, any points scored must be from collecting the number plates. [See **What's All This Stuff About Anoraks?** under 24.1, "Time and the Rani".]

The Analysis

The Big Picture There are obvious cinematic visual reference-points at work, so we'll get those out of the way first. Two then-recent films have flying cars in a traffic-jam in a city – *Star Wars Episode II: Attack of the Clones* (2002) had a chase around Coruscant, the Trantor-like planet-covering city (see below) and *The Fifth Element* (1997) had begun with a similar, more overtly Manhattan-like future city where Bruce Willis drove (flew?) a yellow cab. The Mill's effects bods overtly alluded to Coruscant when devising the shots of the city at dawn. We also have the film-of-the-song *Convoy* (1978), which led to a brief fad in the UK with American-style CB radio – it was more talked-about than talked-on.

However, the most significant factor in this story's genesis is the revelation. As Gareth Roberts wrote in a slightly tetchy aside in his piece on "How to Write for *Doctor Who*" for the 2010 *Brilliant Book*, anyone who thinks that the 2005 marque could say more than the 1963 model is missing a few very large topics that are now off the table, notably religion. This is indeed a cavernous gap in the revived series' repertoire. The earlier version had to deal with it right from the second episode, when sun-worshipping cavemen were being manipulated by a scheming little old lady who used the dead as a source of her authority (until the Doctor's party later turned this to their advantage with skulls and candles). Real religions, in the Hartnell Historical stories, were shown as a source of conflict (1.6, "The Aztecs"; 2.6, "The Crusade"; 3.5, "The Massacre") or a personal choice in the face of the State (2.4, "The Romans").

For the rest of its initial run, the series' characteristic response run is introduced in "The Time Meddler" (2.9), in which a visiting time-traveller shrewdly, brazenly and comically abuses Catholic ritual and the status of priests as fonts of all wisdom. Thereafter, all non-local religions are depicted as half-remembered science from aliens who either posed as gods or were misremembered that way. Most of the time, they were cynical methods to induce sheep-like conformity in the humans, plots hatched by beings with a generations-long plan to achieve a rather squalid or desperate objective. Occasionally, the mythology of cultures no longer around to object provides a disguise for space-opera/ horror movie trappings (13.3, "Pyramids of Mars"; 15.5, "Underworld") or we get a real culture mumbled about so that we can assume that this is what happened (14.6, "The Talons of Weng-Chiang").

Although many *Doctor Who* staples are rooted in the same long-disproved belief-systems that inform most current religious/ spiritual practices (notably, that there is a thing called "consciousness" that has a physical manifestation capable of being transferred, downloaded or re-embodied), the series reflexively rejects religion as a process. Indeed, the closest "Gridlock" comes to making a statement is to depict the communitarian impulse among the drivers as a scam to save everyone's lives by keeping them (literally) in the dark.

The most interesting precedent for that is "Planet of Fire" (21.5), where the priest Timanov is just about the only person who believes in the god Logar, but enforcing his law is the only thing keeping the small society from extinction. What makes this different from most *Doctor Who* based on the same quasi-Von Daniken idea is that there is a genuine threat to the population *as well as* a cynical spacefaring society popping in and playing god. The more usual version is a rumour or half-memory of some terrible threat from outside that will kill the ungodly if they leave the safety of the "protecting" tyrants. (See, for example, 6.4, "The Krotons"; 18.4, "State of Decay"; and 14.4, "The Face of Evil", although that's a weird case as the threat is made by the *same being* that is protecting the Sevateem from monsters and the Tesh

Must They All be Old-Fashioned Cats?

continued from Page 85...

rather than remaining the self-important figure she was in every previous appearance.

Donna is, in one regard, a throwback to old-style companions in that her departure from the series (the last one) involves a wedding. It's her *third* on-screen nuptial, in fact, and hubby isn't even allowed a line of dialogue this time (which only puts him a notch above Lee in X4.9,"Forest of the Dead"). It's interesting that while we've had more same-sex married couples than most dramas (well, two stated ones in Davies stories: the Cassinis and the Russians in X4.16,"The Waters of Mars"), the only wedding ceremonies we see are heterosexual, and in all of these cases it's the mother-daughter dynamic that is fuelling the plot (although we didn't quite know how far that was true in X5.13,"The Big Bang"). Moffat's had a more bizarre mother-daughter relationship built into his stories, and we'll note in passing that the only time a couple seems ever to have had sex aboard the TARDIS is just after they were legally married and – as a result – the Doctor himself acquires in-laws. Amy Pond is alarming since almost all of her personality, once she's old enough to be played by Karen Gillan, is entirely determined by the two men in her life and their relationships with her are to do with her reproductive capabilities, despite her spending the latter half of Series 6 forgetting that she ever had a baby. However stroppy or "feisty" she may be, she's effectively denied any agency. Look at what she does for a living. Look at all the things she's capable of doing in "The Girl Who Waited" (X6.10), but doesn't, choosing instead to, er, wait. Even the supposedly more pro-active version in "The Wedding of River Song" (X6.13) is primarily concerned with rescuing the Doctor, even though she has no idea why, or who Rory is or anything else. (This whole scenario defies explanation as it breaks even Moffat's own rules on how these things work – see **Is Time Like Bolognese Sauce Now?** under X5.5, "Flesh and Stone").

Of course, Amy's daughter Melody Pond, AKA River Song, is a magic alien baby. She has to be, as no mere woman could possibly marry the Doctor without removing the series' charm for pre-teen girls. This also applies to him acquiring a daughter by putting his genes in a magimix and coming out with Jenny (X4.6, "The Doctor's Daughter"). We're going to delve into this in another essay (**Does He... You Know... *Dance*?** under X4.8, "Silence in the Library"), but it's worth noting that the Doctor now definitely had a childhood and parents and acknowledges having been a father (in, oh look, "Fear Her"). Aliens now have childhoods (X1.11, "Boom Town", for example) but, prior to "Gridlock", the only BBC Wales example of something not conventionally human producing offspring was the Face of Boe's pregnancy. Captain Jack was supposedly from a culture where the imperative to reproduce led to lowered resistance towards miscegenation and (somehow) same-sex relationships, but we never actually saw that in any of the stories in which he appeared (despite a hint in X3.11, "Utopia"). Moreover, after over a century on Earth he appeared, by the time of *Torchwood: Children of Earth*, to have fathered exactly one child (plus a vague hint in *TW: Everything Changes* that he was once pregnant himself). We would never now get a story such as "Kinda" (19.3), where humanoids are living in a (generally) happy and functional polygamous clan structure. As with their terror of questioning religious sensibilities or showing the effects of violence, the BBC Wales version is more timid and unimaginative.

We must also reconsider the programme's odd attitude to marriage. While death, reproduction and consciousness are all technologically mediated when the plot needs it, and time-travel makes relationships complicated, the Doctor and River's wedding vow alters the nature of spacetime itself ("The Wedding of River Song") – even though the Doctor is already married to Elizabeth I ("The End of Time Part One"; X7.15, "The Day of the Doctor"), Cleopatra (14.1, "The Masque of Mandragora"; X2.3, "School Reunion"; "The Husbands of River Song") and Marilyn Monroe (X6.0, "A Christmas Carol") and she has two other husbands on the go in one episode (plus a baffling reference to Stephen Fry). This, in a story that suggests that this is uncommon even in the fifty-fourth century, despite so many other mores being shown as arbitrary when it strikes the author as funny.

River seems to have got about a bit even after marrying the Doctor, dating androids ("Silence in the Library") and apparently hiring her crew to investigate the Library on their looks rather than ability; he in turn has some sort of past with Tasha Lem (X7.16, "The Time of the Doctor", although much of the dialogue indicates that she was invented at short notice when Alex Kingston was

continued on Page 89...

from the Sevateem.)

Seen through this lens, the significant absence in "Gridlock" is the notion we would sometimes get in old *Who* that there is a counter-myth; you might expect there to be someone – an elderly lady, usually – who recalls the old ways, and is treated as a witch for casting doubt on the official version. Think about it: every time we hear of a "legend" of the Time Lords, or a fairy-tale the Doctor was told as a Time-Tot, it turns out to be literally true, while the recorded, "canonical" version is a masterpiece of spin and obfuscation. Not once or twice... *every time*. So, in a story that partakes of so many of these trends in older episodes, we get the Doctor lying about Gallifrey and then coming clean (while omitting the bit where he apparently blew up his own planet and wiped out his people). It's interesting that the establishment of a holding-pattern saves the New New Yorkers; it's analogous to the Time Lords' favourite method of sweeping things under the carpet, a time-loop. And that the person who reveals the truth to the Doctor is an old lady (but being a cat and in a society where longevity seems to be a given, Novice Hame doesn't look like, say, Martha Tyler from 15.3, "Image of the Fendahl" – the mother-lode for so much of Davies's work – or Olive Hawthorne; 8.5, "The Daemons").

We're not claiming direct influence so much as that Davies has imbibed a whole tradition of *Doctor Who* that's as much a part of it as Yeti-in-the-Loo or running up and down corridors. The BBC world-view of the 60s, 70s and 80s was resolutely non-denominational – which, in Britain, means secular. Religion is what other people do, we just have "values". That unexamined assumption was less tenable in later years and at present the Corporation has guidelines on not causing offence or making unwarranted all-embracing statements about something called "us".

BBC guidelines prevent an overt statement such as "There is no God and anyone who says otherwise is trying to sell you something", but they also prevent any endorsement of a specific faith. (Steven Moffat's approach to this topic has been surprisingly sensitive and nuanced – see X6.11, "The God Complex"; X5.4, "The Time of Angels"; and any story set in River Song's era. Indeed, his entire time on the series has been grounded in a notion of Predestination and Free Will being equivalent.) Both Moffat and Davies proclaim their atheism, but they happily raid the scrapbook of past religions for story-ideas, images and what seem to them to be logical progressions of ideas. Whereas the previous generation of *Doctor Who* writers could assume a linear development from superstition to science and that the future was rational, the new lot have been raised on Hollywood effects-movies and seem to have preferred the pretty pictures drawn from earlier ages to the bother of learning science at school. (If nothing else, we will see how this tradition blighted Davies's story-telling ability at the end of this year and thereafter.)

The two films mentioned above seem like Science Fiction, but they have plots reliant on mediaeval beliefs and end up validating the viewpoints of quasi-monastic orders over biologists and engineers. *Star Wars* essentially peddles the Divine Right of Kings and a weird idea that clones lack souls like regular folks, while even the title *The Fifth Element* presupposes a flat Earth with the Sun being pushed around it by angels. With the BBC Wales stable taking their inspiration from the pretty pictures in other visual media, themselves derived from 30s magazines, themselves taken from musicals (check out "Petting in the Park" from *Gold Diggers of 1933* for the brass bikinis that Margaret Atwood seems to think are SF's defining feature), coherent world-building has slid down the priorities of programme-makers, if not viewers. Collaging is so much easier, and the placement of religious iconography – or symbolic representations of a religion – makes a faked-up world seem more complete if you only have 42 minutes to tell a story and depict an unfamiliar culture. (Or not, if it's X7.8, "The Rings of Akhaten")

Mentioning 30s musicals takes us back to Manhattan. The image of the skyscrapers, the bustle and the melting-pot was the key twentieth-century icon. All those RKO and Warner Brothers films were made in Los Angeles but set in New York, but a more New-Yorkish New York than location filming could provide. Van Nest Polglase's eye-popping sets for Fred and Ginger's elegant misunderstandings and Anton Grot's realisation of where the logic-defying Busby Berkeley routines happen convey the *idea* of New York, just as the crime-stories of the same studios (and the same Art-Directors, like as not), the stylised downtown inhabited by gangsters, most of whom had priests for brothers (usually played by Pat O'Brien).

The next two episodes will deal with the way

Must They All be Old-Fashioned Cats?

continued from Page 87...

unavailable). Moreover, finally marrying Rory makes Amy not just unavailable to the Doctor (who seems not to actively fancy her, probably because he first met her when she was eight), but capable of rewriting her own past so that Rory was always the only one for her (X6.2, "Day of the Moon"; X6.8, "Let's Kill Hitler") in the face of the evidence ("The Eleventh Hour"; X5.5, "Flesh and Stone"). This wedding-day is stated several times to be, as their daughter puts it, part of the "Base-code of the Universe" ("Flesh and Stone" again). There's a concerted effort to make marriage more than just a legal status and almost as potent as the much-vaunted Fixed Points.

On this matter, the series is poised on a knife-edge of showing family life as we know it to be and sticking to the precepts of 1963. When *The Sarah Jane Adventures* (made for CBBC, the under-twelves channel) is more honest about the realities of twenty-first century Britain than the general-audience series, something very odd is happening. Perhaps they realised that under-twelves in Britain had been exposed to more different types of family-group than are shown in television intended for export to more conservative countries, such as China or America.

Series 4 started to explore alternatives to conventional child-rearing. The Adipose (X4.1, "Partners in Crime") had a nursery planet that went missing, so their humanoid matron began using overweight British customers as unwitting wombs. Apart from the element of consent and the potential health-hazard in the extreme way this was being done, this isn't necessarily a bad thing. With a few checks and balances, it could have been an intriguing story about people volunteering to help a threatened race of cute aliens and the way our society considers fat to be bad but encourages – indeed, depends upon – all the things that promote it. The story-as-made is interesting for what it does say, and hint at, but the emphasis is squarely on the Adipose as hapless threats to normal society, rather than the surrogacy (by men and women) and how this might change things if it went more smoothly.

When the Sontarans finally returned (X4.4, "The Sontaran Stratagem"), the entire story was about making Earth over as a breeding colony, despite its low gravity, but the script completely bungled the idea that these warriors have discarded sex and variation in favour of cloning and conformity. (We'll pick this up in **Who Are You Calling Monsters?** under X3.6, "The Lazarus Experiment".) The notion that they can muster an army in minutes is rather muffled when they need to spend the best part of a year making a nest.

Sontaran war-hero Strax (X6.7, "A Good Man Goes to War") is now a comic-relief foil, and his main characteristic in his posthumous returns in Series 7 is his inability to tell boys from girls. Moffat earlier cut a line from "The Pandorica Opens" (X5.12) sneering at their same-sex relationships, but a gag about "handbags" remains and Strax is shown to be able to suckle babies. However, the Paternoster Gang are the closest we've had to the elective family model since LINDA; there's a cross-species same-sex marriage and a kerr-razy-mixed-up Sontaran butler. In the past, this sort of set-up was pretty much the norm aboard the TARDIS at various stages – and even at the peak of the one-companion period, we had the "UNIT family". These have to be considered the least troubled domestic set-ups of any quasi-familial households in the programme. If there is one scene that shows the ideal nuclear-like family, it's the beginning of "The Chase" (2.8) – if it were any more like the ad-man's idea of a Sunday Morning in 1965, we'd hear *The Archers* or *Two-Way Family Favourites* and be able to smell Yorkshire Pudding.

The only times we ever see a real family all happily getting along, as it happens, is Christmas episodes. And, as we've said, the most radical challenge to this domestic norm as the ideal comes in the supposedly children-only spin-off. The whole point of *The Sarah Jane Adventures* is that parents "don't get it". Alan Jackson finally joins the gang at the end of the first series, only to be written out as his ex-wife hints that she's not as easily duped as she let everyone think. Thereafter, the whole thrust of the series is that genuine, biological parents are no substitute for wise, experienced spinsters who acquire child-allies and save the world before the homework's due. Predictably, single parents are shown to be basically as clueless as any other kind, but Chrissie Jackson isn't quite as grotesque as Jackie Tyler.

Magic alien babies abound in *SJA*, including two that Sarah winds up adopting herself. Most stories are about threats to the unity of this group, with one member per story caused to consider

continued on Page 91...

that 1930s New York has become the default setting for futuristic cities, but the logic of this means that you need Catholicism in the background to stand in for every conceivable ethnic minority's backstory. New New York has blue people, red people, white people, cat-people and people from pictures – but the only *religion* is the cat-nuns, who are nurses first and foremost. (The Face of Boe has dreadlocks, but these might be tentacles rather than a sign that he thinks Haile Salasse was the Messiah. The smoke probably isn't ganja, if it can protect Novice Hame from disease.) The more recent idea of New York – the late-70s cliché of crime, drugs, sleaze and defiance – is also at work here with the most organised and un-hassled drug-pushers in television history. Anyone growing up in 70s Britain would have had this idea in varying strengths, from *Taxi Driver* through *Starsky and Hutch* to American bands coming to London from CBGB's and claiming to have invented Punk. America seemed conceptually absurd.

The kid's comic *2000 AD* was all about ridiculing these exciting situations and locations by reconfiguring them in a very English context. There's a lot of talk about "Gridlock" having borrowed from *2000 AD*, but closer examination makes this claim questionable. In particular, the chap in the bowler hat isn't particularly, as Davies says he intended, a variation on Max Normal (the resolutely square informant in *Judge Dredd*) – he's more like Mr Benn, the secretly-resourceful *habitué* of a magic costume shop from, er, *Mr Benn*. Max Normal was an informer, based on Huggy Bear from *Starsky and Hutch*, whose freakishly square appearance was intended to be as out-of-place as the disco-era clothes worn by Antonio Fargas in the TV series. A character a bit like Sally Calypso was in *Halo Jones* (see 24.4, "Dragonfire" and X4.0, "Voyage of the Damned").

Yet the basic idea, of locating people like the ones we know (either from experience or iconography) inside a ludicrous America-Lite, like Mega-City One, is clearly what's at work here. In this case, the idea that the city was constructed with a slum as a design-feature is less silly than it might be. The idea is usually that such areas, especially when geographically placed beneath newer, more futuristic bits, are left-behind or built-over remnants. This idea was a standard-issue part of off-the-shelf dystopias in the *New Adventures* books, and formed the backstory for Roz Forrester and Chris Cwej: two companions of the Virgin Books Doctor. What's significant is that the denizens of the "Gridlock" Undercity are all standard-model human, rather than being the various analogues for ethnic minorities. (Especially the Cordwainer Smith-esque cat-nuns. Smith's stories called all animal-derived characters "Underpeople" and worked in a storyline close enough to the contemporary Civil Rights movement for people to miss the personal significance, but that's a whole book in itself.)

As we saw in **What was Season Two Supposed to be Like?** under X2.11, "Fear Her", Davies had been playing around with the idea of having the Face of Boe make his final announcement in "New Earth", but had eventually put it off once a third series was confirmed. Re-using an established setting and going into what's under the surface is – as with the treatment of religion – habitual amongst writers weaned on Letts/ Hinchcliffe/ Williams-model *Who*. Similarly, the cheeky re-use of last year's trademark effects shot, as a scripted comment on how things "usually" look there, is the kind of cost-cutting that turns into a plot-point (see, for example, the start of 18.3, "Full Circle").

The emotions-as-drugs concept was worked up from Gareth Roberts's ninth Doctor novel *Only Human*, but didn't really start there (you can bet that if something is parodied in Woody Allen's *Sleeper*, it's officially a Science-Fiction Cliché). It may also be the case that mood-names such as "Bliss" echo MDMA's street-name "ecstasy" (or the David Bowie song "Memory of a Free Festival" in which "someone passed some bliss among the crowd"). Davies's use of it is in synch with his idea of cocaine as an intrinsic part of the New York experience, as used in his own *Doctor Who* novel *Damaged Goods*. Meanwhile, the urban myth about alligators in the sewers of New York was already enough of a standard to have been introduced into both post-apocalyptic London (2.2, "The Dalek Invasion of Earth" – Terry Nation and Dennis Spooner had a peculiar relationship to the mythos of Manhattan, as we will also see next episode) and Thomas Pynchon's debut novel *V* (1963). The low-lying smog at the base of a city's atmosphere, with flying cars hiding in it, is a straight steal from *The Fifth Element*, but that in turn derives from generations of flying-cars-in-New York sequences dating back to 20s pulp magazine covers and the dreadful musical *Just Imagine* (released November 1930, i.e. the month when X3.4, "Daleks in Manhattan" is set).

Must They All be Old-Fashioned Cats?

continued from Page 89...

how long they can keep up with the dual demands of a real family and a good one. (Even then, Rani's lack of an extended family presence is peculiar.) The UNIT stories tended not to have to do this, as the various regulars seemed not to have any lives outside the whole world-saving thing, and never socialised with anyone who didn't know what they did. The Brigadier's occasional Regimental do aside, the only time a serving member was seen to engage with normal life was Benton arranging to take his kid sister ballroom dancing (13.4, "The Android Invasion").

An obvious point to make is that parents are, to most children, fairly boring. That's somewhat out of necessity, since they spend all their time and money on raising children rather than doing anything reckless or fun. Yet every child grows up thinking that their family is the standard against which anyone else's is to be measured, and sometimes the discovery of difference is alarming. Few teenagers believe that their parents have any real idea what's happening in their lives. School and family are interruptions to their true education or social interactions. Dads are, by definition, embarrassing, especially when they try too hard not to be (wearing sunglasses indoors and playing a guitar, attempting current slang, looking smug when they've got it right, etc.).

The regulation husband, wife and 2.4 kids was never the only option, but is increasingly unlike what most households in the UK are like. For most people watching, therefore, *SJA* was the closest any manifestation of *Doctor Who* ever got to reflecting what life was like in a modern family. Nonetheless, mixed-race relationships don't tend to produce children in any form of *Doctor Who*, flying in the face of all real-life experience. Brannigan's interspecies brood is the one example we can find on screen and mentions of others (X4,16, "The Waters of Mars" for example) are scant and infrequent. We have no gay parents on screen, although Jo seems very supportive of her son's choices. (See *SJA*: "Death of the Doctor". Jo Grant, as was, is here depicted as the exception to the rule in that her married life was even more haphazard and exhilarating than travelling with the Doctor, and yet she's managed to raise children and grandchildren while hurtling around saving the world and putting herself and everyone with her into harm's way for a cause.)

Settling down is still the biggest threat to the Doctor. The temptation to give up adventuring and raise kids is obviously strong enough for there to be a story at all in "Human Nature" (the book, and X3.8, and X3.9, "The Family of Blood"), but the series relies on him not having this option. Thus River Song is incarcerated and killed, although the storyline is unclear on what exactly is not being said. Why, for example, does marrying the Doctor make time start up again ("The Wedding of River Song")? The series requires any such "threat" to the Doctor's wanderlust to be countered or neutralised, thus nobody watching "The Doctor's Daughter" should have been surprised that Jenny was killed, or that they resurrected her (they'd used so much else from the end of *Star Trek II: Wrath of Khan*, the slingshot ending had to be recycled too). The Doctor has to remain a bit clueless about children, thinking that whatever he thinks is "cool" must be what they like and missing the point about routines, responsibilities and setting an example.

(See also **Is Kylie from Planet Zog?** under X4.0, "Voyage of the Damned".)

The majority of these depict future-NYC as hellish, but Isaac Asimov, who grew up in Brooklyn, has fun subverting the cliché in both *The Caves of Steel* (see 14.5, "The Robots of Death") and the *Foundation* stories. Trantor, the planet-wide metropolis, has a spaceport that is manifestly Grand Central Station and a population who never even get to ground-level, let alone see the sky. We could also invoke an advert for Norwich Union car insurance from around the time this was being written, in which cartoonish cars floated in streams on a yellow background, with animated big-headed photos of drivers, accompanied by Spike Jones's "Hawaiian War Chant" for some reason. A cited reference that Davies brought up was the computer-animated co-host of early 90s BBC1 Saturday Morning kids show *Live & Kicking*, co-hosted by the marginally less-believable John Barrowman. This was Ratz, a cat in a Biggles hat, but it only appeared on a monitor and from the neck up. No children seem to have been traumatised by floating disembodied cat-heads in leather bonnets blethering about 8-bit games consoles. A similar possible reference is the Studio Ghibli film *Porco Rosso* (see also X1.4, "Aliens of London" and "Daleks in

Manhattan"), where it's a pig who flies biplanes.

We'll just mention that the idea of a population being manipulated by non-existent authority figures appearing on the screens of the masses is hardly original (there was a rather famous one by George Orwell), but also that the clearest example of this particular idea in *Doctor Who* is, er, "The Macra Terror".

Additional Sources The 2005 *Doctor Who* Annual had a piece which told of a mountainside on the planet Crafe Tec Heydra in the Silver Devastation, wherein were carved runes and hieroglyphs telling of a battle between machines and people where one survivor walked away, but with the message *You Are Not Alone* (we will return to this book in 3.10, "Blink"). In another tie-in, *Doctor Who: Aliens and Monsters*, Davies had "translated" a work telling that when the Face of Boe finally dies, the sky will split open and he will give his last secret to a wanderer. The idea that the Macra were kept in New New York's zoo and escaped (a throwaway suggestion by Davies in *DWM*) is now enshrined in print in *The Official Doctionary* (sic) by Justin Richards.

Oh, Isn't That...?

- *Ardal O'Hanlon* (Brannigan). It's Father Dougal! (Or Thermo-Man, if you insist.) A stand-up comedian and compere from Dublin, O'Hanlon was cast in the hit comedy *Father Ted* as the breathtakingly dim young priest Father Dougal Maguire. He also played a superhero married to a normal woman in *My Hero* (until Thermo-Man apparently regenerated), but has been more active in Ireland and smaller roles on other series. He's recently been on stage in well-received straight plays, notably a revival of *The Weir*.
- *Lenora Crichlow* (Cheen). Her breakthrough TV role was in the Channel 4 adaptation of *Sugar Rush*, but she's mainly known now for the early series of *Being Human* (see X2.3, "School Reunion"), playing Annie, a ghost. She was also in Olympic cash-in film *Fast Girls*, one of about five Noel Clarke projects to hit our screens that week. It's customary to mention her father's role in saving the Notting Hill Carnival, but if you've been reading this book from the start and following the footnotes, you'll know all about that.
- *Jennifer Hennessey* (Valerie): had been a reporter in *The Second Coming*, but is now more obviously Bill's adoptive mum Moira in Series 10.

Things That Don't Make Sense A lot about this story only works if we assume that New New York is the only city on New Earth, and that the Overcity is hermetically sealed – literally and culturally – from the rest of the planet. (That way, we can avoid worrying about why nobody's concerned that there hasn't been any fresh celebrity gossip from the Earl of Queens or suchlike. The Naked Lady has a magazine which we assume is a flexible e-reader, otherwise we'd have to posit robot cyclists with big cloth caps delivering newspapers and periodicals.) All right, but that would mean that most people have joined a pre-existing traffic-jam *after* the plague wiped out the Overcity and everyone in the Senate. Where were they before this?

... because if enough of a market-economy remains for Mood-peddlers to flog their wares, there must also be food coming in and the prospect of life outside that one street existing as normal. The Doctor suggests that the authorities have abandoned the slum as if it's quite a new idea. And yet, in terms of New Earth's society, holograms must have handled all interaction with the upper city right from day one, or there's no way the crisis-instituted rules could have been taken seriously. The point being: what was everyone told 24 years ago when the access points closed down? And why has nobody realised that they'd not seen the flying ambulances and police cars except on video? Apart from the Cassini division, every car we encounter is someone who's joined a pre-existing system. Where did they come from, and why did their portion of the Undercity not have any contact with the main metropolis? How did they obtain vehicles? How did those vehicles get channelled into the tunnel?

Besides, why didn't either the Face of Boe or Novice Hame just tell anyone in the motorway what had been going on? Once the virus was gone, there's no reason not to have the inhabitants figure out their own escape; doubly so, to prevent newcomers adding to the congestion. Then again, if the virus did go airborne and the standard quarantine is 100 years in this era, it'd be a good idea to have a confirmation that New New York is safe to live in again from someone besides one dishonoured nun who's been rendered immune by Boe-fumes. (If the Face of Boe *is* Jack, then the "ancient songs" he sings to Hame must include a lot of show-tunes. That must be part of her punishment; in cat-years, she's spent 168 years listening to these.) Hame's been standing around dusting Boe's jam-jar for 24 years. Would it have killed her to hoover the place, remove a few of the skeletons – maybe even conduct a few funerals, which is sort of her job?

So the Doctor hacks into a screen and says: "That's the view we had [during my last visit]". Okay, but why is it on anyone's screens? It's one thing if the motorway people need to be fooled, but the other residents (and we're led to assume there are a lot) might want to go there one day. If it's to pretend that nothing's gone wrong, why not make images than make the Overcity seem crowded, dangerous and costly to keep the Undercitizens from wanting to leave the safety of their genteel poverty?

Come to think of it, whose clever idea was it to even *have* an Undercity? Obviously, New Earth was meant to memorialise the old one, but it's almost like a historical re-enactment project gone horribly wrong, and the Doctor takes it just a wee bit too seriously. That the Undercity risks falling into the sea when the power cuts smacks of a malicious piece of social engineering rather than just bad design. And the Macra certainly aren't a product of Old New York, so either someone introduced giant killer crabs to a city on purpose or they're smarter than the Doctor gives them credit for being. If that's true, there's no good reason for creatures who live off car fumes to try to attack the very machines upon which they're dependent. (The logical solution is that Boe and Hame sent them in as sheepdogs to stop anyone from leaving and finding out the truth, but if *that* were the case, they should have imposed a limit of single-occupant vehicles only in the Fast Lane, rather than let three people get killed each time one of them gets lucky.)

Of course, the Macra, as intergalactic pests, may well have just arrived there on their own. Except... either they got there a while back and survived the extensive terraforming that gave us applegrass and breathable (to us, that is) air, or they somehow didn't get to New (and 14 other "new"s) Earth until after the smog made life tolerable for them, which suggests intelligence – or at the very least some lax customs officials. If quarantine lasts for a century, then the chances of even tiny Macra crabs getting onto the planet via banana boxes (or grape deliveries to the hospital across the bay) are slim. Teleports must be presumed to have filters, to prevent Vincent Price-style mishaps. The alternative is that they literally travelled through space, as seeds or spores or eggs, and flourish on any planets where they find conducive conditions. In which case, they must have been in the Undercity well before the closure of the skylight. Undetected, on a planet noted for its medical facilities. Only reaching this giant size in the 25 years it's taken for the hatches to re-open. Unregistered as a traffic-hazard by the people offering computerised updates. Cyclists in London are more closely scrutinised that that now.

[For the record, Justin Richards claims, in one of umpteen BBC-sanctioned tie-in encyclopaedias, that the Macra escaped from New Brooklyn Zoo. The absurdities inherent in this idea would take a long time to catalogue – just for the moment apply the previous caveats about whether it happened before the ring-road was sealed, when anything untoward would have been dealt with immediately, or afterwards, when nothing could get in or out. Or just try to imagine Macra that size being able to get through the doorway Cheen and Milo use to abduct Martha, and then shutting the door behind them so they don't choke on all that oxygen leaking in. If they made a hole, they must have blocked it very well and nobody noticed.]

Thirteen minutes into the story, Cheen mentions that their buggy has 'self-replicating fuel' (we checked the DVD subtitles on that). O-o-o-o Kay-y-y-y... Why, then, do they need to abduct Martha to get a fuel-ration to change lanes? Why does the entire Undercity have an economy using 'credits', when they can nonchalantly ignore the Second Law of Thermodynamics and make anything they want, for free? Because if you have infinite energy (what this impossible feat of engineering would be) and teleport technology, you can reproduce everything. If you have limitless energy, increasing exponentially from a fairly high starting-point, why is it necessary to wait 24 years before plugging an immortal head into the National Grid to open the doors? If you can power anti-gravs without burning petrol, what is the point of petrol-burning cars? (By "petrol", we mean any fuel would provide smog and propulsion in roughly equal measure.)

The cars' identical design makes it clear that they were built by the one plant; what is it, how does it work, and who's running it? What does everyone need jobs *for*, especially in such locales as laundries and iron foundries? We're in post-scarcity economics here, which is fine if you're wanting to tell Iain M Banks-style stories about decadent immortals (and the various self-parody characters driving in-character buggies look like they come from exactly this milieu[19]), but sits oddly with the mercenary mood-peddlers and grubby downtown vibe. If even young newlyweds desperate for work have this kind of magic technology, *how is anyone poor*? All right, so maybe "self-replicating" means endlessly-recycling, with minimum loss (i.e. zero-entropy rather than minus quantities), in which case the fuel is being re-used ad infinitum – ergo, there must be vents for the cars to suck in exhaust-fumes, so no smog, thus nothing for the Macra.

So let's pretend that this silly line isn't there. If Milo and Cheen really *do* need work that badly, how is six years in a car creating babies a good idea? Moreover, the food and oxygen recycling's a bit haphazard: they process all their waste into rice-cakes but can make pickled eggs, so it's not just algal sewage reclamation (and, parenthetically, pickled eggs and rice-cakes in a confined space must be a test of any marriage). We presume that the water recycling is by condensation of vapour, but everyone seems to be sweaty and there are lots of absorbent surfaces on the furniture and electrical gubbins with exposed wires. The amount of muck Milo and Cheen produce revving up suggests that they are running on something more like coal than diesel – are their fuel-tanks TARDIS-like? The small size of the vans doesn't appear to have any room for even a spare jerry-can.

More to the point, if life in a camper van is capable of decades-long extensions to their journey-time, what of the people who sell moods? If they have gadgets like the drivers, why do they need to sell moods for money? If the gadgets cost money to run, how does the motorway's economy work? Is the pale woman who wanted to forget her parents a lone specimen, or is there more of the Undercity we don't see? And if there is, what happened to the mood-dealers when the roof opened? The Doctor thinks his ticking-off is the reason they all left, but this is improbable (imagine him walking into a crack den and saying "That's very naughty, stop it at once" and getting out alive, let alone having an impact). But if they're gone out of business in half an hour, it must have been more than the drivers who took his message on board, which suggests *another* news network and some kind of public transport, which raises a lot of questions about the story's whole premise.

What's especially odd is that with moods costing two credits, and no work for anyone who lives there (hence the mass exodus to the foundries and what have you), the booths for the mood-pushers are so perfunctorily guarded. You'd expect break-ins and muggings and hold-ups, leading to steel shutters and well-armed stallholders, not wooden whelk-stalls.

The anti-grav isn't switched off when Milo cuts the power, so it must be a natural state of whatever they've made these camper-vans out of in such vast numbers. In which case, how can they change height and move up and down, and why doesn't switching off the power make them float up or sink? Or if it isn't affected by the power being on or off for everything else, isn't it a bit of a risk keeping that one thing on?

Milo and Cheen are obviously as idiotic as Martha says, if they think that living for six years in a confined space with a kidnapped girl is going to make for a comfortable living situation. (We might presume that the citizens of the year Five Billion-and-change have a different sense of time owing to extended lifespans. We know that Cassandra was millennia old. However, Novice Hame seems to be getting on a bit, so perhaps only the humanoids have longer lives.)

Oh, and Brannigan's car only moves a few yards from the doorway in the whole time the Doctor's on board. Yet according to one or other of the Cassinis, 53 cars passed the Pharmacy Town exit in the last half hour.

As we've mentioned in earlier volumes, the idea that Janis Joplin gave the Doctor his coat is odd when you think which previous Doctor it might have been. We first see the item in "The Christmas Invasion" (X2.0), hours after the Doctor finally regenerates into a body where he can physically get into it. The only alternative is that Janis met the Hartnell Doctor, under a peculiar set of circumstances, and that he was wearing platform shoes so that it didn't trail all the way to the floor. (Anyone wanting to imagine the intermediate John Hurt incarnation taking time out from doing terrible things in wartime to pop to the Fillmore can do so on their own time.)

The Doctor doesn't even try to reverse the teleport when he wants to get back to the motorway. We still have no idea what mechanism the sonic screwdriver employs to do this, so maybe it won't work if the device in question really has run out of power. But if they haven't the power to do a two-way teleport, or open a few doors, someone ought to have told Hame how to rig up solar panels. They've got *sunlight*, after all. Yet the entire situation is apparently resolved because the Doctor techs a tech, which goes wrong until the Face heaves a sigh and throws the rest of his life force into it. It rather seems as if the only thing the Doctor actually accomplishes is to inadvertently force Boe to commit suicide to save everybody else.

And... how does Martha know *all* the words to "The Old Rugged Cross"?

Critique The biggest compliment this story got was when Steven Moffat tried redoing it and fell flat on his face. "The Beast Below" (X5.2) is an unholy mess, but is in most essentials the same conceit. There are many reasons why that one failed and this one succeeded, but a lot of it is down to marshalling the resources needed. Most of what we see in "Gridlock" is a reworking of things they had tried last year (even down to the computer graphics of the city) and the one big new prop, the camper-van, was used a lot in this episode and again in "Midnight" (X4.10). Nonetheless, they made sure this was in the same block with a much cheaper and less time-consuming episode (X3.6, "The Lazarus Experiment") in case of emergencies, and made the previous block's two stories revolve around one big digital effect each. The episode is conceptually ambitious, but logistically fairly conservative – there is nothing here they weren't certain they could do well in time and on budget. They even factored in bad weather for the shot-on-location scenes.

Yet even if all the elements are tried and tested, the combination we see here is very novel. The kaleidoscope's been shaken and what we get this time is – for all the New York affectations – a very British tale of ordinary people muddling through and bonding in adversity. Normally such stories are framed as being entirely admirable but, as we've discussed in the essay with "Smith and Jones", there's an undertow of wilful blindness to a terrifying problem and a sullen resistance to any doubt that bonding and muddling-through is appropriate. At the level of individual families, it's endearing and heroic – as a community or nation, it's shameful and stifling. The faith in the social institutions that no longer exist is killing people but keeping the planet alive; the religious ceremony is preserving hope but is entirely fraudulent. That whole "Keep Calm and Carry On" mentality is preventing anyone from asking the right questions and breaking out of this criminal conspiracy. If the BBC hierarchy had worked out what Davies was saying (a lot more deftly and less clunkily than in X1.7, "The Long Game" and X1.12, "Bad Wolf"), the series would likely have been pulled, merchandising windfall or no.

What makes it work, in terms of world-building, is that Martha and the Doctor interact with different sets of people. In many ways, this is the story where Martha finally stops hanging on to the Doctor's coat-tails (at least, metaphorically), even though circumstances force this upon her. She reasons things out slightly ahead of the others. Milo and Cheam look like a real and likeable couple, and while excluding them from the finale after hearing so much about the Doctor was procedurally wise, it seems like compounding the error not to have representatives of the survivors confronting their saviour(s). However, there wasn't really time for that. It's a story in itself.

All of these people have stories of their own. A lot of this episode's charm is that the intersection of all these concurrent lives with the Doctor's is tantalisingly brief. Even the Doctor and Martha admit they barely know one another. This gives us the excuse for a New Viewers Start Here discussion of the Time War, this time in terms of what the Doctor's world was like. That peculiar end-scene led some viewers to think that New Earth would become Gallifrey, but the intention was to juxtapose the dead city's memory living on with the Doctor's loss and the hymn's lyrics. It's the last we see of this world and, but for a coda in One Hundred Trillion AD, the furthest into humanity's story we have ever had. Audiences might have got bored if we'd had a fourth visit to this period, but it's strange we never had any hint of Donna being shown this period. As things stand, this finale is optimistic and open-ended, so we'll take it.

And the Face of Boe dies and gives this year's big storyline a push. It's odd how this prop caught on despite being a background detail in "The End of the World". A big elaborate death-scene for a rubber face the size of a life-raft ought to have been ridiculous, but it works. We are, once again, left to imagine the other things this entity has seen in umpteen centuries and whether future Doctors were involved, but what's important here is that the human(oid) cast sell the scene. It's still not entirely clear what the Doctor and Boe were actually *doing*, and whether the Doctor's actions were needed or if Boe was just hanging on to deliver his message (like Billy Shipton in seven episodes' time) – an uncertainty that makes this story more or less heroic depending on which side you take.

Still, this is the first time in ages that a one-episode adventure has felt like 45 minutes'-worth of story. It's nether stretched nor cramped. The main things that everyone remembers actually take up less screen-time than it seems in retrospect, and this vast and diverse assortment of log-jammed drivers is fewer than a dozen cars. The Macra are only in shot fleetingly. Once we've got the idea of the Doctor dangling from beneath one car and opening the roof of the one below, we don't need to see that – so the rest of the descent is sketched in with fast edits between passengers.

That's one of the most intrinsically *Doctor Who*-ish things about the story: that we pop into each of these places not knowing what will be inside, but it's radically different each time. It's like an accelerated version of *Through the Keyhole,* but any one of them could be creepy or funny or absurd or something between. Then when this has gone on long enough, we get the nasty crab-monsters. Just saying "here comes something scary" all the time lessens the effect when something scary comes. We need a lot of different types of surprises before someone can shout "Boo!" This episode pulls out a stream of them like a magician producing endless silk scarves.

The Lore

Written by Russell T Davies. Directed by Richard Clark. Viewing figures: (BBC1) 8.4 million, (BBC3 repeats) 0.8 and 0.3 million. AIs 86% on both channels. A slight glitch affected viewers in Wales on the first night.

Repeats and Overseas Promotion *L'Embouteillage Sans Fin* (traffic-jam – literally "bottled-up-ness" – without end); *Festgefahren* ("Stuck").

Production

Once the Face of Boe's revelation during the last visit to New Earth was kicked into the long (apple) grass, a third visit to this milieu was more-or-less inevitable. Russell T Davies thought he had at least another story to tell and had a few technical challenges he wanted to try – notably an episode where the actors were encased in a wholly CG world rather than the digital elements being inserted into location or studio footage. After the rough edges of the previous episode on this planet (the one time an effects shot was replaced after being signed off on), the new story would be about the planet's own rough edges. We'd seen uptown (well, a hospital and some long-shots from a beach), so now we got the slums. Terrible weather had blighted the location shoot, so the new script asked for rain. Those elements that had worked (the cat-people masks; the "verticality" of the chase-scene; the sense of a bigger, weirder world of primary-coloured humanoids; standard-model ones and cats living together and getting on with their lives) were amplified and some sourer notes added.

• The first idea was apparently a climax with giant Macra trashing the skyscrapers and threatening the sophisticates in their penthouses. With the next story ("Daleks in Manhattan") involving the Empire State Building, it was thought too close a similarity to *King Kong*, but the main reasons for moving the Macra from main villains to an additional threat were logistical. While bringing back also-ran monsters from a wiped Troughton adventure that Davies had enjoyed as a kid had a perverse appeal, the story's main focus was moving from the elite to the forgotten people in the ring-road. This allowed for a bigger world to be sketched in with, essentially, one main set (the car, redressed for each set of motorists), and The Mill achieving the scale of the world with implicit crowds of people inside thousands of identical vehicles. One complete prop "space-Trabant" was built, by Icon Effects (who'd made the telescope for X2.2, "Tooth and Claw"), but with the base of another so that Tennant could be shot from a number of angles descending from one to another.

• Director Richard Clark came to this after making a number of short films and directing two *Life on Mars* episodes that reached the screen a month before this. Production on "Gridlock" began 18th September at the Temple of Peace (already a very familiar location – see "The End of the World" for Boe's earlier visit, and the essay with X2.12, "Army of Ghosts").

• The make-up for Anna Hope (as Novice Hame) was subtly different from her "younger" appearance last year. Millennium Effects were on-hand for this and the new-improved Boe. The upgraded mouth-movements warranted a small script-alteration to have him die outside his tank, breathing proper air for the first time in ages (as per Anakin in *Return of the Jedi*), rather than telepathically communing with the Doctor as last time. Although those actors requiring prosthetic work or make-up had to start their day in the small hours, most days on this episode were relatively straightforward, with no night-shooting (a big relief after "The Shakespeare Code"). When it came time to film the scenes in the darkened Senate, including Boe's death, Tennant texted Davies about how sad everyone was to be losing this big rubber face. If you failed to spot it, the Senate is the Temple of Peace, again.

• Production went to Upper Boat 20th September. Set Director Malin Lindholm had worked out the most efficient order to redress each version of the car set, and this was supposed to make the detailing more rapid. *Doctor Who Confidential* were interviewing everyone that day, the basket of live kittens proved recalcitrant (see X2.11, "Fear Her"), and the small car set was difficult to film on – which perhaps explains why shooting fell slightly behind schedule. The kittens were coaxed, by a combination of treats and distractions, to make a mouth-movement with which The Mill could work to do a "Mama". Tennant, not really a pet person, picked one kitten to get used to him between shots, so that he could pick this one up without too many delays when that scene came. Ardal O'Hanlon would rather have played a villain, but seemed calm about the amount of make-up work playing Brannigan entailed.

• By now, it had been decided to provide a limited view from each car's window using smog rather than a costly and time-consuming CG image. This completed the bulk of the shots using the Brannigan family's home. O'Hanlon completed his scenes on the 22nd, finishing with the green-screen exterior of Brannigan telling the choking Doctor to come into the car. While that was happening, the car-interior set was being redressed as the businessman's vehicle; Tennant did a bit of work on that (as did Hope) and then had a three-day holiday, although not all of the scenes in that vehicle were completed as planned.

Agyeman returned the 23rd to start the Milo and Cheen subplot in the redressed car set. The majority of this day's work was the scenes early on when the car is undamaged, including their go at singing "The Old Rugged Cross". Monday the 25th was more Milo and Cheen scenes, and the day that Any Effects came to bash the car about; the three actors (who had bonded in the tiny set, as there were no other characters with whom to interact) just yelled and got buffeted. Most of the turbulence is the camera moving (observe Cheem's remarkably still hair when they pull a 360), but a stage-hand walloped the hull as a cue to jerk around like they do on the USS *Enterprise*. The pickled eggs and bead-curtains were replaced by chintz and 50s radios for the same set to become the home of Mrs and Mrs Cassini. May was played by Georgine Anderson, who had been a "May" in Davies's *Century Falls*.

Tennant did the Cassini's scenes, then the opening TARDIS scene with Agyeman while the car set was redressed as the Red Man's vehicle, then given a light redressing before doing Whitey's (as the chalk-coloured man is called in the script). Next day, with Agyeman released again, the postponed scenes with Nicholas Boulter as the Businessman were completed, including one with Tennant. He did the teenager car scene, then did the green screen work of dropping from car to car while the car was again redressed for the naked couple (they closed the set for that shot). The green-screen work involved the car exterior and the floor of the one above for Tennant to hang from. Clark occasionally reworked this in post-production so that the Doctor appeared to drop just before the target vehicle was in place. Each of these drops was shot from a slightly different position to increase the variety, matching the differences between each household the Doctor encountered when he entered each vehicle. Then, after a brief visit with naturists, they had to wait for the Businessman's car to be redressed before finishing main work on that versatile set.

• Location shooting started the next day, the 28th, with the TARDIS materialisation, Martha's kidnap, and the Pharmacy Town scenes to be shot at the Maltings at East Tyndall Street, Splott, Cardiff. This Victorian factory complex was solidly-built enough to pass for the city's foundations, but needed dirtying-up (although it was being turned into flats). It had buttresses and everything, but was very close to main roads, so everyone was alert in case of traffic noise. A traffic warden was given a walkie-talkie to communicate with the crew, and had been detailed to keep Cardiff's motorists from asking too many questions or ruining a take.

This time, the rain had to be provided *manually*, with sprinklers and wet weather gear. Getting the shower to go exactly where needed was harder than anticipated. Lucy Davenport, as the Pale Lady, had spent time in Los Angeles immediately before the shoot and had stayed indoors as much as possible. The monitor shows the effects shot from "New Earth" as well as one of the pre-recorded Sally Calypso inserts. The design team had made price-lists for about 100 moods, including Geeky, Witty, Fury, Pissed-Off, Chipper, Complacent and Weird.

Tennant and Agyeman returned 2nd October to finish "Smith and Jones" while the remaining car scenes were finished; the *American Gothic*-styled Ma and Pa, Javit (the Goth cat with two "Vestal Virgins" aboard), and yet more effects shot of the cars. The ADR dub had the line about the Doctor and Boe being "old friends" added, to fit in better with the tongue-in-cheek admission in X3.13, "Last of the Time Lords".

• On first transmission, the episode was scheduled to go out a bit late due to the FA Cup semi-final between Manchester United and Watford. Contingency plans were announced for an overrun, including delaying for a week and showing "Rose" instead of *Confidential* on BBC3. It was newsworthy, and fanboy topical songster Mitch Benn, on Radio 4's *The Now Show* did a number about this.[20] To the surprise of nobody – except maybe Sir Elton John – Man U thrashed Watford 4-1, so extra time was surplus to requirements, but some people were caught out by the continuity announcer handing over to Sally Calypso as if it were yet-another trailer before the episode.

X3.4: "Daleks in Manhattan"

(21st April, 2007)

Which One is This? There's no business like sow-business. Tentacle-sex across species, a Busby Berkeley-style routine (for humans, sadly[21]) and the proper New York. On no account is this to be confused with the other time the Daleks visited the Empire State Building (2.8, "The Chase"). That was an inept farce designed to cash in on the already-waning public enthusiasm for the Daleks regardless of whether there was a story worthy of them, and written under protest by Terry Nation. This one is by Helen Raynor.

Firsts and Lasts It's the first time we're explicitly told that individual Daleks from one story have survived to pop up in another. This lot are the Cult of Skaro, the ones who time-shifted their way out of "Doomsday" (X2.13). Last time, the Daleks' shells were polycarbide, as per "Remembrance of the Daleks" (25.1). Now, they're "Dalekanium" for the first time since 1964 (2.2, "The Dalek Invasion of Earth"). For the first time in the new series (the last was 26.4, "Survival"), we have a woman writing a story: script editor Helen Raynor (making this the first time an accredited script-editor had written a story since 22.6, "Revelation of the Daleks"). She's actually the first woman to write for the Daleks.

And, this is the first story that's ever had filming done in America (just pickup shots for a sense of the skyline and the Statue of Liberty, but it's the principle of the thing).

Murray Gold's written an original song to be performed in the theatre revue, which makes this time the production team had tried anything of the sort since "The Gunfighters" (3.8) used "The Ballad of the Last Chance Saloon" as both a voice-over narrative and a ditty for Steven to sing. Is this one more memorable? You decide. Gold's also finally given the Daleks a new chant-like theme, which we'll hear every time they appear from now on.

Praise be! For the first time this century, they manage to go a whole episode without mentioning Rose Tyler. We also have the debut of the "Basically... run!" line [see X5.1, "The Eleventh Hour"].

Watch Out For...

• In the finest (if that's the right adjective) traditions of John Nathan-Turner, there's something here to get the dads watching: a parade of chorus-girls in various stages of undress in the pre-credits sequence. We're in the tradition of the Hollywood Backstage Musical, as Broadway is depicted on screen as something very unlike the reality. In the case of *42nd Street* et al, this meant something bigger than life, with at least 200 dancing-girls and a routine that nobody in the paying audience would have been able to see properly. BBC Wales's *Dalekanium-Diggers of 1930*[22] falls rather short of this, or indeed the average school play, yet Martha's disruption of their big production-number is intended to be funnier than the routine would have been if uninterrupted. Leading this legion of leggy lovelies (as Warner Bros would undoubtedly have phrased it in the trailer) is

What Were the Best Online Extras?

In our essay **Was 2006 the *Annus Mirabilis*?** we suggested that one of the underpinnings of all the televised goodies was the role of the *Doctor Who* BBC website(s). At the time, these included a dozen different in-universe websites, loads of games, and everything else down to and including lots of shiny desktop wallpapers made from high-resolution pictures of the cast. In addition to this was all the lovingly built up content from the prior years of the BBC Cult website, in which *Doctor Who* already had pride of place by a large margin, with several ebook releases of old Virgin novels and two fan-written guides to the series as the continuity guide.

Fast-forward to the anniversary year and what's odd is how much of this older material was still on hand to bulk up the site; the version of Pong that was whipped up to make the release of a script page from "The Next Doctor" just a little more challenging than looking at a news article (mercifully easy, but if you lose all your lives on level six you still had to start again) was still to be found in the eleventh Doctor's Games tab, right underneath all the quizzes and "How to Make a Cube". And the link that lead back to something that's recognisably the pre-2005 website was still right there on the main page.

Well, it's a fairly involved and somewhat sordid story, but let's start where it begins: the BBC Cult site. In 1998, someone had the bright idea of using a chunk of the BBC's website assets to cover some of the geekier programmes. In practice, this meant American shows: *Star Trek: Voyager*, *3rd Rock from the Sun*, and *The X-Files*, but also *Seinfeld*, *Larry Sanders* and *The Simpsons*. If you were in Britain at the time, this constellation of series makes absolute sense (except *Seinfeld*, known around these parts as being the thing that allowed you to go and eat something after *Newsnight Review* before *Larry Sanders* came on). A lot of it is the supposed cachet of getting all the American references, and that quintessentially 90s association of "minority interest" with "cool" (see **What's All This Stuff About Anoraks?** under 24.1, "Time and the Rani").

Nevertheless, they knew their target audience; the first British programme to have pride of place on the Cult front page was *Doctor Who* (updated with a snazzy blue background rather than the quick and plain black that they'd been using earlier; pay attention to backgrounds in this account, they'll be important). This was by summer of 1998, just in time to ponder what the BBC might be doing for the 35th anniversary (answer: ditching all continuity in the books range and releasing 5.3, "The Ice Warriors" on VHS), with an invite for readers to write in for the first time by participating in the new *Doctor Who* forums.

But it didn't really get exciting until 2000, when James Goss started heading an off-shoot website that focused solely on *Doctor Who*. New material started coming thick and fast then, with several online webcasts (a reworked version of 17.6, "Shada", and a new Colin Baker story that's remembered largely for overhauling the Doctor's jacket). There was even an overly ambitious attempt to reboot the series ("Death Comes to Time": one of few items that not even the most diligent of *Doctor Who* timeline obsessives has ever, ever managed to coherently explain or fit with any other content and with which few really bothered).

We've discussed the hassle that the various teams fighting it out about who would get *Doctor Who* caused for any of them getting it at all (compare to Doug Naylor's attempt to get a movie made out of *Red Dwarf* and eventually chucking it in and returning to television, or the hassle that Douglas Adams had in making his script go to Hollywood). To cut a long story mercifully short, the failure of BBC Worldwide to get anything off the ground offered an opportunity. Davies had been trying to sell a new version of the show since 2000. This kept falling through for a lot of reasons, not least of which being that Nelvana was trying to work out an animated version of the show at the same time. (See the essay with A5, "The Infinite Quest".)

2003 was a good year if you liked Unbound Doctor stories (audios dramas based on *what if* scenarios and with improbable actors in the lead role – see **How Often Has This Story Happened?** under X3.9, "The Family of Blood" and **Stunt-Casting: What are the Dos and Don'ts?** under X2.2, "Tooth and Claw"). Six of the eight Big Finish stories in the range came out that year, and we can assume coincidence that two of them came out in September 2003, just as the BBC announced that the proper *Doctor Who* series was coming back. This is where "Scream of the Shalka" comes in; it was meant to be the biggest project the Cult site had yet seen, inaugurating the fandom's coming to terms with no televised *Who* ever again, and restarting it in a new format for a new century. Unfortunately, one of the side effects of the BBC's

continued on Page 101...

Miranda Raison from *Spooks*. She's not actually from New York, or even American. Can you tell?

• The Doctor and Martha's first impulse on finding themselves in NYC in 1930 is to visit a shanty-town. One might have expected a trip to Coney Island, the Cotton Club or the Apollo but the executive producer has decreed "no jazz", despite ordering his hireling to write a story in 1930 New York. We will have more evidence of Russell T Davies's lamentable taste in music warping the plot later this year (X3.12, "The Sound of Drums"; X3.13, "Last of the Time Lords"). Anyone who has visited Central Park might be mildly amused at how far short a wet afternoon in Wales falls. As the *Confidential* lovingly details, the production team were delighted to find a wall near a school playground that was a reasonable enough match for the Statue of Liberty base. Cutting between shots of Liberty Island and Penarth Leisure Centre works, just about.

• Conversely, the sets for the work-in-progress Empire State Building are spot-on and make the Art Deco-style Daleks seem perfectly at home in their new bolt-hole. They also reproduce – in moving, colour pictures – the famous Lewis Hines shots of the construction workers, especially the one on a girder over the precipitous drop from near the top.

• Murray Gold's decision, back in "Dalek" (1.6), to give the Daleks a chant like unto Damien's Devil-Dog in *The Omen* means that their annual surprise returns need a more recognisable "theme". Similarly, giving the Cybermen something like the "Dies Irae" (X2.5, "Rise of the Cybermen") means that the Top Monsters also need a tune we can all hum. So the Crouch End Festival Chorus have now been given words to chant, to a tune a bit like the bad guy's theme in *The Magnificent Seven* – but he refuses to tell anyone what those words actually are. Theories abound: the most popular is "These are some boring Daleks", but "This is appalling garbage" also works.

• After their supposed failure with the Slitheen, the tendency when creating monsters has been to pick an Earth animal, make a mask of the head, add a cheap set of overalls and hope nobody complains. This time, as the pig-in-a-spacesuit and squid-in-a-boiler-suit have been done (X1.4, "Aliens of London"; X2.8, "The Impossible Planet"), they do something daring and have a pig in a boiler-suit, and a lot of others with their heads less well-animated. The one who gets the close-ups is credited as "Hero Pig Man". The boiler-suits are Guantanamo Orange, making this porcine malfeasant look remarkably like Chewbacca celebrating Life Day in *The Star Wars Holiday Special*. Older British viewers may also be thinking of Porky the Pianist from *Tiswas*.

• It's been a while coming, but the Welsh series finally got their own bonkers Dalek cliffhanger. In the best old-skool tradition, the *Radio Times* managed to spoil it a week ahead of time (see 9.1, "Day of the Daleks" for a brilliant cover giving away a cliffhanger from two weeks in the future).

The Continuity

The Doctor He likes a nice cold Atlantic breeze [in keeping with his avowed fondness for nasty weather in X3.3, "Gridlock"]. He's keen on the ideal of the Statue of Liberty, and quotes the "huddled masses" line that every schoolchild in America knows. [As we'll see in X3.6, "The Lazarus Experiment", this Doctor likes being able to throw around a quote, but only the most screamingly obvious ones.]

In a thoroughly ill-judged joke, he promises Martha she can kiss him later, then tosses in an offer to the lower-class worker Frank as well. Tallulah thinks that he and Martha are together. [A nice and liberal perspective, given that three-quarters of the country had anti-miscegenation laws in the 30s. So much so that when Martha indicates they aren't together, the singer presumes he's gay instead.]

During a chase by angry Pigmen, he shifts a manhole cover without trouble. When identifying the strange (Dalek) blob in the sewers, he seems to be using something a bit like the "whittling it down" process from X1.5, "World War Three", and identifying the planet of origin as Skaro, as opposed to just thinking "hang on, that's a bit like the various Dalek blobs I've encountered..." [we could make a list, but it's a long one]. He's utterly sick of Daleks by this point, complaining about how he always loses out when they still survive.

• *Ethics.* Upon seeing a group of non-humans in a dark and spooky location, the Doctor decides everyone had best run for it *before* they've even done anything threatening.

• *Inventory: Sonic Screwdriver.* With the help of scrounged rubbish from backstage and radio capacitors, the Doctor rigs up a DNA analysis

What Were the Best Online Extras?

continued from Page 99...

organisational structure (creating lots of little sub-units who had no idea what other people are doing) was that this got lost in the hype over a new television series.

It was an understandable mistake and all parties behaved themselves in public. Almost. When queried on the issue, Davies would dodge by slagging off Richard E. Grant as having phoned in his performance (anyone wondering how an obvious candidate for a guest appearance could have stayed away from the show so long, this may well have something to do with it), writer Paul Cornell played the stalwart fanboy (he was already a shoo-in to write for the televised version, more than enough reason not to rock the boat). So "Shalka" was released at the end of 2003 as a slightly embarrassing oddity and everyone started speculating about who the next new Doctor would be.

(And it wasn't quite as ignored as all that. For one, the interpretation of the Master, played by Derek Jacobi – funnily enough – was, unfortunately for purist Delgado fans, rather more in line with the slap-slap kiss-kiss slash of the new series.)

Meantime, the BBC shook up their websites and shut down a lot, including the Cult websites (a massive amount of internal politicking is going on, and accounts make it seem like the Cult/ technology-friendly crowd are duking it out at this point with the higher-ups for the soul and future of the BBC) as the notorious "BBC Trust" started messing with everything to look as if they were doing something... except, and this is an important except, for the *Doctor Who* website. So James Goss and what's left of the BBC Cult team had nothing else to work on, and we got two years of top-notch website content. This started off with a real-life version of Clive's website from X1.1, "Rose" (which included the two sections we see in the episode, plus a funny, frightening, and downright touching guestbook, with entries sent in by the general public).

For the first two seasons of the show's return, the BBC made a lot of little websites that expanded on the show's existence. These were timed so as to be updated and posted just in sync with the episodes being aired. For the generation of Internet-savvy kids coming to *Doctor Who* for the first time, it became a ritual to look for these as soon as the episode had aired – checking out the full spoiler version of the Fear Factor, see what curious bits of lore there might be in the Fact Files. (Little bits of info – largely just simple continuity explanations for the new fans, but with a couple of behind-the-scenes facts to freshen it up. James Moran saying that the TARDIS-as-an-artwork in X4.2, "Fires of Pompeii" was a deliberate allusion to 17.2, "City of Death", for instance.) There might be a new game, too. (There was a fresh one for nearly every story in 2006; Flash games, but well programmed and sometimes fairly involved – the "Fear Her" one, in which a crayon Doctor has to play connect-the-dots and avoid being erased from existence by the scribble monsters, is considerably more suspenseful than the actual episode if you play with the sound down (X2.11). The backstory behind these: the BBC awarded an external contractor £150,000 to get these done properly, and got their money's worth.)

Goss went in 2007, the website visibly trod water the next year and then went into a bit of a decline. The red-and-gold Tennant design stuck around until Matt Smith, when they gave it a facelift that brought back a colour-scheme like the blue-green Eccleston-era one and tidied up the site in a few other ways. Yet, generally, at that point all the energy started to go into making fancy games. Aside from a few good short stories by reliable *Who* stalwarts, nothing interesting happened there any more – and the URL changed from bbc.co.uk/doctorwho to bbc.co.uk/programmes/b006q2x0 to fall in line with the rest of the BBC programme websites.

The next notable development was the 50th anniversary website, and that was really just a news feed with a giftshop. Anyone looking for information on the recovered nine-episode haul of Season Five clicked on the BBC's official outlet in October 2013 and saw a pre-determined list of ten monsters from which you were to pick the scariest (regardless of whether any of those was the one that genuinely did it for you as a child). In the meantime, a great deal of material on the BBC site is now tricky to find if you don't know just what you're looking for, accessible only through the Wayback Machine, or just gone entirely.

Nevertheless, those two years were a brilliant time to be a *Doctor Who* fan – and that went double for the ones who liked the website – so here's a quartet of the best features from the early days...

continued on Page 103...

device; the final touch is a spotlight to warm up the brain sample. The screwdriver also opens manhole covers [possibly with the electro-magnetic setting we saw in 10.3, "Frontier in Space"].

• *Inventory: Other.* He pops out the glasses, first to examine the Skaro brain in the sewers, then to take a good look at it when he's studying its DNA structure.

The Supporting Cast

• *Martha* comes across as astoundingly insular on her first trip to America, asking why police in 1930s New York don't care about disappearances from a mixed-race Hooverville. [She compounds the error by repeating the question to Tallulah, then decides to be miffed when she gets much the same response.] She doesn't particularly encourage Frank's shy attempt at chatting her up, but hugs him readily when scary aliens march them down a corridor. When he mentions he's been hitching, she quickly says she's been doing the same [not exactly in line with the 30s' American conception of hitchhikers, but he doesn't question it]. She admits to having done some acting before, 'Shakespeare, you know' [see two episodes ago].

She's never been to New York, but she's always wanted to see it. Arriving right after "Gridlock" prompts her to try the "new new new new..." formulation, but she gives up halfway through. She's seen black and white newsreels and thinks they're quaint. She comes off with a high score on the Dalek intelligence scan, right after she's disrupted a theatre performance with a full house and revue in progress [see **Things That Don't Make Sense**].

When Tallulah sympathises about the Doctor being a 'hot potato' (sic) who's 'into musical theatre' (sic), Martha looks ready to say "it's not like that" but stops herself [at long last, she's noticed that he's not showing signs of being interested in her romantically]. When the Doctor volunteers for a potentially dangerous excursion into the sewers, she puts her hand up without prompting, but clearly isn't happy to do it.

For a doctor in training, she's awfully squeamish about the novelty glowing brain. [It's an exercise for the reader as whether Martha can tell just by looking that it isn't a human organ; she also wonders if it's radioactive. The smell ought not to concern someone who's participated in surgery.] Oddly, she seems much less bothered by the Pigmen's appearance, though she promptly assumes they're up to no good. Dalek experimentation on involuntary subjects infuriates her even more than Frank's apparent death by Pigmen [she's still not quite used to this adventuring lark, since shouting 'it's inhuman!' really is just begging for the snarky response].

She recognises the name "Daleks" from the Doctor's potted history last episode, but only seems to realise what she's up against when they name themselves [so they weren't described to her].

The Non-Humans

• *Daleks.* They're noticeably less cocky than usual, even if they do insist they have no concept of worry. One has an actual conversation with Mr Diagoras while ascertaining if he'd be appropriate for the Final Experiment. It knows that versions of New York last through all of history [though we don't learn if its knowledge extends to the year Five Billion].

The skirt panels are removable; we see that the metallic half-circles are actually full spheres, and we have a glimpse of a flat white section where one was removed. They refer to this metal as 'Dalekanium'. Finishing the preparation of a 'chromatin solution' is the last step before the Final Experiment.

So, the part of the plan we know from this episode: for extra manpower, they've created the Pigmen [a 1930s version of Robomen; 2.2, "The Dalek Invasion of Earth"]: mind-wiped drones that are still human-shaped, but with pig heads. They were created by combining animal and human DNA. The Pigmen serve as heavy muscle for kidnapping people – the less intelligent ones are converted into new Pigmen, and the more intelligent ones are brought to the Dalek lab. The Daleks carry out the intelligence tests by waving suckers at people [exactly what they might be looking for, given that Lazlo is made into a pig and Frank is clever-clogs in this system, is difficult to guess].

By use of telepathic transmission, they've convinced Mr Diagoras that they're in league with him [probably mentioning that they're extraterrestrial] and have used his skills as a businessman to finish the Empire State Building on time and send people into the sewers for conversion. [We presume that this entails his handling all the logistical problems such as unobtrusively acquiring equipment for a genetics lab, porkers and people for Pigmen conversion. Picking such a massively

What Were the Best Online Extras?

continued from Page 101...

1. Ebooks

The section dealing with *Doctor Who* books was a large and wonderful place once. There were previews of the ongoing BBC book line, with witty tagline descriptions and extracts from the most recent books (quite well picked extracts, by and large; it's remarkable how promising the first chapter of *Deadly Reunion* seems in comparison with the rest of the novel). There were interviews with the authors, dozens of them. By the time the PDA range was cancelled (that's the *Past Doctor Adventures*: stories about Hartnell to McCoy, and the equivalent of the Virgin *Missing Adventures*), they'd had a rudimentary message board set up for people to discuss the latest release.

This wasn't the best of it, though. What was the best was full copies of various choice Virgin *New Adventures* and *Missing Adventures*, rereleased one by one with fresh new illustrations to boot: *Human Nature*, *Nightshade*, *The Scales of Injustice*, *The Empire of Glass*, *The Well-Mannered War*, *Lungbarrow*, *The Sands of Time* and *The Dying Days*. All of these featured commentary by the writers. (Paul Cornell actually did two, after the television rendering of *Human Nature*; by this point the Tennant main page section of the website, done up in teal and orange, was already being differentiated from the Eccles-and-older areas of the website, which were all in the bluish-green that characterised his TARDIS lighting, with separate main pages for both. So the new site had information on the new episode, and the old site had information on the old book, with easy linkage back and forth...) It was a delightful, evident connection between the old and the new.

These all vanished from the BBC website at the end of 2010. Six months later, the BBC started testing out e-books on demand and these days an increasing number of authors are having their old books getting back into print. Which is good. But these eight were freely available to the public and now they're not there any more.

2. The Actually-Quite-Good Dalek Game

In the interests of strict accuracy, we must note that the pre-Eccleston iteration of the website had some games; an electronic version of Top Trumps (of which we have spoken in Volumes 3b and 6) and a frankly absurd time-travelling tennis game where one could play as John Lennon and Shakespeare at Wimbledon. Those were relatively simple Flash games without much depth to them, sort of like the Google Doodle one for the Fiftieth Anniversary.

"The Last Dalek" was different. It went up on the BBC website just after X1.6, "Dalek", to best capitalise on fan excitement. (As we've mentioned, updates were very closely tied to the broadcast of the actual episodes under Davies; flavour text about all the stories was appearing on Mickey's website up through X1.11, "Boom Town".) It was far more involved than anything that had shown up before: easily worth an hour of play, especially if you took the new game-plus option that let you destroy everything with the big endgame gun. For a generation of kids just coming of age with the Internet, it was exciting and a reassuring sign that the programme-makers were just as interested in what was happening off-screen as on. It looked just right. And you got to play as the Dalek.

We mentioned that for quite a while it wasn't clear whether there was even going to be a Dalek episode, which makes pulling together a solid and entertaining game even more impressive. The continuity was tight, too; it's explicitly presented as a version of "Dalek" with no Rose standoff to get in the way of the Dalek shooting things, so there's references to Van Statten, the alien hairdryer and the Doctor's desperate last stand. The ending, in which a ghostly Christopher Eccleston swears he'll not leave his TARDIS unprotected and tries hopelessly to stop you from making the Daleks the Lords of Time, is at least as affecting as anything broadcast this century.

(It was so solid a platformer, in fact, that they went back and did it again with K9 wandering through Eccleston and Tennant episodes. That version's considerably more surreal.)

3. Weird Associated Websites

Mickey was a godsend for this purpose, as he provided a narrative hook for all this extra content. The idea was, he took over Clive's website after "Rose". (Old-skool fans will have recognised the "fanzine-as-alien-conspiracy" joke inherent in the setup.) In practice this meant a series of exciting, sometimes acerbic, sometimes naive commentaries on the episodes as they happened, with odd tie-ins (an essay by a young Adam, and Mickey's attempts to make sense of the events of X1.8, "Father's Day" 30 years on without even knowing

continued on Page 105...

self-obsessed man must have spared them someone who would ask nosy questions. In particular, he must think they don't have designs on New York, if he intends to take it over himself.]

Fundamental DNA type 467-989 is from Skaro, and requires such clever genetic engineering that the Doctor notices *that* before realising it's Dalek. [We see in the next episode that Dalek DNA has a double helix structure but with spikes, so maybe the Doctor's contrivance with the spotlight and his sonic magnifies the brain enough for him to see if the cells look like conkers or not.]

Like all worthwhile aliens, they have English accents. [Even after an indefinite time spent in America, they still pronounce 'laboratory' with five syllables, and nothing like "lavatory".]

Dalek Sec's plan, which he's held off clarifying to the other Daleks, involves ingesting Diagoras; Sec's casing opens in the same way as it does in "Dalek" (X1.6) and the mutant inside expands and consumes Diagoras whole, then closes and takes several minutes to process. [The other Daleks inject it with something, possibly the chromatin solution they all keep talking about.] After a few minutes, a new creature steps out of the capsule, looking largely like Diagoras and even wearing the same suit, but with a one-eyed tentacle head that's very rude-looking indeed. The other Daleks are dubious about this plan, which they say violates the 'Dalek Imperative' [presumably the in-built drive towards purity].

At this point, they're agreeing with Sec that Daleks need to abandon their casings. [They refer to it as a 'shell' here, as with "Remembrance of the Daleks", though to what extent this is their own opinion rather than a meaningless parroting of Dalek Sec's isn't quite clear. It'll be more so next episode.]

Planet Notes

• *Skaro* is described as 'gone'. [It will be back in X7.1, "Asylum of the Daleks". Then gone and back in X9.1, "The Magician's Apprentice".]

History

• *Dating.* New York's Central Park has a Hooverville, with a pleasant view of the nearly-constructed Empire State Building [not strictly accurate in terms of location, but we'll let that slide]. The building was due to be completed at the end of November, give or take [in real life, it opened to the public on 1st May, 1931]. Martha finds a local newspaper with the dateline 'Saturday 1 November 1930'.

A dollar a day is considered slave wages [quite a lot of Americans were only too willing to work for that sum in the 30s, so perhaps this version of America is suffering from inflation]. The city has numbered and kitschy clean sewers [not quite so silly as 22.1, "Attack of the Cybermen", but very tidy all the same]. There's a 'gamma strike' coming that's 'accelerated', against Dalek expectations [either that or they're hastily making up for miscalculating its arrival in the first place; which might explain everything wrong with the timeline in **Things That Don't Make Sense**].

Solomon appeals to Hooverville's sense of camaraderie by bringing up his experiences of combat in the Great War. [Considering the limits on African-Americans in the military at the time (largely, segregated units relegated to support roles behind the lines), there's only one setup that matches his dialogue and the history books. The 369th Infantry Regiment, the first African-American group to be sent abroad and one of the few to experience combat, was both tremendously successful in combat and very cohesive. They were paired off with French troops, since white Americans wouldn't serve with them; what with having some of the first African-American military officers as well, it's no surprise that Solomon would call upon this memory as an ideal. The regiment having been a reworked version of a New York National Guard unit (hence their nickname "the Harlem Hellfighters"), it had gone back to state service after the war and was still highly respected. (At the time this story's set, they'd just finished building an armoury for the unit in Harlem, but it'd be no surprise if Mr. Diagoras wasn't involved with that.) It explains a great deal about Hooverville's setup if Solomon transferred his experience and authority from the military into organising a cohesive community, and renders everyone's willingness to post sentries and fight at the drop of a hat much more understandable.]

What Were the Best Online Extras?

continued from Page 103...

as much as the Doctor and Rose do). His characterisation on the website is miles ahead of what we got on screen. The version of the site for Series 2 was lighter and definitely more child-focused; Noel Clarke recorded several video messages to introduce the games and explain to the viewer how important it was to chase the Clockwork Robots or break into the Deffry Vale website by acing their aptitude test. For the parallel universe game, you even got instructions from Ricky.

Yet Clive's wasn't the only website: the other function of Mickey's website was to serve as a clearing house for the new URLs. The second one, and one of the better ones, was a UNIT website put up shortly before the broadcast of "Aliens of London". At this point, it played coy with the whole "aliens are our business" angle and only offered little teasers about UNIT being set up in 1968, although there was quite a good joke postdated to 10 March about asking people to please not pirate a file that looked like "something they would most want to download". After the climatic "buffalo" in X1.5, "World War Three", fans rushed off to try out the password (if they didn't get the hint from the episode itself, Mickey had posted it on his website) and were greeting with a serious of deeply sarcastic UNIT message boards, some of which bewailed the existence of Mickey's website. It kept updating until X2.0, "The Christmas Invasion", presumably so that Davies could make his own decisions about how to tell stories about modern-day Britain coming to terms with aliens... which he never quite got around to doing.

There were lots of other websites by the time "Doomsday" aired (X2.13). A couple were educational (the tie-in for "The Christmas Invasion" had some actual facts about space as well as in-jokes about British Rocket Group). By the end of it, they could even do a parody one – Millingdale Ice Cream was a website about a fictional ice cream company that existed merely to play an ice cream truck jingle version of the swoopy Flavia theme and whet viewer's appetites with silly ice cream flavours – satsuma Christmas Surprise and the like. Then the Graphics department thought it'd be funny to use it in the background of X2.10, "Love & Monsters", so "Madame du Popadom" ice cream is probably now canonical.

Goss had hoped for "dozens" of websites for Series 2 – in practice it worked out to about one per episode, with an accompanying game, but that's still more than then we'd had before or since. From "The Christmas Invasion" on, most of the story content on these was written by Joseph Lidster. He'd been hired by James Goss after a chat in a pub and compliments about a Big Finish audio (probably *The Rapture*) and was kept on long enough to write Martha's Myspace, which showed a much more laidback, free-and-easy character than the one we actually got to enjoy on the show. As we said, Goss left soon after that as well, and that's about when this sort of thing ended – they revamped the look of the website, as we said earlier, and kept making games, but a lot of energy was now going into the *Torchwood* tie-in websites instead. For whatever reason, Moffat was never as interested in this form of storytelling (even though Joseph Lidster ended up doing website content for *Sherlock*), so the website under Moffat largely became a clearing-house.

After the end of *Doctor Who Confidential*, this has also been the one-stop location for behind-the-scenes stuff and interviews, but these are less involving. There is, however, a lot of effort put into getting younger users to develop their own games from available components released through the site and unlocked as they appear on telly. This is a remnant of the educational remit of the more complicated professionally-made games we'll get to in a moment.

4. Fear Forecasters

Long before liveblogging became an acceptable way to behave during all new television broadcasts (if it ever did), the BBC website crew came up with a nice and simple concept: shiny new *Doctor Who* was bound to be scary, and parents might want to know in advance what their kids were going to be frightened by, so some sort of forewarning for impressionable families might be helpful.

Enter the Fear Forecasters: Amy, Harry, Samuel and Adam, aged 5 to 13, and their mums and dads. They got to watch the new episode *before anyone else* (and to their credit, the kids always seemed to find this as exciting as it should be), commenting on its scariness throughout, and at the end of it the four children would average out their Fear Factor to offer an estimate of how scary a story was, on a one to five scale. (Theoretically, although in practice nothing scored lower than a two. Since

continued on Page 107...

The Analysis

The Big Picture ("Daleks in Manhattan" and "Evolution of the Daleks") As you will recall from last volume, Stephen Fry was asked to take a few moments from his busy schedule to toss off a script for Series 2. It was set in the 1920s, had aliens and a Major Historical Figure who turned out to be an alien... and was generally too expensive to be made in the time allotted (and was probably not very good).

Nonetheless, the idea of this era as a setting was one to which Russell T Davies clung, so when commissioning a two-part Dalek story for Series 3, he stipulated that it be in the past as a contrast to the future and present-day settings already used. As we will see in **The Lore**, the starting-point was a notion of the Daleks doing Doctor Moreau-style experiments to make servants of the kind they'd had in previous Earth-based stories (the Robomen from "The Dalek Invasion of Earth", the Ogrons from "Day of the Daleks"), and the rest of the story derived from there, with a major detour to avoid speakeasies and Jazz (because Davies is weird and prefers manufactured pop). As Davies himself admits, when he asked Helen Raynor to craft the story he had in mind, he had forgotten that there was any such thing as a Depression. Instead, he was positing a story about glitz, glamour, showgirls and the Empire State Building.

This is odd, as the key source for this impression of 30s New York is Warner Brothers musicals, which made a big deal about the New Deal and used the economic conditions of the time as the basis for their plots. Exhibit A is *Gold Diggers of 1933*, which, in between four songs – one of which bears closer examination – is a tale of hard-up showgirls trying to make ends meet when their show's cancelled, and then trying to salvage a new production that's about the Depression. Until the (heavily revised) end of the film, it's unclear how such a frothy show can be "about" widespread hardship, but the end number, "Remember My Forgotten Man", contrasts World War I parades with breadlines.

Earlier in the story, the Boston blue-bloods who want to prevent the young songwriter/ performer from marrying "beneath" him get tirades (from the various girls they themselves land up marrying) about what a single woman in the Depression might have landed up doing that's worse than showbiz. This, and the chorus-girl-to-star plot of a previous Busby Berkeley film, *42nd Street*, lurks behind a lot of Tallulah's dialogue and implied backstory – apparently Tallulah is the star because Heidi Chicane broke her ankle just before opening night. (It's not a very plausible name, but Raynor and Davies were thinking of Jodie Foster in *Bugsy Malone* rather than bothering to watch genuine 30s films. Tallulah Bankhead didn't play that kind of role, and wasn't famous early enough for "our" Tallulah to be named after her.)

We referred to these two films as "Busby Berkeley" movies, but the only complete film he directed was *Gold Diggers of 1935*: the choreographer is one of those rare filmmakers who has become an *auteur* without being the accredited director. In contrast to the RKO musical-comedies starring Fred Astaire and Ginger Rogers, the Warner Brothers films had their feet on the ground as regards the everyday lives of the audiences. People as affluent and fancy-free as Astaire's usual characters only appeared in the Berkeley films as the threat from outside.[23] Warner Brothers were such enthusiastic advocates of Roosevelt that their other main style of film – aggressive, moralising gangster melodramas – had sententious captions at the start about how society had to deal with the root causes of such villainy, implied to be a mix of self-interest and *laissez-faire* policies such as those Herbert Hoover had tried to use to kick-start the economy. Hoodlums and the Establishment were two sides of the same coin, combining forces to oppress the common man.

However, the more immediate source for the big production-number is the pastiches done in 80s films: the original idea was to use Cole Porter's "Anything Goes", slightly anachronistically, perhaps mainly because it was in the title sequence of *Indiana Jones and the Temple of Doom*. There's a more overt similarity between the song Murray Gold wrote and the Stephen Sondheim 30s pastiches Madonna performed in *Dick Tracy*, and the character of Tallulah seems more like Breathless Mahoney than any Ruby Keeler character from a real 1930s film. Indeed, for all that we're invited to read Tallulah as the heroine of a Broadway musical, the backstage doesn't seem to bear this out and the setup we see is more like the Ziegfield Follies than anything with a plot – lots of pretty girls, a backstage clown and no audience hisses when a dance performance turns into a comedic chase number. If you want a specific film that

What Were the Best Online Extras?

continued from Page 105...

you're curious, X2.8, "The Impossible Planet" scored as the single scariest episode ever.)

And for the first few Forecasts, that was pretty much all there was to it, with a transcriber dutifully taking down minute-by-minute notes about "these aliens are really freaky" and "that's scary!" But it quickly evolved into something rather more special – as close to an unmediated look at a family watching *Doctor Who* as you're likely to get. Amy commenting that the golden cloud in "The Doctor Dances" were obviously faeries, one of the dads stoutly pretending not to have had a crush on Elisabeth Sladen and being teased about it through "School Reunion", the kids recognising Paul Cornell's name for "Human Nature" and cheering... It turned into an uninhibited, rambunctious, enthusiastic record. Endless joy at the opportunities the show offers for scatological jokes, snarky and adoring asides from the dads, lots of crisps and singing along to the theme tune. It's exactly the sort of viewing experience that the BBC was hoping to encourage.

This went on for five years, with the kids growing up, becoming more fannish, and switching from VHS to DVDs (they stopped reviewing at X4.15, "Planet of the Dead", probably for publicity reasons), but the feature hasn't been seen since. Quite why no one thought of doing this for Steven Moffat episodes is a question, especially as scaring small children seems to be his *raison d'etre*. (It is to be noted in his favour that a Moffat episode always went down as being quite scary. Except for the one set in France, anyway.)

But then, with the series being used by everyone in the BBC to prove that their guesses about how to transition synergistically into being a multi-platform content-provider (or somesuch managementese) had turned out right for once, the website started to become almost the justification for the series. When the reworked BBC website became the home of iPlayer, the catch-up service for licence-fee-payers (and a few privileged tablet-owners overseas, mentioned in X7.16, "The Time of the Doctor"), inevitably it was *Doctor Who* that was used to launch it. We saw when discussing the promotion of X4.0, "Voyage of the Damned" how the ability of the public to see it any time in the following week was both mentioned whenever possible and – crucially – included when calculating the final ratings figures. Tennant's last two years were the place where the website bore the brunt of pre-publicity, in effect replacing *Totally Doctor Who*.

Following this, things went into, well, whatever the phase after overdrive is; Piers Wenger, stepping into Julie Gardner's shoes (which may be why all the photos of him seem to show him wincing), pitched the online material as being *as important as what was on telly*. To this end, the computer games of the eleventh Doctor were provided to the British public for free and, we were told, to be treated as canonical. The behind-the-scenes stuff of Matt Smith and Karen Gillan being scanned and modelled was included in *Doctor Who Confidential* (itself largely superseded by the online content and axed after X6.13, "The Wedding of River Song"). Worse, without having played the first of these games, *City of the Daleks*, very little of X7.1, "Asylum of the Daleks" makes any sense. It didn't help that the BBC had another round of website cuts in 2011.

Wenger was gone soon after this, and his eventual replacement, Brian Minchin, was a veteran of *The Sarah Jane Adventures* (the website for which was itself rather fun). Things are changing again, so we'll just take this story up to the big Anniversary bash.

5. Comic Maker

Scarcely a month after X3.13, "Last of the Time Lords," the team rolled out the virtual equivalent of Colorforms – you were given pictures of the Doctor and his companions, backgrounds and speech bubbles and were invited to make a comic out of them. It was a clever way to use the art assets now familiar to children from "The Infinite Quest," of course, but there was more to it than that – RTD gave the press an enthusiastic quote about children using it to make their own *Doctor Who*, and more to the point did a video tutorial telling kids how to do so. As artificial a format as it was, it worked; thousands of comics were made and posted to the BBC website, and eventually you could download and print them for yourself. Julie Gardner observed that something about the show simply made people want to tell stories.

A year on, someone had the clever idea of asking professional *Doctor Who* writers to write their own comics with this software. These ranged from the silly to the sentimental to the surreal. (Keith Temple cheekily did a sequel to the subplot from

continued on Page 109...

combines the Hooverville aspect of 1930 New York and the precarious Vaudeville life, the first three minutes of Peter Jackson's *King Kong* looks like as good a match for this story as any. That has ingenious montages of high- and low-life accompanied by Al Jolson belting out "I'm Sitting on Top of the World".

One thing that might help American readers follow the story's curious logic is that there are few opportunities to study twentieth-century American History until the last point before University, the A-Level (and it's one of a number of options, of which the simplest is nineteenth-century Europe). The main source for kids and ex-kids in the UK is thus the sketchy background provided for harassed English teachers who resort to setting the lowest-ability classes *Of Mice and Men* as the one novel they are made to read, perhaps in their entire lives. Thus, for most people hereabouts, the idea has taken root that the Wall Street Crash began an immediate Depression and that everyone therefore fled to California that afternoon in pursuit of something called The American Dream, which is about owning rabbits. Everyone lost their jobs simultaneously on 27th October, 1929 and most of them threw themselves off tall buildings.

This isn't quite how it happened, of course. Raynor is slightly closer to the truth than the downloadable handouts, but has missed a few crucial details. One thing she rightly drew attention to in the script: there was a shanty-town of some 2000 unemployed New Yorkers at the Hudson River dump in Central Park; in November 1930, it was well on the way to becoming a fixture. This and others like it were indeed called "Hoovervilles" in honour of the incumbent President. Recent research indicates that in the Manhattan area, the percentages out of work in 1930 breaks down as follows: among white men, 19.9%; black men, 25.4%; white women 11.2%; and black women 28.5%.[24] In October that year, New York placed Colonel Arthur Woods in charge of the relief efforts. The police began a survey of the numbers of "needy", while the Salvation Army opened eight food stations. The city paid for 12,000 a day to be fed. That month, Mayor Jimmy Walker had set up an Official Committee for the Relief of the Unemployed and Needy, recruiting the Police and the Board of Education to supervise the issuing of food, rent money and grocery vouchers in the city. Meanwhile, Seward Prosser's committee was set up to look for longer-term solutions.

On 1st May, 1930, President Hoover had declared that the Depression was over, citing the construction boom in New York as one of the signs. In fact, the perceived boom was partly the completion of projects begun before the Crash, but mainly a combination of symptoms of that downturn: mass unemployment cuts down on strikes and wage-bills. Desperate men will work for less, and under worse conditions. That said, one conspicuous sign of confidence was the commissioning of the Empire State Building. Work began on this shortly before Hoover's claim, on 7th April, and it was finished in a year (i.e. rather later than this episode suggests).

Raynor's storyline is fairly mendacious, but contains grains of truth. For example, the controversial "Fast Track" policy meant that work began on the construction before the blueprints for the upper storeys were completed. The spire at the top, which is counted as 17 of the 102 storeys, was a last-minute addition to beat the recently-completed rival project, the Chrysler Building. It was intended to be used as a mooring for Zeppelins and added 61 metres to the overall height, making it the tallest building in the world for four decades. To get around the zoning laws, the building became narrower as it went up, but also less ostentatious once beyond the height that a passer-by could see detail. A canny application of those same laws meant that the top "third" could be as high as the engineers thought they could get away with.

Unlike most previous skyscrapers, it was thus designed to be built from inside out, which was safer and less obtrusive. At the peak of construction, it employed 3500 men, plus ancillary staff (catering and drivers). Nonetheless, it came in considerably under-budget – at an overall cost, with the land, of $41 million ($24.7 million for the building itself). The construction used a method like supermarkets' "just in time" policy, moving in parts and equipment from the sources at exactly the time they were needed with 500 trucks per day to prevent blocking 5th Avenue – according to one source, the rivets came from Pittsburgh still warm from the forges. The topping-out of the 86th floor (the highest occupied part) was in October. This modular construction and the other innovations made the rapid, massive sign of New York's defiance an immediate

What Were the Best Online Extras?

continued from Page 107...

"The Impossible Planet" that they could never have afforded to make for X4.3, "Planet of the Ood"; Helen Raynor wrote the Moxx of Balhoon prequel everyone had expected back in 2005 and Peter Anghelides turned in a surprisingly touching take on post-Time War angsting.) They also added a new treat – the Trailer Maker, which allowed you to cut and paste sound effects, Murray Gold's music, and clips from Tennant (and eventually some Eccleston) episodes to make short trailers. Tennant's fakeout regeneration was a favourite setpiece.

(This wasn't the only time that Goss thriftily reused animation artwork from the children's production he'd produced – that same summer, the website did a competition in tandem with BBC Blast to allow a kid to actually create a game. *Doctor in a Dash*, a pretty bog-standard racing game, came out at the end of the year and had an intro that clearly has the same animated Doctor from "The Infinite Quest".)

But they never got around to updating these for Matt Smith and the software was gone by the Anniversary year, so you can't even read the professionally-done comics. The sole remnant of the trailers is a handful of blurry YouTube clips. (The replacement Facebook app launched in October 2013: sticking a picture of your face into the title sequence. Not the same at all, really.) Those of us too young to recall seeing the now-wiped episodes can experience a little portion of the existential angst this causes, knowing that you once read a comic by Paul Cornell that not even he can see now. Still, it was a nice thought while it lasted, and the Comic Maker did get the website nominated for a BAFTA.

Even this wasn't entirely unprecedented: "Scream of the Shalka" had a website feature with paper doll versions of Alison, the Master and the Doctor that you were meant to print out and colour in yourself, complete with a scan of how to make the "*Blue Peter* Theatre" that was very obviously taken from an old *Radio Times*. It's very sweet.

6. Commentaries/ behind the scenes videos

The DVDs used to come in two forms; the "vanilla" ones just have the episodes and are put out very soon after broadcast to catch the wave of public interest, then the box-sets had a few of the features we've been describing and the now-traditional commentaries and Video Diaries. This ended once Moffat's regime began making so many extras for the website and *Comic Relief*, there was no room even had there been time. However, even by Series 3, the amount of material generated exceeded orthodox commercial exploitation, and the BBC's public service remit meant we got everything they couldn't squeeze onto discs by other means. Who gets to be on the commentary teams for each episode seems oddly haphazard. With the episodes covered in this book there was a solution: namely, recording two sets of commentary and picking one for the DVD and one for online. One of the odd side-effects of this is that we've had a lot of work to do resolving discrepancies between two accounts of the making of a given episode. Another has been that for various logistical reasons, the online commentary hasn't always been playable when we've had the DVD handy to put on or vice versa. Listened to on its own, there are odd gaps when everyone is watching and listening to an episode not included in the feed. Moreso than usual, these chats make the listener feel like an eavesdropper. You also have to remember what's on screen at any given time for the comments to make complete sense.

Because of the timetables of everyone involved, many of the online commentaries were made closer to transmission than the ones on the discs. This allows a few interesting sidelights, as well as reuniting people who've not seen each other for a while. The most cheerful aspect of this is that Freema Agyeman had caught up with her sleep and landed up acting as moderator in some of these, coaxing a shy Thomas Sangster to talk on X3.8, "Human Nature" and refereeing a sort-of family reunion on X3.12, "The Sound of Drums".

One reason for deciding which commentary went where was simply concerns about how safely they could broadcast information about forthcoming episodes. The online commentaries were available immediately after broadcast of each week's adventure, whereas DVD box-sets have generally been fairly comprehensively spoilered. The same logic applied to which interview clips were in *Doctor Who Confidential* and which popped up on the website ahead of the broadcast. There is also the matter of value for money (something the BBC Trust get to make noises about in order to prove that they're worth

continued on Page 111...

icon, even if it took another three years before the offices inside were taken. The "Empty State Building" was a sore point for many, and it took *King Kong* to make Americans embrace it.

Where Raynor varies most alarmingly from the truth is in the people behind the project. Mr Diagoras (the name comes from a Greek poet from around the time of Thermopylae) is a left-over from the original idea of a story set in the docks about pigs going missing but, with the embargo on writing about speakeasies, he is there mainly as a straw-boss. In reality, the main contractors, Starret Brothers and Eken, were one of the more broad-minded teams. Raynor suggests that it took a brutal suppression of workers' rights to achieve a project of this size on time and under budget. She was clearly thinking of later disputes where employers suppressed unions and any sign of workers demanding basic rights with gunfire – there was the Pinkerton mine shooting in the 1890s and Cripple Creek in 1902, true, but the general impression we have of this is that it peaked in the 30s. Henry Ford and Walt Disney are among the famous figures vilified for violation of the Wagner Act towards the end of the decade.

This makes sense: Raynor and Davies grew up in South Wales, where coal-mining was more than simply the main employer, it was the thing that dominated all aspects of life for centuries until the 1984 Miners' Strike and the Thatcher government's remorseless demolition of the industry (see 22.3, "The Mark of the Rani"). It was in South Wales that the nearest Britain has to a Cripple Creek occurred, when the then-Home Secretary, Winston Churchill, sending in the army to suppress rioters in Tonypandy in 1922 was enough in itself to cause a scandal. The mythology in the UK is that America was like that all the time, and with less provocation.

The term "Hoovertown" was put into UK currency in the mid-80s, as the similarity between the Thatcher government's Monetarism and Hoover's failed policies (and their consequences, with homelessness following home repossessions and unemployment in both decades) began to have hitherto unimaginable consequences. Hoover's policies might have worked, if the technology of the time had allowed state-wide or national micro-management, plus data-processing in real-time of the kind used by banks today. His main inclination was to remove governmental controls on the banks at precisely the point that those controls were the main thing stopping these banks from folding. So fold they did, and they took a lot of small businesses – mainly farms – with them. This was where the 1932 Depression that followed these initial problems differed from earlier "Great Depressions", such as that of 1890. The one thing any nation losing manufacturing jobs can do is soak up the excess labour on the farms. However, not only did a record-breaking drought lead to the Dustbowl and all that arose from that, but few banks were willing to loan money to farmers to tide them over this lean patch, and many banks foreclosed on mortgages as a desperate measure to stay in business themselves.

Stories from later in the Depression of the lengths to which people would go to get work – and the ways this need was exploited – merge with tales of bootleggers and their pitiless exploitation of out-of-work men from the immediate post-war period, 1919 and after. Again, Warner Brothers told that story; *The Roaring Twenties* was reissued several times and was often on British television in the early 80s. Through parody and half-memory, a garbled version of this history persists. In this context, gangsters and straw-bosses seemed indistinguishable. However, the decision to remove any taint of Jazz left Diagoras as a character without a purpose, and the clumsy grafting of him onto the construction work compounds the other anachronisms in that part of the story. The profiteering that followed Prohibition, and the lack of tax revenue from alcohol sales, was by 1930 thought by many to be exacerbating the effects of the Crash, and politicians in both major parties were veering towards repealing the Volstead Act. In general, the Democrats were more "wet" and – shortly after this story's supposed date, on 4th November, 1930 – that party had a landslide victory in the midterm elections. Ironically, it was A.E. Smith, failed Democratic candidate in the 1928 election and former Governor of New York, who made the speech nominating Franklin Roosevelt for the 1932 election despite their rivalry. Smith was also the head of the consortium that had built the Empire State Building. (FDR's campaign song, "Happy Days are Here Again", wasn't adopted until that nomination and had been used in five films in 1930, so it being played on the radio so soon before important elections isn't as wrong as some commentators have suggested.)

What Were the Best Online Extras?

continued from Page 109...

funding themselves). Anyone who'd paid for the disc of X4.0, "Voyage of the Damned" would want to hear something more illuminating than Julie Gardner, Phil Collinson and Russell T Davies laughing for a solid minute over the word "jet-ski" and each pretending not to know who the other two were.

With the end of *Doctor Who Confidential*, some ten-minute pieces were posted on iPlayer and the website accompanying Series 8. These closely resembled the mini-pieces on the Series 7 box-set, but were promoted more heavily.

7. Guy Fawkes

The 2010 series had a big publicity blitz for the *Doctor Who Adventure Games*. These were one of the most complicated attempts to hitch the popularity of the series on television to the BBC's bids to diversify. A great deal of stress was put on the canonical nature of the stories, the fidelity of the characterisation of the new Doctor and Amy and the educational bonus of the game-play. Half an episode of *Doctor Who Confidential* was given over to the scanning process and modelling of the game-avatars of the leads. (It was unkindly suggested that the digital Amy had a greater range of facial expressions that Karen Gillan's bog-eyed gawp, and the binary-encoded Doctor walked more naturally than Matt Smith.) Moreover, the first game was a chance to show off their very expensive New Dalek Paradigm design in a context where they looked most at home: software.

The BBC's most high-profile previous attempt at a *Doctor Who* computer game, the 1990s CD ROM *Destiny of the Doctors*, was – it has to be said – a shambles. The game-play was clumsy, the linking material (performed by Anthony Ainley as the Master) was at best perfunctory, and it tried to synoptically include every Doctor and famous alien – supposedly what the fans wanted – and laboriously introduce it all for absolute newbies. It only reminded people of *Doctor Who* when it reminded the critics of why the series had been canned.

The new series of games were written by long-time associates of the BBC Wales series, Phil Ford and James Moran (X4.2, "The Fires of Pompeii"; X4.16, "The Waters of Mars"; X8.2, "Into The Dalek") and had supporting cast from the series, notably Big Finish veterans Barnaby Edwards and Nicholas Briggs. The music cues were retreads of broadcast scores. Much of the gameware came from experienced manufacturers Sumo Digital, but in collusion with the new BBC Interactive franchise. More importantly, it had support from other BBC departments. Sumo's head designer, Sean Millard, began his career with a Dalek game in the early 1990s, but the chief creative brains on the series, called *The Adventure Games*, were Charles Cecil, Phil Ford and Steven Moffat. The look of each game was tried out on the showrunner just as any other design decision for the broadcast series would be. Charles Cecil's formidable CV as a games designer includes *Broken Sword*, so the project had credibility among gamers. The first *Adventure Games* release, *City of the Daleks*, re-introduced Skaro ahead of the TV series (X7.1, "Asylum of the Daleks" and the apparently contradictory X9.1, "The Magician's Apprentice") and led to three others, *Blood of the Cybermen*, *TARDIS* and *Shadows of the Vashta Narada* in rapid succession.

In the case of the last of the games, *The Gunpowder Plot*, the educational remit was pushed in the publicity via more overt links with BBC Learning, makers of what Schools TV as now persists and the "Bitesize" section of the BBC website given to exam revision help. The head of BBC Learning at the time was Saul Nassé, who had previously been editor of the technology showcase series *Tomorrow's World* and, before that, leader of the Bedfordshire Local Group of the *Doctor Who* Appreciation Society. The promotional material for the game had teachers' notes and links to the schools section of the BBC website. It won a special award from BAFTA Cymru. Unlike the other games, it had Rory in it (a popular move among reviewers) and a definite "slot" in between two broadcast episodes in Series 6. It got thumbs-up all around, so why was it the last?

Part of the problem was that it had three barely-overlapping audiences to please. The game was free to download for anyone in the UK, so needed to be for mouse and keyboard rather than adapted for custom-built machinery and have glitch-free download without too much memory being eaten on Mum's laptop or the school computers. (Hard as it is to recall, smart phones and tablets were only starting to catch on when this began.) The gameplay was designed to be simple enough for people who don't play many games (and the early stages have the player being taught to

continued on Page 113...

Mythological New York, as with the last story, is a bigger source than the real one. The disastrous musical *Just Imagine* opened in November 1930 and depicts a future closely resembling the version of the contemporary city in Hollywood. One of the many side-effects of this stylisation of skyscrapers and Art Deco apartments is that this 30s bravura still works as shorthand for "futuristic". Raymond Cusick's designs for Skaro and various other space-cities in 60s Dalek stories were derived from the lack of right-angles in many of the landmark buildings of this period, notably some of the ones Frank Lloyd Wright was beginning to devise. The most overt melding of technology and building-design was the big rival to the Empire State Building, the Chrysler Building, which incorporated the shapes of car-parts into its décor and the characteristic ziggurat shape at the top.

The other manifestation of the myth is yet another re-run of the alligators in the sewers. Davies is at least keeping with the traditions of Terry Nation and Dennis Spooner (see Volume 1), and comments on this as a notion he wanted to suggest in "Gridlock" (X3.3). Of course, the Daleks had been to the Empire State Building once before, in the single most embarrassing part of that monumentally embarrassing story, "The Chase" (2.8). Davies cited the Morton Dill scene in that story as a possible reason why the Daleks might have known of this edifice. Similarly, the use of sewers under a theatre isn't unprecedented (14.6, "The Talons of Weng-Chiang"), as we are firmly in *Phantom of the Opera* territory. The pre-credits scene's use of a wooden pirate in a dark cellar is almost identical to Jago being spooked by the totem-pole left behind by Six-Gun Sadie in the 1977 Robert Holmes story. That had a Music Hall over a sewer leading to the fugitive time-criminal's lair and guarded by genetically-altered beasts. Sound familiar?

Meantime, Gareth Roberts (X3.2, "The Shakespeare Code") had written the first Quick Books novel, published in spring 2006; this was an initiative to encourage youngsters who didn't enjoy reading. Entitled *I am a Dalek*, it dealt with the idea of human-Dalek hybrids by making the guest companion in the story one herself (see X7.1, "Asylum of the Daleks" and then everything with Clara in thereafter). As we mentioned above, there's a hint of *The Island of Doctor Moreau* in this story, as there will be in the next one (X3.6, "The Lazarus Experiment"), which is where we'll develop this theme. But the icon of the pig-hyena that is the main threat in the three film versions is what's being used here, rather than the book's more complex debate.

To get really obvious, there's a guy called "Solomon" whose first significant act is to resolve a dispute over a loaf of bread by tearing it in half – you may remember this from 1.Kings 3:25 – and whose last act is to ask flying, heavily-armed space monsters if they recognise compassion or God (see George Pal's version of *War of the Worlds*).

Oh, Isn't That...?

• *Hugh Quarshie* (Solomon, de facto Hooverville leader) plays Ric Griffin on *Holby City*. He'd thus worked briefly with Agyeman before, re-attaching her arm or something. Practically anyone with an Equity card has been in this or the parent series, *Casualty* (see Volume 6), but he's a regular fixture. In 1987, he was criticised in the tabloids for asking why nobody was thinking of a black Doctor to replace Colin Baker. You may also have seen him in *Star Wars Episode I: The Phantom Menace* as the pilot who first identifies R2-D2.

• *Andrew Garfield* (Frank, Hooverville resident) er... you *do* know he's been Spider-Man in two huge feature films, don't you? He was also in *Never Let Me Go*, a film everyone steadfastly pretends isn't science fiction, with Carey Mulligan (Sally Sparrow in X3.10, "Blink") and Keira Knightley (who was Padme's decoy in *The Phantom Menace*). On television, he appeared in *Red Riding*, based on David Peace's grim novel and starring David Morrisey (X4.14, "The Next Doctor").

• *Miranda Raison* (Tallulah, stage-performer) was in hit BBC action show *Spooks*. (Apparently, it had to be renamed *MI5* in America, but that's as if someone decided that *The Mentalist* ought to be renamed *Sacramento PD* in the UK to stop anyone thinking it was about a maniacal Alan Partridge fan.)

• *Ryan Carnes* (Laszlo, Tallulah's boyfriend and mutated pig-person) was sporadically in *Desperate Housewives* as Andrew's love-interest.

What Were the Best Online Extras?

continued from Page 111...

manipulate an avatar of Rory before the main narrative begins).

Yet when looking up reviews for this piece, we found that most of the comments are from American gamers (who had to pay for it) unfamiliar with the series or the key incident of British history at risk from Sontaran-Rutan interference. Luckily, if you manage to get through the game without learning anything about 1605 London, you'll have picked up a lot of *Doctor Who* lore. Both the programme's history and that of Jacobean geopolitics are presented as plot-coupons for the individual player, although it's the stuff in the TARDIS that's useful for defeating aliens. That's right, the game's designed for single players, but it comes with class-notes.

Assuming, however, that you are ten years old, a UK resident and have never played a computer-game before but want to know all about programme-lore and Robert Catesby, the main feature that would strike you is that there are a set number of tasks to complete with little (optional) info-dumps along the way. However much you might want to just explore this odd-but-almost-known city or talk to people about something other than doctrinal differences, this is all as rigidly-plotted as a 45-minute celebrity historical, albeit less mendacious than of late. There is a preferred route through the game, with no option for history to go any differently if you make different choices given the information at hand. This has been a perennial bugbear of history teachers with regard to software, the notion that whatever in fact happened was the optimum outcome. There is a walk-through online that enables the story to unfold in the smallest possible time, just over two hours, without ever encountering a Silent. (Although their gimmick is amnesia, these eldritch horrors are somewhat perversely employed to help players learn. They offer additional information without affecting the run of the game, so are absent from the walk-through.) Nonetheless, our hypothetical child player would have a feel for wooden London and the dawn of the modern age, and would have been thoroughly briefed on the functions of Black Rod. What an adult would notice on getting to the end is that the voice-cast includes pretty big names: Phil Daniels, Ralf Little and Emilia Fox. (Little has, subsequently, been in broadcast *Doctor Who*; X10.2, "Smile").

However, it's thought that reason this marked the cessation of the project was the internal ructions in BBC Wales. By the time this game emerged, almost 18 months after the first, the series was down two Executive Producers. The *Adventure Games* project had been closely associated with one of these, Piers Wenger, who had succeeded Julie Gardner as BBC Wales' Drama boss but soon took over a bigger plum job as head of Channel 4's drama department. Beth Willis, the other departing Exec, returned to her lucrative berth at Shine. By the time the flurry of replacements and other complications settled, all three of the lead actors had left. BBC Worldwide, now in overall charge of the games associated with BBC series, moved all of its gaming operations to the US and games manufacturers moved from consoles to smartphones. The shambles of *The Eternity Clock* might warrant more commentary in a later volume, but the current state-of-the-art is *Doctor Who Legacy* (a free download along the lines of *Candy Crush*, but incorporating all Doctors for once) and tie-ups with Lego and Minecraft.

8. Adventure Calendar

Can you see what they've done there? It's like an Advent Calendar but counting down to the *other* big event on December 25th, a new hour-long episode. Every day, from December 1st onward, they pop a new morsel on the site. Sometimes, these are games. (The run-up to "Voyage of the Damned" had such delights as a jigsaw of starship *Titanic* that you completed to win a glimpse at a page of inconsequential script, plus the *Su- Doc- Who* pun everyone had already made came to fruition, with nine faces replacing the nine digits and a mugshot of Tennant as the prize.) Sometimes, it's behind-the-scenes photos. Occasionally, a new short story would be serialised, tying in with a recent episode (so Rupert Laight gave us the full story of the anecdote about Charlemagne, Madonna and a mad computer – X4.7, "The Unicorn and the Wasp").

2012 was notable mainly for the sneak preview of the new "Magic Roundabout" TARDIS console and interviews with Moffat where he all but admitted that the New Paradigm Daleks were a blunder. With the demise of *Doctor Who Confidential*, this is our main opportunity to see the cast giving each other tacky presents or chatting backstage. 2013 was the year when the fall-

continued on Page 114...

What Were the Best Online Extras?

continued from Page 113...

out from the Anniversary allowed them to almost completely ignore the forthcoming episode for the first two weeks, instead telling us about the Zygons (and claiming that the Savoy Hotel is in Paris, which is news to anyone who's taken a short-cut to Charing Cross station past the tradesman's entrance).

Admittedly, about 2/3 of this stuff would fail to make the grade as DVD extras or Easter Eggs, but the whole point of Advent Calendars is that you don't know what you're going to get each morning; the cumulative effect of the ritual is part of getting into the mood for the big event on Christmas Day. And, as with most things about Christmas, by December 28th it already seems an impossibly long time ago...

9. Bonus Material Superior to the Broadcast Episode Whence It Came

We discussed the *TARDISodes* in Volume 7; they were one-minute long clips made especially to be played on phones that could play video, usually prologues to the broadcast episode. In general, they were intended to widen out the story beyond the confines of wherever the Doctor and Rose had materialised, so that the people who found the ancient writings about Krop Tor were shown on a different planet discussing whether to investigate ("The Impossible Planet") or the events depicted in a wood-cut were shown to us with brief but effective special effects (X2.2, "Tooth and Claw"). Gareth Roberts did the scripts and they were neat, punchy and sometimes rather more interesting than what we got in that week's show.

This sort of thing came back in the Moffat years with bits of prolepsis (backstory, in other words) from Series 6, showing Nixon receiving his first nuisance call (X6.1, "The Impossible Astronaut") and so on. One to note is the clip for X6.3, "The Curse of the Black Spot". It's moody, it's tense and acted to a Tm and gives a real sense of being on a ship far from any hope of aid – everything the broadcast episode failed to manage.

Series 7 went one better, with a mini-serial of one-minute episodes stripped across a week. "Pond Life" is, as the name suggests, what Amy and Rory did between adventures, with the Doctor popping in and out and disrupting their semi-normal lives (she's an international model, he's a nurse...) in, well, wherever they were living this year. (Didn't anyone think this through? See Volume 9, where we have to try to make sense of this.) Chris Chibnall wrote this, and X7.4, "The Power of Three", and to be honest the stuff about Rory walking in to the bathroom and finding an Ood sat on his toilet deserved screen-time more than the rather trite ending of the episode. (An Ood in the loo... maybe they live in Tooting Bec now.) Most of this material in fact looks to have been made as part of that episode, suggesting that they selected some scenes for the montage of a year passing and some for the website; the incident with the unseen Zygons at the Cafe Royale is of a piece with the Doctor fleeing Sontarans in "Pond Life" and less spectacular-looking. If we take it that the six months or so of "Pond Life" is in the year where he's popping in on the Cube in "The Power of Three", then it makes a bit more sense that Brian is also on hand to monitor the Cube when the Doctor's away.

By late 2013, this was itself part of the overall plan of the broadcast episodes. In between Strax reporting on various ingredients in the big show, we had two mini-episodes that help make sense of what we saw and one of these, "Night of the Doctor", was an event in itself. If you didn't know, this is the hitherto unseen story of how John Hurt's character comes into the story and stars Paul McGann. He is recognisably the same Doctor from the TV Movie (although when naming former companions, Grace and Chang Lee are conspicuously absent) and has been trying to avoid being in the Time War until one person too many dies and he resolves to change. Fortunately, he's dying (or dead) on Karn (13.5, "The Brain of Morbius", although that adds another can of worms to the problem of numbering the Doctors) and so the Sisterhood help him pick a suitable new persona to end the War. It sounds like a Big Finish audio, and looks like one of the cheap episodes of *Babylon 5* set on the Drahzi Homeworld, but the presence of McGann and their ability to have kept is a surprise fed into the buzz surrounding "The Day of the Doctor". For some viewers, the expectations it raised were unmatchable by any single episode.

10. *The Five(ish) Doctors Reboot*

For all that the BBC's carpet-bombing of the British media in the week leading up to November 23rd 2013 stressed the whole 50-years-ness of it all, they were mainly preoccupied with the eight most recent years and all the things from it they

What Were the Best Online Extras?

could sell. There was Mark Gatiss' *slightly* mendacious play "An Adventure in Space and Time", which teased us with sets and costumes from missing episodes that the rumour-mill said weren't as missing as they had been, but was notable mainly for suggesting that Paddy Russell was a man (3.5, "The Massacre"), that Sydney Newman and Mervyn Pinfield stuck around until 4.2, "The Tenth Planet" and that Heather Hartnell was also married to Leggy Mountbatten from *The Rutles*. There was an edition of the resolutely middle-brow BBC2 puff-programme *The Culture Show* in which Matthew Sweet went on at length about 17.5, "The Horns of Nimon" and the allegations in Richard Marson's book *JN-T* about 80s producer John Nathan-Turner (see Volumes 5 and 6) whilst supposedly investigating how this series had managed such a grip on the national imagination. By and large, though, this was a series whose real history began in 2005 if the coverage was any guide – you had to go to local radio to get anything more. Then, on the BBC's digital Red Button and the website, a small note of protest was heard...

Peter Davison had already mentioned a few times that the term "Classic" for anything made before 1990 was a bit offputting, but the real surprise about his half-hour film *The Five(ish) Doctors Reboot* is how game everyone was to parody themselves. The plot is that he, Colin Baker and Sylvester McCoy are desperate to be in "The Day of the Doctor" (as is Paul McGann, but he won't admit this) and, after pestering Steven Moffat with phone calls, decide to take matters into their own hands. Around this simple storyline are sardonic comments on everything from Olivia Coleman being in every television drama that year (X5.1, "The Eleventh Hour") to the steep-admission fee for the guided tour of the studio complex. To list all the surprise cameos would be beside the point, but there's one who couldn't be in it (hence the name) and they manage to allude to a previous no-show by the same performer (see 20.7, "The Five Doctors" for a hint).

The film was written and directed by Davison, and produced by his daughter, Georgia Tennant. Her pregnancy was alluded to in the script, as was Colin's stint on *I'm A Celebrity... Get Me Out of Here!*[25] and the peculiarly long shoot on *The Hobbit*. It's in-jokey, as might be expected, with on-screen gags about Adric, the regeneration in 21.6, "The Caves of Androzani" and lines from old scripts. The most interesting feature is that it did indeed use the sets for the 2013 Anniversary special and ends with a strong hint that one scene in the finished version actually did have the old Doctors hiding in plain sight. (Sadly, the dates don't work for this to be true.) The episode landed up vying with the official Anniversary Special for the Hugo award.

This was (partly) made and promoted by BBC Wales as part of the anniversary, yet is critical of it. It has the Anniversary Episode at the centre of the action (and thus was kept until after broadcast of that) and – as with John Hurt's Doctor slagging off the other two for catch-phrases and gimmicks – seems at times as if Moffat is aware of how corporate the whole series has become and what he would think of it all if he were just a viewer. It also crystallised a feeling a lot of people had that, with Moffat giving interview after interview, and the renewed focus on Hartnell (through the Gatiss play and his status as the original) and Troughton (with rediscovered episodes going on sale a month earlier amid a whole lot more hoo-hah), someone else was being unfairly sidelined.

Oh, you know... Big bloke, a bit camp, Welsh accent...

X3.5: "Evolution of the Daleks"

(28th April, 2007)

Which One is This? Wrath of Caan. In the absence of a hunchback called Igor, the Doctor assists Dalek Sec in an experiment to create new life with a thunderstorm, a tall building and a lot of sparking machinery.

Firsts and Lasts One thing's remarkable: this is the first time an attempt to take over the world is seen to begin in Manhattan, rather than the Home Counties or a remote village in Pigbinshire or Scotland. Outside tie-in books, the nearest precedent for this is "City of Death" (17.2), which is mainly Paris but also Florence, Rome, Greece, Egypt and the middle of the Atlantic, and isn't really a takeover as much as it's a prevention.

Oh, and we have the revived series's use of a title expressed as "[noun] of the Daleks", and its first internecine dispute between Daleks over purity. That's as reliable a plot-device as jungle-planets and surgically converting humans into their drone-like slaves. It's also the first time we've seen them remove panels.

The Daleks mention "Skaro" by name and do a countdown in "Rels" (an old piece of Dalek lore used in Nation's tie-in books and the second Cushing film).

Watch Out For...

• Although they've had to cannibalise their own travel-machines to build their mad-scientist lab, the Daleks have enough spare parts around to mass-produce authentic period plasma-bolt-firing tommy-guns for their semi-human minions. Both sides shoot it out in a theatre, with the Dalek Sec-Diagoras hybrid in chains on stage, lit by the footlights, as both Frankenstein's Monster and the Elephant Man were. You won't see this combination of images anywhere else.

• ... neither will you see two Daleks conspiring against a third and looking around to see if anyone's eavesdropping (the gossipy Cybermen from 19.6, "Earthshock" finally have competition).

• ... nor a lot of pig-men in a lift politely not making eye-contact.

• For once, Martha has a chance at some genuine doctoring. It'd perhaps have been better if she'd had any screen-time to do it properly, but considering how often she's allowed to be genuinely clever, even a quick bout of bandaging comes off well. She also manages a miraculous catch, as the sonic screwdriver falls three storeys and she apparently just pops her hand out, in a thunderstorm (of sorts), and grabs it.

Even more miraculously, she works out exactly what the Doctor intends her to do with the psychic paper and does it (we'll see this again before the year's out). That said, what it transpires she did with it off-screen is, um, remarkable (see **Things That Don't Make Sense**).

• The Doctor is up on the pylon of the Empire State Building when he drops his screwdriver, doing something or other involving his DNA, lightning and a coaxial cable (see **Things That Don't Make Sense** for what they *say* he's doing). You may recognise the pylon from its guest-role last year as Alexandra Palace (X2.7, "The Idiot's Lantern"). It'll be back later this year. You may also recognise the strange Dalek science, based on static electricity and an ability to convey personality-traits thereby, from the works of the very first script editor (see **What Planet was David Whitaker On?** under 5.7, "The Wheel in Space" and **What are the Silliest Examples of Bad Science in *Doctor Who*?** under 10.4, "Planet of the Daleks"). Indeed, we're struggling to think of a single plot-beat here that Whitaker didn't use in 4.9, "The Evil of the Daleks".

... oh, found one! Unlike "the final end", but like every other Dalek story ever since the first one, the last Dalek escapes and runs away to fight another day. Just like "Doomsday" (X2.13), it yells "Em-er-gen-cy tem-por-al shift" and vanishes to another place and time, but it's different this time because... err... (In fact, it turns out to have been very different, but wait until their next appearance in X4.12, "The Stolen Earth" for that. Older UK viewers may also be thinking "I deny you the Nidus", but that's a different story.)

The Continuity

The Doctor Seems to have acquired a death wish, for whatever reason – there's no trick up his sleeve when he screams at the Daleks to kill him during the attack on Hooverville, and Dalek Sec's change of heart temporarily floors him. [This, as opposed to the way he seems sure the Time Lord hybrids won't shoot when they redo this scene 20 minutes later.]

Which are the Most Over-Specialised Daleks?

In the hype about "Asylum of the Daleks" (X7.1), we were promised that we'd see every single type of Dalek ever. True, if you pause and look carefully, you can see the Special Weapons Dalek (25.1, "Remembrance of the Daleks") sulking in a corner and a Parliament on the Mothership (sadly, lacking George Clinton and Bootsy Collins) which has both the New Paradigm "Teletubby" Daleks (X5.3, "Victory of the Daleks") and the good ones. Special also did whatever Daleks do instead of twiddling their thumbs in X9.1, "The Magician's Apprentice" and X9.2, "The Witch's Familiar", but when they needed a big gun to zap the TARDIS, they used a glorified chandelier. The New Paradigms have colour-co-ordinated job-titles ("Scientist", "Drone", "Eternal" – whatever that means – "Strategist" and "Supreme"), like Power Rangers or Care Bears. These fashion-victims, the charcoal-grey trial runs and some blue-bobbled 60's throwbacks were all milling about in orbit over their planet-sized cupboard under the stairs too. There were, however, some pretty significant gaps. The Emperor(s) would have been a welcome touch, especially if they got all three to pose for photos (see 4.9, "The Evil of the Daleks"; "Remembrance" again and X1.13, "The Parting of the Ways"). The Glass Dalek (22.6, "Revelation of the Daleks") was also conspicuously absent.

However, for anyone who's been watching this series a long time, and who'd seen every extant episode (and maybe a few that aren't currently around), a few glaring omissions were obvious. Here, then, are a few of the most entertainingly niche Dalek designs *not* to have been asked along for Reunion of the Daleks...

The Streaker Dalek (21.4, "Resurrection of the Daleks")

Generally, when a Dalek loses its shell, or is forcibly removed, it skulks away and dies. "The Daleks" (1.2) makes a big thing of this dependence on the life-support machinery, and "Destiny of the Daleks" (17.1) has one wandering around Skaro before dying in a little burrow it made for itself. Not so the hardy individualist at large in the warehouse where the Movellans have hidden their virus. Perhaps as a response to the viral attack on the electrics of the shells (see **Soft Porn Daleks**, below), one Dalek has trained in naked combat. Fans have slagged off this sequence for being a flagrant *Alien* rip-off, right down to the cat, but maybe we should think of this as a trial-run for *300*.

By the time of "The Witch's Familiar" we see Dalazar, the Dalek city on Skaro, pulled into the ground by a slithering horde of elderly, naked Daleks who've been in the sewer/ cemetery without even cribbage or daytime television to while away their retirement.

The Jean-Paul Gaultier Dalek (2.2, "The Dalek Invasion of Earth"; 9.1, "Day of the Daleks"; 10.4, "Planet of the Daleks"; "Resurrection of the Daleks")

Once you've enslaved a planet's population, you want to humiliate them, break their spirit. What better way than forcing those who work directly for you to wear ludicrous space-age couture? Well, there's torture and mind-control drugs, of course, but they're less funny on screen.

No, the optimum way for the Daleks to assert their supremacy is to design outlandish clothes that make the humanoids wearing them look sillier than Daleks. (And when the Daleks in question are wearing dish-antennae and talking like bored actors wobbling their fingers inside their lips when speaking, this is a tall order.) You need helmets that look like the petrol-tank of a 50's motorbike with little hatches cut into them for the face to poke out of, and with tiny dish-antennae so that the Robomen don't feel left out.

Later on, when your twenty-second-century conquest has gone a bit better with more preparation, you can force everyone in your office to wear grey Nehru suits, grey make-up, grey shoes and grey nail-polish. The lower orders can wear leather helmets a bit like the Roboman hats, but with orange jumpers and brown leather waistcoats. Without the helmet, this looks like you're one of the dancers of a Saturday Night light entertainment show, and would rather be doing high kicks with Lulu or Cilla Black. Invisible slaves need to be more noticeable, and warm in the cavernous recesses of your pet icecano, so you equip them with furs. Lurid purple furs. And, like night-club bouncers, you deny entry to anyone in the wrong shoes.

When you hire space mercenaries, you have to give them screamingly early-80's leatherette tunics (charcoal, with red or yellow-trimmed patch pockets and epaulettes) and cute little forage caps with peaks that go down to the chin – all that's missing are lime-green wraparound shades and a red and black chequered kerchief around the neck. Anyone can get space-mercenaries that look like extras from *Mad Max*, Daleks go the extra Rel

continued on Page 119...

He's still trying to take on the alien threat without getting anyone else involved, twice telling Martha to stay in Hooverville – the first time so she can attend to the wounded, the second makes clear that he simply wants her out of the way. [Of course, this is after he allowed Solomon to have a go at talking to the Daleks and watched the man die for it, so he's possibly more sensitive than normal on this point.]

He taunts the Daleks about their perception of radio chitchat. ('A simple little radio... What's the point of that? Oh, with music, you can dance to it, sing with it, fall in love to it. Unless you're a Dalek, of course. Then it's all just noise.') [This resembles no Dalek story so much as the fifth Doctor's 'well-prepared meal' speech in "Earthshock". The Daleks' perplexity at music is also analogous to Cyber-humour-failure, as per 25.3, "Silver Nemesis".]

He's surprised to hear Sec-Diagoras say that any deaths could be wrong and, after much sarcasm, comes around to thinking Sec-Diagoras might just be something new. By the end of the story, he's saying that Sec-Diagoras was the cleverest Dalek who ever lived, and is outraged by his death. Nonetheless, he promises Dalek Caan that he's willing to help so as not to cause yet another genocide. It bothers him immensely to be turned down. [With Capaldi-enhanced hindsight, the Doctor's enthusiasm for cocktails of Dalek, human and Time Lord genes is remarkably weird. See Series 9 for more; arguably, X9.02, "The Witch's Familiar" is wholly incompatible with this story.]

He can stabilise the pig-man Lazlo's condition, but can't do plastic surgery to restore his face.

• *Background.* He says 'First floor, perfumery' when a lift opens [so he's seen *Are You Being Served?*].

• *Ethics.* The Doctor apologises when he asks Martha to stay behind and fight rather than follow him up to the roof [compare with X3.13, "Last of the Time Lords", where both of them think the idea of him asking her to kill the Master is hilarious]. Transmitting Time Lord DNA to mind-wiped humans intended to receive an infusion of Dalek DNA – an entire new species either way – seems like a good idea. [But contradicts X4.6, "The Doctor's Daughter". Conversely, he doesn't seem more outraged by these hybrids' genocide than he would about the deaths of any independently-minded species, so maybe the smidgeon of DNA doesn't make them all *that* Time Lord-ish. We don't hear a peep from the Doctor about any Pigmen other than Laszlo, so either Dalek Caan offed them as well, or the Doctor takes Sec at his word that they can't be helped.]

• *Inventory: Sonic Screwdriver.* The Doctor repeats the electronically magnified sound trick from "The Runaway Bride" (X3.0) on the Daleks. And he can light a Bunsen burner more flamboyantly with the screwdriver than a simple match.

• *Inventory: Psychic Paper.* Martha's use of it takes us into Jedi Mind Trick territory [again, see **Things That Don't Make Sense**].

• *Inventory: Other.* The wireless he was repairing last episode was in his pocket. It still plays music, but smashes after the Doctor's first escape.

The Supporting Cast

• *Martha.* Under the impression that a gamma strike will be a lightning strike, she comes up with the idea to roast all the Pigmen (save Laszlo) by running a lot of electric conductors to the elevator. She's sickened by her role in killing them, but accepts Laszlo's argument that the Daleks had done that ages before. The Doctor outright ordering her to go back to Hooverville yet again has her complaining that he's just like a Dalek [an uncharacteristically tactless statement, even if he has been side-lining her all story]. Having worked out that the Daleks have an energy collector somewhere on the Empire State Building, she still takes ages to realise it's on the top.

She seems to know *The Prince and the Showgirl* [1957, starring Marilyn Monroe and Laurence Olivier], calling Tallulah and Laszlo 'the pig and the showgirl'.

The Non-Humans

• *Sec-Diagoras.* At first, he's enthusiastic about having access to all the human talent for destruction and war, but the genetic splice quickly goes off and has him feeling compassion and respect for the courageous – so much so, he invents a transparent excuse not to kill the Doctor. The other Daleks mysteriously keep Sec alive after the mutiny, but shoot him mostly by accident when he pleads with them on the Doctor's behalf.

• *The Cult of Skaro.* They escaped Canary Wharf ["Doomsday"] with an Emergency Temporal Shift; the Doctor thinks this would have drained their power cells. They believe themselves to be the only Daleks remaining in existence [as if].

Notably, Sec says – and the other three confirm

Which are the Most Over-Specialised Daleks?

continued from Page 117...

and doll theirs up as dancers from *Xanadu*. For excursions into enemy territory, they add helmets that look like baby Dalek domes, each with an eye-stalk handle so they can take it off quickly or, more reluctantly, put it on. And bobbles all around the base, like Dalek hemispheres. This intimidates the other side, the same way that Highland regiments going into battle without underwear was supposed to make them seem more fearless and terrifying – nobody who is prepared to be seen wearing a hat like that would be daunted by anything, and would never be taken alive (see **The Streaker Dalek**, above).

We also have to ask why the Dalek High Command went for such bold colour-schemes. In addition to the controversial choice of red for the Drone (a colour which, as any fan versed in 60's tie-in books would know, is invisible to Daleks), we now have the New Paradigm's other exciting liveries for Strategist, Sporty, Ginger and Baby. (See **What are the Great Merchandising Disasters of the Twenty-First Century?** under X5.3, "Victory of the Daleks").

The Esther Williams Dalek ("The Dalek Invasion of Earth"; 2.8, "The Chase")

After a hard day's conquering, what's better than a nice swim? One Dalek clearly thinks that this is one of the perks of invading Earth and is under the surface of the Thames, just minding its own business, when the Robomen report that The One They Call The Doc-Torr has shown up and is griping again. This is clearly one specially adapted for sub-aqua work, as it talks less like a normal Dalek and more like an Aquaphibian from *Stingray*. Further proof comes when a regular everyday Dalek dives off the side of a boat, cracking open its shell in mid-air. It's not chasing anyone (there being nobody left aboard the *Mary Celeste* to chase when this happens), and it is not pushed by anyone or anything else. What happens on screen is that a Dalek finds itself on a boat just off the Azores and thinks to itself "that water looks lovely".

It doesn't stay in its shell, though, as the impression we're clearly supposed to get is that this is not somewhere a Dalek shell ought to be. This is in the very next Dalek story, by the same author, and was written six months later. Surely, Terry Nation could remember his own cliffhangers? The obvious conclusion is that there is one Dalek who loves to swim and has been adapted just for this task and another, equally splash-happy Dalek who is in a standard-issue shell and just opts to get out and have a dip; otherwise, we'd have to conclude that Nation's just a hack who got lucky.

There may still be a Dalek who went overboard in the Atlantic and has been wandering around the sea-bed since the 1860s – which would make the lack of any interference in the affairs of Atlantis (4.5, "The Underwater Menace") rather odd. It's easier to assume that, as we saw the shell splitting in mid-air, the occupant either drowned or was swallowed by a whale. But then again, Professor Zaroff might have kept it in a tank as company for his pet octopus, and it could have crept into his room at night and whispered hints about drilling to the centre of the Earth.

Pointy-Headed Stunt Daleks (4.3, "The Power of the Daleks"; "The Evil of the Daleks"; "Planet of the Daleks")

Just as Jon Pertwee's head seems to expand when he does anything dangerous or strenuous (i.e. whenever Terry Walsh replaces him for the action scene), so the Daleks have a habit of going into film and becoming more perfectly conical when they are called upon to do anything risky. This Euclidean development is also noticeable when the crowd-scenes become too big to do in a small room with those curiously static spearholders (see **Flat Pack Daleks**, below) and require a large arena. Thus, when the Daleks get into mass-production and set up an assembly-line inside their seemingly tiny spaceship in the lab on Vulcan, or when they start running into landmines and shooting each other in battle-scenes too big to be executed at Television Centre, or when a cavernous subterranean base houses a secret army of ten thousand (all swamped in gooey turquoise liquid ice), they all straighten up, abandoning the forward thrust of their skirts and adopt a geometrical rectitude hitherto only seen on the Denys Fisher "Tricky Action" Rolykin toys, on sale in all good toyshops in the mid-60s.

The Soft Porn Daleks ("The Chase", "Resurrection of the Daleks", and laterally "Abducted by the Daleks")

While the fusion of Dalek Sec and Mr Diagoras results in a one-eyed snake in trousers, the real smut is to be found at the end of the first episode

continued on Page 121...

– he 'created' Caan, Jast and Thay to serve him. It's perhaps for this reason that they initially adhere to his orders [however strange they might appear], but eventually default to the tried-and-true Dalek belief system, and mutiny against Sec. Upon learning that the Doctor swapped in his own DNA to make Time Lord-Dalek hybrids, the Cult decides they're intolerable and kill them all. Only Dalek Caan escapes, with yet another Emergency Temporal Shift [see "The Stolen Earth"].

One of the Cult whines about the urge to kill the Doctor being irrepressible, when given opportunity to do so. [Given that Daleks don't traditionally express desires to kill, so much as explaining that's what they're going to do without bothering about motive, this seems new.] According to Sec-Diagoras, Daleks haven't felt pain of the flesh in thousands of years. [Presumably, he means it's been that long since the Kaled race gave way to the Daleks, way back in 12.4, "Genesis of the Daleks".]

Splitting the atom is a useful standard of comparison to use for a Dalek about the extent of human development. They count time in 'Rels' [which appear to be pretty much like seconds], and 'minutes' [which vary in length according to how close to an exciting set-piece we are].

• *Pigmen* live a few weeks at best. They've been trained to kill with their teeth.

• *The new Time Lord-Dalek-Human hybrids* have increased serotonin levels before they start asking awkward questions. They all dress the same way. All of them die when Dalek Caan throws a hissy fit about them being failures and activates a kill-switch.

Planet Notes

• *Earth.* The Daleks seem to know a lot about solar activity in the Sol system, claiming that the coronal mass ejection of November 1930 would be the biggest for a thousand years. [So it was less a matter of detecting one than of having some kind of almanac, possibly from the 2012 edition of Wikipedia (X1.6, "Dalek"), and knowing when one was scheduled. Sadly, their base of operations will be pointed away from the sun when this occurs. Solar flares and coronal mass ejections such as this are slower moving than light, so the Daleks can observe the signs even without satellites, and make preparations for the arrival of the useful energy two or three days later.]

Things That Don't Make Sense ("Daleks in Manhattan" and "Evolution of the Daleks") Well, the biggest contradictions follow the retconning, since "Doomsday", of how the Cult of Skaro functions – not just that they have a clear hierarchy but that they now refuse to think the unthinkable. Which was, y'know, their whole *raison d'etre* last time.

It's also weird that the Daleks seem to have taken to putting Doctor-thwarting deadlock seals on things such as lifts, but neglect to put them on the all-important Dalekanium plates on the Empire State Building's spire. And there's Martha's incomprehensible response upon seeing Lazslo – instead of just going round backstage, she wanders onto the stage in the middle of a show and causes a major peacock pileup. And there's the Doctor's out-of-left-field offer that the Daleks can kill him if they end the attack on Hooverville. It's the Daleks, why on Earth wouldn't they just shoot him and murder everyone anyway?

But all of this pales into insignificance before Martha's use of the psychic paper. You know the drill: the Doctor confirms the general impression he gives that he's allowed to be somewhere, with credentials appearing in front of the eyes of an official or guard in keeping with what that person expects to see. Sometimes, this surprises the Doctor himself (X2.7, "The Idiot's Lantern"). What has *never* happened before – and won't again – is that the paper over-rides what the guard is seeing and hearing. Just try to imagine this (unscreened) sequence: Frank (a hobo), Tallulah (dressed – well, semi-dressed – as a show-girl) and Martha (wearing men's clothes, black and female and from London) somehow persuade the security detail at the Empire State Building – *in 1930!* – that they are an architect and two engineers. This is no longer mere psychic paper activity, this is the most powerful perception filter yet seen in the programme's history. We're beyond Obi-Wan and into Roger Delgado territory (see Volume 3), and can only conclude that Martha has more forceful mental power than a Time Lord and more control over what happens. All of this without ever having seen this wallet before now, and not being given the slightest hint of how to use it when the Doctor hands it to her. So the real surprise about the end of "Last of the Time Lords" (X3.13) is that Martha doesn't become Prime Minister when they re-set history.

It's a pseudo-historical set in the relatively

Which are the Most Over-Specialised Daleks?

continued from Page 119...

of "The Chase". The sand on the planet Aridius stirs, and a gasping, groaning slightly distorted voice is heard. As its panting and sighing becomes more ardent, so a dome breaks the surface, followed by a longer, thinner shape supporting it. The moans become more energetic still as the shape rises, proud, achieving full height as the voice fades out in a dying fall under the end music.

This was as explicit as Dalek filth got in the monochrome years, but by the mid-80s, as the BBC banned Frankie Goes to Hollywood for using the verb "to come", Davros and his converted guards had an unfortunate reaction to the Movellan virus. Even though it was just a return to the Troughton-era standby of the Foam Machine (see Volume 2 for more examples than we care to enumerate), this was so – um – on the money that the victims of this virus tended to respond by crying "aaah-aaah-aaaaaaaah!" and raving arms or plungers about in giddy abandon while gushing until spent. Yet Mary Whitehouse neglected to complain, which is why *Doctor Who* wasn't taken off the air for another year.

The less said about "Abducted by the Daleks" (2005), an independent sex parody smacked with a cease-and-desist order, the better. The Daleks kidnap some strippers, but little happens beyond a bit of plunger-fondling. It's not even good porn.

Assorted Carney Daleks ("The Chase"; 11.3, "Death to the Daleks"; 20.7, "The Five Doctors"; "Remembrance of the Daleks")

There comes a time when the similarity between Dalek technology and fairground rides becomes overpowering. The arrival of a Dalek task-force at the Festival of Ghana is notable mainly for how at-home they seemed. All right, a few items presented difficulties (there was a large staircase they avoided, although this ought not to have daunted them) and the Frankenstein's Monster Animatronic display used one as a ghetto-blaster, but overall they seemed literally part of the furniture. Thus when they went to Mechanus and fought odd robots who seemed even more like carriages on tea-cup rides from 1965, the graphics and visual style is classically fairground. The Daleks themselves, as was noted right at the start, give off a smell of Dodgem cars.

It's thus no surprise at all that when the Daleks are denied the use of their guns, their scout-ship has, apparently fitted as standard, a set of air-pistols and a lot of china TARDISes to shoot at. What's impressive is that, unlike most fairground shooting galleries, the sights aren't off and they don't win a stuffed toy for destroying every one. Inevitably, the lone Dalek on Skaro's Death Zone shows up at a Hall of Mirrors and tries some fancy shooting. With this tendency the one thing the two warring Dalek factions agree on, the visit they both make to London in 1963 is noteworthy for the mutual decision to switch off their shock-absorbers and treat the old roads of the city as a cake-walk, wobbling around and completely missing any other Dalek they shoot at during the course of the day.

Swiss Army Daleks ("The Daleks"; "The Dalek Invasion of Earth"; "The Chase"; 3.4, "The Daleks' Master Plan"; "Day of the Daleks"; "Planet of the Daleks"; "Resurrection of the Daleks"; and the two Peter Cushing films in the Appendix to Volume 6)

That all-purpose probe – the one that looks like a sink-plunger – is good for almost all technology the Daleks have designed for themselves. For anything else, they need to call in a specialist. Writing letters requires a whole set of skills they no longer have (as we'll see shortly), but constructing anything fiddly must be a pain. Yet we are told, time after time, how sophisticated their technology is.

Consider the stolen time-travel equipment the rebels have in "Day of the Daleks". This includes small knobs to operate it, a mini-Dematerialisation Circuit and a shoulder-strap. All right, the strap may be a human addition, but the technology is – we're told – all Dalek. Even assuming that they built these things for the Ogrons to use, the circuit is a smaller version of something the Doctor was having difficulty repairing with his opposable digits (fewer than a Lamadene). Similarly, the Dalek operating the transmat into Coal Hill School needs Mr Bronson to do the rewiring, yet this equipment must have been installed before they implanted mind-control devices into school staff.

What the BBC Wales episodes have confirmed is something we saw in "The Dalek Invasion of Earth": a specialised Dalek whose job it is to write graffiti all over time and space. The lions in Trafalgar Square have angular tags drawn in what appears to be marker-pen, or perhaps Banksie-style stencils were used (combining the advanced technology of the **Holding-a-Piece-of-Paper**

continued on Page 123...

recent past, after the invention of sound-recording, so of course there's anachronistic or misprised dialogue: in the space of one scene, Tallulah refers to the Doctor as a 'hot potato' (presumably thinking "hot tomato", but that's generally girls being described) and says he's 'into musical theatre'. For starters, a 'hot potato' is how one describes a problem or task one doesn't want to be left holding. It dates from the 1850s, whilst the use of "into" meaning "enthusiastic about" is mid-1960s Californian. (In 1930s New York, to be "into" a person or organisation means large sums of money are owed.) Later, she calls the Daleks 'aliens' in the current sense, as opposed to simply querying their immigration status. That "how [blank] is that?" thing comes back to haunt us too (see X1.8, "Father's Day").

Indeed, there's a fairly hefty anachronism inherent in the idea that the Doctor being 'into musical theatre' implies anything about his sexual orientation in the 1930s – girls showing their legs and cleavage was strangely popular amongst heterosexual men too, especially when they were live and thus in colour rather than the monochrome images on a screen. (We had a look for any idea that the male audience for such shows was more gay than not before 1970 – not a sausage!) The cliché to which Tallulah alludes is about the dancers on stage and we don't see any male dancers in this show, just a couple of juggling clowns backstage. That cliché was the flipside of a real observation, that gay men were more comfortable when working in showbiz and thus a bit more visible but – as with 80s *Doctor Who* fandom – just because a social grouping isn't heteronormative and the gay members are making more of a splash, that doesn't mean it's statistically significantly more likely that any given member is gay than in the outside world. Ah yes, and that the Daleks call a lift a "lift" is unsurprising – but Frank and Laszlo, as Americans, do it, whereas Martha refers to "a service elevator".

More broadly, it's a story that hearkens back to *Doctor Who* of yesteryear in that the more one considers the Daleks' plan, the more one wonders whether they actually *have* a plan. Fair enough, Dalek Sec has a solid idea of what he's doing, but he doesn't road-test a highly dodgy procedure until hours before the critical gamma ray strike. The other Daleks know little of this, judging by their quickness to mutiny once he's spelt out the plan properly. And Dalek Thay thinks that, once they've got a lot of human Daleks, converting the rest of Manhattan will be easy. Given that the initial conversion required a highly infrequent gamma ray strike, exactly *how* are they going to go about this?

Never mind that if the Daleks went to this time and place to cash in on a specific solar flare (let's leave aside the fact that history says they're a bit late for one). Why are they working to such a tight schedule? Everything seems to happen in the last 24 hours: the Dalekanium going on the spire, Sec ingesting a New Yorker and they're *still* recruiting people for the final experiment. Being time travellers, did they not have advance warning? Or are we to believe they were opportunistically cashing in on the solar flares and the Doctor's arrival? (If they could make them happen to order, even with just four Daleks and everyday household items, they could conquer Earth much more efficiently than this loopy plan to breed badly-dressed drones.) Ultimately, nobody seems sure from one scene to the next how rapidly the Daleks have had to implement their (ahem) Master Plan. There's one scene where the impact is 11 minutes away and everyone's just talking about this plan as if they've got weeks. (If we stop to ask why an impending Coronal Mass Ejection of this size hasn't caused Manhattan to be covered in forests, we'll start to cry – see X8.10, "In the Forest of the Night", if only to upwardly revise your opinion of Helen Raynor by comparison.)

So, it would seem, to Dr Science's dismay, that "DNA" is now a sciencey buzzword used about as accurately as "constellation" in Tom Baker stories. We're obliged to point out that it does *not* travel via wires when propelled by gamma rays – any more than those people with smart-phones who post pictures of their lunch with the caption "om nom nom" can expect anyone to be able to eat the image. Also, the picture we're shown of Dalek DNA makes it look like barbed wire. If it's DNA, it has four bases (Guanine, Adenyne, Thymine and Cytosine), traditionally represented by coloured balls on the outside of models of that double helix. They don't look like that under a microscope.

However, if Dalek DNA really is deoxyribonucleic acid (and Davros's whole career seems based on this premise), it'll be the same GATC sequences in a different order, not something totally different represented by images resembling a goth's tattoo. If the Daleks want to configure their com-

Which are the Most Over-Specialised Daleks?

continued from Page 121...

Dalek, see below, and the Thals' "Liquid Colour Spray" from "Planet of the Daleks").

As the BBC Wales episodes have these cryptic messages appearing in various colours, it can't be just scorching concrete. The most famous example is the one on the fly-posters at the start of X1.8, "Father's Day", which is alleged to say "Bad Wolf" in Dalek, so maybe all of these owe to that cosmic vandal Dalek Caan – see **Bad Wolf: What, Why and How?** under X1.13, "The Parting of the Ways". If the ones we see in Trafalgar Square are the work of Caan, then we have to wonder whether the Daleks who arrived on Earth in 2257 saw these messages and thought "Uh?" Then we have to wonder whether the timeline that has these Daleks-with-dishes is one Caan was able to access, and *then* whether these Daleks would have known that moving Earth was easier with a magic tractor-beam... and that way madness lies. It's easier to assume that the scribbling on national monuments was the work of naughty younger Daleks on their first tour of duty. Maybe it's just directions for how to get to Forbidden Planet.

Most obvious of all specialisations has to be those Daleks rebuilt to have something other than plungers. We know of the Special Weapons Dalek, but more common are the ones with flame-throwers, blow-torches or pincers on their left arms. It could be that the plunger-probe is detachable and can be replaced with whatever tool is most appropriate... but the on-screen evidence is that they have to send off for a special Dalek with one of these appendages wired-in and ready. If the Daleks had a ready supply of interchangeable arms on a rotating display, or outfitted their bases with handy dispensers throughout their bases (in case you need fire, break glass), the Doctor and his chums would have been killed in every single encounter. There is one whose job it is to hold a Detector, first identified in "The Chase" as "Seismic Detector", that can apparently feel humanoid foot-prints and breathing from miles off. It also makes a loud ASDIIC sort of noise, so if it's that sensitive, it would detect its own readouts and set up a feed-back loop until it goes bang. However, this device is carefully gymballed and cantilevered so that the read-out is always visible to viewers but never to the Dalek holding it. No Dalek has an eye-stalk long enough to read something it's holding.

Having to cut laboriously through metal doors in bases that the Daleks themselves constructed must be embarrassing as well as time-consuming. This leads us to wonder what a flame-thrower Dalek does when not on a job. Do they barbeque? We know that the food they grow by artificial sunlight includes aubergines. (Look carefully at the champagne-bucket of food they leave for Temmosus and his pals in "The Daleks". They've got eggplants on Skaro, even though they think all other life is extinct, so there must be a market-gardener Dalek, with a watering-can built in.) Maybe they fire pots (sink-plunger hands would be ideal for any Dalek who has ceramics as a hobby). If they sleep between visits from Time Lords, they must think all Dalek bases are vulner-able to attack all the time. So how *else* could the Daleks penetrate their own security without such a delay? Well...

Flat Pack Daleks ("The Daleks"; "The Dalek Invasion of Earth"; "The Chase"; "The Power of the Daleks"; and theoretically "The Daleks' Master Plan" and "The Evil of the Daleks")

... the alternative is that you slip a very thin Dalek under the door. There are a lot of very thin Daleks on hand, able to perform such limbo-dancing manoeuvres. They attend big meetings. We see them filling out crowd-scenes, although they don't say much. From certain camera-angles, they look for all the world as if someone has made life-size cardboard cut-outs of one Dalek and propped them up to cover the fact that they have only four fully-operational Daleks handy. At the start of the scene with the **Rather Uncertain Dalek** (see below), one is seen either descending to the Bridge in a lift or being run off on a giant photocopier.

This has been suggested as the Dalek equivalent of the end of *Beau Geste*, where the four remaining Legionnaires augment their apparent numbers with dummies and corpses. This is, of course, a damnable slur. There is an obvious reason for these giant-sized Weetabix giveaways (see **Why Was There So Much Merchandising?** under 11.4, "The Monster of Peladon") – the early experiments with time-corridor technology must have led to dimensional anomalies. If the Daleks in the Time War were assaulting all realities, as the end of Series 4 suggests, then they must have gone to the realm of the Graffiti-Monsters from X8.9, "Flatline".[26] The irony is that close examination of

continued on Page 125...

puter simulations to show that they're so bad-ass their very nucleotides are sharp and spikey, why not depict the puny human base-pairs in pastel cotton-wool blobs or *Hello Kitty* heads? Obviously, this graphics package is standard Dalek field ordinance. (Maybe it's the same one Jennifer Aniston used in those L'Oreal ads where "here comes the science part" denoted "we think you're stupid – give us your money".)

Moreover, the Doctor gives Sec the immensely confusing advice that he should: "...split the genome and force the Dalek-Human sequence right into the cortex". Basically, he's proposing a sort of brain-surgery with new, home-made cells implanted into the dead brains of the abducted humans. All right, that *might* work to hot-wire corpses... but the Doctor's ludicrous Time Lord "DNA" delivery wheeze relies on the idea of altering every single cell of the zombies, not just an implant in the brains of otherwise unaffected humans. Assuming that he means "genome" when he says "cortex" and "nucleotide" when he says "genome", we're almost up to *Star Trek* levels (i.e. magic with the names of real things – see next episode), but Sec would have said "Uh?"

Why do the Daleks create Pigmen, anyway? Pigs aren't known for being obedient animals, and how is this an improvement over a simple lobotomy? The Daleks control Robomen because they're wearing those whopping great skiffy helmets – do Pigmen just accept orders from anyone? All right, yes, the main thing about pigs *re* human biology is the similarity of the major organs and the relative ease of transplants without tissue rejection, but how did this happen as an offshoot of research into grafting Dalek genomes into humans? Did they try to make Pig-Daleks? (Come to think of it, that's a *much* better story right there, with a chase through the meat-packing district and references back to Mr Sin. They could have set it in 1950 and thrown in references to *View from the Bridge*, the one Arthur Miller 50s play not stirred into X4.10, "Midnight".) If the Daleks can splice DNA to make Pigmen without benefit of massive amounts of gamma radiation, why do they need it to make human-Dalek hybrids? In fact, gamma radiation is almost the *last* thing you need to make stable genetic modifications that behave predictably. The whole point about atomic mutations is that they aren't controllable. Nor does brain surgery really need a big dose of Roentgens.

For that matter, the three-ply mutants experience an increase in seratonin levels, which makes them start asking awkward questions. So they get blissed out, and *that* makes them curious and uncomfortable? Maybe it's not cause-and-effect, then. Maybe getting faxed Time Lord "DNA" includes bonus levels of Triptophan (see 22.3, "The Mark of the Rani") akin to a giant banana milk-shake. (Then again, the Doctor has the ability to make bananas appear out of nowhere – X1.10, "The Doctor Dances"; X2.4, "The Girl in the Fireplace"; and consider the Banana of Reasonable Comfort in X6.7, "Let's Kill Hitler" – so let's not discount it just yet.) The wider point is that the writers have now started using "DNA" as shorthand for some mystical force of self-hood, possibly derived from the loopy "Morphic Resonance" scam from the 70s or homeopathy (see X4.16, "The Waters of Mars"; X7.6, "The Snowmen").

There's also the problem of why the Daleks separate people according to their level of intellect, take the superior ones for the Final Experiment and then, er, wipe their brains. If intelligence is any one thing, it's the ability to apply learning to novel situations. This is probably as much acquired as inherited (and if it's inherited, messing with their DNA to this extent removes that as well). Nonetheless, if their minds are blank slates, then the ability to walk, fire guns and speak English with Brooklyn accents must result from either Dalek or Time Lord genes. So maybe it's the episodic memory (personal ones) that goes, and not semantic memory (facts and abilities). That's neurologically suspect, but more worryingly is that they intend to include this sort of thing in the revised Dalek blueprint. Why bother, if they're going to ditch the things that make humans different from Daleks?

The mysterious disappearances in Hooverville, it would seem, owes to the Pigmen kidnapping people in the dead of night. But the Pigmen attack by biting, the most usefully aggressive specimens would likely get their throats ripped out. The Doctor warns Solomon that everyone in the Hooverville has to leave, because the Daleks need a breeding stock. Surely New York is filled with people who could be used the same way? Besides, where did the Doctor get this idea?

A related point is that the Daleks abduct *a thousand people* for the final hybrid experiment, plus all the pig-slaves they're burned through, all in the space of a few weeks. With the police and

Which are the Most Over-Specialised Daleks?

continued from Page 123...

the sucker-probes of these 2D pioneers reveals that the specific Dalek chosen for the experiment is one with an affinity for flat surfaces...

The *I'm Holding a Piece of Paper* Dalek ("The Daleks";"The Chase";"Planet of the Daleks")

Yes, the Skaroine terrors have an individual Dalek whose job is to hold pieces of paper flat, so that the viewers can see what's written or drawn on it. It's clearly very proud of this ability, as it pokes the paper into any nearby TV camera and waves it about with merry abandon, as if to say *Look. Mum. I'm. On. Tel-ly*. When denied use of a piece of paper, this one shows off the special rectangular attachment in its probe-sucker that gives it the edge in stationery-manipulation, which is how we can tell that it was this specific Dalek who was cloned and mass-produced in 2D form (see above).

The Rather Uncertain Dalek ("The Chase" – specifically the third episode, "Flight Through Eternity")

Time travel, even with the time-corridor technology they used to use, brings with it inherent instability to the timelines and all sorts of niggly quantum effects. Daleks are rather dogmatic and can't deal with doubt or overlapping probability-states. Their scanners show space-time to be a series of nested black and white rectangles, rather than the complex striations and clouds we know from various title-sequences. On the whole, it's probably best to make this the responsibility of one specific Dalek and not bother the ones making the big decisions with such hazy maybes. The usual fate of such abominations (such as Dalek Caan after naked time-surfing) is a sort of quarantine, or indeed a planet-sized Asylum full of improbable survivors of previous episodes.

However, when they built the prototype DARDIS, they needed a navigator whose presence on the bridge was a given, even though this would annoy the Black Dalek. The higher mathematical functions involved in calculating eigenvalues for negotiating the space-time vortex must be on another plane altogether, as this Dalek finds it difficult adjusting to the clarity demanded by normal Dalek life. When asked to convert a measurement of time in the Dalekian Scale into Earth measurements (just in case any humans were watching), it seems very unsure and mumbles, saying "err..." and generally sounds as if it were counting on whatever toes a Dalek might still have.

Salvation Army making a census of the needy, so that the city's leaders can calculate how many soup-kitchens or work programmes are needed, this is possibly the first time in decades that this kind of mass abduction *would* be noticed.

Dalek Caan adopts the post of battle-commander and plugs into the strategy computer – which was to have been Dalek Sec's job. But Sec is now wearing a suit and spats, not a Dalek shell, so how could he have interfaced with the computer? And in the tradition of Restoration Comedy, it's assumed that if two people are whispering off to the side, no one else can hear them. This applies even to Daleks, who should have advanced sensory abilities.

So, you're Daleks, and you've been sulking because your commander banned you from killing your mortal enemy, and eventually you get tired of this and mutiny. Your mortal enemy stands around for a couple minutes looking slightly awkward. Does it occur to you to *shoot him where he stands*? No, it does not. Worse, the Doctor's unmotivated and silly "shoot me!" scene in Hooverville has Sec ordering his underling not to kill the Doctor, which doesn't account for at least five occasions prior where they could have just gunned him down when they had a chance. And these Daleks met him in Canary Wharf – they're probably going to recognise him, aren't they? Also, going by the markings on each unique Dalek, one of them is simultaneously flying down to Hooverville *and* talking to Sec back at the ranch.

We have a huge problem with Frank's backstory: why is he in New York at all? He's from Tennessee, a place to which city-dwellers fled for work on farms in the period before the Dust Bowl. He's the eldest boy and his father died, so was therefore one of the few people in America *guaranteed* a job. (It's possible that an early draft had him coming to the more gay-friendly Big Apple to escape prejudice, but that's not in the dialogue, and Andrew Garfield plays him as nervously trying to pick Martha up. It's almost definite that an early draft had the story set a few years later, and thus mildly more plausible that someone in Frank's position fled elsewhere to get work... but California or Florida were the usual choices for Okies. If the bank foreclosed on his mother – improbable, with a son old enough to run things and a mess of brothers – it would only be after trying at length to get their money's worth out of the property. We're only just a year on from the Wall Street Crash; it wasn't until harvests began failing that the agricultural sector seized up. It's theoretically possible that this might have happened before the next tax-year after the harvest after the Crash but that would be a more unusual story and Frank would have told it.) We'll generously assume that he's been in the big city for a while and his accent's changed.

# # #

[Before our next set of (fairly hefty) geographical quibbles, we ought to state that the fault here is less Helen Raynor (whose first trip to New York was, apparently, for *Doctor Who Confidential* some months after submitting the finished script) than with generations of parochial Manhattan-based authors and film-makers who blithely assume that everyone not only knows all the geography of this city, but what each street and district "means" culturally and with regard to income, attitudes and background. People outside New York can feel justifiably pleased with themselves for following any more than three-fifths of what Woody Allen, Paul Auster, Stan Lee or Thomas N Disch (and hundreds more) had to say on the city. If a film can be released called *Crossing Delancy* and not bother to *explain that title anywhere in the dialogue*, we're all within our rights to make up stories about this place without bothering to check, just like Hollywood does about London. However, it's not beyond the means of most people with access to the internet, a few books or friends who've lived there to find out the basics – especially with flogging this series to the Yanks as such a high priority for BBC Wales. This is not difficult. Even a Cardiff-based production team who can't get Chiswick right might have picked up on the following...]

Liberty Island is not only one of the worst places to land the TARDIS if you want to show Manhattan to Martha, it's a pretty lousy view of the Statue of Liberty (Robbins Reef Island might have been better). Then again, this may be to hide from her the odd way the glass flame in Miss Liberty's torch has turned to gold. To get to and from the city from the island, you need to take the ferry – which entails a round-trip from Battery Park (a long queue) and getting a round-trip ticket each. So getting *from* the island after materialising there is going to be a trick. Let's assume psychic paper chicanery, but this still leaves getting back again, which makes the heartfelt farewells at story's end a bit silly as the first ferry leaves at 9.00am. It's November and the sun doesn't rise until 8.00 and there's that queue, so the Doctor and Martha obviously just leg it once Frank's persuaded Hooverville to take in Laszlo. Besides, the Doctor's promised Martha a fun time in the Big Apple but they leave before she's seen anything a first-time visitor in 1930 might have wanted to see.

Because the storyline is that the Doctor takes her straight to Hooverville from Liberty Island via Battery Park. That requires them to use public transport or taxis, either of which would need current currency. That's a bit more organised than the Doctor usually manages to be (even if he at least went to the city deliberately this time). Martha's going to need cash or subway tokens for the story's later parts (not just for herself, but probably Frank and Tallulah too), when they go to the Empire State Building – again, not impossible, but slightly out of character for the Doctor to have provided a bag of cash and explained use of the things that look like washers from a bathtap. In order for this story's timeline to function without benefit of teleportation, it's sensible to assume yellow cabs all round, and no traffic jams. (The words "yeah" and "right" spring unbidden to mind.)

Or, if they're using the subway, let's assume from the ambitious musical number that Tallulah's theatre is on 42nd Street. This cuts down the walking when the Doctor's party return to warn Hooverville about the Daleks, but also allows the Daleks to shut down the subways by zapping the switching-station at Grand Central Station, just around the corner. (There's a subway tunnel under 42nd Street, intersecting with the IRT, but that was never used – this might have made a better location for the Dalek lab than the basement, where all the construction bricks and steel for the skyscraper were kept.) The trolley-cars, if they were on a separate system, might still have been running that late, as might the buses. If the Hooverville is near Columbus Circle, they can get to within a block of the Empire State Building on one bus/ trolley, so there wouldn't have been a convenient break where Tallulah could change her clothes and pick up some ready cash.

Right, so everything works *if* Tallulah is the star of a hit Broadway show... less so if she's just some hoofer. Well, her first name's in lights, and on the posters, but there's no surname (so she's like Madonna or Semprini). In which case, isn't her disappearance after a peculiar incident in her big production number going to stand out in a news cycle so slow, a few hobos vanishing gets front-page coverage? In 1930s New York, you'd get radio and late edition papers (and those boys in big caps shouting "Huxtray! Huxtray!"), so when she showed up on public transport with a guy in workman's clothing and a black woman in jeans and a leather jacket, people might well have told the police. Not least if they've spent several hours in sewers, with giant pigs and are now in a confined space with other passengers.

So – all right – maybe she's not such a big star, and can date a pig without it becoming a scandal. *Maybe* Martha's party can get to the Empire State Building without anyone batting an eyelid. *Maybe* there's a handy sewer-exit near Central Park big enough for the Daleks to fly out of without anyone spotting them and *maybe* they can fire energy-weapons at night and make explosions happen without the authorities investigating. Fine, but none of that accounts for the supposed time-frame. If Tallulah's not a star, she's going to be sacked considering she ran out in the middle of a revue – but this is never brought up again, so Heaven knows what's going to happen to the showgirl and her pig in Depression-era New York. If they hang on for a few years, they might make good money at the 1939 World's Fair, but the immediate future is a bit Todd Browning.

The theatre isn't so close to the Dalek base that they can just pop between the two, as it seems they do at the end of the second episode. A Dalek and half a dozen pigs escort the Doctor from Hooverville to the lab – even if the sewers are empty and in a perfectly straight line, it's still quite a walk. And *still* nobody spots anything, even after all those explosions in Central Park. A bigger problem is at the climax, when first the Doctor's party leave the 86th storey of the same building where the Daleks are working without them noticing, and get to a theatre. Next, the Doctor summons the hybrids to that same theatre and – lo! – the Daleks are on stage with Sec. Let's be even more generous than before and assume that the Daleks teleported, despite all this talk of low energy reserves. The alternative is that they have somehow squeezed themselves through the man-hole cover, down those tight backstage corridors and up on the set past all those ropes and curtains. (Never mind stairs, this is something we'd all like to have seen the Daleks do.)

# # #

[And now to return to business as normal...]

The people of Hooverville have – literally – a shedload of rifles. You might think that a couple of thousand unemployed men (and a few women) in a borderline-illegal camp with all that artillery might have been a bit of a risk, what with all those banks and grocery stores in Manhattan, but the police don't seem to mind. And, if those two guards ran to Solomon's tent with a tale of pig-men attacking, would such a canny leader and war-hero have forgotten to tell them they ought to post replacements on sentry-duty, even if he didn't believe the Doctor's story of flying space-beings in electric tanks? And the well-armed sentries we do see don't think to shoot the pigs dressed as escaped prisoners.

As with "The War Machines" (3.10), it's improbable in the extreme that a New York paper has nothing better to put as a banner headline than missing cases from a shantytown. (Admittedly, the paper the BBC mocked up – which was posted on the BBC website – claims it's a sham designed to garner funds and public sympathy. This still doesn't explain why the typo "Citiys" turns to "Citys", without the possessive apostrophe it requires, in two different shots.)

It's the Depression, and a dollar a day isn't bad pay for the time. So the coffee Solomon chucks onto the fire must be *really* off, if he can throw it away without there being someone prepared to drink it.

The Pigmen didn't have any direct contact with the scaffolding that Martha and Frank use to conduct what they think is lightning. As we know that it isn't static electricity, but gamma-radiation-with-a-hint-of-Gallifreyan, even if they had been hit, they would just wake up talking very fast in mockney accents. But if it's just lightning and they were touching a metal floor, then Martha would have been a bit frazzled too. She's actually hugging a steel girder when she tells everyone to stay away from metal.

So the Doctor tells the Daleks off for putting their attempts at new Dalek mutants in the sewers to die. He has a point, even if we later learn from Missy, in "The Witch's Familiar" (but not *The Dalek Pocketbook & Space Travellers' Guide*), that they have the same word for "sewer" and "graveyard", and it would have been more secretive to incinerate those as medical waste. (Then again, perhaps the one green blob the Doctor finds is just one unfortunate escapee. Now, if we'd seen a giant clam anywhere...) And you know, it's been a while since we've seen sewers as tidy as these (see 22.1, "Attack of the Cybermen"; 25.2, "The Happiness Patrol"), and the steel manholes are lighter than they ought to be. Worse, it's treated as if the Pigmen are shut out when Solomon slams down a sewer lid, but they easily open it up later when they feel like kidnapping Martha. What's even odder than the Doctor romping around a sewer in plimsolls is that Martha only starts gagging at the smell when she encounters the Dalek mutant.

Small goofs abound in the set-dressing: the elevator goes to 100 floors, but the building only has 86 usable ones. A decal of the completed Empire State Building silhouette is next to the buttons, despite the Daleks announcing only that morning that they need to add a mast. (Production designer Ed Thomas can't be blamed for this; the script specifies that we first meet Mr D on the "102nd" storey.) The posters in the theatre can't decide whether it's the "Laurenzi" or "Lorenzi", but they agree that all productions are "staring" Tallulah rather than "starring". Quite how she's been on the posters for three or four previous shows despite Heidi Chicane only just having had her unfortunate accident is another matter. (One of those posters is based on an Alphonse Mucha poster, *The Arts: Dance*, from 1898, and therefore still under copyright in 1930 as he was still alive.)

The Daleks are so short of supplies that one of the bronze Daleks has to sacrifice his panels to make the solar-flare collector. However, Dalek Sec has abandoned his buggy and is walking around in a suit and tie, so why didn't they just cannibalise his travel unit? (Unless, of course, the black casing for Sec's go-kart wasn't Dalekanium at all but something else, which raises so many questions we don't know where to start.)

A error with hindsight... the way that the Doctor subverts Sec's plan by using space-lightning to send Time Lord DNA down a pipe is even weirder now we know that he originally fled Gallifrey because the Matrix gave him a telepathic scare telling him about an all-destructive Hybrid – widely assumed to be Time Lord-Dalek (see "The Witch's Familiar" et al).

Finally: you're a writer, you want to have a solar flare scene and you decide it happens at night. No wonder the Doctor and Martha confuse it with a lightning strike; at least those aren't affected by which side of the planet you're on.

Critique ("Daleks in Manhattan" and "Evolution of the Daleks") Daleks are like monosodium glutamate: they give a lift to a story that's already good, but you can't just eat a spoonful of it and think "This is great!". There *are* reasons that this story has to be about the Daleks rather than Gubbage Cones, Voord, Snot-Men of Neptune (X9.9, "Sleep No More") or A.N. Other Monster, but they aren't enough to outweigh the sense of them being window-dressings.

After London had been invaded in past, present and alternative history, it was an obvious move to pick another time and place familiar to viewers and chuck Daleks at it. It was also worth putting the Daleks in a story that wasn't a season finale and exploring the enigmatic Cult of Skaro. It could have been a lot worse, or a lot better, but ultimately what we're given is a tale of the Doctor's on-running battle with a familiar foe, with a few period dressings to make it look a bit different but sound like same-old-same-old. Essentially, we're in the same territory as "The King's Demons" (20.6) or "The Mark of the Rani" (22.3).

One of this story's key weaknesses is the same one we get in Celebrity Historicals – rather than sketch in why actions or observed greatness make so-and-so famous, we just have the Doctor repeatedly telling us that so-and-so is brilliant and then saving the world by being brillianter. In this story, Manhattan is the celebrity and everyone, even Dalek Keith (it's one of the non-black ones, but they get muddled up – see above), keeps saying how great the city is when quite obviously standing in front of a green sheet in Cardiff. There was no chance of a battle-scene of a hundred Daleks flying down 42nd Street and blowing up vintage cars, so why bother even trying?

Yes, there's a momentary *frisson* of seeing a Dalek in an Art Deco setting that isn't Ray Cusick channelling Frank Lloyd Wright (1.2, "The

Daleks"; 2.8, "The Chase"), but everything in this story that purports to be 1930s New York is taken from third-hand. The dance routine was originally going to be "Anything Goes", suggesting the production team's research began and ended with *The Temple of Doom* rather than even actual 1930s films (themselves an exaggerated Californian version of the city). Russell T Davies vetoed speak-easies and jazz, so what was left, exactly? Soup kitchens and Broadway. All right, that's *still* an interesting starting point, and Helen Raynor is to be commended for finding a way to broach the subject... but it's all done so maladroitly, and now leaves a slightly nasty taste in the mouth. One dead giveaway is that the pre-credit sequence has a scene taken almost wholesale from "The Talons of Weng-Chiang" (14.6) and the plot develops on remarkably similar lines. New York in this story is as mythologised and garbled as Victorian London was in 1977. The difference is obviously that the mythologising began in visual sources still popped on by BBC2 when they aren't expecting many viewers, and therefore readily available to the viewers. We can all see 1930s Manhattan as it really was any day of the week – and, quite honestly, a damp bit of Wales isn't going to cut it.

Meanwhile, the story's other term is that we're supposed to be so excited by the Daleks coming back that we don't really need much else. They made this mistake in the 60s and 70s and, again, Raynor avoided being too obvious or making a story that could have used just any old aliens. And yet, that's where it really falls down. Sec talks about the Daleks lacking emotions – but that's the Cybermen; Daleks are motivated by violent emotions such as hate, anger and xenophobic terror. Even if an individual only started watching in the Eccleston Months, the repertoire of Dalek reactions is pretty well fixed. So much so, we go in whistling most of the tunes. Everyone knows full well that any attempt to change the Daleks' basic nature is doomed to failure, because they have to come back same as always next time. On the other hand, making this story about the Cybermen, the Voord or the Bandrils would have materially changed the premise. So there's an interesting Dalek story struggling to emerge here, as well as a potentially good story about the Depression in New York, but they aren't doing each other any favours.

In particular Dalek Sec, in hybrid form, is insubstantial as an antagonist. Denied the Ring Modulator and with an American accent, there's little in the dialogue to suggest the most intelligent Dalek wot has ever been. Neither is there much of Mr Diagoras's ruthlessness and charm left. The look of the mutant in the suit is arresting, but the lines needed more of a tug-of-war going on and maybe a touch of vocal treatment. We never really get any sense that the Cult fear this creature too much to just shoot it, but despise it too much to obey their former leader. There are hints of this, but then we abruptly get told "Oh, by the way, we have 11 minutes to resequence the DNA of a thousand victims". A countdown, even one in Rels, needs a build-up. The story's pacing is strange in other ways, even with a November setting to make daylight hours shorter.

In order to make this work in under three hours of screen time, the Doctor has to act *very* weirdly. He begs a Dalek to shoot him (for some reason), then chummies up to Sec-in-a-suit to see if he can make a revised version of the race that he thinks wiped out his people (except in episodes when he thinks he did it), then does *something* to the Dalekanium panels that he later claims was his plan all along – even though he was apparently hoping to be killed (and thus strand Martha 60 years before she was born, in a battlefield) before he knew enough to formulate such a plan. We lurch from set-piece to set-piece with only a hazy idea of why anyone is doing what they do.

A lot of this incoherence owes to the big narrative innovation of this year: that episode two of a two-parter is *almost* a new story rather than a linear continuation of the first one. Here, "Daleks in Manhattan" is a pastiche of Warner Bros backstage musicals and "Evolution of the Daleks", appropriately, is stitched together from lumps of 30s Universal horror films. If they'd gone with this a little more boldly, it might have worked, but the visual style is more homogeneous than the scripts. Director James Strong makes most of the ambitious shots work, but the slapstick of Martha disrupting the set-piece musical number falls flat, and the "reveal" of the emptied bodies suspended from the ceiling is squandered.

Maybe it needed Expressionist lighting and old-fashioned lap-dissolves and wipes between shots, maybe everyone needed to have re-watched *The Public Enemy, My Man Godfrey* and *Bride of Frankenstein* (Mark Gatiss could have lent them a copy[27]) rather than *Bugsy Malone* and 80s Dalek stories. If this seems a bit out-of-keeping with *Doctor Who*, watch "The Girl Who Waited" (X6.10) and "The God Complex" (X6.11) for examples of exactly the sort of techniques a 1920s/ early 30s film would have yoked into service without seeming even slightly out of place. Ernie Vincze at least gets the lighting right for the sewers and cellars. There's still not much of a sense of place or time, however much they dub on "Rhapsody in Blue" or an oddly-chopped "Puttin' on the Ritz".

Enough of the period details ring true for the ones that don't to stand out, just as enough of the performances are sufficiently plausible for Tallulah to look like a big mistake compounded by a dodgy accent. As we've indicated above, there are a lot of easily-checkable things they got wrong, but they also caught in time many things that could have been as bad. If that's damning with faint praise, so be it. This is a hard story to get worked up about.

The Lore

Written by Helen Raynor. Directed by James Strong. Viewing figures ("Daleks in Manhattan"): (BBC1) 6.7 million, (BBC3 repeats) 1.1 and 0.5 million. Viewing figures ("Evolution of the Daleks"): (BBC1) 7.0 million, (BBC3 repeats) 1.0 and 0.4 million. AIs 86%, 85%. (The BBC3 repeats were almost the same, but the less-viewed showing of the first half on the following Friday got 88%; presumably those people who bothered liked it a lot more than the mass audience had.)

Repeats and Overseas Promotion Germany used the English titles, but in French these were *L'Expérience Finale* and *DGM Dalek Génétiquement Modifié*.

Production

The initial plan seems to have been to give Steven Moffat first refusal at one of the two-part stories for this year; with his workload on *Jekyll* mounting, this was dropped and an idea from Tom McRae (X2.5, "Rise of the Cybermen" et al) was considered. "Century House" was kept on a back-burner and later talked about in Series 4's discussions, but by then Moffat had written a one-episode cheap double-banked story, "Blink" (X3.10), which seems to have been too similar for the McRae story to have a fair chance. Instead, a 1930s story was put together. Davies largely devised this from a number of items he wanted to include, and tasked Helen Raynor with making it all work in the space of two episodes.

Raynor, then ending her stint as script editor, was entrusted with doing a period Dalek story to match the far-future and contemporary stories, one set in America in the 1930s and with pig-men and showgirls. She and Davies originally discussed using the West Side's meat-packing district (which even now looks enough like the grotty bits of the Cardiff Docks – see X2.7, "The Idiot's Lantern"; X2.10, "Love & Monsters" – for a low-cost fake) for a sort-of hybrid of *On the Waterfront* and *The Island of Lost Souls*. One idea vetoed from the start was any hint of Speakeasies or Jazz, a feature in the shelved 1920s story by Stephen Fry (see **Was Series 2 Supposed to be Like This?** under X2.11, "Fear Her"). This meant that Mr Diagoras became a rather nebulous "fixer" rather than any clearly-identifiable type of entrepreneur.

• Raynor brought in some ideas of her own. She thought to include the construction of Empire State Building as a plot-point (which moved the story to a specific date). The spire's look seemed to justify altering history so that the Daleks, if they didn't actively commission the building, at least interposed their needs into the plans (in keeping with those 60s tie-in books where they were credited with building the Pyramids and Stonehenge). Rather than merely contrast Broadway and pig-slaves, she introduced a *Phantom of the Opera* subplot and looked at the home-lives of showgirls, drawing on her own theatrical background. Crucially, Davies had completely forgotten that the Depression happened and that Hoovervilles existed. Raynor re-watched 80s Dalek stories to get a handle on their obsession with genetic purity, and how it conflicted with their urgent need to survive at any cost. She also found that the contrast between Solomon and Diagoras, both affected by the Great War, gave the story a shape.

• Two of the guest-cast were actual Americans, with little idea of what they were letting themselves in for. Ryan Carnes, once a State Champion in a pig-hollering contest, had to be fitted for the Laszlo's pig-dentures before leaving for Wales, and had trouble explaining them to customs. Eric Loren (Diagoras) took time out to buy DVDs of old episodes, including "Genesis of the Daleks".

• James Strong, who'd directed "The Impossible Planet" and "The Satan Pit" (X2.8-2.9) the year before, plus Block Three of *Torchwood*, was asked back for the Dalek two-parter. After hearing that

Doctor Who Confidential was going to New York (with Raynor, apparently researching the story after she'd written it), Strong asked Phil Collinson if it a skeleton crew could be sent to shoot scenery as well, instead of relying on stock footage. In the event, Strong, Collinson, Dave Houghton (special effects) and a cameraman flew to New York as part of an eight-person team for both productions. Locations had to be cleared with the New York authorities, as with any filming in the city post-9/11. Confirmation came three days before the Tone Meeting (Strong attended this in a bit of a haze, as his son had been born in the small hours of 22nd September, just before he boarded the train to Cardiff). On 13th October, they did an early morning shoot at the top of the Empire State Building – Collinson, on his first visit to the city, admitted to a fear of heights at exactly the wrong moment, when they get into the lift. The 14th involved a trip to Liberty Island, to get shots of the Statue of Liberty and long-shots of the Empire State Building, before returning to Manhattan to obtain some shots looking up at the skyscraper from in front of a Fifth Avenue bar. The next day was the Majestic Theatre, which, appropriately, was then home to the Broadway production of *The Phantom of the Opera*, and finally Central Park, specifically the Sheep Meadow, with particular attention to matching period buildings and merging in their Empire State Building plates.

• By this time, the proposed street-battle had been removed, with Davies intervening to make the cliffhanger less ambitious than the projected scene of Daleks and Pigmen on the city streets (with period cars and extras and all), bringing the cost for these two episodes below the budget-busting first estimates.

• Production on Block Four started in earnest Monday, 23rd October, with a set at Upper Boat serving as Mr Diagoras's office for the Dalek crew (Barnaby Edwards and Colin Newman, with Nicholas Briggs on voices). This time around, specific actors were assigned individual Daleks. Paul Kasey was once again the creature-in-boiler-suit lead, this time as Hero Pig Man, and he and Loren were needed for all the scenes of Daleks trundling around the Empire State building in the first episode. (Edwards and Briggs would eventually ask Loren to work with them on a Big Finish audio, "Assassin in the Moonlight", dealing with Lincoln's murder.) At one point, Nicholas Pegg had to substitute for Edwards, who had to rush to London to record a BBC Digital trailer.

On Wednesday, they did the TARDIS scene (later dropped), after which were the *Children in Need* clips for that November's festivities. The leads weren't in character, but it was a first glimpse of Agyeman in her red jacket ensemble on the TARDIS set (it's not quite clear whether her first day with the Daleks was Tuesday or Wednesday, but RTD sent a text message).

Tennant stayed late for a photoshoot on the 30th, then he and Agyeman took off the next day for the National Television Awards. The Dalek operators were needed that Tuesday, though, for the start of the Transgenic Laboratory scenes; these took place on location at the NEG glass site in Trident Park, which was dusty and loud (Tennant, in the DVD commentary, recalls that the building was being demolished as they were filming), and many scenes needed redubbing because of the gas-bursts and effects.

• Due to a misunderstanding, the costume department had provided Loren with black leather gloves, thinking that Millennium Effects had only provided the Sec-Hybrid head; as it turned out, Sec-in-spats was also accessorised with mutated hands. It was decided relatively late in the day to mess up his nice pinstripe suit.

• After scouring South Wales for suitable rusticated masonry, the Penarth Leisure Centre had the Statue-of-Liberty-esque wall that so delighted *Doctor Who Confidential*. The crew shot there Thursday, 9th November (two units in fact), and took advantage of unexpected good weather that matched Strong's New York shots. The unit got much of this done before school was out and Tennant was mobbed. The site is popular with dog-walkers, and strays, so everyone had to look where they were stepping, and dogs occasionally used the TARDIS prop as a toilet.

From the TARDIS exterior scenes (and green-screening to make Wales look like New York Harbour), they went to Bute Park, where the Hooverville sets doubled for Central Park. The set was complex and labyrinthine, and in a nook of the woods so that it wasn't immediately visible from the main roads – somehow, the production team had managed to keep this four-day location in the city centre more-or-less secret despite all the explosions. This was the second site they had chosen: the original idea was to use a part of the main park (as used for the walk in the autumn leaves where the Doctor explains Hooverville), but the spot picked was the breeding site for a rare newt and thus protected at such times. The replacement woodland site was inside the grounds of University of Wales, Cardiff.

• The episode two Dalek attack on Hooverville was recorded on Monday the 13th, mostly at night. Danny Hargreaves of Any Effects was on hand to make things explode, although only two big set-piece pyrotechnics were detonated and shot from various cameras (another of Collinson's cost-cutting decisions when this story looked like bankrupting the series). The same location was used the next day, with heavy rain making the cast and crew fairly miserable. (Tennant's health suffered, as we will see; he had been hoarse after the NEG shoot, but some of these scenes also needed redubbing in post-production.) Between shots, Raison hid inside the tent where Briggs was doing Dalek voices. The eye-line for people talking to flying Daleks was achieved with a long pole on which was a toy Dalek (instead of a tennis-ball as is customary).

• On Wednesday, 15th November, they had the use of a theatre – the Parc and Dare out in Treorchy (a mining town famous for its Male Voice Choir) – for Tallulah's performance. They had four days, since the theatre would shortly thereafter be staging the usual Christmas panto. Murray Gold wrote a song for the occasion. The original plan to use "Anything Goes" was, to use a period phrase, nixed, as the song hadn't been written when the story happens. The originally-scripted scene of Laszlo seeing Tallulah looking like an angel (as in their first scene together) meant that her costume had to have the wings and halo, which fed into the song's lyrics.

The dancers and Raison had rehearsed in a London studio, and spent the Monday before the shoot getting used to the stage's dimensions. (There had been an earlier rehearsal, but choreographed to "Anything Goes".) Strong and Ailsa Berk worked out how to make the routine look bigger, and use the camera the way Busby Berkeley had. Raison's guide-vocal was one she'd recorded in a hurry at Gold's studio. (That last series of rewrites sent out on 27th October had included a slightly reworked scene of the Dalek examining the Dalek brain.) The revue scenes were finished the next day, then the finale. Meanwhile, work started on "Blink" after a read-through on the 16th – Tennant had to miss it, as he was saving his voice for the evening.

• Everyone had the weekend off (although Tennant, Edwards and Briggs were booked for the *Doctor Who* gala concert that Sunday), and work resumed Monday, 20th November at our old friend Headlands School in Penarth (X1.3, "The Unquiet Dead"; X2.2, "Tooth and Claw"), for Tallulah's dressing room and the backstage corridor. Tennant was in London's Pinewood Studios to record the *Weakest Link* special (won by Camille Coduri), shortly after recording his Easter Eggs for "Blink". It was noticed that the scene of Tallulah telling Martha about the theatre had to be accompanied by the starlet screwing her earrings on rather than using more modern pop-studs. A number of sequences had to be dropped for lack of time, so they finished recording the dressing room scenes on Wednesday the 22nd, before moving to the cellars. David Tennant finally came back the 23rd November for his electrocution on the mast at the Cardiff Heliport where they'd built the mast for the Empire State Building – we saw it last year as the roof of Battersea Power Station (X2.6, "The Age of Steel") and Alexandra Palace ("The Idiot's Lantern").

• A few scenes were trimmed: Tallulah is upset about being out in Central Park at night in November (a sequence included on the box-set); after Martha's bravura use of the psychic paper, Tallulah claims that her costume-design means that she ought to be the architect, as "this cleavage takes work" (can't imagine why that was dropped); an intriguing passage has the Doctor wondering if he and the Daleks are doomed to keep meeting rather than it being a coincidence; Sec, just before dying, reveals that he knows exactly how many beings he's made suffer as he is now suffering.

• Oddly enough, the effect that The Mill found most laborious is the one the effects teams in the 60s did almost nonchalantly: lightning. To make a convincingly snakey strike, each shot is done by hand, frame-by-frame. It has to be matched to the flashes on set, so the old method of inlaying a spark-generator shot by another camera (see, for example, 5.1, "The Tomb of the Cybermen") isn't enough now. This technique, painstaking as it is, allows lightning to course over Tennant's face. Compared to this, the first wholly CGI Dalek mutant was a breeze.

• The *Radio Times* gave Dalek Sec a cover, which irked some fans on first broadcast, but by Christmas the Dalek Sec Voice Changer Mask was one of the best-selling toys.

X3.6: "The Lazarus Experiment"

(5th May, 2007)

Which One is This? TV's Mark Gatiss fights the seven signs of ageing by becoming a giant CGI scorpion, and chasing the Doctor up and down lots of corridors.

Firsts and Lasts For the first time since 12.3, "The Sontaran Experiment", someone who's written for the series is acting in it (last time it was Glyn Jones, author of 2.7, "The Space Museum"). Mark Gatiss finally lives his childhood dream and plays a baddie in *Doctor Who* – and he's brought along his own wig from an earlier project (you *can* see the join, alas). He's the first former writer to have appeared naked. Yet, despite his involvement and the fact that the last 20 minutes is a straight steal from *The Quatermass Experiment*, this was written by someone else. No, really.

For those of you who were following the ins and outs of the late 80s attempts to remove any hint of sex from the series, the fact that we see Martha's laundry and observe her undies drying is a marked contrast to the hoo-ha over whether Ace wears any. (See 24.4, "Dragonfire". Whether Amy has anything on under her nightie when floating around in space or meeting the Queen – X5.2, "The Beast Below" – is still debated by people who aren't sure if Steven Moffat's entire term as producer will turn out to all have been a dream.)

Richard Lazarus turns himself into something even nastier than he was, making him and it the first physical human-to-monster transformation of the BBC Wales years.

And the Doctor's "reversed the polarity" for the first time since 20.7, "The Five Doctors" (or, chronologically for the Doctor, 17.2, "City of Death"). He comments that he's a little out of practice.

Watch Out For...

• Richard Clark, who directed this and "Gridlock" (X3.3), has a knack of inserting cutaways to small unscripted details that make a scene. There are many to choose from, but note, for example, that the string quartet playing Murray Gold's Martha-music look peeved and disappointed when someone tries to evacuate the building because of a ferocious monster. Observe, also, that there are scenes that go for over 30 seconds with no cuts, and one or two where it's obvious that one take was used for the majority of the dialogue with just a few inserts, completely unlike the majority of scenes since the new series began. This is especially noticeable when compared to next week's frantic episode (X3.7, "42").

• There's a woman called Martha and a man named Lazarus, so of *course* he comes back from the dead. But, oh dear, they really have gone and asked too much from The Mill this time, haven't they? Vogon spaceships, Elizabethan aliens, and building-sized Macra have all more-or-less worked as impressive *wow* moments, since the scripts haven't lingered on them, but this time we get a ropey-looking CGI monster that needs to dominate proceedings for the sake of the plot. UK viewers could have been forgiven for thinking it was the spider-monster from the 1998 "Lynx Effect" advert with the cave-women. The scorpion's face is probably supposed to resemble Gatiss, but looks more like David Bowie – was this an elaborate "Glass Spider" joke?

• This contrasts with one of the better bits of location shooting they've managed this series: the gorgeous shots of Southwark Cathedral (except that it's bigger on the inside – see **The Lore**) matted in to Cardiff locations seamlessly. Combine that with reminiscing of the Blitz more effective than entire stories set in World War II, and we have a scene that seems to have been grafted from a much better episode.

• If you have a story set in a castle, a TV station or an old hospital, you shoot it in one of Cardiff's hospitals, obviously. But if you have a story about a futuristic medical facility, you have to go to the Millennium Centre, just across the road from Torchwood's supposed location, and use their foyer (X2.1, "New Earth"; X6.10, "The Girl Who Waited"). If you are doing something in a clean-looking lab, you need an old glassworks such as this one or "The Runaway Bride" (X3.0). Either way, you get into a bit of trouble if the script has people looking from either of these locations towards identifiable London landmarks.

• That lab is blown up in a way that any schoolkid could copy; none seems to have done so, which is either testament to the maturity of the nation's youth or proof that school labs are alien and un-used places to the kinds of kids who might want to cause that kind of trouble. Either way, we're a long way from the era when Mary Whitehouse could gripe about the Doctor showing us how to make a Molotov Cocktail (13.6,

"The Seeds of Doom") and be taken seriously. Maybe the British Public thought that this scene was as scientifically reliable as usual in the revived series (see **Things That Don't Make Sense** for every single episode since X1.1, "Rose").

The Continuity

The Doctor At long last, he breaks down and admits that Martha's been a proper travelling companion all along – but not before he convinces Martha that he really is leaving her for good in her home time, to the point of dematerialising in the TARDIS before coming back for yet one more escapade. When she protests about this treatment, he shrugs off her frustration and anxiety, but smoothes it over by saying she was never just a passenger. [It can't escape comment that this Doctor is damned inscrutable as to when he decides to keep Martha on. For Mr. No Second Chances, he's either giving her lots of them, or he's conflicted about whether to stick her. No one's dithered this much about TARDIS travel since the fifth Doctor era, only this time it's the Time Lord who can't make up his mind. If, as Gatiss and David Tennant speculate on the commentary, this whole story is Martha auditioning for full-time status, then the thing that swings it for him is her decision to act as bait. In that case, why isn't her sister Tish along too? Maybe Martha's ability to divine the right setting on the screwdriver tips the balance in her favour.]

We're starting to sense this Doctor's impression that Time Lords can live too long; at Southwark, he refers to lengthened lifespan as a curse [compare with his similar remarks in X2.3, "School Reunion"]. Cocktail nibbles get him excited.

He's [predictably] read T.S. Eliot's "The Hollow Men", and can finish off the first and second most famous quotes from the poem. On the other hand, he has to have the word "geek" explained to him [which means he cannot possibly have been UNIT's scientific advisor in the 80s, as some chronologies claim]. He's wearing his unlucky tux, and is not unpleased by being compared to James Bond. [NB: this is not the cheap suit he wore as a waiter in X2.5, "Rise of the Cybermen", despite what cut dialogue might suggest.] He retains his Converse All Stars.

Martha hasn't told him anything about her mother, or else he's forgotten. [Since we've no evidence that there's any unchronicled adventure since X3.1, "Smith and Jones", it's probably the former.] He now trusts Martha to get people to safety while he teases the baddie into chasing him. He's not happy about Francine slapping him, extrapolating from a two-mum survey sample [including Jackie Tyler, obviously] that they do it every time.

• *Background.* The Doctor notes that Lazarus's type of regenerative process is seriously energy-draining. [See also X2.0, "The Christmas Invasion" and X5.1, "The Eleventh Hour", in which new-born Doctors stuff their faces at the first available opportunity, and also X4.17, "The End of Time Part One".]

Beethoven [when he was older and partially deaf, apparently] taught him a few things about playing loud. [We hear more about the Doctor's relationship with Ludwig in a weird pre-credit confessional at the start of X9.4, "Before the Flood".]

• *Ethics.* As so often happens, the Doctor's job is to declare "Everything has its time and everything dies" at someone bent on slipping death a mickey. [The question of whether he'd still be so adamantly opposed if Lazarus's doohickey had *worked* is skipped over lightly, which is a shame, considering that opposing people-eating monsters is a brainlessly simplistic choice. But he's even more unhappy about it when Lazarus makes his commercial intentions clear – perhaps it's a timeline concern that bothers him, but he doesn't say so. Then again, *Doctor Who* rarely takes a favourable view of immortality; see in particular 13.5, "The Brain of Morbius" and "The Five Doctors".]

He deliberately kills Lazarus with a blast of screwdriver-augmented organ music, and doesn't seem a bit regretful [Lazarus has made it obvious that it's either him or Martha]. Martha herself shows no sign of concern about the Doctor's actions [well, killing Lazarus *is* done in self-defence]. Earlier, he tried blowing the creature up with a gas-tap and a rejigged light-fitting.

• *Inventory: Sonic Screwdriver.* The Doctor uses it on the controls when Lazarus's experiment looks like it's going to explode. [It's one of those stories with no explanation for what the Doctor's screwdrivery "magic" actually entails. Apparently, if he doesn't do an unspecified *something*, the whole room will explode.] He plugs it into the church organ to create a sonic wave capable of downing Lazarus. It can also detect the energy patterns of fluctuating DNA. Setting 54 opens locks. Martha

Who are You Calling Monsters?

Last volume, we voiced a few concerns about the handling of non-humans in the re-awakened series and its derivatives (**Is the New Series More Xenophobic?** under X1.3, "The Unquiet Dead"). This time, by contrast, we're interested in some of the other options the new series has available that the original didn't, and why some of these have seemed more fruitful than others when people began writing the current model.

For newer readers, a word about fashions in horror. As we've been arguing since Volume 1, the period from 1963 to date is one where distinct phases in what audiences find terrifying can be identified. We have observed how alienation, in its widest sense, was the most terrifying aspect of that immediate post-Kennedy era, when adults were encouraged to find children unsettling (especially children brighter and more attuned to the modern world than they were). Not fitting into a society was the worst thing that could happen, other than being *made* to fit into one.

Then we enter a long period where depersonalisation (brainwashing, amnesia and the removal of the "soul" by surgery, drugs or broadcast "waves") was tied to the idea of replacing an individual with someone (or something) that nobody else could identify as not the original. From the mid-70s, the fear is of being treated as, or reduced to, mere meat. After all, status and intelligence don't matter when you're being chewed by a shark or having an alien bursting from your chest. In these phases, and the ones that followed, it was less that every single horror was replaced in each specific film or series, more that the centre of gravity in the film/ TV market shifted perceptibly. After all, the mid-70s was a peak era for a hybrid form where daemonic forces arranged "accidents" to remove anyone preventing a plan, so that individual held a visceral fear of being squashed under a lorry or beheaded by a random pane of glass – but on a wider level, it was a conspiratorial "other", this time the Devil rather than aliens, vampires or commies. *Doctor Who* was in an increasingly strange relationship with Hollywood trends as we smear into the 1980s. While there was a vague sense that going back in a "horror" direction was what fandom-at-large and the general public wanted, the BBC hierarchy and some well-placed fans had completely different ideas. Scenes reflecting what was happening in major films of the time were spotted into stories, rather than the entire scenario capturing the public mood as before.

Instead, we had the attitude of the comics-fan prevailing, in which team-ups were intrinsically exciting and an old character or race could be brought back with renewed success. When old monsters were revived, they were placed onto the screen with little or no contextualising, nor any attempt to take what had made them successful in the first place and reconfigure it for the new circumstances. "Warriors of the Deep" (21.1) places the Silurians and the Sea Devils in a futuristic base, in a Cold War parable where pretty much any other monster would have served just as well. (We know this to be true, since Mark Gatiss told almost exactly the same story with an Ice Warrior in X7.9, "Cold War".) The thing that had made the Silurians effective (see 7.2, "Doctor Who and the Silurians") was that they were both the primal fears of our pre-human ancestors and antagonists who had a better claim than humanity to call Earth theirs. They were also physically formidable, able to stare holes in walls and survive in conditions deadly to mammals. The thing that had made the Sea Devils work (9.3, "The Sea Devils") was that they had the Silurians' characteristics, plus the home advantage in the sea and unusual agility and speed on land. None of these features was utilised in "Warriors of the Deep". Whilst the sort of psychological horror that the original Silurians evoked was no longer on the table in 1984, nothing in the new story took its place. *Doctor Who* was by now an action-series, not intrinsically "horror".

When we first considered this change, in Volume 4, the idea that *Doctor Who*'s primary purpose had ever been to scare was considered laughable in some quarters. The success (both critically and within the industry) of Steven Moffat's work for Russell T Davies removed this taint and once Moffat was in charge, the emphasis shifted almost exclusively towards this aspect of the series' repertoire. Moffat's restrictive definition of "scary" brings its own problems, of course, but it has made the new series directly comparable to the perceived "Golden Ages" of the mid-60s "Monster Era" and the mid-seventies "Gothic" phase. Such a comparison brings up many interesting features.

First, and most obvious, is that the actual word "monster" has been relegated to a few stray comments in dialogue (X2.4, "The Girl in the Fireplace" being the most obvious) and one episode-title (X2.10, "Love & Monsters"). Yet, by order of the head honcho himself, the writers and production

continued on Page 137...

figures out the setting that over-rides security lockdowns [somehow].

• *Inventory: Psychic Paper.* [We haven't seen the Doctor demonstrate its "plus one" capacity to Martha, but it's perhaps used to get him in without someone asking for his ID. Tish takes credit for it in a cut scene.]

• *Inventory: Other.* The glasses are pulled out for examination of the computer screen. [In a cut scene, the Doctor finds the first draft of the US Declaration of Independence in his tux; he suggested adding "... and the pursuit of happiness".]

The TARDIS The Ship lands precisely on target in Martha's flat [even though we've not seen her tell the Doctor where she lives; that presumably happened off screen].

The Supporting Cast

• *Martha.* After four adventures [that we're shown, at least], finally she realises that the Doctor's modus operandi is to end up in increasingly dangerous situations. She's dismayed when the Doctor's brought her to her own flat and seen her drying undies.

She pardons Lazarus's forwardness in kissing her hand, so that she can collect a DNA sample. She can read and comprehend a close-up of DNA. [We're never told what field of medicine Martha intends to specialise in, so this is a possibility. On the other hand, the computer graphic display seems designed to explain DNA to six-year olds. The *Torchwood* episode "Reset" has Martha discovering genetic anomalies in murder-victims and the next one, "A Day in the Death", shows her following Owen's transmogrification. So she seems to specialise in Space Opera Genetics.] When her brother is badly hurt in the chaos, she's calm and collected in her diagnosis of concussion.

If her sister's complaints are anything to go by, one of Martha's jobs as self-appointed family anchor was policing Tish's boyfriends. [Given that Tish is trying to cosy up with a man who just *killed* his partner, Martha's instincts are probably better in general. As a matter of fact, Tish's delivery of the line is downright jealous.]

Perhaps as compensation, Tish insists that Martha is dreadfully unsocial. [Considering that she's in the final stages of qualifying, this is at least a short-sighted belief. Still, Tish is so thoroughly unsurprised to hear that Martha's friend is a science geek, it sounds like Martha's prior romances have tended towards the more cerebral side of the spectrum.]

Martha trusts the Doctor enough to set herself up as bait while he sorts out a plan, even though it previously perplexed and upset her to find out that he's improvising. She eventually puts her foot down and insists that the Doctor stop promising her "one more trip", then happily hugs him when they've resolved their little standoff. She owns at least one LBD and [seeing the kind of footwear she uses at work in a hospital] her collection of high-heeled shoes is predictably impressive.

• *Francine.* She tacitly airs suspicions that the Doctor is having it off with her daughter, and thinks Martha is unfocused. [Contrary to pretty much all of Martha's characterisation before or after. In fact, Francine thoroughly mistrusts the Doctor even at the start.]

At a crucial moment, one of Mr. Saxon's men talks with Francine about how dangerous the Doctor is – this works so effectively, she ends the episode begging Martha to come back home immediately. [Exactly what this conversation could have entailed, we have no idea, but it's tempting to speculate about Adeola's fate in X2.12, "Army of Ghosts". If Francine had some inkling about the danger inherent in the work that Martha's cousin was doing, then accepting the word of a stranger about a man you've barely said "Hullo" to becomes rather more credible. Double points if the Master dug CCTV footage out of Torchwood showing the Doctor doing something that looks disturbingly lethal.]

She's still pushing Martha to complete her training, nagging that she isn't a doctor 'yet' and won't be if she slacks off and gets a life [see **Things That Don't Make Sense**]. Whatever she does for a living [see next story for an educated guess] she can afford a fairly recent posh frock. [The alternative is that Tish got it for her as part of her work, but Francine would have had to have got a fitting at remarkably short notice.]

The Ex-Humans

• *Professor Lazarus.* A nasty piece of work even before his DNA starts shifting; conniving, venal and a misogynist to boot. He was deeply traumatized as a child by the Blitz, and wanted to develop a way to stop death. He has cynically manipulated Lady Thaw to get her money and contacts, but – once rejuvenated – he discards her in favour of chatting up Tish. As a younger ver-

Who are You Calling Monsters?

continued from Page 135...

staff were to avoid using it when possible. The non-human characters are "aliens" most of the time – Russell has spoken, this is the law. This was a profound change and part of a number of other potential problems the series has had to face (or pretend aren't there, depending on who's in charge). "Monster", as we'll see, denotes a tension between an idea of "human being" and what is before us. "Alien" is simply about geographical origin.

Whilst, these designations overlap to a degree in traditional *Doctor Who*, they are not directly interchangeable. Not everything that isn't from around here is a monster and not everything that the Doctor feels obliged to stop is from off-world. However, the perverse insistence that today's audiences can't handle any story where humans on another planet aren't from Earth (see **Is Kylie from Planet Zog?** under X4.0, "Voyage of the Damned") makes this equation pretty exact for most purposes. The last time the series was so reflexively afraid of otherness was the Troughton era, and it's worthy of note that the Doctor then used "alien" to mean "wrong" even when he's one himself. (See, for instance, 6.2, "The Mind Robber", where he describes the sound afflicting the TARDIS in episode one – as if anything is more or less at home in a white void outside the universe – and then in the next story, 6.3, "The Invasion", electronic circuitry is somehow too weird to work. Both uses of the word are in episode six – once to describe the logic of the Cybermen's circuitry, the other for how they can't handle emotion in a human-designed electronic device.)

But what's changed is that the sixties stories tended to define "a human being" as not just the standard of acceptability, but within fairly inelastic terms. Apart from the Doctor, who played down his origins so well that the Daleks tended to talk about him as a human who'd travelled and got more wise (see, for example, 4.9, "The Evil of the Daleks"), not only was "human being" confined to anything that looked humanoid, but it wasn't even all of them. Anyone "processed" was no longer eligible. Anyone who had the right shibboleths of humanity, regardless of origin (such as the Thals or the Gonds – 1.2, "The Daleks"; 6.4, "The Krotons") was accepted into the club. It was all down to "passing" (see **What are the Dodgiest Accents in the Series?** under 4.1, "The Smugglers" and **Is *Doctor Who* Camp?** under 6.5, "The Seeds of Death"). The hallmarks of humanity in most cases – empathy, imagination, the "big picture" and a lack of egocentricity – are almost indistinguishable from those of literacy (see **Why Doesn't Anyone Read Any More?** under X1.7, "The Long Game").

Egocentricity and its close anagram geocentricity are at the heart of both the BBC Wales series and phases of the programme's earlier history when the series' spirit (and budget) made most stories revolve around London and/ or the companion-of-the-day's immediate relationship with his/ her family or the Doctor. Whilst the series' most literate phases were also the ones with fewest ties to present-day Britain, we can't make an exactly opposite case. Andrew Cartmel's term as script editor, for example, increasingly resisted stories wholly set on other worlds, but was among the most bookish and allusive in its long history. Conversely, Troughton's last year had precisely one story set in contemporary London ("The Invasion"), in which a machine designed to replace book-learning was the main anti-Cyberman weapon, while the other stories varied wildly in their interest in life in 1960s Britain (his companions were a pre-literate Highlander and a post-literate future-girl, both of whose basic knowledge differed from story to story). On the other hand, this year saw the first space-story not to have any non-humans (6.6, "The Space Pirates", by monster-maker extraordinaire Robert Holmes) and the one story from this phase genuinely interested in reading ("The Mind Robber") was compromised by a subplot about a plan to invade Earth. In that story, the link between literacy and being a fully-fledged "human being" was made explicit, and the always-present threat of being made less-than-human was pushed to the extreme by characters either becoming stereotypical bundles of pre-scripted traits (i.e. fictional versions of themselves) or cardboard cut-outs.

This is important: removal of flexibility, of options for change or potential for development, is one of the main ways that monstrosity has been characterised throughout *Doctor Who*. The most extreme reduction of potentiality is, of course, death (and we'll be looking at how this has been diluted and reconfigured lately in **Why Can't People Just Die?** under X4.9, "Forest of the Dead"). Any active character with curtailed options is,

continued on Page 139...

sion of his old self, he has a blond mop and is dressed sharply [he evidently picked his wardrobe in advance, with some idea of how he used to look].

'Hypersonic' sound waves enable the Professor to set up a resonance field that supposedly restores him, but sends his genetics haywire. With his unstable DNA consuming vast amounts of energy, he requires intensive consumption of life force (the Doctor actually calls it 'life energy') to survive. Appropriate sonic resonance seems to realign the base-pairs and wake up some of the "junk" DNA that constitutes a large part of the genome. The Doctor hypothesises that Lazarus's scorpion form is the result of a dormant genetic path that the Professor accidentally activated, accessing other options not taken in our evolutionary past [oh Lordy – see **The Big Picture** and **Things That Don't Make Sense**]. Thus, whenever his DNA shifts, he converts to the alternative life form. It retains Lazarus's face, more or less, but in other respects is close to a scorpion's legs and sting with an almost-empty, exposed human rib-cage that's double normal size.

The face, while still capable of speech, is characterised by a smaller nose than in human form and a jaw that bisects into insect-like mandibles. The sting is more complex than that of a terrestrial scorpion. [Indeed, it resembles a Fendaleen (15.3, "Image of the Fendahl"), which may account for a lot of odd features about this being's ability to absorb life-force from humans. Many similarities exist between Lazarus's apparatus and Professor Fendelman's sonic time-scanner (sic) – both are only used at night, but in Lazarus's case, this might just be showbiz rather than solar flux causing interference. The Fendaleen seem to acquire more bulk, from somewhere, than the humans they used to be hitherto had. These beings absorb life-energy and, as with the Toclafane, were bogey-men from a Time Lord's childhood. As Mr Saxon provided some degree of technical assistance, this makes in-universe sense if not actually working.]

The creature that Lazarus becomes can leap across long distances, climb walls and run along ceilings, and withstand explosions.

History

• *Dating.* At a guess, it's Tuesday morning on Election Week when the TARDIS comes back [see X3.12, "The Sound of Drums"]. The Doctor says they've only been away 12 hours after "Smith and Jones", and Francine confirms that Leo's birthday was the day before. The cocktail party seems to take place that night.

English Lessons

• *Blue Plaque* (n.) Round blue signs erected by English Heritage (that's an actual agency, not a tendency) to mark sites associated with notable figures. The list includes people from Winston Churchill to Jimi Hendrix, but the basic requirement that the recipient be dead means that Lady Thaw is being exceptionally thoughtless.

• *Southwark Cathedral* (n.) As you'd expect, it's a church in Central London, right next to London Bridge, the new version of Shakespeare's Globe (X3.2, "The Shakespeare Code"), St Thomas' Hospital ("Smith and Jones") and Borough Market. The basic building is 800 years old, rebuilt in the late nineteenth century, but Lazarus's speech makes more sense with the knowledge that it's only been a cathedral since 1905. (NB: Southwark actually has two cathedrals, the other being the Catholic one half a mile away. And it's pronounced "suth-uck", the first syllable like the start of "mother".)

The Analysis

The Big Picture There's a notorious episode of *Star Trek: The Next Generation* entitled "Genesis" (NB: not to be confused with the Genesis Device from *Star Trek II: the Wrath of Khan* – Stephen Greenhorn won't pilfer that until this time next year). In this, comedy-nerd Reg Barclay contracts some kind of alien flu, so the ginger doctor gives him a special artificial T-Cell that makes all the un-used genes in his double-helix come to life and turn him into a spider-man, and then everyone else gets it and turns into other things. Six episodes later, the series ended after seven successful years. This episode's wonky science made any molecular biologists watching hide behind the sofa, as was often the case when *Trek* tried to do anything about genetics and evolution. (See **What are the Silliest Examples of Bad Science in *Doctor Who*?** under 10.4, "Planet of the Daleks". By the way, despite various comments over the course of the *About Time* series about *Star Trek* fans, one thing that unites these people and experienced *Doctor Who* fans is wishing that a story called "The Chase" had never happened.)

Who are You Calling Monsters?

continued from Page 137...

effectively, one of the walking dead. As a fundamentally uncanny story-element (using "uncanny" in the technical sense, the closest translation of Freud's term "Unheimlich"), this is enough to unsettle the status quo and make a story happen, but *Doctor Who* writers have reflexively used these as part of a story of recruitment: they want you to be like them. This therefore makes an aspect of normally-defined "humanity" that they lack become the focus of the whole story. Whilst an individual character with something missing or deadened is still a character, as conventionally understood (and capable of either change or a terrifyingly extreme form of obsessive behaviour – see below), a group of them become monsters.

Webster's Dictionary, following St Isidore of Seville, derives the word "monster" ultimately from *monere*, the Latin root of "demonstrate", "remonstrate" and "admonish", basically meaning to show or prove. These beings are warnings. The OED differs slightly, finding twelfth-century French origins meaning a marvel, prodigy or super-human (we get this sense in one colloquial use, as in "a monster hit"). There are more instances of the former use than the latter, but even appealing to etymology doesn't give us a clear distinction. The earliest uses of the word in something recognisably like English are in Chaucer and the Wycliffe Bible, usually for Greek mythological half-men fought by Hercules or Ulysses. Chaucer's version of Boethius's *The Consolations of Philosophy* has Fortune described as a monster for being inhumanly perfect. There's even a citation in the OED for a 1440 piece describing Jesus as a monster for being born perfect, from a virgin.

While we're in Dictionary Corner, let's remind ourselves that "hybrid" and "hubris" both come from the Greek word for crossing a line. Although combining traits is – as any gardener knows – a way to restore the vigour of a species, there remains a nasty undertone of racial purity as an end in itself whenever hybridity is treated as a menace. While a monster can be supernatural, a hybrid is merely animal, never quite "complete". (We have an echo of this etymology in Series 9, but it never quite gels.) One of the clichés of the Davies stories is beings that are obviously humans with animal-masks, and these are never more-than-human.

Greek myths give us the first important use of monsters in storytelling. Characteristically, their monsters were half-human, half-something-else. That something else can be any other animal, and the animal chosen can be anything, usually an animal that has supposed characteristics that are being exaggerated. Each of these half-humans is thus a representation of a trait, much as the Egyptian gods were, and thus a symbolic way to tell stories about abstract concepts. In many ways, this has been how the Davies stories have worked. Suppose, for example, that someone wanted to suggest dunderheaded, officious police with a blinkered view of their duties. Obviously, you sketch that it by having cops who are half-human, half-rhino (X3.1, "Smith and Jones"). See how this works? Let's try another: you want blindly obedient servants who can do things with opposable thumbs that their masters can't and are easily identifiable by viewers as vicious and loyal. What could be more logical than half-human-half-pig? (Well, almost anything, but you did a pig-man a couple of years ago and people liked it – X3.4, "Daleks in Manhattan"; X1.4, "Aliens of London".)

As we said a few paragraphs back, the mass/mob nature of the Pigmen makes them monsters, while one who is still capable of speech becomes a sympathetic character. This use of the herd (and the word is unusually apt here) comes just as the Daleks themselves become characters with names for the first time since the Doctor nominated "his" Daleks and a human voluntarily became a Dalek in human form ("Evil of the Daleks" again). Here is where it gets interesting: Laszlo retains his sense of self and former attitudes but, apart from Tallulah being repulsed by his new look, his main problem is a curtailed life-span. As we saw in many of the "Gothic" stories of Philip Hinchcliffe's term as producer, many of the most memorable antagonists the Doctor has faced had the same problem. There was a period between symbolic "death" and literal when the abused villain, kept alive by hate and ambition, was even more single-minded than before. Laszlo is the first such character neither bent on destruction and revenge, nor begging for death. The nearest we got to such a figure before was the mute, inglorious George Cranleigh, a character and story so badly botched that we had a whole essay on it (**Do Mutilation and Entertainment Mix?** under 19.5, "Black Orchid").

So while a monster is a deviation from conventionally "human" defined as much by mental attri-

continued on Page 141...

Thus, in the script for "The Lazarus Experiment", there was a one-line attempt at a rationale for what was happening that sounded a bit like the explanation Data gives for his cat turning into an iguana. Oddly, this version omitted the *Trek* script's misappropriation of the term "intron", although people in the UK are more familiar with these due to the early 90s scare over the variant Creuzfeld-Jakob Disease: the notorious "Mad Cow" neurological infection that led to sweeping changes in agri-biz 20-odd years ago.

Pulling back from this one line, though, the bulk of the episode is manifestly indebted to Nigel Kneale. It begins with scientific hubris, because curiosity inevitably causes trouble in his works, and then goes through a ministerial conspiracy, a panic at a public event and then a monstrous giant beastie climbing up a church and crashing to its death after being given a stern talking-to about what it means to be human. Even if Stephen Greenhorn wasn't a big fan, a lot of these things were around at the time he was writing.

As we noted in Volume 7, a live remake of Kneale's *The Quatermass Experiment* was made in 2005, with Tennant, Gatiss and Jason Flemyng, plus Tate Modern standing in for Westminster Abbey. As a follow-up, there was a remake of the Kneale-Lite serial *A for Andromeda* by Fred Hoyle (the original was long-since wiped, except for tiny clips, so the DVD release of the sequel needed a push). What strikes one watching these, especially the latter, is the lighting and digital camerawork. The early twenty-first century has taken for granted that biological horror takes place within places with lots of pale-green, glassware, fluorescent lighting and corporate logos. *A for Andromeda* 2006-style (made by BBC Wales) cast redheads for both of the female parts, but generally looks like Mint Imperials being dissolved in milk. That brings us back to "New Earth" and the decision that white should be treated as a positive colour rather than an absence. One key and memorable shot from "The Lazarus Experiment" is fugitive guests silhouetted against the giant green-on-white backlit glass logo. Partly this is in all the previews because it's a good shot; partly because it establishes the Lazarus Industries logo ahead of "The Sound of Drums", where it's on the Master's ring, but mainly it works to sum up the category of story this is: medical horror.

So the visuals, while seeming to pull away from the content (since we've already had the look of the 50s *Quatermass* evoked in X2.7, "The Idiot's Lantern") are in synch with earlier attempts to update that sub-genre of British TV SF. In many ways, this media representation of very expensive biological experiments derives from cosmetics ads of the late 90s. The laboratory they've taken as their model is Laboratoire Garnier, which wasn't really a lab at all and was asked not to call itself that, and the jade, turquoise and white look crops up there (and in the branding of the UK high street chain Superdrug). Actual biology – although increasingly in the news through the simplistic reporting of the Human Genome Project and Dolly the Sheep – is too hard to put into sound-bites. Commercial interests have relied on this to put advertorials into the media as "news" items, and reporters need to become better at questioning these.

The GCSE exam has increasingly been more about evaluating claims based on evidence than about performing experiments or dissections (see "School Reunion"). The interesting thing about the PR launch is that it *is* a PR launch rather than a peer-reviewed paper, or series of published results in the official journals. Nothing about this episode makes any sense from that point of view (as we'll see in the appropriate section), but if we evaluate the story on its own terms, the *really* odd point is that Lazarus announces that he will "change what it means to be human" – as if his stunt will start the debate rather than contribute to it. That debate, in the circles in which Lazarus has to have been working for decades, is further advanced than the rather simplistic "Nature Vs Nurture" of pop culture; even if we take genes as the base-mark, which ones matter? The whole division between introns and exons comes into play, as does the role of mitochondria – this isn't exactly obscure, and it's an informed layperson's first hint about how blurred the lines will get.

Within *Doctor Who*, the debate has been about whether "humanity" is cultural or genetic, and often has the altered people deciding to retain personality traits. As we will see in this story's essay, the assumption is that anything that looks "monstrous" has to fight to be as good a person as they were. The converse isn't true, however – in 9.4, "The Mutants", Ky achieves a sort of angelic state but uses his immense psychic powers to zap the Marshal to death rather than, say, bliss him out and make him see the error of his ways. The main sources for this debate are the basic stories about

Who are You Calling Monsters?

continued from Page 139...

butes as physical appearance, the tendency has been to use the altered human's physiognomy to denote the internal changes. This is a legacy of fairy-tale and mythology where, as we have seen, a character's similarity to an animal traditionally ascribed particular personality traits to the exclusion of all others as a form of shorthand. This is also true of machinery. Characters who look like machines think like them too, QED. The problem with machine-people or beast-people is that they are also formidable physical presences – superheroes as well as supervillains. In the 1980s, writers got so hung up on the Cybermen being better than humans in appearance and abilities, they lost sight of the original "lack" that had made them monsters. The surgical/ mummified walking-dead of "The Tenth Planet" (4.2) became enhanced, unstoppable supermen almost indistinguishable from the freakishly muscular film-stars in vogue then. What's fascinating about the Series 2 reconfiguration of the Cybermen is that the basic fear that made them such a potent symbol in the 1960s was almost completely forgotten (there being relatively few tranquilliser-zombies these days), but a new, aligned fear replaced this: people-as-merchandise.

As with ATMOS (X4.4,"The Sontaran Stratagem"), the technology is the human-scale interface of a vast unaccountable network of commercial entities. These agencies sell convenient consumer-tech to people in return for both money and personal details, and the customers surrender control of aspects of their lives almost without realising it. Lumic turning his customers into Cybermen is merely completing a process that hapless members of the public entered into voluntarily. Far from being citizens who buy products, as consumerism moves further from government or public oversight, we become the product to be sold to advertisers: "content providers" and data-miners. The gadgets do the thinking for them. They become physically metal and depersonalised, but the real change happened long ago.

In an odd way, 2006 is almost the last time this particular fear can be visualised in this way. The old Romantic commonplace of technology and reason making people less human, and more machine-like, has become an obvious fallacy now that social media technology has made people seem more irrational, hot-tempered, insulting and (well) anti-social than at any time in recent history. Consumer tech has revealed a widespread fear about anything that makes people more "human" (as hitherto understood, see above) – be it long, detailed discussion, actual science or keeping your thoughts to yourself. However, as is amply proven by "The Bells of St John's" (X7.7), the problem for television drama is that typing on a tablet is no more watchable than typing on a laptop, and the effects of engaging with social media are no more telegenic than the processes of reading books or writing with pens ever were. People have to physically transform as a result of whatever technology is absorbing their attention, and this needs either factories making Cybermen out of hypnotised customers or viewers having their faces illogically sucked off and trapped inside TV screens (X2.7, "The Idiot's Lantern" or indeed "The Bells of St John's"). Representing current fears is a lot harder than when you could have paranoia represented by a metallic object screaming "exterminate" in a distorted voice, untrustworthiness by gold-skinned perfect people who don't blink (8.3, "The Claws of Axos") and moral turpitude by being a slug (22.2, "Vengeance on Varos"). That story's identification of looks and worth is made complete by the "Transmogrifier" ray. (See also **What Were Josiah's "Blasphemous" Theories?** under 26.2, "Ghost Light".)

The tendency to use similarity to or difference from orthodox-looking humans as quick-and-dirty characterisation is easy, but it's also treacherous. We are only a small step away from the bogus sciences of Phrenology, Physiognomy (determining who was likely to be a criminal by facial features or body-parts – the gap between a woman's big toe and other toes supposedly indicating a tendency towards prostitution, for example) and Racial Profiling. We're supposed to know better now. Just as pre-natal influences and miscegenation are no longer automatically trotted out to account for villainy, polite society frowns upon assuming that injury or deformity is indicative of personality. We are a long way from the *Dick Tracy* era of bizarre-looking criminals whose criminality and looks were one and the same. When debating fictional other species, these tendencies have a longer tail-off, since the main point of making up aliens is that they look exciting and odd. Apart from their very presence in a previously established normality making arresting images (and, in

continued on Page 143...

making a person from scratch: *Frankenstein: or the Modern Prometheus* by Mary Shelley; *The Island of Doctor Moreau* by HG Wells and the Asimov "Robot" stories. What's interesting about these is the ways that the role of education forms the main thrust of each. Lazarus is rebuilding himself rather than making a new being, but we're back in the realm of Original Sin, with a strong hint that Lazarus is made to become ugly because his soul is ugly (see **What Were Josiah's "Blasphemous" Theories?** under 26.2, "Ghost Light"). We've already seen how Russell T Davies regards the endless quest for perfection through surgery (X1.2, "The End of the World"). Narcissism and a fear of ageing underlay the plot of *Queer as Folk*. If we think of Lazarus's project as a form of extreme cosmetics rather than an investigation into the karyotype, we get closer to the ethical debate being enacted here.

The question is framed as being about whether extended life is necessarily better, but the on-screen events between the set-piece speeches make it seem to be about whether anyone – however brilliant or determined – has the right to consume someone else. We saw a lot of that kind of thing in Tom Baker's term, with shrivelled corpses having their life-force drained hither and yon (13.2, "Planet of Evil"; 14.1, "The Masque of Mandragora"; 14.6, "The Talons of Weng-Chiang"; "Image of the Fendahl"; 17.5, "The Horns of Nimon"; 18.4, "State of Decay"), but the only other time this happens in the new-series episodes is "The End of Time Part One". (There was a near-miss in X10.10, "The Eaters of Light", but with Vitamin D.)

Richard Lazarus is presented as a creepy old man letching after Tish but, when he is rendered younger-looking, she sees no problem with it. She explicitly invokes Michael Douglas and Catherine Zeta-Jones (a topical gag with Davies's fingerprints all over it, especially after their honeymoon in Swansea).

As we will see in **The Lore**, the original idea was for the climax to take place in St Paul's Cathedral, rather than Southwark, because making it St Paul's Cathedral rather than Westminster Abbey makes it a *completely* different thing from *Quatermass*, doesn't it? The administrators of St Paul's, as has been shown by the controversy over how much they charge the public to enter and the unpleasantness over the Occupy demonstrations, see the building as holding a special place in the nation's iconography beyond the ostensible function as a place of worship, and are very protective of their image (although X8.12, "Death in Heaven" was a bit of a change of policy here). If we try to imagine the end of the episode taking place there instead of Wells-as-Southwark, obvious logistical changes would have been required because of the layout of Wren's church. However, the notion of Lazarus sheltering from the Blitz in St Paul's makes more sense, even if neither cathedral was really used much for that purpose. St. Paul's Cathedral, despite being a major target for German bombers, survived the Blitz intact. There are many photos of the dome rising above searchlight-illuminated smoke.

Oh, Isn't That...?

• *Mark Gatiss* (Professor Richard Lazarus). You may have heard of him for writing "The Unquiet Dead" (X1.3), "The Idiot's Lantern" (X2.7), as well as several stories that aired after this one and umpteen tie-in books and audios. Outside *Doctor Who*, he's best known as one of the writer/ actors for *The League of Gentleman*, a horror comedy sketch show, in which he played 1/3 of the 40-odd characters. He's as well-known for performing as himself, with appearances in countless docu-dramas about people from the 50s on BBC4, self-written documentaries about old horror movies (the sort of thing Peter Capaldi parodied in *The Cricklewood Greats*) and interviews about things he's written. He is co-producer of *Sherlock*, in which he appears as Mycroft Holmes and writes episodes. He still does the occasional real feature film (such as the notorious dud *Sex Lives of the Potato Men*, which isn't about Sontarans). Oh, and he pops up, from time to time, in *Game of Thrones* as an envoy from the Iron Bank of Braavos.

• *Thelma Barlow* (Lady Thaw). She's Mavis Wilton off Corrie. We don't really need to say more for British readers (she lasted 26 years in the role), but she had odd things afterwards, including a gig in *Dinnerladies*. But, yes, playing one of the most famous characters in *Coronation Street* meant that only massively different roles, such as this, would really do (see next episode for more of the same).

• *Bertie Carvel* (Mysterious Man) was doing a lot of television around then. A lot. More recently, you may have heard him on the soundtrack album of Damon Albarn's *Dr Dee* opera. He was also Miss Trunchbull in the stage musical of

Who are You Calling Monsters?

continued from Page 141...

the past, cliffhangers), they are there to disrupt. Whereas in older *Doctor Who* and *The Sarah Jane Adventures,* this was often the end of it, and the disruption wasn't of necessity malign, the new series' one-episode format often results in the story being compacted to:"bad-thing-arrives-and-has-to-be-defeated". So "odd-looking" is almost invariably "bad".

When this is assumed without there being much justification for it, the most common way of handling it is a "fixer" sequel (X4.3, "Planet of the Ood"; X1.11, "Boom Town" and any story with Strax – see below). Otherwise, the series leaves the unpleasant taste of making the same assumptions that lay behind Nazi exhibitions of "inferior" racial types. It also assumes that human is the only body-shape appropriate for any other world. Anthropocentrism is understandable in a drama using human actors, but it's far from being the only option. These days, there are computer-generated beings far beyond what the old series could muster: what's interesting is how rarely they've done anything that isn't in some way tied to the humanoid form.

The last "great" monsters (as generally listed by the BBC, if not any one fan or viewer) of the original series were the Sontarans, and these provide a handy example of how they did things differently back then. Robert Holmes was reading about the causes of World War I, and came across descriptions of how the caricature of the Prussian officer we all grew up with was grounded in real-life examples. John Friedlander (mask-maker in the mid-70s peak of mask-making) and James Acheson (costume designer for many of the key stories of the same period) wanted to do an alien whose head exactly fitted the space-helmet it wore. This idea suited Holmes's satirical intent when creating a race of pragmatic warriors who saw everything in military terms. To rationalise such a physically-diminutive character being so forceful, the script posited a high-gravity home-world, which led to this powerful individual not having the strength to break free of ropes. To make fun of the new companion's contempt for sex-role stereotyping, Linx came from a race that had even got rid of sex; this led to a notion of them as clones and – by implication – the Probic vent as the one weak-spot. All the things we know about the Sontarans and their culture derive from attempts to account for their nature, even though this nature is a parody of a human personality-type as manifested in a set of individuals most people in Britain only knew from old cartoons in *Punch*.

Nonetheless, Holmes saw things through to their logical conclusion once he devised a reason for things to be so, and knew how to derive other consequences from the same cause. Comparison with Davies is obvious: a race such as the Judoon are the way they are to speed up storytelling by simply presenting a race of officious space-cops and saying nothing more about them. They are there to tell the story, but nothing would have made the story different if they'd been space-cows, space-mooses or space-aardvarks. Change anything about the Sontarans' backstory, and you change "The Time Warrior" (11.1) and "The Sontaran Experiment" (12.3) in important ways, and forestall any of the developments of these ideas that allowed them to come back in different types of story.

Yet, when this core idea is rejected, forgotten or just not identified, there is enough about the Sontarans as a species to make them almost impossible to get too wrong. Helen Raynor came as close as anyone has to messing up completely, making them male and sexist and annoyed at humans poking fun at their height, but she (or more likely Davies) managed to keep faith with the original idea ("The Sontaran Stratagem"; X4.5, "The Poisoned Sky") and Moffat has restored a lot of the original comic potential, albeit with flaws of his own.

But it's worrying that whilst Holmes went back to first principles to account for what he wanted to write about, and derived other logical consequences of these, few if any of the current generation of writers has any experience of literary SF and the sort of thought-process that Holmes, Terrance Dicks, Douglas Adams and to a lesser extent Christopher H Bidmead applied to monster-making. Instead, the tendency is to borrow cool-looking beasties from other sources (including older *Doctor Who*) and find reasons for these to be in the story, as opposed to making the story hinge on why they're the way they are. Turning the Sontarans into a race of short men with short-man syndrome is disappointing to some, but at least makes a sort of sense. With hindsight, Linx, Styre and the others we've seen (except in the hopeless

continued on Page 145...

Matilda, but recent television includes playing a sympathetic version of Nick Clegg in the political docu-drama *Coalition* and a cynical PR for the police on *Babylon*. Even more recently than that, he was one of the title characters in *Jonathan Strange & Mr Norrell* – the first, in fact. You might spot him in *Les Miserables*, but definitely couldn't miss him in *Doctor Foster*.

Things That Don't Make Sense One advantage of this story being so openly (let's call it) "inspired" by that *Trek* episode is that the majority of the science-fails have been adequately (indeed, copiously) covered elsewhere. Still, if we were to summarise...

You cannot inherit genes from anyone or anything from which you are not a descendent. There are, therefore, no bits of chromosome that can be reactivated that would turn anyone into anything from which humans did not descend. Whilst changing conditions produced many peculiar adaptations, and several cataclysms made hitherto-unpromising mutations pay off and eventually produce humans, none of these was a scorpion, a spider or an earwig. They were all on different branches of the family-tree.

So the only way that Richard Lazarus can possess *any* scorpion DNA is if he ate one just before going into his magic shower-cubical or popped one into his pocket – we can't believe that he did this willingly, so maybe a rival who'd seen *The Fly* tried to sabotage the scheme. (Well, maybe. Presuming the tissue-sample to be rejuvenated has to be alive, a living scorpion in his clothing would have been more easily detected, given that scorpions are not native to the UK. And it can't be any old nearby genetic material, otherwise the leather and cotton in his clothes would have conjoined with him; see X1.9, "The Empty Child". We should also assume that the process is unlikely to reanimate something he ate. Maybe olives *are* dangerous...)

More to the point, why is Lazarus *only* flipping between Mark Gatiss in a wig and Killer Earwig from the Dawn of Time? If his DNA is in this much flux, why would it fixate on the scorpion form for shifting? And trying to get round the problem of how a relatively compact humanoid-sized mutant turns into a giant killer scorpion is only highlighted by the Doctor's comment that Lazarus has "spread himself thin". We can certainly forgive a certain amount of artistic licence (especially once the mystical "life-energy" has been invoked), but if scorpion-Lazarus is light enough to walk on ceilings, it's odd that he isn't significantly skinnier each time he reverts to human, especially as he's eating so little and doing so much running around. (As a side point, The Mill seems to acknowledge the mass-problem by rendering Lazarus's scorpion-form as skeletally thin; one wonders whether it could have consumed anything other than life force. And, let's not forget, Lazarus started out with an old man's body-mass. And yet, he's had some suits tailored for his youthened self, despite not being able to get measured for them until after he turns into that person.)

Martha, fresh from her innovative use of the Psychic Paper last episode, immediately figures out how to use the Sonic Screwdriver and invents a new use for it. Most public buildings are designed to let people escape in a hurry if there's some kind of accident, so the hassle that Martha goes through to evacuate the building is a puzzle. Never mind how Tish handles the PR afterwards. And once again, we have the problem that – in the UK at least – if Lazarus is allowed to call himself "professor", he must still be attached to a university. Did they have any say in this? Is there any kind of oversight from the faculty, at all?

Aside from mentioning the fact that "hypersonic" means "faster than Mach 5" – so this sound travels five times the speed of sound – and that problem we had last week about computer-illustrations of DNA reacting as if they were somehow photos responding to real changes they couldn't perceive, Dr Science is going to abandon trying to make sense of it all and just leave the building. Which leaves us to get on with the basic logical flaws and inconsistencies...

Martha has a mobile phone and an answering machine. Ten to one that if she sometimes ignores the answering machine to screen her calls (and she must, judging by Francine's order to turn on the telly), they'd call her mobile instead. But the Doctor doesn't turn it into a Magic Phone until next episode, so you'd think she could receive calls in her own time period at least. Her service-provider would update her mobile within a minute of getting within range of a tower, which in London is almost everywhere. (In all fairness, the script addressed this and had Martha switching her mobile off when Leo called. Yet with all the worry about what Martha's been up to, nobody

Who are You Calling Monsters?

continued from Page 143...

case of 22.4, "The Two Doctors") almost make more sense with this as a factor in their behaviour.

There's another paradox here: the older stories had more episodes in which to get beyond first impressions and look into motivation, background and complexities, but usually didn't bother. When they did, they couldn't guarantee than any one viewer would stay the course and watch the whole story (we're looking at you, Sir Salman – see below). These days, not only is the screen-time for a first story of any new or reclaimed alien limited, but the resources used to make any one mask or costume are far greater and thus more of an investment. If a species makes its new-series debut, it'll likely be back within a year, usually more than once if the budget's being squeezed. The real surprise of X7.14, "The Name of the Doctor" was that there *wasn't* an Ice Warrior in it. In some ways, the old way was better, in that it made the Universe seem a lot bigger and more varied. These days, especially when the inventor of a new race gets the rights every time they appear, there's no such thing as leaving the audience wanting more (X7.5, "Angels in Manhattan" for example). This has led to less complexification of these races than might have been expected.

Traditional *Doctor Who* monsters come in two basic flavours: once-human(ish) aliens who've had a personality-trait removed (often literally, by surgery or genetic tinkering) and humans who've become "contaminated". These are both such clichés that Salman Rushdie's mis-remembering of the plot of "The Mutants" (9.4) is significant for how far he thinks it conformed to type. The actual story has the twist, rather shocking for its time, that the "mutation" is pupation and the humanoids are the larval form of glowing, angelic psychic beings. Normally, deviation from human-looking is seen as a decline or indicative of a moral lapse. Other than these two trends, the main source of monstrosity is being designed as henchbeings for someone else, or resembling something to be found in nature (an obvious example of that would be the embryo-like Zygons: 13.1, "Terror of the Zygons"; X7.15, "The Day of the Doctor" and Series 9).

Sometimes even this is part of the transformation, as most obviously happens in 12.2, "The Ark in Space". The Wirrn are manifestly based on a terrestrial species, as the Doctor makes a point of noting just before the average viewer thinks to complain. There is thus a logical reason for the Wirrn to resemble wasps physically and in their behaviour (making a nest in someone's home while they are asleep, laying eggs), and for the insect-like conformity and over-specialisation of the defrosted humans to make a link with this; thus Noah's somatic transformation into an insect isn't purely symbolic or crassly literal. Conversely, although Richard Lazarus is also transformed into something yukky after being revealed to be a nasty person, there's not any attempt to affix what he becomes to who he was. (X3.6, "The Lazarus Experiment", if you hadn't surmised this from context.) The scorpion/ earwig/ spider thing is something that they thought The Mill could make look good when it chased Tennant and Agyeman up and down lots of corridors.

Which brings us to the biggest paradox of all. They have so many options available to them, and yet this one is only used in a story where the logic of doing so is at best questionable. There is *no* reason for Lazarus to turn into something from which no human is descended, but this is the one and only time that The Mill has been asked to devise a completely inhuman-looking being. They have never again done a story about a human becoming anything else. (Unless you stretch a point and have Rory being an Auton for a while in X5.12, "The Pandorica Opens", albeit he's still Arthur Darville with an occasional prosthetic hand; or the Flesh-Jennifer becoming a giant alabaster whippet – X6.6, "The Rebel Flesh".) They've not done any other non-bipedal beings (except Tricey in X7.2, "Dinosaurs on a Spaceship", which was on their hard-drive already). What makes this more bizarre is that the main place where Tennant's Doctor has met genuinely innovative and interesting-looking aliens has been the animated tie-ins, "Dreamland" and "The Infinite Quest" – where, for technical reasons, the execution is less well-rendered.

It is the production team who have been fearful of making any innovations, not the public. The original concept for the Abzorbaloff, after all, was for something the size of a double-decker bus, but Davies opted to make it Peter Kay in latex ("Love & Monsters"). With the technology at their disposal, expensive though it is per minute of screen-time, the live-action series could be less conservative than it is (See **Is Animation the Way Forward?** under A5, "The Infinite Quest"). The choice of crea-

continued on Page 147...

complains that her phone hasn't been working.)

As it's only been 12 hours since "Smith and Jones", why is Francine so alarmed about Martha hanging out with a strange man, given that just *four hours before that* she was on the Moon with space-monsters? Francine was keen to defend Martha against accusations of lying the previous night, so all she has to say is "Mum, this is the guy who saved me from the space rhinos and got the hospital back". Also, there's something decidedly off about how Martha spends her day. If it's 12 hours since she left her parents ("Smith and Jones"), by the time she and the Doctor go to Lazarus's press launch, some eight to 12 hours have elapsed. There isn't time for Martha to have done a full shift at work and got home; neither should we presume she spent the whole day deciding what to wear. Yes, she had to go into town first thing to pay the rent, but there's a reliable bus and tube network, so it wouldn't have taken *that* long. As the story ends with her making the Doctor either take her on full-time or not, has Martha incautiously gone in and quit, or does she spend a whole day trying to watch telly with a bloody great police box in the way, or taking the Doctor to Tesco to pick up groceries – or what? (This isn't Rose Tyler not having a shop to go to we're talking about; you'd think that the hospital staff would be crying out for help with all these already-ill people now suffering the after-effects of oxygen deprivation, in addition to the usual patients. The *real* surprise, actually, was that she was released to go to her brother's party. If, on the other hand, everyone involved was given sick-leave to recuperate while they rewire the electricity and plumbing, we're back to the initial question.)

Tish is a terrible PR director if she's reduced to inviting all her family members to the supposedly exclusive cocktail party. Mind you, Martha's surprised to hear about Tish's job (and you'd think that working for one of the UK's greatest experts in regenerative medicine would have come up in conversation beforehand), so they must have sacked the last one only recently – like, shortly before the TARDIS arrived and Francine rang Martha to tell her Tish was on telly – and yet she's been in the job long enough to contact the caterers and know the security procedures.

Speaking of which, why is this event almost entirely attended by young, pretty people, when the more obvious people to invite are rich, old folks such as Lady Thaw? And why is the first-ever use of Lazarus's "youthening" technique in front of an audience, rather than – y'know – on test-subjects? There has apparently been no trial-run, no experiments on real or figurative guinea-pigs, nothing published in *Nature* or *The Lancet* and no peer-review of any kind. One might have expected at least an observer from the British Medical Authority or the National Institute for Health and Care Excellence (NICE, the people who decide on how much taxpayers' money goes on specific treatments on a cost/ benefit basis). Nobody from any of the major pharmacological groups (GSK or Pfizer, for example) seems to be there.

And why is nobody doing the minimum amount of looking around you'd get at the average stage-magician's show where one person goes into a box and another comes out? There isn't even any kind of medical test before and after comparing the general health of the subject(s) – perhaps they're saving the checks on his heart-rate, breathing, kidney-function and other age-related conditions for later, but just the state of his hips and knees would make this a worthwhile test. Plus, if the technique is genetic a simple swab test before and after would confirm that it's the same person and indicate anything worrying, such as... just to pick an example... activated introns likely to turn the subject into a giant scorpion every so often. (Yes, we can accept that it would be dull to watch, but there's less rigour here than in an infomercial.)

Like Lady Thaw, Richard Lazarus ought to have been evacuated in the Blitz – nobody sheltered in churches as he claims. They have spires, so were a nice obvious target for aerial bombardment, and Southwark is right on the bit of the Thames that the Luftwaffe could identify by its shape (see X1.10, "The Doctor Dances"). St Paul's Cathedral, the one really obvious target not damaged (Battersea Power Station got a small ding), was unscathed despite the relentless bombing – but nobody would have known this in advance. Even if we accept "Southwark" as a last-minute rewrite for "St Paul's", there are no records of anyone using Southwark Cathedral as a shelter – it's close enough to Waterloo Station for the tube to have been a handier bolt-hole with a higher chance of survival.

So, the Doctor's "inspired" plan to undo the Lazarus effect is to play a cathedral organ with a screwdriver as an amp, which *eventually* works,

Who are You Calling Monsters?

continued from Page 145...

tures, and the types of stories in which they appear, have been restricted by choice. Steven Moffat's term as executive producer has been characterised by fairy-tale bogey-men or walking corpses rather than any attempt to make aliens from other gravities, atmospheres or climates. Technically, as make-up and CG effects, these have generally been pretty accomplished, but there is a certain sameyness to them. Spoonfaces and Smilers, Whispermen and the Silence, Monks and Fisher Kings and statues and snowmen and mummies that creep up on you... it all blurs into the same sort of thing after a while. (Especially if you remember *Buffy*.)

The Richard Lazarus storyline – a human infected or otherwise combined with other genetic material and becoming something else – was used more in Philip Hinchcliffe's three-year term than in the whole first four Doctors since BBC Wales got the gig. For older fans, therefore, "The Lazarus Experiment" looks fairly familiar, even routine, and yet another knock-off of *Quatermass*, but for the new audience of that period it was – and remains – at time of going to press, unique. Other than this, the only traditional-seeming "monsters" made by BBC Wales are those brought back from the 60s and 70s. Old monsters come back as much as anything because the production teams have less faith in their own creations than the London-based teams had. The perceived failure of the Slitheen (X1.5, "World War Three" in particular) chastened them into simplistic animal-head-on-boiler-suit designs or reaching back into the 60s and 70s. The tendency to bring back old monsters isn't for the benefit of the general public, who just want novelty, but for precisely those older fans who object to them getting it "wrong". Those old monsters belong to the same assumption of what "human" looks like that made the Thals obviously benign because they were blond and blue-eyed.

(See also **Wot? No Chelonians?** under "The Pandorica Opens".)

but the discords that do the trick come after a lot of horror-movie music. Does the Doctor think that the endangered Martha and Tish need a bit of Vincent Price mood-music to make the situation more scary?

A really picky point: to look at Martha's flat, why do all companions have a postcard from the Isle of Man depicting that island's three-legged flag stuck to their fridge or notice-board? And a not-so-picky point: why, exactly, is Harold Saxon so keen on warning Martha's family about the Doctor, potentially causing word to get back to her? If she'd actually listened, his Paradox Machine would have been even more mucked up than before. It might be to make her more amenable to having her phone calls monitored (see X3.7, "42"), but all the information he gains from that he already knew from when Martha told Professor Yana. From Saxon's point of view, this intimidation and meddling is one more risk on top of the ones he's already taken and is only possible because he knows all about Martha's family already. It doesn't even get him closer to taunting the Doctor, which is the only motive he'd have for doing something like this.

Critique It's a story about a man who takes mortality personally and wants to do something about it. This is interesting and sharply-written in the first 20 minutes, despite the increasingly strange way the Doctor's blowing hot and cold over Martha's status as a travelling companion. Then the nasty scorpion-thing trashes a cocktail party and things deteriorate. We go from a character-study that only *Doctor Who* can do to routine chasing, explosions and monsters (the things people think *Doctor Who* always does and therefore *has* to do).

After ten minutes of this, it seems to be over... and then it starts again in a different building. The exchanges between the Doctor and Lazarus are theatrical in the best sense: abstract ideas made biographical and personally important. It's as close to Tom Stoppard as you're going to get on Saturday nights before *Any Dream Will Do*. However, these are punctuation between the stuff with the scorpion-monster-with-the-face-of-David-Bowie.

In between these, we also have the increasingly implausible Jones family and their strops. On first broadcast, this was a slight annoyance as it looked like it was going somewhere. But it became less than the sum of its parts, so they tried again next year with Sylvia Noble. With hindsight, therefore, it just gets in the way – but with *more* hindsight once the Ponds have come and gone, this family's reassuringly spiky and fractious. It still seems a bit grafted-on, although not as badly as in the next episode. If we'd got a second year of Martha, her family might have been worth persevering with (especially Leo and his baby and girlfriend, whoever they were). One of the biggest problems of near-future or present-day settings for *Who* is that the viewers measure what they see against what they know. The Jones family's inconsistencies are part of this, much as the frequent errors of basic London geography in other stories, and the odd scene where it seems to be simultaneously daylight in Delhi and New York. You need this family to put the Doctor and Martha in the action relatively easily, but it makes little sense for the PR director of such a prestigious do to conscript her family to make up the numbers.

We've discussed the idiotic science-fails at length already; it was as easy to have got it right as wrong, and if they absolutely *had* to have a scorpion-creature instead of a hybrid of pelycosaurs and anthropoids or whatever, they could have justified it with a few lines. There's the obvious precedent of *The Fly* to fall back on, and surely there must have been earlier experiments with animals. The point of the monster – apart from exciting small children – is to get across when Lazarus needs to kill again. *That's* the threat, not what the critter looks like. The story-as-written seems to have focused more on his belief that he is allowed to ingest "inferior" humans, but this is lost along the way. The flimsy justification for the transformation into something yukky looks suspiciously as if they didn't care why it happened so much as how cool it would look. The lack of attention to this (as with the sloppy logic of Tish's CV, Dalek Sec's plan or phases of the Moon) makes it look as if nobody cares.

There's sometimes a gesture towards justifying this approach, by claiming that attention to detail can get in the way of a good story. That's fine, if you've got a good story to tell, but in this case what we get is lightweight and negligible. This episode is especially frustrating as the talky bits give lip-service to a genuine dilemma for the Doctor, as well as a problem he couldn't fix by shoving his screwdriver into something and running up and down corridors. It looks as if the author considered a better, more exciting and genuinely intractable problem, then rejected it in favour of making children's television.

To be fair, it's good-looking children's television. The keyword was "classy", and it has a lustre that transcends its status as the cheap episode (look at the cast-list: nine speaking parts, and one of them's the Olive Woman). As director, Richard Clark has held things together (apart from that ropey monster) and slips in odd surprises. However much better the storyline could have been with a bit more time (or a bit less interference), the finished episode is at least smarter than it ought to have been (or would have been in another series). It's brisk, occasionally gorgeous and with, at least, different types of explosions and monsters from usual.

At the heart of it is Mark Gatiss, who is adequate as an old man, entertaining as a nasty one and prepared to push himself for the sake of the story. Unlike, say, Simon Pegg (X1.7, "The Long Game"), he never looks as if he's thinking *Hey, wow! I'm being a Doctor Who baddie for real at last!* A couple of his vowels are a bit too northern for someone supposedly in Southwark in 1940, but we'll let that rest. His prostheses are about the best ageing make up we'll see for a while (and, at risk of a spoiler, we have two more coming up later this year). Thelma Barlow, as Lady Shaw, simply doesn't look like Thelma Barlow.

So as with the last two episodes, there's a calm competence about it all. There could have been more, but for anyone watching week after week – or on a box-set or streaming binge now – the variety of styles and settings is more alluring than any one episode. They can do *this* then *this* then *this*. Series 3 upped the ante for that range of formats and sub-genres, but each individual specimen adheres more to a house-style than to the needs of each story. They've killed off the old public perception of the *Doctor Who* look and sound – squeaky Radiophonic Workshop music, wobbly sets, rubber-suit monsters and iffy CSO included – but the new formula risks being just as take-it-or-leave-it.

The Lore

Written by Stephen Greenhorn. Directed by Richard Clark. Viewing figures: (BBC1) 7.2 million, (BBC3 repeats) 1.0 and 0.5 million. AI 86% for BBC1, 85% for BBC3.

Repeats and Overseas Promotion It's *L'Expérience Lazarus* in France (only two weeks on from the Final Experiment), but *Der Pries der Jugendd* in Germany.

Alternate Versions The version shown on BBC1 first time had a different end-credits sequence: instead of the "throw-forward" to the following episode, the remainder of Series 3 was trailed in a specially-made sequence using the voice-over from "The Family of Blood" and a pause in the "Strange Strange Creatures" music to allow the Master to drum on the desk in Ten Downing Street. It had been made for the BBC's "Red Button" digital-only extras feature, but given an airing as an emergency measure. As with the Christmas episode end-trailers, it hadn't many computer effectsm but showed off the guest-cast, prostheses and explosions.

Production

Apparently, a different story was scheduled for this slot until very shortly beforehand. Stephen Greenhorn, a Scottish writer hitherto best known for the "Karaoke Musical" *Sunshine on Leith* (now a minor feature film), was asked to come up with a biological horror story. (We have, as yet, no details of this "lost" script, but logically it must have connected to the "Doctor Dobby" subplot of the season finale. It's unlikely to have been what had become X2.11, "Fear Her", although that had originally been pencilled in for Series 3.)

Greenhorn was working on an adaptation of Jean Rhys's novel *Wide Sargasso Sea*, itself a reworking of *Jane Eyre* (and which was broadcast in late summer 2006 – it was produced by Julie Gardner, which is how he came to the team's notice). Russell T Davies planned from the start for this story slot to include more characterization of the Joneses, and so he provided Greenhorn with the script of the first episode. At this stage, details of the family's situation by the series finale were unclear, so the script was to have small portions that could be amended nearer the shoot. Greenhorn's first thoughts were a story about the Thames Barrier (sadly, Davies had just used the same idea – see X3.0, "The Runaway Bride") and a sentient skin-graft that controlled the host (worryingly close to what everyone thought *Spider-Man 3* would be about). Finally, a story about a "Professor Anger" who made a Faustian pact to grow young proved to be a good starting-point. The name had to go, so they opted for the only marginally less obvious "Professor Lazarus". The script apparently began life as "The Madness of Professor Lazarus".

• Once Mark Gatiss was confirmed for the title role, Richard Lazarus's childhood home over a bookshop was amended to being over a butcher's, as a wink towards *The League of Gentlemen*. The opening scene was added last, less than a week before the read-through. The name "Harold" for the mysterious Mr Saxon was still unresolved, and was dubbed in post-production months later.

• "The Lazarus Experiment" was the second story in Block 3; shooting started at the prestigious location of Wells Cathedral, Somerset, on 3rd and 4th October. Gugu Mbatha-Raw (Tish) and Gatiss were needed along with the two regulars and a SteadiCam crew. It was also more practical for Adjoa Andoh (Francine), Mbatha-Raw and Reggie Yates (Leo) to record as many of the scenes of Martha's family in one visit to Wales as possible, so they had been shooting the pub row at the end of "Smith and Jones" the previous day. Agyeman was pleased to be out of her red jacket for a change, but Gatiss was either in just a flesh-coloured jockstrap and his wig, or swaddled in a blue onesie (or "babygro" as we called them then, and Gatiss does in the interviews). The wig was in fact the one he had been fitted for when playing Dr Chinnery, the hapless vet in *The League of Gentlemen* (a performance and character not a million miles away from Peter Davison in *All Creatures Great and Small*, except more slapstick/grand guignol). Others they'd tried looked even worse (see the Sideshow Bob abomination he wore in *Nighty Night*, the first choice here, before you condemn the final decision).

• As stated, this story was commissioned and made in a bit of a hurry. Wells was chosen because it looked plausibly like the interior of Southwark Cathedral, but was easier to get permission to work in – earlier plans for St Paul's Cathedral had fallen through. Everything at the Cathedral was shot at night; Wells Cathedral is used by worshippers and visited by tourists even in October. (Tennant and Gatiss recall the hotel they were using, in nearby Shepton Mallett, being a bit noisy by day when they were trying to sleep.)

• The 5th saw a move back to Cardiff to the quasi-futuristic setting of the National Assembly for Wales building (the Senedd, pronounced "sen-neth"), where they shot the younger Lazarus's reception room scenes. The building was only opened a few months earlier and security was tight. These scenes were also all done at night, partly because it was scripted as such, but also as it's a public building.

• On Monday the 9th, Gatiss was made-up as Lazarus's older form, involving a three-hour make-up process he had to endure every day for the rest of the week. (David Tennant found it "freaky" seeing his friend looking like this, although he'd have old-age makeup twice himself this series.) Each day needed a new prosthesis. Millennium Effects worked mainly from a cast of Gatiss, but some of the wattling was derived from a bust of Vincent Price (appropriately for a story so much like *The Fly*). Gatiss found the reduced visibility from the rheumy contact lenses slightly awkward. The 10th saw the Lazarus-Doctor meeting, showing off Lazarus's rejuvenation device (itself a rejuvenated prop that had once been the descent pod from "The Impossible Planet" and "The Satan Pit"), and Martha helping everyone out of the building, although a lot of this material was cut. Bertie Carvel, eventually credited as "Mysterious Man", did the scene with Francine becoming very concerned about the Doctor. (This had been added fairly late, to tie in with Davies's plans for the series finale, so Greenhorn's on-set presence might have been partly to smooth out last-minute rewrites.)

• At the end of the episode, the "Next Time" sequence was dropped in favour of a compilation of moments from the latter half of the series. This was possible because these episodes were closer to completion than they had been when "The Runaway Bride" was aired and it was necessary because the following week's planned showing of X3.7, "42" was forestalled for a week to allow the Eurovision Song Contest to be broadcast.

X3.7: "42"

(19th May, 2007)

Which One is This? Set the controls for... well, as far away from the Heart of the Sun as you can manage. The orangey-looking one with Cindy Beale and the trivia questions about Elvis and Happy Primes (not to be confused with any of the other orangey-looking spacey stories...).

Firsts and Lasts This is the first *Doctor Who* script by Chris Chibnall – who'll become something of a mainstay of the Moffat years, if not exactly a highlight, and take on a bigger importance with Series 11. As a "utility" writer working on cop-shows and anything that pays the bills, dropping in quick science lessons when he thinks nobody'll notice, he can best be compared to, um, Pip and Jane Baker. (See Volume 6, especially 23.4, "The Ultimate Foe", or **The Lore** below for the piquancy of this.) If you're looking at this story for clues about how he'll handle his new job as Boss of *Doctor Who* from 2018 onward, it's not much help.

A bit of music written for this episode became the unofficial Series 3 Theme and was used in the trailers, cliffhanger reprises and every subsequent episode this year. However, more noticeably, we have the first moment since they relaunched the series where absolutely no sound – music, sound-effects or dialogue – has been used.

This is the only *Doctor Who* episode with a written prologue, which the BBC debuted on the website. It bears the somewhat unimaginative name of "42 Prologue", is written by someone else (Joe Lidster), and goes into detail about Erina's backstory and the crew's inter-relationships.

This was intended to be the first story set entirely inside a spaceship since the 2005 return; but instead they put in the stuff with Francine and Mr Saxon's aides. It *is*, however, not only the shortest episode-title ever, but the only one entirely in digits.[28]

Watch Out For...

• The running-time for a new-series episode, without ad-breaks (as BBC viewers would see it on first broadcast) is 42 minutes, unless it's the show-runner splurging. There is thus a hint that there's an attempt at the Aristotelian Unities, with the on-screen time matching the time the charac-

How Long Should an Episode Be?

Those who want to drive a wedge between the new series and old would like us all to think that only two options are on the table: 25-minute sections of a longer serial, or self-contained 45-minute adventures. Closer examination, as usual, reveals a lot of variety between these two allegedly "pure" positions.

At the heart of this debate is an idea – echoed so often that it's never examined – that the pace of storytelling has accelerated, and that modern viewers take in information faster. The first problem here is the idea that only information-reception matters, rather than mood, atmosphere or excitement. If the *speed* of storytelling is what matters, then the synopses available online spare you the bother of watching the story at all. The most information-dense story was probably "Ghost Light" (26.2), but a version of that with the cliffhangers removed, and any redundancy for viewers who'd missed a week trimmed, would be too rich a mix for anyone who thinks that everything made so far has been leading to Series 10. "The Crimson Horror" (X7.12) has a neat synoptic "story so far" sequence that condenses what would ordinarily have been 20 minutes of screen time to five minutes, but "The Name of the Doctor" (X7.14) has very little actually happening and one thing that *does* is shown to us three times. A key incident that would have illuminated much about that episode was relegated to a DVD extra, but the episode as a whole seems over-long, padded and all aimed towards the cliffhanger – which has to come after 45 minutes regardless of what they show to fill that three-quarters of an hour. Those of you who read Volume 7 will recall is how often the early Eccleston episodes under-ran because they had misjudged how much material was needed to fill the new length of episodes. In this volume and the next, we'll see the writers and directors confront the opposite problem – having too much for 45 minutes.

Nonetheless, this duration has been accepted as "right" for the current style of story and all deviations from it are considered to be problems, as the main object of the exercise seems to have become overseas sales.

When people talk about the accelerated pace of storytelling, what they so often mean is that specific conventions have become accepted to eliminate the need for verbal exposition. Other conventions that served this purpose have fallen into disuse over the last half-century and now seem just as odd as today's cinematic tics inevitably will. Season Four, in early 1967, has a lot of voice-over relaying of thought-processes, a habit that now seems strange and kitsch (a relic of 50s Hollywood, especially so-called "Women's Pictures"). The jumpy editing of flashbacks when Tommy is figuring things out (11.5, "Planet of the Spiders") may look odd now, but it was closer to standard for 1974 TV drama than a lot of the other things in that story. Every generation has a repertoire of non-naturalistic storytelling devices that people shrug and accept then, a few years later, see in reruns and think 'uh? Already, some of the editing fads of the late 90s that resurged in the first two years of the new series look as dated as making the picture wobble when you go into a flashback (see X4.7, "The Unicorn and the Wasp" for a sardonic use of that tic). What is forgotten is that any of these is a matter of choice.

The current editing conventions and use of multiple sources, scenes that might be subjective impressions and visual ellipses (the equivalent, in montage form, of "...") mean that "Love & Monsters" (X2.10) could have been 25 minutes or an hour, depending on how fast they wanted to tell this story, and indeed could comfortably have lost the less-than-popular scenes with people in latex playing monsters. Just because certain options are available, it doesn't follow that they have to be used at all, or certainly not all of the time, any more than the techniques of the 1960s *nouvelle vague* or early 70s split-screen trickery were compulsory for Troughton or Pertwee stories. (Watch *Easy Rider* with someone raised on modern blockbusters, if you think film-grammar has accelerated in 40 years.) Buried in the archives are many British TV dramas that attempted to keep pace with what could be done in cinema. They have aged less well than the bread-and-butter soaps, classic novel adaptations and crime series with which we have to lump *Doctor Who* in any given year. (Aggressively "now" dramas such as *The Corridor People* or *Rock Follies of 1977* act as a sort of core-sample of what's left unwiped.)

If you are looking for a period when the pace of narrative – in terms of information given to viewers in *Doctor Who* – picked up appreciably, try Colin Baker's term in the mid-80s. Compare any story made in the three years before 21.6, "The Caves of Androzani" (itself peppered with slow, moody sequences and fourth-wall-breaking asides) to any made after 24.1, "Time and the Rani"

continued on Page 153...

ters experience second-for-second. Actually, that's not the case here, so the only space-opera to have achieved this remains that *Babylon 5* episode where Sheridan's arrested for saving the Galaxy again ("Intersections in Real Time"). So the title's a complete cheat? Well, suffice to say, they make a lot of fuss about how they will collide with the Sun in 42 minutes (see **Things That Don't Make Sense**), but they start saying that about five minutes into the episode.

• Fans of earlier iterations of the series might feel cheated on other grounds – this story's premise and conclusion are *very* similar to 13.2, "Planet of Evil", but with the glowing-eyed mutants reproducing by line-of-sight with the star (so actually more like 15.2, "The Invisible Enemy" with a bit of 14.1, "The Masque of Mandragora") and using their infection mind-control to get a ride home (as per 14.2, "The Hand of Fear") and drumming that episode's catch-phrase in ("Burn with me", cf "Eldrad Must live", "Contact has been made"). So it's a Bob Baker/ Dave Martin rip-off masquerading as a Louis Marks rip-off? Well, not quite (see **The Big Picture**, below).

• Other things making a comeback: the Doctor puts on a spacesuit like the one in X2.9, "The Satan Pit"; he does this to do a space-walk to operate controls for a spaceship that the designers imprudently placed on the outside (10.3, "Frontier in Space"); the spaceship's name is that of the transmat component that went missing in 12.5, "Revenge of the Cybermen" (the "Pentalian drive" was around Kelman's neck); Martha has a blinding revelation that her mum won't know where and when she died (X3.3, "Gridlock") and the spaceship's captain is almost the last person you might have expected to get to be cast (19.6, "Earthshock").

• After three years, they've finally decided that not all orange sparkly fairy-dust is intrinsically benign. Perhaps as a legacy of supervising *Torchwood* Series 1, Chibnall has given us evil, vicious orange sparkly fairy-dust.

• The story is, generally, cut very rapidly, with even exposition dialogue edited as briskly as the action-sequences in last week's episode. This makes the lingering shots of Martha's escape-pod drifting towards the sun, and the Doctor watching it from behind an air-lock door, more remarkable. The pod's interior is lit in blue, whereas everything in this ship seems to be red or orange, as if the manufacturers knew it'd be involved in some solar skulduggery.

• Even aside from the pleasant acknowledgement that space does not come with a Murray Gold soundtrack, you'll want to watch the escape pod launch scene here to fully appreciate the parody version in X4.1, "Partners in Crime" (though Russell T Davies had actually been sitting on that scene for a few years at this point).

• When was the last time you encountered, as the Doctor does here, anyone explaining Happy Primes on prime-time television? Not even Johnny Ball did that.[30] BBC4 has Marcus du Sautoy to do whole hours on the stuff this episode introduces and leaves in under a minute. It's especially refreshing that the Doctor assumes the rest of the universe should be as clever as he is about something the viewership might genuinely have heard of before the episode.

• The spaceship is a long corridor for the Doctor and his chums to run up and down, but there are hatches you have to open with trivia questions, plus occasional lateral-thinking challenges and menacing men in helmets. This is oddly familiar for anyone who recalls either *The Crystal Maze* or the various me-too gameshows – notably one called *Scavengers*, set on a spaceship full of booby-prizes, where middle-management types pretended to be space-mercenaries. That had an ex-*Blue Peter* presenter pretending to be in a Hollywood space film, rather than an ex-*EastEnders* regular.

• As occasionally happens with the worst-written companions, a story manifestly written for "Generic Girl" can do them some favours (see 24.3, "Delta and the Bannermen" for a good example). Thus, for one week, everyone ignores the Martha's-crush-on-the-Doctor subplot and Freema Agyeman shares more chemistry with William Ash (crewman Riley Vashtree, who's stuck in an escape pod with her) than we've seen her display with David Tennant.

• They wanted Bertie Carvel from last week's episode back, but he was busy, so they replace "Sinister Man" with "Miss Dexter". Davies's dad knew Latin.

The Continuity

The Doctor He likes the idea of teaching recreational mathematics in schools and can identify a happy prime sequence when he hears one. He doesn't know whether Elvis or the Beatles had more No. 1s. [See **History** for why he's confused.]

How Long Should an Episode Be?

continued from Page 151...

(where the speed of the direction in shots-per-minute is at odds with the laborious scripting, which makes sure every single detail is explained twice, except the ones we most need to make any sense of it all). The calendar says that only five years separates "Terminus" (20.4) from "The Greatest Show in the Galaxy" (25.4), but it looks more like 15. It's not just plot delivery; the visual cues and sound-design "texture" are richer and denser, allowing a more complex story with different moods and subtexts in the same amount of screen-time, although this could be said to be a function of the early 80s stories' stripped-down, low-cost approach. *Doctor Who* in the early 80s was behind most BBC drama in terms of pace (because most other series were in well-established locales or genres, so you didn't need to spoon-feed viewers as you would with a new planet in a period of history not shown on any other series).

Oddly, only "prestige" dramas retained the leisurely pace of the 70s (something like *Tender is the Night* or *Edge of Darkness* will serve to prove this). Stuff intended for domestic consumption accelerated. Even the allegedly lowest-common-denominator TV of the 80s, *Dallas* and *Dynasty,* were matching each other on the number of edits per scene and scenes per episode (and hiring people with stopwatches to check out the opposition), and *Miami Vice* was cutting a cop show like a pop video. BBC drama took the hint. By 1988, it was possible to drop viewers into a *Doctor Who* story faster, partly because the few people still watching were "on-board", and partly because the script editor tended to use Earth history or the present as a setting – the few alien worlds the McCoy Doctor visited were sketched in with very broad strokes and were allegorised England like as not. (The more formulaic *Star Trek: The Next Generation*, starting at the same time, was considerably slower to begin with, even though it was using a well-established formula from the 60s.)

It is now possible to tell *simple* stories faster, on average, but anything of any depth or nuance takes as long as it ever did. The standard unit of television narrative these days is, after all, the box-set. We'll come back to this in detail later but, for now, it's worth considering that the most rewarding "one-off" single-episode stories of the new series have been ones relying on the audience already knowing half the story when they started. After a point, *Doctor Who* stops making the slightest concession to the viewer whose first episode this might be. Imagine watching "The Magician's Apprentice" (X9.1) as your first-ever exposure to the series – the "shock" revelation of the young boy giving his name as "Davros" might have prompted established viewers to bounce up and down and make small puddles but, as the titles began, newcomers would have been baffled as to what all the fuss was about. Series 10 began with good intentions in that regard, but the cliffhanger to the penultimate episode of the run (X10.11, "World Enough and Time") relied on everyone knowing who the man with the silly beard was, why Missy knew him and why she was so exercised by the spaceship coming from somewhere called "Mondas".

Back in the mists of time (1984), when BBC Video began releasing old stories, the cliffhangers were clumsily removed and in one or two cases the plot was "simplified". There was an hour-long edit of "The Brain of Morbius" (13.5) that retained all the plot "beats" (as those crass textbooks on writing blockbusters call them), but had removed all the reasons anyone would have wanted to watch the story. A genuine "good parts version" would probably skip a lot of the "beats" and be a compilation of scary moments, funny lines and the occasional good set or effect – but of course make a lot less sense. If a change of pace can make a fairly dunderheaded story such as that one worse, imagine what a story that relies on incremental developments and the establishment of a mood, such as "Inferno" (7.4) or "The Seeds of Doom" (13.6), would have been like.

Sometimes, such a process was a revelation: the omnibus repeat of "Planet of the Spiders" was clearer and better-paced, as the jiggery-pokery to make the cliffhangers happen on time was removed and almost all of episode one was trimmed away. It's possible that this was the first story conceived of as being amenable to an omnibus showing: it was directed and largely written by the producer, Barry Letts, and was his penultimate story in charge. The inevitable post-Christmas repeat of a recent story was scheduled for the day before his swan-song: the debut of Tom Baker as the new Doctor. Therefore, configuring the story in such a way as to work (just about) as six episodes leading up to one TV "event" (Pertwee's

continued on Page 155...

He seems utterly terrified [arguably more than we've ever seen him before] when the star-entity possess him, as he realises he might kill everyone on the ship, including Martha, if he can't stop himself. He hasn't explained regeneration to Martha yet. Still, he's working overtime to treat her as a companion this story [perhaps to apologize for dithering over it so long]. He's getting used to her fondness for hugs, and even initiates a non-ironic one himself this time.

After nearly roasting to death, he fancies ice-skating on the mineral lakes of Cuhlhan. [Some sources spell this 'Kul-Ha', which is a bit more Marvel Comics-ish.]

• *Ethics.* At first he tells Captain McDonnell that he doesn't know whether he can restore her husband. After she insists that he not give her false hope, he confirms that there's nothing he can do.

He screams quite a bit at McDonnell for not scanning the star before scooping fuel out of it [Well, that error *did* cause the deaths of most of her crew, and him undergoing intense agony. It's not clear how she should have known about the possibility of a sentient star, yet there's a distinct lack of surprise on the crew's part when they learn of it. This might very well explain why fusion scoops are illegal in the first place.]

• *Inventory: Sonic Screwdriver.* The Doctor once more uses it to give Martha's phone Universal Roaming. [X1.2, "The End of the World," though he seems to have refined the jiggery-pokery since then. It only needs a quick buzz, not opening up the back and fiddling with the SIM card.] He uses it as a medical scanner to diagnose Korwin's body temperature and condition [X1.9, "The Empty Child"; X6.7, "A Good Man Goes to War"].

• *Inventory: Other.* Every time he's trying to read the *Pentallion* computer screens, he whips out the glasses, then whips them off again to emote.

The TARDIS The Doctor lands on the *Pentallion* because the TARDIS had picked up a distress signal. The exterior shell handles temperatures of 3000 plus, with nary a scorch mark.

The Supporting Cast

• *Martha.* She goes wibbley upon realising she's within spitting distance of a star. When there's an opportunity to volunteer [as with X3.4, "Daleks in Manhattan" especially], she takes it. The Doctor here augments Martha's mobile [as with Rose's] to Superphone status that can call the twenty-first century, and gives her a TARDIS key.

Francine is surprised to have three calls from Martha in one day. [This is a complete turnabout from everything we've learned about Martha's relationship with her family so far, although we *might*, in a pinch, interpret this as irritation that Martha's been out of contact for a couple of days.] She's a bit rude to her mum when lives are on the line – her response to Francine's concern upon hearing someone screaming in agony is to hang up her. This isn't like her usual self, at least not to her mum's knowledge. [Given Martha's intended profession, her need to snap orders to nurses in life-threatening crises is probably at odds with the nurturing voice of reason she cultivates for her family.]

Once again, she's keen on physical intimacy under pressure, hugging crewman Riley when it appears they'll both die. She shows signs of being slightly attracted to him, though not enough to want to stay in the era [à la Jo Grant or Sarah Jane Smith continually running into sympathetic supporting blokes and letting them down nicely]. At the end, she scores a rather big snog and tells Riley she's sure he'll find someone to believe in eventually, but eases off when he looks hopefully at her.

• *Francine:* She's not at work on Thursday mid-morning. [So we might imagine that Trevor's still paying for the house. Martha lives elsewhere, as we know, and Leo's got a small child and a flat with his anonymous partner – so either Tish has blagged a lot more well-paid jobs we didn't see, or Francine works shifts doing something incredibly lucrative for four hours a day. There is, of course, one occupation who get a day off work when there's an election – maybe she's a remarkably well-paid primary school teacher and is off because her school's the local polling station. A teacher in 2008 would probably have a better computer, as it's a work expense.]

Planet Notes They're halfway across the universe from Earth, again. [We presume this is an estimate; see also X2.4, "The Girl in the Fireplace".] It's the Torajii system, which is inhabited.

The Non-Humans

• *The Star.* The crew of the SS *Pentallian* have, in essence, stolen some promethean fire from a conscious entity – to whit a star – and that which remains can possess a human who looks at it. An

How Long Should an Episode Be?

continued from Page 153...

departure, not watched by as many people as they hoped) *and* as an hour-long warm-up for another piece of "appointment television" made sense. The main point is that it was nearly unprecedented. *Doctor Who* was made to be watched one episode a week, until 1982, with little or no prospect of re-watching.

Indeed, some younger reviewers trick themselves into thinking that the old stories were "hacked into" half-hour segments, suggesting that they think everyone watched the whole story in one sitting with just the (non-existent) BBC ad breaks. That wasn't an option when the stories were made. There's that constant worry that the viewers might have missed an episode (or never have seen the series), and so a variety of ways in which the story so far is sketched in that, if the whole story is swallowed in one bite, seems a bit wearisome. So is the reprise of the previous episode's ending and the set-up of that week's big finish.

In some weeks, the amount of unrepeated material was fairly small; episode five of "The Mind Robber" (6.2) comes in at 18 minutes and 12 seconds, but the titles and reprise take 48 seconds and the end credits begin at 16:48. That's just over a quarter-hour of new material. "Meglos" (18.2) has 17 minutes in episode four, but covers it by playing the end theme slower. There are obvious differences between these two episodes, but the main one is that "The Mind Robber" has enough incident, changes and sense of escalating crisis for the final phase to warrant a whole episode rather than trimming the earlier ones to make it a four-parter (had such a move been financially possible – see Volumes 1 and 2).

These examples aren't typical, but people who prefer the BBC Wales output point to the amount of *any* old-style episode that is devoted to setting-up or coming out of a cliffhanger. The very term is controversial – the scholars who put together *Doctor Who: The Unfolding Text* (see **The Semiotic Thickness of *What*?** under 24.4, "Dragonfire") wanted everyone to switch to calling episode-endings "suspended enigmas". But the silent-movie terminology tells us something important – namely that the primary purpose is to get people back in front of their tellies for the next episode by any means necessary. Don't imagine for a second that Russell T Davies or Steven Moffat were above such ploys.

What critics of this format claim is that the bulk of an episode is therefore padding between cliffhangers – an accusation that could also apply to "The Name of the Doctor". There is a grain of truth in this in some stories, notably Peter Davison ones and some of the Pertwee UNIT six-parters, but the majority of stories use the end-of-episode phase to make a transition between phases of a story. Pertwee and Davison were both Doctors during the most soap-like phases before the new series, and so the better examples of their cliffhangers are illuminating. Soap cliffhangers, and indeed the progression of story within an episode of a soap, follow a clear logic of who knows what about whom at any stage. It's expected that viewers will keep tabs on who is aware of what within an episode or a longer strand, and why it matters that someone is trying to prevent someone else from finding out.[31]

"Day of the Daleks" (9.1) is very soap-like in this regard, with the three episode-ending-revelations conforming to this pattern almost exactly. (The "shock" that the Daleks are in control in the terrible future is weakened by having a cameo by one earlier and – it so happens – by the story being called "Day of the Daleks", but this is no worse than pre-publicity for a soap making the return of an old character an "event".) We get confirmation, at least, that the Daleks are back and causing trouble in a future whence came guerrillas trying to kill someone in our time; the Doctor sees a Dalek; the Daleks figure out that this "Doctor" is *the* Doctor. Each cliffhanger, as well as putting someone into a precarious situation, changes the rules and moves us into a new situation.

The same is true of "The Green Death" (10.5), but something else is going on there. Each episode moves the relationship between UNIT, Global Chemicals and the Wholeweal Community around a bit. Along the way, the number of supernumerary characters who live or work in Llanfairfach is whittled down. The drama shifts from being recognisably like most 70s television set in contemporary Wales (as episode one is, aside from an interlude on Metebelis III) to something more clearly rhetorical, with a mad computer and soldiers shooting at monsters underlining the urgency of the Doctor's psychedelically-lit debate with Stevens.

Similar generic shifts come with every episode-

continued on Page 157...

afflicted person undergoes a rapid rise in temperature and glows fiercely through the eye-sockets [rather as those infused with Mandragora Energy did – "The Masque of Mandragora"]. Using a blast-helmet, they can keep this hidden and only reveal the energy when infecting or evaporating others. The control this energy has over humans (and a Time Lord) weakens when the host body is chilled.

History

• *Dating.* [Details in later stories make "42" seem contemporary with the Ood saga, meaning it's the forty-second century, though no one actually says so in the script. Apart from being yet another gag on the eponymous number, the decoration and technology aren't that far out from "The Impossible Planet" (right down to the reuse of the Doctor's orange spacesuit, although this was substantially refitted and was actually red now), and the *Pentallion* crew is either all-human or close enough (certainly, someone on the ship was familiar with twentieth-century UK pop music). If it's the same era, Martha's complaints about rebound trips ("Gridlock") are resoundingly justified.]

Wives and husbands taking each other's names is optional in this time period. Fusion scoops are illegal. Deadlock seals might be standard issue even for cheap and nasty ships [or else a handy safeguard for smugglers interested in a massively overcomplicated security system]. The Beatles are counted as "Classical" [see 2.8, "The Chase", yet again].

Martha's phone calls to Francine take place on 'Election Day' back on Earth (a Thursday).

[Actually, why does Francine get the call when she does? The Doctor diddles with Martha's phone at the start of the episode, with the TARDIS in flight, so there's no obvious calibration to her body-clock. How long, therefore, does the Ship think Martha's been a passenger? It can't be using her first time aboard as the datum-point, because she's been to 1599 for at least two days, Five Billion for about eight hours, 1930 for over thirty-six hours and then at least a day in her own flat. If the TARDIS returned her home as long after leaving as it felt like to Martha, they would have missed the election.

[If we take the simplest explanation other than this, that T-zero is when the TARDIS leaves at the end of "The Lazarus Experiment" and that Martha's just changed out of her frock into a cardigan, jeans and vest-top, Francine would be grumbling that her daughter got her out of bed to cheat on a pub-quiz in the small hours. But it's light and we know it's Thursday after 10.00am because the polls are open. Miss Dexter asks if Francine has voted yet, so that puts it somewhere between noon for the question to be valid, and 9.30pm, for it to be possible if she hasn't already cast her ballot. It doesn't look like 9.30pm.

[On the other hand, if we factor in that "The Infinite Quest" is supposed to have taken place between stories (see A5 at the end of this volume), Martha's had a week to ten days of fungus, frost-bite and faeces and the Doctor spent an additional three years on a bird's shoulders at some time before this story starts. Martha's Magic Phone would have had a material impact on the plot of the animated serial, so it must be set before the start of "42". For any of the previous stories to have happened as they did, the TARDIS and/ or the Doctor must be landing at the right time of day for Martha's sleep-cycle to function normally (as normally as a junior doctor in A&E ever does, at least), so went to the Globe at roughly the same time of night as they left Leo's 21st. The alternative is a jet-lagged Martha dozing through entire stories. This must be why the TARDIS landed in her flat in the early daylight hours rather than immediately after they left the previous night. We know it was the previous night because Tish makes a joke about Martha going out two nights in a row.

[Occam's Razor suggests that "The Infinite Quest" could have happened immediately before "The Lazarus Experiment" (despite the dialogue there stating that they've had one trip to the future, one to the past and a detour to New York) and that Martha-time is synched to Francine-time when the ceremonial handover of the phone and key takes place. Alternatively, for the 'Monday' mentioned in the stage-directions of "Smith and Jones" to work, that set of adventures is all within one day of Martha-time, however long it took for the Doctor or Kaw, and the phone was fixed for her on Thursday morning, two days after the TARDIS landed in her front room and Francine range up to tell her Tish had a new job. After giving up her 'heart's desire', Martha caught up with her sleep and explored the TARDIS wardrobe and kitchens then got given a new phone in what felt like mid-morning. There are still some **Things That Don't Make Sense** about these scenes but they can wait.]

How Long Should an Episode Be?

continued from Page 155...

ending of "Terror of the Zygons" (13.1), going from spooky Scottish werewolf tale to Doppelganger/spy conspiracy, then from that to Harryhausen-esque monster-stomping then something more like *The Man from UNCLE*. Each episode "sells" a different component of the story to a casual viewer rather than asking that viewer to accept a lot of implausible developments at once. [Watch the opening of the Peter Cushing *Doctor Who and the Daleks* for what would have happened if they'd tried that in 1963 or 2005. Series 1 made a point of slowly drip-feeding all the aspects of the series to new viewers over the first six weeks. Each new TARDIS regular has to be introduced to us, then to the Doctor's world, then to the Doctor, all in an episode that has a shallow learning-curve (so is probably set in present-day Britain with a relatively minor threat, such as an escaped convict: X3.1, "Smith and Jones", X5.1, "The Eleventh Hour" – shop-dummies or a puddle – X1.1, "Rose", X10.1, "The Pilot"). Then a few more episodes ease us (and the newbie) into the rest of the programme's repertoire. To do it all from scratch in three-quarters of an hour needs absurdly credulous characters, ugly info-dump dialogue or clunky plotting – sometimes all at once: see X5.8, "The Hungry Earth".]

In each of these 70s cases, the process from one episode-ending to the next is what's important. The logic by which we get from A to B is characteristically *Doctor Who* and cannot happen any faster without making the story stupid, the characters stick-figures and the world in which they are working a schematic, one-dimensional place. Sometimes, it's like that anyway, but the caricature Welsh, Scottish or Futuristic Dystopian gestures are made a *bit* more complex and life-like than they could have been, and surely no worse than the travesty of Hooverville we have in "Daleks in Manhattan" (X3.4), for example. In any given episode, they develop the world, the story and the situation as far as it can go before changing one, some or all of these, then the abrupt transition is the cliffhanger that gets us watching what happens next.

Surprisingly, this is the same fundamental decision that made the later two-part BBC Wales stories seem so radical. Once the production team saw that they could move the story on more than just "now get out of that", we started to have the latter half beginning in a new situation that stems from the previous episode's end, but doesn't immediately follow. "Last of the Time Lords" (X3.13) shifts to a post-Toclafane world a year later. It takes five minutes longer than a standard-length episode but, as we will see, some of that was so irrelevant in purely plot terms that it was cut overseas without harm. "Forest of the Dead" (X4.9) pulls a genre-switch on "Silence in the Library" (X4.8), but resolving this to the earlier storyline takes less than the whole length of the latter episode and – to the unsympathetic viewer – results in a final 20 minutes that is barely different from the notorious running-up-and-down-corridors that killed so much time in the early 80s. However fast the edits are, however many shots per minute we get now compared to then, it's the same amount of story per minute in this kind of sequence.

What's missing in many cases is the gap between episodes and the room for the cliffhanger and everything before it to "breathe". We'll elaborate on this point elsewhere in this volume and the next, but a look at the fevered online speculation about the end of "The Stolen Earth" (X4.12) indicated that the pause between transmissions of part of a story makes the communal experience more vivid. (We cover this in **What Were the Strangest Online Theories?** in Volume 9.) This is analogous to what happened between every episode in the 60s and 70s and, to a lesser extent when the broadcast schedule was changed, the 80s. School playgrounds and workplaces were the place where incidents in the episodes took root. Viewers on first broadcast only had a day to get excited about whether the beings abruptly revealed at the end of episode one of "Earthshock" (19.6) really *were* Cybermen, but it still made more impact than if the two episodes that week had been amalgamated (as they were for the unexpected summer repeat). Twenty-five minutes is as long a tease as writers and directors can get away with before viewers get jaded (and for the first episode of a Terry Nation-scripted Dalek story with "Daleks" in the title, the attempt is especially irksome). If that's all you think an episode of *Doctor Who* ought to be, then this is a problem. For most people watching in Britain, it ought to be entertaining on its own terms.

It's not as if Steven Moffat has stuck religiously to the 45-minute format. Davies splurged on Christmas Specials but, in his first year alone.

continued on Page 159...

###

For the rest of the History section, we shall turn our attention to a historical detail which we thought *at first was more explicable, but (it turns out) is actually a quagmire...*

[When the Doctor and Martha are confronted with the trivia question of "Who had the most No. 1s, Elvis or The Beatles?"... well, we can't file the scenario under **Things That Don't Make Sense**, because the ultimate answer of 'Elvis' was logged by a drunken crew-member who, rightly or wrongly, expected *they* would know the answer when the time came. But for anyone wishing to work out the genuine answer to this vexing question... hrm, please note that it's not specified whether we're to go by the charts in the US, the UK, on Draconia or what. Nor do they mention *which* UK chart, American chart or Draconian chart (assuming the Draconians have more than one – maybe females have their own).

[In America, the industry standard for music charts is *Billboard* magazine, which has been publishing Hit Parades since the 1930s. However, they only started keeping track of the Hot 100 (single sales and radio airplay) in 1958, which misses much of Elvis but includes all the Beatles; this means that in the "official" version, the Fabs have more US No. 1's than the King. *Cashbox*, which tallies just sales of bits of plastic (or vinyl, and now downloads) often had completely different figures. Then again, the sales of specific types of music are listed in different charts. By contrast, airplay wasn't logged as part of the UK chart the way *Billboard* did it. (Well, the pirate radio stations – see 5.6, "Fury from the Deep" – did, but they practically ran on payola.)

[So maybe the absent question-setter picked the UK charts and was just talking about vinyl unit-shifters. Err... that's even more complicated. The first UK chart, in November 1952, was a Top Twelve, compiled by someone at the *New Musical Express* taking time out from selling ad space in the mag to phone 50 record shops. In those days, each record shop sold only those recordings and sheet music produced by the company to which it belonged (EMI, Decca, HMV...), so getting a good enough sample while avoiding pluggers working out which stores were being polled was tricky. Three years later, *Record Mirror* launched its own chart, using different shops (as far as anyone knows), and *Melody Maker* another one a year later. They almost tallied, but not quite. *Melody Maker*'s chart polled shops in Northern Ireland, which the others didn't (and Northern Ireland is part of Britain, and gets BBC television and all that).

[When the BBC tried to do music programmes based on sales (because by now the charts were becoming like trainspotting or cricket, something where stats were an extra source of fun), they polled these three, sometimes coming up with a No. 1 that none of the others had (we could explain their reckoning system, but it's really beside the point). Other people compiled their own, including, in 1959, one very dodgy set of figures from a now-forgotten paper called *Record Retailer*. This is the one that the compilers of the *Guinness Book of British Hit Singles* have, bizarrely, used as their baseline before either Gallup or the British Market Research Bureau were called in (the BBC wanted a reliable chart after the week in August 1968, when three records were somehow at No. 1).

[The thing is, depending on which chart you believe, Elvis had a No. 1 or 2 with "Devil in Disguise" and the Beatles with *Please Please Me*. The BBC's chart was itself occasionally wrong, being tampered with by pluggers or, in June 1977, the BBC itself to prevent the Sex Pistols getting to No. 1 with "God Save the Queen" in Jubilee week. So, assuming that the people setting pub-quizzes in the forty-second century are relying on the dodgy *Guinness Book* stats, rather than actual sales, and are thus assuming the UK charts to be the only ones that matter (which is the consensus in most countries in Europe, apparently) and the US charts are too messed-up to be reliable (see **What's Happened to the USA?** under 4.5, "The Moonbase") and that the charts in this universe are the same as in ours despite Kylie, Billie, Cribbins and Doddy going unrecognised... what *is* the right answer?

[Thanks to reissues and pre-releases of singles nobody had yet heard (which plummeted from the charts once they got air-play), Elvis Presley had 17 No. 1s in his lifetime. Add to this five posthumous ones (including the one loitering at the foot of the Top 20 the day he died, "Way Down"). The remix to which the Doctor alludes is Junkie XL's "A Little Less Conversation", which was a No. 1 in 2002. The Beatles had 17 in six years, and might have had one more if the BBC hadn't removed "Real Love" from the playlist after

How Long Should an Episode Be?

continued from Page 157...

Moffat had an opening episode that brandished its running-time in the title (X5.1, "The Eleventh Hour"), a third episode that was conceived of as a 75-minute Bank Holiday special (X5.3, "Victory of the Daleks"), the penultimate episode (X5.12, "The Pandorica Opens") was 50 minutes and then "The Big Bang" (X5.13) was 55 minutes. It wasn't just his own episodes: "Vampires in Venice" (X5.6) was also over-length.

Latterly, excess material has been put online or in box-sets, and the episode-length brought down to what the BBC1 bosses can schedule in between shiny-floor shows. In his previous work, Moffat was a master of pacing everything to work out in 28-minute farces, scrupulously providing all the information needed within the episode, disguised as autonomous jokes. If he chose, or if the episode-length had been set as half an hour, or ten minutes, or an hour, he could have worked with that with just as much – or little – aplomb. Certainly, the protracted exegesis of "Heaven Sent" (X9.11) only really needed ten minutes of screen-time, but the sense of endless repetition was part of the point.

Traditionally, the make-up of the viewing population included a lot of small children and was a cross-section of the public. As we keep having to point out, the original "point" of the series was something everyone could watch *together*. Sustained communal viewing is something that needs short bursts. The BBC doesn't have commercial breaks within programmes and only has "interstitials" (trailers, continuity announcers, reminders of the line-up for the evening) between programmes. The 45-minute format is designed for export to other territories, where there is punctuation inside the narrative, but they seem to have different ideas about which demographic it's intended to serve. (We'll expand on this in **How Does This Play in Pyonyang?** under X4.1, "Partners in Crime", but BBC America's resolute focus on 18-49 year-olds seems perverse to anyone familiar with the British public – while Japan's reaction was, um, interesting.)

Even if the attention-span of the five-year-olds who are the bedrock of *Doctor Who*'s long-term appeal had somehow doubled between 1989 and 2005, the duration of episodes has forced a "shape" on episodes (described by Murray Gold as 20 minutes of set-up, 20 minutes of running and a tag). It's also encouraged incidents to happen roughly where foreign broadcasters (or commercial UK digital stations – UKTV Gold used to re-run the Eccleston episodes while we were waiting for new Tennants) put adverts. If you've watched *Doctor Who* with small children and no adverts (as pretty much everyone in Britain has), you'll observe that the plot is less of a factor than the visual or auditory appeal of what's happening moment-to-moment (see **Does Plot Matter?** under 6.4, "The Krotons"). For the kids (who grow up into committed viewers, or don't), *Doctor Who* isn't so much a story as a "place" you visit once a week; a visit like that is better for being brisk. (Parents of excitable children would far rather have a half-hour a week than get them over-tired and stroppy after a 45-minute sojourn.)

The only reason that 45 minutes became standard is that everyone else was doing it, so BBC Wales could export *Doctor Who* to be used in-between all the US shows the same length. When John Nathan-Turner was thwarted in his ambition to make such an export drive, and had the number of episodes per year halved, he opted instead to make stories as long as they needed to be and as many as he had the resources to make. The three-parters of Sylvester McCoy's term were partly a budgeting exercise, making two stories out of a six-episode production block, but they were also tidier than the four-part ones as narratives. As we saw in Volume 6, the four-part stories of that final year suffered greatly from being too complex and plotty to fit into 25 minutes a week, and needing to be re-edited for video and DVD release.

Four-part stories could be coerced into working as US-style 45 minutes and it has been argued (not entirely convincingly, but by people in the "loop") that opting to make three-part stories killed the series as a commercial venture just as it salvaged the quality of the scripts and production. The three-parters, however, wouldn't have bothered the PBS stations – they either showed *Doctor Who* an episode at a time, or in a story-a-week omnibus that ran to whatever length was required. (6.7, "The War Games", being a staggering ten episodes, got broken into two five-episode chunks. Every other story ran as long as it pleased, with the six and seven-parters gaining a bathroom break – a chance for the network to show in-house promos, with a notice saying "*Doctor Who* will return in a few minutes" – between episodes four and five.) But the three-parters would never have sold

continued on Page 161...

it entered the chart at No. 4.

[So that seems like a slam-dunk, until you ask what "pre-download" means. If it's the BBC's now gold-standard chart, then the use of downloads was tallied with the sales of physical recordings in 2007... but they were permissible as long as a physical copy was also on sale from several years earlier. The first record to get a No. 1 on downloads alone had been *Crazy* by Gnarls Barkley, which dominated the charts during Series 2, i.e. Spring 2006. There had been an industry-regulated download chart since 2003, but not in the BBC's listings. This change was the reason there was a campaign to get Billie Piper's *Honey to the B* back to No. 1 shortly before this episode was first broadcast. (They changed the rules *again* in 2017, after a month where 16 of the top 20 "singles" were tracks from the same Ed Sheeran album.)

[However, other sources tallied downloads for at least ten years before this, so if, *if*, someone setting a pub-quiz on a spaceship in the forty-second century was being specific enough to stipulate "pre-download" in the question and meant "before downloads were included in the charts compiled by The Official UK Chart Company on behalf of the BBC" rather than "before downloads were possible", then the answer is "Elvis Presley". They may, of course, not have known that, being drunk when they set the questions, and their knowledge of "Classical Music" may have been so poor that Elvis Costello was added to Presley's score while Wings, the Plastic Ono Band or George Harrison might have been counted with the Beatles' totals – but let's assume not. So then the biggest question is why Martha didn't know this, what with the Radio 1 chart countdown being presented by that nice Reggie Yates, who looks so much like her brother that it must have been a family joke.]

The Analysis

The Big Picture The clearest way to get a handle on this is to look at the rejected ideas. Chris Chibnall's first idea for the story, once Davies provided the "glowing eyes" and "space-walk" elements, was for this to be a research station that had been examining the star for some time. A precedent for that notion, either or both of the film versions of *Solaris*, provides a lot of the other components too: the unknowable entity being studied responding by probing the scientists' minds; the marriage knocked out of shape by prolonged spells orbiting another world; the cryogenics and the suicide of something that may or may not be married to one of the crew... Stanislaw Lem's original book elegantly satirises the scientists' motives for examining something "alien" merely to find something that reflects themselves back in a flattering light. Andrei Tarkovsky's long, mesmeric film – from 1972 but looking utterly unlike anything made in the West that year – used to get shown on Channel 4 when it was still arty. The Steven Soderberg film, from 2002, was an hour shorter and more about the people than the genuinely inhuman consciousness they try to fathom.

Davies suggested it would take too long to explain what a solar research station does, and they should just jump straight in with the action. Thus the nature of the entity trying to pull the *Icarus* (as it was called then) to its doom is now just another brain-teaser for the Doctor, like Happy Primes. (We could, at a pinch, dignify the idea of a sentient star being tortured for profit by claiming it was derived from Frank Herbert's novel *Whipping Star*, although it's unlikely that anyone involved had read this.) Similarly, production designer Edward Thomas's first thought for the ship's design was to have a barrel-shaped rotating hub to provide artificial gravity. This was trimmed away to save on the studio set-building by just converting a paper-mill into a spaceship as usual. Meanwhile, Chibnall trimmed out an idea that the Doctor would scale the whole outside of the ship to get to a clamp that could apprehend the escape pod, and made the controls be just out of reach on the hull's exterior. Everything was subordinated to the gimmick of the real-time narrative, botched as that was.

Nonetheless, the thinking was that the story's locale, the spaceship, ought to be as real as was affordable without spending ages on explanations. It thus became industrial-looking. The reference for the costume designer was *Alien*, but we can claim first dibs on this, as there were earlier attempts to remove the antiseptic and military look of space-travel right back in *Doctor Who*'s past. The very first spaceship in the series was in "The Sensorites" (1.7), and that was based on a McDonnell-Douglas Dakota. Consider that both "42" and "The Space Pirates" (6.6) can claim to be the first space-story in each iteration of the series to have no conventional monsters. Consider that Robert Holmes's professed starting-point for the

How Long Should an Episode Be?

continued from Page 159...

to a bigger network in that format – presuming there was any serious danger of that happening, and presuming the BBC had been minded to even try back then. The appeals to the Drama department to allow 30-minute episodes for 26.3, "The Curse of Fenric" were rejected, hence the multiple edits doing the rounds and the slightly confusing exegesis in the middle.

The BBC's unaccountable decision to hide Series 8 at 8.30pm after a very unpopular gameshow was offset by some of the most child-friendly episodes we'd seen for a while; repeating the experiment the following year allowed the writers to attempt a more "adult" direction, but we landed up with stories that were also less amenable to being hacked about to include adverts. "Heaven Sent" was at once the least child-friendly episode and the least BBC America-ready (it was eight minutes longer than usual and relied on slow, sustained accretion of details, a process deflated by people yelling about Chevy Malibus or new episodes of *Luther*). Those people who saw it seem, on the whole, to have adored it, but it seems actively to have repelled the general public in both territories. The format fell between two stools. Looked at with hindsight, a lot of 25-minute episodes, especially first parts of stories, seem like exercises in keeping a mood going almost up to breaking-point (e.g. 2.7, "The Space Museum" first episode; 14.3, "The Deadly Assassin" Part Three; 12.2, "The Ark in Space" Part One; 7.4, "Inferno" Episode Six...) Changing gear in mid-episode in a one-part story is a lot harder, so we have had more homogeneous stories (X2.10, "Love & Monsters", "42" and "Heaven Sent" being perhaps the outstanding examples – not perhaps anyone's favourites, but outstanding nonetheless). Some overshoot and try to continue past the natural end of this mood, but if you have adverts before that you can skip this and come away thinking it's well-paced.

Indeed, the overseas distribution has had trouble fitting ad breaks into even episodes written (as much as anything) with these in mind. BBC America puts them in the oddest places, and ruthlessly excises anything that takes the running-length over 42 minutes (this radically improves X4.15, "Planet of the Dead", but devastates X3.0, "The Runaway Bride", for example). It has emerged that "Heaven Sent", with a running time of 53 minutes on BBC1, was scrunched into the BBC America format by the simple procedure of cutting the number of frames-per-second by 5%, taking 57 seconds for every minute on screen on BBC1. Luckily, there wasn't that much dialogue, but what there *was* had been hard enough to follow even at the right speed.

However much Davies took US television as his model, even to the extent of "sweeps" episodes in a country that doesn't do ratings sweeps (X1.6, "Dalek"), the placement of the story-phases to emulate how a US 45-minute (or one-hour, there) is sequenced is imprecise. Watching a rerun on BBC America or Disney XD is often frustrating. The momentum is lost, and they choose to pause almost at random. Even a transmission of the consciously US-friendly "Vengeance on Varos" (22.2) messed up the best cliffhanger of the 1980s by editing it out and pausing the action five minutes later. The black-and-white episodes had recording breaks for the benefit of the cast and set-dressers, but these served as commercial breaks in the hundreds of stations to which these stories were sold. Sydney Newman was aware of the export potential of the series he created, however much the effects and demands on the actors dictated the episode-length. Dennis Spooner spoke of the "dramatic W" where there is a mid-episode peak, and one-story script editor Victor Pemberton was consciously aiming to place breaks in the plot-development for New Zealand (or whoever) to put in station breaks (5.1, "The Tomb of the Cybermen", a story with many other odd features seemingly designed to make it exportable).

The strange irony is that the first 45 minute episode, episode one of "Resurrection of the Daleks" (21.4), is one of the better examples of a four-part Davison story where the three scripted cliffhangers were game-changers. The circumstances that made this story have to be remodelled between completion and transmission needn't detain us, but the immediate impact was to make Season Twenty-Two the first year where in which the episodes were scripted to be that length. The interesting part is that the script editor, Eric Saward, took advantage of the change to do the things that today's viewers think of as padding – delaying the arrival of major characters, investigating the worlds in which the stories take place, giving characters a chance to be more than plot-functions.

continued on Page 163...

latter was imagining a space-faring tramp-steamer set against all the chrome-plated space corps ships. This became the core of the series as it moved into the post-Apollo era, with people treating space travel as a job like any other, and a general assumption that nothing quite works right.

In "Planet of Evil" (13.2), to pluck an example from the air, the focus is less on the power-struggle between the experienced Vishinsky and the ambitious Salamar, and more on the blue-collar workers who schlep the futuristic equipment on and off ship. By the time we get to "Resurrection of the Daleks" (21.4), this is taken so much for granted that it's a surprise to see people in white uniforms that stay white. Of course, the sweaty-woman-in-a-grubby-vest cliché hadn't fully consolidated in 1984 but it was on the way, with *The Terminator* adding Sarah Connor to the growing list of female tough-guys that would include a lot of John Carpenter characters. (As far as Hollywood's version of blue-collar spaceflight is concerned, *Dark Star* was there first; see 18.5, "Warriors' Gate"). By the time Sigourney Weaver appeared in the various *Alien* sequels, the character of Ellen Ripley had become the inspiration for many imitators, to the extent that the casting of Beryl Reid as one such avatar[32] (19.6, "Earthshock") seems perverse now.

The twenty-first century saw a sub-genre of films (parodied by Adam Buxton as *They Crashed From Space There*) with grubby, industrial spaceships run by cynical capitalists, usually just called "The Company", who treat their employees as expendable – see, for example, *Moon*. That spawned a sub-genre of *Doctor Who* stories like the films: X10.5, "Oxygen" is the most recent and least thought-through (see also X6.5-6.6, "The Rebel Flesh"/ "The Almost People" and many more.) "Ripley" is only a letter away from "Riley", but he's the kind of character you'd see in the more recent films. (Incidentally, around the time this episode was written there was a lot of press about 60s folk-fugitive Vashti Bunyan emerging back into the spotlight with *Diamond Day*, recorded decades before but now used in adverts.)

We can cite so many 70s and 80s *Doctor Who* stories in this section for "42", because the entire story derives its form and content from them. We mentioned in the **Things to Notice** that there are overt, knowing allusions to a lot of Tom Baker stories; the one element that is specific to the BBC Wales series is the decision to use a derelict factory as a location, giving them a corridor that is genuinely long enough to run up and down at top whack – as opposed to the stalling needed to make a Davison-era set look bigger while seeming to move around it more rapidly than anyone actually is. That's like something we saw last year (X2.8-2.9, "The Impossible Planet"/ "The Satan Pit") in a story that was itself Hinchcliffe-by-numbers.

Therefore, the most obvious resemblance is to "Planet of Evil", in which a mineral that binds matter and anti-matter is found on a planet supposedly at the edge of the Universe (don't ask how, we did two essays trying to figure that out). By day it's safe, but when night falls an invisible force attacks people, draining their life-essence. The scientist in charge, Sorenson, has developed a concentrated form of this mineral but is imbibing it, and its effects include making his eyes glow. The Doctor says that the forces on this world will not allow any of the material to be taken, so the spaceship is pulled back when it tries to leave, and will crash if they don't remove every trace. But Sorenson's got it in his blood and, when the young, insecure captain attacks him with an ion-charged ray, an army of glowing "anti-men" walk the ship, killing the crew. The Doctor has communicated with the planet's enigmatic resident intelligence, and tries to get all of the mineral back before the ship crashes and/ or the anti-men kill everyone. The glowing eyes effect is one of the better specimens of 70s CSO, but Davies had just seen something like it in *Hex* (see X1.7, "The Long Game"), and put it in the list of things he wanted Chibnall to include in his story. We could also comment on the way a series of locked doors opened by answering questions was used to pad out "Pyramids of Mars" (13.3) and "Death to the Daleks" (11.3), although these were a bit more interesting, visually and conceptually, than a pub quiz.

One thing that marks this story out from these (except maybe "Pyramids") is the way the incidents in what is (probably) the forty-second century have consequences in the early twenty-first. But even that has a sort of precedent in a rejected notion said to have been discussed for the Matt Jones script, with Rose being possessed and chaos being unleashed in the Powell Estate as a result. The means by which this is effected here is by the pub-quiz extended gag. We had a go at explaining

How Long Should an Episode Be?

continued from Page 161...

The fact that he thought of this as an either-or deal is curious. The Hartnell historical stories were primarily about exploring worlds, with the characters – at best – being part and product of those worlds. That was what *Doctor Who* was conceived of as being *for*. The advantage of shorter episodes in the early years was that the episodes were made week-by-week and, even aside from the stress of learning a script in five days and making the episode in one go, the sets could be changed from episode to episode as needed. Once the move to set-by-set production was completed (in the mid-70s), this was no longer imposed on writers and producers. It was, however, a handy way of breaking up a story into phases, so that no one story lacked the things anyone watching thought ought to be there, but no one episode was obliged to have all of it.

That's the most significant difference between then and now. What is thought to be necessary for a weekly episode is everything an old-style story would have had, on a tick-box approach: the reasons for the pretty pictures, stunts, one-liners and effects are very rapidly alluded to, but in the broadest strokes. The paradox is that black-and-white episodes seem to be more filled with incident than modern ones, and events seem more motivated even in the first episode of a four-parter, but we can't in all honestly say that the characterisation of the regulars is any more consistent or nuanced. The difference is, these days we *expect* it to be better, and have the whole sales-pitch of the series on the companions and their "emotional journeys". We've examined some of the inherent risks already (**Are We Touring Theme-Park History?** under X2.7, "The Idiot's Lantern"; **Why Doesn't Anyone Read Any More?** under X1.7, "The Long Game"), but compared to other series that tried to do everything in under an hour, *Doctor Who* Welsh-style comes off rather well. The formulaic nature of any television designed to tell a story in that short a time, with so many "necessary" items, isn't any different now than it was when "segments" of US television were made to be shown in any order. Anyone who gripes about the colour episodes of *The Avengers* being a string of set-pieces and always the same plot every week has to accept that this is what *Doctor Who* has become.

What's different *now*, and has changed even since "Rose" (X1.1), is the idea of television narrative being made for both week-by-week and box-set-binge viewers. When we look at the differences between Davies and Moffat, the extent to which communal "appointment" television in a family and a new approach – split between delayed-action individual immersive viewings and online comment during the thing's initial broadcast – is as abrupt and fierce as the alleged chasm between 25-minute and 45-minute episodes (see **Appointment Television?** under X4.14, "The Next Doctor"). If the end of an episode doesn't answer a question, it's because it's part of a bigger story that might not be finished by the end of the series. Episodes are more self-contained by becoming less self-contained.

The problem there is that, in order to show one episode a week and not have it annoy more viewers than it pleases, the stories must have all the relevant information for the end of that episode to make sense inside that very episode *but not the solution to the longer-term riddles*. If these plotlines are why a viewer has specifically tuned in, well and good, but the British Public, who've been paying for all of this whether or not they watch other "cult" shows, may have other reasons for watching (see **Stunt Casting: What Are the Dos and Don'ts?** under X2.2, "Tooth and Claw" for one aspect of the pre-publicity) and deserve more.

Most of the time, to be fair, they get it – but we can end up with episodes where the ostensible story seems like killing time between the hints of the wider storyline (e.g. X1.7, "The Long Game"; X3.6, "The Lazarus Experiment"; X7.8, "The Rings of Akhaten") and casual viewers, whose millions make up the ratings that justify all of this now, feel short-changed. And yet, BBC Wales's research indicates that only one viewer in ten now watches religiously week after week. Killing time in an effects-led show is a bigger problem than in almost any other kind of drama, and when the costly (if cheap-looking) digital and prosthetic effects in "The Rings of Akhaten" were make-weights for the low-rent story of how Clara's parents met, the justification for taking up 45 minutes trying to do both is hard to see.

Neither does that episode feel "story-shaped". Without getting into the murky realm of Griemas, the Russian Formalists or Lacanian film-theory (nor yet the Scott-Meredith formula of the 30s pulps), the movement of a plot towards a sort of

continued on Page 165...

this in the notes for "Love & Monsters" (X2.10), but it's worth noting how many of the common reactions of these are here, the "how are we supposed to know that?" accompanying something familiar to us but not to them, the condemnation of anyone using a mobile to cheat and the way something someone finds ridiculously easy is impenetrable to others even when explained.

The main thing everyone knows about this story's origins, though, is that the gimmick of using the countdown to a disaster (see **Things That Don't Make Sense** for our thoughts on the precise nature of the catastrophe) is a nod to the US series *24*. That had a clock running through each episode, to the bemusement of BBC viewers who saw it jump when an ad break was skipped and a supposed hour-long episode lasted, well, 42 minutes. Chibnall knew the series well enough to get James Moran (X4.2, "The Fires of Pompeii") to write a *Torchwood* episode, "Sleeper", that had Captain Jack suddenly turn into Jack Bauer. Once this format had been decided on, everything else was subordinated to it.

Oh, Isn't That...?

• *Michelle Collins* (Captain Kath McDonnell) was Cindy off *EastEnders*, or Stella from *Coronation Street* (depending on your taste in soaps). In between these two roles, she was one of those ex-soap stars whose name was enough to get any drama made, so there was a period when anything on ITV1 that wasn't a soap had her in it, unless it was something with Ross Kemp or Sarah Lancashire ("Partners in Crime") or Martine McCutcheon. Collins had been Cindy Beale, whose desperation to get away from her tedious husband Ian, the chip-shop magnate, led her to hire gunmen and flee to Spain. Or Italy. Or something... (The plotlines in this phase of the series drove a lot of casual viewers away, so we can't find anyone who remembers it clearly and can't be bothered to investigate. Or rather, we could before we looked, but reading just the first few pages of the Wikipedia entry made our eyes glaze over.) Anyway, she'd had the title role in *The Illustrated Mum* and been in an episode of *Sea of Souls* (the latter produced by Phil Collinson, who took over *Coronation Street* and cast her as Stella).

• *Elise du Toit* (Miss Dexter, Saxon's security agent) was a graduate of *Hollyoaks* and *Dalziel and Pascoe*, but has been around a lot since, including as M's assistant in *Skyfall*.

English Lessons

• *Mobile* (n). It's a mobile phone but, in the UK at least, not necessarily on a cell system as in the US – so we've not taken to the term "cell-phone". Neither do we pronounce it like the place in Alabama.

• *Universal Roaming* (n.): the ability to use a phone on a number of networks, including abroad. This didn't use to be standard, so it was a big sales-pitch once mobiles and "beginner" tariffs were almost at saturation for the UK market.

• *Pub Quiz* (n): a specific type of trivia contest, played in teams but, more generically, what people now call any kind of trivia quiz (regardless of venue or time of day). If it had actually been in a pub, as was more likely in 2008, this would be a weird time for Francine to have received the call and be asked if she'd voted.

• *Go on, my son* (sl.): what people say when a long kick looks like reaching the goal unimpeded; by extension what people say to encourage inanimate objects.

Maths Lesson

• *Sierpinsky Sequence* (n.): Riley's bid to lock Ashton out of the escape-pod controls uses a pattern of prime numbers. We could transcribe the technical definition(s), but explaining that would take a while. (It's the same Sierpinsky who devised that perforated triangle-made-of-triangles you used to see in textbooks about Fractals.) Thing is, there are three possible sequences of numbers this guy defined and categorised and the second is of what's called "composite" numbers. (The smallest currently proven is 78,557 – huge amounts of software have been devoted to finding one smaller than this that can be proved to satisfy the criteria.) This is, in our world, postgrad stuff. We therefore have to ask why Riley could do this off the top of his head and not know what a Happy Prime was.

Things That Don't Make Sense *Paging Dr Science, Paging Dr Science...*

As the Doctor asks, it's 42 minutes until... what, exactly? The Captain says that's when the ship's going to crash into the sun, but they're *already inside the sun*. The precise boundaries of hydrogen plasma can't be drawn. What everyone's looking at, the big orange swirly ball, is the photosphere, which is visible but less hot than the area outside it, the chromosphere, and that's a lot less hot than the almost invisible layer outside, the corona,

How Long Should an Episode Be?

continued from Page 163...

equilibrium usually follows a four-stage process of problem, complications, crisis and resolution. There are more than practical reasons why four-part stories seemed right to many viewers, even if the third episode was often fairly static plot-wise but had all the memorable moments that weren't cliffhangers. The BBC Wales solution leaned toward the first of these stages being the pre-credits, then... well, many stories moved the timing of transitions around, leading to episodes where the amount of screen-time given to each was noticeably different. They also had the post-match material assume equal or greater significance, so that the "end" of (to pick an obvious example) "Tooth and Claw" comes long before the episode concludes, because all the "arc" stuff about Queen Victoria setting up Torchwood has to come afterwards. (See also **What's a "Story" Now?** under X1.13a, "Pudsey Cutaway".)

If watched one episode a week, older-format stories are more varied, atmospheric and amenable to being discussed in the intervening days than newer ones. If watched a series at a time, the newer ones are more likely to benefit than older ones (if anyone has time and inclination to watch all 39 extant episodes of Season Six in a sitting, they deserve all they get). Indeed, the reception Series 7 (the one that starts with "Asylum of the Daleks" in September 2012 – or, arguably, "The Doctor, the Widow and the Wardrobe" nine months before that – and ends with "The Time of the Doctor" a whopping 15 months later) had from seasoned fans and the Licence-Fee-paying public indicates that watching a week at a time (even without a nine-month gap between the first two episodes, then four months between episodes six and seven, then four months again) was frustration. People like incremental story-telling. Ever since Scheherezade, audiences respond better to teasing than to "Spoilers". If the series reverted to 25 minutes, using the skills (and audience competence) of today, there would be complaints but the majority of the public wouldn't object.

One casualty of the move to one-episode stories has been the Doctor's ingenious escapes from prison-cells. To hear the new-series showrunners talk, you would think that the whole process of locking the Doctor up was merely to kill time until the scheduled cliffhanger, as if he and he alone makes plot happen. The sonic screwdriver and the psychic paper serve to avoid such sequences, but these bits were an integral part of the storytelling. Literally, in some cases (as this was where anyone who'd missed an episode got a conversation explaining the story so far), but it was a handy method of demonstrating Our Heroes' bravery and cleverness in getting out of situations we could identify with. Sometimes, admittedly, it got silly, as with the overpowering of a Primitive with naff conjuring tricks and Venusian Aikido (8.4, "Colony in Space"), but as such it was part of making each episode have a bit of everything you'd want in a *Doctor Who* episode. Any episode might have been someone's first.

The procrustean 45-minute format is a commercial decision rather than being in any way artistically or logistically determined. The economic arguments behind many of the strange decisions about the scheduling of Series 6 and 7 would have been unnecessary had these stories each been shown in pairs of 25-minute parts rather than one 45-minute lump, as there would have been enough time between shooting and broadcast to do all of the effects and slide into a new financial year, making the on-screen exposure prolonged and sustainable rather than the quick bursts we got.

With the interest in online catch-up services (as a means to bolster ratings as much as anything else), this would have been a genuine success rather than a damage-limitation exercise. If at some point the Netflix/ HBO model of television distribution becomes the industry standard, and everyone makes half-hours or two-hours or some other currently unwieldy and unsellable length, *Doctor Who* will adapt and a new generation will wonder how anyone had the patience to watch 45 minutes where not much happens, and the characters are stick-figures by whatever standard is by then applied. For the majority of the BBC Wales era to date, the arbitrary imposition of this episode-length, however much it appeals to people used to it, has led to a lot of stories that fell between two stools – either too long or too short for it. It has also led to an emphasis on precisely the "boring" elements that seemed to get in the way of what viewers in the 60s and 70s watched *Doctor Who* to get – sidelining of all the fun, flavour and atmosphere that made the ritual of tuning in on Saturday teatime more potent than anything any one episode could contain.

(We're going to come back to this from another angle in three episodes' time: see X3.10, "Blink".)

which is where the spaceship is already frying. So they should already be vapour, if they're ever going to be. The plasma and radiation extends beyond that layer, growing steadily thinner but not ever really ending with a precise physical cut-off point. (Using our own sun as an example for the moment, there is an agreed "end" of magnetic force and ionised particles, the heliopause, but that's a hundred times further from the Sun than Earth is – *Voyager 2* hasn't got there yet, despite being launched around the time of 15.1, "Horror of Fang Rock".) Moreover, the corona isn't a nice regular sphere, but a constantly-changing irregular zone – like a splash happening in three dimensions for billions of years. So the *Pentallion* is 42 minutes away from phasing out of the very hot bit into a visible but less-hot layer.

How hot? Well, let's take the visual evidence at face value and assume that, like the majority of stars we know about, this is a red dwarf: slightly smaller and less vicious than our sun, but still pretty mean. This makes the temperature of the photosphere a mere 4125 degrees Kelvin, on average, compared to a toasty 6000 or thereabouts for Sol. Our sun's corona is anything up to two million K. The corona of a K-class star, as far as anyone can tell, only one and three quarter million. (Kelvin? You probably learned this in school, but to refresh your memory – it's a scale in units identical to degrees Celsius, but starting at Absolute Zero, so just subtract 273-and-a-bit from the number to get the temperature in Centigrade. K-class stars are the next-down on the Hertzsprung-Russell classification from G-class, which is our sun's category. That's like being able to identify English regional accents as basic Fan-lore.)

Just suppose, for the sake of argument, that this star's oddness (being intelligent and able to possess humans and that) means that the photosphere is hot and nothing outside it is. It's still basically plasma: hydrogen fusing inside magnetic fields can be considered a gas. How do you "collide" with a gas even if you've not evaporated on the way in? How do you measure the time before your ship "smashes" into it so precisely? How does the increase in temperature that will be what wrecks the ship not kill you long before then? (And we presume that casual viewers will have noted that the production team doesn't take the "42" countdown all that seriously, aside from chucking in the timer every so often when they think a scene's over-running or about to have a conversation about the wonky logic.)

And to be clear... this isn't just science pedantry for its own sake (enjoyable as that is). There's just been a story a couple of episodes back where the Daleks were rather relying on the Earth being inside the heliopause to power their experiments. Two years ago, there was a story about the Sun going nova (X1.2, "The End of the World"). Chris Chibnall is enough of a fan to pick up lore from the old series and pilfer plots and spaceship-names from Hinchcliffe, so the fact that there's an episode of "The Daleks' Master Plan" (3.4) called "Coronas of the Sun" – a title that made generations of kids look up what that meant – might have been a clue. Stars are different from planets and positing the whole sales-pitch of the story – up to the title and arbitrary deadline – on an idea that a star is a solid sphere is asking for trouble. This is hardly obscure or arcane knowledge (we had a look around online: the *Old Farmer's Almanac for Kids* has the basics Chibnall lacks, albeit in Fahrenheit.) When your science is wonkier than that of Dennis Spooner, who wrote for *Fireball XL5*, it's time to rethink your career. When even Russell T Davies has written a story with more accurate solar science, we wonder why Pip and Jane Baker weren't giving this episode a good kicking.

Moreover, once they've ejected their fuel and stopped being pulled into the sun, the crisis is over... somehow. And they can overcome the gravitational pull of a star even when they're right next to it. With no fuel. And at least 40 minutes'-worth of momentum in the other direction, towards a body which, as basic Newtonian physics suggests, gets more gravitationally-attractive the closer you get. (Even if they weren't about to "crash" into a star, they've been accelerating rapidly for over half an hour and then they slam on the brakes and start to reverse, which takes energy. This time, not even the explanation in a cut scene can save them.) Once the sparkly orange fairy-dust of doom is jettisoned, not only does the ship stop heading towards the star, but all that temperature-increase stops and everyone's comfy again. All that magnetic flux hasn't trashed the ship's controls, neither has the heat affected the metal buttons and knobs (even on the outside – don't imagine we've forgotten that). No, the ejection of the fuel and the captain makes the sun seemingly just... go away. When *Thunderbirds* did an episode with the same premise ("Sun Probe"), it was more accurate than this.

This star's attractive force is entirely by the magical power of the intelligent plasma inside the ship, and nothing to do with it having a mass about 30 million times that of Earth. That's handy, because it means that you can pull back an escape capsule just by switching on a magnet (of course, stars have colossal magnetic force too, but Dr Science is now curled up in a foetal position under our desk). Less handy, the spaceship seems to have been designed specifically to make everyone's lives *stupidly* difficult. The controls for the escape-pod over-ride being on the outside of the ship *ju-u-ust* beyond reach of a human(oid) arm is only the start. Since the ship apparently consists of engines at two ends and a long corridor with 29 doors in the middle, it's hard to tell where they put the cargo. Maybe there was an idea that the core of the ship was to have containers attached, as appears to be the case with Briggs's ship in "Earthshock". If so, from what we can see, there isn't any cargo attached.

Every shot of the *Pentallian* approaching the star has it spinning on its lateral axis, *except* when it decides to eject a pod in a nice straight line to the star, and then when the Doctor needs it to hold still for a bit to pull that pod back in an equally straight line, both operations taking a lot longer than expected even if it that bit of the ship just happened to be pointed the right way. It's also improbable that the escape pod launch procedure is quite that protracted when everything else seems to lack sensible safeguards.

How do these stasis chambers supercool or heat anything when they're non-enclosed? The Doctor's covered in frost, while Martha isn't even shivering or wishing she'd kept her cardy on. Three feet of air isn't that good an insulator. (One has to wonder the purpose of such a device under normal circumstances. Perhaps cryogenic suspension to save on the food bills. Or maybe they grow more peas in their hydroponics section than they can eat.) It supposedly freezes things to Absolute Zero, despite the effect this would have of making the ship cease to exist. Martha not only avoids sticking to the metal when her exposed skin touches it, but burning herself on all the other exposed metal she encounters and clings to in the very hot spaceship. Captain Cathy, like Martha, is wearing a vest-top – and yet with bare arms she manages to manhandle Ashton into the fridge and set it for Absolute Zero, which is even more alarming in this context than it would normally be. However, in doing that, she puts her own arm in with no ill-effects and her breath doesn't even mist. If this odd containment were to cut out, they could easily survive in the star's heart just by switching up the air-con, at least until all matter dissipates as a side-effect of the energy-drain at -273 Celsius. (Dr Science is back, after we threatened to make him watch X7.8, "The Rings of Akhaten".)

The vent chamber is a room on a ship that has breathable air until the heat-systems kick in, at which point the temperature increases 3000 degrees in about 30 seconds. What does it do and how does it work? With the use of an illegal fusion scoop and generally cheap and shoddy equipment (there's no independent medical generator?), Riley's concern that the Doctor and Martha might be police, and the way that the crew don't even know how to work their own ship, it's almost too tempting to think that the entire crew is in on a smuggling scam that they never get round to mentioning. Then again, they hardly seem competent enough to pull that off (though it would lend all the "we have no secrets from each other" dialogue piquancy).

And now back to more mundane silliness...

The Doctor wastes valuable time and energy repeatedly shouting "I WILL SAVE YOU!!" to Martha as she plummets ever so slowly into the Sun. She's got a phone. He's got a phone. Both phones carry signals through time and space, and we know that solar flares aren't a problem, since Martha calls her mother in the twenty-first century. Even if he hasn't got his phone on him, somehow, he's got the ship's comms and a screwdriver. Instead, we have the whole palaver with the external controls. Ah well. Apart from anything else, the problems we had last time he put a spacesuit on remains: why is it still baggy on him when the air's been pumped out, and why can we see his face – and some lightbulbs to make sure we can – when he's stepping out into face-frying sunlight? Real astronauts have sun-visors for exactly this reason.

At least Martha can make phone calls, since she's not trying to operate teeny-tiny keys while wearing hefty gloves. Ashton's not so fortunate. Even if they get the right answers to the trivia questions, they'd run out of time. Francine has an old laptop that needs a separate mouse, but this isn't plugged in even though the machine's on. Come to think of it, is her mum the only person capable of using Google in Martha's entire social circle? Why not call someone who is presumably more savvy about such things, such as her brother Leo? Or Tish, who's just lost her job and might need a call anyway?

[NB: younger readers, please accept that when the story was made, in 2006, Martha's Nokia was top-of-the-range. She couldn't have googled the answer for herself even if she could type on that tiny keyboard. She certainly wouldn't have been able to access the ship's computers, because the whole trivia contest is a security measure. Remember, Rose's mobile only acts like a current model in an Evil Parallel Universe where Cybus Industries has pre-empted Android by at least five years. Of course, the Doctor could have slipped Martha a later model and rigged it to work on the mobile networks of her own time before 3G was established even in Britain, let alone the rest of the world. Then he'd have to explain about swiping left or right, what apps are and so on. We're still in The Land Before Samsung, but it's weird that a doctor from 2008 doesn't have a Blackberry. Even if Martha could jump from phoning a friend to looking it up online from her own time, would her phone only have given her internet material from the day she left Earth?]

We expended a lot of thought in *Dating* about why Francine picks up the call when she does rather than several weeks after the election – and about what the correct answer to the Elvis/ Beatles question ought to be. We still have to wonder why Francine thought that Martha had skipped out of hospital to take part in a pub-quiz in what's probably the early afternoon (it's notionally possible and gets more likely if she's using "pub quiz" as the generic term for trivia challenges it has become) and why she's home from work on election day and not doing anything but the real puzzle is... where's Tish? She was unemployed on Monday, apparently, and her boss died the previous night after trying to eat/ seduce her, in such a way that the whole company she was working for has had to close down. If she's not too traumatised to do anything (in which case she'd be at home), she'd be all over the media; as PR for this disastrous company, she's the last woman standing and the public face of the debacle. You'd think that would have come up in the conversation. Alternatively, she might be getting interviewed by the Saxon campaign for her next new job tomorrow morning. That would have been worthy of a comment too. Either way, she hasn't had time to move out so Francine would know all about it.

Scannell, the only vaguely sensible crewmember, is right that we don't know how the infection spreads. In any four-parter (like the ones this wants to be; see the accompanying essay), there'd have been a scene where crewman Korwin stares out the window and has an odd moment before breaking down entirely ten minutes later... but since we don't see this happen, it's difficult to understand what aspect of the star's mode of possession leads it to sometimes kill crewmembers rather than infecting them. The obvious thing for malignant light to do, when separated from Martha and Riley, is look at them through a window and infect them, rather than – inexplicably – launch them away in an escape pod. If the ship is still this close to the star, the crew can't have taken the fuel on board that long ago, so why hasn't someone besides the Doctor deduced that the fuel is the source of all the problems?

The star's motives aren't too clear, either. (How often does one get to write a sentence like that?) It's clearly unhappy about having bits of itself taken away and used as fuel, but you might think that a sentient star would have the wherewithal to attack the ship much more directly – say, by shooting big solar flares at it. Even if it does want revenge, guilt-tripping the captain is an oddly human method of going about it. Why not just issue an ultimatum first? Telling people they've pilfered part of a conscious star and broiling a non-essential item as proof of ability ought to have done it.

So our homicidal star decides not to kill the Doctor after the fuel tanks are emptied – even though it was killing everyone on board regardless of their connection with engineering. Nice for the Doctor and Martha, not so good for the rest of the crew.

But the really obvious is: with all of Russell T Davies's contacts in the media, and The Mill's knowledge of the special effects for any film in production, and Andy Pryor's feelers in the casting world (and the same production block as this featuring Chipo Chung in X3.11, "Utopia"), how did anyone involved in this production not know that Danny Boyle had been making *Sunshine* since 2004, and that it would be coming out days before this episode's expected transmission date?

Critique It begins with the TARDIS locking onto a distress signal, just like "Planet of Evil" or "The Invisible Enemy". They land up on a grungy spaceship where one of the small crew is infected with something that will start picking off the others, just like *Alien*. Most of the rest of the episode is between these two poles. In place of the white Formica and brushed nylon leisurewear of Tom Baker-era spaceships, we have oil and singlets like aboard the *Nostromo*, but the story is 70s vintage *Who* in almost every other respect.

Almost, because they use the new series' obsession with mobile phones to get Martha and her mum arguing in the midst of this. It's not quite played for laughs. The film-look video and rapid editing make what is quite a talky episode seem to skip along like an action movie, but a lot of that is in the scripting as well. What's interesting about the pub-quiz sequence is that it's happening in four places and two centuries. This is a methodology of television writing that wasn't really available to scriptwriters in the 1970s. (The nearest example within a BBC context is when writer and director are liaising on a film or – very rarely – are the same person. 11.5, "Planet of the Spiders" is as near as we see in *Doctor Who* of that vintage.)

If we consult that *vade mecum* of the trade, *Writing for Television in the 1970's* by Malcolm Hulke, we'll see a lot of sound reasons why this wasn't practical and stacks of handy hints on how to avoid having to do it. Even when they started making series entirely on film (the BBC eventually following Euston Films' lead with *Target*, for which see Volume 4), the writing wasn't as supple and scenes tended to be longer however rapidly-edited they were afterwards. You can date an episode of any long-running series to within 18 months with a bit of practice, and spot the vintage of almost anything made before 1998. However much a fan-cum-screenwriter might be (to put it politely) working in the traditions of the old series, it's impossible now to write exactly like they did then. As we will see in Series 7, Chris Chibnall and Mark Gatiss develop ways to bring their own voices to the fore while writing stories even more indebted to the past than their first two attempts each. The acceleration of the storytelling means that they don't try to sell the premise to new viewers, but get on with the plot – as if it's obvious that as they're in a spaceship in trouble, there *must* be an infected human sabotaging the engines and killing the crew, because that's how things work.

There's even something a little 70s about Martha's relationship with crewman Riley. The story ends with both of them assuming that they won't see each other again. But the new series doesn't have that fitted as standard. Granted, it's nice that Martha gets a whole episode not mooning over the Doctor or listening to comments about how Rose would have done it differently. Instead, Martha's mainly written as a combination of Jo Grant (romancing a cute guy she'll dump at the end, because she has to get back to work in a different century) and Sarah Jane Smith (somehow knowing how all this future tech works at a glance – see "Planet of Evil" in particular). Offsetting this refreshing change is three calls to her mum (not Tish, asking whether she still has a job; not Leo, checking on his concussion; just Francine even though Martha knows how each conversation will go and can't get her mum to accept that working in a hospital means people she's not introduced to the family and the occasional offstage scream). It's a stark contrast to all the orange and metal and sweat and running that Francine gets to sit down in a kitchen, but it comes close to killing the momentum of the episode, which is its primary asset. Once you've decided to do a race-against-time in a spaceship, Graeme Harper is the obvious director for the job.

One day, the range of regional English accents in the cast will date it as much as the relative homogeneity of accents in a 70s episode does now. (It sounds, from that perspective, like an entire crew of the "comedy" underlings in the Television Centre version of spaceflight.) For some UK viewers, having Cindy Beale as a spaceship captain is less plausible than a talking star and a ship "colliding" with it at a definite point. However, if you can ignore Michelle Collins's past life, there's nothing anyone in the cast does to put a foot wrong. William Ash's pronunciation of "Bee-attles" makes this far-future world more remote than any holo-projectors or teleports would have (it's an old joke, one used in *Help!* and a Victoria Wood sketch about posh idiots playing *Trivial Pursuit*, but it does the job).

A big advantage it has over last year's trip to this era is that the characters are given to us and only *then* sketched in, rather than a laborious process of introductions and trying to make us care about the obviously doomed ones. This script lacks even time for the time-saving info-dumps and relies on the dialogue and acting to make the people and their relationships solid. Compare Erina to Scooti

("The Impossible Planet") and the difference is clear: we haven't got any "poor Erina she was so young and cute and a mascot to us and so indispensable, why did she have to die, *why her?*" faffing about, just a brief exposure to her, Ashton asking her for things, her grumbling, her death, Ashton wondering where she is as he is himself attacked, the discovery of her death and shock. We're not ordered to feel for her, just left to, after Rebecca Oldfield made one brief impression and Erina's death another. Chibnall and Graeme Harper trust us in ways that Matt Jones and James Strong didn't entirely. That's also more like a Tom Baker story than a normal BBC Wales one.

There's one thing decidedly not-70s about the deaths; the first two people attacked by Korwin are young women, who are killed, then Ashton gets converted. That wouldn't have happened even in the late 80s, even if the crew had been mixed (unless it's an "everybody dies" story). Moreover, although the episode is in distinct phases, it's hard to assign episode-numbers the way one can to many other stories in this phase; the Doctor being infected might have been a cliff-hanger, as might the pod being jettisoned, but they almost overlap and most other significant developments are incremental. Most one-episode BBC Wales stories, supposedly, are 20 minutes of set-up followed by 25 minutes of running. This one begins with the running and then moves outward. Oddly, this makes it look as if they stop caring that the ship's about to "collide" with a star, once they realise there's an alien infestation.

The sequence where the Doctor has to go *outside* to use the spaceship controls is where this sag begins – apart from the sheer stupidity of it, this looks as if they've lost faith in the story's premise and its ability to keep the audience hooked. Yes, the Doctor becoming infected allows a scene where he depends on Martha, but it's not as if she hadn't got anything to do before then – Scannell can suddenly be spared once she's doing medbay duties, which makes it look as if one of them was idle before that. We don't get any more of the pub-quiz stuff once they have drained it of any reason for Martha to be doing it. The speed with which the crew reach the control room in the second half reveals how contrived the first half really was. As with the last episode of "Pyramids of Mars", this is an author playing for time.

Unlike that sequence, though, this doesn't look quite so cramped and studio-bound. With all the derelict factories they've been changing into alien labs or space bases, it's starting to look a bit samey (and will get worse in the 2010s), but this is probably the definitive version.

The Lore

Written by Chris Chibnall. Directed by Graeme Harper. Viewing figures: (BBC1) 7.9 million, (BBC3 repeats) 0.9 and 0.3 million. AIs at 85% for BBC1, but BBC3's less-picky viewers gave it 89%.

Repeats and Overseas Promotion We've mentioned that France called it *Brûle Avec Moi*; Germany stuck with *42*.

Production

After a long spell toiling in the routine police procedural dramas that keep so many actors and writers in work, Chris Chibnall had scored a job on *Born and Bred* (produced by Phil Collinson – see X1.6, "Dalek") and was lead writer on the first two series of *Torchwood*. He had also completed scripts for *Life on Mars*, the 70s-set cop show (see X2.11, "Fear Her" and X3.11, "Utopia").

However, as we imagine you probably knew, his earliest brush with TV was on a live daytime discussion show, *Open Air*, where he and his young chums from the Merseyside Local Group of the *Doctor Who* Appreciation Society slagged off Pip and Jane Baker to their faces (see 23.4, "The Ultimate Foe"). Their comments on his subsequent career are not recorded. (Fandom, however, recalls his review of 23.3, "Terror of the Vervoids" in *MLG Megazine*, where he berated the Bakers for an unchallenging story consisting entirely of running up and down corridors in a spaceship being chased by silly monsters.)

• Chibnall wrote much of "42" with his torso in plaster after a fall downstairs. His script-conferences were mainly by phone. His original brief had been to have a spaceship, a space-walk, the sun and someone with glowing eyes, but it was strongly suggested that he could take the story of "The Impossible Planet"/ "The Satan Pit" on another stage and show Ida and Zack on a planet, probably encountering the Ood (see also X4.3, "Planet of the Ood"). Many of the team were keen to have Claire Rushbrook back as Ida Scott (hence, perhaps, Rushbrook's appearance in the *Weakest Link* special recorded shortly after this).

One early idea was that the setting should be a base studying the star, and that the occupants had been there since birth. Davies eventually admitted that they couldn't afford that, so Chibnall was asked to write a story just in a spaceship with corridors and no aliens.

• It was tacitly agreed that the ship's look should be consonant with that of "The Impossible Planet" and set in the same time-period. (Another reason for the "42" being that it was the forty-second century – for a brief while, it was thought that the pods might be smuggled Ood; this went by the board, but the idea of conveying them in containers took hold when they came back.) The time-limit gimmick came very early on – partly as a hook to differentiate this from other episodes, but also as a spur for the author. Korwin was named after a friend of Chibnall's, Riley's original surname was "Kincaide", as in Chibnall's godson (but then Davies used it for X3.3, "Gridlock"), and Ashton's original name, "Motta", sounded confusingly similar to "Martha".

The sequence with Francine and the Sinister Woman was finalised later than the rest, when the storyline had been resolved. The spacewalk, and possible zero-G sequences, were curtailed to opening a door so that the Doctor could pull a lever. The "Peony" system looked good on paper, but when said aloud was too much like "penis", so became Toraji. After supervising *Torchwood* Series 1, Chibnall was fairly punch-drunk but managed the whole script – rewrites and all – in six weeks, as long as he would usually take on a draft. This was fortunate, as the production schedule was revised at short notice and this story was made earlier than expected.

• One design idea was that the ship would have a drum to provide gravity, making it look like a concrete-mixer (as per *Babylon 5*). With the story's evolution from SF to generic action, the design of the SS *Icarus* (still called that until well into the shoot, hence a few redubbed lines and a cut where Martha thinks the people who named her ought to have known what would happen) became more linear and industrial. Early ideas that the ship's gravity would shift and the passage to the auxiliary control room would be a climb were abandoned, so that the bulk of the episode could be made in abandoned factories (just for a change). The designers made sure as much orange and yellow was used in the built sets and redressed locations as possible, and that the two blended seamlessly. The computer model's basic look was worked out in time for the graphics and set departments to devise on-board diagrams of the layout.

• The mighty Graeme Harper had been given Block 7. Since his four-episode marathon last year, Harper had worked on the new BBC *Robin Hood* and was even more in-demand than before. This block was composed of "42" and "Utopia", and started work Monday, 15th January, on what was scheduled to be the first week after the end of Block 6. (In fact, it wasn't, largely because bad weather and David Tennant's voice problems had held up Palmer's production a few days.) There had been a good deal of uncertainty as to the production order, but Derek Jacobi's schedule eventually called for "42" to be shot first. Thus the cast, crew and location had to be assembled and prepared in a week, including construction of the ship components to be taken to the location and made to look as if they belonged there. Tennant, still with throat-lurgy from Hooverville, skipped the read-through and was replaced by Gary Russell.

• The shoot began on Monday, 15th January. Tennant was back, his voice fortunately recovered, and Harper's first order of business was the Upper Boat TARDIS scenes for both "Utopia" and "42", except for the Master's regeneration. After that they began work on the escape pod sequence. A trial run with make-up to make Agyeman look hot brought her out in a rash, so a more orthodox blusher was used thereafter. The spacesuit Tennant wore was indeed the one from "The Satan Pit", but with a modified collar for ease of use and re-dyed red (although in all the orange lighting, this doesn't show). A large fan (the sort that increases air velocity, not the sort that amasses DVDs and such) simulated solar-storm activity. The tight shot conceals how close Tennant was to both the floor and the edge of the door-set. One take resulted in the handle coming off in his hand (see also 4.8, "The Faceless Ones").

After this, he and Agyeman went off to do the TARDIS scene for Palmer's 1913 two-parter, while Michelle Collins (Captain McDonnell) began her stint on the programme at the end, doing the airlock suicide with Matthew Chambers (Korwin), then the floating-in-space scene against a green screen. (This was also the day of the very last shot for "Smith and Jones": the notorious door-lock scene, which had to be redone without the sonic screwdriver. Since Charles Palmer was filming Tennant and Agyeman that day anyway, he took care of this snippet as well.) Collins had spent some time in the gym, knowing that she'd be in a vest for most of the episode. However, she had just returned from a holiday in Bali, and found standing in a factory in Cardiff in January in a vest hard to acclimatise to quickly.

• The next day, the production moved to the St Regis Paper Company mill in Caldicot, Monmouthshire. This would serve as location for the *Pentallian* set proper. There were practical comms units with ship-diagrams that lit up according to which section was being contacted. Filming a story where the ship was supposedly frying meant that takes where the actors' breath was visibly misting were unusable. Collins, in her vest-top and with baby-oil on her exposed skin to simulate sweat, was especially uncomfortable, and also found the oil on the floor of the factory caused her to slip. (Tennant and Agyeman were in a nice warm recording studio elsewhere in Cardiff for the first two sessions of A5, "The Infinite Quest".)

• A number of scenes had been rearranged, for some reason, when shooting resumed after a short break on Monday, 22nd January – but the reshuffling probably wasn't just so that Chris Chibnall could enjoy his on-set visit, with the scene where the Doctor and Martha are first saying hello to the crew. The Thursday to follow was given over to the Riley and Scannell corridor sequences, and both scenes in the steam room where the TARDIS lands. This is another genuinely industrial part of the factory; the ship's engineering section was beneath the vast steel rollers used for the paper. Dry-ice "steam" was vented through leftover components of the factory's workings. The bulkhead doors were added digitally.

Friday the 26th saw the return to Upper Boat to do all the medbay scenes on the set they had there. This scene needed a practical prop, sliding the patient in and out, and thus couldn't be made on location (they were re-using the MRI machine from earlier in the season, in case you hadn't guessed). On Monday the 29th, during the Doctor's initial freeze, some of the buttons came off this console too. The Doctor's spacesuit was coated with a form of make-up spray, while Tennant's face and hair were coated in gel to which a dusting of small plastic crystals was applied, then a few larger ones and finally some bigger ones. Making him up took hours, for a shot that took minutes. Freema Agyeman later commented that she saw the scene where Martha freezes the screaming Time Lord as Martha's first properly companion-esque moment.

• The pre-credit scene was to have ended with Martha saying "We're stuck here!" It seemed less dramatic than the shot of the sun, so the scene was redubbed and the old one's music cues were re-edited to suit.

• As the broadcast date approached, it became obvious that Eurovision would cause a delay in transmission. Rather than move from the usual slot and lose half a million viewers (as the last two such episodes had done), it was proposed to use the change in Martha's status as a natural break and give Scooch (the hapless manufactured band sent to lose for Great Britain with an overtly camp, innnuendo-riven ditty suspiciously familiar to fans of *The High Life*) centre-stage. It was also increasingly clear that the impending release of the feature film *Sunshine* – in which a spaceship called *Icarus* was heading for the sun and the crew were being bumped off by someone who'd looked into the star a bit too often – might cause trouble. As it was, the film's reception was mixed, but Davies obviously took careful notes for future reference (see X4.16, "The Waters of Mars").

X3.8: "Human Nature"

(26th May, 2007)

Which One is This? *Superman II* done as a period-drama. Someone who looks like the Doctor dances and the universe almost ends. *TV Comic* gets recycled again, although this story's "Martha the Maid" doesn't thrash any Quarks. Instead, we have walking scarecrows, cricket-ball shenanigans and *Ripping Yarns*. And Ferb.

Firsts and Lasts For the first time, we have a *Doctor Who* episode that's intentionally and explicitly a televised version of a previous story from a non-telly format (just ahead of Moffat doing it in X3.10, "Blink").

And, we have our first on-screen evidence of the Doctor's previous incarnations being the ones we're familiar with from pre-1989, as the Doctor's human self – John Smith – has helpfully been sketching his earlier incarnations (even the one played by Paul McGann; see X3.11, "Utopia" and X7.14, "The Name of the Doctor").

At risk of spoilers, this is the first use of the

Why Should an Alien Love Cricket?

Since the first draft of this essay – written for Volume 5, but discarded in the course of things – both cricket and *Doctor Who* have gone from being sad fringe interests in Britain to resuming the importance that was theirs by right, then losing it again. Moreover, some attempts by people in other countries to account for the global interest in either have been, at best, more revealing about the attitudes of the authors and their native lands than the subject-matter. The odd thing is, if you go looking for hard and fast evidence of cricket being used as a tool of imperialist oppression, all that ever shows up is people citing other people who simply state it as fact in passing and move on. If we want to talk about the role of cricket in liberation politics, start with CLR James's book *Beyond a Boundary* and examine the career of Learie Constantine – and indeed the sport's role in putting pressure on Apartheid-era South Africa and helping the healing immediately after Mandela was voted in.

We can go into that later, but first we have to attempt something long held to be impossible. Let's quickly explain how cricket works.

The first thing to note is that the person bowling the ball can't bend his (we'll use male pronouns for now, but keep reading) arm more than a few degrees when bowling, but afterwards anyone throwing can chuck it. Usually, the ball is bowled overarm (a legacy of the ladies' game in the era of crinolines) and across a distance of 22 yards, generally bouncing just ahead of the target. That target is a wicket, three upright sticks (stumps) on which are balanced two smaller batons (bails) and a couple of feet in front of those is someone with a bat. (That bat isn't just a stick, it's four different pieces of wood, two different woods, engineered for very specific performance.) There are two wickets, one where the bowler releases the ball (with a batsman waiting for his go) and another defended by the batsman on strike.

Now, that ball is cork covered in leather, and it begins its working life as a sphere with a seam (the stitching) – so when it bounces, its change of direction is fairly predictable, but it moves at about 90mph. This leaves the guy on strike less than 1/16 of a second to guess its path and hit it away: if he hits it to where the bowler and his captain (assuming they aren't the same person) have placed waiting fielders to catch it, he and his opposite number run between the wickets as often as they can (they have cumbersome leg-pads); if the ball goes to the edge of the field (the boundary) without hitting the floor on its journey, that's counted as six runs and they don't need to actually run; if it rolls to the boundary, that's four; if it's thrown back to the wicket and either hits the bails or is used by the wicket-keeper (poised behind the wicket) to knock off the bails, the batsman based at that wicket is out.

So it's essentially getting points (runs) for out-witting traps. The bowler gets six balls in an over, then another bowler attacks from the other side and aims at the wicket that was the first bowler's base of operations. After 80 overs (in most cases), there is a new ball on offer, since the ball has become interestingly scuffed. If the bowlers are careful, one side will be smoother than the other and the ball's aerodynamic properties will allow slower bowlers more options for trickery. A spin bowler can use different grips and wrist-actions to make the ball bounce alarmingly. There are 11 players per side, of whom some are better bowlers than batters, and some have faster reactions and can field the ball very close to the wickets; once ten of them have been bowled out, caught out or committed a technical offence, the other side go in to bat, two at any time, and the former batting side all stay out bowling or fielding.

Unlike baseball (which is sometimes played – called "rounders" here – by small girls), there are four or five different formats of cricket, at different lengths and requiring different skills. The most prestigious is the Test Match, the five-day international game, usually in a series of five or six (this is the version interrupted in 3.4, "The Daleks' Master Plan"). The most commonly played is the village afternoon match, 40 overs per side (we see this version in 19.5, "Black Orchid"). A bigger version of this is played between professional county sides, and the players in these are often reconfigurations of Test players, working together as, say, Yorkshire or Somerset, then playing against each other later in the week as, say, India or New Zealand or England. This is where the selectors find the national sides. These days, there are also One Day Internationals, with almost the same line-ups as the Test sides, but not quite. And the latest adaptation the Twenty20 format, which is cricket on amphetamines, and in India is mutating so rapidly it may well become a separate game. (Bollywood-style cheerleaders is only one of its odd aspects.) This is very popular with betting syndicates, but lacks any prolonged sense of tension.

continued on Page 175...

Chameleon Arch technology, the apparatus by which the Doctor rewrites his very cells and makes himself human (here we're not told if the Doctor created it himself or if they're standard-issue TARDIS technology).

And this is the first BBC Wales episode not to have been produced by Phil Collinson. Instead, he gets credited as "Executive Producer" for the first time.

Watch Out For...

• The scarecrows are coming! The Family of Blood's "soldiers" have been choreographed to walk as if they have no knees. The result's as unlike *The Wizard of Oz* as you can get. (It is a bit like the way the second Doctor was written out of *TV Comic* though; see **The Big Picture**.) Look at the crowd scenes, then see how many of them they made. Then look again.

• It's 1913, and the companion of the moment is played by someone of Iranian-Ghanaian extraction. Paul Cornell, this story's author, has the bad guys chuck out a couple of racial slurs in a bid to acknowledge the era's general ghastliness, but tries to cast the snobbery in class terms. The author and director seem rather enamoured of the period. However, Martha's so annoyed about not being allowed to drink inside the pub, she goes a whole scene with Jenny and forgets to mention the Doctor. That's right, a scene where the Suffragettes are dismissed as dreamers is the one occasion where Martha passes the Bechdel Test.

• As cost-cutting measures go, an invisible spaceship's one of the better ones. More experienced fans may be thinking of 17.6, "Shada" in this sequence, but now that we've seen this sort of thing done less well (X5.10, "Vincent and the Doctor"), it's notable how effectively it's done here.

• Absurd as it is, the scene in which John Smith lobs a cricket ball – thus causing a chain reaction that prevents a piano from falling upon a passing mother and child – is helpfully ambiguous as to whether there's anything innately special about John Smith, or if he's just clever when he's attentive. (It took the production team ages to get right, but we'll talk more about that in **The Lore**, and also cricket in general in the accompanying essay.)

• Older viewers may find the reflexive naming of the Family of Blood's members ("Mother of Mine", "Son of Mine" and so forth) reminiscent of *Spike and Tyke* or Neil Reid's ghastly single from 1972. The "recruitment" of the hapless humans to serve as hosts is effectively creepy: so much so that one was cut before transmission. But look at the way they try to suggest someone else is inside those bodies. Some of it is the use of odd lenses, but most of it is down to the performers. This is the story where they tried to do everything the way they made *Doctor Who* before computers.

The Continuity

The Doctor The Doctor secrets his genetic code and memory inside a Victorian watch by use of a device, a Chameleon Arch, which transforms him on a cellular level into a human – imaginatively called "John Smith". The TARDIS creates a whole new personality and past for him. [See the entry for Smith, below.] Admittedly, he has little time to work out how Martha should look after this alternative personality, but his 23-item list of instructions doesn't cover his human self falling in love. The last thing he does on that list is to thank her.

John Smith's comments lead Joan to suspect that the Doctor has an eye for the ladies [see **The Supporting Cast**].

• *Background.* "Human Nature" picks up at the end of an unspecified adventure, one that that culminates with the Doctor and Martha them running into the TARDIS. The Family's chasing them, but they failed to see Martha's face. [The BBC set up a MySpace account for Martha that said they were at the 2007 Eurovision Contest; this was written by Joseph Lidster, the author who usually does their fictional websites, so we'll take it into consideration on the same level as the Millingdale Ice Cream info.]

• *Ethics.* He's taking a risk that the Family – who will die in three months without a life-upgrade – won't try going after anyone else if he vanishes [there are plenty of long-lived species in the universe besides a rogue Time Lord; it's lucky that they never encounter Jack], but he's willing to sacrifice months of his time and Martha's to avoid killing them outright. If they catch up with him, the plan is for Martha to restore him so that he can handle the situation personally. In the instruction video, he explicitly tells her it's her choice of whether or not to open the watch, as the Family will then be able to find him. [This could be, depending on how you want to look at it, more cruel and terrifying – and far more responsibility and trust than he ever thought of giving Rose.]

• *Inventory: Sonic Screwdriver.* It's been in the

Why Should an Alien Love Cricket?

continued from Page 173...

Tension is the key word here – the optimum situation is one where the two sides are poised so that if the batting side get a few more runs, they will win but have one wicket left and the amount of overs left are dwindling. If they get out the other side wins, but they have to take risks. Sometimes not doing anything, resisting temptation, is the smart strategy. How this differs from most other team sports is that the actions of any individual on the pitch can make more difference to the overall game than in football (yours or ours). As a game of maths and strategy, it's more sensitive to small fluctuations.

Here's where it might help to have read all those early 90s books on Chaos Theory. The dead giveaway is that Nate Silver, the US statistician whose number-crunching is sought by politicians and the media, baulked at the prospect of calculating the outcome of the Ashes series. (The significance of that particular grudge-match we'll come to later.) Watching a match thus requires a constant low-level attention, punctuated *at almost no notice* by intense involvement. This is also how fielding, except at close quarters, affects the brain. It's a sort of Zen state.

The game physically happening is an approximation of the game(s) unfolding in the minds of the spectators, captains, bowlers and batsmen; they are all evaluating strategies and remembering precedents, but as anything actually occurs (or a plan is thwarted), this is adjusted. It's like a more pragmatic, athletic version of chess. Crafty bowlers and inventive batsmen alter the dynamic. Again, baseball has some of these features, but it's more mechanical and linear.

You may be beginning to see the appeal to the Doctor. By now, it's already clear (we hope) that the clean-cut, guileless fifth Doctor was a fast-bowler by temperament as much as ability, whilst the more cryptic, worldly fourth Doctor was revealed – to nobody's great surprise – to be a spinner (16.1, "The Ribos Operation"). The other Doctors have been less explicit; his comment in "The Daleks' Master Plan" can be taken as complete ignorance of what's going on, but – listened to in context – could equally well be an ironic comment to the clueless Steven and Sara. The "Well played, sir" line in "Death to the Daleks" (11.3) sounds like a member of the MCC – we'll pick that up in a bit – and, this being the Pertwee Doctor, is in keeping with that character but no indication of genuine interest. There's not much else apart from the whole Davison era, but compared to the other sport supposedly universally adored in Britain, it's a flurry. Prior to Matt Smith's two brief allusions to his former career (X5.11, "The Lodger"; X7.4, "The Power of Three"), all we have is Mickey's interest in pub-lunches and what satellite packages the TARDIS has, and the Doctor carrying an old-fashioned rattle (14.1, "The Masque of Mandragora"), to show for football's much-hyped status as an omnipresent obsession everywhere except maybe America.

To an outside observer, this might look like the Doctor associating himself with the elite. Actually... no. Football, despite the tendency of the last 20 years to use it as a means for middle-class men to act "authentic", i.e. working class and blokey, became big business a long time ago. It's been a handy tax-relief investment for foreign billionaires, so that a game between Chelsea (owned by a Russian Oligarch) and Liverpool (owned by the man who bought the Boston Red Sox) is almost the modern equivalent of those 70s middle-east wars that were Cold War proxies. Cricket began as a game for shepherds, with the bat an adapted crook, the wicket self-evidently derived from fences and gates and so on. It was primarily meritocratic, although time to practice often accompanied a private income or a spell at university. Until as late as 1963, there were separate changing-rooms for "Gentlemen" and "Players", but the distinction was mainly between people who had a real job for most of the year, only turning pro when the loss of income in touring Australia or wherever instead of working in a mine was reimbursed, and the amateurs, who had private incomes. Both were in the side on merit.

Fiction has found this distinction useful for suggesting class tensions or dramatising other personality clashes or ideological splits, so this has been the main way that non-cricketing nations (well, one in particular) have seen the game represented. Often, these sequences were the comic highlight of a generally angry novel, but this didn't transfer to the big screen. (See, for instance, Joseph Losey's rendering of LP Hartley's *The Go-Between* – but note that the screenplay was written by cricket-addict Harold Pinter – or A.G. MacDonnell's *England, Their England*, the screen adaptation of just the cricket bit was produced by Innes Lloyd,

continued on Page 177...

Doctor's coat for two months. Martha retrieves it after the watch goes missing, thinking it might remind John who he really is. [Oddly, it's included in the Journal of Impossible Things sketches, so he does remember it after a fashion. He knows it's sonic, but can't think of the screwdriver part.]

• *Inventory: The Watch.* It's a silver pocket-watch, in a hunter-case with engraved Gallifreyan symbols [quite why they're there, given that the person on whose behalf it was created won't be able to understand them, is a different issue]. A Perception Filter [X3.12, "The Sound of Drums"] prevents John from noticing it until the pre-set time period is up.

When a schoolboy, Tim Latimer, opens the watch, it doesn't release the Doctor's consciousness into either of them – but it does create a trace that the Family is able to scent. The watch communicates with Tim to some extent. [We'll find out there's a good reason for this, but it's rather dangerous for a watch like this to attract attention to itself so readily.] His opening it releases a golden shimmering ray simultaneously with random memory access; these are largely recent flashbacks, with several images of Martha. [What we see is not a literal rendition of the Doctor's memories, since one of the images is a full-on shot of the Doctor himself. Whatever technology's involved is at least theoretically capable of transferring the information to someone besides John Smith, or we wouldn't have a story.]

The TARDIS [The extent to which the Doctor has programmed the TARDIS and the Chameleon Arch for this sort of contingency isn't clear; if the Doctor put this program together post-Time War for his own purposes, that would explain why, unlike most of the programs on the Ship, it doesn't involve a personalised companion-friendly hologram.]

The Arch equipment resembles no bit of TARDIS tech [but brings to mind a less stupid version of the helmet/ torture device the Master plugged the Doctor into back in the TV Movie]. Its wiring suspends from the ceiling [as it's never been apparent in the long-shots, we assume it's in the same hatches that provided gas-masks in X2.5, "Rise of the Cybermen"]. It has three nodes, like small light-bulbs, which touch the subject's forehead. The process affects the lighting and seems to hurt. There's a plug-in for the watch on the console.

When the Ship is on emergency power, the console room lights are largely off, and we don't see Martha using anything but the instruction video.

The Supporting Cast

• *John Smith.* So... technically, he's a fictional construct the TARDIS put together while the Doctor's memories have all been siphoned off into a watch. He doesn't know this, nor that in another month he's meant to stop existing.

Smith wears a bow-tie and tweeds [but refrains from going on and on about how cool this is]. He lives in a book-lined study with certificates on the wall [including Pitman's Shorthand – how the TARDIS fabricated those is another matter] and invites boys in to borrow history textbooks, mainly about the Napoleonic or Boer Wars.

According to his memories, he was born in the Radford Parade district of Nottingham, on Broadmarsh Street [not quite what real Nottingham's like, but it's what the script says]; his mother was named Verity and was a nurse, while his father was a watchmaker called Sydney. [Volume 1 explains for all about Verity Lambert and Sydney Newman.] Smith stoutly denies being Irish; he's not from Gallifrey, but does think he learned art there [the original reference is to 14.2, "The Hand of Fear"].

He writes down stories of his adventures, in a book he calls the *Journal of Impossible Things*, but treats it as a dream journal. [We see Martha in the opening scene, but he never mentions having seen her in his dreams, although he drew her alongside them; perhaps he assumes his mind simply filled in a familiar-looking person, but it's curious that he never seems to bring up the point with her. Or he's simply embarrassed.] He has terrible handwriting, but is a gifted draughtsman.

He's been teaching history at the Farringham School for Boys for two months when the story opens, and has fallen for Nurse Joan Redford very hard. As a teacher, he seems to be at least competent [unlike the novel version, there's no hint that innate Doctorish characteristics are interfering with his duties – noticeably, and without batting an eye, he grants permission for a student, Hutchinson, to give Timothy a beating].

After an improbable rescue of a baby in a pram from a falling piano with a cricket ball, he becomes rather more self-confident and asks Joan to the dance. Once the ice has broken, he pro-

Why Should an Alien Love Cricket?

continued from Page 175...

for whom see Volume 2.) The real action of cricket, the mind-games and bluffing, isn't immediately filmic the way baseball is, which is why films involving the game have to focus on the associated culture and lore. (If you've seen John Boorman's *Hope and Glory,* you'll appreciate how something intended to be poignant and significant can be baffling if you don't know what a googly is[33].) Admittedly, the percentage of bright lads who got to university before World War II was smaller and from a less broad spectrum of society, so playing for Oxford or Cambridge gained a patina of privilege, but that stratum was more racially-mixed than England as a whole back then, definitely more than football was until 1985. For the reasons outlined above, cricketers have a tendency to be more bookish than average, and this brings with it a lot of other connotations and quirks that form a halo around the sport itself.

For anyone alive now, and especially over 40, the main source of information and heritage has been BBC Radio's *Test Match Special*. The biggest name associated with this was one of the few commentators not an ex-player: John Arlott. He was a former policeman and, at one time, the head of the BBC's Poetry department (he, as much as anyone, fostered the career of Dylan Thomas, another cricket-buff). Speaking slowly and with a perceptible West Country burr, he succinctly described the play when it was happening and the minutiae of the ground when it wasn't. In some matches, listeners found themselves hoping for an interruption so that he could talk about pigeons or the efforts of the grounds-staff to keep the pitch dry in a light drizzle.

Other commentators brought reminiscence and differences of opinion, punctuating their oblique insights and comments about the cakes sent in by listeners with sporadic mentions of the game unfolding. (We refer you back to New Year's Day 1966 and "The Daleks' Master Plan": a police box materialising on the crease sends "Ross" looking through the archives for how often this has happened, but the commentators are more concerned with how it will affect play than how bizarre it is.) Until very recently, one had the sense that every cricketer was a frustrated novelist – this persists in the newspaper columns by former players and the differing styles of commentary on different media. Television coverage was, for most of the last 70 years, the responsibility of the BBC (one of the "crown jewels" that they had to cover, by law, free to air with no commercial breaks), then the Blair government caved in to pressure from Rupert Murdoch and it eventually went behind a paywall (see **Why is Trinity Wells on Jackie's Telly?** under X1.4, "Aliens of London"). The radio coverage continues, and has its global cult following as much for the odd mix of characters doing the commentary as the play. Generations of people in the UK associate *Soul Limbo* by Booker T and the MGs with the start of summer, after its use as the TV theme for over a quarter of a century and subsequent adoption by *TMS*. Why this record?

The 1970s was the decade of the West Indies team. The various Caribbean islands had their political differences and internal difficulties, but by judicious choice of players from as many islands as possible, and the advent of a generation of big hitters and terrifyingly fast bowlers, they cut a swathe through the international game. With the growing numbers of second-generation Afro-Caribbean British citizens – especially in Brixton, Leeds, Nottingham and Birmingham (sites of major cricket grounds used in Tests) – these guys were icons. (The interested reader is directed to the 2010 film *Fire in Babylon*, explicitly linking cricket to wider issues, hence the Bob Marley-esque title. See also the essay with X3.2, "The Shakespeare Code". The film ignores the way England adapted to the Windies' game after 1976, and thus beat the dirty cheating Australians, whose only tactic was injuring the other team's batsmen.)

More to the point, they made the other Test sides (England; India; Sri Lanka; Pakistan; sometimes – but not right now though – Zimbabwe; sometimes, but not between 1968 and 1991, South Africa; Australia; Bangladesh; and New Zealand) buck their ideas up. The game accelerated to the point that when Australia unveiled a slow spin-bowler, Shane Warne, and got through the defences of the batsmen who'd only faced pace-bowling (except on moist pitches, or where the teams used a spinner to kill time until the new ball), it was treated as a revelation – or shenanigans. That was the 80s, when Australia were in their pomp. Unlike America's idea of a "World Series", cricket is a global game. Test matches are a means by which the best national sides take turns at humiliating England, or each other, but there

continued on Page 179...

ceeds to kissing quite readily. When Joan's speculating on his similarity to his fictional alter ego, he self-deprecatingly laughs off the idea that he could be a ladies' man. His line, 'I've never, er...' suggests that he's never kissed anyone [so the TARDIS must not have fitted him with such memories]. He doesn't know if he can dance, but quickly discovers he can do a fine waltz with Joan at the village hall.

Smith has a maid named Martha whom he "inherited" from his family. He seems dimly aware that he has to retain her services no matter what, but not why this should be. When she charges in, panicking about aliens planning to destroy them all, he assumes that she doesn't understand fiction ('cultural differences'), and starts trying to explain it in a slow and highly patronising manner. He then fires her, after she slaps him, and fumes about how ridiculously fantastical she is.

The Perception Filter works so well, he doesn't remember even owning a watch. Seeing a big alien ray gun doesn't set off anything either. [The *Journal* says that he was the "eccentric oldest son who was meant to inherit", which could mean lots of things. Given the Davies-era version of the Doctor's family, it may even be true. It sounds worryingly like the rejected Leekley script for the TV Movie. There's quite a bit more text where that comes from, as Cornell wrote up text for a version of the *Journal* that was flogged to the hardcore fans. It includes more-or-less confused versions of just about every new series story up to this point (the version of X1.7, "The Long Game" with the Jagrafess as a gargoyle is rather touching). Original series information largely didn't make it in, save for one page of breathtaking fanwank with the description of Gallifrey from "The Sensorities", the hermit from "The Time Monster" and the absurdity of his being made President. (He indicates he's been around long enough to have been dancing in the city towers, which sounds like nothing so much as 15.6, "The Invasion of Time".)]

• *Martha.* Has spent two months scrubbing floors as a maid at a boys' school. She has an awkward relationship with John Smith – even after two months, it's not in her to hide the casual familiarity that she enjoyed with the Doctor, even though Smith finds it increasingly upsetting.

It hurts her cruelly that someone who looks and acts so much like the Doctor can fall in love after all, much less with somebody else altogether. Joan's treatment of her as a servant doesn't improve matters. Boys making racial slurs are ignored with quiet dignity, but it seems that in two months, she's only become properly friendly with Jenny, another maid.

She's told Jenny to think of her as a Londoner [although Jenny talks about 'your country']. It's only now she's grounded in 1913 that an enthusiasm for travel is coming to the fore; she's been holding on to her dream of seeing the stars again for months. At some point, she's been shown how to operate the scanner and play the Doctor's instructions.

After running out of ideas to convince John of his true identity, she gives him a good slap and attempts to drag him off to the TARDIS bodily. She's quick enough on her feet to ask a leading question when Jenny begins behaving oddly, as Mother of Mine has taken over her body. She apologises to Joan for her plan to change the Doctor back.

The Non-Humans

• *The Family of Blood.* There are four of them (Father of Mine, Mother of Mine, Sister of Mine and Brother of Mine; the nouns of direct address shift depending on who's talking to whom), and they do seem to be an actual family of sorts. They have some kind of hunting mechanism that depends on scent [and seems to involve the olfactory organs of their hosts, since they all sniff a lot]. They have short lifespans in others' bodies, but could maintain themselves for much longer if they absorbed the Doctor's regenerations.

Their spaceship is invisible when parked until touched, at which point a green-lit force field lights up; the inhabitants have a way to open a door into their ship at will. This seems to be part of their native technology or an innate ability; they have guns that fire a similarly-coloured light. Perhaps as a safety precaution, their ship's approach resembles a falling meteorite.

They're capable of animating scarecrows to act as heavy muscle [probably all local ones, or else they cart around a hold full of scarecrows across the galaxies]. They're clearly not fussed about taking lives, even apart from taking over other people's bodies. They can access a few memories of the people they inhabit, enough to get by temporarily without being noticed, but not enough that Mother of Mine can act entirely convincingly around Martha, or know that sardines with jam is ridiculous. ['This body has traces of memory',

Why Should an Alien Love Cricket?

continued from Page 177...

are international sides for the Netherlands[35], Canada, Afghanistan, Ireland[36] Kenya and Scotland. Even France is beginning to catch on again, although they are officially the reigning Olympic silver-medallists (it was last an Olympic sport in 1900).

The women's game is even more interesting, as there are fewer full-time players in any of the national sides, and they are almost always more evenly-matched. There have been American teams, too: pre-War, there was a Hollywood side of actors from cricketing nations, notably David Niven, Errol Flynn and Boris Karloff as wicket-keeper. These days, there's a Compton Cricket Club, "Homies and the Popz", who were due to play against Afghanistan's fledgling team as there are few other US sides to give them a match. America will never take to a sport that can't sell saturation advertising spots, though, so the slow-motion version of football where the ads are punctuated by bits of sport now and then will prevail. Nonetheless, the first-ever international cricket match was Canada vs America (Canada won, since you ask).

The objections of people who only know about cricket from disparaging kneejerk comments about snobbery, Imperialism and privilege and miss the most important point about it (at least for this book's purposes) – that it has a three-century span of global culture caught up in it, much of it to do with turning an opponent's apparent strengths into opportunities for improvised brilliance. Does this sound familiar? It's a set of practices bound by codified procedures and accepted behaviour, both of which are important but sometimes run up against each other. There's the letter of the law (the MCC's handbook: 42 Laws – not "rules" – with endless sub-clauses) and the spirit; something can be legal but "not cricket". Since 2000, this has been codified in the preamble to the rulebook, but they were assumed until then to be self-evident.

That Spirit of the Game (and they use those capitals) was always understood to be about maturity and respect: fair play, obviously, deferred gratification and harmonising individual gifts towards a collective aim without being simply part of a machine (as is often the case with other team games). The ethos of the game is a system for surviving adolescence. It discourages the obvious. Again, this has a resonance for *Doctor Who*. In life, as in civil disobedience, obviousness is fatal. Most opponents know how angry mobs will react and have mechanisms in place. Having something ready or available that hasn't been anticipated, and yet is entirely within the rules, has been a successful methodology for all underdogs and survivors. Such things often require observation, experience and hypothesis-testing.

At a very basic level, this is a subject one either gets intuitively or doesn't. The kind of people who never will, and don't even try, have much in common with the kinds of people who tend to be the bad guys in *Doctor Who*. The winning-at-all-costs mentality has a habit of causing mistakes that lead to opportunities for anyone playing for the love of playing. The Laws contain many clauses that discourage a kind of play that is boring to watch or over too soon – important now that box-office takings form such a big part of the income for professionals, but always a significant part of the conduct of play. In many ways, these guidelines subordinate neurotic adherence to the Laws to an aesthetic sense of what's right and just and entertaining.

One legacy of the use of the Empire to spread the game – thinking of it as a "tool" of Empire is like thinking that Jazz, a by-product of slavery using all the surplus military band instruments made for World War I, was a "tool" of German expansionism or the Confederate States – is that cricket provides an international language for exiles and expatriots. A shared passion gives people from any background a link in a strange land. India and Pakistan seem to have been either at war or preparing for the next one at any stage in the last half-century, but people raised in those countries living next to each other in Leicester or Toronto or Boston can compare memories and watch together.

The twenty-first century game bears all the signs of having adapted to wildly different circumstances, both where the game is played and by whom. The conflict between two radically different approaches adds to the aesthetic and conceptual appeal of any given game. Even if we accept the (largely unproven) assertion that the Empire used the game to normalise the British subjugation of very hostile environments and their native populations, it would have been impossible to impose such a game onto people who didn't want to take time and effort to learn how to do it. Let's be honest: basketball is a much more efficient mechanism for economic and cultural infiltration.

continued on Page 181...

Mother of Mine says next episode.] Whether it's memory-tapping or their own tech that gives them a command of idiomatic English isn't clear.

We have little idea of their true form, although Mother of Mine manifests as a green smoke, temporarily occupying a glowing globe, when possessing Jenny by entering her mouth.

Planet Notes The Family have somehow acquired a Time Agency vortex manipulator. [This is possibly a more sophisticated model than what Jack seems to have, given that it's capable of transporting an entire spaceship with crew. Then again, this may be how the Chula ship navigated to 1941, but not the ambulance – X1.9, "The Empty Child". See X5.12, "The Pandorica Opens" and *Torchwood* Series 2 concerning the ubiquity of vortex manipulators without any sign of the actual Time Agents attached.]

History

• *Dating*. As the posters indicate, the village dance that John and Joan attend was Tuesday, 11th November, 1913. Martha says that she's been there for two months, so they probably arrived at the start of term. [As mentioned above, we can probably date the opening TARDIS scene to 12th May, 2007. Perhaps in Finland. It's possibly for this reason that John Smith dreams of being an adventurer "in the Year of Our Lord two thousand and seven", even though Martha's native year is 2008.]

The Boer War appears to have happened on schedule, including the Battle of Spion Kop (January 1900). Joan's husband was killed there.

English Lessons

• *Playing silly beggars*: a child-friendly form of "playing silly buggers," which simply means to act foolishly. "Bugger" is a much ruder word in Britain than America, meaning something very specific.

• *Fob-watch* (n.). So let's clarify one thing; a fob-watch is a watch with a leather strap rather than a chain, which this evidently isn't. The one that John Smith has is in a hunter case, i.e. a case that springs open when the catch is released. The word "fob-watch" isn't used in the dialogue, except in one "filler" scene with Martha and Joan. Martha might use a looser term (she does so in "Utopia"), but not Joan. The person who keeps calling it a "fob-watch" in commentary is Russell T Davies.

It's easier all round to call it a pocket watch.

• *Rozzers* (n. sl.). East London term for police, with lots of theoretical explanations but already old-fashioned by 1903, so a Public School boy might use it semi-ironically. Perhaps.

• *OTC* (n.). Officer Training Corps. The British Army traditionally made a distinction between enlisted soldiers (who were conscripted or signed up to join) who could be promoted up to a point, but officers were commissioned at a fairly exalted rank and promoted from that starting-point. To receive a commission was as much as anything to do with schooling and family background (if one's father was in the same regiment, and grandfather and his father and so on). Much of the regime at a public school (see below) was conceived with this in mind, especially sport (see the accompanying essay), hence the much-quoted but misunderstood line of Wellington's that Waterloo was won "on the playing-fields of Eton".

• *Public School* (n.). To reiterate from earlier volumes, in England the term "Public School" denotes the ones set up in the middle ages for the education of people whose parents weren't royalty. This came to mean, by the time of the 1844 Education Act, an elite who actually ran the country. Despite attempts to make them less significant in the life of the nation, the handful of these institutions (still technically classed as "charities" and thus tax-exempt) have provided a disproportionate number of the students to the most prestigious universities and thus the cabinet, civil service and such. Eton, the most exclusive, with the most long-running and incomprehensible traditions and entrance criteria, gave us the majority of the Conservative members of the Cameron government, as well as such fixtures of US television as Hugh Laurie, Damien Lewis and Dominic West.

There are a lot more that *act* as if they were the source of the cream of the nation, but are just as shut-out as grammar-schools and comprehensives. Farringham (named after the village where Cornell lives) is one of these, it seems. They did, however, provide a lot of military officers and inept schoolmasters.

Why Should an Alien Love Cricket?

continued from Page 179...

Such a programme of imposition of British values onto subject nations would have ended as soon as the local sides started literally beating the Empire at their own game. Each national side developed their own style of play, and took turns at humbling the England team on tour or in England. Each style of play conveys a sense of cultural distinctiveness, as identifiable as an accent.

It was this sense of bringing part of "home" with one that led to the spread of the game everywhere the English went. It spread as a meme rather than being imposed, although it was played in the schools where those selected subjects who passed exams and seemed like good prospects for the burgeoning bureaucracy had been sent. As these individuals were such a vanishingly small percentage of the population, this cannot account for the rapidity of the game's growth in the Raj or other colonial outposts. Yes, the sons of maharajahs may have gone to the elite public schools in England, or universities, and even played for England. They also played polo, and that's never really caught on except as a show of conspicuous consumption. Yes, the majority of the first clubs set up overseas were military to begin with, and employed locals first to collect balls and keep the grounds, but the speed with which multi-racial sides sprang up isn't just sucking up to the masters. It has to have been something in the game itself that led it to such intense global popularity.

The story has gone around that the British purposely used it to impose "their" values on their underlings. The take-away values that people got from cricket were diametrically opposed to the processes and apparatus of imperial control; what happened instead was that, as with using the Bible in schools, it gave the oppressed tools to organise and articulate grievances and stick it to The Man. (We refer you to **Is This Any Way to Run a Galactic Empire?** under 10.3, "Frontier in Space".) Cricket didn't change the plantation-workers and functionaries, it was changed by them.

Every generation has a national side that completely reinvents the game and everyone else has to devise a response. When new techniques wipe out any other side on the pitch, the characteristic response is to learn from it and fight back. However, the more in-keeping response is to reach back into the past and find something that's been half-forgotten and try that. Here is one other way that cricket differs from most sports: although the show-offy fast-bowlers and big-hitters have a relatively short career, those who rely on guile as much as athleticism tend to endure, to outlast the newcomers and let experience tell. Not falling into traps is largely a matter of recognising those traps, and setting them yourself for impetuously aggressive players requires intelligence and maturity.

Balancing these two tendencies has been a constant process of micro-adjustments. And, of course, the other team's players are trying to second-guess these, and everyone knows this, and knows that the other side knows this, and that side knows this and... The ludic autonomy of the game-as-played rubs up against its links to all of the folklore, pragmatic politics, inherited techniques and other matters in the dressing-room or stadium, but not out at the crease. The technical innovations may derive from a combination of these extramural factors, but you can't dwell on it when you're focussing on split-second changes and long-term strategy simultaneously. The time for that is practicing and coaching.

Which is how all the different versions of cricket link up and form a cohesive entity, developing from the English game of the eighteenth century (the one mentioned in *Northanger Abbey*) and the street games with tennis-balls and tin-can wickets played in any side-street from Durban to Durham (except, maybe, the USA). If we take this essay's title at face-value, these "aliens" love cricket because it's part of childhood and a native land. The one specific alien this book's about probably didn't play it as a child (although, if we take another reference in "Black Orchid" seriously, he may have wanted to drive a steam-train, so we can't rule it out), but he will have seen it played in so many ways by so many types of people, he could easily have latched on to it as a topic of conversation before ever attempting to play it himself.

What Americans think of as "quintessentially English" is often just un-American and to be found all around the English-speaking world. There is an element of the bucolic idyll about one manifestation of cricket – the village match with beer, tea, sandwiches, church bells and the much-talked-about crack of leather on willow (the bats being well-preserved with linseed oil rubbed into them over the winter). The versions played in Mumbai, Trinidad or on Bondi Beach lack nearly all of these

continued on Page 183...

The Analysis

The Big Picture ("Human Nature" and "The Family of Blood") There's a temptation to begin with the book version of this story, published in 1995 as one of the *New Adventures* range, and featuring the seventh Doctor and Bernice Summerfield instead of the tenth Doctor and Martha. But actually, the *first* and most obvious thing for us to say is that this story is a lot like "Mawdryn Undead" (20.3). A series stalwart loses his memory and teaches in a minor public school, while some manipulative aliens who want to become Time Lords need the Doctor's life-energy to achieve their ends. An alien schoolboy in a wing-collar occasionally steps into a cupboard or alcove to commune with a higher power, denoted by his face being lit from below. There's a vintage car or two. The key scene the story wants us to wait for is the anamnesis, when the hidden past of the key character comes back in a flurry of fast-edited clips of old episodes. Then, it was the Brigadier and a range of sepia-tinted monochrome images from 1968 to 1975. It was beings who'd already stolen the power of regeneration, and been condemned to immortality and stasis for their crime. And it was the Doctor who was manoeuvred into (potentially) sacrificing his future to save everyone.

Moving the focus away from the decision the Doctor *has* to make to one he made in the pre-credit sequence (or before the book version of this story started) entails a plot-device with an even longer history. For most people in the West, the earliest introduction of the Slavic stories of Koschei the Deathless was in Stravinski's 1910 ballet *The Firebird* (Murray Gold seems to be flagging this up with small hints in the scarecrow massacre music). It goes back a fair way before this, but the ballet spread the tale of the wizard whose mortality/ soul was hidden in an object safely lodged a long way away. In the ballet it was a crystal egg, but other stories have more elaborate things-inside-things-inside-things. James Branch Cabell, who's responsible for vast amounts of patchouli-scented fantasy, used the idea in the 1920s. (The use of the name in a different *New Adventures* context needn't detain us here, but keep an eye on X3.11, "Utopia".) We also have it in *Neverwhere*, but more of that anon. What's important is the reification, making a concept a physical object that can be hidden, stolen and used as a MacGuffin.

The choice of a public school in 1913 as a hiding place seems, at first sight, to be the ideal Doctorish smokescreen. For the print version of Sylvester McCoy's Doctor it may have been: for Tennant's Doctor, less so. What's noticeable about the two accounts is that John Smith is, for once in the BBC Wales phase of the series, entirely a product of his time. As we saw in **Are We Touring Theme-Park History?** under X2.7, "The Idiot's Lantern", most adventures in Earth's past make a point of denying that what might be called local conditions affect anyone's upbringing or attitudes, preferring to make everyone seem "just like us" in defiance of recorded fact. Paul Cornell's book was scrupulous in giving this human avatar of the Doctor appropriate period attitudes and a comprehension of the world and England's place therein that reflected the real past (and the umpteen fictional representations of it). Much was made, at the time, of the book's use of the OTC training Smith gives his charges – making the schoolboys practice with weapons as part of the curriculum. The principal visual reference for this and its links to bullying, privilege and institutional brutality is Lindsay Anderson's film *If...* This associates a lot of ideas in the air in 1968 (especially the Paris student riots) with the operations of such a school, and ends with what might be a dream-sequence (the title has this potential of "what if?" as well as the Kipling allusion), with an armed insurrection against the teachers.

Schoolboys in quaint uniforms operating machine-gun emplacements is also a handy and well-worn metaphor for World War I, which began in the school holidays of 1914 and seemed like an adventure, at first. It's become a cliché to look back on 1913 as the last innocent year and use the popular fiction of the time to highlight how misled everyone was. This is all in the vocabulary of modern day school-story parodies, pre-eminent amongst which is *Tomkinson's Schooldays*, the pilot episode of *Ripping Yarns* (op cit) which is mainly following Thomas Hughes (it seemed as though *Tom Brown's Schooldays* was being adapted about once every two years by the BBC or Hollywood), but also links up with polar exploration[34].

That sort of thing was done straight even after Palin and Jones had reduced it to rubble, often on Sunday nights on BBC1 in the late 70s. One such, *To Serve Them All My Days,* was what Matthew Waterhouse was doing when he got cast as Adric,

Why Should an Alien Love Cricket?

continued from Page 181...

features, only the bat and ball remain constant (unless you're in the street or on the beach using a tennis ball or one you'd throw for the dog to fetch), but each has different rituals. What they have in common is less of a vocabulary of such elements as a grammar. Those thought-processes are shared and understood among cricketers and spectators.

Some people might claim these to be specific to the British, but this just makes applying them better all the more satisfying. Embarrassing the English national side (the MCC[39]) has been a source of amusement since 1882, and the first defeat by Australia on home turf (there was a mock obituary posted in *The Times*, which led to a faux-cremation; the small urn of ashes is symbolically played for between the two sides every two years). Newly-independent former colonies established their self-hood by this ritual. In the 1930s, it was Australia; in 1950, it was the legendary "Calypso" series, the first after the Empire Windrush had brought immigrants from the Caribbean; a generation later came the "Blackwash".

Off the pitch, then, the game connects up to issues of race, class, politics and good conduct – yet when immersed in a game, the main concern is... the game. As we said, ethics roughly equate to aesthetics, even to the extent of knowing when to disregard even this. WG Grace, for example, only ever disagreed with an umpire once: it was a charity match and he towered over the hapless official, saying "they came to see me play, not to see you umpire". He was a practicing doctor, and once knocked up a quick match-winning century (100 runs) and got himself out deliberately in order to rush off and deliver a baby.[40]

Larger-than-life characters such as this abound, but there are figures in the present-day game potentially as much the stuff of legend. England players these days try to seem like ordinary blokes just doing a job, but future generations may speak of them differently; we can confidently predict that Sachin Tendulkar's 100 centuries in international matches will make this seem like a golden age. He's been controversial in the past, but people are beginning to forget even this. The immediate past tends to become more like a story when feats such as this occur. The classic example in English cricket prior to the 2005 series was 1981, when the flamboyant all-rounder Ian Botham was made captain and it all went wrong, with two Tests in an Ashes series lost badly. Relieved of the post, he almost single-handedly won the series, against a swaggeringly potent Australia (*almost* single-handedly, as we have to acknowledge Bob Willis's bowling which, under normal circumstances, would have been the most extraordinary feature of any series).

... which brings us back to the incident in this story to which we've attached this essay: John Smith's piano-haulage rescue-by-cricket-ball in "Human Nature". This was a scene that the production team fought hard to retain and make happen as written, even in face of the technical complications involved. Story-wise, it's clearly denoted as the first complication – the first expression of pure Doctorish instinct, in what's so far seemed like an idyllic situation for Smith. It's the image that everyone remembers from that story, and everyone concerned knew exactly what they were doing equating cricket with the Time Lord. In the original novel, the vehicle the Doctor used to preserve his personality was a cricket ball. This seemed intuitively right, just as the watch used in the broadcast version – being visually effective as something that can be opened and symbolically apt, connected as it is with time – was right for the television rendition.

In short, then, everything about the Doctor's personality, approach to problem-solving, knack of winning and empirical examination of the world(s) around him seems consonant with how cricket is played. "Talking the opposition into their own traps" is what Clara describes as "Doctor 101" (X9.10, "Face the Raven") and is as good a summary of how cricket works as any. All the things he values are connected with the wider culture around cricket. Many of the people he admires and name-drops were fond of it (even Benjamin Franklin – X3.1, "Smith and Jones"; X3.6, "The Lazarus Experiment"). It's a good fit for someone who seems like a Victorian Englishman, but is very far from home, and it also works for someone who seems like a twenty-first century bloke who has no home left.

so fandom was aware of it even if nobody can remember anything else about it. We've mentioned *Goodbye, Mr Chips* under "School Reunion" (X2.3). Films set in such places were constantly re-run, so generations not born when boarding schools were considered a ludicrous anachronism knew all the clichés and parodies, including St Trinian's (see X4.18, "The End of Time Part Two"), long before the Rowling juggernaut came along.

This is especially true of the boy's papers of the era (see 6.2, "The Mind Robber" and 6.7, "The War Games"). In 1940, George Orwell wrote an essay accusing Amalgamated Press of exerting disturbing dominance over the minds of susceptible youth by inculcating stolidly conservative, it's-always-1910 ideas of the world through years of selling papers with lots of cheap school stories. He chose *The Gem* and *The Magnet* as the most successful and popular examples of these, only to find out that the "Frank Richards" who had signed off on 30 years of stories wasn't a newspaper construct but a perfectly real person who held a fondness for the Edwardian age. Understandable, given that he got the decades-long gig on these papers in 1907.

Between then and the Great War, Richards lived it up in Europe, sending in copy by day and gambling at French casinos by night – yes, really – oblivious to the approach of war. His subsequent stories lack any indication that anything significant had changed. Billy Bunter, the greedy, overweight, cowardly sneak, became a pop-cultural icon between the wars. Result: a writer who was already deeply fond of endless paeans to the joys and trials of public schools ended up doing these for a half-century in one way or another, helping to cement the genre of *Tom Brown's Schooldays*, *Goodbye, Mr Chips* and *Stalky and Co.* as a genuinely popular cultural touchstone. Television picked this up in the late 1950s (see "Shada"). There was also a parody on BBC TV, *Whack-o!*, which was revived in the early 70s despite some *very* dodgy subtexts. Bunter was still relevant enough in the 60s for Richards's estate to send the BBC letters about "The Celestial Toymaker" (3.7) using a naughty schoolboy named Billy as a villain.

One especially effective pastiche of this is issue #25 of the comic *Sandman*, entitled "In Which the Dead Return; and Charles Rowland Concludes His Education". In this, Rowland, a boy unable to go home in the school holidays, meets a boy murdered in 1916 in the same school (there's sort of a baggage-handlers' dispute in Hell, and Death is run off her feet). The lonely outsider finds he has more in common with the dead boy and opts to stay with him rather than go to the afterlife when he is himself killed. *Sandman* was written by Neil Gaiman: it's hard to discuss Cornell's early work without this name cropping up. A recent piece by a Gaiman expert who came to *Doctor Who* late makes the case that the finale of this story, where the Doctor exacts mythological revenge on the Family of Blood far outside his usual repertoire, and the script insets a second voice-over narrative to mediate this, is the single most Gaiman-ish thing in *Doctor Who*, like, evah.[37] Even X6.4, "The Doctor's Wife" is, at best, second (and that was written by Gaiman himself). The vocabulary of this sequence and Tim's "He burns..." aria have more in common with *Sandman* than anything we have ever seen or heard in *Doctor Who* up to this point, even the storytelling framing-device of X1.8, "Father's Day".[38]

We might at this point also mention Shivering Jenny of the Shallow Brigade, a deity who manifests as a small girl with a red balloon, from the same story (collected as *Sandman: Season of Mists*) as the schoolboys and Death. Gaiman also used Koschei, directly and in the storyline of Rose Walker, the causal nexus in the shape of a teenage girl, and – as we said – the motif of hiding one's life inside a keepsake cropped up when the Marquis de Carabas (see X1.12, "Bad Wolf") was killed and came back in *Neverwhere*. Death's sibling, Despair, is said to look out at us from every mirror (although, to be fair, Gaiman lifted that conceit and quite a bit else from Jean Cocteau's *Orphée*; see 18.5, "Warriors' Gate"). And Gaiman used the idea of a powerful entity (Death) becoming human for one day per century to experience our lives.

That's actually rather an old idea, and there's a whole testament of the Bible about one such incident, but the thing about Jesus is that he had a pretty good idea what he was doing. Many of the pop-cultural versions have someone losing sight of the celestial and getting on with a mortal life. There was a lot of this in the late 80s and early 90s: Martin Scorsese's film *The Last Temptation of Christ* focussed on the idea that it would have been easy to give up messiahing and raise a family with Mary, and the Devil knows this, sending him glimpses of a satisfied ex-saviour getting old and enjoying domesticity (Cornell's confirmed that he had this in mind). Wim Wenders's *Wings of Desire* and *Faraway, So Close* are about retired angels taking part in Berlin's adjustment to the Cold War and its ending. (The former of these was remade by Hollywood as *City of Angels*; it took all the Walter Benjamin references and cameos by Nick Cave and the Bad Seeds and replaced them with Nicolas Cage and Meg Ryan apparently re-running the McGann movie, less entertainingly.)

However, we have to admit that the big one everyone has in mind here is the first release of *Superman II* (see next episode's essay for more on that). Cornell's online notes on the novel would have it that he started off wanting to do a version of this in the *Doctor Who* universe. He'd also read Peter David's *Star Trek: The Next Generation* novel *Imzaldi* and was impressed; for non-*Star Trek* fans, this was the book that broke all the Paramount rules about character limitations and garnered a reputation for being a particularly Profound and Romantic too-deep-for-the-small-screen story.

Britain has a long tradition of stories set in public schools; the sudden break between comfortable Edwardian hopefulness and a war that no-one had expected led to a lot of elegiac literature in the aftermath, as well as more aggressively modern art-forms as Europe and the World acclimatised to the changes. Juxtaposing these eras for a tragic love story was so obviously mete for Cornell's purposes that he ended up writing it twice. Cornell had talked about setting the novel just before World War II, but he and *New Adventures* editor Rebecca Levene decided the war needed to be a "genuinely meaningless" one instead. He based the school in the novel on his own experiences, with a touch more brutality and the OTC training chucked in (which goes a long way towards explaining any little errors about British schoolboys you may have noticed). The girl's red balloon was taken straight from the novel, but the nursery rhyme that's Sister of Mine's accompanying theme is a play on the Dalek-controlled girl in 25.1, "Remembrance of the Daleks" (possibly by way of *A Nightmare on Elm Street*).

Being trapped for eternity behind mirrors might also pick up on Kilgore Trout's famous theory that mirrors are leaks into other universes, a notion so common *Lost in Space* did it in the first year. In the Cornell novel, the balloon was so much a part of the Sister of Mine analogue's adopted persona that it reacted as if part of her, a trick borrowed by Moffat in "The Eleventh Hour" (X5.1). And... *New Adventures* writer Kate Orman is credited for helping Cornell with the novel, but Steven Moffat had a hand in it as well, and warrants a cameo as a curly-haired Scotsman who makes fun of Sylvester McCoy's dialect and may or may not be having it off with the local barmaid. His contribution to the story was the journal that John Smith is writing, for which you'll have to read next episode's essay. (We note, in passing, that a teacher calling himself "John Smith" telling fairy-tales that are more true than anyone realises is the framing narrative for George MacDonald's *Adela Cathcart*, from which we get "The Light Princess" and others; this was what inspired Lewis Carroll to try publishing his stories.)

Smith's stories of the Doctor are – obviously – not just stories, while Smith himself is one. This paradox is familiar from 19.1, "Castrovalva" and the sources we cited for that (Borges in particular), but the most obvious is Philip K. Dick, most clearly in *The Man in the High Castle*. The literary conceit of a fictional hero being more real than the author is as old as *Don Quixote*, but crops up in Lewis Carroll.

For the record, the scarecrow army is knowingly taken from the means the Time Lords use to apprehend the *TV Comic* version of the second Doctor, after he evaded them to move into a five-star hotel and guest on panel-shows between "The War Games" and 7.1, "Spearhead from Space". (See **Are All the Comic-Strip Adventures Fair Game?** under X4.7, "The Unicorn and the Wasp" and **Is There a Season 6B?** under 22.4, "The Two Doctors".) We might also note Cornell's former colleagues Keith Topping and Martin Day and their BBC Books entry *The Hollow Men*. The way the first scarecrow beckons to the farmer is noticeably like the gesture made by a scarecrow in *The Singing Detective*. There was also the end of the first series of *The League of Gentlemen* (op cit throughout this book and Volume 7) in which one character ended up being made to work as a scarecrow. The look of these ones owes more than a little to the Oogie-Boogie in *The Nightmare before Christmas*.

Additional Sources Well, in case you missed it, this has a lot in common with the Virgin *New Adventures* book *Human Nature* by Paul Cornell. There was also that fake MySpace account for Martha. One of the most famous deleted scenes of the Davies era is the long version of the instructions that Martha here fast-forwards through, in the course of which he asks her to make sure he doesn't hurt anyone, not to worry about the TARDIS, not to become involved in major historical events, not to allow his human self to abandon her, not to allow him to eat pears (another novel reference, it's on the written list of instructions for Benny) and demonstrates the same inability to stick to a coherent listing scheme that we'll see in X4.0, "Voyage of the Damned". He then spends a minute wibbling on about a Housemartins gig in 1990 (it's one of David Tennant's favourite bands, and he needed a no repetitions, no hesitations minute of continuous babble for the video) and wraps it up by reconfirming that if they are found by the Family, she knows what to do. This isn't *quite* what happened, but everything except the pears and the Housemartins gig appears in the broadcast episode – though observe that we cut to Smith eating a pear – so we can assume that's more or less valid.

Whether the tenth Doctor's favourite gig ever actually was the Housemartins is an open question, but we'll never hear anything more canonical on the subject. On the DVD box-set, you can see the whole of the message to Martha (but, mercifully, no Adam Faith), John Smith humming Bananarama to himself while shaving and the girl who becomes Sister of Mine being lured into a trap and killed by scarecrows.

Oh, Isn't That...?

- *Thomas Sangster* (schoolboy Tim Latimer; these days, he goes by Thomas Brodie-Sangster). He was a minor during the filming *of Love Actually*, so we won't blame him for appearing in that (he was doing his A-Levels when he played Tim in this story). He played the young Paul McCartney in *Nowhere Boy,* but basically, he's Ferb. Anyone unfamiliar with *Phineas and Ferb* (the only watchable thing on Disney Channel) just needs to know that there's an odd-looking kid who usually gets one line per episode, and his Englishness is part of the effect.[41] He also did voice-overs as two of the Tracy brothers in the new *Thunderbirds are Go!* He's also been in *Game of Thrones* as the relatively sensibly-named Jojen Reed, plus the recent film version of *The Maze Runner.* He can also be spotted in *Star Wars Episode VII: The Force Awakens* as a First Order Officer – again, not saying much. Oh, and he was in *Wolf Hall.*
- *Jessica Hynes* (Joan Redfern) had, until this episode went out, been Jessica Stevenson, the other half of Simon Pegg's acting and writing partnership in *Spaced* (and thus the special "surprise" guest in *Shaun of the Dead*). She'd worked with Davies before on *Bob & Rose*, and voiced Mafalda Hopkirk in *Harry Potter and the Order of the Phoenix* (Sophie Thompson actually played the part in *Deathly Hallows*). Shortly before this, she'd had a moderate hit with a timid sitcom called *According to Bex* (we mention this simply because it was seen more on US telly than here), more recently she was in *The Royal Family* and *TwentyTwelve* (see X2.11, "Fear Her") and the film *Son of Rambow*. We'll discuss other projects of hers later.
- *Rebekah Staton* (Jenny/ Mother of Mine). Breakout star of BBC3's sitcom *Pulling* which, as the name suggests (if you're English, anyway), is about single girls looking for shags.
- *Harry Lloyd* (schoolbully Jeremy Baines/ Brother of Mine) had been in an adaptation of *Goodbye, Mr Chips,* but is now mainly known for playing Will Scarlett in the me-too *Robin Hood* (see the essay with X4.10, "Midnight") and is another of the growing band of *Doctor Who/ Game of Thrones* crossover actors. He was Daenerys Targaryen's brother, Viserys, who gets to wear a crown of gold.

X3.9: "The Family of Blood"

(2nd June, 2007)

Which One is This? The Last Temptation of Doctor Who. Alas for Smith and Joan.

Firsts and Lasts We have our first official confirmation that dwarf star alloy exists in the Doctor's universe (since its introduction in 18.5, "Warrior's Gate" technically happened in a bubble universe). Steven Moffat will borrow it again later.

This is the first time that we've seen any reference to Remembrance Day, other than possibly the title of "Remembrance of the Daleks" (25.1), and certainly the first time anyone has poppies.

Watch Out For...

- After this episode, nobody has any excuse not to be able to name all the bones of the hand.
- It's always a bit difficult to tell with Paul Cornell to what extent he's written a scene like Latimer's description of the Doctor as "fire and ice

How Many Times Has This Story Happened?

The summer blockbusters of 2013 included two odd specimens: *Star Trek: Into Darkness* was amusing – if annoying – for the decision to make an English actor the Most Evil Person in History (again) and to give Noel Clarke one line of dialogue after ten minutes of quality scowling, while *Man of Steel* has an English Superman defeating an American General Zod, rather than vice versa as in 1980. Both were rebooting a well-established film franchise derived from something that was even-more-established before the first film. Yet both were aberrant remakes of earlier film manifestations (the first sequel in both cases), which seemed to rely on the audiences knowing the originals well enough to spot the connections, paraphrases and differences. The sting in the tail is that *Man of Steel* takes most of its shape from *Superman II*, a film which exists in two radically different forms anyway. Inevitably, when the subject of "Human Nature"/ "The Family of Blood" comes up, we'll be talking about *Superman II* quite a bit – but the question we ought to consider first is what the producers of *Into Darkness* thought they were doing, and what that tells us when evaluating the relationship of the novel *Human Nature* to the televised... well, is it a "version"?

The 2009 *Star Trek* film from J.J. Abrams devoted a lot of time and effort to establishing a time-paradox storyline, which freed the new chronology and cast from the need to develop in the same way as all the TV series and subsequent films, spin-offs and books that came before. (Maybe they were worried that Lieutenant Arex from the cartoon series would take up most of the effects budget.) Then *Into Darkness* bust a gut contorting logic so the plot and characters (and occasional embarrassing dialogue) from *Star Trek II: Wrath of Khan* could recur in this exciting fresh universe. The result is conceptually like "Rise of the Cybermen" (X2.5), but without the possibility of the Bad Wolf manipulating the timelines to create a parallel universe so conveniently story-friendly.

Where the first film in this line cast everyone to look as if they could feasibly grow up into the *Star Trek* actors we recall from the 60s (or the 80s films), *Into Darkness* tried to sell the idea that Benedict Cumberbatch's Khan would, if allowed to live, turn into the one portrayed by Ricardo Montalban (neither was especially convincing as a Sikh, but never mind). The alteration to history that made the first film divert from the timeline that leads to *DS9:* "Take Me Out to the Holosuite" and *ToS:* "The Way to Eden" has also, it seems, affected events two centuries beforehand that – on the strength of *Star Trek: First Contact* – seemed to lead to warp drives and the Federation. This all seems to be a rather perverse move, to spend so much time and effort on a film that riffs on another film that a fair percentage of the potential audience already know (and obviously love), and the rest need to know to get all the plot-twists and in-jokes. The film could be considered to be a fantasia on the plot of *The Wrath of Khan* and *ToS:* "Space Seed" or – to be generous and imagine how anyone a few decades from now will see it – a Bad Quarto. Or, conceivably, this one will be the *ur*-text and *The Wrath of Khan* might be thought of as a trial run, the way Michael Mann's *Manhunter* relates to Brett Rattner's *Red Dragon*. (Or maybe *Star Trek* as a whole will be thought of as a corrupted text of *Blakes 7*. It could happen.)

The problem is that these two recent *Trek* flicks tried to have it both ways – to be respectful of, but distinct from, the accepted time-line *and* to be a wholesale remake with modern blockbuster plotting and set-pieces. *Doctor Who* looked like doing the latter in its first year back from the abyss, but then admitted to being part of the same basic sequence of events as before, and this caused a lot of trouble. On first broadcast, it was possible to accept "Rose" (X1.1) as a remake of "Spearhead from Space" (7.1), but if the latter is now inescapably part of the Doctor's past and England's history – and with the Master and Sarah Jane Smith coming back and talking about old times, it has to be – then the plot of "Rose" becomes a bit silly. Similar problems apply to "The Android Invasion" (13.4) and "The Christmas Invasion" (X2.0) – mutually-exclusive stories about British probes into the solar system with long-term consequences we *have* to accept for several recent episodes of *Doctor Who* and the whole of *The Sarah Jane Adventures* to exist (see **Was There a Martian Time-Slip?** under X4.16, "The Waters of Mars"), while the whole messy business of how much of *Torchwood* can be said to have "happened" in the Moffat era is one for a whole essay later.

Back in the 80s, fandom convulsed itself in disputes over the twin-headed monster of Continuity and Canon (both thought worthy of capitals and used as either noun or adjective). We devoted a lot of Volume 6 to trying to draw a line under it with a common-sense approach, and illustrated how the new-series crew were being pragmatic and inclu-

continued on Page 189...

and rage" because that's the sort of thing he's known for doing, or whether Russell T Davies did it as a Cornell pastiche. It's either tremendously effective or you'll laugh yourself off the couch. The flash-forward, where John and Joan see a whole future that is denied them, is like this but even more so.

As high-stakes gambles go, the inserted narratives we get this episode were the boldest move since the series came back. Director Charles Palmer takes his cue from this and includes a few daringly impressionistic scenes, notably the overlapping images of the scarecrow army, and carefully grades the image for the Doctor's reprisals against the Family to make it uncertain whether it really happened as we see it.

• The episode's climax is like a sick inversion of *Bagpuss*: when the Doctor wakes up, all his enemies have to stay awake forever. For some reason, possibly connected with who's got the author credit, the Doctor abruptly becomes fashionably "dark" and punishes the Family with astonishingly sadistic and impossible fairy-tale living deaths. Even by Whitaker-Science standards, audiences may be forgiven for snorting "fiddlesticks and flapdoodle" as a girl is made to hide behind every mirror ever like in *Sapphire and Steel*.

The Continuity

The Doctor Spends his first actual scene pretending to be John Smith, so that he can make the Family's ship explode (after asking them to stop bombing the village). Afterward, he somehow contrives to pack them all into his TARDIS and sentence them to various ghastly fates. [We don't need to regard Son of Mine as a reliable narrator on this score, but we're probably intended to believe the part where the Doctor does all of this without a trace of anger.]

The Doctor asks Joan to come with him, saying that he's capable of everything that John was. [How seriously or honestly he's speaking, given that someone who's just as in love with him has been pining away for eight episodes, is an open question. Especially given that he wants Joan to be a companion rather than wife.] It puzzles him to be turned down. He shows no sign of reaction when Joan says John was braver than he is. When she asks whether anyone would have died if he hadn't come here on a whim, he doesn't argue the point.

Once he's reverted to his Time Lord self, he can use 'simple olfactory misdirection' – 'an elementary trick in certain parts of the galaxy' – to fool the Family into thinking that he's still human. He falls over himself to agree that Martha made up her disclosure (to Smith) about being in love with him. Son of Mine claims that the Doctor visits Sister of Mine every year, and thinks he might forgive her some day.

The Doctor tells Joan that he could change back into John Smith, but that he won't. End of discussion. [Towards the end of the story, the Doctor – or Smith, or perhaps the actor David Tennant – narrates a short description of WWI over the scene with wartime Timothy. We refer you to **Who's Narrating This Series?** in Volume 6 and the essay with X3.10, "Blink".]

• *Ethics.* [Hoo-boy.] After waking up to find that, in his absence, several people have been murdered, two women have fallen for him in the explicitly romantic sense, and his distraught human self has been rectified the situation by committing suicide, the Doctor goes on a rampage and sentences the Family to eternal nothingness. [For crimes not tremendously different from plenty of other monsters he's encountered – the main difference is that they survive unlike, say, the Slitheen, because the Doctor went out of his way to ensure that. One way of interpreting this is that – owing to the personal stakes involved – the Doctor has simply been pushed too far on this occasion. No second chances.]

There's a strong hint that the timeline's been changed when Tim survives the shelling. [We never see the end of his original prognostication, but with Murray Gold blasting triumphant music everywhere and Thomas Sangster shouting "Thank you, Doctor!", it's a fair cop. It was definitely a timeline change in the novel, at any rate.]

• *Inventory: The Watch.* It gives advice to Timothy [but isn't helpful enough to suggest he go to Martha before battle is joined]. Tim's able to open it and direct a golden memory ray [of the Racnoss genocide in X3.0, "The Runaway Bride", to be specific] to mentally overpower Sister of Mine for a moment, or to lure the Family with the Doctor's "scent". John can sense the Doctor's mind "sleeping" in the watch, but Joan can't tell anything about it. [Martha never touches it, so it might have any effect on her. In the original novel, the MacGuffin starts turning Tim into a Time Lord and the Doctor all on its own. It would explain

How Many Times Has This Story Happened?

continued from Page 187...

sive. However, we were forced to admit even then that there were odd points where this became hazy, and television stories reworking material from other media by the same author had already accumulated a lot of screen-time. Add to this the material than made it onto television that was freely (or not-so-freely) borrowed from the other versions of *Doctor Who,* and the question again becomes vexed.

Between 1990 and 2003, there were any number of self-appointed "continuations" of *Doctor Who* which – in the absence of a BBC television series – were all roughly equal in status. The *Doctor Who Magazine* strip had seniority; it had started in 1979 and developed its own continuity and autonomous storylines. The Virgin Books *New Adventures* had the imprimatur of the BBC; they could claim the heritage of Target novelisations from 1973, and the three reprints from 1965. Then BBC Books took back the rights after the botched TV relaunch in 1996. Big Finish audio, the relative newcomer, had actual actors and music and sound effects, so felt more like television adventures. There was also a comic strip in the *Radio Times*. BBC Online put out *The Scream of the Shalka* just in time for this to not be "official" any more, as its ninth Doctor (played by Richard E Grant) lost out in the canon-sweepstakes to the Christopher Eccleston version. We'll examine the specific echoes of *TV Comic*'s strip in Gareth Roberts's stories, Roberts reworking his *DWM* strips for television and the complex relationship the strip "The Flood" has to a number of Davies projects in a different essay (**Are All the Comic-Strip Adventures Fair Game?** under X4.7, "The Unicorn and the Wasp") and allude sideways to *Star Trek* again, and a different comic-strip, shortly beforehand (**Is This the *Star Trek* Universe?** under X4.6, "The Doctor's Daughter"). So, for now, here are a few general comments to set out our stall...

In essence, anything that happened in print, on audio, online or in pictorial form between the last original-series story, "Survival" (26.4) in 1989, and the first new-series one, "Rose" in 2005, is, by virtue of having been licenced by the BBC, just as available to be reworked as any broadcast episode. (The special case of the TV Movie is one for Fox's lawyers to resolve; see X3.11, "Utopia". And the BBC keep forgetting that Studio Canal own the rights to the two Peter Cushing films.) The executive producer can choose which specimen of which sub-franchise he can include, just as that post confers the right to pretend that such-and-such an earlier broadcast episode never happened. (Or, more commonly, to forget the details and cause a mess in the middle of an attempt to simplify continuity – we weep to think about it, but almost all of Volume 9 will provide examples.) However, for anyone attempting an in-universe account of (deep breath) what consequences come from acknowledging events in one or other of the mutually-exclusive narratives being cherry-picked (exhale), there is – brace yourselves – a get-out clause of nested "universes" and aberrant time-lines.

In superhero comics, there was a strange distinction made about the main narrative and "Imaginary Stories" (sic), where alternatives were tried out behind a sort of fictional quarantine. Big Finish tried this when they wanted to use actors they thought *ought* to have been the Doctor, and it allows partial acceptance of parodies, unauthorised fan projects, pet theories and the like. The *Star Wars* franchise did something similar, swapping round *The Empire Strikes Back* so that Leia trains under Yoda, for example. Each of these is a one-off, a side-line from the main course of events as told in the "real" story. Thus, in *The Scream of the Shalka,* the ninth Doctor on offer was played by Richard E Grant, *after* he'd been a tenth Doctor (A4, "The Curse of Fatal Death") and in a project where Sir Derek Jacobi was the Master *before* he was Professor Yana.

In **Where Does "Canon" End?** under 26.1, "Battlefield", we tried a different tack, arguing that access to a particular manifestation of *Doctor Who* might be the gold standard. This has obvious problems if you argue that the television version must of necessity be paramount, since we have less access to, say, "The Macra Terror" (4.7) than to the various short stories on the BBC website. Here we have to admit a small problem: we have no idea how many people have read *Human Nature*. The book sold at least eight thousand copies, as they all did on average, possibly three times that many. This is largely because a lot of people had them on order as a matter of course and there's no guarantee that any copy sold was read. Conversely, the books were a regular feature of children's libraries in the UK and there was a brisk trade in second-hand copies via Oxfam, jumble-sales and

continued on Page 191...

Martha not keeping the watch on hand herself, if continued exposure to it could have this effect on a time traveller in the televised version.]

Somehow, it's able to give both Joan and John an image of what their lives could be like, with the two of them marrying, having children and grandchildren, and John dying a quiet death of old age in hospital. [Only after this is John brave enough to open it, so it performs its function perfectly.]

Once Smith's opened the watch, it's emptied of all Time Lord-related content and becomes a normal pocket-watch – which the Doctor gifts to Tim as a souvenir. It's still telling time when Tim consults it in a muddy foxhole. The Doctor comments that Tim was accessed the Time Lord mind within because he was born with a low-level telepathic field (an 'extra synaptic engram casing').

• *Inventory: Other.* He has glasses in his pocket when he comes on board the Family's spaceship, so he can put them on for the reveal. [Since he's still wearing the clothes that John Smith had at the dance, where the glasses came from is a puzzle.]

Dwarf star alloy chains are either kept in the TARDIS boot cupboard, or the Doctor interrupts his methodical vengeance to collect them from somewhere. [Halford's, perhaps.]

The TARDIS Can, it seems, be parked on the edge of a collapsing galaxy's event horizon without being pulled in. [Good brakes. We're forced to presume that the TARDIS time is synched with that of the Family's Time Vortex manipulator, since there's no point having the Doctor spend three months waiting for the Family to die off if only five minutes have passed for them.]

The Supporting Cast

• *John Smith* is bloody terrified to find out that all the aliens and fantasies he's been writing about are real, particularly when he finds out about his alternative self; it takes his best friend and his lover most of the episode to talk him into accepting the watch. He doesn't even recognise the name TARDIS. Only after seeing it and having Joan point out that it's mentioned in his journal does he start seriously contemplating being the same person as the Doctor he's been writing about.

He makes for the school right after the dance, even though the Family have indicated that they aren't interested in anyone else. [No one quite plays it as though John is selfishly endangering a school full of minors, save for Joan's comment that he should know it's wrong.] When the little girl shoots the Headmaster in front of him, he immediately takes command and orders the boys to retreat. Smith holds a pistol when the scarecrows besiege the school – but never fires it.

He's horrified that the Doctor didn't even conceptualise that falling in love was a possibility. He contemplates simply giving the Family the watch, but accepts Joan's argument that it would be more terrible to allow aliens to run riot with its powers across the stars. Eventually, he's brave enough to open the watch and change back to the Doctor.

• *Martha.* She grabs Baines's gun and pulls off a convincing bluff that she's willing to use it. Upon finding that John has been standing around with his girlfriend being confused when everyone else has fled in panic, she tells him he's rubbish as a human.

She admits to being in love with the Doctor while trying to explain him to John [it's not her fault under the circumstances, but that's hardly a recommendation to a man who's just discovered the tender emotions]. When he remembers the exchange as the Doctor, she fumbles her way through a cover explanation and is tremendously frustrated when he takes her at face value yet again. She asks if she ought to go talk to Joan after it's all over. [Joan is the only woman Martha knows capable of understanding what she herself is going through; at the start of the episode, she explains that she's not a romantic rival to Joan in an even more painfully awkward scene.]

As usual, she starts hugging people when under stress; Timothy's the only one who'll accept one from her, so he enjoys two. She explains she's a doctor to a disbelieving Joan, and names and demonstrates the bones of the hand.

When they leave Timothy, she has a black jacket on that's noticeably more subdued than the red leather she's favoured all year [it's the one Tim sees in a flash of her running when he accidentally touches her].

The Non-Humans

• *The Family of Blood.* In their travels, they've picked up enough Earth history to know about the coming war [it'd be an obvious datum to anyone tracking down a time trail and correcting for a few years difference either side]. They also know the word TARDIS, and identify the police box [they were shooting at it last episode, although

How Many Times Has This Story Happened?

continued from Page 189...

library sales. Moreover, the book was posted on the BBC's *Doctor Who* site in November 2002 and relaunched to tie in with Series 3 five years later. How many hits were the same people over and over is unknowable, but the book was removed in late 2010. The broadcast episodes were officially tallied at 7.7 million viewers for the first and 7.2 million for the second, but – again – how many of those people were just in the room while it was on and how many watched with the intensity that a reader reads is unmeasurable. And we can't dismiss the book for being "merely" a book. After all, the Daleks had two goes at tunnelling to the Earth's core from Bedfordshire, one of which was shown once in 1964 and the other several dozen times after a cinema release worldwide. Even the Doctor seems to remember this version rather than the telly one (12.4,"Genesis of the Daleks"; cf 2.2, "The Dalek Invasion of Earth" and *Dalek Invasion Earth 2150 AD*).

Instead, let's get back to *Superman II*. Here we have the classic Imaginary Story scenario – Lois Lane finally figures out that Clark Kent and Superman are the same person and they get romantically involved, requiring him to surrender his powers and live like one of us. To keep it from contaminating other stories that have the basic set-up everyone knows, they have to press a hefty reset button to curtail any threat of – you know – consequences. Due to the weird nature of this franchise's custody in the late 70s, the first two films have two directors (sort of) and two sets of script: the end of the first film was written for the second and the start of *both* films had similar depictions of the trial of the Zod squad (see 2.8, "The Chase" and 20.7, "The Five Doctors"). The 1980 *Superman II* release, credited to Richard Lester but bearing few of his characteristic touches, is 2/3 of the version directed by Richard Donner. The 1978 original *Superman* is credited to Donner, but has some scenes by Lester and both of these first films were substantially shot at the same time. The 2006 edit of *Superman II* is supposedly Donner's director's cut, minus a few scenes never shot and with a lot of re-worked scenes from the 1978 film. Got that? The big difference, for our purposes, between Donner's *II* and Lester's is that the cop-out ending is changed – Lester has it that everything we've seen really happened but that Lois is made to forget it all with a magic kiss and reverts to her factory settings (see X4.13,"Journey's End"), while Donner has the whole story made never to have happened by Supe flying around the world really really fast (see X3.13, "Last of the Time Lords"). Can we apply a similar distinction to the 90s sources of twenty-first century TV *Who*? As it happens, we can.

Sometimes.

The last official *Doctor Who* tie-in that Virgin produced was Gareth Roberts's *The Well-Mannered War*, which closes off everything after 17.6,"Shada" by having the 80s television episodes and all subsequent manifestations confined to the Land of Fiction (6.2, "The Mind Robber"), hence the Doctor's increasingly costume-like clothing from 18.1,"The Leisure Hive". However, the penultimate one, *The Dying Days* by Lance Parkin, takes advantage of a loophole in the contracts and has the McGann Doctor and Bernice Summerfield team up with the Brigadier and UNIT in an adventure that, with Marc Platt's *Lungbarrow*, sets up Summerfield's own borderline-rights-infringing Virgin Books series which toward the end got involved in a storyline about beings who created pocket-universes and fought a war across time. Some of what that entailed resulted from Lawrence Miles (by his own admission) misinterpreting Terrance Dicks's *The Eight Doctors*, thinking that the Virgin novels and the BBC ones took place in different continuities and then trying to codify the idea in two of his works: the Benny novel *Dead Romance* and the BBC Books two-parter *Interference*. The idea that the *New Adventures* and the *Eighth Doctor Adventures* didn't share the same universe never really caught on, *but* some of that storyline seeped into those franchises (they used a lot of the same writers), and the ability to traverse the boundaries of these fictions/ cosmoses/ continuities became more and more important.

Then Big Finish – in a bid to convince the BBC that they could, in fact, make pro-level audio stories – got the rights to the Summerfield character and re-told a lot of the early, funny Benny novels in audio form... which meant changing the details than made the connections to other in-house versions of earlier stories potentially muzzy. So, if you want to make a Venn Diagram of "realities", then you can put the Virgin Benny books *inside* the Big Finish audios, but right up against the edge, the *New Adventures* touching where the Virgin Bennies border the Big Finish stuff, the Big Finish

continued on Page 193...

how they know its name is another matter].

The Family can telepathically communicate, as evidenced by the green-glowing effect used last episode. Dying while in the form of their hosts is a danger to them. They've used 'molecular fringe animation' to turn the scarecrows into an army. Their ship has sufficient bombing armament to destroy an English village.

As alluded to last episode, Mother of Mine can access 'traces of memory' from her host body, but it's akin to her looking something up in its mental database; the Family, quite clearly, doesn't have full command of their hosts' memories and personalities all the time. [Son of Mine, certainly, forgets all of Baines's grammar when taunting the Head: "You have an army," he says, "So do we" (sic). So, apart from the various murders Son of Mine has committed, he deserves to be obliterated for incorrect auxiliary verb-use.]

To summarize their various fates: Father is wrapped in dwarf star alloy chains and chucked down something like a deserted elevator shaft; Mother is tossed into the event horizon of an imploding galaxy, to spend eternity in her dying moments [see **What's With All These Black Holes?** under 10.1, "The Three Doctors"]; Sister is entrapped in all mirrors everywhere and Son is frozen in time as a protector over England, in the same scarecrow getup as the ones they were using as soldiers.

History

• *Dating.* There's a female vicar at the Remembrance Service. [So the final scene is 13th November, 1994 at the earliest; that's the first year the Church of England had them. If we presume that Timothy was neat enough to have been born in 1900 – and he must be about that age, if he was a schoolboy in 1913 – he'll have to be 94 by then, so let's assume it was the first year.] The shot of Martha running is obviously nearer our time, and has her in the black jacket from the end of the story, so we will assume an unseen adventure in the early twenty-first century [although probably not in the four days between her meeting the Doctor and Saxon becoming Prime Minister; see X3.12, "The Sound of Drums"].

English Lessons While we're here, we should discuss poppies. It's traditional in Commonwealth countries to wear red poppies to memorialise veterans and victims of war, and raise funds for their dependents; this is a Remembrance Day tradition along the lines of Memorial Day in America. [Only less politically charged, despite the efforts of some politicians. In the 80s, the wearing of white poppies stirred up a degree of controversy; this was a symbolic "memorial" for any soldiers or family of soldiers who might be killed or injured in any future conflicts. For what it's worth, Margaret Thatcher despised the concept of white poppies, so the fact that they've had a look-in in recent years is probably an overall plus. Still, they haven't been so widespread that Martha and the Doctor wearing red ones needs to be interpreted as anything other than a gesture of respect to Timothy.]

Things That Don't Make Sense ("Human Nature" and "The Family of Blood") [A caveat here that many of the biggest issues were forced by the demands of the adaptation; by this logic, we can handwave the TARDIS being able to create a solid 1913 identify for the Doctor from scratch, his two-month courtship of an Edwardian lady and the whole question of why the Chameleon Arch gives you amnesia, because Paul Cornell and Russell Davies are having to stuff an entire novel into the equivalent of a four-part episode. (At least the gaffe from the book about mayonnaise coming in jars in 1913 has been expunged.) Nevertheless, we're reviewing the episode that aired rather than the novel, and on its own terms...]

This would be a one-episode story if it hadn't been decided, somehow, to keep the watch in John Smith's study where anything could happen to it. Why not just leave it in the TARDIS? Or, why doesn't Martha just keep it on hand for three months (unless continual contact with it would have her turning into the Doctor)?

We should also ask who decided that Our Heroes should hide out in a very small village in rural England in 1913? Did the TARDIS select it? Did the Doctor? If the rationale was that present-day London would be the most obvious place to look for the Doctor, why pick the third-most-likely hiding-place instead? After all, if you're looking to hide from beings that can be a *bit* confused by Farringham's tiny population, and if both Martha and a police box would be conspicuous in such a setting... why not go to Notting Hill in the late 60s, or one of the umpteen planets colonised in future by vast numbers of racially-mixed people with English accents? If the TARDIS

How Many Times Has This Story Happened?

continued from Page 191...

Benny books inside the audios, the *DWM* strip just lightly touching the *New Adventures* causing an Abslom Daak-shaped bruise (see X8.5, "Time Heist")... and, well, eventually, you find they can all be argued to be inside each other.

So whilst Davies and Moffat can exercise *droit de signeur* over anything someone else wrote for Virgin, Big Finish, BBC Books or Marvel/ Panini, and be allowed to get away with it, the relationship between any given source material and the TV story that emerged from it (such as the audio *Jubilee* and X1.6, "Dalek"; the audio *Spare Parts* and X2.5, "Rise of the Cybermen"; and more) isn't always the same. If we define canonicity as simply "this adds something to my enjoyment or understanding of what I'm watching", and apply a rule of thumb that any televised adventure readily available to Joe Public overwrites any wiped episode or tie-in work, we might finally be getting somewhere. Thematically, *Jubilee* has a lot in common with "Dalek" – but it doesn't explicitly contradict it; they are both available to anyone who wishes to detach them from the format/ franchise whence it arose. The BBC Wales series has contradicted Big Finish a few times – but then again, it's also contradicted earlier iterations of *Doctor Who*. It's also given us migraines trying to resolve Moffat storylines with Davies ones. We're getting paid to try to make all the televised adventures work together as one coherent whole, but you can choose what you include.

We've been here before. In **Who Narrates This Series?** (under 23.1, "The Mysterious Planet"), we entertained the notion (familiar to hardcore Sherlock Holmes fans) that the account we have is a lightly fictionalised version of real events with a few details changed. The BBC has vouchsafed the Doctor's exploits and is retelling them in melodramatic form with actors who look vaguely like the real people, and scripts that attempt to make sense of bizarre events that no sensible writer would make up (hence the unexpected and apparently random casting changes and plotlines that make little or no sense). If we assume that a sequence of events like the two stories of John Smith in 1913/14 really happened to a Time Lord called the Doctor, and that Paul Cornell has tried to explain it in two different formats, reconciling it awkwardly to the narratives of the Doctor's life that surround it in both cases (hence both Professor Bernice Summerfield and Martha Jones being on hand and the Doctor's "soul" being hidden in a cricket-ball *and* a pocket-watch), we might be able to make both stories equivalent, like shadows on the wall of Plato's cave both cast by the same real-but-inaccessible object. We could extend this idea ad infinitum and have Benny Summerfield, Iris Wildthyme and River Song all be *roman a clef* approximations of the same character, but that way madness (and A3, "Dimensions in Time") lurks in waiting.

The specific case of "Human Nature" is complicated because in the television account of that name, we have the person who is working on a fiction that we sort-of remember as real events. In the novel with the same title, John Smith's made-up story – co-written by Steven Moffat – tells of an inventor whose wibbly-wobbly timey-wimey adventuring rewrites his own past. He creates a whole race of god-like time-travellers with two hearts and becomes one of them, forgetting that he was ever a nice old man pottering around in a home-built time machine. If we take this at face value, the "canonical" adventures star Peter Cushing and the whole television series and various others are Imaginary Stories. Let's not rule out Moffat using this to resolve all the complex storylines he's started and can't seem to stop (see Volumes 9 and 10). If everything in *Doctor Who* is "inside" a story told by someone whose other stories are what we know to be – within the overall narrative of the series – "true", can we disregard it?

Concerning Cornell's opinion on the canonicity of "Human Nature" as against *Human Nature*, he started off with the premise that the telly version would be canonical, and that the NA version had been run over by a Time War. He also included "Genesis of the Daleks" and 14.3, "The Deadly Assassin" in his reckoning of what didn't count any more. There's a problem even with that: any other author who'd adapted a Virgin book for television might have been able to argue this, but Cornell, as author of "Father's Day" (X1.8), had the Doctor explicitly state on screen that he and Rose can remember an incident that was removed from time (see **The Reapers, er... *What?*** under that episode). Moreover, both Davros and Sarah remember having met in Skaro's early days ("Journey's End"), even if the details vary a bit. (Davros apparently recorded all of his chats with the Doctor, to play back in X9.1, "The Magician's

continued on Page 195...

has nostalgically picked gilded-age Earth because it fits with the first five Doctors' personae, it couldn't have chosen a *worse* locale that this unless they somehow tried to smuggle Martha onto one of Shackleton's polar expeditions without the lads noticing. If it's to minimise potential casualties, a small but diverse community in a period the Doctor doesn't visit much (the 1990s would be a good bet) might have been wiser. And all of this presumes that even if the Family didn't see Martha's face (or skin colour, or else they could easily pick her out among a village full of white people), they didn't catch a whiff of her in the opening scene when she was running for her life and sweating a bit.

In fact, given the haste and panic of the teaser, and that the plan to turn the Doctor human is made up on the fly, *when*, exactly, does he record the instructions of how Martha should look after him? Yes, the TARDIS systems can make a Doctor-shaped interface, but this is obviously very specifically recorded and done on the scanner, rather than appearing like Susannah York in *Superman II* (to pluck an example from the air) as happens in the very next story and many others. Oh, and as at least one person connected with this guidebook has Nottingham links, we should mention that John Smith's made-up memories of his childhood are complete gibberish. Radford's a village in the Rushcliffe district west of the city, just next to Saxondale, a long way from Broadmarsh Street (in the city itself, south of the city centre, with one of Britain's oldest shopping malls slapped on top of it and near the main railway station). Perhaps this was a deliberate ploy in the script to make us think Joan would get a map and check, leading to the questions about where Smith played as a child, but it's just as likely to be a mistake by the author or Davies. And how exactly does Joan get out of her ball gown and into a nurse's uniform so quickly?

The Chameleon Arch is fairly unhelpful at hiding anyone on purpose, given the way that John Smith can't seem to shut up about adventures that are a dead giveaway to any nefarious aliens who might be hunting him. (Possibly, it's another indication that the Doctor rigged up this system for an entirely different purpose once.) The watch, meanwhile, is running a clips compilation for that small percentage of latent telepaths among the population, who can overhear it yelling *I contain the soul of a Time Lord, yo!* Except... if the watch is operating a catch-up service of the Doctor's adventures, where are Smith's dreams coming from? He has no reason to remember being the Doctor because the Doctor, such as he is, lurks inside a mechanical device. The only way this works is if the TARDIS, or the Arch, has shoddily fashioned a human body with the same one-in-a-million genetic quirk as Tim's. And how crap is the watch's perception filter, if Smith draws the watch several times in his journal alongside the TARDIS? The Ship also flags it up by having Smith "remember" that his dad was a watchmaker.

[All right, there are two options for this... either every TARDIS has a Chameleon Arch, for some unaccountable reason, and they can be set for any species. Or, the Doctor made one for his personal use and calibrated it to "human", because he's the Doctor. The dialogue and direction suggest that the Arch defaults to human, but under what circumstances would the Time Lords normally have any need for this gizmo? Even leaving aside their ability to resurrect dead Time Lords in the Time War, why they would want such a facility? But if the Doctor had it custom-made and set to our species, possibly to allow him to forget his (apparent) destroying of Gallifrey, is it pure coincidence that the Master did the same?]

There's a scene where Martha and Jenny are outside the pub drinking halves of bitter, and Jenny thinks Martha's got her head in the clouds for wanting to drink indoors like women in That Lunnon. Quite apart from women getting beer *at all*, rather than being fobbed off with port and lemon (as would have happened as late as the 1970s), Martha seems to have managed to get served despite her skin-colour and lowly status as a skivvy. We might imagine this is more of her Jedi Mind Trick mojo with the Psychic Paper (see X3.5, "Evolution of the Daleks"), but she doesn't use that item at any of the key moments where it would have been really, *really* handy.

According to Hutchinson, his assigned Latin translations include the poet Catullus. This is 1913. Given the activities we associate with Public Schools, wouldn't his teachers have found something a bit less explicitly homoerotic?

So you're fighting monsters that are, to all appearances, ordinary scarecrows. It's a week after Guy Fawkes Night. Does it occur to you to set the straw men on fire with the candles, gas-lamps and coal-fires available (never mind that all the adults smoke)? No, you go for a hackneyed illustration

How Many Times Has This Story Happened?

continued from Page 193...

Apprentice", except 17.1, "Destiny of the Daleks" and "Spack off!")

Even if the first iteration of *Human Nature* were over-written, the Doctor has done it before and would remember the problems with Joan Redfern. So, obviously, the best way to make that problem go away is to remove "Father's Day" from the canon. But can we, given that this gave us Pete Tyler? Maybe, but we can also claim that the situation since then has changed, if the absence of the Reapers popping up after all of the other big temporal anomalies in subsequent stories is the result of the Bad Wolf, an intervention which causes other problems we'll deal with as they arise. (See **What Constitutes a Fixed Point?** under X4.2, "The Fires of Pompeii", **How is This Not a Parallel Universe?** under X4.11, "Turn Left" and **Is Time Like Bolognese Sauce?** under X5.4, "The Time of Angels".)

The other *New Adventures* novel to have been plundered so comprehensively was *Damaged Goods* by Russell T Davies, which fed into *Torchwood: Children of Earth*. Elements of Cornell's first book, *Timewyrm: Revelation* have shown up in Moffat scripts – several times – but never all in the same one, and not with the same connections between events. Many of the other books in the series were contradicted outright. It is possible, should you choose, to accept *Human Nature* alone of all the Virgin books as being canonical but, if you do, the implications of the buried fairy-tale about the Doctor's true origin mean that neither this, nor any book, nor any TV episode can really be canonical in the accepted sense... because Peter Cushing is the One True Doctor. Please, nobody tell Studio Canal.

It's probably safest to take the novel as just another Imaginary Story, but one *about* Imaginary Stories.

of the stupidity of war by machine-gunning them in slow motion instead. (The surprise is that they don't break off and play football in the mud for a bit, exchange Christmas cards then return to the slaughter.) Later, the Head is shot dead by what appears to be a schoolgirl with a ray-gun who's accompanied by a clearly hostile Baines – but no matter how bad things get, nobody seems to contemplate shooting this obviously dangerous couple. Not even trigger-happy Hutchinson.

The Family's tactics aren't all that clever either – given the pressing need to track down A) an ordinary human and B) a school boy with a watch, they just start bombing the village, at risk of killing the very people they need. We joked feebly about the scarecrows being brought to Earth by the Family, but there are an *awful* lot of these raggedy soldiers. We're still looking at a catchment area rather bigger than can be seen from ground-level (and their ship's in a valley). Their recruits are spaced out over several miles, one per field. Even if they have a Scarecrow Animator Ray, they have to nip out over the horizon and point it at each scarecrow in turn, which is only marginally less risky than two of them popping out at night and stealing scarecrows for conversion on an operating table. And we know it's muddy, so they can't use bicycles or a wheelbarrow. Yet they seem to have put together an army of flippy-floppy scarecrows in less time than it takes Joan to do up her corset. (They might make them from old clothes and straw, using the one they found in a field as a model, but then we have to assume that they came to Earth with a jumble-sale and some silage on their ship. This indicates remarkable foresight.)

Why is the TARDIS fully powered-up when the Family manhandle the Ship to the school, whereas Martha left it on tick-over as part of the silent-running routine? Why is the TARDIS in a field when the Doctor trudges up to it and chats with Martha at story's end? Then suddenly Tim's there. (Maybe his OTC training includes camouflage.) How did the noticeably not-very-tall Tim get signed up, even in the jingoistic ferment of August 1914, and even if he managed to lie about his age?

Setting aside for now whether the Doctor's punishment of the Family seems disproportionate to the other foes that he's faced (see **The Doctor**), we should ask how literally we're to take Son of Mine's account of the Doctor's wrath... because, if he has such abilities and resources at his command, a lot of other stories would have been over a lot earlier. Just sticking to the David Tennant episodes, "The Satan Pit" (X2.9) seems like a bit of a waste of time if he's got dwarf-star alloy chains and can hurl people into the event horizon of a collapsing galaxy. He could have chatted to Rose at the end of "Doomsday" (X2.13) for months on end if he can park the TARDIS there. And how did the Daleks destroy a race whose one surviving member can put someone behind every single mirror? Holding someone frozen in time disguised as a scarecrow would have prevented thousands of deaths, if he'd done it to John Lumic or Dalek Caan. A Doctor who can pull that kind of stunt isn't going to be daunted by a bunch of no-marks like the Silence. Imagine if he'd been that stroppy in earlier lives and made Gavrok (24.3, "Delta and the Bannermen") have to be in Test Card F for all eternity.

Because of all we've said in the last essay and what we know of the original novel, it almost feels weird to point this out, but... why has anyone got a cricket-ball on his person in November?

Critique ("Human Nature" and "The Family of Blood") It seems perverse to describe anything set about a century before as "retro", but in this case it's entirely justified. Partly as a budgetary discipline, but also as an aesthetic choice, this was made with as few computer effects as possible. In order to establish the Family of Blood as eerie, eldritch or uncanny, we are shown them in close-up through wide-angled lenses – a trick that was fashionable in the late 1990s. Other scenes use theatrical methods of lighting from below or simple synchronised movements. It has longer, wordier scenes and an emphasis on the boy soldiers who would be sent to the trenches.

That last bit is the most significant. In the kind of BBC drama this most closely resembles, that aspect of the Great War is almost a given, and there have been more plays and films about the hitherto less-often-told stories. The last major BBC work to tackle the usual story of "it'll be over by Christmas" had been *Blackadder Goes Forth* (1989), after which it had been one-off plays about the Angel of Gallipoli, the Christmas Eve Football Match or Queen Mary. In the 1970s, this sleepwalk into a catastrophe was ticking away behind any of the umpteen school-based period dramas or "trouble at t'mill" tales of class conflict. In many ways, therefore, *Doctor Who* was doing what it always used to: going slightly against the grain of mainstream television drama while using its resources.

One thing definitely against the mood of the times then (less so now) is having so many speaking parts for actors with Received Pronunciation. There are three speaking parts who don't (three and a half, if you count the Doctor's Gor Blimey affectation) and the two female ones are outsiders, inferiors (apparently: *we* know Martha's hiding) and the other is a local landowner who resents the school. All the rest have an aura of privilege and contempt. We gather that actor Harry Lloyd is rather a decent sort in real life, but Baines is utterly contemptible and convincingly played.

More experienced fans would have noted the definite *New Adventures* tinge – not just to the story many had read, but the portrayal of the Doctor as an elemental force playing at being a whacky character from a family TV series. There is also the way that the story refuses to simply end with the explosion and punishment, but adds tag-scene after tag-scene. This was something Paul Cornell brought to the book series that became almost *de riguer*, along with prologues and preludes and other such parentheses for what would have been "the story proper", had it been a four-parter in 1988. He did it better than most (and we note that when Martha and Jenny go to the landing site, we can hear an owl – another of the author's habits), and here it gives a sense of the focus pulling out, showing us a wider picture each time. It's not just an under-running episode being stretched. The Doctor coming back and thwarting the Family isn't the end of the story – it's left to us to decide if what we see and hear happened and, if it did, whether this was John Smith contaminating the Doctor with vindictiveness.

That this story seems out-of-keeping with Series 3 is perhaps appropriate, but what is sometimes said – that this resembles the sort of production designed to win BAFTA awards (the earnest dramas, often by Stephen Poliakoff, that get put on in Autumn on Sunday nights) – isn't entirely right. It's not really like them and it has different ambitions. At a pragmatic level, the key difference is that the majority of such pieces are about uncovering a family secret or a similar concealed truth. We go into this story knowing who John Smith really is and why Martha's so keen to protect him, the emphasis is on how resuming the usual run of adventures will affect people around them and Smith himself. The story, like the novel, is part of a sequential series and thus cannot be considered in isolation. There is no real risk that Smith will stay put.

Martha, meanwhile, is a fish out of water and has to take abuse and incomprehension stoically. In the novel, Benny had a life of her own and rather enjoyed 1913. In this version, as with Rose every so often, Martha goes undercover as a servant, but – with the whole skin-colour issue hitherto largely ignored – as soon as Martha dressed as a maid, it raised hackles (especially among American fans). The unfortunate reality is that women of any colour having as much agency as Benny gets in the book is anachronistic. To have done anything else on screen would have been insulting and weird – this is what 1913 England was genuinely like, and real people had to endure this sort of treatment and worse. Making Martha's version of the story just like Benny's would have stretched credulity and made the ducking of the race issue in the two previous trips into the past even more uncomfortable. Above all, the audience-identification figure (more than in any other story, she is the one person who knows what *Doctor Who* normality is like) is on the back foot because of prejudice. Rose would have faced it for her accent and being female; Martha gets a triple-whammy. With every effort being made to get the on-screen period details right (and we only found one small error, women getting served half-pints), this is a salutary reminder of how far we have come in a century.

If we're actively searching for things about which to gripe, maybe David Tennant keeping the sideys and not acquiring a moustache as Smith makes it harder to accept that he's a different character this story. Perhaps a bit of a Nottingham accent might have helped too. He is engaging and not so puppyish as Smith. The village dance waltz tune doesn't sound quite right for the period; a bit too 1930s, and there's an accordion on stage we can't hear in the score. There's one car they try to have in shot as often as possible (a constant problem with period dramas, one that nobody who recalls the French and Saunders spoof of *House of Elliott* can ignore). As you can tell, we're reaching now. We can't find a specific actor to single out for praise or a bum note (not everyone is happy with Thomas Sangster's Tim, especially in the 1917 flash-forward, but it rings true and there's only one line where we think of Ferb).

Seen now, in isolation, it works as a piece of drama, but the angsting over whether the Doctor is a good enough man to justify Smith's seeming death is a bit like contractual obligation. Dark's easy; any sulky teenager can write Dark. What makes this story interesting is the restraint from wallowing in it. It's still a bit out-of-synch with the rest of the story – in the second half, neither Smith nor Joan recall the way they thought of the Doctor as a paragon last episode. The whole don't-get-too-close Byronic stuff has been hammered into the ground since then; it lessens Martha's case that she never mentions his inspirational effect on everyone or all the people from her time who will suffer if there isn't a Doctor protecting this and other planets. People talking at length about how terrible the Doctor can be is a Virgin Books legacy we could have done without in the new series. So's the rather protracted end, with a series of epilogues and postscripts and codas. Nonetheless, this is by default the premier example of a type of *Doctor Who* that hadn't been done for decades, and hasn't really been tried much since.

Opting to make a 90-minute *Doctor Who* that could have been made in 1995 might be seen as a gamble (or another sneer at Michael Grade), but it's a reminder that the budget and advanced effects we by then assumed to be standard weren't the sole secret of the programme's current success. Placing it after one of the most dynamic and fast-edited episodes – one that proclaimed the pace of the new series in its very title (X3.7, "42") and showed how the staples of 70s episodes could be made to look and feel contemporary – was a smart move. As we'll see, it allowed a further development and redefined the Doctor/ Martha relationship. In the context of Series 3, it's the latest in a string of episodes that nudge at the edges of what the series does these days. Even the Dalek two-parter seemed like routine *Doctor Who* stuff done a bit differently.

Getting a drama of this kind onto Saturday nights on BBC1 (opposite an ITV elimination/ casting show plugging a West End revival of *Grease*) was an achievement. Doing it as part of a bigger series was remarkable.

The Lore

Written by Paul Cornell. Directed by Charles Palmer. Viewing figures ("Human Nature"): (BBC1) 7.7 million, (BBC3 repeats) 0.9 and 0.3 million. BBC1 AI: 86%, BBC3 AI: 88%. Viewing figures ("The Family of Blood"): (BBC1) 7.2 million, (BBC3 repeats) 0.8 and 0.3 million. Same AIs as last episode, apparently.

Repeats and Overseas Promotion *La Famille du Sang; Smith, La Montre et le Docteur; Die Natur des Menschen; Blutsbande.*

Production

As we've mentioned, the script derived from a novel published in 1995. In this, the Aubertides were after the Doctor's essence, but the Doctor had hidden it in a cricket-ball while physically becoming human and having the memories of "John Smith", a teacher in a school in (note the slight year change) April 1914. Smith began an awkward romance with the school nurse while the Doctor's companion, Benny Summerfield, had adventures of her own and hung out with Suffragettes. Russell T Davies had requested a screen version of this. He pencilled this story in to be episodes four and five of Series 3 and, while the character of Rose's replacement was still in the works, had toyed with the idea of Martha coming from this time-period (see Series 7 for a similar last-minute change and the unwieldy consequences).

The script went through a spectacular number of rewrites even for the Davies era, clocking in at 18. The first version was a straight-up adaptation, cutting out the subplots, but with Martha's family visiting her (at this point, she was still going to be from 1914). An early decision was to literally cut to the chase; the book has a lengthy build-up to the Family's literary precursors arriving. The timescale of the 1913 component, compared to the book, was curtailed, with the potential problem of Smith and Joan's tentative relationship having to blossom in under a day. The author and producers knew that John and Joan's relationship ought to go on for as long as it had in the novel, to be plausible for the time period, but there was concern that this made the aliens a bit useless, really. During this protracted scripting process, Helen Raynor had left her post as script editor to write the Dalek two-parter and Lindsay Alford took over.

Davies had deliberately refrained from rereading the novel, to maintain perspective (he recalled an incident in the book where the school turned to glass), but found he kept urging Cornell to make the adaptation more like the original, as did everyone else. Cornell had tried out a version that started with Joan and John already married. Cornell credits Davies with the decision about replacing the cricket ball hiding-place with a watch, as well as the inevitable monster baddies: the scarecrows. No one seems to know why Tim Latimer changed so much between the book and the script (in the original he's a conscientious objector, is driving an ambulance in that scene on the Somme, and is very pointedly wearing a white poppy in the analogue to the telly war memorial scene). On the other hand, Joan's racism from the novel was retained, though she refrains from insulting Martha. (Yes, she uses the n-word in the book, in a different context. Removing it from the BBC website version appears to have been the single editorial change anybody asked for when they were still putting up e-books.)

• The plan, as with the simultaneously-made "Blink", was to go for an "organic" look with as many mechanical special effects as possible. The spaceship was to have been buried (see 8.3, "The Claws of Axos"). One idea taken from the book was to include the girl's balloon as part of Daughter of Mine's physical form (this was eventually abandoned, as they couldn't figure out how to make a balloon on camera attack people convincingly).

It was obvious early on that the ambition they had for doing a whole story without computer effects or green-screen was going to be hard to realise. The invisible spaceship idea was part of this plan, albeit one that eventually needed The Mill, but many of the key decisions about how to tell this story – from the use of a simple green light to denote a telepathic conference, to the purely actorly ways of indicating aliens inside the stolen bodies – are a legacy of this wish to do "trad" *Doctor Who*. What was possible, with this restraint in place, was using a specific garish green for everything Family-related without causing CSO difficulties. Later, they decided to give the Family rather curious weapons, so "zap" effects were in fact needed. These weapons, designed by Peter McInstry, were intended to suggest a non-humanoid form for the Family (hence the awkward grip, which would give Freema Agyeman some difficulty) and to imply a biological technology – supposedly, the gun contained a creature that exuded energy-pulses in response to being pricked by the trigger.

• Late changes included Daughter of Mine's original fate (being turned into a statue) being changed to avoid similarities to "Blink" (similarly, "Wainright" became "Cartright"). She had been the narrator of the punishment round-up sequence, rather than Baines/ Son of Mine. Smith became less Doctorish, and ceased to be a doctor in his own right, but Joan got to find out the Time

Lord's true name. Cornell sat in on earlier read-throughs to get a handle on Martha.

• With the decision to make this as Block Six, concurrently with "Blink" as Block Five, this story became the responsibility of Charles Palmer, the director of Block Two, and Susie Liggatt, previously producer of *The Sarah Jane Adventures* pilot and several other dramas (notably a production of *Our Mutual Friend*). Jessica Stephenson (as she was still styled then) had been dropping increasingly overt hints that she'd like a part in the series. Wednesday, 29th November saw Tennant's first day on the production, on location at Treberfydd House way out in Brecon, the main school location. The team would be there for nearly two weeks, but plans to use this more were shelved when travel time was taken into consideration (the dance scene was to have been shot here, it seems). They began with corridors and the entrance hall, including hapless Smith's fall down the stairs (a stunt that required a crash mat), and the exterior shot with the rented vintage Peugeot. During breaks the series armourer, Fauja Singh, trained some of the boys in shooting a genuine Vickers gun.

• The scarecrows were outfitted with bladders, like the ones used to fake blood spurting from a bullet-wound, to shoot straw. As usual, Ailsa Berk was on hand to coach the actors in the monster-suits on how to move, in this case a loping walk with movement from the hips rather than the knees. She would do more orthodox choreography later.

• 7th December was Paul Cornell's set visit, and he got to see Smith's study set at Upper Boat, where they did various episode eight scenes requiring Agyeman, Hynes and Tennant. He claims to have been just to the right of shot in the pre-credit sequence of Smith waking up. Many of the books were authentic period hardbacks, and there were faked vintage photos of Tennant as a schoolmaster and a Pitman's Shorthand certificate. According to DVD commentaries, the prop newspaper Martha hands Smith is the same one with the Hooverville report, but with an altered front page. The *Journal of Impossible Things* was drawn by a trainee at the Art Department. Tennant popped over to the TARDIS set for his list for Martha (the full version is a DVD extra).

• Wednesday, 13th December was for the footage of the local village, for which they needed the period buildings at St Fagans National History Museum in Cardiff; most of the shoot was spent on the cricket-ball-and-piano scene. This was complex, as the location was extremely delicate. St Fagans is a collection of old buildings that have been painstakingly moved to one site and is a visitor attraction, thus everything has to be preserved. So, no explosives could be used for the gunfire leading up to the episode's end, no redressing was possible, and everything had to be cleared out for when the site was open to the public (note how often they take Saturdays off in this shoot). A phone box was covered over, but otherwise the location had to be untouched.

• The next day required more pick-ups of the piano, then the dance scenes, including the cliff-hanger. These were shot upstairs inside the Miners' Institute building. Tennant and Hynes had been coached by Berk in the car-park between shooting scenes, so the waltz went relatively smoothly. (This was a tango in one draft, until research revealed that this had yet to cross over from Argentina to rural Herefordshire in 1913.) By now, Tennant's illness was noticeably changing the mood, as he was saving his energy for takes rather than joking with the crew and cast as usual.

• Friday, 15th December was the last day before Christmas holiday, and they completed all of the village hall material plus the scenes outside it. Tennant was off to promote "The Runaway Bride" (X3.0) for the next three days. Agyeman had one more day of vacation than Tennant, who was called back Wednesday, 3rd January for the Family spaceship interiors at Upper Boat (actually inside the Torchwood Hub standing set), but he had the next day off (to do *The Friday Night Project*, in which he dragged up as Billie Piper for one misguided sketch and pranked uber-fan Andrew Beech in another).

• Main filming should have wrapped on Thursday, 11th December, on the Upper Boat TARDIS set, complete with *Doctor Who Confidential* and Paul Cornell on hand. They only needed the scene of Staton being thrown out of the TARDIS and the opening Martha/ Doctor scene, but Tennant was so ill, he was given extra time to recover and only the first of these were done. (The next two days were spent on the readthrough for Block 7 and script for "42", so that's what Agyeman was doing.) The much belated scene was completed Wednesday, 17th January, with Tennant coming straight from his exterior space-suit walk for "Utopia", even as Graeme Harper shot footage of Michelle Collins.

• A lot of the dialogue needed to be redubbed

with ADR due to rain and traffic (the pub scene was especially inaudible, apparently). On the music dub, a piece of nonchalant whistling was to have accompanied Martha on her bike to the hidden TARDIS but, although Julie Gardner approved, it was left until the inevitable soundtrack CD issue before Jake Jackson's gifts as a *siffleur* became known to a wider audience.

• Both this story and "Blink" were later nominated for Hugo awards for Dramatic Presentation (Short Form). The Hugos are nominated by SF fans at the annual WorldCon (whereas the Nebula Award is awarded by professional writers only, so is more analogous to the Oscar – only one *Doctor Who* episode, "The Doctor's Wife", has won this), and the shortlist is drawn from the five or so most-nominated specimens of each category. Since 2003, the "Dramatic Presentation" has been split into Short and Long, which is roughly feature films and television episodes. (But not just those: the winner the year before Moffat got one for X1.9-1.10, "The Empty Child"/ "The Doctor Dances", was Gollum's MTV Award acceptance speech. Other nominees have included one of those Pixar shorts they put on, because their movies are so brief.) As you probably know, "Blink" got the nod over this, a *Torchwood* episode and two US series, but among those rooting for Cornell was Neil Gaiman. As we will see, the success of this story and the general "buzz" around both *Doctor Who* and Gaiman led many to wonder how long it would be until he wrote an episode himself (see next volume if you don't know). Cornell eventually got his hands on a Hugo at the 2010 ceremony in Australia – briefly (see X4.16, "The Waters of Mars") – before acquiring a timeshare in a couple of them as part of the podcast SF Squeecast. No, really.

X3.10: "Blink"

(9th June, 2007)

Which One is This? Scary statues. And Carey Mulligan. And scarcely any Doctor.

Firsts and Lasts First appearance of the Weeping Angels (they'll be back). Here, they're mysterious and reasonably frightening. It's also the start of two popular refrains: "wibbley-wobbly timey-wimey", and – in stories in which the Weeping Angels return – some derivation of "Don't blink!"

It's the first time we've had a female director in the new series (and a female director at all since 22.3, "The Mark of the Rani"). And this is the first story to have been adapted from something in a *Doctor Who* Annual, although we might stretch a point for "The Fish-Men of Kundalinga" and 4.5, "The Underwater Menace".

It's also the first time this century we've seen the Doctor defeat baddies by, in effect, ducking when they are aiming from all around – something similar happened with two Gundans in 18.5, "Warriors' Gate", but making the TARDIS dematerialise so the Angels all neutralise each other is what he lands up doing with Gallifrey in 7.15, "The Day of the Doctor".

This is the start of Security Protocol 712, using a DVD to activate the TARDIS autopilot and a hologram of the Doctor as a user-interface, rather than pre-recorded messages from the Doctor himself.

Watch Out For...

• It's a Steven Moffat episode and once again he's consulted his Bumper Book of Things That Scare Children. This time he's found... Victorian masonry. The Weeping Angels are statues, except when you're not looking. Except, for most of the time, the ones in the episode aren't statues but dancers staying very still. One or two shots use polystyrene maquettes (see if you can tell which). It's lucky they look so effective, as using the same plot, scripts and directing with garden gnomes or traffic-cones would have been ridiculous.

They're statues, but they chase people. In the hands of a less-skilled director, this could have been embarrassing. This is the sort of conceit that 80s Italian horror films either got very right or very wrong. While in later return-matches, the Angels get more complicated abilities that no director could ever have managed to make work on screen, this time around they are conceptually simple enough to allow director Hettie McDonald, the cast and the design team to enlarge on the script and make even these characters engaging.

• David Tennant is in this for four short scenes, but dominates the episode. One of these scenes is a pre-recorded Emergency Protocol hologram and another is a short film clip of him answering questions we can't hear. The latter plays several times and seems, at one stage, to be the answers to anything the one-off protagonist says, by accident, and on another go-around deliberately answering

How Messed-Up Can Narrative Get?

This is a return to matters raised in the essay **Who Narrates This Programme?**, which we ran with 23.1, "The Mysterious Planet", and **How Long Should an Episode Be?** under X3.7, "42". As with a lot of the essays in this volume, the habit of online commentary to split between "in-universe" and "real-world" pieces isn't really helpful here, especially as this essay is about where those two overlap.

To summarise for those of you just joining us, the set-up of "The Trial of a Time Lord" (which took up all 14 episodes of Season Twenty-Three, but seemed much longer) indicates that everything we'd ever seen presented in 25-minute segments on BBC1 was a slightly partisan version of the Doctor's life as the Gallifreyan afterlife/ central computer, the Matrix, relayed it to the High Council or any other interested parties. In *Doctor Who*, we have examples of overt selection. The TV episodes we see tend to omit some information and keep potentially useful facts from us until a particular moment (such as when 20.7, "The Five Doctors" shows a pair of gloved hands manipulating the Timescoop, but not that it's Borusa behind it all – we only learn that when the Doctor himself finds out). We have music added, not all of which the characters in the story can hear, and decisions about which point-of-view is selected at any given moment in the story.

The fact that it *is* a story (with a start, developments and a finish of whatever kind) is itself something that *someone* has chosen and, if we agree for the moment that everything in *Doctor Who* is "real", the identity of that narrator is something occasionally touched on within the narrative (notably in Season Twenty-Three, where it's the basis of what passes for a plot). There is selection going on, possibly slanted. We came to a tentative conclusion that the source of all the images was the TARDIS, but *who* is selecting *what* bit to go *where* was left open, in the hope that more evidence would emerge.

Well, it has, but it doesn't help much.

By the time we get to "Sleep No More" (X9.9), it's evident that the provenance of the story is part of the story, with a facsimile of Reece Shearsmith arranging found footage (not all of it created when the narrator records the links) into a *Doctor Who* episode as clickbait for anyone interested in the Morpheus process so he can transmit his lethal meme. In this one case (with a freaky shrunken title sequence and where the source of the very images we're seeing is the Doctor's biggest clue), we've got a self-cleaning narrative – because there's no way this tale can reach us on the terms afforded by this conceit. Yet one shot of Clara letting herself into the TARDIS is from the Ship's perspective, and the way that we find out about all of this is – by virtue of the narrative's source being a plot point – inconceivable without intervention from the last conscious entity on the station as it splashes into Neptune's upper atmosphere.

However, drawing attention to the way the narrative is collated simply makes all stories where they *don't* do this a bit more dodgy, epistemologically, because we can't know for certain if there is any one person or intelligence mediating it. Two episodes later, we have the Doctor telling a story to Clara despite admitting that he has no way of knowing anything about her, so he is inferring her role from the gaps he notices. There's a strong hint that what we see in the flashbacks that make up the bulk of "Hell Bent" (X9.12) are "real", and an accurate account of what occurred, but there are many reasons to doubt this. One is that the bulk of the episode happens in isolated "reality bubbles", one of which is around the Cloister and affected materially by Matrix-hallucinations. Another is that, if the whole episode is narrated by guesswork by an amnesiac Doctor, all bets are off about whether any of it happened until the bit when we see Ashildr and Clara in their TARDIS. If it's collated after the fact by someone (possibly that self-same Matrix), there isn't a lot of time to do it, as the episode comes to a head five minutes before the total and utter end of everything, ever. BBC Wales has made stories with more varied exceptions to the norm of the original series, but the norm is itself quite weird when you stop and think about it.

We even got someone in "The End of Time Part One" (X4.17) calling himself The Narrator, but his testimony is messed up six ways from Sunday. For starters, he's retrospectively commenting on a story that was still happening while he was telling us all about it, as if it had passed into legend. Then it turned out he was one of the key players, and addressing a lot of other interested parties, rather than simply telling BBC1 viewers a story. Then it got really fuzzy as his narrative began with him telling us about the actions of two key players, despite the plot requiring him to not know about said actions. (The mysterious Woman in White is

continued on Page 203...

her questions. He's going to do something similar in Moffat's next episode too (X4.8, "Silence in the Library").

• Back to the design. They can't have real films being said to contain the Doctor as an Easter Egg, so they've made up 17 titles and put posters for some of them in Banto's shop. In keeping with the theme in Moffat's last two episodes, one is called *Banana Smugglers*. The Doctor's "Timey-Wimey" detector (and boy, are we going to get to hear that phrase a lot in the next few years) is a lash-up of 60s consumer electronics worthy of Jon Pertwee or Sylvester McCoy.

The Continuity

The Doctor Somehow, he's able to put together a colour clip of himself in 1969 [film, not video] and give it to Billy, a future DVD-maker, for use as an easter egg. He cheekily recommends no swimming for half an hour if one's been travelling in time without a capsule.

While stuck in 1969, he enlists Martha to do the dirty work in a shop to make some cash. [Anyone familiar with the era's *TV Comic* strip will know that more imaginative ways exist to support yourself in 60s Britain. According to the same questionable MySpace page we mentioned last story, the Doctor and Martha only spend a few weeks in 1969, in which time they contrive to get a flat together. (So presumably they're not renting. It's 1969 – and they're not married, and of mixed race... landlords back then took a dim view of either, but both at once would have been unspeakably bohemian even in London. The Doctor apparently spends most of the time watching *Coronation Street* and moping on the sofa. Still, the tenth Doctor has more reason than most to avoid drawing Torchwood's attention, so what Martha sees as him slacking may simply be hiding.]

• *Background.* He's brought Martha to see the moon landing four times. [If she's not exaggerating, it's tempting to think this is what blew a hole in the universe in the first place. See X6.2, "Day of the Moon" for more.] He says he's rubbish at weddings, particularly his own [given the highly improvised nature of the ones in X6.13, "The Wedding of River Song" and 7.15, "The Day of the Doctor", he has a point].

When Our Hero for this story, Sally, actually meets the Doctor for the last time, he's in the middle of an earlier adventure with Martha with a selection of disparate elements. He and Martha are armed with bows and arrows, and she reminds him that migration's started and they only have 20 minutes to 'red hatching', and it involves four things and a lizard. [One of them, most likely Martha, had taxi-fare handy.]

The Doctor trapped in 1969 has read and memorised the whole of Sally's dossier on the Easter Eggs and his graffiti messages.

• *Ethics.* [Given that the Doctor is made to carry out a series of predetermined actions according to a folder that Sally hands him, it's difficult to judge the Doctor's morality for such things as, for instance, his telling Billy precisely how long he's going to live. Then again, Billy might have demanded such answers in exchange for carrying out his part of the loop.]

• *Inventory: Glasses.* Worn to read off an autocue.

• *Inventory: Other.* He's constructed an exciting Heath Robinson "timey-wimey" detector that boils eggs at 30 paces – alarmingly, he seems to have discovered this inadvertently, and blown up some poor unsuspecting chicken with it. Its proper function is to *ding* when temporal anomalies happen.

• *Inventory: TARDIS Key.* [Either Martha or the Doctor must have lost their key to the Angels (we checked; the one the Doctor gives Martha in X3.7, "42" is on a thin and shimmering metallic chain that looks like a necklace, whereas the one Sally finds is looped through thick twine that frays and snaps when she pulls at it. So the Doctor probably mislaid his.]

The TARDIS It's possible to make a DVD that will set the Ship on a pre-programmed flight path. Entering the console room with an authorised control disc automatically triggers Security Protocol 712, which causes the disc to glow until inserted in an appropriate spot on the console. The disc leaves Sally and Larry behind, as well as the Angels outside the Ship. [See also X1.13, "The Parting of the Ways" when the TARDIS materialises around Rose and a Dalek to bring them into the console room. X8.7, "Kill the Moon" retroactively explains that Sally and Larry were left behind because they weren't touching the central console during take-off.] Billy confirms that the TARDIS lock's current manifestation is that of a Yale lock. He also suggests that the proportions are all wrong and the phone's a dummy [but omits

How Messed-Up Can Narrative Get?

continued from Page 201...

somehow able to contact Wilf, a trick that could have been handy if any of the other High Council members knew about it.) At the time of telling us certain of the events in "The End of Time Part One", the character played by Timothy Dalton was speaking with a certainty that Part Two's developments show he cannot have had. In the following week, we see the President of the Time Lords, also played by Dalton and addressed as "Rassilon" by the Doctor, learning part of the story he had already told us and asking the scabby Soothsayer's advice about possible ways out of the pickle they were in.

It gets worse: the sanest way to account for Part One's narrative gimmick is to assume that it's Rassilon telling the Time Lords *why* his brilliant plan backfired, retrospectively after the events of Part Two. But then the whole hype about "humanity's last day" only works if you are in that part of the story where the Master has become everyone, and that was over and done with by the time we think the Narrator was speaking, and he would have known that (because we saw him undo it all himself). And then the same character (er, we think) is in "Hell Bent" as if none of the earlier story happened.

There's a very noticeable gap in the provenance of voice-overs. If Rose is telling us all how she sort-of died from within a parallel universe shut off from the TARDIS (X2.13, "Doomsday"), how are we hearing this? Now, admittedly Rose came back and the Ship was able to drop her, Jackie and the spare Doctor off, but if the "I died" sob-story came from this encounter, it is evidently no longer even as true as it was in "Doomsday". It could, of course, be a side-effect of the link-up at the end of that episode that somehow had the Doctor able to see the shoreline and Mickey. However, it's all in the past tense, as if told to us by someone who experienced the signal shutting off.

The basic problem with all retrospective first-person narrative is that the narrator needs, at some time, a chance to tell someone – us or an implied audience – and therefore to have both witnessed the bulk of the events and lived to have told the tale. Inserting such a narrative, or fragments from it, into the ostensibly neutral omniscient third-person account we've come to accept as standard means that we've had to ask the narrator of that section to tell us about it with hindsight. When we get a sequence like the wrap-up of "The Family of Blood" (X3.9), told to us by Son of Mine, we're in deep schtuck because he's supposedly in temporal stasis as he says this. We're left to assume that he was unable to assist his relatives when the Doctor picked them off one by one, in front of him and in various preposterous fairy-tale ways, and that these things *really did* happen as we are told. (There's potential mileage in this narrator sounding more like the original Baines than Son of Mine, if we want to make his stasis merely physical, with their two minds spending centuries awake and conversing. Yet, once again, why this narrator was asked for a statement at any one time rather than another is never explored – although it's the sort of thing Paul Cornell used to win prizes for when he did fan-fic, so someone must have thought about it.)

This multi-voiced narrative can be used well, especially if it's implied that there is a controlling intelligence, an "author" (not necessarily the one credited at the start of the episode) who is either selecting who gets a say or is at least refereeing a group of competing texts, channel-zapping between narrators or sources. It can also be used effectively when there is an "official" account and "interruptions" that burst in and add a commentary or correct it. Used badly, self-consciously Dialogic drama or prose can be an unholy mess. Anyone who recalls early 90s "Yoof" television or the efforts of ad-men to emulate Hip-Hop will know what we mean. *Doctor Who* has never quite fallen so far short of aiming high as *Glen or Glenda* (although the last two episodes of 6.3, "The Invasion" resemble Edward D Wood more than is usually admissible when discussing Douglas Camfield's directing – not a criticism of Camfield, but a recognition of what could have achieved with more resources). Nonetheless, the interruption of uniformly standard TV editing and image-quality, and the change in who is ostensibly being addressed – is it the companion, is it us at home, is it a possible bug relaying conversations to another character in the story? – occasionally discomforts viewers who just want jokes, explosions, scary monsters and running up and down corridors.

A more drastic rupture of this pact has been the twelfth Doctor's habit of talking to the viewers in an otherwise empty TARDIS. When the apparently rhetorical question of why people talk to them-

continued on Page 205...

the big problem: that it's all wood instead of just a wooden door in a concrete shell].

The Doctor thinks that if the Angels gain control of the TARDIS, they'd be able to feed on its time energy [possibly Artron energy], and that one of the side effects could include blowing out the sun.

The Supporting Cast

• *Sally Sparrow.* As with Elton [X2.10, "Love & Monsters"], she's the protagonist of the story with the Doctor and companion firmly in the background. We're told nothing about her occupation, but she has an interest in photography and – it would seem – breaking into dangerous derelict houses. Sally ends the story running a used book and DVD shop with Lawrence "Larry" Nightingale, and seems to pair off with him at the end. [But no one's mentioned either of them again.]

Before then, she spends this story interacting with a series of clues that the Doctor prepared for her benefit in 1969, culminating in the moment where she and Larry send the TARDIS back to that year, and thereby tricking a quartet of Weeping Angels into forever staring each other immobile [see **The Non-Humans**]. Sally claims that sad is 'happy for deep people', and only owns 17 DVDs – the exact ones that feature the Doctor's Easter Egg. Her best friend appears to be Lawrence's sister Kathy, but Sally doesn't know much about her, and seems only perfunctorily concerned about her disappearance. [Truth to tell, being asked out by a young cop seems to make her forget her grief.]

• *Lawrence Nightingale* has hidden talents, including Pitman shorthand and grief counselling. He has a full-time job at a video store and a complicated hobby: participating in the 'Egg Forums' about the Doctor's messages. Eventually, he and Sally take over the shop, and turn it into an antiquarian bookshop with DVDs as a sideline.

• *Martha.* As a follow-on to working as a maid for two months [X3.8, "Human Nature"], somehow she's working in a shop supporting the Doctor while they're stuck in 1969. Unsurprisingly, this annoys her. [You could argue it's a piece of character development in context, since it was only last story that she explicitly stated about how much she enjoyed travelling in time and space.] She's very excited to have been to the Moon landing four times.

She wears different clothes from normal, including a blue-grey Alice-band. [In the ending scene in the modern day, she's wearing a hot pink headband that neither suits her nor resembles anything we've seen her wear before. Also a leather skirt.]

The Non-Humans

• *Weeping Angels.* Silent assassins who disguise themselves as inert statues when anyone's looking at them. The Doctor informs us that they work on a "quantum lock", which means they can only move when someone's not looking at them. They appear to move perfectly silently. [The entire point of the "don't blink" business is that there's no other way of establishing their reality. This makes their decision to go vocal in X5.4, "The Time of the Angels" all the stranger.] The Doctor says they're 'as old as the universe, or very nearly', and considers them psychopaths.

They feed off the potential energy left in a timeline when someone is removed from it and sent backwards in time. [A methodology so close to the Trickster's creatures in *The Sarah Jane Adventures* and X4.11, "Turn Left" as to be suggestive. The part where Billy dies at exactly the same time(ish) as he was taken from history is presented as causal, but might not be a coincidence. It would make some sense if the Angels displaced people the length of time that they're "intended" to live – that might also happen to Kathy, although she's sent back to a much earlier era, and ends up dying some 20 years before she departs. Conversely, the story itself suggests that the time passage differs depending on what angel is involved, with the Doctor guessing that the same monster attacked him, Martha, and Billy. See X5.4-5.5, "The Time of Angels"/ "Flesh and Stone", for how their mode of attack seems to change from "eat" to just "kill".]

When Angels look at each other, they freeze for good [and, perhaps, die]. It appears they must touch victims to attack them.

There is absolutely no way of telling from this story whether they're intelligent creatures or instinctive hunters. ["The Time of Angels" confirms that they're the former, but that's on an alien world far in the future. Those Angels are so different, they may well have evolved between appearances. The Doctor's word 'assassins' suggests that they are selective in whom they harvest, and might imply that they were created for this purpose. It's possible, as they seem not to like Time Lords, that they were Dalek-forged weapons in

How Messed-Up Can Narrative Get?

continued from Page 203...

selves when they're alone came in "Listen" (X8.4), it had the option of being the Doctor addressing his hypothetical specimens of Perfect Hiding – but it sounded for all the world as if writer Steven Moffat was chewing over a series convention for our benefit. This got more pointed in "Before the Flood" (X9.4), which lectured us about the inherent problem (in many Moffat scripts) of an idea coming from nowhere in a temporal loop. On the one hand, it's possible this is the conclusion of the conversation the Doctor was having with Clara at the end of the episode, but *that* scene ends with the Doctor looking down at the camera and shrugging, for our benefit.[42] The convention of the Doctor talking to himself (and us) but not other characters has been there from the start. The Hartnell Doctor was doing it from the pilot episode, but it was accepted television discourse back then.

The *Moonlighting* stuff in "Before the Flood" only differs from the Doctor's conversation with a not-there Borusa in "The Invasion of Time" (15.6) in that it's about the difficulties of scripting *Doctor Who,* and openly acknowledges a problem half-mentioned before in Moffat stories, but not offering a solution or even any excuse. This, in the jargon of media fantasy, is called "lampshading": making a problem obvious by attempts to disguise it badly, like hiding a corpse by putting a lampshade on it and failing to persuade anyone it's a standard-lamp. (It's also, in the jargon of proper, written-down SF, called "A Message from Fred", an author inserting a grumble about the difficulties of writing this stuff.) Some find this an unsettling break in the Fourth Wall, others think it's innovative, but 30 years earlier it was a familiar television trick. (If anyone remembers later episodes of *Roseanne*, a series hitherto praised for its grit and no-nonsense plausibility compared to more aspirational sitcoms, the Becky saga is the classic example.)

The target audience for 2015 *Doctor Who* grew up with *Spongebob Squarepants*, where the problem of things underwater catching fire is pointed out but never resolved. People who consider that *Doctor Who* ought not to be directly comparable to *Spongebob* (or *Boston Legal*, a series whose metaphorical lampshades were its *raison d'etre*) baulk at this, but this is one instance where a traditional aspect of the programme's storytelling since 1963 has come in and out of fashion. When flagrantly done while the fashion is for jaw-clenching earnestness and bourgeois realism (see **Is "Realism" Enough?** under – where else? – 19.3, "Kinda"), it irks anyone new to the series. Perhaps if the Doctor's console-room soliloquy from the end of "The Massacre" (3.5) came back into the archive, it would be more palatable to that portion of fandom (the biopic "An Adventure in Space and Time" has a reconstruction of it). In "Heaven Sent" (X9.11), the Doctor paused the action to talk to an imaginary Clara (and us) in an imaginary TARDIS: a purely theatrical device for plot exposition, and one that varied the pace a bit in a long episode of an old man tottering around a lot of corridors. It's very like the protagonist-in-a-coma episodes of most US dramas this century (if *CSI: NY* has done it, it's officially A Thing), but with a crucial difference. There seems to be no good reason why we are following this particular iteration of the Doctor through his discovery that he's just one of billions.

We've now had a Fiftieth Anniversary story where the Doctor addressed us for the first time since... well, was the monologue at the start of "The Face of Evil" (14.4) aimed at us or himself? If it was just thinking aloud, then the last time we were spoken to directly inside an episode was "The Feast of Steven" (episode seven of 3.4, "The Daleks' Master Plan") and that prologue to "The Deadly Assassin" (14.3) – presuming that was the Doctor speaking, and not just a Gallifreyan chronicle that Tom Baker narrated. And then we get into debates about whether in-character appearances in other series count, and that leads us to the *Disney Time* incident (13.1, "Terror of the Zygons") and *Animal Magic* (17.1, "Destiny of the Daleks"). Plus we have television conventions such as freeze-frame (14.2, "The Hand of Fear" and two in the next story) that have fallen from favour lately.

Audiences in the 70s (except for Mary Whitehouse) weren't as unsophisticated as some younger commentators seem to think. We've had voice-over thoughts in the past, notably "The Moonbase" (4.6) and "The War Games" (6.7), although that was itself a fashion that directors left behind. However, there was a scene in "The Family of Blood" in which the Doctor – or at any rate David Tennant not sounding Scottish – tells us about World War I. It could have been John Smith or a clip from a documentary narrated by flavour-of-the-month TV star Tennant. That epi-

continued on Page 207...

the Time War. The one time all three races were in the same episode, X7.16, "The Time of the Doctor", great care was taken to avoid the Daleks and Angels meeting.

[Rassilon mentions the Angels (X4.18, "The End of Time Part Two"), but they seem to pre-date even Gallifrey. However, we never encountered them before, despite them being almost the perfect Hartnell-era time-glitch, so perhaps the War has altered the nature of space-time (see **How Can Anyone Know About the Time War?** under X4.13, "Journey's End" and **Is Time Like Bolognese Sauce?** under "Flesh and Stone") and allowed them in.]

It would appear that there are only four Angels in Wester Drumlin, an uninhabited house, and that they're been there for two years. [When Sally takes the TARDIS key from one Angel, it crumbles slightly in exactly the fashion you might expect when removing a piece of string baked into plaster. Possibly River Song should have shown up to the *Byzantium* with a bazooka.]

[NB We will round up a lot of the apparent inconsistencies and logical lapses connected with this race and their various, seemingly mutually-exclusive abilities in **What's With These Angels?** under "The Time of Angels".]

History

• *Dating.* The Doctor spends most of this story sometime in the first half of 1969, since he's looking forward to the Moon landing. [See also X6.1, "The Impossible Astronaut". Martha's MySpace suggests dating around March/ April, since they watch Lulu win the Eurovision Song Contest. Three other people won it too. You'd think she'd get the hint to avoid Eurovision, as it always seems to lead to trouble for them. Also, it would be nice if one of them had bothered to video 6.6, "The Space Pirates" for us to find.

[As for Sally Sparrow, the main part of the story takes place '38 years' after 1969, so it's commensurate with the story's broadcast year, 2007. Kathy confirms that this was the year she left behind. The final scene with Sally giving the Doctor the folder takes place a year after the rest – it says so on screen. If it's the same week as the rest of Series 3, they might have caused problems with Martha's mum phoning but – just this once – nobody mentions "Saxon" or a hospital on the Moon. The script said that three years had passed, which would explain why nobody's using "aliens" as the obvious explanation and no-one online has heard of the Doctor, but this seems unlikely from the way it's directed.

[We have little evidence for where in England this story takes place, but everyone has northern-ish accents (except Billy), and it looks like a medium-sized town that can support an antiquarian bookshop-cum-DVD exchange, has a Victorian police-station and lots of statues, and apparently only one identifiable council estate. Nonetheless, Kathy claims to have been 'in the middle of London' when the Angels grabbed her. The types of shop and the sort of hilly roads we see might make this Crystal Palace, Crouch End or – at a pinch – Blackheath, but then we have to ask why a Victorian house of that size has gone undeveloped for so long in such a desirable and costly neighbourhood. And why almost every speaking part is from oop north.]

Larry cites *Scooby-Doo* [see also X2.6, "Age of Steel" and X2.12, "Army of Ghosts"].

The Analysis

The Big Picture In case you hadn't heard, the 2005 *Doctor Who Annual* had a story by Steven Moffat called "What I Did in My Christmas Holidays by Sally Sparrow", in which a 12-year-old told us about finding a message from a stranded Eccleston Doctor under her wallpaper and effected a rescue. The name "Sally Sparrow", although very like the Roald Dahl-ish names Moffat gives all female characters when he takes over the series, is also suggestively like that of the dead narrator of *The Lovely Bones* (X2.12, "Army of Ghosts"), Susie Salmon.

However, the notion underlying most of this story is the Copenhagen Interpretation. We've gone into this in a few earlier essays (notably **What *is* the Blinovitch Limitation Effect?** under 20.3, "Mawdryn Undead" and **What Makes the TARDIS Work?** under 1.3, "The Edge of Destruction"), and we'll return to it and the rival/ complementary Many Worlds theory later in this book, so let's be brief. At a very basic level, properties of particles seem to be affected by being observed. Photons seem to "decide" to be either waves or particles, depending on who's looking and at what. Not everyone bought that idea. Erwin Schrodinger, himself responsible for theorising many peculiar (but probably right) phenomena, baulked at the notion and proposed a

How Messed-Up Can Narrative Get?

continued from Page 205...

sode sets a new record for the number of inserted narrators and possibly-not-quite-real shots.

So voice-overs and on-screen captions have become less objective (to the extent that we have had two saying "A very long time ago" – X6.8, "Let's Kill Hitler" and X7.14, "The Name of the Doctor" and a positively chatty typewriter making date-stamps and comments in X9.7, "The Zygon Invasion"), but this isn't as bold a switch from the norm of the original series as we might imagine. So let's revert to the position we left this topic in with the Volume 6 essay and look more carefully at what – if anything – is unprecedented.

We'll assume, to start with, that nothing's changed and the "rules" are just as before, and that two basic rules are being followed. One is that the character we're following is the same Doctor we followed from Totter's Lane (1.1, "An Unearthly Child") to Horsenden Hill in Perivale (26.4, "Survival"). Other Time Lords were "resurrected" to participate in the Time War, but this didn't befall our protagonist: his memories of the past seem to chime with episodes we've seen. (Even if those around him appear to have had slight edits done), and he thinks of these badly-dressed people calling themselves "Doctor" as himself. There's an obvious caveat around John Hurt's character in the Anniversary Special, but we'll get to that.) The other rule is that the Time Lords are out of the picture (to the extent that Gallifrey coming back was a threat) and thus the Matrix – their repository of all information about cosmic affairs including the bits of their own world's future they can't directly observe – is no longer available as the obvious selector of which bits of TARDIS input we get to see or hear. That's obviously messier now than when the stories in this volume were broadcast, but we'll stick with it for the moment.

The most noticeable change is that the decision on which incidents in the Doctor's life warrant television episodes and which don't is increasingly hard to justify. Whereas there are a few occasions when time elapses off-screen inside a story (notably the two weeks between the defeat of WOTAN and Ben and Polly coming aboard the TARDIS in 3.10, "The War Machines"), the new series is littered with alarming gaps of up to two centuries (X6.1, "The Impossible Astronaut") and indeterminate spells in which whole lifetimes are skipped (X7.16, "The Time of the Doctor"). Why whatever befell the Doctor, River and Jim the Fish is memorable enough to be talked about but not shown, when something as lacklustre as "The Curse of the Black Spot" (X6.3) was given 45 minutes of screen time, is unclear. The beginning of "The Caretaker" (X8.6) was studded with the ends of much more televisual incidents than the *Waterloo Road* stuff that comprised the bulk of the episode. Considering that the entire life of the Doctor between "The War Machines" and "Spearhead From Space" (7.1) might conceivably have taken two weeks, the gap between scenes at the end of "Death in Heaven" (X8.12), this becomes all the more remarkable. All of this indicates a "need to know" rationale for later big developments, as opposed to deciding what would interest viewers of some hypothetical television serial about the Doctor's real-life adventures, as determined from a cache of (say) stolen UNIT files or Matrix records.

If we go with the idea that the TARDIS is collating all the sensory impressions and media output in a hazily-defined "collection area" (as mentioned in Season Twenty-Three), we can account for about 80% of what we've seen on screen. As before, why some bits are chosen and not others, and the sequencing of these revelations, is a question we may never get answered – but we can't find many gaps where nobody involved is able to have their minds tapped for information. (Except, oddly, 3.2, "Mission to the Unknown", where the only conscious being still alive when the TARDIS lands several months later is a Dalek who showed up at the end of the story and killed everyone. And we're only assuming that the *same* Dalek was in "The Daleks' Master Plan". Other than that, we have the end of 18.5, "Warriors' Gate", where Romana's in a whole different universe after the Doctor's left for N-Space, and can no longer monitor her activities from the TARDIS. "Dead" Rose in "Doomsday" is another matter; we'll get to that.)

This, when considered in conjunction with the sheer number of temporal anomalies and timey-wimey paradoxes where the Doctor "remembers" an idea he never actually had, might indicate that the version of events we have here is slanted away from how an objective narrative would present it, making the TARDIS benign or neutral rather than the manipulative, evil mind-parasite than makes the Doctor endure regular torments and makes entire people come into existence for her benefit.

continued on Page 209...

reductio ad absurdam, now known as Schrodinger's Cat.

What if, he said, the both-and-neither vacillation of a particle was used to influence something manifest on the everyday scale? Would something as naked-eye noticeable as a cat hover between two states? If you had a cat in a sealed container and a bottle of noxious fumes that could be uncorked by a yes/ no detector of one single particle, would the cat be both alive and dead until someone looked? The maths said yes. Nobody seems to have tried it – partly because of animal welfare concerns, but mainly because whatever you do, you would need to not look at the result and look at it at the same time. And if someone has tried it, until everyone in the world is aware of the fact it's still both happened and not-happened and so on, until you have to have the whole universe on a live feed and then the speed of light becomes a limiting factor and then...

Let's just agree that nobody's done it. However, the physics behind it is what makes DVDs work (light-as-waves is what makes those rainbows when you hold them in a strong light, light-as-particles makes the lasers that read the information off the disc), as well as all electronic devices invented since the Transistor in 1947. There have been a steady stream of popular science books explaining quantum physics, especially since the mid-80s (around the same time that the media trend-mongers decided that science was "sad", and so the steady sales of these books must have been entirely under-the-counter). Moffat would probably feign ignorance of all of this, but we tend to evaluate by results. The situation in "Blink" is so closely patterned on the Copenhagen Interpretation, it would be a remarkable and uncharacteristically un-deterministic coincidence otherwise.

Determinism, in the philosophical sense, is one of the hallmarks of Moffat's work. We saw in "The Girl in the Fireplace" (X2.4) how his plots demonstrate a rigidly causalistic logic regardless of the chronological sequence of those causes and effects. Time paradoxes can be made to work in this belief-system, because human agency is irrelevant. We could trace this idea through Calvin, Schopenhauer and Leibniz, but for our purposes just think about "Time Crash" (X3.13a) and ask whose idea the solution was. In religious terms, this idea connects to the Protestant belief in the Preterite (the un-saved) and the Elect (those pre-selected for salvation at the beginning of time) and how nobody can change their status.

In this story, even the Doctor is bound by what has been written (by Sally) and what might happen if he or Billy try to change the script. The Doctor – the man who can talk his way out of anything – has to read off an autocue. Hitherto, with maybe two exceptions (2.7, "The Space Museum"; 18.5, "Warriors' Gate"), the Doctor's abilities as a Time Lord allow him unique liberty within otherwise pre-set events. After Moffat takes over as executive producer, the limits to this and the Doctor's efforts to bend the rules form the main plot-arcs and motivate individual episodes (see **Is Time Like Bolognese Sauce?** under X5.5, "Flesh and Stone" and **Did Series 6 Need to Happen?** under X7.1, "Asylum of the Daleks"). Scots Presbyterianism is to *Doctor Who* in the early 2010s what Buddhism was for the early 70s.

Now we've mentioned Pertwee-era silliness, it's worth thinking about the furthest-fetched of the Barry Letts pet projects: 9.5, "The Time Monster". In this, we meet a "chronovore", a being that feeds on time, and – in the course of its duties – deprives a young scientist of his expected lifespan (leaving a badly-made-up actor with white hair and wrinkles and modish early 70s clobber). This lad, Stu, is half of a sitcom couple from their era, the other half being a short-haired female scientist who grumbles about men thinking they're in charge. These two, like the Naval personnel in 9.3, "The Sea Devils" and the aliens in 9.2, "The Curse of Peladon" and 9.4, "The Mutants", see the already rather formulaic Pertwee-UNIT from outside, as Sally does here. Two of the three contemporary-set stories in Season Nine are timey-wimey, so that mixture of ordinary people encountering the Doctor's world and a temporal paradox messing with everyone's heads is hardly novel.

We should perhaps mention that there is a conversation between a bewildered protagonist and an apparently pre-recorded television commercial in Chapter Ten of *Ubik* by Philip K Dick. Comparing things in famous books to things that happen in *Doctor Who* episodes doesn't necessarily prove causality (it comes just after someone goes into a shop to complain about a dead parrot; although we know Terry Gilliam's a fan of PKD, nobody's ever suggested this as a "source" for the *Python* sketch), but – as we will see – it's far from being the only theme or incident in a Moffat script to strongly resemble something from that novel.

How Messed-Up Can Narrative Get?

continued from Page 207...

(See X4.6, "The Doctor's Daughter"; X6.7, "A Good Man Goes to War"; **Are Steven and Dodo Related?** under "The Massacre"; and **Why Do Time Lords Always Meet in Sequence?** under 22.3, "The Mark of the Rani".)

In **Where Does "Canon" End?** under 26.1, "Battlefield", we explored the extent to which the series can be said to be a single narrative, with "subsidiary" ones such as the *Doctor Who Magazine* comic strip and Big Finish audios taking a partial stake within the main one. This too has become more complicated in recent years. We have had an online-only clip (later included in the DVD of the Anniversary episode) which tells of how the Doctor (played by Paul McGann) changed into the not-really-a-Doctor Doctor (a brief shot of John Hurt circa *I, Claudius*). Quite apart from the vexed numerical status, there was a lot to wrestle with concerning the way the Doctor mentioned most of his Big Finish companions, but not Grace or Chang Lee nor any from the books (see **Does Paul McGann Count?** under 27.0, "The TV Movie") and the way this rebirth was facilitated by the Sisterhood of Karn (see **Who Were All Those Men in Funny Wigs?** under 13.5, "The Brain of Morbius").

Reconciling even the various things that call themselves *Doctor Who* is hard, even without spin-offs contradicting the main series (see the essay with X4.5, "The Poison Sky"). Just on television, there was a more-or-less consistent house-style for *Doctor Who*, *Torchwood* and *The Sarah Jane Adventures* and a degree of internal consistency about each of those not tripping each other up, nor yet deliberately contradicting, the earlier version of *Doctor Who*. (Accidental, apparent or negligent contradictions are still happening, hence these books.) Within the supposedly-objective narrative (itself questionable when looked at in detail), it's become increasingly common to embed or weave together other subjectivities, voice-overs from specific characters or point-of-view shots of things they saw or experienced. It slipped out of the routine house style of the series, but was never ruled out.

A common assumption is that using various modish narrative devices is a clear sign of a schism between the old series and the BBC Wales version. Closer examination (albeit tempered with the imprecise recall of viewers who saw now-missing episodes) shows that there is very little new about it. Most of the narrative devices currently used in *Doctor Who* were there from the start – we mean the *very* start. Watch "An Unearthly Child" if you think flashbacks and subjective camera-shots are recent developments. We had "Marco Polo" (1.4), with the eponymous protagonist grumbling about his unwilling passengers in a voice-over with animated maps and on-screen graphics. The end of "The Massacre" is depicted with contemporary illustrations. Viewers were addressed by characters in trailers for Season Five stories (5.3, "The Ice Warriors" and even more overtly 5.5, "The Web of Fear", where the Doctor told us – specifically BBC1 viewers under ten – all about the new-look Yeti) and on other occasions within the story-as-broadcast. There's the Doctor's toast to the viewers at home in "The Daleks' Master Plan" and his looks to camera, especially at the end of "The Invasion of Time", plus more subtle and "permitted" nods towards us in stories as diverse as "Nightmare of Eden" (17.4), "Vengeance on Varos" (22.2) and "The Five Doctors". Deliberately non-realistic graphics began and ended specific stories. (Notably the season-ending episodes – 2.9, "The Time Meddler"; 1.8, "The Reign of Terror"; and see Susan's departure in 2.2, "The Dalek Invasion of Earth". But look at the custom-made titles for stories as diverse as 7.4, "Inferno"; 4.2, "The Tenth Planet"; and "The War Games"). We've even had a Hollywood-style screen-crawl and the Doctor telling us the story ("The Deadly Assassin").

As with the clever *Sherlock*-style on-screen text in, say, "The Bells of St John's" (X7.7), it's obviously *Doctor Who* using whatever tricks viewers are comfortable with from every other current TV drama. The inserted date-stamp captions Moffat's pinched from *Heroes* for Series 8 and after will, one day, look as dated as the graphics for the TARDIS in flight in "Colony in Space" (8.4) or the slow-motion bat superimposed over Aukon's face (18.4, "State of Decay"). What's changed, and changes continuously, is the patience of the average viewer with this kind of jiggery-pokery, so that what were brief "artistic" moments (or rather desperate ways to tell a complicated story with limited resources) are always part of the standard repertoire of all TV drama being made at the time. Nonetheless, they are all things that nobody within the story-world is actually seeing.

[Actually, we don't know that the whole series from day one hasn't been filtered through one

continued on Page 211...

(See "Silence in the Library"; X5.13, "The Big Bang"; X6.0, "A Christmas Carol"; X9.0, "Last Christmas"; X9.8, "The Zygon Inversion"...)

As we mentioned in **Things to Notice**, the set-up of apparently static objects moving when one isn't looking is a basic childhood fascination (think of *Toy Story* or 8.1, "Terror of the Autons") and one exploited so often in horror films, it's hard to think of a first example. It was certainly enough of a cliché by 1999 for *South Park* to ridicule it in their second Hallowe'en episode, "Spooky Fish in Spooky Vision". Many of Moffat's cited inspirations are similarly commonplace. He found the children's game Grandmother's Footsteps scary as a child, while the look of the statues is derived from a number of similar tombstones, especially a World War I memorial in Belgium. The term "Weeping Angels" denotes memorial statues that are not looking at the visitor to a tomb, but instead seem to be mourning on our behalf. There was a considerable vogue for them at the end of the nineteenth century and beginning of the twentieth; the earliest seems to have been William Wetmore Story's carrera marble monument to his late wife, in the Protestant cemetery in Rome.

The name "Wester Drumlins" was where Moffat had lived once. There were deserted houses that looked dangerously ruined and creepy and, above all, the Victorian fad for tombstones looking like mournful angels included some with their hands covering their faces. A few of the London cemeteries have guided tours on Sundays, notably Kensal Green and Highgate. (We have to point out that the connection between Grandmother's Footsteps and Victorian funerary decoration had been made in 1980, with the PoW escape plan sequence of *Sir Henry at Rawlinson End*. Anyone coming to this film after Series 7 will find the main theme a bit familiar too...)

It may be relevant that there is an overgrown graveyard in Hull – of all places – that local kids used to claim had clear paths through the brambles, because the statues used to go for walks at night. The leering face of the Angels as they approach reminded many people of the Medusa. In that case, as you will recall from mythology (or 6.2, "The Mind Robber"), it was the burning curiosity and need to look – rather than the need to not stop looking – that was fatal (turning people to stone if they opened their eyes... Moffat will invert this inversion for "Flesh and Stone" and X8.4, "Listen", plus the Moffat-influenced X9.3-9.4, "Under the Lake"/ "Before the Flood").

And, as we have already cited it in connection with X2.7, "The Idiot's Lantern", you may already have seen the *Sapphire and Steel* story (usually referred to now as "Assignment 4") where people are chased by a faceless man and sent back to be part of old photos. We'll pick up on this when the Angels turn out to be memes next time. That's also what most people think happened at the end of Stanley Kubrick's film of *The Shining* (see X6.9, "Night Terrors"; X6.11, "The God Complex"; and 5.4, "The Enemy of the World" and 5.5, "The Web of Fear").

Incidentally, the "why don't they go to the police?" point is a line that comes up quite often in the documentaries included on DVDs of Alfred Hitchcock's films. It's frequently reported to be the starting-point for his rewrites of novels.

Fundamentally, though, this story is where Moffat's notion that primal childhood fears – supposedly universal and interchangeable – are the *raison d'etre* of the series comes to the fore. As you may recall from Volume 4, this was a minority view among active fans in the 1990s, but now it is a policy being aggressively pursued, with Moffat as the attack-dog. In providing a knowingly low-cost, Doctor-lite episode in lieu of the two-parter he was unable to do through other commitments, Moffat was almost self-parodically furnishing a script with his trademarks: temporal paradoxes, flirty women and ooh-scary. This time, at least, he remembered to include a story as well.

Additional Sources As mentioned, the story "What I Did in My Christmas Holidays by Sally Sparrow" was in the 2005 *Doctor Who Annual*. It was later put on the BBC Website. The Sally in that story is a pert 12-year-old, apparently with a charge-account at Claire's Accessories, who finds an SOS from the Doctor behind her wallpaper from before she was born and rescues him. He then shows her a news clip of her as an adult reporter covering a huge scoop. Martha's MySpace account claims that the Doctor is watching *Coronation Street* in 1969 and feeling sorry for himself, but doesn't specify which is cause and which effect (early 1969 was mainly Ena Sharples slagging off Minnie Caldwell, and Elsie Tanner packing her bags and leaving for good every three weeks).

How Messed-Up Can Narrative Get?

continued from Page 209...

person's perception. This might be why the 1970s stories seem always to have the same henchmen getting beaten up or falling off things, regardless of what period or planet they're on. Occam's razor makes this a more likely reason than Davros having a cloning plant for Terry Walshes and Alan Chuntzes (12.4, "Genesis of the Daleks"), or every big government scientific base in the UNIT era hiring the same security grunts who were made redundant when Jon Pertwee blew up the last one. However, now that the seeming popularity of BBC English across the universe is merely a side-effect of the TARDIS, and all humanoid bipeds are descended from Earth colonists, appeals to narrative convention when BBC Wales has expended so much time and effort in removing the need elsewhere seem almost churlish.]

Where this becomes interesting is when something looks, at first sight, like standard-issue TV narrative practice but turns out not to be. A handy example, because a character loudly and repeatedly comments on this, is Donna's dream-life in "Forest of the Dead" (X4.9). The elisions between cause and effect look exactly like the normal editing from any sitcom, drama or *Doctor Who* until Donna *says out loud* that there ought to have been a few months between meeting someone and getting married, as opposed to 1/25th second. We've had moments like this before, such as the way characters can't deviate from their scripts in "The Mind Robber" (6.2) or "Carnival of Monsters" (10.2) and previous dreamscape stories (notably 23.4, "The Ultimate Foe"), but – perhaps surprisingly – they weren't laboured as heavily as this one is. As with Elton's first-person narrative in "Love & Monsters" (X2.10), a deliberate transgression makes us aware of the number of times we've been told to "just go with it".

Speaking of which, there are two possible ways to think of what's "real" in Elton's story. One is that, as with any *Doctor Who* narrative, it comes from some main source (whatever that is) and then footage from elsewhere – subjective impressions, TV feeds, people remembering the events years later – are pasted in. The other is that only Elton's pieces to the camcorder can be relied on, and the rest is his very selective, very subjective recollection, so that the internet "exploded" and his PC went bang, that his mum faded away on saturated 8mm film to an ELO soundtrack and so on.

If we work with the latter account, then we have to ask where the shot of Ursula on his table talking from inside her slab came from. If we assume the former to be right, because it works for every other episode, then we're stuck asking how much of anything we've ever seen was misremembered, imagined, heavily-partisan or just wrong. This goes double for "Last Christmas" (X9.0), which the author tells us is only "real" in the end-sequence (although this contradicts several things we see on screen, notably the other dreamers in the story waking up in places where the Doctor isn't). While the writers routinely use idiot-beams (or "Perception Filters", as they're called in the dialogue) as a cop-out for characters not thinking clearly enough to avoid obvious cliffhangers or what's in front of them, we're in a position of wondering whether *anything* in the series is "real". (See also **How Much of This is Happening?** under X5.6, "The Vampires of Venice".)

An option hitherto denied directors and writers is the degree of control over the image. In the past, there were two basic grades, film and VT, and things that could be done to distort either of these. Between "Rose" (X1.1) and "The Next Doctor" (X4.14), they used a form of video-tape that could be processed to resemble film. In that processing, and moreso with the newer HDTV equipment, the degree to which an image is reconfigured is entirely a matter of choice. Take "Blink" (X3.10) as an example; the Doctor's piece to camera had to be manipulated to make it look as if it was A) done to camera on 16mm film in 1969 and B) being relayed to us via a portable DVD player in a gloomy room. The majority of such interventions have been to denote subjectivity, much as the *Top of the Pops* style of effects in the 70s and 80s episodes were, but rather than draw attention to their televisuality (e.g. "Kinda"), they seek to resemble earlier forms of visual media. The obvious instance is the flashback-in-a-flashback in "The Unicorn and the Wasp" (X4.7) that looks like a hand-tinted silent film of the Folies Bergère (and the similar catch-up sequence in X7.12, "The Crimson Horror", both scenes influenced by Canadian borderline-steampunk detective show *Murdoch Mysteries*).

But look at the multiple types of image for different forms of viewer-prompt in X3.12-3.13, "The Sound of Drums"/ "Last of the Time Lords". Some flashbacks were slightly darker and less colourful, when it was a quick insert from an earlier episode

continued on Page 213...

Oh, Isn't That...?

• *Carey Mulligan* (Sally Sparrow). She'd been on *The Amazing Mrs Pritchard,* but then came *Bleak House* and the start of her film career. She was Oscar nominated for *An Education* and was in the Baz Luhrmann *The Great Gatsby.* Her most recent outing at time of going to press was *Suffragette.*

• *Lucy Gaskell* (Kathy Nightingale). The usual: a stint on *Holby City*, a part in *Cutting It* and she's been a regular on *Casualty*. She also appeared in the notoriously poor comedy *Lesbian Vampire Killers* with James Corden, of whom more next volume (X5.11, "The Lodger" and X6.12, "Closing Time"). The surprisingly decent straight-to-DVD sequel to the not-very-good feature film *Dungeons & Dragons* has her in as a saucy sword-wielding elf (with a Mancunian accent).

• *Michael Obiora* (Billy Shipton) was a very camp bellhop in the wretched *Hotel Babylon* (the comedy-drama, not the even worse "zoo" format show with Dani Behr).

• *Louis Mahoney* (Old Billy Shipton). For our purposes, he was the newsreader in 10.3, "Frontier in Space" and crewman Ponti in 13.2, "Planet of Evil". He's done so much else, including *Fawlty Towers*.

• *Findlay Robertson* (Larry). Actually, not a lot: he did forgettable Channel 4 drama *NY:LON* (about cross-Atlantic relationships and stuff) and that's about it. He just looks a bit like a lot of other actors who got similar roles.

English Lessons

• *Pants* (n): Underpants. Generations of British schoolkids have laughed at inadvertently funny things Americans have said about this.

• *Hull* (n): Seaport on the East of England, on the Humber Estuary, technically in Lincolnshire but effectively where Yorkshire begins. It's been officially designated City of Culture 2017. London-based comedy writers make play with the similarity of the name to "Hell", but in the local accent it sounds more like "Hool", so that only works on the page.

• *ITV* (n): The second TV network in Britain and the first to be funded by advertising. In the early years of the twenty-first century, they were reliant on a few blockbuster talent-shows and *Coronation Street*, and their drama was lamentably formulaic. There was a horticultural-themed murder mystery series called *Rosemary and Thyme* (see X4.7, "The Unicorn and the Wasp"), so the idea of investigators called "Nightingale and Sparrow" is, indeed, "a bit ITV". (And their odd treatment of Agatha Christie adaptations can wait until "The Unicorn and the Wasp", but these days, with *Downton Abbey* and *Broadchurch*, they are recouping lost ground. Most of Davies's early hits were for ITV.)

Things That Don't Make Sense So, let's get this straight: Sally is good enough friends with Kathy to invite herself in at one in the morning, let herself in using her own key, start making the coffee and rouse Kathy from a dead sleep. Lawrence is comfortable enough in the same flat, which he shares with his sister, to have put monitors everywhere and wander around naked. How is it that Sally and Lawrence haven't met yet? (Kathy's letter is also a little strange, in that it implies that Sally – if they're such good friends – doesn't know that her parents are dead.)

Even for a show that came up with the Ood, the evolution of the Weeping Angels is improbable at best. The Doctor says that they freeze into stone – all right, so perhaps the type of stone is changeable, and they could in fact manifest as boulders or flagstones, which would at least explain why a species supposedly around since the start of the universe look like Earth gargoyles. But that would mean that this lot go out of their way to appear threatening when they're actively hunting someone. And they seem to weather badly. (So much so, the mob on Alfalfa Metraxis in "The Time of Angels" are almost powder, despite not having been looked at for centuries.) But if they *actually become stone*, then their 'most perfect defence system', as the Doctor names it, really isn't all that, because a simple sledgehammer ought to do them in. Or just a decade of being rained on.

Moreover (and we touched upon this in **The Non-Humans**), there seems to be very little coherent pattern to when and where the Angels send people. Notably, the same one that got the Doctor and Martha grabbed Billy, which is apparently why he's catapulted back to 1969 with them, in the same city. (Presumably, the Angel could have sent the Doctor to live out his days any time up to a thousand years ago, but perhaps picked a relatively recent date to grab all of Martha's expected life – which isn't good news for her given how relatively recent 1969 was.) Their modus operandi seems to entail the victims living out the lifespan they ought to have had when the Angel

How Messed-Up Can Narrative Get?

continued from Page 211...

(e.g. Professor Lazarus or Creet); one, for which we have no external verification, was a lyrical description of Gallifrey as it had been, with a purely conjectural image of the Master being infected by something coming through the Untempered Schism. (See "The End of Time" for an eventual answer that retrospectively confirms the Doctor's account, even though he wasn't there.) Every image we see in the post-2005 episodes has been processed, but most have been made to look like unprocessed film. We're encouraged to trust these as "true". The picture-quality is part of the information we're given to work with and, however subliminally, helps us figure out what's going on.

This could open up a whole new way of making *Doctor Who*... if anyone dared. With a few scant exceptions used for budgetary reasons, the BBC Wales team makes almost all of the footage used in any current episode. You might get (to continue using that story as an example) stock footage of Air Force One stitched into a fake news item and a scene shot at a disused airstrip, but anything purporting to be "found footage" has been manufactured (again, "Sleep No More" showed the problems inherent with this rhetorical device). Directors, producers, editors and DoPs control the process. That's why, when something slips through that wasn't planned, we mention it in **Things That Don't Make Sense**.

But what if they went the other way? It's entirely possible to make something that's *Doctor Who* simply by editing together genuine found footage and constructing a series of connections that require the involvement of a time-travelling alien. Some of the LINDA meetings came close, and Moffat-era scripts have had purely verbal jokes about the police box at Earl's Court tube station ("The Bells of St John's") and the Easter Island statues ("The Impossible Astronaut"). Our basic knowledge of the Doctor allowed most of "Blink" to work without any overt explanation. Going the whole hog allows all the "accidental" details that inevitably seep in unless you are making the whole story in a computer or animating it (see the essay with "The Infinite Quest") to become "deliberate", or at least available for multiple interpretations. Just as Mina Harker's obsession with Dracula makes the newspaper reports of zoo animals part of a narrative, so a pseudo-documentary *Doctor Who* where a construction is placed on apparently disparate archive material could work. (Something like Orson Welles's *F for Fake* for example, or David Blair's *Wax*. In theory, it could even be done in the trademark style of Adam Curtis, whose documentaries reconfigure old adverts and cartoons to weave a sardonic commentary around his calm voice-over.) Or it could be *Glen or Glenda* all over again, and just look like someone talking cobblers over apparently random stock clips.

One odd detail unlike anything we saw prior to 1996 is the use of TV news that nobody in the story is watching. When added to rapid inserts of web-pages that no character is consulting (e.g. X4.16, "The Waters of Mars"), we have a new way of info-dumping. News bulletins were a common method of relaying information (for example "The War Machines" and 4.2, "The Tenth Planet"), but we generally went into these from the viewpoint of a speaking-role within the fiction (at least until 9.1, "Day of the Daleks"). The newer method was tentatively introduced in "Aliens of London" (X1.4), but with a cover-story that the Doctor was monitoring the news on Jackie's telly. By Series 3, we were so used to channel-hopping updates that we could go into one, then get an unexpected clip (Tinky Winky dancing) and pull out to the Master watching *Teletubbies* the way he'd enjoyed *The Clangers* several lifetimes before.

All the most effective uses of that kind of technique required an unseen narrator to bind the disparate elements into a cohesive story. Narrators can be characters within the story or outsiders. There are precedents for both in *Doctor Who*, either planned (as with Messire Marco's account of the journey to Cathay or kids singing a rubbish nursery-rhyme, "Marco Polo" and X6.9, "Night Terrors" respectively) or the BBC announcers doing "The Story So Far" with Seasons Twenty-Three and Twenty-Four, or Howard da Silva on 70s American showings of Tom Baker episodes. A narrator who is outside the narrative is given a strange sort of power, an assumed omniscience that a participant cannot, by definition, have (even when narrating posthumously, as with *Lovely Bones* or *Dangerous Housewives*, or indeed River Song in X4.9, "Forest of the Dead"; see **Why Can't People Just Die?** under that episode). To date, most BBC Wales episodes have opted instead for multiple narrators from within the story, or adjacent to it (as in X6.12, "Closing Time" and those kids giving eye-witness accounts, apparently to the

continued on Page 215...

touched them – but how does that work on a planet where the near-future keeps changing due to time-travelling invaders? Can they tell who's going to avoid being hit by a bus or zapped by a Dalek? If so, why grab the Doctor or Martha at all, as they're not going to be part of that timeline for very long anyway? All right, it's possible that they can sniff out people who might have made a difference and feast on the absence of that difference-making potential, but *that* would predispose them towards people with a lot of ties to this timeline. Instead, the Angels home in on single people with one friend who aren't especially missed. (But they are missed a bit, so that can't be the criterion for selecting victims either.)

They send Kathy to a point where she can live until around the time she was born (which is more sensible), but send Billy to 1969, so that he can be in two places at once in the same city. Obviously, the Doctor would know to avoid paradoxes, but would any given human refrain from visiting their younger self, and causing the sort of thing we saw in X1.8, "Father's Day"? Or, is Billy somehow unique in having lived twice in an overlapping chronology? Apparently not, as the events in X7.5, "The Angels Take Manhattan" make this issue much more complicated. Besides, what if – lacking the guidance from the Doctor that was, apparently, all that prevented Billy from making the Sun explode – a victim were to send a message to their younger self to prevent their meeting a malignant statue in the first place?

Who chucked the flowerpot at Sally's head in the teaser? The Doctor? (If so, he's taking a huge risk going back there with Angels around.) The Angels? (Why would they make someone look *at* them?) Hooligans who, purely at random, have nothing better to do than chuck flowerpots into abandoned houses at the exact spot where someone is standing (and have avoided being abducted to 1978)? (And..."Wester Drumlins"? Even though it's named after a real place, what kind of a name is that? It sounds like a wholesale paper towel supplier, not an old house.)

And we are confronted with the question of how paranormal assassins from the Dawn of Time landed up in a residential area, stuck for decades in one house, rather than rampaging through Earth's population (see also X10.4, "Knock Knock"). They've had *two years* and – if Billy's haul of abandoned vehicles is any indication – have touched a number of people. Later in "The Time of Angels", the relatively small number of soldiers accompanying River Song is enough to charge up a whole planet-full of these beings.

In their anxiety about whether the lighting will fail at Wester Drumlins, Sally and Larry don't stop to wonder why there's any electricity *at all* in a house no one's inhabited for at least two years. Perhaps the Doctor arranges that as part of the paradox as well (see **The Lore**). But if the Angels can make lights flicker, why not switch them off altogether and have done with it? Sally and Larry could have avoided a whole lot of Larry-as-Shaggy stuff if they'd just put that large mirror in the hallway in front of the Angel he's forced to look at without blinking. (Moffat finally does exactly that in "The Time of the Doctor".)

A problem we'll have in all subsequent stories with these things: the Angels remain as stone when anyone is looking at them. Unfortunately, there are scenes when no character in the story is looking, and yet they still look like tombstones. (This will get ridiculous when it's the Statue of Liberty taking a walk and nobody in the whole of New York is giving it a glance.) And why is vision the only thing to root them to the spot? What's wrong with touch? Is the ability to smell petrichor (X6.4, "The Doctor's Wife") not enough? They even make a trademark noise; handy, so you know they're around even when not looking. There must be thousands of blind people flung into the past, leading to packs of abandoned guide-dogs. (And here we'll assume, in light of later episodes establishing that "the image of an Angel becomes itself an Angel", that Sally simply lucked out and didn't photograph one in the house at the start. Well, that, or the Doctor rids himself of her folder after tidying it up, or there's a rogue Angel somewhere in the Ship's library.)

Why *were* that many people going to Wester Drumlins anyway? Over two years there amassed a haul of a dozen cars, some with engines still running. Did someone honestly mistake it for an off-licence or post office? If, as we speculated under **History**, the large abandoned property is in an affluent bit of London, you would expect a lot more people to have been to inspect it, more efficient security to stop Sally getting in and out and borough surveyors from the fictional London City Council to have taken measurements. On the other hand, as the property seems to have been condemned, and brownfield sites like this are at a premium, why is it still standing after so long? It

How Messed-Up Can Narrative Get?

continued from Page 213...

Silence). The obvious comparison for this style of storytelling is, of course, *Rashomon,* but with the picture-grading and jiggery-pokery available now a better analogy might be Zhang Yimou's 2002 film *Hero,* in which the colour-scheme alters depending on who's telling the story and what axe they have to grind. If they dared, they could go as far as *Sin City*.

Between the two poles of A) a wholly-animated, controlled and entirely rendered story, and B) one made of found-footage, edited pseudo-documentary style, are a number of options as yet untried. The series has made momentary use of narrative techniques from other genres and types of television, but the basic assumption is that everything we see happened to the characters, that a causal link exists between events (albeit not always straightforwardly linear, but timey-wimey and asynchronous – we *assume* that "Blink" happened to the Doctor and Martha after "The Family of Blood" and before X3.11, "Utopia", but there are no cues other than the placement of a story mainly set chronologically before the Doctor met Martha) and that some kind of narrative closure is going to happen... one day. In episodes such as "The Impossible Astronaut", we get the start of what may be five different stories, some of which will sort of-end with "A Good Man Goes to War", some with "The Wedding of River Song" (X6.13), some with "The Time of the Doctor" and one or two may not actually get finished because the threads were (apparently) forgotten. We peeped into this vexed issue in Volume 7 (**What's a "Story" Now?** under 1.13a, "Pudsey Cutaway").

A particularly awkward example of this assumption messing things up might be the apparently accurate flashback in "The Waters of Mars". We see and hear roughly the same incident: a Dalek swoops down on Adelaide's attic bedroom then, unexpectedly, looks her in the eye and leaves. Adelaide's account is spoken to the Doctor, even though he brought it up and appears to know a lot about it already. Her version is that the Dalek looked into her and then decided to spare her, although her parents were "lost". Her memory is presented just the same way as everything else in the story, without the effects used for flashbacks in, for example, X1.11, "Bad Wolf" (a montage of clips of Rose hearing the words "Bad Wolf", including one she couldn't have heard but never mind, superimposed on the image of the space-time vortex from the end credits) or X3.12, "The Sound of Drums" (rapid monochrome images from earlier episodes).

Unlike the pictures accompanying Baines's account, the picture-quality isn't any different. It's given to us as "real". It is, however, mediated. There's music, echoing the score of X1.8, "Father's Day" (itself deliberately a minor-key reworking of "Some Day My Prince Will Come", but sounding like the theme from *The Long Goodbye*). The sequence leading into this is the Doctor telling Adelaide about how important that day's events on Mars will be to future history, a sequence using rapid edits of BBC News web-pages of events even further in the future, just as they have been showing what will be remembered about this Fixed Point throughout the episode. As we'll see, a lot hinges on whether this 50-year-old event happened precisely as shown (see **What Constitutes a Fixed Point?** under X4.2, "The Fires of Pompeii"). The Doctor seems to be going by the official historical record as much as any personal experience, but he still requires confirmation from an eye-witness: one who was a child then and is now pushing 60. Either the images we see or the narrative we hear might be considered highly suspect and subjective, but we get both at once and are invited to accept this seemingly-preposterous incident as true.

Flashbacks are certainly more common now. With the exception of "Planet of the Spiders" (11.5), the majority of original-series episodes had cliff-hanger reprises and that was about it. After the renegotiated deal with Equity, it became common to include montages to re-introduce old characters (19.6, "Earthshock"; 20.3, "Mawdryn Undead") or emphasise the Doctor's long television past (18.7, "Logopolis"; 21.4, "Resurrection of the Daleks"), but an episode such as "Last of the Time Lords" uses half a dozen, amounting to about a minute of screen-time. The previous episode uses bespoke retrospective footage – that is, inserts that aren't from previously-transmitted material (the Master's childhood, the escape from Malcassalro) alongside bits from recent episodes for anyone just joining, but also makes a point of introducing new concepts without any warning or build-up. The intent is to have all viewers on the same page, regardless of whether they knew about Professor Lazarus or Harriet Jones, whilst

continued on Page 217...

ought to have been flats by now. Or a Tesco Express.

If you haven't already, read the essay with X3.2, "The Shakespeare Code" or talk to anyone who was in Britain in 1969. Then imagine Martha just getting a job in a shop all anyhow.[43] And imagine how easy someone with psychic paper and a detailed knowledge of that year could have blagged a free flat, a string of winning bets on horse-races or next week's No. 1 record, or a cushy job managing a club, a pop group or a stable of promising young painters and photographers. Most people reading this book would, if stranded in 1969 London, make a killing. And yet, if they've been there a couple of months and are short on cash, wouldn't Martha's high-maintenance hair have started to grow out into something a little frizzier? If she's only got the clothes she was wearing when she was nabbed, they can't be on a high enough income to get her a triple-process, at 1969 prices, even if she can find someone who can do it in Britain.

An obvious one, in light of other episodes: has nobody on these supposedly world-wide Egg Forums heard of LINDA or been contacted by Elton Pope ("Love & Monsters")? If, as we are to believe in a few episodes' time (X4.1, "Partners in Crime"), Donna Noble's been looking for the Doctor online, has she not said anything to them? Unless these DVDs all came out in a very short space of time, wouldn't Torchwood have been interested? Or Harold Saxon? Or UNIT, or Mr Smith? We could go on... The Doctor doesn't name himself in the Easter Egg, but he does admit to being someone who travels through time in a blue box. *Surely*, that would have garnered some attention from certain parties.

Two last awkward details... when the TARDIS dematerialises, look at what the Angels are looking at. The two farthest from the camera aren't being looked at by the two nearer ones or each other. Finally, Larry says that the 17 DVDs with the Doctor's Easter Egg are "totally unrelated" but we later find out they're the whole of Sally's DVD collection. Does she have no consistent tastes and interests or just purchase them with maximum randomness in mind? Even if she'd acquired them by other means (like someone else moving out of the room Kathy moved into, or well-meaning aunts giving her discs when she didn't have a player), there would be something to connect at least two out of 17 and probably at least half. Larry is active in the online groups that discuss these things and yet not only has he not got a pet theory of what links the discs, but the process of theory-making isn't the primary activity on any Forum he's on. Seriously? It's almost as if nobody involved in this story's production had ever met anyone who was a fan of anything.

Besides, *you* try making a list of 17 films that have absolutely nothing in common. Once you get past five or six, it becomes exponentially harder with each additional film. (We've tried.[44]) Has she even watched them? As she has no idea what "Easter Eggs" means in this context (allowing Larry to explain it to older viewers), and as her encounters with the message from the Doctor are all from Larry's collection anyway, and the Doctor selects these discs to use as conduits merely because that's what Larry's transcript says he did... what does Sally's collection of DVDs have to do with anything anyway?

Critique (Prosecution) Now that his halo is considered tarnished in some quarters, there are many who find fault with Steven Moffat's methodology, repeated tricks and overall attitude. There are others who are willing to believe that it will all come out right eventually once he's provided the all-embracing "answer" (something still not entirely present after the long continuity conversations in "The Time of the Doctor" and, at time of going to press, with precisely one episode left to get it all in). On both sides, there is a phrase that keeps coming up: *but he wrote "Blink", I'll give him that*. For those who take this line, there is an obvious question: *have you watched it lately?*

Reviewing it now is like appraising 1.7, "The Sensorites", in that its breakthroughs now look stale and the only unexpected bits are small flaws and period details. As with the original *Star Wars*, we have a self-contained work that takes a few risks, gives us things we've only read about on screen and occasionally surprises us with self-mocking humour. Likewise, the sequels, prequels, spin-offs, knock-offs and wannabes taint the experience. Seen again after the shambles of Series 8, or the semi-season latter half of Series 6, the things that went right for this story are clearer to see.

Like Douglas Adams, Moffat is someone who responded brilliantly to crises or limits and improvised innovative solutions to apparently intractable problems. Given a seemingly-impossi-

How Messed-Up Can Narrative Get?

continued from Page 215...

pulling the rug from even the most devoted and scrupulous viewer by abruptly introducing Archangel and *Valiant*.

[An aside about the official record: to come back to the arguments in **Are We Touring Theme-Park History?** (under X2.7, "The Idiot's Lantern") and **Whom Did They Meet at the Roof of the World?** (under "Marco Polo"), we have had several adventures set in what is given to us as "real" historical incidents, but is – historians now say – questionable. (We could also include 3.8, "The Gunfighters" and X5.10, "Vincent and the Doctor".) Although the *Doctor Who* version of events always carries the promise/ tease/ conceit that what we're getting now is the unrecorded version, what "really" happened, there is always a degree of winking at the audience based on our ability to asseverate or confirm any details. "The Chase" (2.8) or "The Myth Makers" (3.3) are spectacular versions of this jape, the latter parodying not just history but mythology-taken-to-be-vaguely-like-history. "Robot of Sherwood" (X8.3) makes the most of this ambiguity and gives us the twist ending that the ludicrous Hollywood Robin Hood was a real person, despite the Doctor's misgivings.]

Most of the agreed conventions of television narrative come from 1930s Hollywood. Looking at film from other cultures or before the techniques hardened into rules opens up other possibilities, but each one would seem weird first time. Almost all conventions of this sort begin as attempts to be more "natural" than what has gone before. Any cinematic or televisual device goes from *Uh?* to *Ah!* to *Oh* fairly quickly, so that the edit of Sylvia fussing around the kitchen behind a static Donna in "Partners in Crime" (X4.1) is as intelligible as the dissolve from the clock at the Adipose call-centre saying 8.00 to 6.30. Nonetheless, the pretence has generally been upheld that this is what in a novel would be called a third-person omniscient narrative. Punctuating it with first-person subjectivity has happened before and after 2005 roughly evenly, although the 70s stories kept it for special occasions (it's used in "Planet of the Spiders", Jon Pertwee's last story, more boldly than usual) and the 1980s almost entirely eschewed it. However, apart from "Love & Monsters", it appears as if an entirely first-person story has never happened... unless we discover one day that the whole series has been one.

[This appearance isn't entirely accurate, however. "Turn Left" (X4.11), if narrated wholly objectively, would consist mainly of a few minutes of Donna standing up and twitching while a large scarab beetle tries to secure itself on her back before falling off, dead. Similarly, X7.11, "Journey to the Centre of the Tardis" (sic) would be three minutes of faffing about in the console room and a seemingly irrelevant snack on a space truck – this might have been preferable for many viewers.]

Yet the decisions of when to reveal or withhold information we might need are still apparently someone's; in "The Day of the Doctor", the narrative flits about within the Doctor's own past in sequence of when he remembers things, but we get to see things that the plot – and indeed every episode since "Rose" – needs him to have forgotten utterly. Quite apart from the handy coincidence of him seeing two paintings in the right order for everyone watching at home to follow the unfolding backstory, the previous episode ("The Name of the Doctor") provides details we need to know, but not the one we were hoping to get: how exactly the Doctor and Clara get out of this apparently intractable situation. Nor do we see why the seemingly anonymous character played by John Hurt – the one the High Council call "the Doctor" – managed to slip even the Tennant Doctor's unconscious mind while it was stuck in a watch whispering to John Smith (X3.8, "Human Nature") or the records of the Daleks (who would have good reason to know this person at least as well as the Hartnell model) according to "The Next Doctor". Only such information as is supposedly good for us is ever given, so we don't find out until "The Time of the Doctor" what his phobia was behind Door 11 (X6.11, "The God Complex"). Steven Moffat took the on-screen dates from *Heroes*, but his main template has been *Lost*, and some of the minute details that look like standard narrative strategies gone slightly wrong are – in fact – tremendously significant for the attentive viewer.

Only *some*, though. Some, including the embedding of the transmission dates of key old series episodes within the set design or incidents (see, for example, the Doctor carving "23/11/63" in the wall of the Tower of London for Clara to use as co-ordinates centuries on in "The Day of the Doctor") may be a red herring. Yet the first of these, the date of "Time and the Rani" (24.1) on the bulkhead of

continued on Page 219...

ble brief, he made something personal and universal. Like Adams, once indulged and feted, he let the quality of his work deteriorate. "Blink" is the last appearance of Moffat as Sun-era-Elvis, hungry and dangerous, as opposed to the Vegas-era, Karate-and-flares Moffat of Peter Capaldi's Doctorate. Seen for the first time, this story starts off as a haunted house yarn then takes reckless turns and – with Tennant largely absent – chucks new characters into a situation that even the Doctor couldn't handle, without a safety-net. If you've come to the series lately, after Tennant and Davies left, this might seem stripped-down and taut, if a little over-familiar. "Stripped-down" is "under-developed" for polite people.

There are a lot of things that went very right here, a great many of them in the script and either amplified in production or not impeded. Just simple things like Martha's three tiny appearances using her to undercut the Doctor make a lot of difference. It's not just the absence of that dreary storyline about her crush and the family's dealings with Mr Saxon; this Martha is a positively different character from the Moffat version of Rose, one we could have stood to have seen more of had things gone differently. As with the two-parter before this, we have an episode with almost no digital malarkey, one that could have been made in 1990, 1975 or at a pinch 1965 (although the Easter Egg concept would have had to have been adapted for 8mm films rather than DVD, but *Torchwood* managed that the following year). Making the regular characters fresh is a bonus, but they're not in it much and their stand-ins are the start of the trouble.

There's a photogenic young couple who "meet cute" and bicker; she is attracted to someone else who proves unavailable and so she resolves her difference with the supposedly-unlikely pretty boy. We know this from umpteen rom-coms, the main difference being that she has to serve the triple function of audience-identification character, author's mouthpiece and mildly-kooky-all-purpose-fantasy-girlfriend while he has to be comic stooge, sympathetic best friend and the focus for authorial self-loathing. In *Coupling*, Moffat split these into three separate characters per sex and let it run on for six half-hour stints of therapy per year. Here, he has one 45-minute shot and has to put *Doctor Who* monsters in it.

Sally Sparrow is that kind of quirky, perky female character Moffat always does: the ones who motivate nerdy blokes into doing things and who probably seem to the author to be positive female roles but are, if such people existed in real life, the sort of woman you'd cross the street, or indeed a lava-floe, to avoid. For all that Sally doesn't seem to have any kind of job or a home-life that makes a lick of sense, this is closer to a realistic domestic set-up than anything we'll see again from this author. (Madame Vastra's is as close as he gets – ask anyone who knows a teacher how ludicrous Clara's "normal" life was, even before an Iraqi orphan showed up in her hallway). Indeed, the gulf between how people act in television and what would really happen is emphasised by Banto the DVD shop owner, and, however implausibly helpful the police are here, it makes the plot change direction usefully. Sally never quite says "This isn't *Doctor Who*, it's really happening", but it gets close.

She gets honorary Companion status by Murray Gold reassigning the 70s electric piano usually reserved for Martha to her for this one week, but is still in all other regards an outsider trying to make sense of it without the Doctor constantly assuring her it's how things really work. Sally is messed-up enough to be more than a stick-figure, albeit in unlikely ways (in reality, a woman who says "Sad is happy for deep people", photographs derelict houses and has only 17 DVD's would be either a Goth or an out-patient), but not a psychopath or neurotic. She is, however infantile her behaviour at times, a fully-grown woman so the time-paradox will have none of the unpleasant aftertaste of "grooming" we'll get with Amy, Clara, River, Bill and even Rupert/ Danny. There's no hint of a longer-term story going on. For the lay-viewer, as the majority of that first-night audience was, this is a plus. With a decade's hindsight, it's a relief.

The problem here is the same as the problem with 21.6, "The Caves of Androzani". Both were refreshing changes from the usual run and, consequently, enormously successful, but people made an unholy mess trying to make lighting strike twice. Everyone drew the wrong ideas about what had worked. Moffat himself got it into his head that things that just stand around but *might* do things while you're not looking are intrinsically scary – and that "scary" is an end in itself, not a momentary side-effect. As a result we got years and years of the same thing: Vashta Nerada; the Silence; the Snowmen; the Whisper Men; the

How Messed-Up Can Narrative Get?

continued from Page 217...

the *Byzantium*, came in the same scene where Amy's wedding-day was the "base-code of the Universe" (X5.5,"Flesh and Stone"). These cropping up hither and yon may just be a whim, and occasionally something that looks like a huge clue in an earlier episode turned out to be a genuine cock-up ("The Curse of the Black Spot", a clumsy edit making a "vanished" pirate reappear unharmed). That episode with the base-code and the two dates also had an apparent mistake about the Doctor regaining his jacket, but transpired to be tremendously important and dead clever. We retain the hope that "Sleep No More" and "Hell Bent" are unreliable-narrator accounts, and that close examination will reveal a true and more interesting version if we interrogate the discrepancies – the way Nabokov's *Pale Fire* or Wolfe's *The Book of the New Sun* work – but so far we've not seen anything to support this.

However, the series is intended to be watched by families on BBC1 on Saturday evenings, and sold to a worldwide audience who may or may not be as invested in it as all that. We could never seriously expect *Doctor Who* to turn out like *The Wire*, a series that spent its first year educating viewers in how to watch it before embarking on more ambitious narrative than hitherto attempted. Moffat's approach during Matt Smith's tenure was criticised for not taking the casual viewer sufficiently into account, although – to be fair – the ratings held firm, and a noticeable viewer defection only occurred once the Doctor became Peter Capaldi. Still, Russell T Davies erred on the side of caution in this regard (see **Is Kylie from Planet Zog?** under X4.0, "Voyage of the Damned") and made every episode resemble the most widely-known forms of TV and film drama possible. Nonetheless, it was Davies who wrote "Love & Monsters" and the Series 4 trailers with Donna telling stories by a fire. Moffat's whimsical use of on-screen verbiage is less of a house-style feature than with *Sherlock*, and is, like all such trickery in every age of *Doctor Who*, about five years behind the avant garde.

Regardless, this is quite tricksy enough for most viewers and potentially a problem. Imagine if the first episode of *Doctor Who* you had ever seen was "The Day of the Moon" (X6.2). The cliffhanger to the previous episode was resolved in flashback in amongst a complex pre-credit sequence supposedly three months after the previous episode, but obviously occurring at a number of different times and places (unless Canton had a transmat or there were three of him). Then, if you were watching this anywhere other than Britain, there was a voice-over and more flashbacks where Amy explains who the Doctor is before the titles run. So she's supposed to be narrating, right? Well, not really. The rest of the episode has her discovering things that happened to her that she forgot, up to and including having a baby (because that was the real Amy and we're following her Flesh copy this episode... aren't we?) and seeing so many Silence that she ran out of wrist and had to keep tally on her face. For the casual first-time viewer, the nearest to an audience-identification character is, er... Richard Nixon. Who has an invisible brass band playing "Hail to the Chief" whenever he walks into shot.

And the episode doesn't so much end as stop: the questions raised aren't answered for weeks or years (or maybe ever) and bits that looked quite sensible are later revealed to be impossible when the alleged "solution" is announced. (This eventual exposition takes place in a tremendously unrealistic chat with a hitherto-unseen character who is uncomfortably like River Song supposedly explaining everything in one minute – "The Time of the Doctor" – but raises a lot of bigger problems when the earlier episodes are re-examined.) No one thing in any individual episode is beyond what is acceptable in standard TV drama but, cumulatively, the storylines become almost impenetrably tangled, and the more anyone tries to account for all of it, the less sense it makes. (Of course, how much the millions of casual viewers on initial broadcast actively worry about such things or are thinking much deeper than "How long until *Strictly*?" is another matter.) Series 10 gestured towards a Year Zero approach at the start (but ended up with an episode that didn't bother explaining who the guy with the beard was, why the Doctor's hands were making orange sparks or why the name "Mondas" was so significant.) The plummeting ratings (especially on first broadcast, where casual viewers were prevalent) and taking a year out for some reason forced the issue. Earlier, more widely-watched seasons, especially Series 7, could get away with more.

Within that phase of the series, the revelation that Amelia Williams became a novelist and guid-

continued on Page 221...

Smilers; the Spoonfaces, Half-Face and his gang; Monks; whatever it was in Rupert's bedclothes; various forlorn attempts to make spacesuits ooh-scary and annual returns of the Angels themselves. All doing the "they're coming to get you... eventually... any day now" thing. In between these we had other writers trying to do Moffat-by-numbers, plugging away at the idea that stories made up of waiting and waiting in children's bedrooms (or similar) with the lights out were more worth watching than a story where something happens every so often and you can see it when it does. He even did a story with a planet full of immobile Daleks, on the basis that these are infinitely more terrifying than the ones that move around and kill people. Eventually we had X7.4, "The Power of Three", which it is hard not to see as a putative successor to Moffat saying "enough already!" Anyone seeing "Blink" for the first time after all of this will (and, anecdotally, has) come out with a verdict of "Meh!"

It functioned in 2007 because it was unexpected. A simple idea was taken for a walk, with characters who were out of their depth and the person who'd normally explain it all restricted to cameos. It could have been a half-hour episode of an anthology series; there's certainly not 45 minutes'-worth of material in this story. At an hour long, it could have allowed light and shade, longer pauses for reflection and characterisation. At a crisper half-hour, it might have been better to stick to the tension-building and skip the romcom stuff. (Moffat himself now says that it might have been better if Sally had voluntarily gone to live in the past rather than settle down as a second-hand bookseller with Larry.) The script falls between these two stools (too short to explore the situation and characters, too long to just be spooky escapism and maintain tension) like many Tennant episodes; a rare lapse for the one writer who'd paced his previous episodes perfectly so far.

Apart from anything else, that extraneous last scene, where they try to make out that all statues are potentially lethal, is gratingly out-of-key with the preceding episode. It hints at what will go wrong with the Angels once they undergo mission-creep. This is the start of the slide towards (metaphorically) poking the audience with a pointed stick and ordering them to be scared of the scary thing. What compounds this repetition is that Moffat had got himself an enviable reputation as an inexhaustible fount of ideas, largely on the strength of this one episode.

The Weeping Angels began as a clear idea and, back then, a good one. Their success was down to the simple fact that we hadn't seen anything quite like them before. Once practically every episode was either Angels coming back or umpteen Angel-analogues by Moffat or his epigones, it was just as samey-wamey as all those Troughton-era Base-Under-Siege, Pertwee/ UNIT Yeti-in-the-Loo and Invasion-of-the-Month or Baker/ Hinchcliffe Defeated-Tyrant-Makes-Comeback plots. In many ways this story resembles most closely "Dimensions of Time", the first episode of 2.7, "The Space Museum". If that had been taken as the gold-standard and emulated again and again, *Doctor Who* would have ended before the end of the third year. What's most impressive about Series 3 was the variety, the way it reflected all the things *Doctor Who* can do. In that context "Blink" is just another example, another type of story, but one that didn't go as badly wrong as "The Lazarus Experiment" or "42", but not as out-there and entertaining as "Gridlock" or "Utopia". Some have used this episode to introduce the programme to newcomers, which would work if every single story were like this one. As an introduction to one specific strand of the programme's potential and MO, it's adequate (for those viewers who are reassured that Sally won't be back), but constricting it to this formula has – contrary to received opinion – been a mistake. Moreover, it relies more heavily than many people realise on knowing the ground-rules of *Doctor Who*.

There's a little too much of the sitcom gag where someone comments on the second-most-odd thing that happened instead of the oddest, so Sally marvels at Larry's shorthand ability rather than the fact that the Doctor is talking to her directly and Larry comments on Sally only having 17 DVD's and not that the Easter Eggs are intended for her. And so on. Quite apart from the writing (although this has the usual flaw of people behaving like characters in a romcom, making Freudian slips and seemingly thinking "What would Meg Ryan do?" rather than "How am I going to get out of this alive?"), the performances are brisk rather than deeply-felt. It is hardly surprising that Carey Mulligan was later Oscar nominated, after making Sally bearable, but Finlay Robertson deserves a medal for making Larry work. They are only as annoying as the sorts of characters in long-running ad campaigns (UK

How Messed-Up Can Narrative Get?

continued from Page 219...

ed the Doctor towards telling her younger self all the stories we'd seen might have worked if *Doctor Who* had begun with "The Eleventh Hour" (X5.1) and ended with "The Angels Take Manhattan" (X7.5) – but we know it didn't. Had Moffat been in complete charge of the series from inception, as he was with *Press Gang* or *Sherlock*, he would have had more leeway to be adventurous. This is, after all, someone who wrote half an episode of *Coupling* in Hebrew with subtitles. (It was in the first series, called "The Girl with Two Breasts", for reasons that made sense at the time.) We will be examining the concept of a viewer "churn-rate" in later essays (especially **Does He, You Know... Dance?** under X4.8, "Silence in the Library"), but there is a traditional assumption that the majority of casual viewers can only remember episodes made by the current team, but remember those in minute detail (see 6.7, "The War Games", specifically the last episode).

However, in one regard, Moffat's tenure on *Doctor Who* has been more radical than any before. The Doctor's personal narrative has been messed up, repeatedly. The Matt Smith version has first reconfigured his own past (X5.13, "The Big Bang") and lightly tweaked everything that happened since the night he crashed in Amelia's garden. Then, halfway through Series 7, he first created his meeting with the future Brigadier by stage-managing the Great Intelligence's next few assaults on Earth (X7.6, "The Snowmen" and 5.5, "The Web of Fear"), then the Great Intelligence went to Trenzalore and opened the dead Doctor's timeline, rewriting it from scratch, then Clara re-re-wrote it all, perhaps changing a few significant details ("The Name of the Doctor", but see also X6.4, "The Doctor's Wife" and 16.2, "The Pirate Planet") and met an unrepentant War Doctor who recalled having destroyed his world, even though the very next episode had him not do this and regenerate immediately after so this encounter could not have happened (and for the Smith Doctor and Clara, it seems not to have done as they're back on Earth in the TARDIS as if nothing happened, although they mumble about half-remembering it), and then the next episode after *that*, the whole Trenzalore thing is prevented from ever having happened anyway ("The Time of the Doctor") and the episode after *that* has the Paternoster Gang back safe and sound from being stranded inside the Doctor's tomb-that-won't-now-exist (X8.1, "Deep Breath"). Plus the Doctor rewrote his own past *twice* in the same episode – first by popping back to the end of the Time War to hold the not-Doctor's hand as he commits genocide, then deciding on a better course requiring all the Doctors to have *always known* about the Time War and arriving near Gallifrey at the same time after doing sums in their heads for a couple of thousand years.

What's funny is that, extreme as this seems, the Doctor got off lightly compared to his companions in this incarnation, as we'll examine in Volume 10. Even if we assume the Moment's intervention was within the Doctor's past, but he didn't quite remember it properly, what exactly happened between the end of the second spasm of Series 7 and the Anniversary is murky in the extreme. Perhaps Moffat had a plan that didn't pan out, as with the scheme to have Victorian Clara as the companion and the two kids with anachronistic teddy bears visiting the future and meeting Porridge and the Cybermen (X7.13, "Nightmare in Silver"). Series 9 ended with Clara "dead", and probably out of the series, but with half a dozen plot-threads about her unresolved. Series 10 did the same for Bill.

However, the main point for us now is that a final arbiter of what happened – a single retrospective narrator of the entire series – existed, the various timelines that have been changed would not have been in the eventual chronicle of the Doctor's life any more than the Peter Cushing film was.[45] The fact that these un-happened events are known to us indicates that the Doctor and/ or the TARDIS is telling us this (see **He Remembers This *How?*** under X1.5, "World War Three"). If we ever find out who's telling us it will be, in effect, the end of *Doctor Who*. Until that point, we have to take it on trust that all narrative chicanery, stylistic flourishes and fashions in editing and dubbing will eventually turn out to have been justified.

readers who've somehow not seen this episode might think of the BT Broadband flat-share soap). That's still pretty annoying. Although Larry turns out to be accomplished and bright, Robertson plays him as comedy foil throughout – a performance perhaps more in keeping with late 70s *Who* or *Rentaghost*. It's good for what it is, but the story needed something else (his last scene hints at this). It takes seasoned veteran Louis Mahoney to make an empathetic character work in this outlandish situation.

Despite the damage it caused, this was an inventive episode and one of only two with an instruction in the title that doesn't suck (the other being X4.11, "Turn Left"). If you enjoyed it in 2007, hang on to that feeling. Re-watching doesn't do the episode any favours.

Critique (Defence by Lars Pearson) More than any other new-series episode, "Blink" is the one that gently lays its hands upon our temples, and cocks our heads to the side so we can't see things straight. Fandom's reverential tones for this story, combined with its status as the second-most popular New *Who* episode (bested only by the 50th Anniversary special), and also the eye-raising phenomenon of showing it to *Doctor Who* virgins *first*, means that we keep staring at this bit of television again and again in isolation, divorced from everything around it.

... a purpose that, of course, "Blink" was never forged to serve. Rather, it's intended as Series 3 episode ten: a change of dance number between the historical two-parter and the three-part finale that begins, at the end of time, with special guest star Derek Jacobi. "Blink" is just one of many vital components of a revived *Doctor Who* that – back then – you genuinely felt could go anywhere and do anything (and, in any given story, probably would). The "Next Time On..." tacked onto "The Family of Blood" is pretty instructive here: on first viewing, you couldn't help but think, "Damned if I know what it's about, but it stands a good chance of being *awesome*". So, funnily enough, "Blink" is probably best experienced within a rewatch of Series Three – but that horse has long since bolted the stable.

There is, of course, a long tradition among SF TV fans of trying to seduce newcomers to a show with an "extraordinary" episode. *Star Trek: The Next Generation* fans regularly fished for love with "The Best of Both Worlds", *Buffy* fans trotted out "Hush" and (more problematically, given the pre-knowledge required) "Once More With Feeling", etc. It's easy to apply this strategy to "Blink" – it's self-contained, with Sally Sparrow at first knowing nothing about the Doctor, and the viewer learning as she does. (Side note if you're watching with that tortuous breed of TV watcher who insists on asking questions while the episode is playing: politely, and with great tact and dignity, advise them to *shut the hell up and keep watching*, and let the episode provide some answers.)

Deflowering newbies with "Blink" is far from bulletproof (particularly if it's over-hyped, raising expectations to absurd levels), but it's hard to argue with success. You can easily find long-term new-series fans (let's call them the Tennant Generation) who'll tell you, "I watched 'Blink' first, then devoured all the rest of the show". By the same token, it's hard to deny that if you chat with the Tennant Generation for long, they're just as likely – perhaps even more so – to reference the Weeping Angels before the Daleks. That would be the Weeping Angels, who instantly became an iconic monster, and impacted upon British culture, more than any monster (Cybermen included) since the Daleks.

Separate eco-system aside, however, what *does* make "Blink" so captivating? It skirts the line between science-fiction and urban fantasy. It's genuinely unsettling – appropriately for a series about time-travel, time is weaponized. (Even though Kathy and Billy live out full, rich lives as a consequence, one Angel-touch means you'll lose everything you prize in the present day.) It moves *fast*, and keeps monkeying with your expectations – Sally and the Doctor's "conversation" via DVD, in fact, is a small miracle in that we've cruised through most of the story thinking, "Well, *somebody*'s got a grip on this situation", and suddenly the Doctor's Easter Egg finishes, and that comfort goes away. The script is imminently quotable – not just "Don't Blink" and "Wibbly wobbly, timey wimey" and "The Angels have the phone box" (although, good grief, those alone...), but even "They just send you back in time and let you live to death", "the only psychopaths in the universe to kill you nicely", and [your favourite quote here] are useful, in the right time and place.

And, crucially, it's a puzzle *du jour*. Steven Moffat grounded much of his *Doctor Who* tenure in puzzles, but with "Blink" the answers aren't as sprawling, and take less effort to parse (or you simply don't care about poking such things with a sharpened stick). Granted, puzzle-stories can lose some of their lustre on repeat viewings, which is why – from where I'm sitting – much of my colleagues' criticism of this story composts down to "Familiarity breeds contempt". But puzzle-stories remain comforting if you let them. All sorts of *Star Trek: TNG* fans have watched "Clues" seven times over, but still find it soothing – and "Blink" moves about five times quicker than "Clues", with three times the content. Tat and Dorothy also pondered making "Blink" longer or shorter, when in fact it's just about the perfect 45-minute tale. Add to it, and you hamstring the pace. Try deleting a scene entirely, and the whole story structure falls apart like a Jenga block. You could maybe trim out the sitcom bits, but then you'd be left with a gaggle of character-void people going through some plot mechanics. Like them or don't like them, Sally and Lawrence wind up as real and vivid as any one-off *Doctor Who* character you can name, despite only having 45 minutes of life.

That brings us to something that isn't often talked about: how one's reception of "Blink" will greatly hinge on the – let's face it, highly subjective – issue of whether Sally rubs you the wrong way or not. Personally, I've no beef with her. She's clever, grounded, and, most importantly, learns as she goes along. *Of course* she's going to stumble in places, and act a bit juvenile; for pity's sake, it's not like she's a seasoned UNIT operative. Sally is... how old, exactly? Carey Mulligan was the ripe old age of 21 when she played the part, and, although we learn very little about her life, Sally comes across as a New Adult. You'd expect lines such as "Sad is happy for deep people" from a pretentious 21 year old; in *Buffy* terms, Sally's cookies aren't done baking yet. Her best moment, in fact, is probably when she verbally grabs the Doctor by the tie and wrenches him on-topic with: "I'm clever, and I'm listening – and don't patronize me, because people have died." She's young, and young people should be allowed to figure themselves out.

If there's a disappointment with "Blink", actually, it's that Sally and Lawrence end up as a couple. However much warmth actor Finlay Robertson endows Lawrence with, keeping a potential stereotype in the realm of "helpful scruffy nerfherder with a good heart" rather than "insufferable geek boy", the final scene paints the character as horrifyingly needy, with a spine-numbing lack of intellectual curiosity... and yet we're made to watch Sally go, "All right, I'll hop on", once she's checked "Give dossier to the Doctor" off her Bucket List. Rose dumped Mickey's sorry ass over a comparable lack of courage, and we cheered her on. But even if the "Sally and Lawrence Forevah!" detail is lamentable, "... and they all lived happily ever after" is almost always a cheat. We never hear from the pair of them again, so we could just as easily believe that she later binned their relationship, opened up a detective agency (preferably with Veronica Mars), exposed many baddies and engaged in several ill-advised and torrid, but at least *interesting*, affairs. Certainly more interesting than life with Mr Nightingale could ever be.

I have, I must confess, struggled with writing this Critique because there's a certain type of story that's so self-evidently good if not great, it's exceedingly hard to detail *why* that's the case. You frequently get this with Seasons Twelve to Fourteen, when Tom Baker, Elisabeth Sladen, Louise Jameson, Philip Hinchcliffe and Robert Holmes produce such solid work, as a reviewer you're often left sitting there, impotently going: "It's pretty great, isn't it? There... there it is. There it is. Enjoy." That "Blink" raises the bar as high as the Hinchcliffe-Holmes era – meaning it's a little bewildering as to how someone could fail to concede that it's not objectively "good" (even if, fair enough, it's not their cup of tea) – is a remarkable accomplishment. It shouldn't work, but keep this story in your trap alongside "Rose", "The Eleventh Hour" and/ or Jodie Whitaker's first episode as a bit of cheese for the next generation. Anything that actively gets people into *Doctor Who* against the headwinds of *Game of Thrones*, the newest Netflix series and so much more can only be viewed as a result.

The Lore

Written by Steven Moffat. Directed by Hettie MacDonald. Viewing figures: (BBC1) 6.6 million, (BBC3 repeats) 0.8 and 0.4 million. The AIs were 87% first go, 89% for the second, then 86% last showing that week. We should note that as per usual back then, Moffat scored a Hugo for the episode.

Repeats and Overseas Promotion *Les Anges Pleureurs, Nicht Blinzeln.*

Production

As with last year's X2.10, "Love and Monsters", Davies was planning a Doctor-lite story to double-bank the packed production schedule. In the meantime, Steven Moffat was now a fixture (he'd locked up Hugo wins two years running), and it was unthinkable for him not to have at least one script in the new series. At first Davies was hoping that Moffat might do the year's two-parter Dalek story, but Moffat's own schedule on *Jekyll* put the kibosh on this. The slot proposed was early in the recording schedule, but it crept later until it became the double-banker towards the end of production.

Thus Moffat got to write the episode with barely any Tennant/ Agyeman presence and almost no money left to make it. Although he had pitched an idea about a spooky library occupied by malicious statues, the two concepts seemed to work better independently, so the statues got given their own story (to Davies's mild annoyance, as he was planning something similar for his Christmas episode – see X4.0, "Voyage of the Damned" for his own angel-statue menace).

Moffat was also keen to retain his record for only having characters die from natural causes, so this became the perverse method of execution used by the Angels. He saved time by rewriting his story "What I Did in My Christmas Holidays by Sally Sparrow". This had been in the Eccleston Doctor annual. Several of the plot devices are the same – the wallpaper, the video transcript (in this version, the Doctor's trapped in 1985, videotaping himself on a home recorder). Sally's 12 years old in this version (so there's no breaking-and-entering or romance subplot). Moffat saved money by making a story about solid objects, requiring minimal computer-aided chicanery. After the technical challenges of "The Girl in the Fireplace" (X2.4), this was a way of resisting getting a reputation for over-ambitious scenarios.

Moffat included the line about the erroneous TARDIS windows as a joking reference to a thread on then-popular *Doctor Who* forum Outpost Gallifrey, where they'd been having a conversation on precisely this topic. With time so short, the plot and much of the dialogue is almost unchanged from the early drafts – one change was prompted by Davies picking up on a suggestion that they rename the episode "Blink", causing the phrase "don't blink" to have to be seeded in the episode. The episode's climax came into focus when Mark Gatiss suggested that there was probably a good reason for Moffat having specified four angels and linked it to the four sides of a police box. There was some debate about whether the Angels could make the light-bulb swing on its cable (until it was realised that electricity in a derelict house was odd enough, so drawing attention to it would strain viewer-credulity).

• Hettie MacDonald had been assigned to direct Block Five's one episode, which would run concurrently with Block Six (X3.8-3.9, "Human Nature"/ "The Family of Blood") and parts of Block Four (the Dalek two-parter). Tennant and Agyeman would make brief appearances, but Tennant would also be directing, writing and hosting that week's edition of *Doctor Who Confidential*. Phil Collinson oversaw production while Susie Liggett ran the 1913 tale. MacDonald's track-record included the feature film *Beautiful Thing* (she had directed the original stage-play, which is how she got the gig), complex drama *In a Land of Plenty* and episodes of *Poirot* (notably the last one) and *Casualty*. Amid other episodes being made 7th November (they were *still* doing inserts for X3.1, "Smith and Jones", plus the screen images or X3.3, "Gridlock" as well as the TARDIS scenes for X3.6, "The Lazarus Experiment" and Gatiss's Hulk-like jacket-rip effect), the first shot of "Blink" was actually the TARDIS hologram of the Doctor.

• Work didn't start in earnest until Monday, 20th November, when the National Westminster Bank (West Bute Street) served as the police station exterior and the front desk (you will recall that a nearby bookshop had doubled for a bank in X3.0, "The Runaway Bride"). West Bute Dock was used for a scene of Kathy calling Sally from a pub (cut before transmission) and Sally's call regarding the DVD extras. David Tennant had a day out of the Dalek block on the 21st, for shooting at the Coal Exchange, Mount Stuart Square, although they don't seem to have used him for anything except the "don't blink" video tape.

• They eventually cut a bit where Sally is hooting at the idea that Kathy could have died 20 years ago, which is perhaps why Malcolm storms off in a huff as soon as he's done being Mr. Plot Exposition.

• All had the Sunday off, then everyone got back to work Monday, 27th November (two productions, in fact; Charles Palmer started work on the Paul Cornell two-parter that day, with Agyeman doing Martha's solo TARDIS scenes at Upper Boat). The "Blink" crew were still on location, going from the Oddverse Café on Charles Street, Newport (where Sally read her friend's letter) to Diverse Vinyl across the street, just the place for Banto's shop (someone had the clever idea of putting an episode of *Gangsters* on his telly; see, of course, 22.2, "Vengeance on Varos"). On Tuesday, 28th November, they redressed the shop a little bit to make it "Sparrow & Nightingale", for the ending scene of Agyeman and Tennant meeting the story's main couple. (Tennant seems to have had a long weekend after finishing work on "Evolution of the Daleks". Whether these were scheduled or added after his voice problems worsened is unclear.) Production for the stars wrapped up with their meeting-Billy-in-an-alley scene, at Charterist Tower.

• Tennant progressed from the video-diaries he'd been keeping of production to directing a whole edition of *Doctor Who Confidential*, about old-series fans who were now making the programme. To that end, he and Moffat broke into a studio in Television centre – then used almost exclusively for the prestigious *Newsnight* – to discuss all the key moments of *Doctor Who* shot there (notably the Pertwee-Baker regeneration). The interview had to be curtailed abruptly when the current-affairs journalists came to work.

• In production, Macdonald was using Gregorian plainsong as the soundtrack for the Angels; in the final version, Murray Gold added skittering string sounds (like those used for the spiders in *Raiders of the Lost Ark*) and a plaintive oboe. Another soundtrack-change was that Michael Obiora had to redub all of Young Billy's dialogue to make his normal Estuary accent more like Old Billy's Jamaican one. Although she went on to have great success in a number of other series, it would be eight years before MacDonald returned to *Doctor Who* (with X9.1-9.2, "The Magician's Apprentice"/ "The Witch's Familiar").

• The first broadcast of the episode was at 7.10pm, like the previous two. Moving the start-time and taking a week off for Eurovision were making slight dents in the expected ratings, but the series was still making headlines. By this time, the press were convinced that Agyeman had been sacked. Word was already leaking about Kylie Minogue doing the Christmas Special, but to deny that Martha was being written out entailed spoilers.

Shortly after the episode came the final of *Any Dream Will Do*, in which applicants for the title role in a West End show (this time *Joseph and the Amazing Technicolour Dreamcoat*) were whittled away and trained as is the fashion these days. John Barrowman had been one of the coach/ judge panel. (We could list all the Saturday Night shows Barrowman was doing then, and the other series on which he was a guest, but the world-count for this volume is getting worrying as it is.)

• Predictably, the sort of websites that make money by selling fannish T-shirts took Moffat at his word on Larry's claim to have made one saying "The Angels Have the Phone Box", and started selling them almost immediately.

• In the wikileaks "Vault Seven" file concerning hacking tools developed by the NSA, it emerged that, alongside "Sontaran" (for the Siemens OpenStage VoIP phones) and "Sonic Screwdriver" (for Mac firmware), there was an especially sneaky way to get Samsung smart TVs to use their cameras and monitor wi-fi even when the set appeared to be switched off. It was called "Weeping Angel", because it was most effective when nobody was looking at the telly.

X3.11: "Utopia"

(16 June, 2007)

Which One is This? The Master's back. Isn't that a pip?

Firsts and Lasts See above. It's the first time we've seen the Master – or indeed any Time Lord besides the Doctor – since "The TV Movie" (27.0) more than a decade before (or, in the series proper, since 26.4, "Survival"). Captain Jack gets to meet this version of the Doctor for the first time (and makes up with him much more easily than many fans had anticipated).

It's the first time we see the TARDIS getting to the end of the Universe, chronologically rather than geographically or owing to imminent destruction in our time (13.2, "Planet of Evil"; 18.7, "Logopolis"). Oddly, next time will be completely different (X8.4, "Listen").

It's the first time that someone with a knighthood's appeared in front of the cameras: to whit, Derek Jacobi.[46] Meanwhile, a *Blue Peter* viewer won a competition to appear in a small role (he's Creet, the young child-aide who tells Martha that the skies are "made of diamonds"), making him the first non-celeb non-actor to get a line of dialogue since another young prize-winner in 14.4, "The Face of Evil".

And they have to retime the captions, to put John Barrowman's name in with the other two.

Watch Out For...

• For all that he's barely in this episode, John Simm gets a better post-regeneration sequence than any new-series Doctor has yet enjoyed. But it's obviously all about Sir Derek, who's delighting in playing a part that looks – on first viewing – like an affable old grandad who can make a spaceship from cake ingredients (and, indeed reminds older viewers of the old *Mr Kipling's* adverts) and on second viewing like a diabolical mastermind. Other things to spot on a repeat viewing (now that we've made a fairly hefty spoiler of the surprise ending) include the resemblance of Yana's lab to the Peter Cushing TARDIS set and Jack's complete lack of any reaction when the Doctor and Martha discuss the Face of Boe in front of him. (Not sure why he should? Hang on for two more episodes.)

• Meanwhile, Captain Jack hitches a ride *on* the TARDIS. The Ship's so pleased to see him, she runs right to the end of the Universe to try and shake him off – facilitating a pre-credit sequence that looks for all the world like John Barrowman's trying to shag a police box in the space-time vortex.

• It's tempting to imagine Russell T Davies and Julie Gardner looking down a checklist of pulp cover-art clichés and saying:

Cat-women with big guns, check.
Black Hole with Satan in, check.
Space-squids – gotta keep Margaret Atwood happy.
Pig-Slaves in sewers, A-O-K.
Rocketships with Fins – thank God for Matt Jones.
Flying car traffic-jams, sorted.

Hang on... we haven't done insect-people or nomadic warriors with tattoos and motorbikes... so our first glimpse of the logic-defying Futurekind comes in the pre-credit sequence, so they can go from a shot of John Barrowman clinging to the TARDIS in flight to the nearly-identical opening shot of the title sequence without confusing anyone.

• Annoying as it is, the verbal tic of Professor Yana's assistant Chantho (begin every sentence with "chan", end it with "tho") goes a long way to suggesting a lost culture she's trying to keep alive. Yet when Martha gets her to dare to break it and be "rude", this isn't seen as a betrayal of her dead race, but as a bit of a giggle. It's an engaging girlie moment, but reinforces how little interest the new series has in anything that isn't pretty much like early twenty-first century Britain, except as a bit of exotic local colour. (Perhaps appropriately, Chantho looks like the love-child of Iggle Piggle and Upsy Daisy, both of whom say their names over and over in lieu of conversation.)

• Talking of colour, this story's retro feel extends to a visual palette familiar to movie-goers between 1980 and 2005, the now-unfashionable orange-and-teal (see "The TV Movie", but also X7.6, "The Snowmen"). What makes this more noticeable is that while director Graeme Harper and Director of Photography Ernie Vincze shot the first half of the regeneration, the end and all subsequent TARDIS shots were on a different block with Colin Teague directing and Rory Taylor as DoP. Their "usual" TARDIS look is less lurid (see also X3.0, "The Runaway Bride", where where they reshot an entire scene to avoid this problem).

• This week's excuse for Our Heroes not knowing anything about the world, indeed the universe, that they've supposedly grown up in and needing someone to spell it out for them: the Doctor, Jack and Martha are hermits, having a hermit get-together. It's apparently just an engagingly silly throwaway joke, but is also pretty much what Utopia purports to be.

• And it doesn't really make sense in story terms, but Freema Agyeman plays it as if this is the episode when Martha decides to leave. The last straw is Jack and the Doctor – a hundred trillion years into the future, and shortly after the former has come back to life before her eyes – ignoring her and their bizarre situation to talk about bloody Rose. If the companion is supposed to be the audience-identification character, Martha's really earning her keep by getting utterly hacked off with this.

The Continuity

The Doctor Noticeably, he spots Captain Jack running toward the TARDIS during a brief stop-over in Cardiff, and sets the Ship in motion to leave the man behind again, without a word to him. After Jack hitches a ride anyway, the Doctor is deliberately cool towards him, except when they're swapping anecdotes about Rose. The Doctor

Why Hide Here?

If you've been following *About Time* from the start, you'll know that whenever we do science-ish essays, we're trying to resolve three things: 1) what present understanding and thinking has to offer on the subject, 2) what the consensus and most interesting variants were at the time the episode in question was written, and 3) what a TV scriptwriter working on a low-budget family show thought would make a fun story.

In pieces such as **What Does Anti-Matter Do?** (13.2, "Planet of Evil"), **How Can the Universe Have a Centre?** (20.4, "Terminus"), **How Many Significant Galaxies are There?** (2.5, "The Web Planet") and **What's With All These Black Holes?** (10.1, "The Three Doctors"), we have landed up giving the Hacks of Sol III credit for at least doing a bit of homework. Most of the goofy ideas on display owe to the designers and directors approximating things that the writers culled from the popular science works of the day, each stage of the process adding slight misunderstandings or distortions. And, of course, the writers can't be blamed for the facts changing after they did whatever background reading seemed adequate. (Mark Gatiss being unable to google Mars, or even use Google Mars, is another matter.)

But it remains amusing (and ironic) that the most belligerently pro-science script-editors (Christopher H Bidmead and Douglas Adams) and the author who became a TV science pundit (Dr Kit Pedler) committed the most grotesque blunders concerning things anyone with a library-card and three minutes to spare could find out, and most bright ten-year-olds at the time could have told them. We now have the wonders of online, so any such mistakes are either deliberate because they want to use an effect that looks "cool" (X2.8, "The Impossible Planet"; X4.0, "Voyage of the Damned"), or accidental because someone at The Mill wasn't paying attention (endless fun and games with "Earth from space" shots and inconstant Moons) or Neil Cross is writing the episode (X7.8, "The Rings of Akhaten"; X7.10 "Hide", but we gave the former a vaguely plausible gloss in the essay with X4.3, "Planet of the Ood").

Other things are so weird we've had to devise explanations for them that also account for other apparent goofs. We'll be revealing the fruits of our labours in Volumes 9 and 10 (forthcoming attractions include yet more on the Silurians, to account for Madame Vastra's apparent ability to play in the snow if she wraps up warm; see **Reptiles With Tits?** under X5.9, "Cold Blood"). The point is, there is no longer any excuse for botching known science – it has to be acknowledged or deliberately contradicted.

To his credit, admitted science-duffer Russell T Davies did get a lot of the basics right. The dates he gives for the creation and end of this very planet are about what the consensus says (X1.2, "The End of the World"; X3.0, "The Runaway Bride"). The depiction he gives in "Utopia" of the heat-death of the universe is as close to some of the known details as you can get, and still have people around to tell us about it. There are small anomalies, some of which we cover in the **Things That Don't Make Sense** listing, but there is a bigger concern. That scenario is only one of a number supported by the observed data and most-likely models, and it's the one least likely to allow time travel. That's not actually a problem. In fact, in some ways, we can see it as partially consolidating an idea that's in this and the next two episodes; that the Master hid in the one place where neither side in the Time War could find him – a future that is only possible if there were no Time War.

At present, the ability to predict the precise fate of the cosmos is beyond us. Observational astronomers, theoretical physicists and *Doctor Who* scriptwriters can only partially back up their claims, not really refute anyone else's. However, informed conjecture at least sets parameters for what might occur if the as-yet-unknown amounts of theoretical entities are in differing proportions. The big known unknowns are Dark Matter (like regular matter/ energy – baryonic matter – but as yet undetectable because of a few quirks, up to and including not being anything like normal matter) and Dark Energy.

Both of these terms are sort of shrugs; the precise details of things that can't be directly observed lead to a shorthand that, unfortunately, catches on and causes confusion when the term spreads into general use (see X3.13a, "Time Crash" for Steven Moffat's inability to grasp the basics of black holes unaided – eventually his teenage son came to the rescue, which is why X10.11, "World Enough and Time" is less stupid than "The Impossible Planet"). Because both of these names came to the public attention at the same time, in the same basic context ("the universe and all that surrounds it"), they seem almost interchangeable. After all, Einstein told us that matter and energy were essentially the same thing. These probably aren't.

continued on Page 229...

explains that he left Jack behind on the Game Station [X1.13, "The Parting of the Ways"] because from the moment Rose brought Jack back to life, he became a 'fixed point in time' that seemed 'wrong' to the Doctor's Time Lord gut-instinct. Nonetheless, he sounds genuinely surprised when Jack describes him as being 'prejudiced'. [They never really resolve that plot strand. It's somewhat suggested that the TARDIS rather than the Doctor decided to leave Jack behind in 200,100, but he didn't struggle to override it or bother to return. (In X1.13a, "Pudsey Cutaway", the Doctor claims that Jack's busy rebuilding Earth – which *might* have even been true for a time, but he couldn't have known that.)]

He goes to pains to argue that he's got the best time travel device in the room; that his 'sports car' TARDIS is much better than Jack's 'space hopper' vortex-manipulator. He finds Jack's flirtatious greetings as annoying as he did in his previous life. He has a low opinion of blogging, using the term to describe Jack and Martha's bitching [see X7.15, "The Day of the Doctor" for more haziness about the terminology of this flurry of consumer InfoTech]. Jack has to remind him that the usual reaction to hearing about someone's destroyed home is sympathy rather than punching the air about having guessed the local terminology correctly.

The fact that he has travelled to the year One Hundred Trillion intrigues him without setting off any alarm-bells [see this episode's essay for what's afoot]. He's initially uncertain about leaving the TARDIS this far in the future. [This very much resembles 21.3, "Frontios". In that case, it was partly because he was breaching the Time Lords' embargo on that era (which might explain why the Ship was so abnormally vulnerable to meteor-impact). However, since then we've seen the Doctor take Rose and Martha to a much later period. Even when stranded in the wrong universe with no power – X2.5, "Rise of the Cybermen" – the Ship was invulnerable, so that cannot be the whole reason he is concerned.]

The human race's survival instinct, even at the end of the universe, prompts another speech about indomitability. [Do we need to point you in the direction of 12.2, "The Ark In Space"?] In a similar vein, he claims [off-screen] to be a Doctor of 'everything'.

• *Background.* He's horrified rather than pleased when Martha tells him about Professor Yana's chameleon-arch-related watch [similar, of course, to his own from X3.8, "Human Nature"], rightly guessing that it might be a Time Lord who'd be better left inside. [If anything, the Nightmare Child speech in "The End of Time Part Two" makes it sound as if the Master might be one of the less dangerous candidates for a post-Time War entrance.]

• *Ethics.* He agrees with Professor Yana that it can be better to leave people in hope rather than tell them the truth, then contrives to make both happen. [This turns out to be exactly what the Master needed, but we'll wait two episodes before elaborating on that.] He thinks to ask Jack whether he wants his curse of immortality lifted. [Nothing in this episode makes it look as if Jack is anything less than glad to be alive, but anyone who saw *Torchwood* will know that he's spent the last century-plus moping around Cardiff and experiencing various horrors.]

• *Inventory: Other.* The glasses go on just in time for him to declare 'I'm brilliant!' [Perhaps he thinks that, slappable as he is at that moment, nobody will hit a man in glasses.] Martha says that the Doctor keeps 'that medical kit' relatively close to the front door of the Ship [possibly installed on her insistence].

The TARDIS Apparently doesn't object to rogue Time Lords regenerating inside or indeed making off with it, but it does go all the way to the end of the universe to shake off the fixed point that's Immortal Jack. [Evidently not the *exact* end of all time as there's still a universe something like a hundred years after this episode, if the rocket's ETA is any clue. Either the Ship landed once it detected that Jack was dead enough, or there's a cut-out that allows the occupants a bit of time to do things once they're there – save planets, get married and so on. See this episode's essay.] A flip of the door-latch can lock the door so that even a TARDIS key or sonic screwdriver won't open it.

[Oh, and the Doctor's upgraded the charging systems since "Boom Town" (X1.11), when even with the extrapolator it took a day to absorb enough power. This time it seems to take about 30 seconds (there was going to be a proper touristy Cardiff scene, but the episode was overrunning and it was simply cut out). Running a powerline through the door to charge the rocket is a 'little bit of a cheat'; the Master consequently stealing the Ship is exactly why the Doctor doesn't usually do

Why Hide Here?

continued from Page 227...

So, just quickly: Dark Matter is the material that *has* to be present in or near galaxies, because they spin around like pinwheels too fast to stay together without a lot more mass than they appear to have. It could be unlit star-sized entities (super-Jupiters or Brown Dwarves) or fairly hefty particles that don't interact with anything else, like neutrinos on steroids, or any combination of these and other things – black holes in far greater abundance than hitherto suspected, for example. The handy thing is that, it having mass and thus gravitational effect on light, anyone looking at far-distant (i.e. very old) objects can infer the influence of such matter through gravitational lensing (more Einstein). The good news is that there's solid evidence (so to speak) from this that enough Dark Matter to make the sums come out right is there, to the extent that it's three-quarters of the matter around and that normal matter (like galaxies and planets and things we can see) is just detritus that's coalesced in nooks the other stuff has created, like dust-bunnies.

Dark Energy is altogether different and a lot odder. In between all that Dark Matter and the occasional galaxy is a lot of empty space. Empty space, however, is pretty active. Particle-antiparticle pairs are springing up and self-annihilating all the time and, indeed, have to just to make sure that the emptiness isn't too predictable for Heisenberg's Uncertainty Principle to apply universally. Dark Energy is another such phenomenon and seems to be mainly characterised by generating negative gravitational pressure. (As always, physicists are using an everyday word – in this case "pressure" – in a specialised way: gravitational pressure is the scrunching of spacetime caused by strong gravity, as with black holes.) In other words, it makes more space. More empty space means more Dark Energy (but this is *not* contravening the basic Law of the Conservation of Energy – honest!). More Dark Energy means... you get the picture. If the effect of the Dark Matter outweighs, in a literal and figurative sense, the effect of Dark Energy, then the universe will most likely end a particular way. If it's the other way around, a totally different and weirder one will result, and if they balance pretty much exactly, we get a third scenario.

More detail in a moment, but first a quick reminder of the situation we actually see in "Utopia". The Universe is, first and foremost, still there. Time is running forwards. All the stars have gone out and the light from them has stopped reaching Malcassairo. Nonetheless, kettles still boil to make the coffee that is miraculously still available, so the process of energy doing work is still just about happening; no changes to the Second Law of Thermodynamics or any other inconvenient laws of physics. At risk of stating the bleedin' obvious, food makes people go and fuel makes engines work. In the scenario where Dark Energy substantially overwhelms the effects of Dark Matter, this isn't necessarily going to be the case come One Hundred Trillion AD.

Following on from our comments in the introduction, we looked at Davies's most likely source for the details in this episode: the June 2006 wikipedia entry on the "Ultimate Fate of the Universe". (There was a point later on when the article offered to redirect to "The End of Time", the BBC Wales two-parter, but also complained that some of the material in the main entry was unconfirmed. We'd love to know what source they would accept as authoritative about something a hundred trillion years hence.) That item took it for granted that Dark Energy is responsible for the observed acceleration of the expansion of the universe some five billion years back, something that other models, notably String Theory, couldn't account for otherwise. Indeed, such an observation could itself have a number of causes, including the known fact that our "local group" of galaxies is in a patch of space with unusually low energy-density (see, again, the essay with "The Web Planet").

The idea underlying that piece is a bit counter-intuitive, but simple and interesting – just the sort of thing that would make a wild scenario for a post Time-War universe. Dark Energy has an effect inversely proportionate to the local density of energy and matter; in the early universe, everything's scrunched up in a fairly small space, so the density is high enough to make Dark Energy behave like the normal kind. Then, at a critical period, the density dropped below a break-even point and the negative pressure kicked in, amplifying the expansion significantly. Thus stars and galaxies had enough time to form the way required for beings like us to be around, then all of those galaxies began to move apart faster as the space between them was left for the Dark stuff to

continued on Page 231...

this; but see, for instance, 8.3, "The Claws of Axos" or 3.1, "Galaxy 4".]

The Time War The Doctor tells Jack that Rose turning him into Captain Scarlet ["The Parting of the Ways"] was "the final act of the Time War". He tells Martha that all of the Time Lords 'died' [see, of course, X7.15, "The Day of the Doctor" et seq].

The Supporting Cast

• *Martha* doesn't object to Jack's patented "greetings", and is obviously very sick of hearing about Rose. When not nursing dead Jack, she's largely making comments that imply she's contemplating going home soon; she refers to the Doctor's companions as 'stray dogs', and is frustrated by the Doctor's coolly lackadaisical behaviour towards them. She finds Jack's manner of ordering her to do the same task faster the second time a bit odd [even though she's spent years in an A&E department, with lives depending on rapid execution of complex tasks]. She can't do shorthand.

She's awkward around small children, not quite knowing what to do with herself when talking to Creet [strange, given that she's an elder child from a moderately sized family and a trained healthcare professional]. She's more relaxed when talking with Chantho, and comparing her own position vis-à-vis the Doctor as much as learning about someone else.

The Doctor's hand-regrowing physiology [X2.0, "The Christmas Invasion"] fascinates and nonplusses her, but she still doesn't know about regeneration yet. When the regenerated Master speaks at the end, she recognizes his voice [see the next episode].

She's wearing earrings again, but has a nice long coat so she can stride around like the Doctor and Jack.

• *Captain Jack Harkness.* [We here encounter Jack following the end of *Torchwood* Series 1, when he heard the TARDIS's arrival noise and sees a glow on his 'Doctor detector': the Doctor's hand that was chopped off in "The Christmas Invasion" and fell into the Thames. The best explanation we're given for Jack's newfound immortality is that – through Rose's agency in "The Parting of the Ways" – he's become a 'fixed point in time and space'. Presumably *not*, however, in the same way as Pompeii, X4.2, "The Fires of Pompeii", or else he would recover from each death thinking he's in a space-station full of Daleks and wondering who that boggle-eyed Welsh bint is. Our nearest analogy is the mutants in 20.3, "Mawdryn Undead", whose immortality is linked to the TARDIS's ability to travel in time, hence Nyssa and Tegan ageing or getting younger as the Doctor tries to escape their ship. We're going to have to discuss this further, clearly; see **What Constitutes a Fixed Point?** under "The Fires of Pompeii" and **What Actually Happens in a Regeneration?** under 11.5, "Planet of the Spiders".]

It turns out that Jack has lived out the entire timespan between 1869 and 2007 waiting for a future version of the Doctor to show up [for more detail, see *Torchwood* 2.12, "Fragments"]. After Rose resurrected him aboard the Game Station ["The Parting of the Ways"], he used his Time Agency vortex manipulator to go to twenty-first century Cardiff, but overshot the mark, arrived in 1869, and thereby burnt it out. [He doesn't say that the location was wrong, so it's tempting to conclude the manipulator was pulled off course by the Rift's opening in X1.3, "The Unquiet Dead" and he just misses meeting the ninth Doctor and Rose, as paradoxical as that would be.]

He first learned that he was immortal in 1892, when he got into a fight on Ellis Island and was shot through the heart. Since then, he's experienced death by 'fell off a cliff, trampled by horses, World War I, World War II, poison, starvation, a stray javelin'. In the 1990s, he visited Rose's council estate a couple of times to watch her grow up, but avoided contact for fear of polluting the timelines. He saw her listed as killed in the Battle of Canary Wharf, but learns from the Doctor that she's merely trapped in a parallel universe [X2.13, "Doomsday"]. Jack doesn't object to Rose making him immortal; it's the Doctor's actions that bother him.

He largely keeps his temper in check even while accusing the Doctor of abandoning him and being told that's exactly what happened. [He's in a very forgiving mood at the moment; just about the last thing he does before leaving Cardiff – see *Torchwood* 1.13, "End of Days" – is to grandiosely absolve his Torchwood team for nearly obliterating the entire planet accidentally-on-purpose, and shooting him dead to boot.] He seems uncertain when the Doctor asks if he wants to die, then claims to have been inspired by the hope of people living at the end of time. Reflexively, he slips back into a supportive role to whatever the

Why Hide Here?

continued from Page 229...

do its thing. The further they separate, the more this effect will be allowed to increase. Then another critical phase begins and, on the 2006 wikipedia timeline, this is dated at – oh, look! – about a hundred trillion years hence.

In this third, "flat" expansion rate, this is where the negative pressure (what we roughly compared to anti-gravity, but it's not actually anything of the sort) gets to the point where it doesn't just push ex-galaxies apart but makes gravity, electromagnetism and the Strong and Weak nuclear forces unable to do their jobs. Matter itself ceases to work (an effect Davros will later replicate with 27 planets, a stream of Z neutrinos, the Medusa Cascade and a small aubergine; X4.12-4.13, "The Stolen Earth"/ "Journey's End"). Moreover, the space available for this to occur in is expanding ever faster, outstripping the ability of light to get anywhere. (It's not that anything, any *thing*, is travelling faster than light, it's that light-speed is no longer enough to cover the expanding distance.) Thus, even light from long-dead stars isn't getting to wherever you might be, so not only have the galaxies gone but news of them will never reach you. The wavelengths red-shifted beyond the ability of anything to apprehend them anyway. This is what we see, or fail to see, in "Utopia". These, and the throwaway reference to the "Dark Matter Reefs", are pretty good evidence that Davies was going from this entry and its cited sources when devising this script. In commentaries, he's offered the idea that the date is not the absolute end of the universe, but just about the time when life ceases to be possible.

Thus the readily-available background reading on cosmology made a wondrously Victorian-sounding bleak far-future seem justifiable, especially with two mighty armies messing with the physical nature of creation as part of your backstory. Documentaries of the time, especially the more gosh-wow ones (still available on YouTube, and we'll be billing Mad Norwegian for the aspirin we needed afterwards) illustrated the three models with gaudy graphics and lots of whooshing noises. A lot of special pleading accompanied the flat expansion described above, and the two other more comprehensible models – exponential expansion (shown with a graph looking like a Pringles chip) and finite expansion (a sphere) – were given more screen-time. Exponential acceleration of expansion would follow there being a universe of almost all Dark Energy with a tiny froth of matter and Dark Matter. In that version, the expansion of the universe accelerates as we said: exponentially and, with finite energy spread over much more space per year, things cool down faster. So fast that atoms stop cohering. Jack's conjectured force-bubble protecting the fugitives from the cold would need to be more like a pocket universe containing just that world. With nowhere outside the planet following our version of physics, that rather rules out the jaunt to Utopia.

In the opposite case (where there's as much Dark Matter as people think there ought to be, but not enough Dark Energy to counteract its gravitational effect), by now the universe ought to be thinking about slamming into reverse and contracting, maybe sending time into rewind and probably with enough of a snap to cause an inversion of the Big Bang, thus starting things off again. We've seen a lot of things in *Doctor Who* to make this scenario the one most favourable to maintaining the continuity – not least that this is the situation more useful for a series about time travel. If the universe is "closed" by that much mass, it is a sort of fourth-dimensional loop and all the interstellar flights and causality violations we've seen can be retained. (See also **Why's the Doctor So Freaked Out by a Big Orange Bloke?** under X2.9, "The Satan Pit" and **Are All These "Gods" Related?** under 26.3, "The Curse of Fenric".)

In a lot of ways, then, the version we see in "Utopia" is the worst-case scenario: the universe peters out, but the space in which nothing happens just goes on expanding. It might be worth noting that this model is, with certain caveats, also proposed in the second-most-likely source for Davies to have used: the popular science book *Bang* by Brian May, Chris Lintott and Patrick Moore.[47] The rest of this essay will discuss why the Master picked it as his bunker, but after this story was written, things got interesting and we can take some comfort in the fact that Russell T Davies's choice of a sullen, enfeebled future has been substantiated to an astonishingly high confidence-level and people have got Nobel Prizes for confirming a lot of what we saw. Twenty-one thousand far-distant galaxies were monitored for Type 1 supernovae, and, yes, the expansion of the universe has accelerated in a way that matches the theoretical version. Observationally, the uni-

continued on Page 233...

Doctor's up to, taking his coat without being asked. When the Doctor's busy, he reverts to being the head of a small band of misfits with expertise and barks out orders to Martha and Chantho.

His attempts to "greet" people become a running gag, but where Martha's concerned he seems happy to stick with light banter and mutual Doctor-baiting. He regards the Doctor's latest regeneration as 'cheeky'. The Futurekind spark a Beastie Boys quip.

Jack "survives" clinging to the outside of the TARDIS as it traverses all of remaining history, although he's dead on arrival and needs a bit to revive. This whole story occurs because the TARDIS reacts badly to Jack, and launches into the far future while trying to shake him off [but by X4.13, "Journey's End", he'll be happily operating a panel of the console with no hard feelings from the Ship].

The Supporting Cast (Secretly Evil)

• *Professor Yana.* He was found as a small child at the Silver Devastation, with only a pocket watch that he's never bothered to open, and no understanding of his origins. His name, as it turns out, stands for "You Are Not Alone" [per the Face of Boe's cryptic message in "Gridlock" (X3.3)].

He's adopted the title 'professor' in the absence of any official body to award [or deny] one. He wears a Regency-style waistcoat and blouson shirt, with a large bow cravat [as a result looking like either Peter Cushing as Dr Frankenstein or the Hartnell Doctor]. He's spent his adult life hopping from one refugee-ship to another. As an old man, he has a tendency towards cynicism and gallows humour, drinks coffee, and has established himself as the resident expert on all things technical. Yet, it seems, he doesn't know something very basic ('Chan I am happy drinking my own internal milk tho') about his 17-year companion's internal biology.

He's genuinely enthusiastic about meeting a real scientist besides himself, and enjoys the Doctor's admiration of his genius... and has apparently *been* that clever, creating sophisticated computers out of food and bits of string. Somehow, he's acquired a wind-up gramophone. He's been living with the sound of drumbeats in his head for all his life [an explanation for this will arrive down the line; see X4.18, "The End of Time Part Two", although this doesn't account for why the human Yana also hears it], and the drumming gets worse when the TARDIS crew drop comments about time travel and regeneration. He's initially reluctant to open the watch, but does so almost as soon as Martha's suggestions break down the perception filter. As soon as he opens the watch, in mind he becomes...

The Supporting Cast (Not-So Secretly Evil)

• *The Master.* He goes downright sociopathic, murdering Chantho in sheer pique because she never alerted him to his pocket watch [which she cannot have possibly known was important] then removing the navigational matrix for the rocket, and finally methodically arranging for a band of Futurekind to attack the Doctor and company.

He fled the Time War, apparently by using a Chameleon Arch to turn himself human and hiding out at the end of all life in the universe. [Possibly in a different time stream than the one everyone else knows about; see this episode's essay.]

Chantho shoots the Yana-Master in her final moments, and he finds being killed by a girl 'inappropriate'. Nonetheless, he manages to hijack the TARDIS and regenerate, becoming...

• *The Master (A.K.A. Harold Saxon)*... who outwardly seems to be in his early thirties, has short blond hair and a northern English accent [see X1.1, "Rose"]. Before leaving, he insists that the Doctor call him by his 'name'. He's finally gone up a level in genre-savvy, and is keen to *not* explain his plan to conquer the universe this time round. [Mind you, much of the next episode will consist of data-dumps about the precise details of such plans.] His immediate post-regenerative state is boyish, boisterous and playful: this is pretty much how he'll be from now on.

Indeed, he claims to have consciously decided to have a young body to match the Doctor's. [This indicates more control over the process than his rival ever had – or certainly *conscious* control; see also X9.5, "The Girl Who Died".

[Here we have to consider the Master's, for want of a better word, 'plan' of turning himself into Professor Yana. We're never told the full circumstances behind his becoming human, so we can't really file it under **Things That Don't Make Sense**. It's safe to assume that it was a desperate move by someone too egotistical to kill himself, but unable to face life in the Last Great Time War. We know from the next episode and "The End of Time" that the Time Lords resurrect anyone they

Why Hide Here?

continued from Page 231...

verse is 73% Dark Energy, 24% Dark Matter and 4% things like Cardiff and Andromeda. In short, we have a flat expansion ahead of us.

The thing is, whilst our universe is notable mainly for existing, it's not necessarily the one that we'd have at the end of a Time War as described in earlier and later stories. Either of the other two proposed far-futures, one that stopped expanding and contracted again before the supposed date of the story, *or* one that had already ceased to have any matter in it by then, is a more likely outcome of wielding the kinds of powers we hear about. Although the details of this are sketchy and the one piece of it we've seen is fairly conventional-looking (the Fall of Arcadia looks disappointingly like the *Star Wars* prequels – X7.15, "The Day of the Doctor") and the Moment is apparently the bomb from *Dark Star* rather than a glitch in time itself as hinted in "The End of Time Part Two" (X4.18), we hear of a lot of things that can't be shown at prime-time or perhaps can't be shown at all. Nonetheless, the implication is that it was a war using time as a weapon in itself, rather than a war merely *for* time. This has largely been taken to be the routine Fritz Leiber sort of thing, with one side changing the past and another changing it back again, or changing it earlier so the first change never happened and neither did the people doing it, et cetera. As we saw in the **Big Picture** entries for "The End of the World" (X1.2) and "Rise of the Cybermen" (X2.5), this kind of story has a long history and has almost infinite room for reworking. One strand that has become fashionable in the last 20 years has been using the conjectural physics we've been describing in this essay as a basis for conflict where the universe's very nature is malleable.

The mass of the universe is, of course, constant. A Big Crunch will compress exactly as much energy/ matter as the Big Bang started out with, *unless* you popped next door for a cup of counter-entropy (18.7, "Logopolis"). A Charged Vacuum Emboitment is, among other things, a potential Doomsday Weapon. In opening a doorway to a different universe, with a smaller one at a higher energy-state and thus likely to spurt mass and energy *into* ours, not only is the expansion of the universe slowed somewhat – making it risky to do it more often – but the chosen point-of-spurt would be vaporised. (As we said above, we have several issues with "Hide".) Any unscrupulous being capable of opening such a ferociously-powerful doorway could blackmail galaxies.

The universe, therefore, has more mass than it started out with... but did any Dark Matter pop across from E-Space? We'd like to think that, with the near-magical Block Transfer Computation and various off-stage entities controlling the laws of creation, it was possible to set up some kind of filter on the CVE, like a tea-strainer, to catch anything unwanted and just allow in raw energy and the odd Tharil. Nobody involved with writing Season Eighteen, very understandably, was that savvy about things only theorised about in the 90s. So, if either side in a Time War were to nudge the amount of Dark Energy available, maybe with the aid of a CVE, would they prevent their own creation and set up intolerable paradoxes – or, perhaps, could they rig the game so that, after changing time to suit their side, they prevent anyone else, including their own side, from ever being able to travel in time and do anything about it?

We know, for example, that Huon particles have been removed almost completely by the Gallifreyans, without the rest of creation becoming especially unbalanced. This incident took place in the Dark Times, a helpfully vague period that seems to have ended around the time the Earth was created, circa 4.6 billion years back ("The Runaway Bride"; 20.7, "The Five Doctors" and – heaven help us – 25.3, "Silver Nemesis"). That's, um, around the time the expansion of the universe accelerated to its present rate.

Now here's an interesting little detail: when the Doctor was given the task of preventing the Daleks' creation (12.4, "Genesis of the Daleks"), the person who gave him his instructions stated, of transmats, "We Time Lords out-grew such devices when the universe was half its present size". He doesn't give a date, but a scale. Looked at again now, with this story seemingly an opening skirmish in the Time War, the person who makes the Doctor take the mission seems not to be a Time Lord from his own time-line. And then we revisit "Logopolis", which appears to be entirely set in the present-day-as-was, 1981, and in which the universe has already passed the point of Heat-Death. This is highly improbable, as is the way 1/3 of all matter is undone in an afternoon and nobody mentions it again later. (20.1, "Arc of Infinity", for example, or Season Twenty-Three's "Trial of a Time

continued on Page 235...

think could be useful, so hiding is the one way to avoid going through this all again. So we can accept that the Master fell back upon a strategy of Needs Must – or what Americans call a Hail Mary Pass.

[So much so, unfortunately, that he doesn't seem to have prepped a means of his restoration. After all, the Doctor used his Chameleon Arch because he had Martha as an alarm clock, whereas someone found the baby Professor (was he called that then?) in the Silver Devastation, an area that existed way back in Five Billion AD and before. That's a bit of a puzzler: why he regenerated or otherwise turned himself into a *child*, either before or after using the Chameleon Arch. Also, that's three places that have survived, one of them for the thick-end of a hundred trillion years, but let's just go along with that one.

[Anyway, Yana has apparently outlived everyone who was around when he was a sprog. He doesn't know the watch is significant, because there's a perception filter around it (not for the last time, we have to wonder if "perception filter" isn't a polite way of saying "idiot-ray"). The point being: there's not even so much as a Post-It note to his future self. So one of three things *should* have happened: 1) he could have lived as Yana and then died, without regenerating, since he's in a human body, 2) He could have lived as Yana and gone on to Utopia, then died horribly along with everyone else, 3) He could have left his watch lying around near a kid with a slight genetic quirk, who then abruptly started going "heh-heh-heh" and making stupidly over-complicated plans to rule what's left of the Universe. He really is *extraordinarily* lucky that the Doctor turned up, shortly after Martha found out about these watches, or he'd never have made a return.

[Moreover, Yana isn't a young man, and his memory lock has worked well enough his whole life. Before Martha mentions it, he has no inkling of any mysterious past. (We are, sadly, denied Yana's *Journal of Impossible Things* where he sketches Adric manacled to a climbing-frame and loving it; Concorde; Cherry Bakewells; a bottle of Moroccan Burgundy; luring an old enemy toward Ravensworth Colliery because a plan to conquer the universe was going too well and he needed an excuse to dress up as a scarecrow... see Volumes 3, 5 and 6 for the Master's gonzo schemes.)

[One lingering detail in this is what became of his own TARDIS – presuming he even still had one as he exited the Last Great Time War – and if there's another time machine hanging around in the year 100 trillion. We saw in "The Keeper of Traken" (18.6) that he has occasionally had a "burner" TARDIS in reserve, but all the dialogue hints here, and in the next two episodes, suggest that the transformation into Yana happened long ago and he was found as a boy decades before the story starts. If he was genuinely hiding, setting his Ship to deposit a human boy in the Silver Devastation and then either fly back to earlier on auto-pilot or self-destruct seems more in character. Or perhaps he's had a whole lifetime as Yana to misplace it.

[Whatever the case, it's surely out of the picture, or else – as Saxon – he could have just taken the Doctor's destination-limited TARDIS back to the year Five Trillion, retrieved his own Ship, and gone anywhere in time and space unfettered. And yet, without explanation, he's in possession of a TARDIS – new or otherwise – in X10.12, "The Doctor Falls". We'll pick this discussion up in the accompanying essay.]

Planet Notes

• *Malcassairo* was once inhabited by the Malmooth, an insectoid species. They lived in a hive-like city structure known as the Conglomeration before dying out, leaving Chantho as the only survivor. [Yana's ambiguous wording might indicate that the refugees wiped them out, though from context it's unclear.]

• *The Condensate Wilderness* lies between Malcassairo and the 'wildlands' and dark matter reefs.

• *Utopia.* The sky there is made of diamonds, apparently. They've been sending out invites that the last of humanity should come there for about a thousand years [see also X3.13, "Last of the Time Lords"].

• *The Silver Devastation.* This is where the young Yana was found. [It's another mention of this enigmatic place; see X1.2, "The End of the World" and X1.12, "Bad Wolf", where it was the abode of the Face of Boe and said to be in the Isop Galaxy – also cited in 2.5, "The Web Planet" and X1.11, "Boom Town"). So the place *must* have been open for business in Five Billion and One Hundred Trillion-minus-sixty.] It has "shores" [typical BBC Wales – even made-up, unseen alien worlds are just beaches].

[By the way, this does not in any way chime

Why Hide Here?

continued from Page 233...

Lord" both have the Time Lords floundering around for an excuse to execute the Doctor and ignoring this.) That kind of cosmic engineering seems to be happening and unhappening a lot even pre-1989.

The obvious thing to do, therefore, is mess with the nature of nature. We've got good evidence that this last throw was planned by Rassilon ("The End of Time Part Two"), so avoiding such a fate would have been tricky had not the Time War been sealed away before he could instigate it. That's not to say it's impossible. All of these timelines are contingent and a TARDIS trying to find one where no Daleks or Time Lords persist would have been tracked down, since if one such time machine can get there, another can. But it's possible to travel into the far future without a time-machine, simply by travelling very fast and letting relativity fight the seven signs of ageing. Assuming that you don't collide with anything and can decelerate eventually (say five trillion years into your flight), it's easy to keep going and avoid everything happening outside. If there is no longer a universe, then you don't know any different and your voyage comes to an end. If the fate of the cosmos is in flux, but you're left alone, then *if* it settles down without either side destroying anything, you can just out-live whoever is left. Whatever the alterations made by one side or the other (removing kinds of particles, adding excess mass or increasing the amount of Dark Energy), the Master could have withstood it in a ship travelling at near lightspeed.

As time passes in whatever contingent future remains after whatever is done to the past, the probability of a resultant state that was uninhabitable after that long a time diminishes. Whoever wins, they'd most likely be extinct by the end of everything. Thus the Master picked a starting-point prior to anything that Davros or Rassilon could do to the universe's physical nature to make it end before One Hundred Trillion, and either A) went in as himself but with a Chameleon Arch onboard, or B) just made like Kal-El: turning into a human baby first and travelling so fast that he was still a kid when they fished him out of the Silver Devastation, so that he could grow up into Mr Kipling. We suspect the former, we've reason to believe that he consciously set up the Utopia scam. Well, all right... there's nothing in the dialogue to *say* Utopia was his plan rather than humanity getting desperate, but both Jacobi and Simm act as if it had been part of the plan from the outset.

Two problems with this: one is that the Doctor's TARDIS was able to get there, the other is that it was able to get back. These are interesting points, as the future that has Yana and the Toclafane in is still possible in a universe where the Doctor has somehow prevailed, but the Time Lords and Daleks are gone (nearly). Obviously, the TARDIS, like our conjectured rocket-powered pram, has gone for the version of the future that lasts longest in order to try to shake off Jack. Or rather, it's gone to the one that has the longest shelf-life, but is still amenable to time travel. The array of potential futures diminishes as time passes (something we have elsewhere suggested is the most likely fuel-source for the TARDIS, the much-discussed Artron Energy – see **How Does the TARDIS Travel?** under 1.3, "The Edge of Destruction" and **What *is* the Blinovitch Limitation Effect?** under 20.3, "Mawdryn Undead"). As we suggested in earlier essays, the role of conscious observers in making this all work seems to be critical, so as the last few sentient species withdraw (or get cut up and stuck in tin cans), the possibility of a time machine working that way also dwindles. This also lends itself to being a good place and time to hide from time-travellers. If either side were still prosecuting such a war, they would be taking steps to make a "flat" universe difficult to maintain for very long – either to score a final victory over the other side by making them never have existed or to keep themselves in power for longer than the universe is currently expected to last.

So the one state of affairs the Master never saw coming was one where *neither* the Daleks nor the Time Lords won but where the Doctor was still around, where the universe was still open for business at the end of their war and where time travel was still an option. If his plan for the Toclafane was to ride to Gallifrey's rescue with a paradoxical army, or to take Gallifrey by force after the Daleks' defeat, he must have got started after waking up in the deep future and finding no sign of either side, or any clue as to who (if anyone) won.

But the Toclafane seem like an afterthought – for all we know, they may have been the work of a different Time Lord that the Master found out about when he got there. His primary purpose in

continued on Page 237...

with the *other* End of the Universe seen in "Listen" (X8.4). This episode's essay will perhaps account for that, although we have no way of knowing if Colonel Orson Pink's twenty-second century is still a viable timeline. Then there's the *other* other End of the Universe in X9.12, "Hell Bent", which is somehow both long after this one – these *two* – and a mere 4.5 billion years in our future, apparently.]

The Non-Humans

• *The Futurekind.* Discount Automart Warriors of the Apocalypse. They look horribly 80s and it's feared – but not confirmed – that the Futurekind are the final human evolutionary form. They have pointy teeth, and like flaming torches, Goth clothing and tattoos. They enjoy hunting humans.

[Though what they do after catching people is anyone's guess – there's a suggestion that it's simply for eating, but it could be for recruitment. Some sort of heightened sensory ability is implicit, since they zero in on the Doctor and company very quickly after the base defences are dropped. The humans in Yana's camp use teeth as a quick method of determining if someone is human or Futurekind, so perhaps this is a form of vampirism and all Futurekind were born human. It accounts for their ability to make fires and drive quad-bikes, plus the way the infiltrator who smashes the launch systems knew what to do and how she got in in the first place.]

• *The Malmooth.* Blue-skinned, approximately humanoid insects with mandibles near a jawbone with teeth and a tongue. On the evidence of the sole survivor, Chantho, they had a cultural tradition that demands all sentences be preceded with the first syllable of the name and ended with the last syllable. [Alternatively, they all used to begin *everything* with 'Chan' and then end with 'Tho' and the humans – especially Yana – have opted to call this one 'Chantho' to avoid a longer, more complex name. Or perhaps just to annoy her. If we assume that Malcassairo and the Silver Devastation are close by, we could be in what's left of the Isop Galaxy, seemingly largely populated in its day by insectoids of various kinds.] They can ingest their own 'internal milk'.

Chantho herself dresses as a human. [In fact, she dresses as Martha, in a low-cut top black top, matching slacks, stack-heeled shoes and a lab-coat.]

History

• *Dating.* The Doctor says that they've arrived in the year One Hundred Trillion. [The TARDIS crew stick to that figure through the episode, but it might be more or less rounded, since none of the locals were around whenever they discussed it.] The universe is now dissolving. No one's ever heard of Time Lords, yet people still say 'oi'. Diamonds still sound exciting to kids [unless we're meant to take that 'the sky is made of diamonds' metaphorically, in which case it's really just about a craving for light]. Yana mentions rumours of there having been time travel 'back in the old days' [perhaps a veiled reference to Captain Jack and River Song's native era], but it's not something humanity can do now.

What remains of the human race *seems* [no one's quite certain anymore] to have all gathered on Malcassairo to take a little trip, on supersonic rocketship, to another refuge-world called [not even slightly pretentiously] 'Utopia'. For thousands of years, the Utopia Project has been working on some way to survive the end of the universe; no one knows their results, but a signal's gone out to all the intelligent life left that everyone should come to Utopia. The Doctor says it can't be on automatic, since the signal is being modulated [that's a complete non-sequitur, but never mind].

The Doctor suggests that humans have reverted to their original form after 'a million years' of evolving into 'clouds of gas' and another million into 'downloads' [but he could just be taking the piss].

[To peg down the opening in modern-day Cardiff, though... well, it's presumably the same day as Jack's abrupt disappearance from the Torchwood Hub (*Torchwood:* "End of Days"), even if the incidental details don't match up. In "End of Days", a gust of wind and a mysterious wheezing groaning sound ((c) Terrance Dicks, 1974) heralded the TARDIS's arrival, and there's side-issue of *how* Jack exited the Hub, given that his teammates are coming through the front door with pizza. Scrutiny of the opening sequence shows that the TARDIS isn't parked on *exactly* the same square as the perception filter it created (see *TW* 1.1, "Everything Changes"), so he might have left via the lift – but could he have done that in the time allotted, and without Gwen Cooper noticing? Alternatively, Jack does like to keep his secrets, and it's not totally insane to believe that he knows of a third way out of his own headquarters,

Why Hide Here?

continued from Page 235...

going that far was hiding, after enabling a future where there was still conscious life. Just because the version of the far future we see here conforms to the predictions of one model in which supersymmetry and string theory are surplus to requirements, it doesn't follow that they aren't somehow in play. Similarly, the rapidly-diminishing options available as matter in the universe fizzles out doesn't mean the end of alternatives. As we saw in the last volume, the Toclafane storyline and the whole Year That Never Was are remnants of what seems to have been an earlier storyline (**Was Series 2 Supposed to Have Been Like This?** under X2.11, "Fear Her"). That wiki article we cited had a lot to say on parallel universes (including, bizarrely, a link to the BBC's weather forecast service when we first checked).

So the Master has hidden himself from himself, but he's also hidden inside a timeline that is very unlikely to stay viable during a Time War. Fortunately, we're going to consider closed-off timelines a lot more very soon. (See **Where's Susan?** under X4.18, "The End of Time Part Two" and **How is This Not a Parallel Universe?** under X4.11, "Turn Left".)

one that's readily accessible unless it goes into lockdown (such as *TW* 1.8, "They Keep Killing Suzie").

[As for *when* this sequence occurs, we covered that matter extensively in **Why the Great Powell Estate Date Debate?** under X2.3, "School Reunion". Suffice to say, it's complicated, and you can quickly lose perspective pondering this sort of thing – on one pass through this, we used Martha's red jacket (the one she's not wearing here, but re-dons in her flat in X3.12, "The Sound of Drums", when she can't access the TARDIS) as evidence that at least one Cardiff stop-over to refuel happens in 2007 (accounting for the date Martha and John Smith keep using in "Human Nature" and the mess of "Blink"). But at the end of the day, it's hard to avoid the conclusion that, if the ninth Doctor meets Rose in 2005, he brings her back a year late in 2006 (X1.4, "Aliens of London") and Series 2 ends in 2007, then *Torchwood* Series 1 *cannot* end before Spring 2008. So it's something of a toss-up as to *when* in that calendar year Jack goes running through Roald Dahl Plass screaming, "Doc-toorrrrrrrrrrrrr", but that year seems a lock, regardless of Martha's fashion choices. It's well before whenever the episodes with Francine in are supposed to be set, because that has to be Autumn 2008.]

Additional Sources The BBC novel *The Game of Death* has a few gobbets about the Silver Devastation, while IDW's comic "Agent Provocateur" makes the claim that humans are one of three species to survive until the end of everything. The other two are the Sycorax and the Uvodni ("The Christmas Invasion", "The End of Time Part Two"). This is also claimed in the *Monster File* complied by Helen Raynor.

Titan's *Eleventh Doctor Year Two* comics establish that the Master was *already* incarnated as a young boy during the Time War, then make a small hash of things by aging him into his older Yana self just before he's found in the Silver Devastation.

The Analysis

The Big Picture We have a whole essay on the problems of relating the version of the Heat Death of the Universe with time-travel, and we discussed the Victorian obsession with Entropy under "Logopolis". In this context, let's start with an 1820 book called *Melmoth the Wanderer*. Oscar Wilde used to book into hotels as "Sebastian Melmoth". It was classic self-pitying last-of-his-kind stuff, about a doomed immortal who sold his soul, and had a big influence on later "Decadent" works. That term, much abused by fake Nazi villains in kid's TV, applied to the *fin de siecle* movement's attempts to somehow become works of art. It's a big subtext of all late nineteenth-century writing and art, and we encountered aspects of it when looking at the Theosophists (7.2, "Doctor Who and the Silurians", the weird German cult of the *Welteislehre* – see 16.1, "The Ribos Operation") and Schopenhauer's influence on Wagner ("Mawdryn Undead"). Another idea that affected how the Victorians saw themselves and the world was the discovery that the Earth was a lot older than hitherto suspected. Combining these two perspectives, HG Wells threw the basic storyline of *The Time Machine* into sharp relief with a coda set on Earth's last day – an aspect forgotten in film versions, but acclaimed at the time as the best bit. We see an approximation of this in both "Hide" (X7.10) and "Listen".

So there's the waning of the universe, the willingness to abandon the crudely human in favour of something more finely-wrought (the most famous expression of the Decadent credo being WB Yeats's *Sailing to Byzantium*) and the whole back-of-the-hand-nailed-to-the-brow sorrow at the inevitability of decay and failure. Set against this, there was the hope for something better and the fear of the brute. Guess what – late nineteenth-century Britain did those a lot too. Although the original Utopia was a sarcastic inversion of everything Thomas More thought was happening in early Tudor England, complete with inversions of the names of things in Greek (such as "Utopia" itself), the real growth of this strand of fantasy was the latter years of the Victorian era. You couldn't move for them. The point of the Utopia that the people of Malcassairo are heading for is that it's not like Malcassairo; they don't really care about the details. That's in itself interesting: the thing that scares them is the hopelessness of their world and the bestial, unreasoning Futurekind, so it's possible that some would voluntarily submit to becoming undying machines (the fate of the fugitives, as we discover in two episodes from now).

The Futurekind may look like leftovers from some 80s film conceived in the wake of *Mad Max* (we're thinking of the kind of tick-box generic fodder that made it to VHS but not DVD – *Spacehunter: Adventures in the Forbidden Zone* can stand for hundreds), but the clues are in the dialogue. This is what humanity's final form will be like, apparently. Leaving aside the fallacious genetic determinism of a definite "future" with no environmental changes to allow variations to thrive or perish, this is horribly familiar from Terry Nation. In his story for the *Radio Times* Tenth Anniversary Special, he claimed that the Daleks were our inevitable destiny, while in what was intended as the last episode of *Blakes 7*, he had woolly anthropoids as a glimpse of what accelerated evolution had in store for us ("Terminal", the end of Series 3). What's looming under this idea is a half-memory, possibly via George Pal's film, of *The Time Machine* and the Morlocks. What such knock-offs ignore is that the Morlocks and the Eloi condition each other – they are class distinctions pushed to extremes into geological time, and neither race would have turned out that way without the other. If Davies had pursued this idea in the storyline, if the eponymous "Utopia" had made the more-nearly-human residents developmentally static while the outcasts adapted to circumstances, there would have been a different story worthy of a whole episode or more – but without any room for Yana and Chantho and Jack and Martha. Instead, the Futurekind are just... there.

As they savage the surviving undeveloped humans for no reason other than mania (albeit tempered with an ability to stop acting like the Tazmanian Devil long enough to go undercover on a sabotage mission), the obvious resemblance is with the Reivers from *Firefly* and the film it spawned, *Serenity*. In *Serenity*, we learn that they were accidentally made into berserkers by a viral mutation of an emotional conditioning (see Gridlock") that affects the amygdala (see X4.3, "Planet of the Ood"). In some scenes the Futurekind are victims of a viral regression, rather than evolution, and that takes us to various zombie apocalypse flicks (notably *28 Days Later*).

Nonetheless, as part of the story's overall rhetorical purpose, the Futurekind are another sort of entropy. In general, the countervailing properties that stave off this inexorable decline are food (living things changing their chemical make-up), structure and information. In the long run, these are all basically the same thing, forms of localised order. As with "Logopolis", there's a strong hint that the wrong kind of imposed order is as much a form of fatal rigidity as the lack of any, so the Master – arch control-freak of the spaceways – is himself a manifestation of disorder. We'll pick this up in the next episode, as the human fugitives become emblems of the inability to change and the Master flips over into being a more contemporary pop-culture figure: the capricious agent of chaos.

Setting the story in what's now called Deep Time is itself rather more modish than it was. Within written-down SF, there was a big movement towards this in the 1990s, especially with British authors. We're in the sort of territory staked out by Alastair Reynolds and Stephen Baxter. Baxter's debut was a pastiche/ sequel to *The Time Machine*, a Morlock-friendly piece called *The Time Ships*. (Ironically, he originally submitted this to Virgin as a *New Adventures* proposal, and reworked it to exclude the Doctor after it had been rejected. See issue 3 of *Vworp! Vworp!*) Reynolds and Baxter have respectively written a Pertwee novel and a Troughton novel for BBC Books, so the gulf between the series and the Hard SF that currently tops the literary carborundum scale is smaller than was thought in the past.

Let's not forget that the whole "sound of drums in my head" subplot is one with which Derek Jacobi would have been amply familiar. It was offered as the rationale for the increasingly erratic and megalomaniacal actions of Emperor Caligula in the 1975 television adaptation of *I Claudius*; that time, Jacobi had to offer a sympathetic ear as John Hurt demanded to be freed from the sound of galloping horses that tormented him day and night. Even without O-Level Latin ("The Fires of Pompeii"), Davies would undoubtedly have seen this landmark series on first broadcast, however stilted he may claim to find it now.

English Lessons

- *Spacehopper* (n.): Like an exercise ball with rubber handles, but more fun. Luke Rattigan (X4.4, "The Sontaran Stratagem") has one in the giant ceramic hand that serves as a chair, next to his teleport and bamboo-plant.
- *Hermits Reunited* (n): an obvious play on the briefly-fashionable website *Friends Reunited*, which wrecked a few marriages and spawned CD compilations of old hits before being bought by ITV, just as everyone who was using it realised that it was most popular with people who'd not really done much since school.

... and it's not strictly a language lesson, but Martha's ability to identify Jack's coat as RAF-surplus is a bit of identification any British student could make, rather than being a spectacular display of fashion know-how. (Back in the 80s, when you could get one for £15, it was a better investment than paying to have the heating on all day.)

Oh, Isn't That...?

- *Sir Derek Jacobi* (Professor Yana/ the Master). Internationally famous Shakespearean stage actor and screen-star. For the general public, his breakthrough role was the title role in *I, Claudius* (as the alleged simpleton who "backed into the throne" because nobody thought he was a threat). When the BBC adapted the whole of Shakespeare, he was Hamlet (with Lalla Ward as Ophelia and Patrick Stewart as Claudius). He then returned to the stage, playing Alan Turing in the play *Breaking the Code* (later adapted for the screen) among other roles. On screen again later, he played (surprise surprise) a famous stage-actor, accidentally stalked by the Crane bothers in *Frazier* and a scientist in one of Gareth Roberts's contributions to the reworked *Randall and Hopkirk (Deceased)* (see X3.2, "The Shakespeare Code"). Lately, he has been rather more noticeable in films and television, including *Vicious*, a sitcom with Sir Ian McKellan (see "The Snowmen") and, as surely everyone knows, narrating *In the Night Garden...* He'd played the role of the Master before (the BBC webcast "The Scream of the Shalka") and starred in the rather atypical Big Finish audio *Deadline* by Robert Shearman (X1.6, "Dalek"), so was already a familiar name for any hard-core *Doctor Who* fans who'd somehow missed all of this. Even better, he later read the audiobook version of *The Mind Robber*. And later, ten years after Jacobi played the Master on TV, Big Finish had him reprise the role in the *War Master* audios.
- *John Simm* (the Master). Fresh off his most famous role, Sam Tyler in *Life on Mars* (see X2.11,"Fear Her"), he'd previously been in Paul Abbott's *State of Play* and archetypal rave-movie *Human Traffic*. He was sufficiently convincing as Bernard Sumner in *24 Hour Party People* to join the real one in New Order gigs and had been in *Spaced* and *The Lakes*. He then engaged in a big project, *The Village*, and a semi-regular laddish crime drama *Mad Dogs*.
- *John Bell* (Creet). On the strength of winning the *Blue Peter* competition to appear in this episode, he's shown up in a few other things and even snagged the part of Bain in the *Hobbit* movies.

Things That Don't Make Sense We can perhaps set aside the *astonishing* coincidence that Professor Yana's name is an acronym for a cryptic message from the Face of Boe ("You Are Not Alone"), on the grounds that the message isn't a coincidence at all but something tailored after the fact to cue the Doctor in to Yana's true identity. We can certainly, however, wonder why on Earth – unless there's a "preservation of the timelines" angle to this in play – the Face didn't say something more altogether helpful, such as "Professor Yana is the Master".

But if we're looking at things that *really* don't make sense, there's pretty much everything about the Futurekind. They're intelligent enough to understand language. They can drive, maintain and (bafflingly, given the lack of resources in this future locale) fuel quad-bikes. And people are afraid of turning into them... somehow. What makes this more than usually silly is the Doctor's claim that the "proper" human race has reverted to the bipedal, hairy, opposable-thumb-equipped form we all know and love *despite* having, in the intervening aeons, been all sorts of other permutations the effects budget wouldn't cover. So it's looking like whatever the BBC Wales Casting Department could muster *is* the final form for mankind and the Futurekind are a subcategory of that... which means, once again, we are using a definition of "evolution" derived from Terry Nation rather than Darwin. After all, nothing on this planet really provides much of a niche without recourse to some kind of protective bubble (see below), so it's a mystery how the Futurekind are any more or less well-adapted to life on this miraculously-preserved world. (Perhaps whatever eldritch force makes people look like humans again failed slightly, but that contradicts what we're told. Or – a wild stab in the dark, if that's not too appropriate a phrase – perhaps the Futurekind are native Malcassairians who came to resemble the refugee humans; see, quite naturally, 18.3, "Full Circle".

(Incidentally, notice how the Doctor says that the signal from Utopia keeps modulating, "so it's not automatic", and yet radio stations do that all the time, especially those ones where everything's pre-recorded – which is more of them than you probably realise. The "M" in "AM" and "FM" is "modulation".)

And now, Dr Science is going to put on a Terry Riley LP and impersonate Peter Jones as The Book...

The planet Malcassairo is a stable planet with an ambient temperature suitable for half-dressed Futurekind to charge around, and Martha to be less cold than in New York in November or Farringham in a *different* November, because it appears to be shielded from the effects of a starless universe at nearly Absolute Zero. This happens without the shield itself being frittered away by such effects and taking exponentially greater power to keep going, up to the point where there is not enough energy even in a conventional planet with a molten core and radioactive materials that still have some half-life left after all this time. This is, of course, impossible.

Such a shield not only keeps out the cold, like a draft-excluder, but prevents the disintegration of all matter on the planet, and the planet itself, and is therefore more likely to be a spatio-temporal discontinuity. Nonetheless, signals from Utopia can get in and spaceships can get out. It is, in this case, a bubble-universe with a cat-flap. This is, of course, impossible.

If, on the other hand, the survivors *have* been generating such a powerful force-field for umpteen thousands of years, they must have a lot more power than the rocket requires. With no star to pin them down, they could have propelled *the entire planet* towards Utopia. Instead, they have diverted all the world's resources to building a spaceship that needs a planet-sized mass to kick against with the wondrous gravitic footprint drive – apparently on the say-so of one man, who just arrived out of nowhere and started building a spaceship in his shed or something.

It seems reasonable to assume that Utopia is another wandering world with no star to orbit, but it can still send out a signal, so why not a bonfire or something? (Well, all right, it would need to be a *pretty big* bonfire, but anyone who's sending rockets to another world is defying the supposed universal heat-death by being warmer than the surrounding space, the same way that anyone making a signal that can be detected over the background mush is defying entropy.) It's not said if the ship's "footprint engine thing" is faster than light but, with it taking a century to travel to somewhere they know exists from their instruments, it must be slower – in which case, the relativistic effects of something big travelling so fast would themselves make gravity happen, which would stir up the uniformly lukewarm space around the ship's trajectory. Yana's people would either accelerate the impending end of everything, or reboot a stellar nursery. And for there to be mass *at all* in this scenario is improbable, unless this planet is somehow under someone's protection without the laws of physics being informed. Which means that this one planet has to have been inhabited for an unfeasible long time. As has Utopia. As has the Silver Devastation. All three are safeguarded against the onslaught of runaway entropy by apparently impenetrable shields, but they know of the existence of the others. This is, of course, impossible.

Light, of course, only travels at light-speed, so the Utopians must be sending out an FTL broadcast. And yet, Yana claims that they can only verify Utopia's existence because of its gravitational force. How, then, is gravity – not really any faster than light – of any use to anyone as a long-range navigational tool? The solution seems, from the dialogue, to be that the rocket is pointed at the signal's source, but rooted to the other large mass by a gravity footprint-a-ma-bob, which is why the spaceship's navigation is from a small room in a tunnel rather than (more conventionally) aboard the spaceship. This requires a planet that has no star to orbit staying absolutely still when providing the reaction-mass for a spaceship. This is, of course, impossible... (as you can experimentally prove by standing up in a canoe on a lake and hurling a brick at someone).

And while it seems a very nice idea that the scanners use gravity rather than light, light is still available. Malcassairo itself has lamps. But everyone talks as though light *as an entity* no longer exists, whereas before it was just starlight that was nowhere to be seen. Admittedly, again, to the naked eye any light from nearby worlds (such as the Silver Devastation) would be swamped by the mysteriously powerful floodlights around the complex and the blue light the hive-city seems to emit, but it would be known and detectable. The main question is therefore less how can Martha see Jack before they stumble across the valley of the Melmooth, more why can't we see any light-source by which we can see *them*? It might be simply narrative convention, in the same way that stars are perfectly visible when the programme-makers want us to see them despite the actors being clearly visible in a way that would drown out real location-shot stars. Nonetheless, they can walk near a cliff without falling in and nobody's carrying a torch (well, not a *literal* one). This is, of course, impossible.

Remarkably, although there's no sunlight, meaning no crops can grow, they have coffee after thousands of years. Perhaps as in all post-apocalyptic stories, they're living on emergency supplies – but that probably means supermarket own-brand with chicory, yet it's still drinkable. This is, of course, impossible.

... so if you've done six impossible things this morning, why not round it off with coffee and Mr Kipling's Cherry Bakewell's at Malcassairo, the truck-stop at the end of the universe?

Critique The plan was, obviously, to try to trick us into thinking that this was one kind of episode, then abruptly do a handbrake turn and reveal what was really going on. That strategy best relies on an audience with no inkling of the programme's past, even the previous two years, and any such viewer would have been utterly confused coming to this as their first ever *Doctor Who* episode. All the flashbacks and references would have helped, if only to establish that it all meant something to someone, but this is an episode for regular viewers who were perhaps half a step ahead of Martha by the last third. We were wise to such tricks, after the last time the show-runner did an apparently throwaway episode eleven (X1.11, Boom Town"), that set up a regeneration and a whole spin-off series. Even a hypothetical innocent viewer unaware of who the veteran actor was would know that this was nearly the end of the series and would by now, three years in, have a sense that the whole "Mr Saxon" thing would crop up even this far from home. Even if the supposed teen audience were somehow unaware of who was playing this part, the lack of any other Doctor-sized threat (the Futurekind were a big enough problem to require the Doctor *and* Captain Jack? – get real) made it obvious that this genial old dear had some kind of secret. Calling the following episode "The Sound of Drums" was a bit of a hint too.

Plus, the family audience all watching together, which was the stated aim of the revived series, meant that you'd have at least one person in the room saying *Oh, isn't that Derek Jacobi*? If they didn't know *I, Claudius*, they'd know *In The Night Garden*... With so much effort put into not giving away the ending, the appearance of a theatrical knight was a big part of the pre-publicity. Steven Moffat might fritter away big name actors on nothing-much parts, but Davies deployed his guest stars too carefully for anyone to be fooled. In Series 4, they brought back a popular former regular for three episodes and didn't do much with her. If the return of Jack was the focus, and Yana was a small role beefed up in rehearsals when they got a bigger name than expected, they would have made more of that, so this element was also leading somewhere else (had we gone into this with X4.6, "The Doctor's Daughter" under our belts, we might have been fooled after seeing Nigel Terry frittered away on a nothing-much part). Even on first broadcast this wasn't likely, simply because bumbling old buffer Professor Yana was too ostentatiously cast. How "Utopia" seemed on that stormy Saturday evening in 2007 was that the rocket, Chantho and the Futurekind were window-dressing. Many viewers had half-guessed what was about to happen, not least with all the clips in trailers of John Simm in a suit outside Parliament. Most of what seemed like revelations were confirmations.

The ostensible story, the last of humanity fleeing the impending end and barricading itself from space-greebos, was a bit shop-worn by now. They'd already done it once this year ("Gridlock", by the same author) and the concatenation of this mysterious old man and the return of Jack made it seem perfunctory. As a visceral threat, the Futurekind are an unnecessary refinement for a scenario about the imminent end of everything, but they look all right for the merchandising and at least don't get in the way much. If their condition had been virally-transmitted, as in the obvious sources for this idea, they might have been a more daunting threat – people with funny haircuts going "Grrr" isn't enough to sustain a story. A version of this lacking the "shock" reveal, with a low-key ending of Professor Yana waving off the spaceship he's dedicated his life to launching, would still be watchable in a way that most stories designed for trick endings couldn't sustain interestingly – but you'd wonder why they spent 45 minutes on that. The entire refugee-camp element of the last of humanity gambling everything on a slim hope and a legend could easily have been the focus of a more powerful story, but not the way this episode squanders it.

Fortunately, this is one of the episodes where everything goes more or less right; better versions of any element in it are conceivable, but not without unbalancing the mix. There's almost too much story going on for the timeslot (something Davies seems to have increasingly struggled with after this). Graeme Harper keeps it hurtling along on sheer brio and momentum, but the real thrill isn't the action so much as the process of putting together the pieces from what Martha already knows and second-guessing the script. For about half the first-night audience, the added extra detail she didn't know was the main pleasure. Just as hardly anyone in Britain could watch X1.6, "Dalek" quite the way someone with absolutely no idea about the series might have done, the ideal viewer has to have never wondered (or heard) about an anti-Doctor. This is an episode that lives or dies on one's tolerance for fanwank.

Nowhere is this more apparent than in the characterisation of Yana. He's scripted as how people think the first few Doctors spoke and behaved, tinkering with a Heath-Robinson machine to save humanity, in the face of the odds, then stopping for a sit-down in an old armchair. His dialogue's all "my dear" and "yes yes yes" and even an "Oh my word" for luck. If that had been all there was to it, any actor over 50 could have had a go. The same goes for the few minutes of the Master, being nasty and pompous. For those few minutes, what we have is a pretty generic *Doctor Who* villain. Where the part needed a skilled stage actor with decades of television behind him was the transition between the two, right in front of the camera. For the benefit of any viewers just joining, we get flashbacks to recent episodes, while for those who've been watching since the 70s we get soundbites of Delgado and Ainley, but the effort of getting everyone on the same page adds to the lopsided nature of the story. Even if we're back a fortnight later to find out what happened to the people in the ship, the launch isn't given the same emphasis and weight as Jack and the Doctor discussing a totally different set of continuity points.

But it would take a heart of stone not to find the return of Jack, the culmination of three long-running sub-plots (one of which, this being a series about time-travel, begins here but has had consequences we've been hearing about all year), a spaceship, an alien world, a cute bug-lady and fast-paced action leavened with jokes appealing. As an episode on its own, rather than notionally the start of a three-parter, there are small structural flaws, but the way it ends almost guarantees that people will be back next week. The last few minutes, even with the hindsight fitted as standard for all but a tiny sliver of the audience, change the situation and put the Doctor on the back foot like never before.

For once the Master's reaction to a situation isn't disproportionate; this really is the end of everything and everyone's going to die. His refusal to accept death (the main quality shared between Yana and the Time Lord iteration, even if, critically, on behalf on what's left of humanity rather than himself) is presented as admirable here and aptly so. These days it's less often that a story is so well thematically fitted to a villain as this one was, and the themes introduced here will be played up in the next two episodes with abandon. With so much superstructure of continuity, characters returning and setting up the next two episodes, it's down to the sets, costumes and extras to establish Malcassairo as a lived-in world.

What only becomes apparent in the process of

re-watching the entire Series 3 is that this is the fourth consecutive episode to have been planned to use the bare minimum of CG effects. Even the practical effects are pared down (and two big ones were dropped in the process of shooting). It's all down to the acting and writing. Nobody is bad in this episode, but with all eyes on the regulars, Barrowman, Jacobi and wee John Bell, spare a thought for Neil Reidman in the relatively thankless role of Atillo and Chipo Chung, unrecognisable and lumbered with a gimmicky verbal tic, making Chantho a person rather than a conceit. What's especially interesting is seeing Tennant and Barrowman size each other up, in character and, to some extent, for real. That the nearest Jack ever comes to complete candour is in a life-threatening situation with the Doctor behind a heavy door is entirely in keeping, and the Doctor acknowledging his own shortcomings as a friend is touching.

The handling of Jack's subplot is awkward and not particularly convincing, but about as well as could be managed given the two seasons of *Torchwood* between which this has to be sandwiched, and Barrowman's (relatively) subdued performance helps. Tennant, faced with some less-than-elegant characterisation and matching Sir Derek, almost makes it look effortless. Agyeman seems finally at her ease, ironically just as Martha is losing hers. Jack's appearance lets her blow off some steam and, while the story doesn't hammer away at a comparison between her and Chantho, it's significant that Martha's reaction is to prompt her new friend to think twice about her familiar assumptions. As mentioned, her behaviour here would have led easily into the leaving scene in "Last of the Time Lords" – that there were two episodes and a Year That Wasn't in the middle is awkward, but more a fault of the following story than this.

There's a dangerous precedent set with so much of the episode's force coming from the integration of long-term or medium-term continuity, and the slotting into place of pieces we've seen in earlier episodes. This time they don't just get away with it, they make something unique to *Doctor Who* that unites casual viewers, veteran fans and everyone in-between, and provides pulse-thumping excitement through the action, suspense and anticipation of where this is all leading. As Davies later said, in any other series they would have been facing ridicule for a villain turning slowly to the camera and saying "I am the Master", but it would have been wrong *not* to here, and we have the unique spectacle of a knight of the theatre as a *Doctor Who* baddie – and this not being the most extraordinary thing in the episode. This is a delicate set of judgement-calls on how "big" to go and in every case here they get it right. Muffing just one of these decisions risked wrecking the entire year's efforts (as we will see in two weeks from now). It's tempting to think of this as a *hors d'oeuvres* for the next two weeks, but this episode flourishes on its own more than they do. And it does have the single best cliffhanger of the BBC Wales years.

The Lore

Written by Russell T Davies. Directed by Graeme Harper. Viewing figures: (BBC1) 7.8 million, (BBC3 repeats) 0.8 and 0.3 million. AI score of 87%, then 88% and 85%.

Repeats and Overseas Promotion The name "Utopia", being from Greek, is the same in every language.

Production

As soon as a second and third series of *Doctor Who* was confirmed, Russell T Davies made plans to bring Captain Jack Harkness back. The character's return in Series 3 was proposed to John Barrowman before any plans were announced for *Torchwood*. Davies was even less forthcoming on the Master's return: he actively denied any such plans when asked, sometimes by citing how much he hated the character. Many of the guest-cast, when asked to appear in *Doctor Who*, asked if they could play the Doctor's counterpart. Delaying his re-introduction was a simple matter of establishing all the other things *Doctor Who* could do rather than – as the TV Movie had tried – setting up the Master as an integral part of the format, and the most-likely cause of any plots. Just as with "Daleks in Manhattan" (X3.4), the idea was that a brilliant mind, in desperate straits, was attempting to survive by any means necessary, rather than the tired idea of a moustache-twirling "Cosmic Supervillain" whose sole motive was to humiliate and thwart the Doctor (see Volumes 5, 6 and 10).

Curiously, Davies has claimed that the idea of A) the Master hiding at the latest date where life could be sustained and B) the notion of Jack coming back were two components of his original plot that he couldn't get to match; the penny finally dropped that the TARDIS flying to One Hundred Trillion AD was a *consequence* of Jack hitching a lift. As the name "Yana" would be revealed as an acronym, all the publicity material called this new character "the Professor", because that was somehow less of a giveaway that this was a renegade Time Lord in disguise (unlike, say, "the Doctor", "the Master", "the Rani", "the Valeyard", "the Monk"...). That name wasn't Davies's favourite idea, as there was a character in *Coronation Street* with a similar one. The early idea of using the Chameleon Arch from "Human Nature" (and having Martha stumble across it) was dropped in favour of the watch.

• Although the final three Series 3 episodes were written as a three-part story, they were more discrete than the two halves of a two-parter, and "Utopia" was made as part of Block 7 with X3.7, "42" and directed by Graeme Harper, while the next two would be a different Block with Colin Teague in charge. In the tone meeting for the episode, Davies was keen that Yana's lab "shouldn't smell of wee". The design considerations were to make it almost all studio and have a vaguely TARDIS-like air, whilst the compound where the last humans awaited departure was intended to give an air of lived-in semi-permanence, with personal items decorating each family's bivouac. (This is just about visible if you freeze-frame, but you don't assign Harper to a story and expect him to linger on non-plot-sensitive details.)

• Three designs were considered for Chantho – one was based on a real stag-beetle and was too insect-y; another was too *Star Trek*. The design needed enough motorised parts to make it mobile, but also to be wearable and convey personality. Once the right head was picked, production designer Edward Thomas based the look of the ruined city around aspects of it. For cost reasons, the idea of Chantho's dorsal spines sticking through the lab-coat was ditched.

• John Bell had won a contest run by *Blue Peter* for a young viewer to get a small part in the series. All the finalists had been selected from show-reels sent in, and given an on-screen audition. Then came a final audition on stage at the Globe (see X3.2, "The Shakespeare Code") with a panel including Andy Prior, the series' casting director, and Annette Badland (Blon the Slitheen from Series 1). As with all child-actors, Bell's available hours were limited by law and he had to come to Cardiff during school term-time, so it was of necessity a small role given maximum screen exposure.

• So the story goes that Phil Collinson went to dinner with friends and met Daniel Evans ("The Christmas Invasion"), who was with Sir Derek Jacobi, who said he'd love to do *Doctor Who* someday. He had, as we have mentioned, played the Master in the online curio *The Scream of the Shalka* (see **Is Animation the Way Forward?** under A5, "The Infinite Quest", plus X5.2, "The Beast Below" and "The Snowmen" et seq.), and also starred in the Big Finish audio *Deadline*. The only quibble was what dates were free for him. As it worked if the production schedule was amended to put X3.7, "42" first, which accelerated the design and casting for that earlier story, and condense all of Professor Yana's scenes into a studio session over ten days. As the story didn't involve the Professor only leaving the complex to go into the TARDIS, this was doable. Just. However, the making of this story, "42", the two-part finale and some elements of the previous two-parter all bumped into each other, so timetabling was tight. (We'll try to avoid too much redundancy in this account, but to keep it all straight needs a bit of repetition.)

• John Barrowman hadn't worked with David Tennant before, but immediately fell into the swing of things. Tennant's video-diary on set shows how much Barrowman, after a year as the star of his own series, was enjoying being the guest on someone else's show – his one "starry" activity being having his dog in his trailer (this shows up on screen when, without thinking or asking, Jack takes the Doctor's coat).

• The watch was the same prop that the Doctor had used as John Smith; it had been the starting-point for Louise Page's costume for the Professor, and Davies's notions for hiding the Master in plain sight. The idea was to give a subliminal hint of Hartnell, surrounding the Professor with Doctorish accoutrements such as Edwardian furniture, advanced technology and an adoring female companion. Jacobi immediately went for the first suggestions she made for the waistcoat and blouse, and the fitting had taken under an hour.

• Jacobi and John Bell both enjoyed their first day on set, as did the two runners-up from the contest; Davies had liked their auditions enough to give them smaller non-speaking roles. The *Blue Peter* team were on hand to record all of this, so Andy Akinwolere (the presenter still, sadly, best-known for dropping the glass star from the top of the Christmas tree in Trafalgar Square) did some behind-the-scenes stuff. Tennant and Barrowman found Bell's repetitive lines calling out for someone with a Davies-model silly space-name in an accent so much like their own native ones hilarious, and took to repeating *is there a Kistane or Biltone Shafe Cane?* in squeaky Glaswegian voices over the next few shoots. Tennant took time out for a cast of his right hand, for later in the episode (and yes, this means that the bubbling hand in *Torchwood:* "End of Days" isn't Tennant's; one of the special effects designers stood in, as it were); and there were so many corridor re-dressings, they had to be given numbers for continuity purposes. They had one corridor set to be disguised as about eight different places.

• Tennant, who as a drama student had queued for Jacobi's autograph after a production of *Richard II* (a part Tennant would later play for the RSC), tried not to gush, nor to grumble as Jacobi's ring impacted on Tennant's knuckle in the "good good good good good" scene. It was also the day when Chantho's prostheses got their first work-out, along with the various fanged Futurekind (whose planned metal extrusions were abandoned out of sheer practicality in the tight tunnel sets). The next day, for disambiguation purposes, Barrowman and Bell became "Big John" and "Little John".

• The weekend was off for Harper's purposes (Tennant and Agyeman had the second recording session of "The Infinite Quest", in London this time), so production restarted Monday 5th February on the Upper Boat set of the all-important laboratory, for the scenes that only featured Jacobi and Chipo Chung. Some more competition-winners, this time from *Children in Need*, were witnesses (just about squeezing into the lab set). The next day, everyone was concerned about the sequence where the TARDIS is winched into the lab rather triumphantly. It was technically feasible, as the set could be partly dismantled to allow a crane in and they'd got a crane handy, and most people really wanted to see it in the finished episode. But Collinson reluctantly dropped the scene when time ran out.

• Friday 9th, despite traffic problems caused by snow overnight, was another multi-shoot day; while some of the crew did the faked up BBC news broadcasts for the finale at the BBC Wales newsroom, another lot worked on the green-screen crew from the day before, did some close-ups of the Wiry Woman and the crucial Yana monitor shots, as well as finishing off computer inserts for X3.7, "42". Derek Jacobi, as you might expect, did his half of the regeneration scene on the TARDIS set (getting into a very fanboyish conversation about it and *Coronation Street* with Phil Collinson: the TARDIS set reminding the veteran actor of the knicker-factory in the soap). Every effort was taken to make the regeneration look like the Eccleston/ Tennant handover, so that even young viewers got the message that this was a nasty version of the Doctor. Jacobi did two versions of the last line, one ranting; the other, the sinister quieter version, was used in the finished programme. Then came the start of that first TARDIS scene, slightly rejigged from Davies's original version so that Harper didn't need to send the leads to central Cardiff for the sake of two lines of dialogue. (The first draft had a bit more of a travelogue, introducing the idea of the time-rift in more detail for newcomers or anyone who'd missed *Torchwood*, and the Doctor using his screwdriver on the light on the police box to speed up dematerialisation.) This change wasn't just because of the snow, but that wouldn't have helped.

• Everyone enjoyed a weekend off and reset their body-clocks, because on Monday (the 12th) they moved to location (Argoed Quarry, Llanharry) for the night shoots. They began with the Futurekind, meeting the beleaguered survivor on the run (Padra, as he's called in the script), that sort of thing. The plan to give the Futurekind quad bikes for the chase were abandoned as a potential risk (after dark with contact lenses, steep drops and mud after all that snow had melted), but Harper used the one they'd hired as a dolly for the camera to shoot the chase (a plan similar to his use of the buggies in 8.4, "Colony in Space"). The cast, for once, didn't have to hold back on the running, but needed to catch up with the camera. They were back the next night, with the TARDIS's arrival and the chase scenes. The location shoot moved to Wenvoe Quarry (familiar from the Series 2 Matt Jones two-parter) on the night of the 14th for the last bit of main production; they did all the entrance tunnel gate scenes and called it a night. In case you were wondering, the scaffolding tower by the gates is indeed the same bit that the Doctor climbed up and got struck by space-lightning upon in both "The Idiot's Lantern" (X2.7) and "Evolution of the Daleks" (X3.5).

• On Tuesday, 20th February (while Colin Teague was handling Martha's stunt driving in the finale), Harper had a second unit at Upper Boat to do John Simm's half of the regeneration sequence, matching it with his Jacobi footage. Simm was credited for this as "The Enemy", again as a precaution against spoilers, although rumours were already spreading in the press. He had been approached by Julie Gardner, who was executive producer of both *Doctor Who* and *Life on Mars*, while shooting the latter in Manchester (more on all that in the next story's notes).

• Murray Gold had already sketched out a discordant three-note theme for the Master before reading the completed scripts and latching onto the four-beat motif. He wove both into his scores for these episodes and Tennant's last two-part adventure. In the dubbing process, a sample of Roger Delgado from episode five of 8.5, "The Daemons" and Anthony Ainley's familiar *heh-heh-heh* from the last original-series episode, Part Three of 26.4, "Survival", were included among Jacobi's tetchy mutterings as the Master's mind inside the watch, while legal concerns prompted the decision not to use the TV Movie's Eric Roberts (see "The TV Movie" and X4.14, "The Next Doctor"). As these voices were a last-minute addition Davies wanted, he sourced them from the clips *Confidential* had amassed.

• As we hinted above, the Master's return was almost as well-kept a secret as Eccleston's departure, but, contrary to popular misconception, the anagram of "Mister Saxon" and "Master No. Six" was unintentional. The shot of Simm on College Green, opposite the House of Commons, was in the trailers for the series launch. However, in the "Next Time" segment for "The Sound of Drums", the Doctor and his chums were barely visible, to keep the suspense of the cliffhanger.

• The episode went out at 7.15. At 9.00pm, the first episode of *Jekyll* was shown. This was a modern-day story redoing Robert Louis Stevenson's Victorian bestseller, written by Steven Moffat. He does that sort of thing a lot.

X3.12: "The Sound of Drums"

(23rd June, 2007)

Which One is This? Everyone's favourite evil Time Lord[48] hypnotises the world without once using the words "I am the Master and you will obey me..." and becomes Prime Minister, somehow. He then destroys Civilisation As We Know It on a floating aircraft-carrier *exactly* like Cloudbase from *Captain Scarlet and the Mysterons*. And leading the fight, one man fate has made indestructible...

Firsts and Lasts We have the Earth's first, proper, honest-to-goodness First Contact ceremony with an alien race, broadcast on television to the entire planet. Again. (See 7.3, "The Ambassadors of Death" and X2.0, "The Christmas Invasion".) It doesn't end well.

This is the first appearance of the UNIT airship *Valiant*. UNIT's also given its blessing to an official, planet-wide broadcast of an encounter with aliens – a marked but increasingly inevitable change in policy since the glory days in the 70s, when their main job was to hide them from the public (a process usually involving shooting the aliens to no avail, then doing somersaults when something explodes).

Most importantly, this is the very first time, since his introduction in 1971, that the Master has unequivocally, definitively won. He's already in control before the story starts. He confirms his victory at the end of this week's instalment, but the whole narrative is the fight-back being thwarted. Think about it: every previous encounter has been about trying to prevent him getting hold of something he needs to either blackmail Earth/ the Universe or restore himself to his former state (e.g. 14.3, "The Deadly Assassin"; 21.5, "Planet of Fire"; X3.11,"Utopia"). The nearest we get to anything like this is 10.3, "Frontier in Space", where he's got himself a cushy government job and is using it to stir up a war on behalf of the Daleks, but that's nothing like as total a *victory*, or as complete a humiliation of the Doctor, as what we get here.

Incidentally, this episode is the first to fade to black at the end. (At least, the first since they've made it in colour.)

Watch Out For...

• With one bound, Jack was free... the resolution to last week's cliffhanger is almost a throwaway, but it shoves us right into the start of the story, and a lot of the jigsaw-pieces come together at once.

• And we finally discover what made the Master want to unleash plastic daffodils, sacrifice chickens and put on a terrible French accent. It turns out that he's had the *Doctor Who* theme play-

How Come Britain's Got a President and America Hasn't?

The version of politics we see in this phase of *Doctor Who* looks like a purée of things the writers had seen on other television programmes and big films of the recent past. It doesn't look much like Westminster or Washington as people who watch news or current affairs programmes, or work in government, would recognise it. The sheer absurdity of Harold Saxon becoming Prime Minister without being a party leader (there being no party for him to lead) is more alarming because you'd think someone who grew up in Britain and lived through several of the most peculiar elections on record would be able to get at least the basics right. Saxon's rise looks like a movie version of American politics, while the US president in the same episode resembles an 80s British parody of Hollywood films with presidents in. In both cases, the sequence of events *before* 8.02am on that Friday would be enough to cause wars or long-term consequences. At very least, everyone outside the UK would recognise that the pseudo-presidential campaign and victory by Saxon is nothing short of a *coup d'etat* in Britain. That would make global share-prices collapse even without everything else that followed.

As Christmas Day 2008 – at least within the *Doctor Who* version of events – went by without any significant mishaps except the Queen having to get up and leave the house (and not being in church at that hour, which is itself remarkable), we can assume that Jack and the Doctor used the Torchwood Hub to rewire the Archangel system for one last subliminal message. After all, the Saturday morning after the election had been a bit fraught. The President of the United States had been murdered by aliens at the behest of the UK Prime Minister on a live global feed. Two minutes later... well, as far as the world's population are concerned, some blip happened and then Saxon was shot by his wife, then died in the arms of one of the three most-wanted terrorists. We can't be sure if the cameras were still on or anyone outside that room saw it. Nonetheless, America didn't declare war on Britain and nobody in subsequent stories recalls news broadcasts telling everyone to apprehend the Doctor, Jack or Martha on sight. We can ascribe the lack of any of the most likely feedback to Archangel... but Winters is still dead and Britain hasn't got a Prime Minister.

Moreover, whilst they can fix the public's memory so that only a few homeless people without phones remember who Saxon was by Christmas 2009 (X4.17, "The End of Time Part One"), they can't change the past. Somehow, the Master broke every constitutional law and precedent to get himself elected as Prime Minister, and somehow Winters was succeeded by Barack Obama.

Let's get America out of the way before the tricky stuff. Winters refers to himself as "President Elect". That title is usually reserved for election-winners in the three(ish) months before that person takes office (so, November to January every four years). It's very hard to crowbar the end of Series 3 into happening that late in the year, so we've got to imagine that A) Winters isn't President Elect in the accepted sense, he's just being a bit pretentious, and trying to convey "I'm the elected representative of my people", and B) it's a US election year.

If America went into an election with the incumbent dead, what happens next depends on whether the Vice President – who would automatically become the President with Winter's demise – is running. On past form, unless they were utterly scandal-ridden beforehand, that newly minted President would be a shoo-in. One might expect that such electioneering as happens in the final stretch of the campaign would be fought on the issue of planetary security, what with all the recent appearances and scares. (Remember, the Atraxi have just been as well, X5.1, "The Eleventh Hour", although Crack-in-the-wall issues might have removed that from history along, with the alleged invasions by the Hath, the Ood and some spacesuited skeletons "recalled" in that episode.) Winters acts as though America were the world's major power, but all the aliens want to do is come to London. This might affect the US electorate's view of themselves. Or, knowing the US media, it might not. Regardless of what America thought of the various aliens and the way the UK seemed to be handling this repeated assault so well, the fact that America was being sidelined might have affected US domestic politics in various ways.

The one incursion to have affected the US prior to this story was the "ghosts" and subsequent Cybermen (X2.12, "Army of Ghosts"). It's safe to assume that nobody knew it was all Torchwood's fault, so how would America have reacted to either of these events? Well, in a theocracy such as the US (by European standards), the advent of real ghosts may have offended or empowered the religious communities: as the apparitions seem to

continued on Page 249...

ing inside his head for nine centuries.

• It's the penultimate episode of a series, so here come the pointless celebrity cameos. This time, it's real-life celebs Sharon Osbourne and McFly, as well as ex-politician Ann Widdecombe, endorsing a candidate to be Prime Minister. Not only is this utterly unlike anything we have ever had in British politics, it's not really like European procedure either. (All right, it is a touch American, but this is the episode where the Master's professing complete ignorance of that country.)

• Alexandra Moen's underplayed dippiness as Saxon's posh trophy-wife – absolutely *nothing* like Samantha Cameron, honest – reaches a peak with her inept dancing as the Toclafane arrive, but keep an eye on her in earlier scenes. It'll be a lot darker next week, but this time around she's doing the heavy lifting to make Simm's manic Master plausible.

• In among all the space-opera and political satire is a thriller plot about the entire government and surveillance system turning against our three heroes. While this is almost immediately dropped when the story needs to move on, it highlights the sort of near-future dystopia potentially available to the series, and provides an effective action sequence as armed troops open fire on Martha's car. It's really Freema Agyeman driving for most of those shots. What happens next involves one of the most understated but fascinating scenes, as the fugitives – thanks to souped-up perception filters on the TARDIS keys around their necks – pass like ghosts through London's streets.

• Even those who frown on terms such as "fanwank" and "squee" found it hard to resist the flashback to Gallifrey with the Citadel as it had been depicted in early *Doctor Who Magazine* illustrations, the proper ceremonial robes, the monochrome day-to-day wear and the Vortex being both a spacetime event and a mental state. The whole thing's directed as a promotional film, *Come to Gallifrey, the Holiday of Thirteen Lifetimes*. We aren't supposed to take it as literally true, although subsequent events indicate that most of what we see happened as we see it.

• The Toclafane invasion, which entails their pouring from a hole in reality and butchering a stunned populace still reeling from the death of the US President on live TV, comes with a sign that this capricious new Master is still the same old grammar-pedant. He insists on a precise use of the verb "to decimate", except that he'd only just committed a grotesque solecism. ("Oh wait, I do" modifying a co-ordinate clause with "to have" as the auxiliary verb, is ugly and grating.) Although it's traditional to refer to this Master as like the Joker, John Simm's performance is more like Bugs Bunny, especially with the sticks of dynamite taped to the back of Martha's telly, his demonstration of "Happy" and "Sad" faces, and ostentatiously zipping his mouth. To make sure we get the point, the camera tilts every so often, as you'd expect in 60s *Batman* or 50s Warner Brothers cartoons, and there are a lot of scenes lit in yellow and purple – as would suit either Sylvester and Tweety, or Cesar Romero and Burgess Meredith.

• If you're paying *really* close attention, observe the Lazarus decal on Saxon's ring (X3.6, "The Lazarus Experiment") and the *Valiant* logo (not unlike the British Rocket Group – "The Christmas Invasion") on the gas-mask.

The Continuity

The Doctor He's under the impression that he'd have sensed a Time Lord's presence [as with X1.6, "Dalek"]; the given explanation for his failing to detect the Master is that he's been mildly hypnotised by the Archangel network like everyone else. [Though his merely saying so seems odd to anyone who remembers the Davison era, with Anthony Ainley adopting ludicrous and unconvincing disguises every week and the Doctor being fooled every time.]

The Doctor admits to having been the Master's friend and colleague once; Martha's suggestion that they're brothers is met with the reply: 'You've been watching too much TV'. Both he and the Master prefer it when the other party uses their soubriquets; the Master gets off on the Doctor calling him 'Master' in particular, though he thinks that the Master's chosen alias is a 'psychiatrist's field day'. To the Doctor, it's more of a surprise that the Master married than that he's become PM.

The idea of a companion fancying him is so thoroughly alien, he uses it to explain how the TARDIS-key perception filters work ('It's like when you fancy someone, and they don't even know you exist.'), in a way that doesn't seem deliberately rude. Finding out that Jack's associated with Torchwood annoys him, but not enough to pick a fight over the issue.

At the end of the story, he's artificially aged by

How Come Britain's Got a President and America Hasn't?

continued from Page 247...

be non-denominational, the Religious Right would perhaps denounce it all as a fake or spin it that the "ghosts" were tormented souls who hadn't been "saved". It's intriguing that the situation goes on for two months and becomes normal-seeming: there is a widespread impression in Britain that the George W. Bush administration was rife with zealots who thought that the Rapture was nigh and that this skewed US-Middle East relations. An event that looked so much like the End Times seems not to have triggered actions such as, say, a nuclear strike on Mecca. No, everyone in America seems happy to have dead relatives wandering around. (As far as we can tell, anyway. This being *Doctor Who*, America is mainly noises-off during the ghosts incident, and more weight is put on Derek Acorah and Japanese teenage girls.) No-one seems to have investigated these entities either (the ghosts, that is – Japanese teenage girls are the subject of endless media reportage). Although the story suggests that, the encroaching invaders use sensory hallucinations to persuade individuals that they are their deceased relatives, it hasn't occurred to anyone to use instruments to measure their electrical properties or anything. This is weird, especially if we assume that the Patriot Act is still in force and anyone (dead, living or manifested) who arrives without valid papers has to be considered a threat to Homeland Security. Or worse, illegal immigrants.

This time, to be fair, such paranoia is justified and the Cybemen presumably bust into people's homes in places that aren't Cardiff or Docklands. Such an incursion would resemble all the worst-case fantasies of Hollywood in the 80s. All those "Survivalists" would be toast. The movie cliché of the ruggedly individualist patriarch protecting his family from Russians/ Martians/ Zombies/ a mob/ The Mob/ Trayvon Martin would be proved stupid, and all the assault-rifles they've got stashed away (for shooting deer, honest) would have proved useless. The Cybermen would pluck them from their owners' cold, deleted hands and America's self-image would have taken another knock. Then, to complete the humiliation, salvation comes from London. Again.

It's hard to imagine contemporary American politics withstanding such a double-whammy. All of this has taken place since the 2004 election, so it's very likely that Winters was the President whom Harriet Jones told to leave this to the grown-ups (X2.0, "The Christmas Invasion"). The Sycorax advent seems to have opened up a new timeline, so the circumstances outlined in **Whatever Happened to the USA?** (under 4.6, "The Moonbase") might not obtain. Nonetheless, when we get to the mid-twenty-first century, we have Bowie Base 1 representing almost every major power except the Philippines – while America is represented by two farmers (one from Iowa, ostensibly, but with a Brummie accent) and the wacky Californian robotics geek. It's still there, but it's not capable of mustering a space programme by itself and it's certainly not dictating terms.

Now let's approach US politics from the other direction. Obama clearly ought to be a Democrat – none of the dialogue in "The End of Time" actually comes out and says so, but there's not much point having him in the story *at all* if he's not roughly like the version we're familiar with. (Except, of course, that he's a famous figure – it's Davies's farewell to *Doctor Who* and he's feeling reckless. It's like having the Queen in curlers in X4.0, "Voyage of the Damned".) It goes missing in the crack between executive producers, but Amy's life takes place in a fairy tale haven, so perhaps Obama came up with the miraculous economic policy that restored the planet to an even keel after economic disaster. Alternatively, the media was vastly overstating the President's capacity to do anything. (As we've been assuming that "AMNN" is a thinly-disguised CNN and Trinity Wells is based in London, she would most probably be explaining it to UK viewers and would make this clear. Why else come in to work on Christmas Day when everything in Britain is shut? American media wouldn't hype this deal so much, partly because some of them hated Obama, but the ones that didn't knew that, due in large part to Congressional foot-dragging, the President can't do anything about the global economy or even much about America's. Perhaps the House and Senate during Series 3 were more amenable than in our universe. That would mirror, somewhat, with Obama's election coinciding with a Democrat takeover of Congress in real-life.)

The mere fact that we're not supposed to like President Winters doesn't say anything about whether he's a Republican or a Democrat, per se. Yes, he's cut from the same cloth as a Bush-style

continued on Page 251...

the Master's Lazarus tech ["The Lazarus Experiment"], and ends up as an exaggerated version of what David Tennant might look like in a century or more. [He's far further advanced in years than the scene in X3.9, "The Family of Blood". This is directly comparable to 18.1, "The Leisure Hive", in which the fourth Doctor ages 500 years, but seems more extreme. (The earlier example was the Doctor actually being exposed to time, whereas this is the cellular ageing process, amplified using data from the Doctor's severed hand and by reversing the effect of the Lazarus device.)]

He's recovered enough from Rose to enjoy a bag of chips without getting wistful.

• *Background.* Both he and the Master chose their soubriquets.

Like the Master [see **The Non-Humans**], he was taken to the hill overlooking the Citadel and exposed to the Untempered Schism, then "never stopped running". [This would appear to be connected with "the blackest day of my life" mentioned in 9.5, "The Time Monster" and whatever the hell was going on in X9.4, "Listen".] This ritual is to sound out Gallifreyan children suitable to become Time Lords and, for said candidates, this is the end of their childhood and the start of intensive study and rigorous training.

• *Ethics.* A minute after saying that he and the Master have nothing left but each other, he tries asking if they can 'fight across the constellations' but leave the Earth alone. [So, hypothetically, damaging other civilisations is fine, so long as Earth is spared – unless this is yet-another innovative use of the term 'constellation', and it's actually uninhabited.]

He adamantly refuses to let Jack kill the Master, on the grounds that, as the only other Time Lord, it's his responsibility to handle the situation. [How many people will need to die horribly because of the Doctor's sense of fraternity? See also "The End of Time Part One" and Series 10.] It bothers him far more than the Master that all the rest of the Time Lords are gone.

• *Inventory: Sonic Screwdriver.* Can repair a broken vortex manipulator in 30 seconds flat, and blow up a CCTV camera. The Doctor also uses it on Martha's phone to work out the construction of the Archangel Network [we refer you to the "Auto-hack" app in X3.0, "The Runaway Bride"], and to hotwire the three TARDIS keys into personal Perception Filter devices.

We here discover [after "Utopia"] that the Doctor used the screwdriver to restrict the TARDIS to two time-zones, so it can't be used to time travel anywhere else.

• *Inventory: Other.* The *TARDIS keys* are, in effect, part of the TARDIS and thus partake of its perception-filter glamour. With a bit of tinkering, the Doctor converts the keys and the SIM cards from phones to tap into Archangel, and make anyone with a key around his or her neck imperceptible to passers-by. [And, presumably, CCTV. This is such a potentially useful device, it's curious he's not used it before or since and resorts to a *Gemini Man* watch in X8.6, "The Caretaker". (See **How Much of This is Happening?** under X5.6, "The Vampires of Venice".)]

He has the presence of mind to take Martha's laptop along when the flat explodes. One of the three fugitives is carrying enough cash to buy chips [since Martha comes back with them, it's probably her]. The Doctor also sports a jeweller's eyeglass [see 11.2, "Invasion of the Dinosaurs"; 15.3, "The Sun Makers" and others]. The kerosene lamp in the chips-and-Gallifrey scene is convenient. [He can't possibly have had that in his pockets, or he'd've used it on Malcassairo. Besides, it's a flippin' kerosene lamp.]

The TARDIS The Doctor can sense his Shp's presence in this time zone, but not strongly enough to hone in on her exact location until he's very close nearby. [Besides, the question of how he senses her *at all* is muddled by the TARDIS being rewired into something else entirely.] He seems as surprised as anyone to find the Master's turned the Ship into a Paradox Machine; this configuration looks much like the console room usually does, but with red lighting and some plumbing-work on the time-rotor. It can be programmed to activate at a specific moment; until the Doctor knows what it does, he won't risk tampering with it, as this can blow up the solar system. [By the next episode, though, he's deduced enough to sanction Jack running in and just shooting it.]

To limit the Master's freedom [in the closing moments of "Utopia"], the Doctor locked his Ship's coordinates so it could only travel to the year 100 trillion and Martha's home time, give or take 18 months [either the location coordinates have some leeway as well, or the Master landed right back in Cardiff]. He says this locking is permanent. [Proceed, of course, to **Things That**

How Come Britain's Got a President and America Hasn't?

continued from Page 249...

Evangelical president (the way that he tells the Toclafane, "I will accept mastery over you, if that is God's will", and he speaks with a twinge of Southern – Bush, a Connecticut native, adopted a folksy Southern accent and vocabulary that waxed and waned depending upon his setting), but Winters's characterisation is otherwise composed of fighting with Saxon about who gets the most time in front of the TV cameras and generally throwing his weight around. This is British children's television: *all* Americans are assumed to be like that. (Reading between the lines, it sounds as if he's boned up on UNIT protocol specifically to make nice with alarmed UNIT personnel who have a sense that something's off with this curious new British PM but don't exactly know what.) This is still an unusual position for an American president, attaching himself to United Nations apron strings like this. [Here we're assuming that UNIT retains some connection with the UN, as Series 1 hinted at, but later episode downplayed and was almost denied in X4.4, "The Sontaran Stratagem". See **What Happened in 1972?** under A7, "Dreamland" and **What's Happened to UNIT?** under "The Sontaran Stratagem" for more on this. The United Nations is far more powerful in this universe than in our own, while UNIT's resources extend to a Moonbase (A9, "Death of the Doctor") and gadgets like the *Valiant* that seem well in advance of anything the rest of the planet can develop. Admittedly, they had help with that. This is, again, broadly consistent with the situation in X4.16, "The Waters of Mars", where international cooperation is not only possible for space travel but, apparently, the only way forward – contrary to what's stated in X8.7, "Kill the Moon". (It's also consistent with the oncoming ecological collapse presented in the Virgin Books *New Adventures*, but right now we're only interested in broadcast episodes and the real world.)]

So let's look at Obama's real and fictional elections; the one we experienced in our world was a fair surprise on its own terms (the US actually electing an African-American president – now *that* would have seemed implausibly utopian not so long ago). The turning point came around – oh look! – September/ October 2008, when John McCain's campaign essentially imploded through a combination of his ineptitude on the global financial crisis and his widely-ridiculed selection of Sarah Palin as his running-mate. We've been assuming that Winters is so thoroughly a Bush-analogue that he was at the end of his second term and looking to establish a place in history – maybe a better analogy is Nixon very publicly offering olive-branches to the Soviet and Chinese governments to score favourable headlines as a torrent of self-inflicted wounds (the impeachment hearings, the political fall-out from carpet-bombing Cambodia, an oil crisis and supporting the coup in Chile) threatened to make his legacy look disastrous.

What if, however, Winters is running *against* Obama and trying to look statesmanlike? If Winters' running-mate is as openly derided as Palin, then his/ her failure to get elected even after what ought to have been a sympathy-vote shoo-in is plausible. (By the way, the economic crisis doesn't need to stem from the collapses of ludicrously-named banks after sub-prime lending, as it was here. In the *Doctor Who* scheme of things, the global economy was torpedoed in 2008 by all the share-prices and currency exchange-rates and everyone's bank accounts simultaneously being reset to zero in "The Eleventh Hour".)

Someone *must* have been President in between the events of "The Sound of Drums"/ "Last of the Time Lords" and the 2009 January inauguration but, presumably, unless also a candidate, that VP was on the cusp of retiring. We would tentatively have to suggest some fictional avatar of Dick Cheney, though taking on the job of being directly responsible for a country that's possibly in the middle of an alien onslaught is a prospect probably no less terrifying to him than to anybody else, come to think of it. (But then, maybe Halliburton got the contract to rebuild Downing Street...)

With the death of the one President who'd tried to fiddle with aliens, versus a fresh new politician who's promising to keep America out of this mess, we finally have a scenario where the electorate might not actually vote for the same party as the President who'd just died. (If we're to continue with the "Aliens of London" reading of aliens as a blatant stand-in for Middle Eastern conflicts, then Obama's withdrawal would be a very nice fit for America's apparent isolationist tendencies in later stories.) This doesn't quite fit the situation we saw in "The End of Time", where Obama is using America's clout to fix all world problems, but that's mainly economic clout which America would take

continued on Page 253...

Don't Make Sense; at any rate, the Master either couldn't or didn't lift the restrictions.]

The Ship is equipped with a Perception Filter, which is purportedly why people see a police box [cf. 18.7, "Logopolis" and many other older stories, plus 22.1, "Attack of the Cybermen" and "The Vampires of Venice"]; the TARDIS keys share enough of this quality that hotwiring them into the Archangel Network means people wearing them can do the same. [At some point the Doctor tries and fails to put his key around the Master's neck; see **Things That Don't Make Sense**.]

The Supporting Cast

• *Martha.* Shows the most initiative she's had all season when the Master starts threatening her family; she tells off the Doctor and attempts a dramatic rescue until the police actually pull out a rocket launcher and force a retreat. For the rest of the story, she remains quietly furious. She doesn't believe her parents would ever reunite and says her brother Leo is cleverer than he looks. Before meeting the Doctor, she did plan to vote for Saxon.

Her flat includes a Magpie telly [X2.7, "The Idiot's Lantern"], a backgammon set and an answering machine. It appears to take up half the top floor of a Victorian semi-detached house [such conversions are the most common residences for London singletons]. She drives a P-reg Vauxhall Corsa C, five-doors, silver. She owns a laptop.

• *Jack.* Sympathizes with Martha's unrequited crush on the Doctor. He's also a connoisseur of chips and can make tea. [He must have been given a TARDIS key at some point, presumably during Series 1, as they have three in this episode and there's no time for him to have obtained one in "Utopia".] After the Doctor's plan fails, he makes sure that Martha escapes rather than taking the vortex manipulator himself. [Arguably, Jack – as head of Torchwood Cardiff – would be better positioned to rally opposition to the Master's new regime, so he's taking a leap of faith in the Doctor's solution to the problem.]

He's acquainted with Gallifreyan legends, but doesn't know of the Toclafane, and explains regeneration to Martha properly. [So he's probably devoted some of the last hundred years to looking up details about the Doctor.] To the Doctor's distress, Jack thinks that dealing with the Master by snapping his neck is a plausible solution.

Jack knows that the Doctor was involved with the Racnoss Christmas star. [X3.0, "The Runaway Bride", though quite how he might have worked this out without stumbling across Saxon isn't clear. In *Torchwood,* Jack is clearly reporting to senior politicians and liaising with UNIT, so it's not impossible that he's met Saxon and simply trusted him the way almost everyone else did. In *TW*: "Reset", he claims that a recent experience with a politician made him less trusting.] He claims he liked Saxon as well. [See **Things That Don't Make Sense**. Maybe the comment was intended to reassure Martha without having any basis in fact.]

The cannibalised TARDIS horrifies him almost as much as it does the Doctor [after all, he spent so much time helping to rewire her in the Eccleston era].

• *Inventory: Jack's Vortex Manipulator.* Despite the Doctor having considered Jack's vortex manipulator a 'spacehopper' compared to the TARDIS being a 'sports car', the Manipulator here accurately crosses *ten trillion years* and uncountable parsecs to get the Doctor, Jack and Martha to London in one piece, and more or less at the same time they left. [This is more significant than it seems. The series has consistently told us that travelling "naked" in the vortex is liable to end with the individual sprayed across spacetime – 5.4, "The Enemy of the World"; 9.1, "Day of the Daleks" – and it appears that only those who have been, so to speak, "initiated" by travelling in a TARDIS can hope to survive this. For Jack's device to carry him any substantial amount back or forward, this has to be a more potent and controlled mechanism than was available to Magnus Greel (14.6, "The Talons of Weng-Chiang"). If, as that story suggests, crude time experiments were killing people in the fiftieth century, then Jack and his fellow Time Agents must draw upon considerably more advanced technology, and not use either the Zygma Beam with the Double Nexus Particle. The conclusion seems to be that while Greel is aware of the Time Agents' existence, they are from after his time – *how much*, we cannot say, but the Doctor's comments suggest something in the order of thousands of years. Fifty-first-century time travel is, as we know from "The Girl in the Fireplace" (X2.4), equally haphazard but uses a crude method of ripping spacetime apart and making portals. So while Jack and his chum Captain John Hart may have been born in the

How Come Britain's Got a President and America Hasn't?

continued from Page 251...

a while to lose.

What's *really* unlike our timeline is the lack of any Congressional stalling or gridlock. Perhaps the mid-term elections, coming just after the UN voted to let Britain's acting PM Mr Green launch a nuclear attack against an alien mothership, saw the first sign of this new form of American politics and Winters was the one stuck with no ability to do anything. Extra points if the Cybermen intrusion business has caused the Tea Party/ libertarian/ etcetera enthusiasts to split altogether, in which case the resultant political anarchy in the more conservative branch of American politics might easily collapse in the face of any kind of concerted effort by the Democrats. (The Tea Party, a phrase that makes many people in Britain think of chimpanzees in frilly knickers, are mentioned as a going concern in *Torchwood: Miracle Day*, but that's a very curious story. See **Must All Three Series Correlate?** under X4.5, "The Poison Sky".)

... and with that all out of the way, let's look at Britain.

###

Right, just so everyone's clear on what the problem is with Saxon, we'll state the bleedin' obvious: an election victory isn't just the number of votes cast for a particular party but the number of Parliamentary seats won. There are 650 constituencies in Britain at present (about 50,000 voters in each one, so city constituencies take up less space than rural ones). The leader of a party that wins 326 or more – or a good case that over 326 MPs will act a group even if they're more than one party, as Theresa May was forced to bodge together in 2017 – is (usually) is invited to form a government and is appointed Prime Minister by the reigning monarch. All ministers, including the Prime Minister, are either MPs or, in an increasingly rare state of affairs, a member of the House of Lords. (Hereditary or appointed: most Peers are now ex-ministers or people who've distinguished themselves in some field and got "life peerages" that won't be handed on. The House of Lords is sort of a Senate – but without any of them having to win any beauty contests – and is, bizarrely, more like a cross-section of Britain than the House of Commons, which is filled with career politicians who've never done anything else. See our comments on 14.3, "The Deadly Assassin".)

It is disappointingly rare for sitting ministers to lose their seats unless the entire government is voted out or for the opposition to make up the Shadow Cabinet (the government-in-waiting) from MPs whose seats are thought to be unsafe. To get that ten-minute audience with Her Majesty and then go to 10 Downing Street with the removal van with your fridge and wardrobe following close behind you have to be A) an MP, B) leader of a party and C) surrounded by people who also won seats the night before, who are capable of doing their new jobs as Cabinet members and in the same party as you (or at least not in a different one).

Is that what we see in "The Sound of Drums"? Is it 'eck as like! We've had a whole campaign of posters and TV adverts for Harry Saxon, like a US presidential campaign, followed by him taking power and making a Cabinet out of people from various other parties who opted to side with him (whom he then gassed). That makeshift alliance or coalition seems to have happened in minutes, rather than the weeks of talks and under-the-table deals we've seen with every Coalition government in European history. Oddly, the closer two or more parties are politically, the longer this horse-trading takes, especially in Britain. It took David Cameron less time to strike a deal between his Conservatives and the antithetical Liberal Democrats than Theresa May had to spend haggling with the more-tory-than-the-Tories Democratic Unionist Party (Belfast's hardcore Presbyterian Tea-Party wannabes).

No, the way Saxon forms a government is more like the situation before the Battle of Blenheim and the formation of the whole party system. (That's a big topic but, in a nutshell, Parliament was split between Whigs, who thought that the role of Parliament was to raise funds by taxing the very aristocrats and wealthy landowners who ran the country on behalf of the monarch, and the original Tories, who thought that the monarch, as head of the Church of England, was therefore supreme in all things. These were tendencies rather than memberships until the 1780s, although Tory support for the Jacobite Rebellions – see 4.4, "The Highlanders" – made such tendencies fairly serious commitments. US politics is, in many ways, a snapshot of Britain c. 1775.) To get to something like this from the situation in "Aliens of

continued on Page 255...

fifty-first century (see *Torchwood* Series 2), there is no reason to conclude that the Time Agency is based then, or that they use technology from that era.

[We should also note that it's somewhat predictable for the Doctor and Jack to survive such a journey – if "survive" is the right word for Jack possibly dying several hundred times – but Martha is also undamaged. So either the Manipulator is even safer than one might think, or the Doctor's influence kept both guidance and the integrity of the passengers within safe limits.]

UNIT/ Torchwood For some reason, UNIT has US President Winters as the intermediary for relocating the Toclafane meeting to the *Valiant*. [With UNIT's files noting that Saxon was the Master in X8.12, "Death in Heaven", it's entirely possible that some of the tiny percentage of the population immune to Archangel were in the organisation. Presumably, this comes as part of the same training that enabled Torchwood staff to resist the psychic paper (X2.12, "Army of Ghosts"). Sir Alastair being packed off to Peru – X4.4, "The Sontaran Stratagem" – makes more sense if we assume that Saxon anticipated resistance from Greyhound.]

The UN protocols for first contact were established in 1968 [this looks suspiciously like a reference to 6.3, "The Invasion", broadcast in the same year], and state that it cannot take place on sovereign soil. [The Master having designed *Valiant* himself, and still using it as his base a year later, would be a very odd coincidence otherwise, so he probably knows this already and is playing coy for Winters's benefit.] The protocols are flexible enough for Winters to take over the first-contact duties from Saxon without any Russian, Chinese, French or Brazilian observers. It's suggested that no one is thrilled about the contact being televised but, with the UK Prime Minister having already promised it to the entire world, everyone has to play along.

Per the terms of this protocol, the location for the first official meeting is a UNIT facility, *Valiant:* a flying aircraft-hanger with a conference suite. At the time of the scheduled encounter, 8:00 AM local time, they are over the Baltic [the same co-ordinates as Bad Wolf Bay – X2.13, "Doomsday"].

Despite being a UNIT vessel, much of the *Valiant*'s design was supervised and influenced by the then-UK Minister of Defence, Harold Saxon. [This goes a tremendous way towards explaining UNIT's comparative uselessness in the post-Harriet Jones era. In **What's Happened to UNIT?** (X4.5, "The Poison Sky") and **What Happened in 1972?** ("Dreamland"), we'll examine the probable reasons why things here are so screwy, and what seems to have gone so wrong by the next story they're in. That his next incarnation, Missy, knows that a protocol exists to give the Doctor command of all military resources ("Death in Heaven") and that there's an anti-Zygon gas on hand (X9.7, "The Zygon Invasion") indicates a degree of interest in more detailed forward planning at a Geneva level. According to the background chat on the radio in this and the next episode, UNIT is still based in Geneva at this point.]

Jack insists that after the Battle of Canary Wharf, he rebuilt Torchwood in the Doctor's honour. [He *did* do that, somewhat, but only after a century of doing their bidding; see *TW*: "Fragments". Jack lists his crew as 'half a dozen', so either he's rounding up, or he counts that Pterodactyl as being a team-member. It's certainly as useful sometimes.]

To prevent Jack's Torchwood crew from aiding him, Saxon (somehow) diverts them to the Himalayas. [They did have a base in India in one of the radio plays, left over from the 1920s.]

The Supporting Cast (Evil)

• *The Master: Background.* He explains that during the Time War, the Time Lords 'resurrected' him as the 'perfect warrior'. [From the dialogue here and in "The End of Time", it seems the Doctor and the Master didn't meet during the War itself, or there'd be no need for explanations. This also opens up an aspect of the Time War we'll discuss in **Who Was That Terrible Woman?** under "The End of Time Part Two".] He fled when the Dalek Emperor took control of the Cruciform [there's no way to tell *which* Emperor this might have been, or whether it's related to the Crucible in Series 4], and – out of fear – made himself human so he would never be found.

Following events in "Utopia", he's now been on Earth for long enough [the Doctor and Vivian Rook, a journalist, independently estimate it as '18 months'] to have himself elected as Prime Minister of Great Britain. His official biography includes a Cambridge education, a novel, and competing for "this country" in Athletics. [See **The Big Picture**. We might suppose that the

How Come Britain's Got a President and America Hasn't?

continued from Page 253...

London" needs things to have altered more drastically than the softly-softly imperceptible "nudge" from Archangel could handle.

We saw in **How Long is Harriet in Number 10?** under "The Christmas Invasion" that this version of events has Tony Blair killed by Slitheen and Harriet Jones taking over. She identifies herself as one of the 1997 intake. The dialogue in "The Christmas Invasion" suggests that a landslide election victory confirmed her mandate some time before the end of 2006. The rough dates for Saxon's arrival are "18 months ago" and "just after the downfall of Harriet Jones". Then comes a crisis in mid-2007 with four cabinet ministers resigning in rapid succession (according to the headlines on Victor Kennedy's *Daily Telegraph* in X2.10, "Love & Monsters"). As we speculated, Harriet withstood the Doctor's initial attempt to depose her with innuendo and whoever replaced her copped this flak. Now, for obvious legal reasons and with charter-renewal negotiations in progress, the BBC couldn't come out and *say* that the most evil being in the universe was a member of the Conservative Party without facing a slew of allegations of bias from the Murdoch-owned media (and possibly a prosecution under the Official Secrets Act), any more than they could claim that Saxon was New Labour, for all his Blair-esque affectations of pop-culture savvy and vast numbers of people voting for him without knowing quite why. Yet to have become Prime Minister, he has to have been a party leader (it's not actually on the statute books, but it's so abnormal not to that the "spell" of Archangel would have been severely disrupted) and he couldn't have done *that* and been Defence Secretary at the same time.

Thus, in the interests of balance and scrupulous fairness, the story presents us with a Prime Minister who has gobbled up support from all three major parties and possibly all the minor ones, mutually-antagonistic as they may be. Normally, this sort of thing happens when an election ends with no clear outright winner, as was the case in 1974, 2010 and 2017, or an all-consuming crisis such as a World War. Neither is the case here; Saxon has an almost total victory and even the endless round of alien assaults on the capital and the Beast of Revelations wandering around Cardiff (*TW*: "End of Days") hasn't really affected how people go about their daily business.

The nearest precedent is to be found in 1931. Although the last Prime Minister not to be a party leader was David Lloyd George (mentioned in "Aliens of London"), that was during (and immediately after) World War I. When the "Coupon Election" of 1918 took place, it was on the understanding that any candidate who wished to be in the Conservative-Liberal coalition (comprising half of the Liberal party, but not the half with an official leader) said so on the ballot. No posters, outside his Carnarvon constituency, said "Vote Lloyd George". The Great War and the Russian Revolution were unprecedented crises, and Lloyd George's personal popularity made him *de facto* leader of the Coalition if not of either the Conservatives or the Liberals. What we see in "The Sound of Drums" is absolutely nothing like this. Had the Toclafane already arrived it's just about plausible that Saxon could persuade the country that he could form a government out of a set of already-elected MPs, as Lloyd George did, but it would still be the culmination of circumstances well beyond what Francine and Tish were talking about. Three days before the election, people were still debating if aliens were behind an alleged incident at a hospital. That there even *was* an election is improbable if the crisis were perceived to be as bad as 1916's emergency. And if the analogy were complete, Saxon would need to have been a much more significant minister, and for a lot longer than 18 months, to have been positioned to be asked to form a government. Moreover, he'd need to have been Prime Minister before the election.

It's not much like 1931 either but it's a lot closer. During the first effects of the Great Depression, the minority Labour government had been unable to agree on a budget of spending cuts. Ramsay MacDonald, the Prime Minister, took the usual step of going to the King and tendering his and the government's resignation, to launch an election. This time, George V said no. As any Prime Minister is, effectively, appointed as proxy by the monarch and asked to form a government after the election (usually a formality, especially with a landslide), it's the monarch's constitutional role to assent to such a move, or not. In the June 2017 election, Theresa May managed to lose the majority she'd started with (and called this election to bolster) and had ten fewer seats than she needed to form a government – but she persuaded the

continued on Page 257...

TARDIS created this life story for him, along the lines of John Smith's background and biography, complete with certificates and qualifications, in "Human Nature". Then again, it's more fun to imagine him doing it all as a prank and hypnotising a publisher to get a first novel into print so quickly. And the Doctor's machine would have put in a few more overt goofs to sabotage it.]

His campaign has been very popular, with some celebrity endorsements [see **Oh, Isn't That... ?**]. In terms of things he's actually done, he was procurement minister, then Secretary of State for Defence and authorized the Racnoss destruction [X3.0, "The Runaway Bride", which possibly explains the shoot-to-kill policy that British forces adopted there, but see X4.11, "Turn Left" for identical events in a Saxonless world].

He seems to have some idea of when the Doctor and Martha will leave to release his past self on Utopia, and then return. [The election and Martha's busy week are perfectly aligned, which can't be coincidence.] As such, he's been keeping tabs on Martha's family – arranging deals with her mum, getting Tish odd jobs ["The Lazarus Experiment"] and all that sort of thing; here, on his pre-planned orders, they're all arrested and flown to the *Valiant*. He's also done some research on Jack, enough to know about his immorality.

As PM, the first thing he does is scold his entire cabinet, in apparent sincerity, for abandoning their own parties and principles to jump on his bandwagon – and then gasses them all to death. [They're in seclusion and his plan comes together at eight o'clock next morning, so it's conceivable no one would be expected to immediately notice.] Otherwise, he's enjoying the role of anti-Doctor, offering his wife jelly babies from a white paper bag [just like Tom Baker's in the 70s] and calling her his 'faithful companion'. They cuddle behind closed doors, though in public he's known for liking a 'pretty face' and chucks Tish under the chin right in front of Lucy. On the airstrip, he wears a scarlet-lined black coat not unlike something the third Doctor might have worn [the Doctor will eventually adopt something similar from X8.1, "Deep Breath" onwards].

He responds to the Doctor's plea that they're the only Gallifreyans left with: 'Are you asking me out on a date?' [cf "Deep Breath", where Missy calls the Doctor 'my boyfriend']. He gets a vicarious thrill asking 'how did that feel?' about the Doctor destroying both the Time Lords and the Daleks. [Interestingly, with all the time he's had to investigate, he's not found anything to convince him that the Time Lords are well and truly gone until the Doctor confirms it. He apparently hasn't even checked.]

There's a strong suggestion that the Master has become incapable of listening to the Doctor's pleas owing to a constant drumbeat that haunts him constantly. [Indeed, the implication is that he's operating under diminished capacity, with the drumming being responsible for all the many nutty schemes that he's tried out over the years – such as, say, plotting to blow up the very planet on which he's trapped in "The Mind of Evil" (8.2).] Here, it's suggested that the head-drumming began when he looked into the Untempered Schism [see **The Non-Humans**] as a child. [A flashback shows that he was wearing a "War Games"-style robe when this happened (6.7; see "The End of Time Part One" for more).]

He thinks the Doctor naming himself 'Doctor' is sanctimonious. He once more enjoys watching children's BBC [9.3, "The Sea-Devils"], in this case *Teletubbies*. [And the 'we've flown them in all the way from prison' sequence suggests he's been watching Eamonn Andrews presenting *This is Your Life* in the 70s.] "Voodoo Child" [a hit from around the time "Doomsday" was on air] strikes him as appropriate music for ordering the literal decimation of the population. [If he, rather than the Toclafane, picks the targets for attack, then London and Geneva going first would take care of some very old grudges.] In passing, he mentions that he uses aftershave.

One aspect of the plan that wrongfoots the Doctor is that this isn't the Master's usual hypnotism, but a more insidious whispering campaign. [As the Doctor deposed Harriet Jones with a more orthodox one, this may have appealed to Saxon's sense of humour. The dialogue makes it seem as if the Archangel buy-out of all other mobile phone carriers was part of the Master's plan, but the timescale makes it possible that this was almost in place beforehand. Certainly, setting up the launch of 15 satellites without anyone noticing would have been harder than anything else he achieved.]

- *Inventory: Laser Screwdriver.* Gold-coloured and bulkier than the Doctor's version; among other things, it has genetic manipulation equipment from Richard Lazarus's experiments. [See "The Lazarus Experiment" as well as **Things That Don't Make Sense**. The Doctor's screwdriver is,

How Come Britain's Got a President and America Hasn't?

continued from Page 255...

Queen that her alliance with the DUP was more plausible than Labour leader Jeremy Corbyn's proposed coalition of practically everyone in Britain who hates the Tories (i.e. well over half of the new Parliament), even though the numbers stacked up equally well if not better. In 1931, the King recommended that MacDonald form a new cabinet from whoever was willing to serve, regardless of party affiliation. (With both of the two biggest parties split roughly evenly over Brexit, this was also on the cards in 2017.)

[Quick constitutional aside: It is the nature of a Constitutional Monarchy that the reigning sovereign has to pass every law – a process called the Royal Assent – and consult with the Prime Minister every Tuesday, when possible (they both have to jet around the world at short notice). That's basically the Queen's job, to read every single piece of legislation and put a literal seal of approval on it. All that stuff with state visits, opening prestigious buildings and garden parties is more public, but her life's mainly paperwork. On the other hand, it means that the Prime Minister of the day has a database of experience dating back to Churchill, someone who's pretty much seen it all. Prince Charles has been deputising for his mum long enough to have a fair bit of this as well. What this means in practice is that a deadlocked situation such as happened in America in November 2000 is impossible here. The equivalent of the US Electoral College is a woman in her 90s who'd been trained practically from birth to do this and has done it since 1952. As with the two elections of 1974, various Wartime cabinets and the three National Governments of the 1930s, the monarch has the right to say, in effect, "you, you and you, stop mucking about and form a government". The role of Prime Minister and the Cabinet system, at least as we have them now, is mainly a legacy of the emergency expedients necessitated by George III having a ten-year leave of absence from the middle of his 50-year reign due to health problems and thinking that he was a tree. If you want to be really technical about it, the salaried post of "Prime Minister" only came into existence in 1937.]

The analogy with 1931 breaks down because this "National Government" wasn't supposed to fight an election. MacDonald was kicked out of the Labour Party but remained Prime Minister. MacDonald formed a National Labour Party, with his successor as the original Labour Party's leader, Arthur Henderson, becoming Leader of the Opposition. People who had worked together and been in the same parties months before were now on opposite sides of the House. The election, caused by the Conservatives, resulted in that party getting a majority of votes, but not of seats, and candidates being voted for on where they stood on the National Government issue. It split the Liberal Party in three, and almost completely drained them of resources. They never recovered, and after 1987 practically ceased to exist (see below for more about the SDP). The MPs returned to Parliament were overwhelmingly in favour of continuing with this arrangement, so it can be counted as a landslide in that regard. This is a very tenuous comparison for the Saxon landslide, but bear it in mind.

If anything, the government of the day would have looked more solid for dealing with the Christmas Star, and Saxon's main impact on politics would have been to forestall an election. Yet whatever party he's with crumbles and politics reconfigures itself over whether or not any given MP supports this person. We have posters saying "Vote Saxon". Not mentioning a party or policy to align your specific MP to or from, just his assumed name. All of those (technically illegal) TV ads are about Harry Saxon, not what he stands for or why any candidate has chosen to support him. The only things we know about his campaign platform are that he talks about aliens a lot and there's a bandwagon. Maybe his entire appeal is that he promises an end to cover-ups about this. That could explain, for example, the pre-credit sequence of the first episode of *Torchwood* Series 2, where a little old lady in Cardiff is unimpressed about a big SUV with a stern logo pulling up and asking if she's seen a sports car driven by a fish-head. "Bloody Torchwood", she mutters as they zoom off.

There is always the possibility that Saxon has formed a new party and that, with Archangel quelling the doubts that would normally follow such a move, he's named it after himself rather than what it stands for – especially as it doesn't stand for anything other than him anyway. It's implausible in the usual run of things (but this isn't the usual run of things) and it might have been slightly too disruptive for the subliminal message

continued on Page 259...

increasingly as the show goes along, suggested to be an extension of the TARDIS systems, so the Master may have got the Doctor's vessel to make one to his own specs. The screwdriver certainly wasn't with Yana's effects when he was found as a baby; if he'd had a gadget like *that* on Malcassairo, his gravity footprint engine would have been up and running before the episode started.]

The Non-Humans

• *Time Lords.* The Doctor tells Martha and Jack that they're taken from their families at the age of eight, to be shown the Untempered Schism: a 'gap' in spacetime allowing free access to the Time Vortex. This is how potential Time Lords are tested and initiated. [We later discover that Gallifrey is home to two billion children (X7.15, "The Day of the Doctor") and yet the Time War has so depleted the Time Lords' ranks, they evidently resurrect recruits from across their own history to serve in the Time War. The implication is that barely any of the tested children make the grade. The alteration that this ritual begins in the genes of the appropriate subject are, according to the Doctor (X6.7, "A Good Man Goes to War") part of what enables regeneration and time-sensitivity.]

Save for the child Master, the Time Lords seen in flashback all seem to be old men, of various races. The mental effect of the initiation ritual is highly variable; the Doctor implies that the sight drove the Master mad.

Time Tots are told children's stories with the Toclafane featuring as Gallifreyan bogie-men. Upon finding out that they're involved, the Doctor acts as if he'd had been told that the Three Billy Goats Gruff were plotting to destroy the world. (Given recent experiences with walking scarecrows, this might not have been unwarranted.)

• *Toclafane.* Flying killer metallic death balls of DOOM! They have knives, needles and zap-guns that extrude when needed from a basic spherical metal body, hovering in mid-air. They can appear at will, and have formed an attachment to the Master. They speak like psychotic children, enjoying inflicting slow painful deaths or rapid-fire slaughter equally. Their arrival from space in droves includes a rapid descent from a crack in the sky that opens over the *Valiant* [as the location is the same as the weak-point that allowed the Doctor to talk to Rose in "Doomsday", this may be another time-rift]. There are, we're told, six billion of them – about the same as Earth's population before the instruction to decimate humanity.

Planet Notes

• *Gallifrey.* [NB: Everything we're shown here of the Doctor's home planet is highly subjective, as his flashback to the Master's initiation is impressionistic and the Doctor wasn't actually there. The dialogue is full of 'some say...' constructions. Granted, subsequent episodes confirm a lot of what we get shown here, but there is room for doubt.]

Gallifrey used to be called the Shining World of the Seven Systems. The Citadel of the Time Lords [15.6, "The Invasion of Time", although the image we see here is from *Doctor Who Magazine* – see **The Big Picture**] was on the continent of Wild Endeavour in the Mountains of Solace and Solitude. The images we get are of a golden-hued world [per the description in X3.3, "Gridlock"], with Time Lords in formal robes. [As we first saw in "The Deadly Assassin", but with sigils more like the new-series Gallifreyan writing than the Prydonian Seal that became their trademark in the 80s. Contrary to what Rodan said in "The Invasion of Time", these Time Lords and their young probands were out on the wild windy moors to conduct this test, so are not safely within the Citadel from birth to death.]

History

• *Dating.* It's Friday morning after the election [UK elections are invariably on a Thursday], and into Saturday. The detail of the sun being up before 8.00am London time when they teleport to a flying aircraft-hanger over Norway, but not when they left the UK seconds earlier, implies late spring or early autumn.

[See our lengthy discussion about this under **Why the Great Powell Estate Date Debate?** in Volume 7. Saxon was Defence Secretary at Christmas ("The Runaway Bride"). The following year, Elizabeth II was in Buckingham Palace. This doesn't leave us much room for manoeuvre. If we're looking at early autumn for the election, we're either running straight into the party conferences in September or the usual Summer Recess, where Parliament is only recalled for emergencies. If we've had the conference season, then an election campaign of three weeks, we're into early October, the latest it can be and still have the sun come up before 8.00am in Norway. Then again, the election seems not to have been run on party lines, so is agreeing a manifesto that big a deal for anyone?]

How Come Britain's Got a President and America Hasn't?

continued from Page 257...

to cope with, but let's go with it for now. Saxon-the-party might be perceived as the way out of stalemate. A comparison worth trying here is with mid-80s Britain and the Social Democratic Party. Post-Falklands, the Conservative Party lurched further to the right and became emboldened in making sweeping changes to every aspect of life, treating every service as part of market economics in accordance with the theories of Milton Friedman. The Labour Party saw its best chance as being in providing a clear alternative, and not only refused to head for the centre-right but went further left (if those terms apply to policies and situations unprecedented in British life).

Three former Cabinet Ministers, one of whom had left Westminster to become an EEC Commissioner, thought that this was an error and set up, with a colleague, a centrist movement. There was already a centre-left party, the Liberals, but they were as much as anything a protest vote in this radically polarised era and were the crucible for what would later become the Green movement. The Social Democratic Party, as the new movement became, also attracted those in the Conservative Party appalled by Thatcherism's lack of regard for what had been the party's values in earlier decades. (The "Tory Wets", as they were termed. Inevitably, the SDP were referred to as the "Soggies"). After the 1987 election, which the Liberals and SDP fought on a non-aggression pact to avoid contesting seats where the other had a better chance, it seemed clear that with the two main parties becoming increasingly intransigent, persuasion was no longer possible and a cohesive image was proposed as the magic solution (it *was* the 80s). Thus the SDP engulfed the old Liberals, the party of Gladstone and Lloyd-George, and the Liberal Democrats were born. Over the years, it became obvious that the traditional, nineteenth-century definition of "Liberal", meaning *laissez-faire* economics, outweighed the twentieth-century definition to do with social justice and, as the 1990s closed, it was hard to tell much ideological difference between them and so-called New Labour. In many ways, the Blair landslide was the true legacy of the SDP's first few years, when it became obvious that a bandwagon effect was possible just by seeming to be different – but not being clear on what you were *for*, just what you were *against*.

Tony Blair's "presidential" style was commented upon when he succeeded John Smith (no, really) as Labour leader in 1994. In removing Labour's last vestige of genuine Socialism, Clause IV of the Party Constitution (about securing a share of the profits for the workers and a degree of worker control, or at least representation, within management), Smith and Blair made New Labour distinct from the party that had alienated the SDP's founders, and Blair consciously made voting Labour a consumer choice rather than an ideological stance. The Party Political Broadcasts of his era were more mood-pieces about how society ought to "feel". They had celebrity cameos (Geri Halliwell, formerly one of the few pop stars to admit to voting Tory, serving tea in an old folks' home, that sort of thing), and are as close as we ever got to Sharon Osbourne endorsing a candidate, as we see in "The Sound of Drums". The makers of *Doctor Who Confidential* obviously made this connection when they used the 1997 campaign song "Things Can Only Get Better" by D:ream (s:ic) under a montage of Saxon clips.[50]

Yet even this was within limits that Saxon clearly does not experience. The constraints on an individual's ability to act like a party mean that a Ross Perot-style one-man campaign to become the elected leader is impossible. Mattheo Renzi's rise in Italy was the first time any parliamentary system in postwar Europe had come close to the Master's campaign strategy, and even he had the PD behind him (quite a long way in the background, if you were to follow the media coverage). Renzi's personality-cult fit the Italian system. (He was, after all, hailed as the antidote to Berlusconi's "sultanate", a corrupt media baron's long reign as president reinforced by owning almost all the private media and then, as President, running the state ones.) That ended in disaster. In France in 2017, something similar happened with Emmanuel Macron's *La Republique en Marche* movement, which he made every effort to present and then run as a movement (akin to 35 years earlier, with the SDP) rather than a personality-cult. France has a President who is unconnected with the Parliament (they are elected separately, a few weeks after the second and final round of Presidential elections). It's not uncommon for the country to look at who got in as President, think *Merde! What have we done?* and elect a totally different style of candidate for their local constituen-

continued on Page 261...

There's a picture of Edward Heath in the portraits of former leaders in the staircase at Downing Street. [So he was definitely Prime Minister at some point – see **Who's Running the Country?** under 10.5, "The Green Death").]

English Lessons [For the benefit of non-UK readers, please note that the timeline for the Master moving into Downing Street the day after the election is the one part of the Master's election in line with what you'd normally expect. The rest of it is, well, deranged enough to get a whole essay.]

- *Wet* (adj.): as used by Margaret Thatcher, it denoted anyone not as hard-line as her, i.e. puny humans. "Wet" as an insult is, oddly, a legacy of all-male Public Schools. Saxon condemning his opportunistic Cabinet as 'wet, snivelling traitors' before gassing them like badgers is a dead give-away as to his party affiliation before he formed his own. Thatcher identified her supporters as "dries" and potential rebels as "wets". (The sarcastic use of 'rejoice' at the climax of next week's episode is another reference to her, a call-back to the sinking of the Belgrano – see "The Christmas Invasion" – and Thatcher's response to this war-crime.)
- *Sunday Mirror* (n): A real newspaper, the Sunday edition of the *Daily Mirror*; the second tabloid to begin and less right-wing than most. It was the *Sunday Pictorial* until 1963. This was the paper that broke the Profumo scandal (25.1, "Remembrance of the Daleks"). Vivien Rook was cast to look vaguely like Eve Pollard, the first of six female editors out of 14 to date (although the name 'Rook' suggests the astringent Jean Rook, notorious for slagging off Robert Holmes – see Volume 4 – who is herself not to be confused with Wanda Ventham's character in 4.6, "The Faceless Ones"). Odd, given recent court-cases, that something about phone-hacking should have come to their attention and been seen as worrying.
- *Lorry* (n.) The proper term for a truck.
- *Rugby Blue* (n.) Saxon (purportedly) played for either Oxford or Cambridge University rugby teams, against whichever of these two he wasn't at, in Varsity matches. Probably as a Fly-Half, as he's not built like an Ice Warrior.
- *Roedean* (n): A girls' public school, very exclusive. Verity Lambert went there.
- *Out of the Unknown* (n.): A 60s anthology series on BBC2, mainly adaptations of short stories. It was the other result of the 1962 document by Alice Frick that led to *Doctor Who*.
- *Chemist* (n.): What Americans call a pharmacist.
- *Chips* (n.) For the benefit of anyone who's not seen the last volume, it's the UK term for what Americans would think of as steak fries. (Well, sort of, but the traditional tourist guide claim that British chips are American fries is slightly simplistic and certainly no one in their right mind calls McDonald's products anything but "fries"[49].)

American Lessons

- *Grits* (n.): It's singular rather than plural. This is a sort of polenta. Because Americans use the word "corn" exclusively to mean maize (corn-on-the-cob in the UK) rather than wheat or rye or barley, the suspicion has been voiced that someone read the recipe for porridge and jumped to the wrong conclusion. This is, of course, incorrect. Porridge has never been made with chicken-stock; even Scots would find this unappetising. The maize-husks are boiled in stock and served as a side-dish, alongside or instead of mashed potato. The weird name is possibly derived from "groats", as in wheat, barley, rye and so on (another term derived from this is "grist", as in what you take to the mill to get turned into flour, so this is plausible). The popularity of this side-dish is contained within the southern US states, leading the rest of the country to associate it with specific sets of attitudes and soul music.

The Analysis

The Big Picture ("The Sound of Drums" and "Last of the Time Lords") As we hinted in **How Long was Harriet in Number 10?** under "The Christmas Invasion", the beginning of this story makes a lot more sense if, instead of Saxon being Prime Minister, he is Mayor of London.

London has only had an elected Mayor since 2000 (there's a Lord Mayor, the ceremonial one-year head of the City, i.e. the financial district, and that job's been around since the middle ages). Only two people have been Mayor of London, and neither is entirely popular within the party he represented. When the post was created, Ken Livingstone (see X4.11, "Turn Left"), who had been the head of the Greater London Council and only ceased to be when the Thatcher government did away with that body (apparently out of spite) was the most popular candidate – but not with

How Come Britain's Got a President and America Hasn't?

continued from Page 259...

cies, from whom the President has to select a government. Instead, La REM swept the board in Parliamentary elections because the opposition were running around like headless chickens, and anyone who thought about voting for one of the other parties stayed at home. He invited more experienced politicians from other parties who'd retained their seats to join him, but they were almost all forced to quit within days because of the very corruption scandals that had made Macron seem like a breath of fresh air. Yet these, even Berlusconi's trial run for Trumpism, were far in excess of what Blair might have dreamt of – he needed Alastair Campbell, after all.[51] And even Macron's meteoric rise from nowhere in a matter of months is a long way short of what Saxon gets away with here.

You will by now be getting the broad shape of our argument. The situation we see in "The Sound of Drums" requires the Master to have concocted the Saxon persona and backstory, and indeed to have been a successful businessman to fund the next few stages. He tends to a dying minister and marries his daughter. He then gets himself elected as a Member of Parliament (perhaps just a matter of getting adopted as a candidate, then arranging the unexpected death of the incumbent) and begins destabilising the government of the day, first by stage-managing the resignations of four cabinet ministers and then by replacing one as Defence Secretary. Somehow, possibly by having been Defence procurement Minister first, he gets the *Valiant* redesigned to his specs – if this is September 2007, then the advent of Daleks, Cybermen and the Christmas Star may well aid his case without him planning for them.

And then things get tricky as he has to form a party of his own, or at least a body of opinion that cuts across party lines so that the next election is fought on whether people are with him or against him. (There was almost an unfortunate precedent for that in the controversy stirred up by Enoch Powell in 1968, after which Union leaders, traditionally left wing, claimed to be "with Enoch" and caused strikes and walk-outs over management hiring non-white staff. See earlier volumes. Conservative leader Edward Heath kicked Powell out of the party. Similarly, divisions over Britain's membership of the EU aren't confined to the Tories.) What happens next requires a combination of circumstances that combine the SDP's initial bandwagon effect, a Blair-like feelgood personality-cult and an election where the Queen is persuaded that Saxon ought to be Prime Minister and form a government out of whoever has still got a seat in the House of Commons when the dust settles.

Well, okay, but this *still* isn't quite right. The posters don't say "Vote for anyone who supports Saxon" – they don't say, for example, "Sir Bufton Tufton your Conservative candidate: he's with Harry!". They simply say "Vote Saxon".[52] The public are being exhorted to vote for a person as Prime Minister, not a party that happens to be led by someone you may or may not think is Prime Ministerial material. There are precedents, such as Pitt the Elder and Pitt the Younger, but that was before the public could vote. Lloyd George, by allowing working class men and well-off women over 30 to vote, prevented anyone from following in his footsteps.

The situation we see requires another change to have happened while we've been away: an alteration to the electoral process more drastic than any politician has ever dared propose in one move. Again, not impossible on its own, but this and everything else that we infer must have happened all *in 18 months* whilst building a Paradox Machine and ferrying six billion killer cyborgs from One Hundred Trillion AD needs Saxon's hypnotic signal to have been working on absolutely everyone, phone or not, at such a pitch that they wouldn't have noticed anything untoward – and if any more aliens were planning an attack, that would have been the perfect time to do it. (They were, but somehow Sarah, Luke, Clyde, Maria and Mr Smith dealt with them all. In that case, it's lucky so many of their mobiles got smashed.). The backroom shenanigans and blackmail that these early stages required would have been fun to watch, with the Master as an even more malignant Francis Urquhart from *House of Cards*.[53]

We didn't see any of that, but had to make do with X3.6, "The Lazarus Experiment". Archangel relies on the Master simultaneously being inconspicuous and very public, rewriting the UK constitution without anyone noticing and grabbing the headlines. If the Canary Wharf incident led to as big a change in British government as the July 2005 attacks, there might have been emergency provisions in place, but we don't see any sign of

continued on Page 263...

the Labour Party he ostensibly represented. The Conservatives, running scared, deployed a former minister, former MP and bestselling author Jeffrey Archer, now Lord Archer. In his capacity as the "Stop Ken" candidate, he received endorsements from entertainers and even Labour figures, notably the TV arts pundit and radio polymath Melvyn Bragg.

However, the public resented the underlying tone of these pieces, which suggested that anyone who thought Archer was dishonest, creepy or unable to tell when he's lying any more was just prejudiced. Thing is, the public were right. Whilst his party were trumpeting their "family values" credentials, he was one of many who turned out to be less-than-pure. Archer was finally convicted for perjuring himself when giving evidence in an earlier trial where he sued the press for a claim about soliciting prostitutes. (Even his admirers admit he was probably doing so, on behalf of someone else – we can't say more in print – but the real damage was caused when one of his advisors gave the woman in question £2000 to leave the country and this was covered up, rather ineptly.) Monica Caughlan's testimony was easily verifiable, but the lawyers did what they could to avoid doing so. (Her subsequent death is probably not connected, but you get conspiracy theories anyway.) A lot of friends who had testified for Archer changed their stories and his secretary admitted to falsifying diary entries.

Archer's detractors, of whom there are many, enjoy seeing his self-aggrandising stories being exploded and so this was hardly surprising. He had apparently falsified his school results to get in to Oxford (and, although the teacher-training course is associated with Brasenose College, this doesn't exactly make him an Oxford graduate in the accepted sense), made rather a lot of money for himself while raising funds for charity (cannily getting the Beatles involved in an Oxfam campaign) and competed in athletics events as a Blue (the only extant footage is of him making three false starts). He became an MP at 29, but he and his wife, scientist Mary Archer, lost a fortune in a dodgy investment – not his fault, this time – and he recouped it by writing the first of many thrillers in 1974, *Not a Penny More, Not a Penny Less*.

He came back into front-line politics in the Thatcher years, rubbing up Tory grandees the wrong way with his unshakeable self-belief, and was an easy target for satirists (his novels weren't much more than workmanlike). Assorted minor scandals and close investigations into his charity accounts were accumulating, but when the perjury trial began, despite his characteristically bullish response (writing and starring in a play, *The Accused*, in which the audience voted on the result every performance), the new Tory leadership dropped him and his mayoralty bid ended. He served four years in prison, but didn't relinquish his peerage. The first trial over the Monica Coughlan affair had seen the judge show his hand by commenting on the "fragrance" of Mary Archer, as if nobody with such a wife could possibly be guilty. All those who had endorsed Archer now wonder whatever possessed them.

Saxon's endorsements by a peculiar cross-section of celebrities is also a link to the start of the Thatcher era. Although nothing like what we see here would ever happen, the use of advertising techniques, including paid ads in cinemas, was one of the innovations of the 1979 campaign and was the work of Saatchi and Saatchi. Nonetheless, the most advert-intensive election had been the 2005 one (see "Dalek"). The traditional method of addressing voters is with the Party Political Broadcast, a ten-minute slot across all terrestrial channels (at least until recently) with low production values and either a vague feelgood message or some hefty stats. Attempts to seem up-to-date were often painful and risible (the worst, oddly unavailable on YouTube, was Dr David Owen's baffling attempt to do Max Headroom for the SDP in 1987 – see this episode's essay for more on them). The 2005 campaign had used broadcasts more like the tearjerkers deployed by charities in daytime commercial slots and one of these, concerning waiting-times for NHS surgery, was so inaccurate as to backfire badly on the Conservatives.

The more normal use of celebrities was at the annual Party Conferences in early autumn and, again, the Conservatives had been more keen to exploit star-power, but more vulnerable when it went wrong. (Notoriously the not-especially-Tory Kenny Everett and a whole slew of DJs and comedians close to Margaret Thatcher and latterly investigated by Operation Yewtree.) Nonetheless, short spots inside commercial breaks where celebs endorse a candidate and not a party have never happened in Britain... but it's feared that this is how things will develop. Such worries have been made public before, most vividly in the 1969

How Come Britain's Got a President and America Hasn't?

continued from Page 261...

that even when the Daleks are obliterating cities a year later. Harriet Jones may have proposed measures to prevent a recurrence of the weird situation that got an MP on an obscure committee[54] into Number 10 by judicious assassinations ("Aliens of London") but that would have required all-party support and the assent of the House of Lords without letting slip that flatulent aliens had infiltrated Parliament and nearly started a nuclear war. (It's theoretically possible that such measures would have included restoring the Lords to their pre-1911 powers of veto and that someone could have become PM simply through their mandate, with no recourse to an election at all, but this isn't the point made in either story.)

It looks as if hefty rewrites to the rules and massive manipulation via the Whips (party "fixers" who co-ordinate how MPs vote in the Commons) forming a loose alliance of ministers and MPs that Saxon has over a barrel is our only hope of making sense of this situation. Yet setting it up and then removing it after the status quo ante is restored requires more drastic action than would have passed unmentioned, even in the frantic start of "The Sound of Drums". What it would need for Saxon to be elected as we see here is for someone like him to have been elected by more legitimate means and completely changing the UK constitution, but without anyone commenting on it or even noticing. In short, the Master has to have been Prime Minister for five years before this for "Harry Saxon" to be elected. Yet nothing about any State of Emergency (the most plausible route by which a normal Prime Minister could force such measures through without Parliamentary consent) is ever mentioned. It would have broken the Archangel spell, in any case. The medical student Oliver Morgenstern (X3.1, "Smith and Jones") would have commented to the press and *Torchwood* would have made a big deal about the special powers. (As it happens, such a change would have made *TW:* "Reset" a bit more straightforward and Jack's actions in stopping alien bombers less controversial with his colleagues but that was all after this episode. *Torchwood* Series 1 is resolutely set in a Wales like the one we knew at the time of broadcast.) *The Sarah Jane Adventures* would have been radically different if restrictions on journalists of the kind usually imposed in emergencies on this scale were instigated.

Had *Doctor Who* not had two spin-offs set in the period immediately before the start of this story, they might have been able to get away with a version of British politics so removed from reality. It's not impossible and it could, just, have all happened without anyone in the many present-day adventures thinking to mention it – but it's roughly as likely to go unmentioned as the Queen converting to Islam or the currency going back to shillings and sixpences. As is so often the case these days, the effort of restoring normality so that the next Yeti-in-a-loo story can happen in a world like ours is a more epic, less plausible story than what's on screen.

satire *The Rise and Rise of Michael Rimmer*, which began as a dig at David Frost's insatiable appetite for prestige, but reached the screens just ahead of the 1970 election campaign in which psephology was an electioneering tool as never before. (It's studded with familiar faces and topical asides and was deemed preposterous at the time, but now looks like David Cameron's training-manual. However, Peter Cook's unnerving performance as the conniving smooth-talker is more like Harry Saxon than it landed up being like Frost. That's at least in part because Frost bought the rights and produced the film, which eventually had a more convincing Frost-a-like character played by Harold Pinter as a sort of narrator.)

In many ways, though, this realignment of politics to being one of many consumer-choices is part of a process that developed all through post-war Western democracies and came to fruition in the late 1990s. Politicians were elected as much on how their image made the voter-consumers *feel* as what they offered in terms of policy. It was something that people feared, and the suspicions of many about Bill Clinton and Tony Blair were remarkable more for how people were alarmed by this, rather than for what happened (or failed to) when they were in power. The extent to which this has become normalised is what worries most observers who comment on it today. Ditto the assumption that everyone, regardless of income or taste, must have a mobile phone.

One odd detail is the way Saxon announces the Toclafane to the viewers, not just the *Little Britain*-style opening ("Britain, Britain, Britain... opened by the Queen in 1972" or whatever, as per Tom Baker's commentary on the sketches), but the phrasing of "A message, for humanity, from beyond the stars". George W Bush's acceptance of the 2004 Republican nomination included the curious claim: "Like generations before us, we have a calling from beyond the stars to stand for freedom". This was shortly after he compared the invasion of Iraq to the Normandy landings. Compared to this on-screen identification of Bush with an evil Time Lord, the portrayal of the fake US President in this episode is fairly tame stuff. He begins a world-wide broadcast "My fellow Americans, patriots, people of the world...", conforming to the basic assumption on British TV that any American who uses the word "Patriot" to mean anything other than guided missiles is probably an idiot and seems, to us, entirely natural in its parochialism and cluelessness about anything beyond America. Winters is killed shortly after bringing God into a conversation with aliens, assuming that they share local beliefs without even asking. (The first thing a genuinely religious man would think to do, really, is find out about this.) As we explore in this episode's essay, Saxon is as much a parody of Presidential-style politics as the fairly obvious jokes about Winters.

He's also just a bit more of a self-portrait when Winters is around. Saxon's suggestion that, "I could make the tea, or isn't that American enough? I don't know, I could make grits. What are grits, anyway?" sounds so much like Russell T Davies on a DVD commentary, it flags up how much else of his dialogue is commentary on the way BBC Wales usually does things – the Master even claims that the Doctor's fugitive trio is "ticking every demographic box". It's in the nature of Lord-of-misrule villains that they comment on the unsayable, including the nature of the medium. It's interesting that such figures are increasingly more likely to be villains than identification-figures these days; compare Tim Burton's *Batman* to Christopher Nolan's *The Dark Knight* and the degree of sympathy we have with the Joker is drastically curtailed. Burton obviously wanted the Joker to win, but wasn't allowed. (*Batman Returns* is more the film he would have wanted to make, with Batman almost acting like the Joker when dealing with clowns running amok, and playfully defusing the Penguin's control-freakery.)

As the name implies, the Master is all about imposing order, his own values, on everyone. The Doctor, on the other hand, was traditionally the outsider able to criticise society and shake things up in favour of the small people against impersonal agencies. For a Master who is more Joker-ish to work, the Doctor must become more of an establishment figure (as sometimes happened with Delgado against Pertwee), but it mainly requires the Master to subvert authority from within. Think of all the uniforms and titles he accrued when taking on UNIT in the 70s.

We could get all Jungian about this, but the dialogue between two characters such as these is almost always a thinly-veiled wrestling between conscience and appetite. We'll see this more clearly when the Master comes back, and spends a whole episode eating frantically and turning everyone into himself. This version is unfettered by concern for others, but is acutely aware of the social nuances and accepted behaviour, which is why he can scandalise everyone so effectively. We can't ignore the extent to which this is the culmination of the Delgado Master's usual MO, doing all the things the third Doctor wouldn't dare, while at the same time being more like how the Doctor himself would usually behave. In among all those references to the 70s UNIT stories (and one solitary mention of Ainley's most characteristically silly moment in "Logopolis"), we get references to stories where the Doctor has taken it upon himself to impose law.

The plot of a politician who seemed plausible and charming (almost) causing the end of the world is familiar from inadvertently-hilarious 1981 Sam Neill embarrassment *Omen III: The Final Conflict* (see below for the way the ending is riffed on) and, equally predictably, *Buffy the Vampire Slayer* Season Three. Admittedly, Davies had already used this more directly with "Boom Town" (X1.11), with the dodgy-but-liked Mayor of Cardiff opening what, for all practical purposes, is a Hellmouth in the city (and thereby setting up *Torchwood* as an *Angel*-esque spin-off), and we'll pick up on the *Buffy* episodes "The Wish" and "Doppelgangland" under "Turn Left". There was, of course, a famous real-life example in Germany in the 1930s, and it's as much a reference to this as to John Simm's recent past that prompts a reference to a "New Order".

In the Gallifrey flashback, we're told of the ritual of exposing promising candidates for Time Lord training to the Untempered Schism. This whole procedure, with the mountains and the robed-and-skullcapped quasi-monastic elders, is very like the procedure for finding the new Dalai

Lama. In this, the reflections on a specific lake are meditated upon, and the birthplace of the next reincarnation is found through looking for clues in the apparent images. The child suspected of being the next Dalai Lama is then presented with objects, some of which belonged to the previous one. The stone gateway has a vague similarity to the eponymous *Stargate* (itself borrowed from CJ Cherryh's *The Gate of Ivrel* – see 26.1, "Battlefield") and various *Star Trek* time portals. There seems to be an echo of Nietzsche's dictum about looking into the abyss and the abyss looks back into you, which might be appropriate. (Some commentators offer the idea that we're back in Rowling territory with the Mirror of Erised, but it's not a compelling comparison.) However, as we've just hinted, there's more than a hint of Damien Thorne about the preternaturally calm, pudding-bowl-haired lad fulfilling an ancient prophesy (more from the earlier *Omen* films, though, particularly the 1976 original *The Omen*).

The sequence with the Doctor, Martha and Jack passing un-noticed through crowds has an interesting literary heritage. The work that tied together these threads into a coherent conceit was Christopher Priest's 1984 novel *The Glamour*, reclaiming the word's older use as a sort of spell that prevents observers from registering what their eyes are glancing at. Such a spell was used, in 30s radio and 70s comics, by the Shadow (Orson Welles's breakthrough role, as well as a dreadful Alec Baldwin film). In one of the *Hitch-Hiker's* books, this was renamed the "SEP field": a psychic shield that made anyone who saw it think it was Someone Else's Problem. Something similar occurs to Lady Dedlock at the end of *Bleak House*, but the most overt uses of it to suggest a supernatural force making certain groups literally invisible (a detail used in Salman Rushdie's *Midnight's Children*) was in the original TV version of *Neverwhere* (see "Doomsday" and X4.2, "The Fires of Pompeii", to say nothing of Neil Gaiman's actual *Doctor Who* scripts: X6.4, "The Doctor's Wife" and X7.13, "Nightmare in Silver"). It later recurred in Gaiman's *Sandman* and *The Books of Magic*. Inevitably, it and the associated memory-wiping (both used by up-to-date vampires, such as in *True Blood*) showed up in Davies's pilot for *Torchwood*, linking the TARDIS's chameleon circuit to the way nobody noticed people emerging from a hidden lift in the middle of the Cardiff's most touristy bit. He'd already used the term "glamour" for a very similar mechanism in his *New Adventures* novel *Damaged Goods*.

Similarly, the Master's insidious telepathic signal is in keeping with many political analysts' ideas on how previously-unthinkable ideas become normalised by a slight but relentless pressure: David Cameron was more overt, setting up a "Nudge Unit", but the concept of "boiling a frog" slowly ratcheting something up so that people don't notice, was common currency. The Saxon message is also similar to the insidious *Keep Calm & Carry On*, a poster devised in 1940 for use as and when the expected Nazi invasion had happened: it was never used, for obvious reasons, but the idea was that a French-style Resistance was to be avoided. (An un-used specimen was found in a junk-shop by Chris Donald, editor of *Viz*, whose previous spoof of such things, *They're Happy Because They Eat Lard*, is far less annoyingly ubiquitous.)

There is a blessed Saint Martha, part of a family that suffered excruciating Roman tortures before all being horribly martyred. The bit that Davies might have remembered later on was the follow-up, in which a Roman woman secretly removed the half-burned bodies to a catacomb. It gives the Viking funeral scene something more of a claim to dignity. In any other circumstances, the name "Vivian Rook" might have been construed as a Celtic/ Arthurian allusion (see 16.3, "The Stones of Blood"), but – as we hinted above – the character seems like a composite of Eve Pollard and Jean Rook.

However, that is just one element of a smorgasbord (or car-crash, depending on your taste) of kitsch in-joke references to late seventies/ early eighties fantasy blockbusters that make up the bulk of episode thirteen's climax. We have the pyre from the end of *Return of the Jedi* for the Master, but the shot of a hand from off-screen taking his ring is the end of *Flash Gordon*. The Doctor and the Master tussle on a cliff-top just like Kirk and Kruge in *Search for Spock*, Earth going into reverse when time is wound back is the original (and proverbially stupid) end of *Superman: The Movie* and the revised end for *Superman II*, a scene routinely offered as the benchmark for idiotic plans in Disney Channel teen comedies. The Toclafane are a bit like the torture device in *Star Wars*, a bit like the killer things in *Phantasm* and – when they start swarming from the sky – just a little bit like the climax of *Glitterball* (the Children's Film Foundation one, not the Derek Jarman home movie). The camera's uncertain following of the

Toclafane down to London or wherever is intentionally a bit like the more recent *Battlestar Galactica,* while the basic idea of *Valiant* is obviously Cloudbase from *Captain Scarlet and the Mysterons* (with an indestructible man and aliens that could be killed with a precise form of electrical shock). There was a similar flying aircraft hangar in the strangely tedious *Sky Captain and the World of Tomorrow*, released shortly before this episode was written. No doubt Marvel obsessives are grumbling that people in Britain – certainly those of Davies's generation – think of Gerry Anderson as the obvious referent instead of that *Avengers* thing that doesn't have John Steed in it. (See X8.12, "Death in Heaven" for a conversation on this intended to distract us from how much like *Iron Man* the rest of the episode was.)

The big one is, as we suggested, the risible *Omen III: The Final Conflict*, which has Damien Thorne – the baby Anti-Christ adopted by Gregory Peck in 1975 in the first film – become President of the U.S.A. in 1984, aged 33 and played by the not-very-American Sam Neill. For a combination of budgetary and last-minute-script-fixing reasons, it's prophesied that his only serious opposition, "The Nazarene", will be born in England. (These films were British-made, hence all the familiar faces who get slapstick deaths in the first two and the *Who*-related stuntmen given speaking roles and over-familiar UK-resident Americans in this effort.) There follows a literal attempt to out-Herod Herod and impose martial law on the UK prior to launching a nuclear war. By the end, the blonde journalist with whom Damien has been having a romance/ hypnotic rape summons the will to stab him in the back with a magic dagger (one of many hidden around the world), and then a big glowing Jesus manifests over the Spawn of Beelzebub to forgive and taunt at the same time.

Because of the character-actors involved and the late-night ITV showings in the early 80s, these films are bracketed in with Hammer and Amicus as part of what a teenager who'd grow up to work for BBC Wales 30 years later would affectionately embrace. (The first *Omen*, by the way, has a memorable daft death for Patrick Troughton as he's spatchcocked by a lightning rod.) Those kids may also have recalled a boy's action-paper called *The Valiant* (rival to *The Victor* and *The Lion*), which contained many strange fantasy-adventure strips as unlike *The Beano* or *TV Comic* as they were unlike Marvel or DC product.

The view of Gallifrey we have includes a Citadel inside a glassy sphere, with pointy towers, taken wholesale from the masthead used in early editions of *Doctor Who Monthly* for their news page "Gallifrey Guardian". The line about keeping the Master in the TARDIS is possibly a callback to the Master's last almost-canonical appearance, in Paul Cornell's webcast "Scream of the Shalka". As we mentioned in the last volume, the Toclafane began as a Plan B for if the rights to use the Daleks were withheld (X1.6, "Dalek") but they have enough in common with the original Cybermen for us to have grounds to think they may have been in the back of people's minds when Series 2 was being conceived – certainly the time-paradox/ alternate universe element and the co-ordinates for Bad Wolf Bay are remarkably similar (see **Was Series 2 Supposed to Have Been Like This?** under X2.11, "Fear Her"). They are an extreme version of the old Grandfather Paradox we've already discussed in this book. The notion of giggly robotic killers with child-like voices is, of course, a slight retread of the Quarks (6.1, "The Dominators"), but without any stage-school kids inside the costumes.

With that kind of fannishness at work, the similarity between the sequence of Martha deducing the truth about the Toclafane intercut with the Master giving his version is noticeably the sort of thing Robert Sloman did for season-finales (8.5, "The Daemons"; 9.5, "The Time Monster"; 10.5, "The Green Death"; and 11.5, "Planet of the Spiders"). We've listed the bulk of the dialogue allusions to old stories along the way.

Oh, Isn't That...?

• *Sharon Osbourne* (herself). Daughter of notorious rock impresario Don Arden, she became famous as the stern matriarch in the reality-soap *The Osbournes*, handling Ozzy's confused state and the strops of Kelly and Jack. Her handling of his career had made her the 25th richest woman in Britain. Then she was one of the judges on *The X Factor* and hosted a disastrous ITV talk-show that was replaced shortly before this episode by *The Paul O'Grady Show* (see X4.12, "The Stolen Earth"). She now divides her time between *Loose Women* on ITV in Britain and the CBS knock-off *The Talk*.

• *McFly* (themselves). Famous as the boy-band that actually played instruments, just as stable-mates and early mentors Busted had been a couple of years earlier and One Direction were later. They had a string of fast guitar-led hits, then teamed up with Busted to tour as "McBusted". They had appeared as themselves on *Casualty* a couple of years before doing the Saxon ad, and performed *Comic Relief* singles. If you care, their names are Tom Fletcher, Danny Jones, Dougie Poynter and Harry Judd and they had seven No. 1s, robbed the Beatles of their record as the youngest band to have a No. 1 album and are big in Brazil. But the film they did with Lindsay Lohan vanished without trace.

• *Ann Widdecombe* (herself). Known to the press as "Doris Karloff" after an incident when, as a junior Home Office minister, she had authorised prison authorities to keep a woman in labour handcuffed to the bed, Widdicombe has sought to rebrand herself as a daffy old eccentric. She has written romantic fiction and made a spectacle of herself on a Kirby Wire in *Strictly Come Dancing*. She was one of a handful of right-wing politicians who left the Church of England when they ordained women priests and is now a Catholic.

• *Olivia Hill* (herself). A real newsreader from the real BBC news channel, unlike the deliberately wrong ones they usually use (X1.4, "Aliens of London" et al). The set she's in is a real one too.

• *Nichola McAuliffe* (Vivian Rook). At last, an actual actor! Star of one of the oddest ITV sitcoms since the 60s, *Surgical Spirit*, which ran for seven years mainly on her ability to deliver put-downs. Other than that, she's had a stint on *Coronation Street* and a couple of voice-overs, notably as James Bond's Talking Car in *Tomorrow Never Dies* and the usual guest-spots.

X3.13: "Last of the Time Lords"

(30th June, 2007)

Which One is This?

Martha's gap-year. Or not.
The Doctor turns into Gollum. Or Dobby.
Then he turns into Jesus. Or Tinkerbell.
The Master takes over the world. Or doesn't.
Jack becomes a familiar face. Or maybe not.
Martha leaves. Or doesn't.

Firsts and Lasts Jack goes back to Torchwood, and this is Martha's last story as a regular travelling companion. In the best comic-book tradition, both will be back later. (And it's almost not worth the space to mention that the Master's death is a temporary sort of thing. However, this time he gets a Wagnerian funeral.)

Murray Gold's initial arrangement of the theme music is completely rearranged after this. (A trained ear can tell that the Tennant version is different and honestly less exciting than the Eccleston one, but the new one will be a proper rework.) Part of the reason is that this is the last time the end credits will be allowed to run this long. The epic-length scroll was already an anomaly in the BBC's rather desperate attempts to get the viewers to the next programme before the last one's finished (see X5.4, "The Time of Angels"). Next year's will be almost as big, but a lot faster.

And, this is the last episode to be accredited as a BBC Wales/ Canadian Broadcasting Corporation co-production.

Watch Out For...

• Infamously, this story entails the Doctor being hyper-aged to become a grey blob (not for nothing is he compared to Gollum) in a tiny suit, but he then gets his old plimsolls back, repels lasers through sheer charisma and floats serenely towards the Master to forgive him for destroying Japan and stuff. This is achieved through Martha having spent a year stage-managing a global simultaneous prayer-meeting, getting everyone to clap their hands if they believe in Time Lords. If ever the term Davies Ex Machina applied in *Doctor Who*, this is it.

• Meanwhile, anyone watching on overseas transmission will have missed a scene where the Master taunts the Doctor with a song by briefly-popular band the Scissor Sisters. It's on most of the edits doing the rounds now, but apart from letting Russell T Davies indulge his music tastes twice in two episodes, it's a scene obviously made to be trimmed for export. It tells us no more than we knew about the Master's relationship with the Doctor and really only serves to distract us from the one significant detail in the scene: Lucy's bruises.

Also potentially trimmable, this story has five consecutive big end-scenes. Interspersed among these are several smaller tag-scenes. Among other things, we have to relinquish Jack and Martha, while keeping the door half-open for these two and the Master to come back. You thought *Lord of the Rings* had a lot of endings? The ones here aren't *that* drawn out, and yet everything after the plot ends takes as long as X3.13a, "Time Crash".

• We've seen signs of it before, but this is the story where Murray Gold goes completely bonkers with the scoring. The Master gets three – count 'em – three themes. However, we get some appealingly old-school electronica in among the orchestral bombast, notably when the Master is walking down a street looking for Martha. Her confrontation with him on the *Valiant* takes the theme she was given into Ennio Morricone choirs-and-guitars grandiosity right out of a Spaghetti Western.

The Continuity

The Doctor He's been living in a wheelchair for a year [since the finale of "The Sound of Drums" (X3.12)], putting up with the Master constantly humiliating him and occasionally having a go at improbable fightback schemes. [The lack of any rebellion would make his nemesis suspicious. There's also a sense that he's been forgiving the Master all year, to the latter's annoyance.] The day before Launch Day, the Master uses Lazarus technology to age the Doctor into a small gnome with manga eyes, and then makes a miniature pinstripe suit for him.

The Doctor's grand plan is for Martha to travel the world telling a story about him, and then – at an appointed hour – the collective belief of the entire planet [or near enough] is channelled through the Master's Archangel network to restore him to youth/ health, and give him super-abilities such as levitation and the ability to shrug off laser bolts. The effect also makes his clothes grow back to normal size.

Despite the Master having ransacked Earth in his bid for universal conquest, the Doctor's stricken by his death, pleading and screaming with the other Time Lord to regenerate. He was convinced that the Master would never have the will to kill himself [he was right that time, and in 14.3, "The Deadly Assassin", which makes X10.12, "The Doctor Falls" even more perverse]. When trying to persuade the Master to regenerate, he mentions Axons and Daleks [8.3, "The Claws of Axos"; 10.3, "Frontier in Space"; 20.7, "The Five Doctors"], while earlier the Master cites the Sea Devils [9.3, "The Sea Devils", of course].

He's starting to think he might have been travelling long enough and that with someone to care for, he'd be all right settling down. [There's no sign of this in the next story and certainly not when he meets Donna again, but this sense of dissatisfaction returns in the Specials.] Both Martha and Jack get invited aboard the TARDIS again, though when Martha asks, he insists he's 'always all right' [see X2.4, "The Girl in the Fireplace" and X4.9, "Forest of the Dead"].

Before Martha leaves, he suggests a few travel destinations, including Meta Sigmafolio and meeting Agatha Christie. [X4.7, "The Unicorn and the Wasp" is, like most of the events in Donna's life, not remotely a coincidence.]

• *Background.* The Master speaks of the Doctor single-handedly closed the Medusa Cascade during the Time War [we'll hear more about this next year, in X4.2, "The Fires of Pompeii" and X4.12, "The Stolen Earth"].

• *Ethics.* He's very insistent about the Master being his responsibility, to the point of persuading Francine not to shoot someone who's destroyed the world and tortured her and her family for a year. Nor has he any qualms about telling the Master he'll be kept in the TARDIS. [The Doctor never seems to consider executing the Master after all the people he's killed and the harm he's done, even at the risk of him escaping and slaughtering people again. The best case scenario, it seems, is that the Master is forever imprisoned within the TARDIS unto mortality, as they sort of attempt in Series 10. It may be that the way the majority of the deaths are made to have never have happened "excuses" the Master, and that the Doctor foresaw this possibility, but that's still a murky way for him to be thinking about this.]

The Master insists that as a Time Lord, he has a right to change the history of the universe; the Doctor accepts the point and talks about how unpleasant all this destruction is instead. In a rare display of gratitude, the Doctor thanks Martha for spending a year of her life saving the universe.

[And as many suspected at the time, the Master's Darth Vader-style cremation is as much to stop Time Lord bio-tech getting into the wrong hands as anything else (see 22.4, "The Two Doctors"; X6.1, "The Impossible Astronaut"; and X1.6, "Dalek"). The Doctor here keeps Hand in a Jar, probably for the same reason, especially after it was used to turn him into Charlie from *Words and Pictures*; see below.]

• *Inventory.* The *sonic screwdriver,* unsurprisingly, can re-fry a vortex manipulator. [After miraculously fixing it two episodes back. The *psychic paper* isn't seen or mentioned, but it's the nearest

Martha – What Went Wrong?

From the executive producers' point of view, it was all very simple. Billie Piper had been a runaway success in establishing the role of the companion vis-à-vis the Doctor; now that she was leaving, they needed a follow-up who could competently prove that Rose wasn't the be-all and end-all of the Time Lord's existence, and that *Doctor Who* would carry on without her. That someone would have an Earthbound family, like Rose, for a ready supply of recurring characters; someone rather more mature and reserved, the better to contrast with Rose's puppyish enthusiasm; and most importantly someone who would have a significantly different emotional relationship with the Doctor, or the fans would cry foul if we'd just had a Xerox of their preferred original. (There was nothing to be done about fans who began badmouthing the new companion as soon as she was announced, so they were, sensibly, ignored.) Consequently, the initial character outlines involved the Doctor still stinging from the loss of Rose, and a companion who would with equal zeal long after him. A medical student, slightly older, with a career and a proven ability to care for people in a crisis.

There were, perhaps, other ways of working around the post-Rose doldrums. Davies could have worked out a character more like Donna (i.e. a standard pre-1989 sidekick), where the cure for the Time Lord's lovelorn moodiness is a good dose of no-nonsense adventure. As the author of one of the more morbid *New Adventures,* he could have just run with the whole concept of a genuinely Byronic hero who's not only physically but emotionally dangerous to be around – which would obviously be inappropriate for a family show unless dripped in slowly. By the time the 2009 specials started, Davies has largely brought the Doctor to that point anyway without bothering to fill in the blanks. That would have made for a much darker and dicier season, ethically, but would have worked with the new companion character as envisioned. It fits much better with the general tenor of Davies-era *Who* – but again, Martha was conceived first and foremost as The Rebound Girl.

The trouble is, it's simply not possible to set up a healthy-sounding relationship with an emotional dynamic that only goes in one direction, in which the two parties are unequal to the extent of 900 years experience. If the medical student had been male, then the unrequited love thing would be so much like Vince Tyler in *Queer as Folk* that Davies would have been accused of only being able to do Mary-Sue characters. As it is, Martha's "This is me, getting out" aria in X3.13, "Last of the Time Lords" is so much like what Vince would say, it's almost jarringly out-of-character for Martha even without the previous 50 minutes of screentime. (Look at it on the page and imagine Craig Kelly saying it, and it's suddenly so much less forced.) To give Martha any more strong character-points would have been risky. The worry was always that any drop in ratings compared to Series 2 would be ascribed, rightly or wrongly, to the new girl not being Billie. Every effort was made to keep Martha likeable whilst making stories that each stretched the formula a tiny bit in one direction but not too much. It wouldn't have been fair on whoever they cast to have done otherwise.

The general disjunction means that Martha's character-arc completely breaks down at the end. In her personal timeframe, she's literally had a year to think about her experiences with the Doctor while singing his praises to as much of the planet as she can walk over. At the end of that, the way that she walks out on him would have made all the sense in the world at the start of X3.11, "Utopia", but fits rather oddly with having heroically rescued her prince hours earlier. Her parting speech doesn't suggest that she loves him any the less, just that she now recognises he's never going to be there for her, and she needs to leave for her own sake. She's not grown any the less fond of the lifestyle; Davies was already pondering ways and means of exporting Martha to *Torchwood* (where, refreshingly, she's a Proper Doctor) when he was writing Series 3. The only way this makes any kind of sense is if we run with the Byronic interpretation, in which case Martha is getting out of a bad situation before it gets any worse. The romantic Übermensch is all very well and good when it comes to saving the world, but you don't want to stay around him too long or you'll get hurt. It's rather ironic that if Davies had just worked through the emotional logic of what he was writing, the concluding image of a woman walking away from an unhealthy relationship and into an exciting, fulfilling career of her own could have been one of the most feminist messages *Doctor Who* has ever portrayed.[55]

... but at the expense of our supposedly family-friendly protagonist, of course, which is probably why Davies didn't. At least, we could have all been honest about what kind of show we're watching,

continued on Page 271...

hope we have of any of this working as a logical narrative; see **Things That Don't Make Sense**.]

• *Inventory: Hand in a Jar.* The Doctor takes it back from Saxon and keeps it in the console room, where it bubbles away for no immediately apparent reason [and behold the Hand's importance in Series 4].

• *Inventory: Other.* He ends the story plus one Superphone, formerly the property of Martha Jones. [She's either one of those organised people who memorises her own phone number, or she wrote it down prior to coming in the TARDIS; this doesn't look like an impulse leave-taking.]

The TARDIS Shooting up the Paradox Machine hardwired into the TARDIS destroys it and reverses all the paradoxical actions that happened as a result, with no signs of irreparable damage to the Ship. [Perhaps Jack has spent his year as Saxon's prisoner working out how to do this properly. Nevertheless, it might make sense of "Time Crash", if the Paradox Machine's destruction leaves the TARDIS's timeline more vulnerable to accident. This also covers the otherwise ludicrous space liner collision at the start of X4.0, "Voyage of the Dammed".]

The Master says that a Paradox Machine can hold together a paradox that covers the entire universe. [This is rather more believable in the wake of X5.13, "The Big Bang", in which it's demonstrated that the Ship blowing up will itself cause the universe to disintegrate. Under certain circumstances.]

The Supporting Cast

• *Martha.* Has spent the last year circumnavigating the globe – Tom, a resistance member, has heard about her having sailed the Atlantic and walked across America. She says she's travelled "the ruins of New York, to the fusion mills of China, right across the radiation pits of Europe". [It's possible that she reached South Africa along the way, but there's no way to be sure.] One of the experiences that haunts her was the burning of the Japanese Islands [depicted in *The Story of Martha* anthology], where she was reportedly the last person to escape alive. Somewhere, she found a disc recording of a Toclafane being killed by being struck by lightning in South Africa.

Depending on your interpretation, she's either confident enough of the Master having plans for her to come out when he starts threatening civilians, or hides until he brings up the Doctor's name [the script suggests the latter, the direction more the former].

On the Doctor's last-minute and tremendously vague instructions to "use the countdown" a year ago, Martha derived a plan to tell the entire world about how lovely the Doctor is. There are lots of rumours about her, including one that she's the only person who can kill the Master. [As this fits with the "there's a gun-in-four-parts that can do just that" theory, she might well have been letting these go as cover for her true plan.]

The scheme involves spreading the word in person and asking for it to be passed on, with an instruction to all think 'Doctor' simultaneously. [Therefore, Martha only has to contact a small percentage of the populace of each country she visits. Nonetheless, she is apprehended on her first night back in England and so, unless she began in a different part of the same country, there seems not to have been time for the people of Britain – Saxon's first and most loyal converts – to have been enlightened.]

She chooses not to travel with the Doctor any more at the end, at first saying that she needs to stay home and take care of her distraught family; the year has also given her self-confidence. After walking out of the TARDIS on that note, she comes back to explain that she'd always warned a friend of hers (Vicky) in a similar unrequited love tangle (with Sean) to get out of the situation, and that she's doing the same. Nevertheless, she presses her superphone on the Doctor so she can call him if needed. [As she does in X4.4, "The Sontaran Stratagem". Martha next appears as a medic attached to UNIT in three *Torchwood* Series 2 episodes, starting with "Reset". There's more on her and Thomas Milligan there and in "The Sontaran Stratagem".]

• *Jack.* Likes fish and chips, doesn't like mashed swede. He's apparently spent most of the year chained up in the *Valiant* and launching unsuccessful escape events every so often. The continued immortality bothers him enough to ask the Doctor if there's anything that can be done – or failing that how long he'll stay young, as he's self-admittedly vain.

The Year That Never Was has made Jack feel more responsible about his Cardiff team, so he declines an offer to travel with the Doctor [and reunites with Gwen Cooper and company, to face their ire at his prolonged absence, at the start of

Martha – What Went Wrong?

continued from Page 269...

and what kind of hero the Doctor is these days. They tried that in "Kill The Moon" (X8.7), with Clara storming out after seeing the Doctor at his most manipulative, but it might work if we know the companion isn't coming back (see 21.4, "Resurrection of the Daleks"). There's a lot of pre-publicity now, so even writing Martha out as a full-timer was less of a surprise than they intended. (They messed that up too, but the press were mainly at fault there.)

Martha's family just fails to make any sense at all, not least because there's just too many characters stuffed into the show. Jackie and Mickey – or Sylvia and Wilf – may have been fairly simplistic characters, but they at least have straightforward motivations, and it's easy to follow the logic of how they interact with our companion and the lead. Martha has about as much screentime and plot function to get through with her family as Rose or Donna, proportionately, but she has two siblings, parents, and her father's girlfriend to juggle. In a series just about a trainee doctor in a busy London hospital, this would be the *set-up* for a drama – but it's a cumbersome backstory for someone whose screen-time will be mainly spent in front of green cloth pretending to see futuristic cities or Elizabethan London. It's also odd on its own terms. We'll leave aside the way none of the kids looks much like each other, let alone their supposed parents (always a problem with casting), and just look at it as writing.

The kind of mid-life crisis Clive's having only really happens in American drama. A middle-aged bloke in Britain, even if earning rather more than Clive seems to be (judging from their house) *might* be the target of a gold-digger, if that's what Annalise is supposed to be. Someone like her *might*, perhaps, gravitate towards the boss (if that's how they met), but it rings hollow. In a childless marriage, he might have taken up with a younger partner simply to have a family, but that's not what's happening here and Annalise doesn't seem especially broody. Generally, a mid-life crisis (if that's what we should call this) is about feeling trapped within commitments and, in Britain, especially for someone from Clive's imputed background (he doesn't sound especially posh, but is definitely a Londoner by birth) would more likely mean travelling the world or extreme sports. If anything, the fact that all three kids now have lives of their own might mean that he and Francine went off on cruises, or each downsized after an amicable divorce. Tish's joke about "spending the inheritance" is just that – a joke. With the kids gone and the marriage apparently crumbling, the logic of hanging on to that house (a fairly modest one, but still a lot of capital) is unclear. The NHS might be largely funding Martha's training, but she could still use the dosh.

They seem to be in a suburb of London, and whatever Francine does, she has Thursday off. (Another odd thing: she can go to junkets at no notice and is at home two days running so maybe, for all her stern lectures on the work-ethic, she isn't actually working herself. This is unlikely in that kind of family. That particular Thursday may be special because of the Saxon involvement, but Martha – oblivious to this – *expects* Francine to be home to take calls about pop trivia; see X3.7, "42".) All the signifiers are of a lower-middle class household (the term "middle-class" in Britain is very different from America's use of the words, and very specific). Any two of the pieces of this jigsaw might fit together, but you can't make all of it work at once. Just at a basic level, if he's got a house like *that*, he wouldn't be able to get a car like *that*. If he's moved out, he seems to be paying for two houses and yet has a car like *that*. If the car's Annalise's (as if), why's he driving?

We mentioned in Volume 7, the extent to which Jackie Tyler was an amalgam of stock traits from Australian soaps, overlaid with the caricature of the "Essex Girl". The same thing is happening here; each of the Joneses is a familiar figure from a different type of British drama, with Clive going through the motions as befitting someone from the Stockbroker Belt (affluent commuter-towns in Surrey and Berkshire, also the domain of rock stars and the odd Russian oligarch), Martha straight out of *Casualty,* and Leo so perfunctorily sketched-in that his partner never gets a line of dialogue or a name (at least on screen). Leo having a baby instead of a degree is the subject of a different kind of drama – and with a mum like Francine, it's almost inconceivable that he's not living in that big empty house of hers... but apparently he is. Leaving out the racial dynamic for now, this family is more like channel-zapping between three series than a plausible home-life for anyone, still less Martha-as-we-see-her.

Remember, at the time this went out, Davies

continued on Page 273...

Torchwood Series 2].

Now for the big revelation... when growing up, Jack says, he was a poster child for the Boeshane Peninsula, and the first one to enlist in the Time Agency. [*Torchwood* Series 2 confirms the part about Boeshane, so the rest of this sequence may not be as flippant as it seems.] Because of this, he claims to have been called 'The Face of Boe'. [The Doctor and Martha, obviously, take this to mean that Jack will, in some distant millions of years, age to become the Face that first appeared in X1.2, "The End of the World" and died after passing them a message about Professor Yana in X3.3, "Gridlock".

[*Should* we take this as gospel? Russell T Davies is on record that it's certainly his intent, and John Barrowman claims – as he always does – to have been happy as a puppy upon finding out. There's some wiggle room, though, in that Jack might simply have taken his inspiration from the Face of Boe, a different being entirely, when he was a lad. Or, he might in fact have taken such inspiration from himself. On the other hand, the Face of Boe showed no reaction to seeing Rose in "The End of the World" and Jack showed no reaction to Martha namedropping the Face in "Utopia".]

UNIT Martha says that the idea of UNIT having a Time Lord-killing gun in four parts with sections in San Diego, Beijing, Budapest and London is silly. [And yet the Master takes it quite seriously; see this time next year for a similar scheme. The most likely part of all this is UNIT having an abandoned base in North London; they *do* have a UNIT Central somewhere, but we aren't told where. It's further evidence that the Master knew quite a bit about UNIT by the time he got started; no word of a mushroom cloud from the Tower of London. He undoubtedly knows about the Black Archive, but this probably wasn't within the Tower back then, as we know from *The Sarah Jane Adventures*. Once time resets, the emergency radio messages hail from Geneva, which must at least be the European GHQ.]

The Supporting Cast (Evil)

• *The Master.* Continuing with the bad pop music theme from last episode, breakfast-time taunting of the Doctor and "Ta-Daa" by the Scissor Sisters [Track Three, "I Can't Decide"] feature in what seems to be the Master's daily controlling-the-world routine. His big plan this time around is building a fleet of 200,000 rockets to invade the universe. In his spare time, he's had lots of ostentatious statues of himself constructed, including his face carved into Mount Rushmore. He turns the Doctor into Gollum largely to annoy Martha. He also compares the Doctor to Gandalf [so at some point he's read Tolkien or seen the Peter Jackson movie adaptation – this being the John Simm Master, we can guess the latter].

He's installed 'isomorphic' controls on his laser screwdriver so that it can't be used against him [see 13.3, "Pyramids of Mars"; X6.0, "A Christmas Carol"]. For some reason, he thought it was clever to install self-destructs for the entire battlefleet into one handy control. That battlefleet includes missiles with black hole converters as warheads. There are 100,000 in Russia alone, twice that worldwide, and 10,000 on the south coast of England. [A simultaneous launch at dawn in the UK would make sense of this.]

In this incarnation, his use of the name 'Master' seems to extend to the bedroom. Lucy emerges with a black eye and seems more traumatised than usual. He's still kissing her as part of the morning ritual, but enjoys getting massages from a selection of women and casually suggests a threesome.

There's not much to suggest he has any particular concerns for the Toclafane, but he refers to them as his children more than once. [If they did this to themselves – see **The Non-Humans** – rather than being his work, it would seem to vindicate his bleak view of humanity, as well as being a detail he kept from Lucy when breaking her will by showing the futility of existence in a decaying universe. (He did this with a day-trip to the End of the Universe, rather than a box-set of *Gotham*.)]

He says he wants 'revenge' on the Doctor, but shows no interest in outright killing him [it's the only leverage Our Heroes have in this story, really]. At some point the Doctor must have spoken about Rose at length, since he makes an unflattering comparison between her and Martha.

Upon the downfall of his plan, he seems almost eager to be shot by Francine, and refuses to regenerate after Lucy shoots him. ["The End of Time Part One" explains the thought process behind this; he's already got a last-ditch plan. Lucy's strangely taciturn in the scene and the glazed expression on her face when Jack confiscates the gun hints at some pre-implanted hypnotic suggestion to do this if everything went pear-shaped.]

The Doctor cremates the Master's body in a

Martha – What Went Wrong?

continued from Page 271...

was being hailed as the saviour of British TV drama and the credit for anything that happened in *Doctor Who* went to him rather than whichever old-series writer he was, um, paying tribute to at any given moment. (We will remind you of this when we get to X4.14, "The Next Doctor".) If you subtracted any one of Martha's relatives, it could just about be made to fit together, although Francine has enough plot functions that it'd be genuinely difficult to write her out of the season. Without Leo, we have the image of an aspiring lower-middle-class family. It's not hard to imagine a rewrite of "Smith and Jones" (X3.1) in which a celebration of Tish's new job is overshadowed by Clive and Francine quarrelling; there's just as much drama there with less explaining to do and "The Lazarus Experiment" (X3.6), the other Jones reunion story, hasn't got Clive in anyway. A Jones family *sans* Tish makes it look as if Francine is hard on her daughter and goes lightly on her son, but this isn't so unfamiliar a situation. It would require the apparently laid-back Leo to be unexpectedly acquiring all these jobs instead (and being fancied by Richard Lazarus?), but as it's all the Master's doing anyway, it might as well be played for deliberate confusion. Instead of the muddle we did have.

Paul Cornell's adaptation of "Human Nature" (see **How Many Times Has This Story Happened?** under X3.9, "The Family of Blood") would have been tricky under the best of circumstances, as the original companion part, paradoxically, required far more overhaul than the Doctor's alternative personality to suit the change to television. Revising Bernice Summerfield's role as sometimes suffragette and women-of-independent-means (who didn't even stay at the school) into the Doctor's maidservant was always going to have awkward class undertones, even before the race aspect was thrown in the mix.

But the race aspect *was* thrown in. Or rather, it was there to be addressed and wasn't. We spent a lot of effort in **Why Does Britain's History Look So Different These Days?** under X3.2, "The Shakespeare Code", explaining that Britain's colonial past and relatively recent racial diversity make it hard to map American experiences or theory onto us. BBC drama is attempting to show the country as it actually is... but that state of affairs is different from how it was in 1989 or 1963. In any other British-made series, casting a minority actor best known for playing the ambitious, conniving hotel chambermaid in *Crossroads* would not cause major rewrites if the part had only specified age and career. (Well, *almost* any other contemporary-set series; the producer of *Midsomer Murders* had to stand down for saying that the fictional village where all these deaths take place is such a never-never version of Rural England that he wouldn't normally use actors from minority backgrounds.) But this character had to go to 1913 and, more bizarrely, 1930s America, and confront attitudes of the era. There was U-certificate casual racism in "Human Nature", but that was perfunctorily ticked off and casual sexism was her big problem. Nobody thought to comment on the semiology of Martha in a maid's uniform – least of all Martha. The lack of comment in "Daleks in Manhattan" is downright freakish and – this being her first trip to a period within living memory and a country where race is always in the news in British coverage of events even today – a deafening silence. What little character Martha had shown up to this point is being contradicted here.

There were a lot of sensible arguments for choosing Freema Agyeman at the time. She'd comported herself so well in auditions, Julie Gardner and Davies had been considering her for the part while Graeme Harper was texting them about her performance as Adeola in "Army of Ghosts" (X2.12). As her subsequent career and interviews indicate, the public like Agyeman and put up with Martha whenever she was allowed to be Freema-with-a-stethoscope. *Doctor Who* has (bafflingly to those of us following it from the 60s), become a flagship series for the BBC, and whoever stepped into Billie's shoes would have been in the spotlight. If they'd skipped a few and cast Karen Gillan, there would be endless comment about how she was the first female Scottish companion and a positive role-model for gingers, so if *that* character had done anything that Rose wouldn't, it would be an outrage amongst that constituency. The point is: Rose was a tough act to follow anyway, without a bundle of extra expectations being ladled onto the character.

All of this leaves the question of whether Martha would have been a better companion if the production team had cast a white woman instead. Agyeman's career took a definite upswing after her appearance on the show, and you could

continued on Page 275...

Viking-style funeral pyre; a ring drops out and is later picked up by a woman wearing red nail polish. [The speculation as to her identity ranged over an astounding number of candidates, sparked off by Davies joking that it was the Rani. It's safe to say that nobody foresaw it being a character like The Beast from *Prisoner Cell Block H* – see "The End of Time Part One" and **The Lore** for whose hand it was really.]

Planet Notes

• *Earth* is out-of-bounds normally, but especially in the current crisis: it is facing 'Terminal Extinction'. Japan has been destroyed. [The tie-in book *The Story of Martha* suggests that the Master did this to eliminate a prior lot of alien invaders, who were annoyed that a Time Lord psychopath was intruding on their own takeover ploy.] London is full of wild dogs. Europe seems to be radioactive, and Russia is one vast shipyard.

The traffic-hazard warning shows the Solar System consisting of nine planets, one of which is Pluto. [How retro! No mention of Ceres or Vesta, though. And not a word about Cassius – see 15.4, "The Sun Makers".]

• *Katria Nova* has whirlpools of gold. [If that's literal gold, the Master's invitation to take Tanya the masseuse there for a triste might be a one-way trip.]

• *Meta Sigmafolio* has a coast [there's a surprise] and a sky like oil on water because of star-fire.

The Non-Humans

• *Toclafane*. Well... the version that we're told by the Master is that at the end of the universe, humanity finally gets to Utopia [X3.11, "Utopia", amazingly] and finds nothing there. Distraught at the ending universe, they cannibalised themselves into and regressed into childlike personalities that shared each others' memories. The Master brought them all back to the twenty-first century, where they were happy to follow his plans of conquest and kill everyone for the fun of it. [If our theory of the Master having set up this timeline in the first place stands, they might well have been set up for universe-attacking from the get-go. This might explain how a society on the verge of technological collapse suddenly has the resources to create billions of identical metallic heads with communications and life support systems, all far more complicated than leaving people as meat. After all, this is exactly what he does ten years later, in screen time, when setting up the Mondasian Cybermen and living out his *Babylon 5* cosplay fantasies in X10.11, "World Enough and Time".]

They seem to be using something called 'Braccatolian Space' as their short-cut to and from other worlds [presumably this is a form of hyperspace, where they've all been hiding, and the crack in the sky last episode was a rift from that dimension].

They can exchange information: the Toclafane that Martha acquires recognises her from Creet's memories, but isn't actually Creet. They're vulnerable to an electrical current of 58.5 kiloamperes, with 510 megajoules of energy.

History

• *Dating*. [The episode entails the Master dominating Earth for a year, then the Paradox Machine's destruction reverse time to a point at about ten minutes on the Friday morning of the election following the 8:02 AM hinge-point. After the reversion, UNIT Central reports that they just saw President Winters assassinated. The various farewell scenes in Cardiff and London take place between then and Christmas, but we can't be sure how long repairs to the TARDIS (including ferrying her down from *Valiant*) might have taken.

[The rest of the episode is dated 'One Year Later' and we have little reason to doubt this means an exact solar cycle (except that the dodgy special effect for the rewind that indicates it's only a month). Quite why it should be exactly 365.26 days between the Toclafane Massacre ("The Sound of Drums") and launching the missiles is unclear, but it's entirely in character for the Master's love of big gestures and countdowns (especially if we take 8.2, "The Mind of Evil" at face value).

[Oh, and since he's had 18 months to assess Earth and plan, we'll have to assume that the Master, off screen, found ways of dealing with Sarah Jane, the Brigadier, etc. and also Torchwood when they returned from Tibet.]

English Lessons

• *Des* (n): In the entry for X1.12, "Bad Wolf", we mentioned *Countdown*, the mesmerically simple game-show adapted from a French maths problem. The original host, Richard Whitely, died around the time of that episode and was replaced, in rapid succession, by raffish sports commentator Desmond Lynam and 60s crooner, 70s standing

Martha – What Went Wrong?

continued from Page 273...

certainly make a case for attempting a competent black companion after the variable writing Noel Clarke suffered. Against this, we have a companion who – particularly in the Davies scripts – is presented as being desperately in love with a protagonist who has just belatedly discovered romance, lost it, and isn't in the mood for noticing it from anybody else. This wasn't going to be pretty whatever the performer's ethnicity. We could argue that the fifth Doctor era was characterised by the same basic dynamic, with Tegan, the professional woman with a crush on a young-looking Time Lord who was missing Romana. But that was a mess, too.

It's a symptom of a soap opera in which, with the Doctor's One True Love having been away from him, the writers were going to define the next person to fulfil the companion role as the one who... isn't. Martha is defined by negatives: A) she's not-Rose; B) she's not going to get the Doctor to fall for her; C) she's not staying after this year; D) she's not white. That last one dominates a lot of the discussion, and anything that failed to work in the character as conceived is now going to look like a straightforward race-fail. However crassly that element was handled, the basic flaws with Martha as a character began a lot earlier, when thinking that the female companion's role is essentially taking part in a romance with an alien. The more *Doctor Who* returned to being like old *Doctor Who* instead of *Buffy* in space and time, the more untenable this was going to become but – for a lot of the new audience back in 2007 – that was the main narrative hook.

The simple fact is that someone has to be first, and Freema Agyeman stepped into a series that had not yet had a female solo companion who wasn't white – mainly because they took the series off the air in 1989 and brought it back in 2005. It's traditional at this point to remind people that the BBC had finally stopped *The Black and White Minstrel Show* in 1978, and had a long track-record of worthy attempts to represent the changing racial make-up of the nation, sometimes faster than the available pool of talent would allow. (Waris Hussein has spoken rather eloquently about being at such a loss for Indian actors, he resorted to casting Caucasian actors for Kipling adaptations in 1964.) There were dull soaps (the 1979 *Empire Road* was notable more for its excellent Dub soundtrack than its characters or plots) and sitcoms (often with the same casts as the soaps, but Channel 4's *Desmond's* and BBC2's *The Kumars at Number 42* stand out), but the main impact was in mainstream dramas attempting to normalise such representation, not just in casting but in the recruitment of writers. Davies was straining against a policy of the BBC only approving of experienced television writers, but Series 3 doesn't show any signs of this coming to fruition. At no stage in the commissioning process was anyone from outside the charmed circle of Davies's chums asked for a script, except maybe Stephen Greenhorn (quite why he was asked at such short notice is a mystery, since there's nobody acknowledged as the author of the abandoned script – we doubt it was Hanif Kureishi).[56] It was all middle-aged white blokes and Helen Raynor. The response by the various other authors to suddenly writing for a non-white actor was generally more muted; Gareth Roberts wove two lines about race into the general introducing-the-companion-to-time-travel spiel and added a gag about Shakespeare's Dark Lady purely for laughs. There are obvious reasons why race might have been an interesting subject in the Manhattan two-parter (X3.4-3.5, "Daleks in Manhattan"/ "Evolution of the Daleks"), but considering the sort of eugenical themes Raynor provided in the plot, it is – on balance – a relief she left the topic alone. Everywhere else the Doctor and Martha go, it's simply a non-issue.

This sounds good and optimistic as it stands. In practice, there is a significant difference between going out of your way to support racism, which doesn't apply to most people on the left of the BNP, and completely failing to grapple with any of the institutional assumptions that act to depower minority groups. It's the difference between fire-bombing houses and hiring John Bennett to play your Fu Manchu parody. Davies isn't guilty of anything quite so egregious, but nobody was especially interested in doing thoughtful exegesis about intersectional ethical issues. The only priority was getting scripts out the door before shooting started.

Should such broader concerns be part of *Doctor Who*'s remit? Barry Letts would have said so. The BBC's regulations say you need a good reason not to. However, given the unholy mess Series 9 made of trying to be topical (egregiously X9.7, "The

continued on Page 277...

joke, 80s chat-show host and twenty-first century icon Des O'Connor. Neither Des is still doing it now.

• *Bexley* (n.): A small town in Kent that's now just within the borders of Greater London. Presumably, if Martha's arrival in Britain was at Dover or nearby, the shortest sea-voyage from France, this would be the easiest way in to the city. Once Parliamentary constituency of Edward Heath (see **Who's Running the Country?** under 10.5, "The Green Death"). Also, bizarrely, the name of an upscale French retail chain specialising in British-style shoes.

Things That Don't Make Sense ("The Sound of Drums" and "Last of the Time Lords") Apparently, we're supposed to find the idea of a gun that can kill the Master being scattered around the world ridiculous – *yeah, right, UNIT have secreted away parts of a deterrent against a dangerous and homicidal alien they've encountered before, as if* – and Martha laughs at the Master for buying it. This time next year she'll again be travelling the world, to unite the components of UNIT's ultimate anti-alien device, the Osterhagen Key (X4.13, "Journey's End").

But our main concern here, as it happens, is Jack's teleport bracelet. When Martha departs the *Valiant* in front of very unconcerned security guards (not even training guns on anyone), she arrives somewhere near Central London. (The landmarks indicate that it's the south, possibly Crystal Palace, but the same landmarks are in reverse order when seen from the Rattigan Academy in "The Sontaran Stratagem".) Why? The last time the bracelet was used, it took Our Heroes to the *Valiant* from an airport within walking distance of Martha's car – itself a short drive from her mum's, which is around the corner from her burned-out flat. Next time, it takes the Doctor and the Master to, er, Siberia (or Neath). In either of these instances, all that happened was someone pressing the "on" switch, not programming in co-ordinates as Jack did.

Eventually, it turns out that the words the Doctor whispered to Martha before she escaped the *Valiant* were: "Use the countdown". Presuming he can reasonably know that a countdown will in fact occur (but all right, the Master is involved, so it's likely to crop up at *some* point), what the hell is that supposed to *mean*? It's a staggering leap from those words to Martha intuiting "travel the world for a year and spread a tale about me, and instruct everyone to revere me at the same moment". (As we've suggested, the only thing that saves "use the countdown" from being total gibberish is if the Doctor later uses the Psychic Paper to give Martha more detailed instructions.) When all's said and done, it seems that the entire planet – with the possible exception of Jack and Lucy, who join in a bit late – were in on the ploy to overthrow the Master by concentrating on the concept of the Doctor. The Master's well enough informed to have heard Martha's bluff about the gun in four parts, but somehow hasn't heard a whisper of this beforehand.

Come to think of it, what is the Doctor's clever plan for dealing with the Master in "The Sound of Drums"? He's wearing a TARDIS key that's been rejigged to let him avoid notice. Somehow, he thinks that getting this over the Master's neck will allow the entire world to "see who he really is". It's odd enough if he's expecting the Toclafane to see the Master as the Master and just go home, but it also requires Saxon to not bother to take off a necklace, or for nobody to notice the Doctor struggling with him. Or, if the idea is that it'll snap the Master's Archangel-induced influence over the voters, that's not going to make a bit of difference once he's won the election and been ensconced as Prime Minister, and his (sorry) master plan is in its end game.

The Toclafane were the result of the Utopia project, to find a way for humanity to survive the eventual end of the universe. They eventually resort to making themselves into cut-price Cybermen. This, after the Doctor tells us that humans became downloads and vapour in ages past, but reverted to the two arms, two legs one head version. Are these optional format-changes not a better scheme? If the technology is lost but coffee and gramophones remain, something must have happened that was potentially even more useful. (This and the fairy-tale name make it seem as though the Master set up Utopia, which complicates Yana's backstory no end.)

It would've been so much cleaner had the temporal rollback affected *all* of the Master's shenanigans, but alas UNIT Central reports still having seen the American president assassinated. We've looked at this obliquely in two essays (under X3.1, "Smith and Jones" and "The Sound of Drums"), but the key point to ram home is that the wind-back of a year is for everything *after* the

Martha – What Went Wrong?

continued from Page 275...

Zygon Invasion"), it's perhaps just as well the Moffat regime normally steered well away from such concerns. However, they rounded off their time on the series with Bill Potts, whose very name and job (all right, she's a *university* dinner-lady rather than a secondary school one – c.f. X2.3, "School Reunion") seems like a bid to remind people of Billie Piper but whose mysterious background (another Moffat staple, the Doctor apparently "grooming" a companion by meddling in her past) and domestic life (the two women closest to her have the same names as the abortive Series 4 companion and her mum, "Penny" and "Moira") look like a sampler of every companion since 2005. Casting Pearl Mackie looked at first like a collect-the-set move, even with the obligatory London accent after experiments with right-Northern and Inverness. Just to seal the deal, they remade "Last of the Time Lords". Twice. However, on screen, Bill isn't just Martha 2.0, she gets to say the things viewers were shouting at the screen in 2007 *about* Martha. Plus, she's so genre-savvy she gets to stand in for American fandom the way the grumpy, forgetful Scottish Doctor articulates the showrunner's complaints.

As we mentioned (**Gay Agenda? What Gay Agenda?** under X1.10, "The Doctor Dances"), at least one minority group is well-represented on the writing team, and this is the one aspect of life in Theme-Park History that is definitively shown to have been worse than today – but even then, it's a momentary lapse in episodes that tend to be romps. Perhaps they were trying to do one group at a time. In this regard, it's worth noting how the story-arc for Mickey Smith developed in Series 2. Although the doofus-to-action-hero plan was contingent on even getting a second series, the character became more interesting once people had seen Noel Clarke's performance and wrote for *that* rather than a vague notion. (In Series 1, the only time he's not written by Davies is the child version in X1.8, "Father's Day", and that's a generic kid-frightened-of-aliens.) Steven Moffat wrote Mickey as his usual nerdy-loser-mate, Toby Whithouse wrote him as Xander from *Buffy the Vampire Slayer* (there's a surprise), and Tom McRae set about finding ways for the character to make more sense alongside an alternate heroic version. With Rose red-shifting away from audience identification, Mickey was more useful and thus more rounded. Nonetheless, his skin-colour and his original uselessness in the first few episodes almost looked like cause-and-effect. Davies did more with Mickey once he'd seen Clarke in action, as in "Boom Town" (X1.11).

By the time the last scripts of Series 3 were being written (and, on the evidence of Greenhorn's being asked to attend location shooting of "The Lazarus Experiment", very hurriedly written at that), the executive producer knew exactly who was playing which role. This is why the Master's comment about ticking demographic boxes in X3.12, "The Sound of Drums" stands out. The Master can't possibly think that the Doctor would find that insulting – the Roger Delgado or Anthony Ainley versions might have scorned the whole travelling-with-apes business, but they'd have hardly used language like "demographic boxes", and it says far more about Davies than the character who's saying the line. Likewise the "Flown 'em all the way from prison" line later in the episode.

Davies thought he was slyly mocking the Simon Cowell *This Is Your Life* special (which had aired just a month earlier) and the unctious Irish presenter of the old series, Eamonn Andrews. In that, unexpected family reunions are foisted upon the unwitting celebrity guest, often including flights from Australia in an era when that was unimaginably costly and laborious. What we actually see in *Doctor Who* is a white psychopath gleefully humiliating a sobbing black family, who were stuffed into a Black Maria and dragged up to the *Valiant* in handcuffs. This is an image far more terrifying than the disco decimation scene. The latter is played as camp, cartoonish villainy that's safely out of the realistic realm and into the sort of stunt that Ainley would just miss pulling off with Concorde or killer trees; the other is entirely too plausible. It would be unpleasant whatever colour they were, but with a racial aspect that by now the writer can't have ignored (or claim innocence over), it is uncomfortable, at least to American viewers, in a "What was he thinking?" way.

Coming back to the Sontaran two-parter, though: Donna points out one awkward fact about the way the ex-TARDIS crew all seem to end up as soldiers. Martha's been in Torchwood and UNIT before going solo, which is, on the face of it, out of keeping with someone who trained to save lives. The idea that anyone who's been in contact with the Doctor becomes militarised extends

continued on Page 279...

Tocalfane descend in their billions. Everyone's seen Captain Jack dying and coming back and it's after he, the Doctor and Martha were announced as Public Enemies 1, 2 and 3 – the people the maniacal Prime Minister makes special efforts to stop after using death globes to kill the US President on live TV. The earliest the transmission could have ended is after Professor Lazarus has been exposed as the dupe of a fiend who blagged control of Britain and then announced the end of the world. Or, if it continued uninterrupted, the whole world saw Saxon shot by his wife after a long and baffling conversation about 70s *Doctor Who* continuity references with a suddenly-younger Doctor (and who has just delivered the rather alarming line "after the President was killed (...) everything back to normal"). What are the viewers at home to make of all of this? (Again, we have to suppose that the Doctor and company used the Archangel technology one last time to make everyone forget that he, Jack and Martha were involved, which is why they can end the story casually lounging about in public without being arrested.)

Aliens are keeping tabs on Earth enough to know that it's in a state of terminal extinction and isn't a tourist destination, but the massively unsubtle build-up of rockets across Russia armed with miniature black holes doesn't seem to bother anyone off-planet. And how exactly they define "terminal extinction", when the place is such a hive of industry, is unclear. Martha dismisses the idea of taking out the Archangel satellites because they don't have 15 ground-to-air missiles... except that there are 10,000 of those ripe for the taking in Southern England alone, each equipped with tiny singularity-bombs. Obviously, Martha has a good reason to need Archangel up and running for a while, but nobody else thinks of this strategy. Or of just pointing one at the *Valiant*.

We have to wonder a bit about the eventual fate of Martha's phone. She gives it to the Doctor shortly after having called Tom Milligan (who's transferred from Paediatrics to A&E overnight) and hung up. Never mind if Milligan was curious and rang her back, presumably *everyone* in her busy social life will be calling the TARDIS. Nonetheless, she apparently tracks down Tom without that phone and they get engaged, so there's a whole stalking storyline involving a woman with access to UNIT's super-whizz-bang computers (see Series 4 and *Torchwood*) that we're perhaps fortunate not to have seen.

If the sun's only been up for about half an hour over Norway, how is anyone in New York sitting in a diner in broad daylight? It's 3.00am there, as even Trinity Wells seems to know. The image of time reversing seems to indicate that months and days are the same length, with the sun and moon whipping around the Earth. (With their many problems on this score – just wait for the Christmas episode coming soon – it may have been worth explaining the heliocentric Copernican model of the solar system to someone at The Mill.)

And Jack tells the Doctor that he, too trusted Saxon, with the implication that he voted for the Master. Is Jack actually *allowed* to vote, given that Gwen Cooper couldn't find any evidence that he exists? Did the people at the polling booths in Cardiff Central not spot an American with an RAF greatcoat trying to vote in council elections, Welsh Assembly seats or for an MEP? (This highlights a big anomaly in *Torchwood*, by the way: Cardiff, cosmopolitan and hip as it is, has a fairly small population and someone dressed that distinctively and looking like TV's John Barrowman would be noticed, especially over 140 years.)

A minor point but signifying a lot that's puzzling about the Master's use of his time over the last 18 months: his CD player skips straight to the second chorus of "I Can't Decide", as if aware that this is going out on BBC1 at prime-time, rather than subject the Doctor to any of the rudeness in the lyrics up to that point. The Master, in between his busy schedule of becoming a Cabinet minister, marrying an heiress, constructing a Paradox Machine and designing Archangel and the *Valiant*, took time out to listen to recent albums just in case he managed to cage the Doctor and needed an appropriate taunting album track. Perhaps he was trying to avoid the bad press Gordon Brown got when attempting to seem *au courant* by mentioning the Arctic Monkeys, but... the Scissor Sisters? Almost the last act to name-drop if you're attempting to avoid anyone spotting anything odd about your meteoric rise.

All right, all right... the whole process of the Doctor turning into first a grey sad-eyed blob then Martha's fairy godmother needs addressing. (Ideally, "addressing" as in putting in a box, taping it up tight and posting to somewhere far away.) First off, why do the good thoughts of millions of people who've never seen him make the Doctor appear as he was beforehand, fully dressed?

Martha – What Went Wrong?

continued from Page 277...

even to *Jackie bleedin' Tyler* in X4.13, "Journey's End". This is another of Davies's *idée's fixe* (explored first in the *New Adventures*, specifically *No Future* by Paul Cornell), and even the attempts to have *The Sarah Jane Adventures* as a counterweight fumbles in this team-up episode. Once the botched romance storyline with the Doctor was over, the only thing to have Martha do was, apparently, have military anti-alien agencies employ her as an ex-TARDIS crewmember. Going back to her *actual* job, the one she's trained for over seven years, wasn't even considered. No matter that her traumatised family needed her to be around and re-establish normality, she's off getting weapons training and swanning off to Cardiff. Rather than have her experiences while travelling a devastated world form a basis for a second year's character-development, they use it as the sales-pitch for tie-in books and have her back, right as rain, a few episodes later.

The most obvious sign that their strategy wasn't working was the haste with which they issued statements that Martha leaving the TARDIS wasn't the end. The plan had obviously been for this character's popularity to slingshot her into *Torchwood* and Series 4's developments, making her return Big News. Instead, her first *Torchwood* episode makes good use of her, but then she's just there while the recently-dead Owen Harper hogs the limelight, whilst her *Doctor Who* revisits are about like when Harry Sullivan was in 13.4, "The Android Invasion". (Both get duplicated by evil invaders, the difference being that Ian Marter finds a new way to do that after the near-identical "Terror of the Zygons", whereas in X4.5, "The Poison Sky", we're supposed to feel sorry for a Sontaran weapon because it's played by That Nice Freema Off The Telly.)

However much this "arc" was planned, it looks apologetic, like an afterthought. There is almost nothing for her to do in "The Doctor's Daughter" (X4.6), so we have the embarrassing subplot of the Hath adopting her as a mascot. In "The Stolen Earth" (X4.12), she's a Londoner in the New York UNIT HQ – a potentially interesting set-up they haven't got time to explore, and instead she jaunts home to mum (who's still on her own in that big house all day; maybe it's Thursday). The rest of the story has the Osterhagen red herring, so she gets lots of heroic stuff and even manages to make Rose feel left out, but all eyes are on Donna when the actual resolution comes. Finally, Martha shows up as a freelance alien-hunter, with a big gun and a fierce new hairdo...and a husband. Under normal circumstances, the fact that the two non-white characters left standing land up marrying each other would be considered unrealistic (in contemporary Britain, at least), but – given how much what they'd each experienced would affect any normal relationship – it's sort of like Ian and Barbara only having each other to talk to.

The lack of any clear thought or directives beyond making Martha not be Rose is the big problem. The idea of a career-woman who earns the Doctor's trust, admits to herself that he's not interested in her and leaves but comes back is – as we've said – Tegan all over again, but she lacks Tegan's stroppiness (just as well, as this would play into another racial stereotype), so almost all her character is her career-mindedness, and that's chucked out once she comes back. Once they realised that anything out-of-the-ordinary, when played by a non-white performer, would be risky, they went all-out to make Martha everywoman, i.e. bland. Then she wonders why the Doctor isn't noticing her. Instead, if they had thought about what a black companion would do differently and how to make this a viable character, with a plausible background, they could have made a worse mess of it – but she would have been more than just not-Rose. The problem, as we have said before, is that the role of capital C-Companion is a job-title, a plot-function or an action-figure audition, but not a character *per se*.

Undoing the Master's magic age-ray is one thing, but providing a shirt, tie, suit and even plimsolls is preposterous. It also makes him able to fly and immune to lasers, even though those abilities weren't part of Martha's tale.

And what actually happened before this? Fair enough when the Master aged the Tennant Doctor to what he'd be like after another century on, but then... the dialogue suggests that by suspending the Doctor's ability to regenerate, they can show what he looks like as a "real" 900 year old. Is that simply adding 800 years to the 100 already piled on, or is the regeneration-suspension retroactive and the cute little grey thing is what the Hartnell Doctor would have looked like if he hadn't transmogrified? And how do we square this against the eleventh Doctor ultimately living about a thousand years without turning into Gollum? (As we will investigate in a later volume, and have introduced in **The Obvious Question: How Old Is He?** under 16.5, "The Power of Kroll", this "900" number is manifestly a fib.)

The Master's message to Martha is from a fixed CCTV camera aboard the *Valiant*, but we see her reacting in horror to the Doctor being turned into a big-eyed grey gnome – something we can see because the narrative switches back to *Doctor Who*-normal, but which would have been out-of-shot for the camera relaying it to Martha. What she would have seen is Saxon pointing a screwdriver at an off-screen wheelchair.

The Doctor insists that he "permanently" locked the TARDIS's coordinates, so it can only travel between 2008 (give or take 18 months) and Utopia. The Master never seems to solve this navigational limitation, and yet the Doctor doesn't seem to have any trouble reversing this later on. And even with a year to think about it, there's a long way between the Doctor not wanting to unpick the Master's alterations to the TARDIS in case of causing bigger temporal problems and sending Jack in there to solve the problem with a machine-gun.

After the trouble the Master's sponsorship of Lazarus caused him, and with previous experience of the Master's faked deaths (notably "The Deadly Assassin"), isn't it a little remiss of the Doctor not to remove the Master's rather conspicuous green ring before cremation? And wouldn't such a ring, after maybe a day on top of a bonfire, be a little too warm for Mrs Trefusis to pick up? (All of that, and we now have to imagine an earlier version of the Master – possibly Anthony Ainley's for maximum comedy value – leafing through a Gallifreyan *Mother Goose* to find a lot of fairy-tale monsters to taunt the Doctor with over the centuries; the Hybrid, the Toclafane, Pikachu, the Underpants Gnomes...)

Critique ("The Sound of Drums" and "Last of the Time Lords") And it was going so well...

If you're looking at this as a three-part serial within a series, then it's a steady decline until the climax of "Last of the Time Lords", at which point it all falls apart. You're watching reruns of this week after week (or day after day, depending upon network scheduling), then the individual episodes in the two-part finale are more different than entire stories in a Moffat series. Certainly, moreso than his own three-part story (one with almost alarming similarities to this, especially X10.8, "The Lie of the Land").

This is, on the one hand, bold storytelling that opens the story's scope and range from Martha's flat to the entire solar system, and shifts the genre from *24*-style conspiracy thriller to space opera. On the other hand, the quality of the scripts plummets between episodes, and the "well, it looked clever on paper" method for defeating the Master was met with hoots of derision on first broadcast. Regrettably, time has not improved it. After the deft way Russell T Davies handled so many conflicting demands on the writing for "Utopia" and "The Sound of Drums", seeing him drop a ball is a bit disappointing. Dropping three or four in rapid succession right at the end is heartbreaking.

Last year's climax had left only one way to go, which was *bigger*. Getting a story larger than Daleks and Cybermen devastating London, and Rose being trapped in another universe forever, would have been hard whatever else came along... and in this regard, there's nothing to fault. Everyone does at least as much as is asked of them. David Tennant, John Barrowman and John Simm are among the biggest stars on British television right now so the story becomes an ensemble piece, especially once Martha takes centre stage. Freema Agyeman shows why the team had such faith in her. Everyone is equal to what the story and dialogue demand, but Alexandra Moen deserves a special mention for going way beyond the scant lines Lucy Saxon gets to glue the end of the story together.

We've been a bit sniffy about some of Murray Gold's decisions in earlier episodes, but here he's tasked with making a story go from relatively light-hearted pranks to a totalitarian regime, and he has played up to the instructions to make it "epic" with restraint and a degree of ingenuity. Imagine Vivian Rook's death scene with the sort of music he gave us in Series 1. We know from the CD releases that he does Big Themes, the way commercial film scores do, but there are moments where his choices were surprising. At this stage, he's capable of doing anything the scripts and directors ask and often adds a bit more.

By ratcheting up the odds against Our Heroes in vaguely-plausible increments across the first episode – presenting each increase in scale to us in turn – episode two sweeps us along briskly, pausing occasionally to savour Simm's cheekiness in the face of the press, his alien collaborators, the US President, the Doctor and then the World. The only time the Doctor isn't on the back foot is when he and his friends are being inconspicuous, the precise opposite of his usual methodology. The last time the two Time Lords were aware of each other's presence in contemporary Earth, but second-guessing rather than debating, was the start of "The Mind of Evil" (when the Doctor had the full resources of UNIT and the Chinese Army, but the Master had a rubber mask and a GPO workman's hut).

Seen this way, the script is a succession of challenges met. How do you top Air Force One? Have Cloudbase. How do you escalate from a bomb in Martha's flat? Have her parents arrested and armed riot-police shoot at Martha's car. How do you go one bigger than the Master as Prime Minister? Have him assassinate the US President live on global television. How do you raise the stakes from a snowstorm of killer aliens cheerfully massacring 1/10 of the planet's population? Er...

And there's the rub. If you take matters this far, no subsequent present-day story will look like the present day *unless* there's a massive cop-out. You only have two choices: a reset button or a series about the post-Saxon world. The latter might have been an option for *Torchwood* alone. Had *Doctor Who* been cancelled, it could have gone out on a massive downer. Next year, they avoid this by having *The Sarah Jane Adventures* firmly set in a world where everyone remembered the Daleks dragging Earth across space and interring the population. It could *maybe* be possible to have everyone mind-wiped by Archangel (and all the deaths and statues inspiring conspiracy theorists for later episodes), but opting for the dumb *Superman* ending was almost as bad as Martha waking up and finding it was all a dream.

Apart from anything else, it's an uneven tone, with so grating and crass an end after so much tension, insight and menace. By the time the Master appears at the start of "Last of the Time Lords", he has stopped being the Lord of Misrule and become a genuine Doctor-sized threat who has to be stopped at any cost. Lucy, formerly a gleeful conspirator, biting the heads off jelly-babies, is now a victim. The treatment of Martha's family goes down really badly in America, but to the home audience it looks like a grinding humiliation and bait for the fugitive Dr Jones, of a piece with the infantilised Doctor in a wheelchair and then a bird cage.

In an odd way, the "Tinkerbelle" ending refutes the idea in "Gridlock" that faith imprisons people, *and* rejects the idea at the end of *The Second Coming* that the mass of ordinary humanity is more powerful and important than any messiah could be. This could be why it seems so awkward; the author isn't entirely sure. On the other hand, using the antagonist's trap against him and goading him into going just slightly too far is a classic Doctor-like move. Everyone on Earth believes in the Doctor – as it's only temporary that could have worked, that belief restores him to normal (again, we need that for the series to continue) then... well, if it had resulted in the Master reverting to Gollum, maybe it might have been in keeping. But giving the Doctor super-powers beyond anything ever seen in the series is deflating. Even then, the plan relies on everyone on a ravaged Earth having faith in a Hero, an alien with amazing powers who'll fix it all for us. It rubs up against the main idea of the Davies series – that the Doctor's main superpower is getting people to live up to their own potential.

This focus on where it went wrong is misleading. Everything leading to that point had been bold and memorable in the right ways, combining images and concepts in a way only *Doctor Who* could do, and extracting the maximum dramatic potential (rather than melodramatic) without it being forced. For all that the seemingly endless string of epilogues get a bit tiresome, they needed to be there, and only go flat because the climax wasn't strong enough to support them. If nothing else, "The Sound of Drums" proved that you could get the whole of Britain – or near enough

– excited by seeing Time Lords in funny collars and a big city inside a snowglobe, something that would have been toecurlingly fannish and up itself in the late 80s. This in an episode with the most grubbily plausible political thriller elements to date and a child-friendly farce about a *Looney Tunes* Time Lord supervillain taking over No.10. The main problem with the "Tinkerbelle" scene is simply that, up to that point, this was about as good as it gets.

The Lore

Written by Russell T Davies. Directed by Colin Teague. Viewing figures ("The Sound of Drums"): (BBC1) 7.5 million, (BBC3 repeats) 1.1 and 0.6 million. AI scores of 87%, then 90% and 85%. Viewing figures ("Last of the Time Lords"): (BBC1) 8.6 million, (BBC3 repeats) 0.8 and 0.5 million. AI scores at 88% throughout, apparently.

Repeats and Overseas Promotion "The Sound of Drums": *Que Tapent les Tambours, Der Klang der Trommeln.* "Last of the Time Lords": *Le Dernier Seigneur du Temps, Die Letze Time Lord.*

Alternate Versions The version first broadcast seemed to lead straight into the Christmas special, with the crashing *Titanic* as the last shot. Then *Children in Need* happened, and a short scene with Peter Davison was inserted between the two; see the entry on "Time Crash".

More significantly, there is a long sequence at the start of "Last of the Time Lords" that was specifically written to be cut-able for overseas broadcasts. The Master gets up one morning, puts on a track by hen-party favourites The Scissor Sisters, and dances around the bridge of *Valiant* taunting the Doctor while singing along to the lyric: "I can't decide whether you should live or die". The short introduction to the episode, of Earth being quarantined by some un-named Galactic agency, is also removed from some versions (notably the French-dubbed one), as are Martha's visits to Milligan and Docherty once time is set right.

Production

Along with the Daleks, every journalist or casual viewer expected that the Master would be coming back as soon as possible. Many actors asked if they could play the role, including most of the guest cast for the first three years. Davies steadfastly denied this, claiming that the concept was a bit tired. His *real* problem was that he believed the character ought to disrupt the series – a large-scale threat requiring the viewers to have some idea of what the Doctor could handle, rather than being an integral part of the show from day one. He had been chastened by the mishandling of the 1996 TV Movie, which put little effort into establishing basic *Doctor Who*-ness (beyond a few meaningless shibboleths for a subset of fandom) before unleashing the Master.

Davies had grown up watching the black and white episodes, so he knew that the advent of Roger Delgado as the original Master had been a shocking change of pace, but he had drifted away from the series around the time Anthony Ainley showed up. However, after steadily ramping up the size and threat-level of the Doctor's adversaries, up to and including a hitherto-impossible Dalek-Cybermen collision in London (X2.12, "Army of Ghosts"), one way to amplify the menace for the third series finale remained. With "Human Nature" (X3.8) having introduced the watch as a method of hiding a Time Lord amid humans, almost all the requisite pieces were in place...

• The Toclafane were, as you may recall, a race devised for Series 1, held in reserve if the rights to the Daleks were withheld (see our educated guesses on what else might have happened in **Was Series 2 Supposed to be Like This?** under X2.11, "Fear Her"). The plans for Series 3 were being finalised as the second was ending transmission in mid-2006, allowing Davies to seed the "Mr Saxon" line in X3.0, "The Runaway Bride". (He'd had the name "Harold Saxon" filed away from an abortive project a decade or so earlier, as it suggested a certain rigidity of thought and steadfastly conservative Englishness, so was ideal for a villain.) "Voodoo Child" by Rogue Traders (featuring former *Neighbours* star Natalie Bassingthwaighte on vocals, and based around the riff from "Pump It Up" by Elvis Costello) was being plugged relentlessly on Radio 1 at the time, so was unavoidable for three or four weeks. The hookline (also the title of their second album, now widely available in branches of Oxfam) was "Here Come the Drums". This and a half-memory of *I, Claudius* fed into the Master's new justification for his mania. (Script Editor Simon Winstone was given the job of securing the rights to use the song but, when the scripts arrived, he noticed that Davies had completely forgotten his original inspiration.)

• The other main concern with concluding the third year was making Martha finally step out from Rose's shadow, saving the world in a way the shop-girl-turned-action-hero couldn't have. This led to the bold step of skipping a year between episodes and keeping secret the surprise slingshot ending where Martha leaves and becomes part of both UNIT and Torchwood. A slight problem arrived when someone realised that nobody had checked if Reggie Yates was actually available for the whole time. As host of Radio 1's chart show, live on Sunday evenings, and a regular TV host and live performer, getting him to play Martha's brother had been a genuine coup even though BBC1 had just cancelled *Top of the Pops* (his other regular berth). As it turned out, he was only available for one day on the second episode's shoot, where Leo ought to have assisted Martha in uncovering the Toclafanes' secret, so it was substantially rewritten and Leo was sent to Brighton to lie low.

• As we said last story, John Simm's schedule was beginning to free up after he had left *Life on Mars,* but this was partially because he was rarely seeing his young son and had a daughter who was born eight weeks before recording for his *Doctor Who* episodes started. Simm was of comparable age and – in TV drama terms – status to David Tennant, so made a plausible match as a sort of anti-Doctor. As Julie Gardner was executive producer on both series, she could discuss with Simm the possibility of him playing the Master without anyone becoming suspicious. The idea of the new Master wearing a leather jacket was quickly scotched as Sam Tyler, Simm's character in *Life on Mars*, was associated with that look (although look at the bridge of the *Valiant* and you'll see a familiar red trimphone). Instead, they mirrored Tennant's Doctor by making Saxon/ the Master "spivvy" with a suit and tie (black, of course), but slightly flashy and untrustworthy. His consort was supposed to carry a slight air of Jackie Kennedy. There were conversations about the Master having a beard; Simm was keen, but Davies thought that the tabloid press would make snide comments and disrupt the Saxon plan. (The recent Fleet Street kerfuffle over Jeremy Corbyn indicates that this was right.)

• Colin Teague had impressed the production team and been given two *Torchwood* episodes to direct, plus the pilot for *The Sarah Jane Adventures*, so it was only a matter of time (specifically, his getting any) before he became the first director to work on all three series. Prior to this, he had directed a few episodes of *Holby City* and a series of low-budget thrillers (*Spivs, Shooters* and *The Last Drop*) with collaborator Gary Young. Teague was responsible for Block Eight, the series finale.

• The script contained a suggestion that Downing Street could be completely remodelled after it was flattened (X1.5, "World War Three"), but the same location they'd used then, Hensol Castle, was available and therefore was used anyway (not that this was inevitable, as it had been so costly and complicated last time). The gas vapour in the Cabinet Room scenes, you'll be happy to hear, was completely harmless CO_2. Later, Hensol Castle was made to look *Friends*-ish when the American students were slaughtered during the "decimation".

• The Toclafane were usually practical props, but their first appearance was CGI. As originally scripted, their method of execution was more savagely playful: hooking victims, lifting them bodily off the floor and shaking them to death like dogs with chew-toys (hence the length of Vivian Rook's dying scream). As the shoot continued, this was one of the casualties of the slight overspend on the sets, but it also saved the time and effort on wire harnesses for President Winters or the customers at the café. As a cheeky cost-cutting exercise and thank-you, the news crew following Saxon around and making his broadcasts for him are the *Doctor Who Confidential* team and the real boom-mic operator from *Doctor Who*.

• Location work on Monday, 19th February, happened at Cwrt-y-Vil Road, Penarth, where they'd found houses for Martha's parents. Colin Teague cast his wife as the young mother watching Saxon on telly (sadly, we don't know who the baby is). Another camera captured Yates's seaside cameo (the Esplanade at Penarth, not Brighton). Then the second unit, with Susie Liggat, headed off to Buckinghamshire for Sharon Osbourne's endorsement of Mr Saxon. The 20th started off at the same Penarth location, for the black van scene, and Martha's memorable stunt driving, down Queen's Road (one of Agyeman's favourite moments in the role). In one of the scenes, practical effects manager Danny Hargreaves was crouched at John Barrowman's feet, detonating the window-squibs for the shoot-out using the dialogue as his cues.

• Thursday, 22nd February saw John Simm at the Millennium Centre celebrating his election and making snide remarks about Doctors. Roundwood, Llanedeyrn had the right suburban shops and underpasses for the scenes of the Doctor and company abandoning Martha's car, plus his phone calls with the Master (it's the same underpass where Elton Pope came with pizza for Jackie in X2.10, "Love & Monsters"). Simm, on his day off, fielded the call from Tennant for the other half of the conversation he'd had at Hensol. Liggat had taken her second unit down to London to record the McFly and Ann Widdecombe endorsements, at Universal Music and the Houses of Parliament.

Work on Tuesday the 27th included the big showdown – which entailed the Doctor's rapid aging via screwdriver, and was captured at five frames per second instead of the usual twenty-five. The relative size of the rival Time Lords' screwdrivers led to ribald texts and comments. Just to reiterate how much things can be shot out of order, Tennant then went off to the TARDIS set and changed his suit for Martha's exit scene. He was back on the *Valiant* flight deck, in old man mode this time, the next day.

• The scenes of the Master wheeling the Doctor around were taken with a camera strapped to the wheelchair, with Simm pushing both. By that point, Tennant was so used to the prostheses that he was occasionally unsettled by the reactions of people who could see him walking around normally in it. Tennant captured the final session of ageing via prosthetics for his video diary – after a couple of days' practice, the make-up now only took two and a half hours.

• On Friday, 2nd March, they blew up Splott – University Place proved a good location for the external of Martha's flat, and then it exploding. The windows were carefully replaced for the propane burst (which was about the only warm thing that day).

• In their final embrace, Simm was slightly scratched by Tennant's stubble, apparently. Tennant was visibly upset by the death of the other last Time Lord (Barrowman's comment to his fellow Scot: "you big Jessie!"). Tennant stayed late that day to record the *Titanic* crashing into the TARDIS set, with a minimum crew for secrecy.

• An early draft had a full Viking funeral with a boat on a lake, as per X6.1, "The Impossible Astronaut", for the dead Master's send off. Ten rings were made for Saxon. Tennant and Simm were genuinely so close to a real cliff when rolling on the ground, Tennant lost a contact lens. (One take was ruined by the sound of an ice-cream van playing "Yakkety Sax" and the leads laughing.)

• The abandoned warehouse where the Doctor, Martha and Jack are eating chips is actually a British Rail warehouse, Cathays, Cardiff, illuminated from outside by 22 lighting rigs. The leads stuffed down cold chips, while the fire that they had going was useful for fiery closeups (needed for the Doctor looking at the Master's pyre). So that's how John Barrowman celebrated his fortieth birthday (well, there was a Dalek-shaped cake and champers after a long night in a damp warehouse).

• William Hughes as the young Master was recorded at Friar's Point (incoming script editor Gary Russell asked that the boy should be done up like the Time Lords in "The War Games"). The ceremonial collars were initially vetoed for cost reasons, as the original fibre glass ones from 1976 were in bits, but the ones from the Exhibition were available and in better nick. Nonetheless, the sparkliness was downplayed. The graphics department devised new sigils to replace the Prydonian Seal on the collars, in keeping with the new series' policy of suggesting lettering and clock components and traces from particle accelerators, although the seal is on the floor of the stone Schism. Tennant and Julie Gardner tried them on for size (as one does) before they left the studio complex. Both of these locations are a few minutes' walk from the locations for the railway siding in "The Doctor Dances" (X1.10) and most of "Delta and the Bannermen" (24.3).

• No doubt you've all heard that it was Tracie Simpson's red-nailed hand pulling the Master's ring out of the fire, almost a year on from her cameo as not-Donna-really to distract onlookers from what was happening on a London rooftop (X2.13, "Doomsday"; X3.0, "The Runaway Bride"). Davies had claimed, probably accurately (when you're the showrunner, lying is part of the job description) that he wrote this tag scene without knowing who or what the female hand was, and why this was happening. He just wanted a way out after killing off the Top Baddie and a release from the episode's general gloom.

• One thing that caused a crimp in production: Colin Teague fell down his stairs and was rushed to hospital with a back injury. (The crew nicknamed the unfortunate director "Tumbling Teague" after this.) Graeme Harper was quickly drafted to finish production. As it happened, the next few days of shooting was booked for NEG Glass again, so nothing unfamiliar to him or the crew.

• Former Gelth voice Zoe Thorne – X1.3, "The Unquiet Dead" – was one of the Toclafane voices. Another was Gerald Logan, Father of Mine in episodes eight and nine.

• The new series began transmission on March the 31st, so the regular cast were hardly able to take a breath with the promotional work they needed to do (not least *Totally Doctor Who*). Neither of the leads was leaving Cardiff for long anyway, as Agyeman was secretly signed up for *Torchwood*.

• Although the budget was so tight that some effects scenes were designated as optional, these were generally the ones the teams were most keen to do. Peter McKinstry had already worked on a view of Gallifrey for the Dorling Kindersley book *The Art of Doctor Who,* so some time was saved. (There were rough plans from Series 1, used more to add cohesion to the look of Doctorish things such as the sonic screwdriver, the Gallifreyan script and, later, the watch from "Human Nature".) Similarly, Neill Gorton of Millennium Effects used the prostheses for Tennant as John Smith aged 70 as a template for the aged Doctor in this episode, but didn't repeat the look. This effect was one of the potentially sacrificial ones, as they had a perfectly good "old Tennant" latex piece.

• As luck would have it, the episode showing a new Prime Minister was shown just as Britain got one for real: after 11 years, Tony Blair stood down in favour of his colleague/ rival/ secret weapon Gordon Brown, who had been Chancellor of the Exchequer for all this time. This resulted in a lot of news coverage of the Blair years in retrospect and live feeds of Ten Downing Street, so *Doctor Who* slotted in almost seamlessly. That week's *Doctor Who Confidential* cheekily used Blair's original campaign song, "Things Can Only Get Better" by D:Ream for a montage of Saxon campaign material.

• The day of the second half's broadcast, the compilation version of A5, "The Infinite Quest" was shown on BBC1. The London Gay Pride march was timed to reach Trafalgar Square just as the episode went out, and they had a giant screen on which to show it. Whereas the secret of the Master's return was barely a surprise on broadcast, Martha walking out on the Doctor was and – with so many half-right press stories about Agyeman's sacking doing the rounds – the BBC had to hurry out a release about Martha's future career, Kylie's Christmas aboard the *Titanic* and the impending return of Donna Noble.

• Agyeman was back on our screens sooner than that: like Simm, she had got tickets for the Glastonbury Festival. BBC3, covering the three-day bash, found her and asked her into the commentary booth for her impressions of the event. Simm and Tennant were later seen at another music event: the *Jools Holland Annual Hootenanny*, broadcast around the stroke of midnight at New Year's Eve, showed them in the audience bopping to Madness, the Kaiser Chiefs, Eddie Floyd, Mika, Paul McCartney and – it being December 2007 – Kylie (see next story for more on her barnstorming comeback).

X3.13a: "Time Crash"

(16th November, 2007)

Which One is This? David Tennant goes *squee* about meeting Peter Davison. For seven minutes.

Firsts and Lasts For the benefit of those who've come in late, it's the first time we've had a multi-Doctor story in the new series. (The last one was A3, "Dimensions in Time," if that counts at all, and the last proper one was 22.4, "The Two Doctors".) And as such it's the first unimpeachable evidence that this is *the* Doctor, not someone who took over his identity in the Time War after the one we were following 1963-89 died. (There was a bit of speculation on that.) Significantly (i.e., we've got a whole essay on what it means), this is the first time both Doctors have apparently come away from such a meeting remembering how it went.

We might also mention that this is the first time the Doctor's ever mentioned shaving; this seems innocuous enough *now*, but means we can't claim complete lack of warning for "Day of the Moon" (X6.2, and see 14.1, "The Masque of Mandragora"). We get a last use of the old arrangement of the theme-tune, although the new one was already being dubbed on to the forthcoming Christmas episode. It's the first time Peter Davison's had his name in the titles.[57]

Plus. This is the one and only time Davison wears a genuine stick of celery in his lapel.

Watch Out For...

• Just to show you how self-aware the show had become, the fifth Doctor asks if the Master still has a rubbish beard and rolls his eyes upon being told "well, a wife!"

• The music's all recycled cues, but the advent of Davison is the occasion for the 80s-style synths to kick in.

• There's no in-text explanation for David Tennant giving Peter Davison a heartfelt look and saying "You were my Doctor"; it's as meta-canonical a moment as the "Happy Christmas to all of you at home" (3.4, "The Daleks' Master Plan") or "after all... that's how it all started" (20.7, "The Five Doctors"). But never fear... since this is for charidee and only seven minutes long, they can get away with it.

The Continuity

The (tenth) Doctor He thinks that meeting his past self is brilliant, and only remembers after a lot of grinning and teasing that these events are likely to destroy the universe in five minutes. He's sufficiently enthusiastic to neglect mentioning that he's the future version of himself, and in fact spends most of the short standing around watching his past figure out what's going on. [This is, after all, how he remembers the incident from the other side.] After they've sorted everything out, the Doctor indicates that many of his current habits (trainers, glasses, going squeaky-voiced when he's a bit agitated) were self-consciously nicked from this particular past self.

Nevertheless, he's ambivalent on the celery: 'Fair play to you, not a lot of men can carry off a decorative vegetable.' He comments on the bone-structure that his younger self will one day be shaving. [This could indicate that regeneration leaves the facial bone-structure largely unaltered, which would explain a lot about the noses they all seem to have, but not the different jawlines. It's more likely the first hint that they'll both remember this encounter, improbable as that seems.]

Despite remembering from his past how he saves the TARDISes, he's not certain at what stage in his life the fifth Doctor actually experienced this scene [and we're not told].

The (fifth) Doctor He's in his usual cricket outfit and celery, but a different hat worn with the back of the brim raised like a trilby. [Except in two shots, that is. Assuming he never changed his clothes in-between stories – if there had ever *been* a gap between televised adventures when Tegan was around – it may be significant that he's not wearing the Gloucestershire B-Team jumper. This makes it unlikely to be any time after 21.1, "Warriors of the Deep". His lack of a sonic screwdriver puts it after 19.4, "The Visitation".]

He's wearing a genuine stick of celery. [Back in the 1980s, Davison spent most of his tenure wearing a Block Transfer Computation-generated stalk of artificial celery; see 19.1, "Castrovalva". This must have smelled the same to him, as his rationale for wearing it is neurochemical – 21.6, "The Caves of Androzani". He swaps this once on screen, in "Enlightenment" (20.5), a story where everything is imagined and rum's main effect is to maintain hypnotically-engendered acceptance of the "reality" of ships sailing in the outer Solar System. If he had ever worn a real stick, as anyone who tried cosplaying the character would know, it would wilt and smell funny within about three hours and he was often trapped for longer than that without the plant seeming to get rubbery.

[These days, within the parameters spelled out in the last paragraph, "Time Crash", for the fifth Doctor, could otherwise occur just about any time that he's by himself in the console room – something we never see when Davison is officially the Doctor, save for his short spell of refitting just before the start of "The Five Doctors". Actually, if both Doctors are fiddling with the console design when this link-up happens, this is a lot more plausible. However, for the fifth Doctor to remember this incident in the same story that "icebergs" of his past are breaking off, and meeting his former selves messes up his memory, is even less likely. See the essay.]

He's heard of LINDA [X2.10, "Love and Monsters"] and seems exhausted with fans who think he's wonderful. [And fanboys *really* must rub the fifth Doctor the wrong way. It's in character for other Doctors to have the occasional bout of shouting 'You ham-fisted bun-vendor' or 'Harry Sullivan is an imbecile!' (or suchlike – 8.1, "Terror of the Autons"; 12.5, "Revenge of the Cybermen"), but hearing this one say 'ranting skinny idiot' sounds a bit harsh. (This is a Doctor who put up with Adric, after all.) In fact, he's considerably more tetchy here than we ever saw in the 80s, which indicates a lot of biting-back when Tegan was getting on everyone's nerves.]

Why Not Mention the War?

There is a tradition that only the chronologically latest Doctor and his entourage remember the events of any multi-Doctor adventure. Certainly, we know from both "School Reunion" (X2.3) and *The Sarah Jane Adventures* that Sarah doesn't recall anything of "The Five Doctors" (20.7), to the extent that she has apparently forgotten that she met Tegan when looking her up (see *SJA:* "Death of the Doctor" in the appendix to Volume 9).

The first two times this happened, there were Time Lords involved. We know from their first-ever appearance (6.7, "The War Games") that memory-wiping is part of their method of making history come out right. (It goes deeper than just cover-ups, though; the mechanism the War Chief uses to abduct soldiers from across Earth's past, and to keep them in their rightful time-zones, is connected to their ability to perceive and remember the truth of where they really are.) In 22.4, "The Two Doctors", we have *three* possible reasons why none of this is familiar to the current incarnation; his earlier self is dosed up with cyrolanamode, then changed into an Androgum – a transformation that rewrites all his future lives until it is corrected – and then the Time Lords take him back out of his own timeline (see **Is There a Season 6B?** with that story). The main purpose of the whole Zygon sub-plot in X7.15, "The Day of the Doctor" is to allow the memory-wipe in the UNIT Black Museum to mess with everyone's heads, even on top of the Moment's influence and the multiple TARDISes and the two earlier Doctors being just ahead of regenerations. Although, typically, this aspect is itself forgotten in the broadcast version (until followed up in a peculiar two-parter in Series 9) and we just skip to the Doctors arranging to lose Gallifrey down the back of the settee.

The more useful point is the way that the most recent Doctor starts to remember the events as soon as the whirly time-slip opens up in the National Gallery. This seems to chime with the sequence of events in "Time Crash", which begins, as usual for this sort of thing, with David Tennant repeating "what?" Evidently, until that moment, the existence of this eight minutes of his past was clouded to him. Nonetheless, the rest of the episode is him observing his former self as if reminiscing. The Cloister Bell sounds, at which point the tenth Doctor says "That's my cue!" That's significant; it's not that he's dimly aware of a former gap in his memory that fills in as he (re)experiences the events, he knows all about it from the second the titles end. Compare this to the situation in "The Two Doctors", where the story ends with the sixth Doctor presumably having just one memory of this, what with all the wiping and time-stream shenanigans. With "Time Crash", we are clearly in a different situation from any other multi-Doctor story.

Or *are* we? The oddest line in "The Five Doctors" is when the second Doctor, encountering the imminently retiring Brigadier, consoles his one-day-to-be old friend about his successor: "don't worry, mine wasn't too promising either". In "The Three Doctors" (10.1), the Doctor manages a sort of telepathic (or trans-temporal) conference to exchange information in a hurry. This presumably includes some basic background about, for example, the third Doctor being exiled with a disabled TARDIS after being apprehended by the Time Lords. It would be peculiar if all three Doctors thus knew the basic plot of, to pick one example of many, "The Claws of Axos" (8.3) and remembered it in such detail that the third Doctor knew exactly what to do and say when finding himself inside that sequence of events. Nonetheless, the second Doctor and the Brigadier reminisce about Omega, so when the first two Doctors were returned to their timelines, some memory of meeting the future Doctor and having the President of the Time Lords beg for his/ their help must have remained.

It's been speculated that the regenerative process includes a mnemonic sweep, and it's certainly true that the third Doctor had forgotten all about recorders, and the eleventh Doctor – bizarrely – seems to have forgotten what cricket even *is* (X5.11, "The Lodger"). Another possibility is that the TARDIS does the cover-up to avoid paradoxes. At the end of "The Ultimate Foe" (23.4), the Doctor and Mel leave together, despite him having not met her yet, and after he has twice seen a future adventure in which she had just taken part (23.3, "Terror of the Vervoids"). Presumably, his memory is manipulated so that when it actually happens (if it ever does), he wouldn't be going by what he saw his future self do (or not do) on the Matrix screen when preparing his defence or watching an edited version in court.

(The multi-Master story, X10.12, "The Doctor Falls", isn't much help here. On the one hand, Missy expects that she won't recall any of this because of some doubletalk explanation of coalescing timelines, even though she remembers where she is

continued on Page 289...

He doesn't recognise his future self at all. [So much for the "Time Lord recognition" the new-series Doctors alluded to in X1.6, "Dalek" and X3.12, "The Sound of Drums". Then again, here the psychic impression is of *himself*, so it would be like not noticing your own BO. Missy never spotted "Mr Razor" (X10.11, "World Enough and Time") even though she, of all people, would identify the smell of latex.] When faced with someone he believes to be a lunatic fan, he agrees he is 'pretty sort of marvellous'. He thinks that creating a simultaneous supernova/ black hole is such a clever bit of TARDIS flying, no one else he's ever met could possibly have done it. [We can only presume that Romana would never have forgotten to put the shields back up in the first place.]

Somehow, the fifth Doctor can work out that the natural conclusions of 'wibbley-wobbley' is 'timey-wimey'. He is perfectly able to figure out all the controls and dials, and initially fails to notice any change in the console layout. [This chimes with something we pick up in Moffat's period as producer: that the physical controls are almost like skeuomorphic icons on a screen representing more arcane and immaterial functions.]

Neither Doctor is particularly impressed by an explosion that's only the size of Belgium.

• *Background.* The current Doctor identifies his predecessor's era with the words 'Nyssa and Tegan, Cybermen and Mara and Time Lords in funny hats and the Master'. [On the Mara, see 19.3, "Kinda" and 20.2, "Snakedance". Nyssa and Tegan were the fifth Doctor's longest-running companions, and the others had multiple appearances but showed up in "The Five Doctors".]

• *Ethics.* The Doctor has no problem mentioning selected bits of future information to his past self, including the Master's continued existence. [This is such a *massively* history-changing piece of information for his past to have (imagine if "Utopia" had started with the ninth Doctor hunting down the only other Time Lord left), we have to assume he's certain he doesn't remember this event *until* experiencing it for the second time. That's not uncommon for multi-Doctor stories, but this is the first time without there being Time Lords, somewhere, to make sure everything sorts itself out properly. The logical assumption: the cricketing Doctor thinks that the babbling wide-boy is only a *potential* future time-line. In any of the near-fatal situations to come, he certainly doesn't act as if he knows he has a definite future, and shows no sign of thinking "oh, of course" when he sees that face. Then again, his reaction to finding the suit and long coat in X2.0, "The Christmas Invasion" is of recognition and satisfaction, as if a crossword clue had resolved itself.

[The other vast spoiler is that the pair o'Docs use a paradox; the Tennant Doctor comes up an idea that the Davison Doctor saw him come up with, but Tennant only *remembered* the idea. In short, this concept seems to have emerged full-born independently of either of them. It's true that the Doctors do tend to give each other ideas that neither or none (depending on the number involved) would have devised straight off. For example, when in a cell together, the Tennant, Matt Smith and John Hurt Doctors complete each other's trains of thought and set up a programme for the earliest Doctor's screwdriver to work on for 400 years, so that the most recent one's has the final answers (X7.15, "The Day of the Doctor"), but the idea there was prompted by the Moment nudging Hurt's Doctor into it. This is not quite what happens here, but there's no attempt to explain or resolve this paradox.

[Given how this story's coda is Tennant standing in for Moffat the Fanboy, it's tempting to think of this as an attempt to consign the annoying question *Where do you get all your ideas?* to a black hole. We'll revisit this tendency of letting the Doctor think out loud for the audience's benefit with the pre-credits scene in X9.4, "Before the Flood". The alternative is that the TARDIS herself is trying to avoid calamity, which opens up a whole lot of questions about how many of the Doctor's ideas are his own (see **He Remembers This *How*?** under X1.5, "World War Three" and X9.13, "The Husbands of River Song" for copying his wife's brain onto a screwdriver because he remembers that he was going to). Admittedly, with the fate of the universe literally in his hands, there's not much incentive for either of them to play nice and avoid causal self-plagiarism.]

• *Inventory: Sonic Screwdriver.* The tenth Doctor offers his to the fifth Doctor, who turns it down. [And there's a hint that the fifth didn't build another one after "The Visitation" because he simply preferred going 'hands free'.]

• *Other.* Both Doctors have their *glasses* on hand; the tenth Doctor refers to them as 'Brainy specs' [establishing a fan-fic friendly term that was much adopted thereafter]. He says that the fifth

Why Not Mention the War?

continued from Page 287...

from one scene to the next. On the other hand, scaring her past self makes him remember, even when he's her, always to carry a spare Dematerialisation Circuit. On that logic, if bootstrap paradoxes count as "logic", she would surely have remembered the much bigger scare of being stabbed, Servalan style. Let's not rule that out...)

The key thing in "Time Crash" appears to be that neither party steps out of the TARDIS. Perhaps the "present day" Doctor only recalls this incident when in the presence of his past self in a neutral time-field they both share. But that means that "our" Doctor could have said or done anything in front of his younger self without any need for self-censorship. This just makes his decision to pull his younger incarnation back for a nostalgic piece of fannish indulgence all the more weird.

Remember, for the earliest Doctor in any given team-up, the later versions of himself are contingent... he could be killed and *not* become any of them. He could be nearly-killed under different circumstances and become a totally different next Doctor; we saw the second Doctor being presented with a menu of charcoal sketches in "The War Games". For what it's worth, the Doctor in the *New Adventures* had good grounds for thinking that his tenth self would be a ginger-haired hippy (see 26.1, "Battlefield"; X2.0, "The Christmas Invasion"; the new Doctor's opening lines in X4.18, "The End of Time Part Two"). He doesn't have to restrict his comments to "Gosh, I was such a big fan in the 80s", talking like Steven Moffat for two minutes.

There is nothing to prevent the later version in this encounter from saying something, some small hint, like "avoid Androzani Minor" or "don't let Davros con you, just shoot him" (21.6, "The Caves of Androzani"; 21.4, "Resurrection of the Daleks"). Or maybe a *big* hint, such as "there's a nasty Time War coming, in which I had to destroy Gallifrey in order to save the universe from the Daleks and what Rassilon had planned." There's no guarantee that the earlier incarnation would take any notice, and the consequences if he *did* are likely to create a paradox in which his source for this information never comes into existence in that form anyway. But while safely inside the TARDIS, such paradoxes are no worse than the one on which the story hinges. If the later Doctor enjoyed being the earlier model so much, and if the Time War and all its associated angst is such a cause of unending grief, what is stopping him from doing this?

We return again to the start of 12.4, "Genesis of the Daleks", and to the Doctor's qualms about sugar in "Remembrance of the Daleks" (25.1). If there is any chance that the Doctor can change the Daleks' future, and if the Doctor thinks that setting in motion the events leading to Skaro's destruction is his decision alone, then we can pretty much rule out the Time War being one of these mysterious Fixed Points. Logically, a war prosecuted by both sides changing history cannot be anyway, but we are only surmising the latter on, admittedly, pretty firm evidence from the dialogue. We later hear that the Time War has been "time-locked" (whatever that means – we have an essay on that coming up in X4.13, "Journey's End") and is inaccessible from this or any consequent timeline. That doesn't seem to bother Rassilon ("The End of Time Part Two") or the Daleks. (X7.1, "Asylum of the Daleks", itself apparently a sequel to a computer game – see the essays with X4.1, "Partners in Crime" and X7.4, "The Power of Three" – in which Skaro was pulled from the Time War to become a base for the new Daleks.)

Perhaps it is simply that he cannot bear to see his younger, more innocent self lose some of that *joi de vivre*. The Doctor of Series 3 is constantly being reminded of everything he's lost. Can it be that he's prepared to forego the chance to retrieve everyone on Gallifrey simply because he can't face disillusioning his earlier life? In some ways that's plausible, in others it's monstrously egotistical even for this Doctor. Previous mentions of the possibility of going back and saving his people have always been agonised "don't you think I want to?" sort of dismissals, as if deliberately messing with Gallfrey's history is off the menu, but here he's in a crisis he remembers from the other way around, so there is a *chance* this one could have worked.

If, as we surmise, this meeting is atypical and there's a possibility the younger Doctor will remember the event after it's over and the timestreams have diverged again, why not risk it? This is, finally, what's supposed to have caused all three Doctors in "The Day of the Doctor" to forget quite where they put Gallifrey, although the explanation for that is a bit garbled, and they somehow get out of the Black Archive with their memories intact and no explanation of what happened at the end of that subplot. In fact, as the episode's climax has

continued on Page 291...

Doctor doesn't really need them and just has them to look clever, with the strong indication that the same applies to him as well. [In 19.2, "Four to Doomsday" the Doctor claimed to be slightly longsighted in his right eye – as per the original Doctor's use of a monocle. In the light of the recent business with the sonic sunglasses, it's possible that the glasses really *do* make the Doctor look clever by providing the much-needed read-out for the sonic screwdriver when it's being a tricorder. It's worth noting how often he puts them on just before running a scan on some alien tech.]

The fifth Doctor is wearing a soft, clean new hat [visually similar to his usual Panama, with the same sort of band]. It appears to be cloth rather than straw/ rattan.

The TARDIS The fifth Doctor refers to the TARDIS's internal configuration and appearance as a 'desktop theme' [again, see "The Day of the Doctor"] and thinks the coral look is even worse than the 'leopard skin' print. [No one's actually attempted to build such a set, mercifully. We know from X6.4, "The Doctor's Wife" that the Ship keeps an archive of old console rooms, including some not yet used but "remembered" from the future. "The Day of the Doctor", a story which is essentially this one with a bigger budget and some Zygons, informs us that these can – much as the aged Davison Doctor is said to here – discharge the temporal differential and change according to which Doctor is using which console. This is almost in keeping with the hints we got in X5.1, "The Eleventh Hour" and 15.2, "The Invisible Enemy" that the Ship sheds them like skins, with prompts and requests from the Doctor about what he'd like next.]

An alarm goes off – the fifth Doctor recognises it and says it's Level Five – to indicate a temporal collision that will create a space-time rift the size of Belgium. Three minutes later, the Cloister Bell goes off, and suddenly Our Heroes realise there's going to be a black hole detonation that actually *can* destroy the universe. [The fifth Doctor made the initial prognosis before he knew that the other half of the collision was his own future TARDIS. The last time the TARDIS threatened to cause a black hole was when the Lock was breached in 15.6, "The Invasion of Time", and the solution was to lock the Ship into temporal stasis. Apparently, 13 versions of the same TARDIS can cause an anomaly big enough to hide Gallifrey in a space-time stasis zone – again, "The Day of the Doctor" – so the problem appears to be control rather than power. All of this makes the Master's plan to save creation at the end of "Logopolis" with two TARDISes making a stable cone of temporal isometry – or something – even more alarming.]

The tenth Doctor explains that he was rebuilding the TARDIS and neglected to put the shields back up. [The rebuilding is no surprise, after the beating the Ship had in "Last of the Time Lords". It's quite possible this is the first vortex trip the Doctor's attempted since Jack shot up the Paradox Machine – we don't see it in the background when the Doctor and Martha discuss the Face of Boe, so they might have taken the train back to London.]

The two versions of the TARDIS coincided while in transit. [We see the exterior shot of a police box in the vortex (blue), suggesting that this is the patch of spacetime where they coalesced. The implication is that the later Doctor leaving his shields down caused this, although logically the early, cricketing incarnation must also have done so. It's possible there's a story where Nyssa wants to go to 2008 for some reason, but we assume that the vortex isn't quite so linear and that the older Doctor leaving Martha behind takes him out of spacetime altogether. But then we have to account for colliding with the *Titanic* in orbit around Earth on Christmas Eve, in the same year he'd just left. It's a bit of a coincidence otherwise.]

The solution to the crisis of a black hole is apparently to create a supernova. As soon as this has occurred, the two TARDISes start separating [and the fifth Doctor fades out of existence in much the same fashion as he did in "The Five Doctors" – or, to be precise, as he would have if they'd had more money to spend].

The TARDIS still has Zeiton crystals [they weren't called 'crystals' as such in 22.2, "Vengeance on Varos"] and a Helmic regulator [12.2, "The Ark in Space"]. There's also a thermal buffer ["Castrovalva"]. If you engage all three in situations of grave crisis, you get a supernova.

The Supporting Cast

• *Nyssa, Tegan, maybe Adric or Turlough or Kamelion.* [In theory, the overlapping TARDISes ought to have left the fifth Doctor's companion/s in some kind of limbo, maybe phasing into older bodies and looking at whatever Ace or Rose had

Why Not Mention the War?

continued from Page 289...

all previous Doctors and a couple yet to come arriving on cue to push Gallifrey out of the universe, *every* Doctor, presumably, must have been told about the Time War and then made to forget it, but left to do the calculations in some corner of their minds from Hartnell's incarnation onwards (the analogy being with the use of a subroutine in the sonic screwdriver's programming earlier in the episode), but consciously forget it until that day. Those days. However, this comes an episode after Clara and the Great Intelligence have both popped into the Doctor's past to rewrite large chunks, so even if it is eventually retconned into making sense on its own terms, it's not much use for Series 3 conjectures. Anyway, as far as we're aware, the Fall of Arcadia might be a Fixed Point that an earlier Doctor couldn't avert, but this is unclear (we refer you to **What Constitutes a Fixed Point?** under X4.2, "The Fires of Pompeii"). The Time War is "sealed", we're told, but this day isn't ever stated to be unchangeable once that state is changed by Dalek Caan.

Having already cited Virgin Books as potential evidence, we can tentatively propose one horribly convincing theory. If, as we suggested in **How Many Times Has This Story Happened?** and **He Remembers This *How*?** (X3.8, "Human Nature"; X1.5, "World War Three"), the Doctor is dimly aware of closed-off timelines and their events, and the actions of his potential other selves, then the obvious conclusion is that Ferret-Boy considers telling Celery-Guy all about the Moment, the Cruciform, the Neither-Nor and the Nightmare Child and then (ulp!) remembers the Past Doctor Adventure *Warmonger* (2002) by Terrance Dicks.

For those who've not read it (which ought to be everyone) imagine "A Good Man Goes to War" (X6.7), but mixed with the kind of continuity-obsessed plotting you got in the mid-80s stories, meaning the worst elements of "Attack of the Cybermen" (22.1) and "Arc of Infinity" (20.1) crop up in a prequel to "The Brain of Morbius" (13.5). Sadly for all concerned, it's not nearly as good as that makes it sound. Set in the gap between "Planet of Fire" (21.5) and "The Caves of Androzani", it has the Doctor becoming commander-in-chief of the kind of army kids used to make with their Weetabix cards (Ogrons, Draconians, Sontarans) to stop Morbius and *his* army of randomly-selected baddies (including Gaztaks; 18.2, "Meglos"). To do this, he has to pop into Gallifrey's past and cause continuity bloopers with young Borusa (14.3, "The Deadly Assassin" et seq) and only semi-reluctantly fend off Peri's lustful advances. The trouble with this as a theory for why the Mockney Doctor chose to avoid it is that *Warmonger* is – on the surface, at least – the book most like what Steven Moffat wants *Doctor Who* to be like, yet we have a Moffat script trying to prevent it. But even if this, or other similar scenarios for the fifth Doctor engaging more actively with Gallifrey's foes, were on the cards, has the later model got anything in his past between these two points that could count as a Fixed Point? Would Arcadia have fallen anyway? As far as he knew at this point it was all his fault, but is any alternative, even this fanwank car-crash, worse?

There's one last option, which is indeed worse. The Doctor doesn't say anything he doesn't remember hearing himself saying. The idea for resolving the universe-destroying glitch seems to come from elsewhere, as if both of him were being prompted. If that's the case, the sinister implication is that the Doctor in the suit is essentially a sock-puppet being operated by the TARDIS, and made to read off a sort of psychic autocue. We've floated similar ideas before (**Who Decides Who's a Companion?** under 18.6, "The Keeper of Traken" and **Why Do Time Lords Always Meet in Sequence?** under 22.3, "The Mark of the Rani"), but this is the biggest indication yet that the Doctor is being manipulated (see also X6.4, "The Doctor's Wife"). Maybe, on the scant evidence of "Forest of the Dead" (X4.9), the Doctor is capable of distorting causality around himself by exerting his will on the events: River Song is copied onto a neural relay in a future model of his screwdriver, the idea coming to him because he remembered having worked out that he will have it (X9.13, "The Husbands of River Song"). The idea originates somehow, apparently because at some point the Doctor will wish *very hard*, and make the idea have come to him outside this loop of cause and effect. In the terms afforded by "Before the Flood" (X9.4), the TARDIS wrote Beethoven's Fifth.

done with the bedrooms. Or they might be out of synch and, not being Time Lords, unaware of anything occurring.]

The Non-Humans

• *Time Lords.* The tenth Doctor indicates that his younger self appearing older than his current self is a normal enough side-effect caused by his presence [to explain Peter Davison being much older – see also "The Five Doctors" and "The Two Doctors"]. Shorting out the time differential will reverse itself once the TARDIS un-knots itself. He physically manhandles his previous self. [The Blinovitch Limitation Effect is definitely not in operation, then, as with other multi-Doctor pile-ups – see **What is the Blinovitch Limitation Effect?** under 20.3, "Mawdryn Undead".] The earlier Doctor's non-involvement in a high-five is through temperament, not fear of an explosion.

History

• *Dating.* [The story occurs in the Time Vortex, so dating is impractical. That being said, the tenth Doctor goes straight from 2008 (after however long it took to undo the Master's damage to the TARDIS) to this collision, to another on Christmas Day 2008 in orbit over England.]

The Analysis

The Big Picture Not that big, really. We discussed *Children in Need* under X1.13a, "Pudsey Cutaway", and we've talked about Moffat and predestination under X3.10, "Blink". This is clearly a topic that he can't leave alone, hence the twelfth Doctor telling us (or someone) to google the Bootstrap Paradox (X9.4, "Before the Flood"). Prior to that, this was the most self-indulgent episode in history.

As such, it sets an interesting tone for what's to come. This is the first story made after Moffat had agreed to become *Doctor Who*'s next executive producer/ lead writer. (What's awkwardly called the "showrunner", although that means slightly different things, depending on whether we're talking about the BBC or US networks.) He wrote the short script while mulling over the offer. So the things that made this one seem fresh are what we're going to get in later stories, where he's obviously thinking aloud on screen.

We get not just a paradox, but a complaint about how using a paradox is cheating; the older Doctor gripes about fans; the younger ridicules much of what was normal in earlier episodes; the Davison model mutters darkly about the TARDIS "desktop theme" and Tennant pokes fun at both the sonic screwdriver and going "hands-free" (X9.1, "The Magician's Apprentice"). For the first half of the episode, Davison gets to be the voice of older fans who were a bit nonplussed by the jittery, jabbering Tennant version, much as John Hurt grumbled on screen about the BBC Wales version's over-use of catch-phrases and gimmicks in "The Day of the Doctor". Above all, it's an air-tight box filled with references to old episodes conveyed in current terminology, and the Doctor voicing the author's thoughts about the entire process of watching (and writing) *Doctor Who*. We're going to get a lot more "messages from Fred" comments in the dialogue about how the story's working (or not), when Moffat takes over properly – but even by this stage, Rose, Reinette and Sally Sparrow have all voiced his concerns.

Meanwhile, according to the tabloids, *Children in Need* and *Doctor Who* were about the only things the BBC could get right that year. The Corporation had made several high-profile blunders and fumbled the damage-limitation. There had been some high-profile casualties, such as *Blue Peter* editor Richard Marson, but the most spectacular shambles was the way Peter Fincham, Controller of BBC1, had mishandled the criticism of the editing of a trailer for a documentary about the Queen, and had been forced to resign hours before "Time Crash" was recorded. Precisely who was really to blame is a puzzle, as is what the problem was for the tabloids (owned by people who hate the royal family), but Fincham was hounded from office just in time to take over ITV's scheduling as it was amalgamated into a single organisation (more or less) and began a concerted effort to win back Saturday nights. Despite the wider available of digital channels and, since 2012, the lack of any alternative to them, British television is still pretty much a two-horse race between what's now ITV1 (as there are now four ITV channels, only two of which make original non-sport programmes) and BBC1.

It's worth reflecting on how the success of *Doctor Who*'s relaunch galvanised the besieged organisation, and showed that their plan for using digital services and co-operating with commercial outfits was at least plausible. Everybody wanted a piece of the series. What we will see over the coming years is a strenuous effort to isolate *Doctor Who* from internal politics and the self-interested assaults by owners of other media conglomerates through their newspapers, while the rest of the BBC mightily does everything it can to milk the series for revenue, and link anything new it tries to this well-known "brand".

You may have already gathered that David Tennant was a massive, *massive* fan of *Doctor Who* even before being invited on board as the Doctor. Moffat had always admired the then-radically-different approach Peter Davison bought to the role. All three had met socially, and this seemed like a good way to acknowledge the series' past. Perhaps the most significant aspect we won't touch on elsewhere in this entry is how far the programme's new-found cachet was slowly rehabilitating the older episodes. Davison had been embarrassed about some aspects of his three years on the series (especially some of the monsters), but was never ashamed of having done it. He was actively involved in the Big Finish audios and the DVDs commentaries. By 2007, anyone who had been ten when "Castrovalva" went out would have been 35, so his generation of fans were now a significant market. He had long said that he'd have liked a second go as a more Hartnellish middle-aged figure, and that's pretty much what we get here.

Oh, Isn't That...?

• *Peter Davison.* See Volume Five. At time of broadcast, he was almost as ubiquitous as he had been when first cast as the Doctor, with a number of hit ITV series (notably *At Home With the Braithwaites* and *The Last Detective*).

Things That Don't Make Sense The repeated references to facial hair raise a slight problem: if "shorting the time-differential" explains why the Davison Doctor looks like Peter Davison circa 2007 rather than 1981, why is his paunch and male-pattern baldness not completed with a beard down to his ankles? It's not as if that's unprecedented. (See 18.1, "The Leisure Hive", and it does appear to grow at a similar rate as a human beard, if not a tiny bit faster, in X6.2, "Day of the Moon" and X6.13, "The Wedding of River Song".) Oh, and why has the earlier Doctor started wearing the back of his hat-brim raised and why is in not raised in certain shots (especially when seen from behind)?

And, yes we know it's a joke, but it's a tiny bit thick of this Doctor to have worked out that his TARDIS has collided with something that looks exactly like it, note that the person standing in front of him can change the TARDIS decor at will, turn around only to have that person say that he's *looking at the back of his own head,* and still conclude that his future self is part of LINDA. (Still, we can't very well blame him for not knowing what to do with a fanboy such as David Tennant.)

Given that a "supernova" and "black hole" are here made to cancel each other out, we might generously assume that Steven Moffat was paying tribute to some of the daftest science-y explanations of the Davison and Pertwee eras, but he's not doing a *Comic Relief* skit of a series that went off the air ten years before (A4, "The Curse of Fatal Death"), this is a legitimate BBC Wales production. Dr Science will show no mercy. So, for this "solution" to reduce the total amount of mass requires the "hole" part to be literally true – or, more radically, some sort of magical minus quantity of mass – rather than an infinitely dense dollop of mass with a fearsome gravitational pull. Even if all the energy of a supernova eventually spirals down into the event horizon, it has not *ceased* to be massive, it's just added the exploding star's mass to the black hole's mass minus a small-but-still-catastrophic percentage that was tortured into emitting from the poles as a stream of hard X rays. So rather than the matter in the TARDIS remaining constant, it's added two huge stellar events to it. Unless, that is, the things exploding and imploding are themselves part of the TARDIS manifest, in which case why comment on the constant mass as though it were an achievement?

Despite what the fifth Doctor here insists, a supernova is rather bigger than Belgium. Naturally-occurring black holes would need a start at least three times the size of the Sun, but this is created inside the TARDIS. Anything compressed to the point that its density makes local gravity misbehave has potential. In fact, with the right motivation (US scientists are trying to do it with precisely-targeted lasers), you can make a black hole with remarkably little mass, a detail half-remembered by those scaremongering about the Large Hadron Collider. Assuming that even Moffat knows that since Einstein, it's rather well-established that matter and energy are the same thing, the *real* question here is where did the amount of it for either of these, let alone both, come from? We don't doubt that there's enough stuff in the Ship to make an explosion the size of

Belgium – it probably included the wardrobe (explaining why Nyssa and Tegan wore the same clothes for months on end). If just under 30 kilos of Plutonium can be turned into a bang the size of a city, then the annihilation of all the mass in a two-bedroom semi would be enough to blow up Europe.

But even if a Belgium-sized bang is happening, and the released energy of maybe an entire shed is being added to the mass of a teensy singularity started off with very compressed photons, it'll *still* release a lot of energy, not least because black holes that small have a shelf-life of moments unless they have a constant supply of matter/energy. So another explosion, the size of Belgium-and-a-star will happen unless the black hole is already very large. (And Moffat should know that you can get energy from chucking things at a black hole, from 10.1, "The Three Doctors".) Ergo, we're back to Square One, and this is something the mass of a naturally-occurring black hole now ingesting any bits of former TARDIS contents that didn't go into making it. So he has obtained from somewhere the mass of three stars the size of the Sun. And a supernova on top of all that. Not the same as the mass being constant, is it?

[To be scrupulously fair, Moffat did get black holes and relativity approximately right in X10.11, "World Enough and Time", but he had a 14-year-old to help him – which makes X2.8, "The Impossible Planet" even less excusable.]

Critique Unlike many contributions to charity telethons, it's not so much *Will this do?* as *Can we get away with this?* Steven Moffat gets to pen a love letter to his favourite Doctor, David Tennant gets to deliver same to *his* favourite Doctor, and Peter Davison stands around looking slightly embarrassed at all the admiration. One does get the impression that nobody could have been as excited about this clip as the production staff. If judged on an absolute scale of *Children in Need* pieces, where normally-staid newsreaders do song and dance routines or the cast of *EastEnders* go disco (as happened half an hour after this was first shown), it's tight and amusing. But from another point of view, it's a bit faffy – not so much a *Doctor Who* story as a meditation on growing up watching *Doctor Who*, as if two versions of the Doctor were doing a DVD commentary as the universe hangs by a thread. That's going to be a challenge for Moffat henceforth – the competing impulses to explain a fan theory about old stories while making a piece of television drama that works on its own merits (see in particular X9.2, "The Witch's Familiar").

Hindsight makes "Time Crash" a worrying precedent. The original transmission had an unspoken criticism from a non-fan viewer: they came out of it to a cheering audience, but the look on Terry Wogan's face was obviously *What the hell have I just watched?* It's not as toe-curling as, say *The Sarah Jane Adventures*'s contribution to *Comic Relief* a few months later, but it needs the indulgence one reserves for "charidee" pieces to enjoy it as intended.

In general, though, it's fine; the first legitimate multi-Doctor story in decades doesn't outstay its welcome. To everyone's relief, they *did* get away with it.

The Lore

Written by Steven Moffat. Directed by Graeme Harper. Viewing figures: 11.0 million (in a programme that got 9.6 million on average over the night), 2.4 million (for the repeat). It was only shown on the *Children in Need* special, but was a DVD extra with the Series 4 box set. The episodeette was repeated at 20 to one the following morning at the end of the telethon, so two million-odd viewers isn't bad.

Alternate Versions The DVD doesn't fade from John Barrowman and Sir Terry Wogan to the start, and has the end titles running for ages, then stopping instead of cutting back to the studio. This is the version available online for the following week.

Production

We've been here before with X1.13a, "Pudsey Cutaway". *Children in Need* is the BBC's own charity telethon, and each year it gets more extravagant. *Doctor Who* had been participating since the big Anniversary bash ("The Five Doctors"), with varying degrees of quality and audience enthusiasm. (Here we can't help but mention A1, "Dimensions in Time". In fact, the earliest-made contribution to the appeal was 17.6, "Shada", when Douglas Adams released the rights for a video release in 1992 conditional on *Children in Need* getting his royalties.)

This year, they wanted something unprecedented and, as Tennant was now a known quantity, the inserted incident would be better if someone else were on the back foot around him. A plan came together slowly and casually over the summer. The team knew Peter Davison socially: he'd popped around for the location work on X2.0, "The Christmas Invasion", and both Russell T Davies and Steven Moffat had dined with him. Tennant had worked with him before becoming famous, and had met him more recently through mutual friend Mark Gatiss (Davison is said to have made a joke about the Blinovitch Limitation Effect – 20.3, "Mawdryn Undead"). Julie Gardner asked Moffat, who was working on his two-part library story for Series 4, to provide an eight-page script with one set (ideally, the TARDIS – it was already built). A multi-Doctor story was practical and Tennant suggested Davison. Colliding the slightly starchy fifth Doctor with the ebullient and self-consciously "street" tenth incarnation was an obvious quick idea, especially as Moffat had been, to some extent, brought back to *Doctor Who* by the abrupt change to what or who the Doctor could be like in the early 80s. Davison had been in a Sue Vertue-produced series a few months earlier. Everyone checked diaries, Moffat phoned Davison and wrote his vignette and that was pretty much that.

• Davison was, as usual, fairly busy. He had just taken over as King Arthur in the production of *Spamalot* running at the Palace Theatre, replacing Tim Curry and thus on posters across London. Many of the big West End shows rotated casts to keep things fresh (and re-publicise a show that had been running for years), so Davison was often on stage, but his TV career had perked up again. He'd kept touch with the worlds of *Doctor Who* through Big Finish audios and recording increasingly sardonic DVD commentaries on his stories with Janet Fielding and the old gang. The beard he had grown to play Arthur was shaved off just before leaving for Cardiff on Saturday night.

• The costume for the older Doctor was a composite. The jacket was the one from the BBC exhibition, the trousers were Davison's Season Twenty-One pair, slightly enlarged for 21.7, "The Twin Dilemma" (which the now less-svelte Davison appreciated), and the hat was bought for the production. The jumper was knitted especially, to match the Season Nineteen one. As the shoot was one day only, they used a real stalk of celery instead of the fabric one used in the 80s.

• Despite being a Sunday and a small shoot, the Upper Boat had a lot of visitors that day. Apart from the *Confidential* crew and Benjamin Cook from *Doctor Who Magazine*, there was a brace of Brand Executives, Davison's young sons (all avid fans of Tennant's Doctor and, to a lesser extent, their dad's), Moffat had come to see the recording and be interviewed (and brought one of his kids as well), and neither Phil Collinson nor Russell T Davies could resist (especially after Julie Gardner's excited texts), although Davies was hard at work reworking the Sontaran scripts and could only make a short appearance. What nobody else knew was that just over a week earlier, Moffat had decided to take over from Davies when Series 5 went into production (well, Davies obviously knew and Cook had been told).

• That year's *Children in Need* was shown on 16th November, and they announced that the relevant eight minutes would be some time between 8.00pm and 8.30. Leading up to that was an evening of bands of the 90s reforming (more successfully than ever in the case of Take That, less so for Westlife or the Spice Girls) and Kylie Minogue, fresh from her two-year cancer-induced sabbatical, performing comeback single "2 Hearts" (see X4.0, "Voyage of the Damned"). John Barrowman, at the peak of his domination of British television, did a number from his new album before introducing the mini-episode alongside Sir Terry Wogan.

At the time the episode was showing, the viewership spiked to an estimated 11 million, making it the most-watched Davison *Doctor Who* ever (at least half a million over the last episode of 19.1, "Castrovalva"; yes, sadly the fifth Doctor's debut was his most popular story). Afterwards, BBC viewers with the right connections could rewatch it online for a week, plus a making-of short. With the Christmas episode just over a month away, this was the start of the pre-publicity for both the event and the new-look online build-up (and digital catch-up).

• In the interviews to promote this, Davison commented on how much the Cardiff production knew each other and loved the show. He said it was one time where the showbiz cliché of the unit feeling like a family was absolutely right, little realising that this would become literally true for him very soon. (See X4.6, "The Doctor's Daughter" if you've somehow missed this part of the story.)

X4.0: "Voyage of the Damned"

(25th December 2007)

Which One is This? Ever wondered what would happen if you crossed *The Poseidon Adventure* with 14.5, "The Robots of Death"? The answer appears to be 24.3, "Delta and the Bannermen" with oak panelling. And Kylie Minogue.

Will Astrid survive and travel with the Doctor? She should be so lucky.

Firsts and Lasts Yes, for the first time someone whom the Doctor has previously cited as a real-world celebrity appears in an acting role as someone else. In X2.7, "The Idiot's Lantern", the Doctor said: "It's never too late, as a wise person said – Kylie, I think", and lo, here's Kylie as Astrid, yet neither the Doctor nor Wilf comment on the resemblance. More significantly for this Doctor, it's the first appearance of one Wilfred Mott: newsvendor, confirmed believer in aliens and all-around good egg. (The Doctor doesn't mention his resemblance to Bernard Cribbins either.)

This is the first time, apart from explicit TV Movies (20.7, "The Five Doctors" and, obviously, the 1996 TV Movie), that an episode has been allowed to creep over the one-hour running-time. It's 75 minutes, as long as three old-style episodes. Indeed, key plot developments happen at 25-minute intervals.

Murray Gold reworks the theme music, with drums, electric guitars and a grand piano. It could easily have been one of those versions from cheap Woolworth's albums of TV hits such as Geoff Love and his Orchestra or Don Harper's Homo Electronica (if you want something like that, stand by for 2014...). There had been several alternative versions floating around from redos of the closing credits, soundtracks, and the like, but this was the first time the opening had been noticeably changed in the new series.

This was the first time the Canadian Broadcasting Corporation declined to broadcast an episode. (A cable-only station took it instead. There was speculation that the multiple mentions of New Zealand was a hint that a new sponsor had been found – note the list of companies backing the *Titanic* on the board next to where the TARDIS lands.)

This is the first time the BBC Wales production staff will dedicate a *Doctor Who* episode to the memory of an important former figure in the programme's long history – in this case the original producer, Verity Lambert, who died on November 22nd. There'll be more of these in coming years. And, as noted in the last two entries, this story begins with the now-traditional festive "what? *what*? WHAT?"

Watch Out For...

• For anyone who lived in Britain in the 1980s, seeing the name "Kylie Minogue" in the credits is even weirder than the initial shock of "Billie Piper" two and three-quarter years before, or "Catherine Tate" last Christmas. We'd had celebrity cameos from John Cleese (17.2, "City of Death"), Hugh Grant (A4, "The Curse of Fatal Death") and the Beatles (2.8, "The Chase"), but this is the most famous person to have a full-blown acting part in the series since its inception 44 years previous. Of course, Kylie was *so* globally-successful and in-demand, Astrid's death is pretty much inevitable – otherwise, she'd have had to have dropped her entire comeback tour to become the companion for the next year.

• It's Christmas, and what did the BBC usually put on instead of *Doctor Who* back when Russell T Davies were a lad? A big 70s Disaster Movie. In fact, Lombard Street to a china orange it would be either *The Poseidon Adventure* or *Towering Inferno*, so he's combined them. Everything's present and correct: the fat lady who plummets to her death; the nice characters dying and the nasty ones surviving and not learning anything; the hero making a speech about how if everyone listens to him, they'll all get out safely – but not everyone doing so, and him beating himself up about it; lots of explosions amid festive decorations; the scene where they stop the plot to plug a song they hope will be a hit; the famous faces, not all of whom are in the main plot; a lot of crawling across very narrow bridges over a burning precipice, and overwrought confessions whenever anything hasn't exploded for a while. We also have umpteen shots of people falling very slowly into a conflagration (well, all right, three such shots – but it seems like more and they all look like Eccleston's death-plunge on *Gone in 60 Seconds* or Sigourney Weaver in *Alien3*.) About the only thing you'd expect to see in one of these films that isn't here is Robert Wagner. Maybe he should have played Max Capricorn (see **The Lore**).

• It's only the third time they've done this

Is Kylie from Planet Zog?

To start with, let's deal with the pedants. No, Kylie is from Melbourne, Astrid is from Sto and *Doctor Who*'s "Planet Zog" is where the bar is in the Sinatra-esque protracted farewell tour from "The End of Time Part Two" (X4.18).

Now let's wind back to the mid-90s, and Channel 4's at-first-refreshing early morning series *The Big Breakfast*. In amongst Chris Evans (the UK one, not the guy who plays Captain America), Liza Tarbuck (see A5, "The Infinite Quest") and general *Tiswas*-like activities were two gravel-voiced puppet aliens, Zig and Zag, from (drumroll) the Planet Zog. Yes, a flagrant *ALF* knock off to some, a blatant *Gilbert's Fridge* steal to others (see X4.2, "The Fires of Pompeii"), but they caught on. As did the term "from Planet Zog" for "out of the loop". (You may recall a cute alien called "Zog" in the stage play *Doctor Who: The Ultimate Adventure* from this time – Terrance Dicks was more likely recalling leftover Hapsburg Ex-King Zog of Albania than riffing on hyperactive breakfast telly, though.) Thus when giving endless press briefings in 2004-5, Russell T Davies repeatedly used the name when discussing whether the viewing public as a whole cared about the same things as viewers of Those Kinds of Programme Featuring Weirdly-Named Characters with Stuck-On Features.

This needs careful examination. On many occasions, Davies stated that there was this thing called "drama" and this *other* thing called science fiction (although he went for baby-talk), and that they are oil and water. Of course, being famous and interviewed by Mark Lawson, what he himself did was obviously capital-D Drama. The strategy had worked before, as it happens, in Chris Carter's cagy efforts to avoid *The X Files* being tarnished with the "sci-fi" moniker (this, despite its healthy diet of aliens, fiendish science experiments and even a monster who was half-human, half flatworm) – a policy that hoodwinked everyone into treating the show as mainstream, and led to surge in viewers once it moved from its "niche" slot on Friday nights to Sundays.

The *other* big problem for *The X Files*, and imported shows you might expect to find in the 6.25 BBC2 "Cult" slot, was that the convoluted long-running stories could seem impenetrable to newcomers. (And, let's not forget, this in the days before you could readily catch up on a show through streaming, DVDs and – ahem – piracy.) That level of investment was, back then, only for a few obsessives. Proper Drama didn't normally do such things; it more often had characters you understand instantly if you're only watching for the first time and situations you've seen umpteen times before. Remember, *Lost* and *The Wire* were treated as a blinding revelation by TV critics who'd somehow not bothered with *Babylon 5*, *Star Trek: Deep Space Nine*, *FarScape* or Cartmel-era *Doctor Who*. We'll come back to this in a moment.

The main manifestation of this attempt to de-skiffyate the most famous British version of science fiction was Davies's repeated claim that "viewers can't identify with people from Planet Zog" (stated so often, we've averaged the slight variations in phrasing). To that end, all human characters would be stated explicitly to be originally from Earth. Now, to be fair, he would often immediately retract and differentiate himself from "viewers" as a species by protesting his deep love of 2.5, "The Web Planet", a story in which everyone other than the regular TARDIS crew were giant insects of one kind or another.

... actually, there's something odd about that statement's sweeping generalisation of "viewers". Apart from the suggestion of research which – as far as we've been able to establish – hasn't happened, the statement is based on an assumption that things have changed significantly since 1964, when the general public were gripped by a story about people on another planet struggling for survival against ex-people in a city on that planet (1.2, "The Daleks"). And it assumes that nobody is playing a blind bit of notice to the caption saying *A long time ago, in a galaxy far, far away* before each *Star Wars* film.

That being the basic assumption of the Davies years, however, it was noticeable that the passengers and crew of the starship *Titanic* were from somewhere called "Sto" and treated a visit to modern-day Earth as a safari. The basics of our lives, and of Christmas, were shown through the distorting lens of Mr Copper's faulty education and seen as if from outside. Appropriately, in a story about a starship called *Titanic*, and which ends up looking as if the Doctor has to go through levels like a computer game, it has a vague whiff of Douglas Adams about it. Adams, as we established in Volume 4, had taken loads from the 50s SF writers: notably Robert Sheckley, Alfred Bester and Frederik Pohl and from earlier *Doctor Who* (wittingly or not, and we think he may have been deceitful about how much he knew). But that view-from-outside thing's as old as *Utopia*, the

continued on Page 299...

(fourth if you count "The Feast of Steven" in 1965), but already the rituals of the Christmas Special are in place. There's a song by Murray Gold and Ben Foster with lyrics that might be about the Doctor. It's called "The Stowaway" and is in 6:8 time and vaguely Celtic, but absolutely nothing at all like "A Fairytale of New York" by The Pogues and Kirsty MacColl, honest. And in the interests of balance, they skip Slade's "Merry Xmas Everyone" this year and have Yamit Mamo sing "I Wish It Could be Christmas Everyday" by Wizzard, the single that vied with Slade's for the top-spot around the time of 11.1, "The Time Warrior". (That's right, they have one of the biggest recording artists on the planet in the cast and *someone else* belts out the songs. Actually, two big recording artists, as Kylie Minogue's there as well as Bernard Cribbins.) As with Dudley Simpson in "The Talons of Weng-Chiang" (14.6) and Keff McCulloch in "Delta and the Bannermen", we can see the composer performing in the band in an unconvincing disguise. That's him with the guitar and stuck-on moustache behind the chantoosie.

• After the hi-jinks with Chantho saying her name a lot in lieu of characterisation (X3.11, "Utopia"), and the tongue-twister alien names of recent years, this story's Jimmy Vee character is a bright red spiky-faced chap in a wing collar and tail-suit who refers to himself in the third-person. A lot. As his name's "Bannakaffalatta", you will either find him endearing or be hoping he dies horribly as soon as possible. He has a significant subplot: he hopes he can remain inconspicuous because he's a cyborg, one of a derided group of outcastes in Sto's kerr-azy upside-down society. In case nobody picks up on the hint of what they mean, we hear that things are improving and they are even allowed to marry now.

• Even without knowing the casting for Series 4, Bernard Cribbins's cameo is an absolute joy; Wilfred in brashly patriotic mode – with Union flags draped up everywhere – is fun enough, but his "then again...", after he's just seen two strangers vanish in front of his eyes after speculating that there's nothing to worry about, is a lovely underplayed touch in an otherwise explosive episode.

• The most ridiculously overblown sequence is the climax, when everything goes into slow-mo, the music goes all Morricone again and Astrid kills the story's baddie by driving into the ship's atomic engines, just before a retinue of haloed angels carries our grieving Doctor upwards. This sort of thing is the flipside of Davies's domestic soap scenes and, while there'll be plenty more such over-the-top scenes in future, he'll never be quite this unself-conscious about it again.

• So a well-known London landmark (Buckingham Palace) is once again doomed to be trashed by an alien spaceship (the plummeting starship *Titanic*); but this time, for budget reasons if nothing else, it's spared. The lead-in to this near-miss involves parodying someone Very High Up who is known to watch the series faithfully. Davies is unshakeably confident in the series and its appeal at this stage, and thinks he can do anything. He's very nearly right, which sets the pattern for the rest of his tenure.

The Continuity

The Doctor Apparently, he's now 903 years old. [When the ninth Doctor said he was "900" in "Aliens of London" (X1.4) and "The Doctor Dances" (X1.10), we might have imagined that he was approximating – but this, nearly three years of real time on from those remarks, cements the idea that he was speaking literally. However, the seventh Doctor said he was "953" in 24.1, "Time and the Rani". The result is a string of falling dominoes that forces the Doctor's age in the original and new series to overlap but not synch up; see also **The Obvious Question: How Old is He?** under 16.5, "The Power of Kroll", **What Happens in a Regeneration?** under 11.5, "Planet of the Spiders" and umpteen references in Volumes 9 and 10.] He's not averse to eating buffalo wings.

He's uncomfortable taking a cruise "on his own", and almost immediately gravitates towards the cute waitress when he stows away aboard [Series 1 Rose would have done exactly the same]; nevertheless, he's not so keen for company as to pick up on Mr Copper hinting for a lift. [There seems to be something special about Christmas for the Doctor; apart from his rhapsodic description of the feast when correcting Mr Copper, we note that whenever he's around on that day, especially on Earth, he acquires companions without any of the tests and auditions Martha endured. Astrid is second only to Clara (X7.6, "The Snowmen") for the brevity of screen-time between meeting and being invited along.]

Despite having been instrumental in several dramatic examples of the general public finding out about extraterrestrial life ["Aliens of London"

Is Kylie from Planet Zog?

continued from Page 297...

Thomas More account of how England in 1515 compares to a made-up alternative. Before that, it was mainly done through characters becoming, or talking to, animals. We have a couple of thousand years of that sort of thing – the Menippean Satire, as the genre's called – and SF took from it what it needed, not least with those diet-SF dramas with actors representing outsiders by having latex things stuck on their faces. BBC Wales's *Doctor Who* in turn took what it thought it could get away with taking from those TV shows. "Voyage of the Damned" uses "they're from another planet" as a catch-all explanation of why we have the set-up of the *Titanic* in orbit around present-day London. And lo! In the middle of all of this tourism in our streets, we get Bannakaffalatta, an outsider with latex stuck on his face so we know he's Not Like the Others. (There's something similar going on with Blue-Faced Humanoids in Moffat stories, but we'll look at that in another essay.)

However, this sequence of tourists in London getting everything about Earth wrong is over almost before it begins, and we're back to the disaster-movie, with no time for satire or alienation (in literal and usual meanings of the word). Nonetheless, the door had been opened. Astrid was a sympathetic character with no hint of Earth ancestry or links to the planet. The point being: it could be done and viewers weren't scared off by it. How much of that was down to Kylie Minogue and how much Davies's craftsmanship, we will never know, because he never did it again.

And in doing it *at all*, he exposed a contradiction. The arguments he'd raised for why he couldn't ever do it in a million years were, on their own terms, fairly plausible. Ignoring the appeal to hypothetical "viewers", he pointed out the implausibility of there being that many species who would look exactly like humans, even on worlds geographically identical to ours. We had to try and reconcile that to the programme's previous assumption of a universe where Earth is insignificant in the original version of **How Does "Evolution" Work?** in the printed version of Volume 5 (the e-book edition has some revisions). That would have been a good case, had he not then turned the argument on its head and used the supposed plethora of human-like species to justify a rhino-like species (X3.1, "Smith and Jones"). It would have been valid as an argument for BBC Wales's *Who*... if he hadn't let both *Torchwood* and *The Sarah Jane Adventures* contain human-like aliens with no connection to us other than the ability to hide here.

There lies the real problem: the shift in public awareness of the basic truth of the universe, that Earth isn't anything special. *The Sarah Jane Adventures* can make a big thing about how vast and varied the cosmos is because the main character can't leave. The Doctor has the option of going to a different galaxy every day of his two-thousand-years-and-counting life and yet, for budgetary reasons as much as aesthetics, he always winds up either in London or a beach near Cardiff. For Davies to justify his decision to keep coming back here, he has reverted to a geocentric viewpoint.

Even Astrid is only in the story because she wanted to see the big wide universe and got as far as St John Street. The plutocrats of Sto want to see Earth because... er... because it's famous, apparently. Or something. In the past, *Doctor Who* went through phases when the whole point was to go to different times and places to show viewers otherness; that was sort of the point back in those meetings in 1962. The most extreme forms of this were in those patches when the companions weren't from around here (or around now), and visits to the present day were oddities. Curiously, those were also often the times when the series was more at pains to stress the virtues of literacy and tolerance. Indeed, when a threat to Earth gets announced at the end of "The Pirate Planet" (16.2), it seems curiously bolted-on, the way the existential threat implicit in "The Mind Robber" (6.2) is weakened by a plan to invade Earth. Geocentricity – or belief that whatever planet and culture we were on in the specific story we were following – was all there was, was what the Bad Guys did.

What went missing was a willingness to assume that audiences can figure things out from first principles without a lot of heavy hints about the similarity of such-and-such a setting to the settings of a lot of other television. This is something that can confuse people going back to examine the series' earlier phases after starting with the BBC Wales version. Television drama as a whole (let alone *Doctor Who*) was less mimetic in 1963. Simply saying it was "like theatre" isn't enough, as we've been trying to explain. Every generation of actors resists the previous generations' attempts

continued on Page 301...

et al], he seems to think that obvious aliens wandering around Central London at Christmas will set off a riot. He says that the pyramids and New Zealand are beautiful. By now he's spent so much time in London he's genuinely surprised that anyone can find it exciting, although this is admittedly when he's worrying about why the street's deserted on Christmas Eve.

He gets far more visibly frustrated about Astrid's fate than we've yet seen from this iteration, shouting 'I can do anything!' before Mr Copper points out he's talking to a ghost. At which point, he calms down and gives it a good snog before leaving in a grump. [His idea of himself as near-omnipotent is going to get him into a lot of trouble later, as we'll see in the next volume.]

He gets lost in the middle of making lists [as with X3.8, "Human Nature"]. Fulfilling upon a long-term wish, [X2.12, "Army of Ghosts"], upon learning midshipman Alonso's name, he can with justification use the phrase, 'Allons-y, Alonso!'

• *Background.* He establishes his authority by declaring 'I'm a Time Lord. I'm from the planet Gallifrey in the constellation of Kasterborous' [the latter bit established in 13.3, "Pyramids of Mars" and reiterated *ad nauseam* in the 80s], even in a context where it means nothing to those present. He somehow [possibly those internal downloads of knowledge of his; see **He Remembers This How?** under X1.5, "World War Three"] is up to date on the Sto soap opera *By the Light of the Asteroid*. At some point, he acquired [from UNIT?] the phone number and evacuation code-words for Buckingham Palace.

He claims to have had 'the last room' at an inn in Bethlehem. [We're obliged to mention the eighth Doctor audio *Relative Dimensions*, in which he says he took Leonardo da Vinci back to the very first Christmas as research for his adoration painting, but that they went out for dinner Leo after Leo chickened out.] The Queen seems acquainted with him – enough to wish him, by name, a happy Christmas [see 7.4, "Inferno"; 12.1, "Robot"; and, alas, 25.3, "Silver Nemesis"].

He's awfully excited to say 'Take me to your leader', and claims, 'I've always wanted to say that'. (In this life, he means – he last did so in 14.4, "The Face of Evil".)

• *Ethics.* Mr Copper comments that the Doctor would become a monster if he could choose survivors. [It's directed as a Foreboding Moment, though we're not going to see much of this until X4.16, "The Waters of Mars".]

He causes a minor panic by exploding a bottle of champagne, to tell off a group of snobs for snubbing the one couple on board who aren't posh and moneyed.

• *Inventory: Sonic Screwdriver.* Busy this go round: aside from the champagne explosion [perhaps he triplicated its flammability; "World War Three"], it recharges an EMP pulse and hacks the *Titanic* systems six ways from Sunday. He has a way to lock the settings so pressing the button on top will open doors automatically. It's no better with deadlocks than it ever was.

• *Inventory: Other.* He's got his tux on again. [X3.6, "The Lazarus Experiment". It really *is* cursed, apparently.]

The TARDIS [See X3.13a, "Time Crash" for an explanation why an otherwise-standard issue spaceship can plough through the Ship and broach its interior dimensions.]

The Doctor's installed a function to make the TARDIS home in on the nearest large mass when 'it's set adrift'; this inconveniently strands the Doctor and company on the failing ship while the TARDIS goes off to Earth, and is therefore not used in this form again. [The TARDIS crashing on planets from orbit, of course, becomes a regular incident in later years. Matt Smith's Doctor is almost defined by his repeated falling-from-the-sky routines.]

The Supporting Cast

• *Astrid Peth.* In the best tradition of *Doctor Who* orphan companions, she wanted off her planet and got off the first chance she had, first by working as waitress at a space diner for three years, and then the same aboard a luxury cruise liner. Insurance doesn't stretch to workers such as her getting shore leave, so she jumps at the opportunity when the Doctor tempts her along. She's touched by the Doctor's sympathy (enough to keep quiet about his being a stowaway). She and the Doctor keep up a not-quite-flirting banter all episode, and when she presses to be allowed to travel with him, he agrees with a minimum of reluctance.

After watching lots of people die, then hearing Capricorn calmly explain it was a deliberate plan and the entire planet below is next, she kills him before anyone can stop her. [A severed brake line makes it a moot point whether she was planning

Is Kylie from Planet Zog?

continued from Page 299...

at some kind of "natural" performance, landing up with a whole new set of mannerisms and shorthand that the next lot reject as corny gesture-coding. The same is true of cinema style, so that the once-shocking use of lens-flare to suggest documentary-like "accidental" reference back to the method of production (which scandalised the original audience for *Cool Hand Luke*) became a cliché that computer-generated sequences and Saturday Morning cartoons fake up from scratch.

These days, made-up television drama has to look like it is happening without any mediation (as did, for a while in the early part of this century, sitcoms). The more something *looks* like television, the less viewers will linger – or so the thinking goes. (We'll pick up this bit of the argument in **What Difference did Field-Removed Video Make?** under X4.15, "Planet of the Dead".) Any new situation has to look like a previously-encountered one for the people making television to feel confident that viewers will "get" it. Thus, the various domestic spaces in "Partners in Crime" (X4.1) were explicitly chosen and remodelled to resemble the dull comedy-drama *Cold Feet*. It's not as if that many people *really* inhabit houses like that, but it's familiar-from-television, much as the conflicting codes used to sketch in Jackie Tyler in Series 1 were. Once generic expectations are safely in place, the story can start adding *different* generic expectations, and make a 45-minute story run smoothly just on this juxtaposition.

Verity Lambert didn't really have that luxury when producing the first run of *Doctor Who,* but there were concerted efforts to at least root individual adventures in similarity with some aspects of conventional (in every sense of that adjective) television drama. The various sub-worlds in "The Keys of Marinus" (1.5) were made to resemble sub-genres of orthodox adventure (togas and Roman statues for Morphoton, then South American jungle, a trapper's cottage, caves and finally a thinly-disguised contemporary Manhattan with Greek Orthodox judges). Coal Hill School was straight out of *Z Cars* (to the extent of the same stock-music on Susan's tranny and in a nightclub patrolled by Fancy Smith in the first episode of each series).

It was almost impossible to make anything made at Lime Grove look like a documentary, and it took an effort of will for viewers to collaborate in making each place visited in any live or as-if-live production. Viewers were able, back then, to accept that, so Planet Zog (or Marinus, or Skaro, or Xeros) was no more or less implausible than Imperial China (1.4, "Marco Polo") or the kitchens of "Newtown" residents in *Z Cars*.[59] Moreover, every individual *Doctor Who* adventure had its own ground-rules for what was permissible as a storytelling device. "Galaxy 4" (3.1) exploited flashbacks and voice-overs, "The Romans" (2.4) flagrantly used stock-footage and jokey captions. (See **How Messed-Up is Narrative Going to Get?** under X3.10, "Blink".) Outright parody of other series only came in the third year, first as a one-off gag (3.4, "The Daleks' Master Plan" episode seven) and then as a cross-generic rooting in the everyday once the TARDIS had *finally* come to spend a whole story in the present day (3.10, "The War Machines").

The BBC Wales version is in a genuine dilemma here. Unlike the days of Lime Grove, the picture-quality and composition are entirely a matter of choice. The use of Betacam and post-production grading makes each episode from this phase look pretty much like the ones either side of it, but it didn't *have* to. The raw material, as can be seen on deleted scenes in the box-sets, is like 90s video, but with too much colour. As with Murray Gold scoring every episode, there is an imposed house style.

The reason for this is clear: they want this series to be palatable to other countries where this is the norm (and one in particular) and, significantly, despite being BBC Wales, they want to look comparable to the other series that US and general-overseas viewers might be expected to compare it with – That Kind of Series – and thus they have made the content as different as is possible whilst still appealing to that market. BBC viewers might see something that starts out like a soap and then goes wrong, but for anyone else it starts out looking at once A) familiar and weird, B) British and yet C) comfortably "real". For the BBC audience, who are paying for it, the converse is true – it's a BBC series but it looks international; filmic and yet homely. The repertoire of things that can be put into this picture-quality holdall can encompass anything from any form of television or feature film... so long as it's almost like something the punters already know.

Thus, off-the-shelf iconography from action-

continued on Page 303...

to go over the edge with him.]

• *Wilfred Mott.* [Not named here, but it's obvious from his later appearances.] He approves of the Queen, and has stayed around in London despite the threat of alien attack [in retrospect, probably because he'd quite like to see one]. The holly in his hat is a tip-off [he'll wear much sillier ones before the Davies era is out], and has a Parachute Regiment badge next to it.

• *Mr Copper.* Officially the ship's Historian, in reality he has a thoroughly muddled understanding of Earth culture that he picked up from Mrs Golightly's Happy Travelling University and Dry Cleaners. He spent his life as a travelling salesman on Sto [doing some dodgy sales, if his ready identification of an EMP transmitter is anything to go by], but wanted so much to leave that he faked his credentials to come aboard the *Titanic*. Unlike most of the inhabitants of Sto, he's familiar and comfortable with cyborgs.

He's very excited about the prospect of a furnished house with a garden and a door. [At risk of spoilers, this isn't the last we'll hear of him (all right then, X4.12, "The Stolen Earth"). Davies had thought about a repeat appearance; see **The Lore** for why this didn't pan out.]

UNIT/ Torchwood No power of Earth, it seems, can defend against a crashing spaceship with a nuclear storm drive. [So the "Death Star" gun from two Christmases ago must be out-of-commission after the Battle of Canary Wharf (X2.0, "The Christmas Invasion"; X2.13, "Doomsday").]

The Supporting Cast (Evil)

• *Max Capricorn* is a cyborg and founder of Capricorn Industries, which he's been running for 176 years. At some point, he's ended up needing a full life-support system [we don't hear if that's normal wear-and-tear or some ghastly accident]. His gold tooth actually goes 'ting' when he says his name. One eye has severe cataracts.

He's apparently rubbish at business, has been fired by his own board and – as the Doctor points out – is such a useless villain that he can't even sink the *Titanic*. He has arranged for his flagship to crash into an unprotected planet with all hands – an act of revenge, as the board will be arrested for murder while he escapes to a quiet retirement on Penhaxico Two: a resort-world with a more relaxed attitude towards cyborgs.

Planet Notes

• Earth is a Level Five Planet [cf. 17.2, "City of Death", X4.1, "Partners in Crime" and, by implication, 16.1, "The Ribos Operation"]. It's all right to send down limited parties to look around under supervision.

• Sto. A humanoid-inhabited planet in the Cassavalian Belt, which is apparently a long distance from Earth. [We don't, as it happens, get any explanation for why they're so fascinated by humans. By the way, for the plot to make *any* sense, we have to presume that Max Capricorn is justified – in accordance with Sto law and precedent – for thinking his board will be charged with murder if the *Titanic* goes down, considering how rarely this sort of thing happens in the UK. Since privatisation in 1996, there have been four lethal rail crashes in Britain, with 50 deaths and hundreds of injuries, and none of the shareholders or directors have been prosecuted.]

The civilisation has serious prejudices about cyborgs, even those who need such technology simply to stay alive – though there's been progress recently, with Astrid noting that they're now allowed to marry. Even super-rich Max Capricorn can't publicly admit to being one, and there's a reference to 'cyborg caravans'. [We presume this is 'caravan' in the original Arabic sense of a convoy of vehicles on a well-worn route, not the British shed-on-wheels towed behind a car, stuck in someone's driveway all year or set up permanently in something like a US trailer-park only less glamorous, for low-cost, dismal holidays near (well, within ten minutes' walk through the rain) seaside resorts.] The non-speaking roles are a cross-section indicative of Britain in 1912 [unlikely ethnic groups in posh frocks], and the Van Hoffs are a mixed-race couple, but this isn't why the other passengers ridicule them.

Their technology entails interstellar ships, teleports and holograms that Capricorn can use to fake his way through board meetings. There is a galactic stock-market, in which Capricorn Industries was once a major player. The currency is 'credits' [just for a change]. Just to emphasise their alienness, they also have doughnuts. People swear by Tov, but worship Vot. Mobiles are referred to as 'vones' and have literal universal roaming, with FTL connections to anywhere [unless blocked].

A passenger, Rickston Slade, sports Edwardian formal wear said to be a 'genuine Earth antique'.

Is Kylie from Planet Zog?

continued from Page 301...

movies (such as the original trailer with Christopher Eccleston running down a tunnel evading a fireball, like any 90s product with messrs Segal, Schwartzenegger, Cage or Willis) can be mixed and matched with off-the-shelf characters and situations from any popular UK TV drama (especially *Linda Green* and *Neighbours*). Unlike the black and white era when the rules weren't as fixed, these all have their limits and boundaries. The Daleks were back as a "design classic" (at least until Moffat was ordered at gunpoint to make a new model to flog more toys – see X5.3, "Victory of the Daleks" and its associated essay), but the conditions that 60s-designer Raymond Cusick worked under, which had led to something so off-the-wall as a Dalek being designed in the first place, were long gone. (See **Who are You Calling a Monster?** under X3.6, "The Lazarus Experiment".) There's a lot of money riding on *Doctor Who* now, so the BBC want broad strokes, situations and characters that can be assimilated instantly, so they can get a new story every week and something fresh to promote and cash in on each time.

In a lot of ways, the treatment of alien planets in BBC Wales's version of *Doctor Who* is rather the same as their treatment of Earth's past (see **Are We Touring Theme-Park History?** under X2.7, "The Idiot's Lantern"). Wherever, whenever the TARDIS lands, it's always to places and times where folks are "just like us". The cosy sitcom family in "The Fires of Pompeii" (X4.2) are as uncomplicatedly familiar as the "old-fashioned cat" and self-stereotyping citizens of New New York (X3.3, "Gridlock"). Davies, again making personal choice seem like acceding to market forces and cultural norms, refused to have anyone in the far future dress any differently from people in 2005 Cardiff (X1.7, "The Long Game"), and claimed the moral high ground over viewers who wrote in to the *Radio Times* ridiculing this decision. As the officially-designated authority on all things to do with BBC science fiction, he could claim that previous attempts at depicting A Future were doomed to date faster than deliberate refusal to do so. That tech-whizz Adam's family had, in a story set in 2012, a tape-based answerphone rather than voicemail could be cited as another example of this.

In the past, however, people tuned in to *Doctor Who* to see not so much predictions (they never once mistook it for the weather forecast or *Tomorrow's World*[60]), but exaggerated, visually-appealing versions of what was current. The recently-recovered episodes of "The Enemy of the World" (5.4) are set in 2017, but the clothes look "futuristic" in other ways – the stark monochrome of Season Five wardrobe choices continues here, but the late-90s look of the underground-dwellers' smocks (we might imagine these in lime green and magenta, looking like that 1997 fad for 1968-as-it-might-have-been you see on book-covers and CDs of dance music) is unlike anything else on television then or now. Apart from making us want to re-write **What are the Most Mod Stories?** (under 2.7, "The Space Museum"), it's a salutary reminder that viewers used to look to *Doctor Who* for various kinds of otherness, including visual inventiveness.

If the locales of *Doctor Who* invariably look and sound like every other drama on BBC1, why bother tuning in? People reading a book such as this might be invested in the stories, but the overwhelming majority of viewers aren't, especially now that the "series of serials" format's been dropped. The occasional wobbly set or horrid piece of wallpaper (again, "The Enemy of the World" has some shockers) was the price we paid for not having every spaceship look like a derelict factory and every alien base a bit of a castle in Gwent. That may not be a trade-off today's viewers are willing to make. However, the BBC Wales team are doing what they can to avoid ever finding out.

Think back to the last time the series was as popular and established as it became under Davies, and we can see many instances of worlds with humans on that have no stated connection to ours. Although some of the tie-in authors came to limit the scope of the cosmos by deciding that, for example, "The Robots of Death" (14.5) was set on a moon of Jupiter, it doesn't have to be; the only on-screen hint of any link to Earth is the synthesized renderings of Delius and Tchaikovsky barely audible at the start. "The Androids of Tara" (16.4) lacks even this, although the character-names are all from classical antiquity or Celtic/ Anglo-Saxon lit. The previous story has a silver woman from Tau Ceti (16.3, "The Stones of Blood"). Viewers simply didn't mind. The Hainish ancestry of "Kinda" (19.3) means that we have two sets of humanoids (plus a Time Lord, an Alzarian and someone from Traken having a kip in the TARDIS), one lot of them *apparently* from a future Earth

continued on Page 305...

[With tins of Brasso and authentic plaques detailing terrestrial companies who've sponsored the ship, it seems that they have visited Earth a lot, probably in the period being recreated. Thus, calling the ship 'Titanic' was probably a macabre joke on Capricorn's part.]

Astrid alludes to a Sto tradition that when a bloke is going into heroic danger, the nearest girl kisses him enthusiastically while standing on top of a box. Or else invents it.

• *Pentaxico Two.* It's got beaches and girls who like cyborgs.

The Non-Humans [It's frustrating; we never get any solid information on whether every humanoid on the ship is from the same species or not, though they do all seem to be from Sto. As to whether the humanoids are human, see **Is Kylie from Planet Zog?**]

Bannakaffalatta is a *Zocci*, small, red-skinned and spiny. The other Sto-residents take him for granted, and it's heavily hinted that he's from that planet. His status as a cyborg is more of a concern to him than his species. [The Zocci are cousins of the Vinvocci, from X4.17-18, "The End of Time".]

History

• *Dating.* It's the year following "The Runaway Bride" (X3.0), so it's 2008, Christmas Eve. [At least, if the Doctor is going by Greenwich Mean Time (as he mentions it being late night 'down there'). It can't be that late when the visitors arrive to witness London's smelly wonders, as Wilf is still selling newspapers. (That would normally be until about 7.30pm, but it's Christmas Eve, so probably not much after four and in most cases about two-ish.) See **Things That Don't Make Sense** for the annual festive timing problems about the sunrise and sunset as seen from space and from ground zero.]

A confused Mr Copper: "[France and Germany and Britain] are all at war with the continent of Ham Erica." The Doctor: "No. Well, not yet. Er, could argue that one." [Your pick as to what part, exactly, the Doctor is correcting here.]

English Lessons

• *Billion* (n.): These days, even in Britain it means a thousand million. That used to be called a "milliard" here [see 13.5, "The Brain of Morbius"]. Sto's currency would have made even less sense if Mr Copper's research had included the old British Billion, a million million.

• *Conker* (n.): A horse-chestnut, the main component of a traditional schoolboy game.[58] In their unpeeled state, they're small, round, and covered in spikes (and green, but we can wait a couple of Christmases for that).

• *Hello, Sailor* (sl.): In 70s sketch-shows, this was how caricature gay men chatted up anyone they fancied; in the 40s, it was how floozies chatted up, well, sailors. It was already a cliché in the late 60s.

• *Good King Wenceslas* (n.): A Czech ruler from the Middle Ages, after whom Prague's main square is named. The Victorian Christmas carol (to a Mediaeval tune) tells of an incident that apparently never happened, where he made big footprints in the snow to allow his page to get to safety (alluded to in 1.5, "The Keys of Marinus"). The opening line, *Good King Wenceslas looked out on the Feast of Stephen* provides the title for the first-ever *Doctor Who* Christmas episode (St Stephen's Day is the older name for Boxing Day), and you can hear the tune in X4.11, "Turn Left".

• *UK* (n.): The United Kingdom, i.e. England, Northern Ireland, Scotland and Wales. "Great Britain" refers to these without Northern Ireland (a bone of contention when the Olympics field a "Team GB" with competitors from Belfast).

• *Boxing Day* (n.): The Feast of Stephen, as we just said. Traditionally, either 26th or the first working weekday after Christmas is a public holiday, and the day on which public servants (postal workers, refuse collectors, that sort of person) get a small gift such as chocolates. It has been a handy way of regifting unwanted items, which lends a macabre subtext to "Last Christmas" by Wham!. It's also the day for odd sporting events such as swimming in freezing rivers or seas, football matches when the FA Cup qualifiers have randomly pitched apparent no-hopers against big, rich teams and, in less civilised times, fox-hunting.

The Analysis

The Big Picture The big Christmas film on telly most years of the 70s and 80s would have been a premiere of a then-recent blockbuster. The blockbuster of 1972 was the start of the Irwin Allen all-star Disaster Movies, *The Poseidon Adventure*, based on a hit novel by now-forgotten bestselling author Paul Gallico. The book, and to some extent

Is Kylie from Planet Zog?

continued from Page 303...

where space-travel is possible, but pith-helmets and blue stockings are back in; and the others, *apparently* native to S14/ Deva Loka, have been there since time immemorial.[61]

The sequel, "Snakedance" (20.2), muddles this further by having Deva Loka as part of an ancient culture across several worlds that experienced three Imperial phases, and long periods between these where chaos reigned. The archaeological finds that Ambril and Chela curate are advanced technology from an earlier cycle. This could all be set *long* into the future, and they could all be from colonies so long-established that Earth's been forgotten even if the hymns haven't (cf. "Gridlock"), but it's Season Nineteen and the Doctor's aiming for 1981 Heathrow every week. Thus, as with "The Daleks", it's tempting to locate "Kinda" as set in the present, but in a different galaxy where there are people who look like us. That's a worry for anyone trying to write guidebooks, but the general public didn't give a monkey's.

What had changed between this state and 2004's fatwa against Zog and her denizens? A key factor was *Star Trek: The Next Generation* and the assorted other series that first appeared on digital TV. The way these series were disseminated in the UK reinforced the Us-and-Them split between the wider public and "sci-fi fans" (see **Why is Trinity Wells on Jackie's Telly?** under X1.4, "Aliens of London"). When they *did* finally get shown on terrestrial, analogue stations, it was generally in a ghetto such as that BBC2 6.25 slot or Channel 4's *T4 Sunday* with the spectacularly annoying June Sarpong. Or really, really late at night, in between sneering shows made of 50s exploitation flicks and dated Public Service films. As with much of *Doctor Who* in the 1980s, the idea got around that nobody you'd want to know watched them. Which is doubly lamentable, since *The Next Generation*, during its initial run in 1987-1994, was shown in syndication but enjoyed strong enough ratings to have mainstream influence. In the US, there were quite a few viewers who tuned in for *Next Gen* week to week, but otherwise wouldn't touch anything that presented itself as "science-fiction".

And there was, it has to be said, a degree of homogeneity among these US series, particularly the ones that tried to replicate *The Next Generation*'s success. They were all set in space, with pseudo-military set-ups for the humans and quasi-religious oddness for the nice aliens. Every so often, they'd go to a planet that had a lot of conifers and be met by peasants in hessian who hailed them as gods or demons. One of the regulars would be impassive and marked out by some kind of make-up or prosthesis. There would also be some kind of long-running conspiracy-theory plotline. They would also have a small pool of the same actors cropping up in each of them.

Davies's ring of steel around *Doctor Who* being *in any* way like these shows was grounded in an assumption that if he let one or more of these features occur, the public would shrug and say "no thanks". He used soap or comedy writers, cast soap or comedy stars as guests, rooted the stories in the companions' boring lives and slowly introduced the space-opera elements as disruptions to a soap version of Normality. He was happy to take what he needed from That Kind of Series, and watched them himself as a fan and as a TV professional, but displaying the outward appearances was – so Davies stated – not an option.

The promotional material for each new series makes the same claim: that *Doctor Who* is Drama, it's about real things and it transcends what they term "sci-fi", meaning... well, their conception is entirely from That Kind of Show rather than actual written-down grown-up SF. That Kind of Show has its own rules and, alas, is a genre the way that prose SF really isn't. These series are, in the worst way, generic. Just as 1970s beauty contests were judged on specific key features – meaning a woman with all of these in place could win without being, in any way, beautiful – so these shows had to have set-pieces and items that were comparable across shows, rather than having any toehold in what life in such a world might actually be like. 80s *Doctor Who* had veered towards this insular state; Steven Moffat aspired to it. In rejecting this, and cordoning off their version from programmes like it, BBC Wales and Davies also removed the approach that had made the series so popular and influential in the pre-Nathan-Turner epoch. It's easier to cut-and-paste things Robert Holmes had already created than to create things the way he did.

Doctor Who in its characteristic moments is closer to the prose form of SF than the debauched collage of 30s cover-art sold to the public as the whole of what's possible. The thought-processes involved were more productively appropriated

continued on Page 307...

the film, are about fate and faith: a fraudulent preacher has to keep the small band of survivors together through their belief in him. Of course, this being a postwar novel for adults, good people die and unpleasant ones live. That set the tone for all subsequent iterations of the formula (notably *Towering Inferno*, *Earthquake* and, um, *The Swarm*). In the film, the most memorable scenes are the fat lady dying and the climb up the Christmas tree. As is well-recorded, Davies saw the film at the pictures in Swansea when he was nine, and the fact that characters in whom he invested were killed arbitrarily unsettled his ideas of the "rules" of drama.

Another lucrative nautical disaster movie of note is the 1997 *Titanic*. We've commented in Volume 7 how many times Davies has riffed on this film and his "discovery" Kate Winslet becoming a huge star because of it. This film, more than the rather more accurate *A Night to Remember*, makes a big thing of the rich people getting away and the loveable ethnic stereotypes in steerage being left to their fate, because it's New Hollywood and people with English accents are protrayed as morally depraved unless female and under 30. The difference between the two films is where this story starts. *The Poseidon Adventure* is about a cross-section of relatively ordinary Americans faced with a literal overturning of their world. *Titanic*, regardless of historical fact, is about a catastrophe caused by arrogant rich English people that afflicts poor, adorable Movie-Oirish and anyone who takes pity on them *but nobody else*.

This change in the "rules" is how "Voyage of the Damned" works. We are encouraged to like the married couple Foon and Morvin, practically *ordered* to love Astrid and expected to find Bannakaffalatta adorable, while Rickston is such an obvious one-note hate-figure, there would have been letters of complaint if he'd been anything other than white and English (albeit played by a Scotsman). Mr Copper is initially ridiculous, then reveals layers and wisdom in a crisis. Then we wheel out (literally) the panto villain, Max Capricorn (boo, hiss), and once again the disaster stems from an insurance fraud caused by a failing tycoon. You may remember this plot, compete with a reference to the Doctor being on the real *Titanic*, from X1.2, "The End of the World". The Disaster Movie rule-book says that we cannot permit a likeable couple to get out of this unscathed and, in a subclause, that if you think such-and-such a character is safe because the person playing him or her is famous, that means one or both characters is going to be toast (literally, in the case of *Towering Inferno*). Thus they could have Astrid flirting away and the Doctor responding, because we all knew Kylie was too busy to be anything more than a one-off (plus, Catherine Tate had been announced as the new companion five months before).

The starting-point for a lot of this was the misprision of Earth's customs and the scene of Astrid finding our domesticity exotic and alien. It's fair to say that anyone who's seen a Christmas Special made by Americans in Britain has experienced this. We'd get Perry Como coming along and making everyone dress like Elizabethans while he was in Pertwee drag, or episodes beginning with establishing shots of Piccadilly Circus circa 1953, and then a lot of American actors in Hollywood failing to do any of our accents and no end of excruciating Dickensian drivel. (And the sound of crickets and cicadas in scenes set after dark. Yes, really.) The *Titanic* being recreated slightly inaccurately and offered as an "authentic" experience to cosplaying rich-kids is rather like the 80s Epcot idea of "typical English". (Things have improved, apparently, especially the food; according to eyewitnesses it originally had a "genuine" Cotswold village with Pearly Kings when it opened.)

The title as it stands now seems to be riffing on the movie *Voyage of the Damned*: a downer of a movie concerning the fate of a ship of Jewish expats from Nazi Germany, who sailed to various countries in an increasingly desperate attempt to find sanctuary. The working title was, inevitably, *Starship Titanic*. Anyone awake in the late 90s would have known that title as the much-plugged Douglas Adams computer game from The Digital Village, around the time Davies was doing *Queer as Folk* and James Cameron's *Titanic* was cleaning up at the Oscars. There was a perfectly wretched novelisation (yes, a novelisation of a computer game – linear plot and everything), but Adams wasn't reliable enough for a company used to deadlines actually being met, so the book was farmed out to one of the game's voice-artists, Terry Jones (he was the Parrot), who stipulated that he had to write the whole thing nude. This was, alas, the one thing the book had going for it. It's a prime example of what goes wrong when people who don't read much SF have a go at writing it. The point is that somehow Davies forgot this, and

Is Kylie from Planet Zog?

continued from Page 305...

than what other people had produced by thinking that way – it was all made from scratch, from fresh ingredients, rather than shop-bought ready-made. For those just joining us, the key point is that SF is not about *content* (spaceships, robots, dystopias and so on), but about *interpretation*. It's a different methodology of reading, one closer to how we all used to read before we learned to skim. Remember how it felt to work out a word's probable meaning from context and how the other words seemed to treat it? SF does that for you again, and uses it to help you conjecture about differences between the world-in-the-text and the outside world.

70s *Doctor Who* did that with images and dialogue and assumed an audience who could play along; the script editors were generally experienced SF readers who'd also worked in soaps. They didn't assume that if you chucked in a big spaceship, the rest of the story would run as normal. Instead, there was an emphasis on making each world (made-up or historically researched) as plausible in how the residents thought of things as in the shape of spoons or what colour sky they had. We got to find out about their world through the residents' language-choices, not lavish special effects. With the occasional exception such as John Smith and Joan Redfern in "Human Nature" (X3.8), this sort of thinking gives writers on the BBC Wales payroll the screaming oopizootics (as Henry Gordon Jago would say – 14.6, "The Talons of Weng-Chiang" being a prime example of both sorts of characters fashioned by their worlds and manifesting it through speech). Astrid Peth may hail from a planet where everything's upside-down but she and the posh gits around her are all off-the-shelf stock figures from... well, from James Cameron's anachronistic *Titanic*. There's no attempt to make Sto a viable society and then derive characters from it, rather the reverse.

A problem that occurs often enough that we ought to know a handy name for it: there is an assumption, especially early on in a franchise, that if any of the features of That Kind of Series occurs in a fictional world, *all* of them must be available. If there are aliens, there must, of necessity, be time travel; if there are alternate universes, there must always be an episode about Jack the Ripper; if they can teleport, they must surely be able to download consciousness into cyberspace; the presence of robots means telepathy *has* to be possible. None of these assumptions follows (see X8.5, "Time Heist" for an especially prime example.)

World-building, laying out the coherent interplay of consequences of a change to the set-up, is here subordinated to a collage-style appropriation of leftovers from other people's work. It's noticeable that *Star Trek*'s first response to a ratings dip was to have an episode where the *Enterprise* visits the 1960s, because it can, suddenly. One of the first things Luke Skywalker asks C3PO to do is arrange a time-distortion or teleport – neither things we can witness in *Star Wars*, but supposedly available as plot developments in the early scripts before Lucas had decided on the rules. The rather mis-named *TV Tropes* website had the rather confusing term "Fantasy Kitchen Sink" (which suggests to British audiences a grim early 60s black and white film about unicorns and elves in industrial Lancashire, probably starring Alan Bates and with Colin Blakely and Leonard Rossiter in there somewhere). Instead, we'll call this "Zog-think".

Doctor Who used not to suffer from this, as each new world visited was discrete and self-consistent. The problem first arises when we started having team-up stories. Indeed, the first observable instance of this phenomenon is episode four of 19.6, "Earthshock" where, out of the blue, the Cybermen can travel in time and aren't worried about the logic of this. This kind of bad faith with the viewers had happened before, occasionally, but it became woven into the fabric of the series ore in the 1980s. Once Tegan had *got* to Heathrow, there was increasingly less reason to set a story in the everyday world of the viewers but, paradoxically, everywhere and every time became increasingly homogeneous. Everyone was up to speed with Gallifrey gossip, so the Doctor's new look and the Master's latest apparent death were dealt with in one line.

This was the mentality that Davies was out to circumvent. Non-Earth-descendant humans were as much a part of the *ancien regime* as cliffhangers, a posh Doctor with a waistcoat, quarries, wobbly sets, electronica and "futuristic"-looking clothes. In trying to reassure the public, to re-emphasise all the many things *Doctor Who* could do and used to do that That Kind of Series can't, it curtailed a lot of other possibilities – things that That Kind of Series didn't know how to do, but which prose SF could

continued on Page 309...

managed not to see the book in every second-hand shop in the land, so he found that he had to change the name of the episode. (He could have got away with it, seeing how much of the game is – let's be tactful – inspired by the same sources and in the same general direction as a lot of *Doctor Who* before Adams's stint on the series.)

One small detail that might be significant: there was a "Lord Copper" in Evelyn Waugh's novel *Scoop*. He was a composite of Lords Beaverbrook and Northcliffe, a press-baron who would fire on the spot anyone who contradicted him. Thus, whenever he made a really obvious mistake, his lackeys would say "up to a point, Lord Copper". The *Private Eye* and many others now use that formula to point out factual goofs in bombastic statements by, say, Rupert Murdoch or the Prime Minister of the day. It's also one letter away from "Hopper" (see **The Lore**).

Furthermore, we have it on good authority that "peth" is Welsh for "thing". It's also worth a quick mention that 1930s handbooks for aspiring writers stated that all rich villains should have two first names instead of a first name and a surname. We're going to encounter lots of these in the series to follow, such as "Klineman Halpen" in "Planet of the Ood" (X4.3), "Kazran Sardick" in "A Christmas Carol" (X6.0) and "Strackman Lux" in "Silence in the Library" (X4.8). Still on names, "Stow" is a suffix on place-names in England, from the Anglo-Saxon for "village", but it's also the Russian number "one". We might also note that the way in which Sto is sketched in from throwaway details that distort the minutiae of Earth happens in US sitcoms, notably *Mork and Mindy* (with Ork described by contraries) and *ALF* (which got into so much detail, there were trading cards with "Bouillabaseball" players). See also "St Olaf" in *Golden Girls* and "Hanover" in *Cheers*.

As we mentioned, the entire Cyborg Rights strand is very obviously a nod towards Gay Rights without saying it out loud. The give-away is that the steward addresses Red 6-7 as "ladies, gentlemen and Banakaffalatta". A story such as this is in a bind, since it cannot represent any minority really existing in the UK as marginal or freakish (note the improbable-for-1912 racial mix of the passengers in the opening scene), but Davies wants to talk about his world.

The Australian Soap theme (this episode was being shot on the same complex where *Torchwood* was playing host to another *Neighbours* alumnus, Alan Dale) is picked up by the Doctor's comments on *By the Light of the Asteroid* being "the one with the twins": anyone stuck watching UK daytime telly in the 80s will recall *Sons and Daughters*. Probably with a shudder, as this was the worst that came to Britain. (The ITV companies passed on *Number 96*, but when we come to X4.17, "The End of Time Part One", we will be discussing *Prisoner: Cell Block H* in all its Sapphic ludicrousness.)

Normally the Windsors would spend Christmas at the Sandringham estate in Norfolk, attending the local church and being left alone by the press, hence the Cribbins scene establishing that the Queen has gone out of her way to spend Christmas in London. That might be expected of her, following her parents' example of staying put during the Blitz, but the show of normality would logically include an early start and a church visit (she's head of the Church of England, after all). The most plausible detail in the scene is the corgi evacuation. Camden is a borough of North London, quite a way from Chiswick (X4.1, "Partners in Crime") and including Regent's Park, London Zoo, the British Museum and the Post Office Tower.

Oh, all right... yes, a lot of the material about the handsomely-carved, supernaturally calm killer robots is taken from "The Robots of Death", including the menacing "Information: you are all going to die", and right down to a scene where Alonso traps a robot's hand in the closing door and it comes off. The joke of the brass head with the sculpted hair repeating "Max" glitchily is a reference to *Max Headroom* (the music-video clip-show and the later dystopian sitcom – see X6.1, "The Impossible Astronaut"). The sequence with the killer Frisbees being batted off with clubs is a straight steal from *Tron* (1982), and that stuff about the Doctor being Max's "Apprentice" and it being a "task" to work out the plot is – as far as anyone in Britain went – a reference to *The Apprentice* (see X2.12, "Army of Ghosts"; X7.4, "The Power of Three") and Sir Alan Sugar (now Lord Sugar, another real-life Lord Copper) rather than to anything involving Donald Trump. (He was widely believed in Britain to be a fictitious character from 80s comedies, until his presidential bid elevated him to being a Boris Johnson wannabe.)

We should also note that many of the jokes about Mr Copper's garbled account of Christmas

Is Kylie from Planet Zog?

continued from Page 307...

and which old-format *Doctor Who* got ten million of people to happily watch. *Doctor Who* is not made for the sort of people who buy TARDIS dresses in Hot Topic, it's made for the British Public, as many of them as possible. Hence Davies's comments about "viewers".

The simple fact is, this is a (relatively) low-budget TV show made with human actors. There aren't many ways around that. Other series that have tried tend to have the same set-up week after week, so can justify the preponderance of the speaking cast being bipedal mammals with opposable thumbs and everything. *Doctor Who* has the potential to be set in a different world, time or dimension every episode. Davies was struggling to afford the few attempts at other planets he *did* include, and offset the cost by making a lot of cheap episodes in-between. Moffat, who was given significantly less money to play with, paradoxically spent less screen-time in present-day Britain, but he and his writers put even less effort into inventing worlds that weren't like (say) bits of folklore, 30s Hollywood's idea of the Middle East or deserted planets with caves and beaches. These are both deliberate choices by the executive producer.

Doctor Who has always occupied an ambiguous territory between "proper" SF and "orthodox" television drama, ever since Sydney Newman's refusal to employ BEMs. *Star Trek* in its original form slightly broadened the vocabulary available to the general viewer, but *Who* producers took what they needed on their terms, not *Trek*'s. Davies narrowed that crossover territory from a sort of marshland, as it had been in the 1970s, to a tightrope. Paradoxically, the clearest examples of the kind of thinking you get in That Kind of Series under Davies happened in *The Sarah Jane Adventures*, a series even less like them in its outward appearances and target audience than even BBC Wales *Doctor Who* (see also **What Happened in 1972?** under A7, "Dreamland"). In keeping with his higher opinion of child-viewers' demand for internal logic, and stories that are more than just pretty pictures, Davies had Gareth Roberts, Phil Ford et al construct watertight plots derived from looking into how people would react if the staples of US space-opera actually happened. Series 1 of the new *Doctor Who* did likewise, but this fell apart through repetition (see **Was Yeti-in-the-Loo the Worst Idea Ever?** under 5.5, "The Web of Fear"). To some extent, "Turn Left" (X4.11) was an attempt to reclaim this lost ground. However, the episode that followed was almost entirely a pastiche of every imported space saga or teen-angst-with-the-undead soap that had been shown in the previous decade.

Any of the options selected by the writers of these other series, and the many others that came before or after them and dealt with human actors in space opera in other ways, could have been selected for a year or so to see what worked. To the casual viewers – and these are the majority of the BBC Licence-Fee payers who fund the series – this would hardly make any difference. They'd just be pleased if we went a whole year where a storyline isn't overly tangled. For most viewers before 1980, *Doctor Who* didn't belong in the same bracket as *Star Trek* or *Space: 1999*, but somewhere between *Jackanory* and *I, Claudius*. When Davies was in charge, it was located somewhere between *Linda Green* and *Horrible Histories* rather than *Battlestar Galactica* and *Lost*.

In his farewell tour of the series between Series 4 and Series 5, Davies gave in and did what he thought fans of That Kind of Series would enjoy as much as he did. The audience expectations were now flexible enough for him to indulge himself. However, the series had become rather rigidly orthodox, largely as a result of his own pronouncements about what it would and would not do. Individual voices were muffled in the rewrites, and any given script would tend towards the mean; now, Davies gave himself co-author credit on two of these Specials. Without wishing to read the tea-leaves too much over who wrote which bits, which we might get as wrong as online guesses over the co-authorship of *About Time*, it's interesting that the portion of "The Waters of Mars" (X4.16) that leads into the regeneration is the last quarter hour, and is facilitated by the awkwardly out-of-place Gadget – exactly the kind of annoying, merchandisable cutesy robot that used to blight US space opera series.

The Vinvocci were similarly anomalous in the two-part finale, although this had a lot of Marvel-like features. Davies's last episode, "The End of Time Part Two" begins with people in velvet fancy-dress burghermeister costumes strutting around epic sets on a CGI world and saying things like "What news of the Doctor?" – precisely what

continued on Page 311...

on Earth mean Christmas in England. Even Scotland is relatively new to Boxing Day as a holiday. We mentioned in "The Christmas Invasion" that the Queen's Speech is the fulcrum of a television Christmas in Britain, and the BBC1 3.00pm showing is the starting-gun for the turkey and sprouts in most homes. Thus her visit to Sandringham for the morning church service and the content of the oddly-unmemorable speeches is headline news on a day when, usually, nothing at all newsworthy happens.

Oh, Isn't That...?

• *Kylie Minogue* (Astrid Peth). Seriously? You'll be asking who the woman with the corgis in Buckingham Palace was supposed to be next.

Well, everywhere outside America, she (Kylie, not Her Majesty) is either a fairly big star or a household name – predominantly for her 25-year singing career, but originally for acting. She and sister Dannii (sic) were child-stars in Australian soaps and Light Entertainment shows. Kylie went on to play Charlene Mitchell, teenage garage mechanic, in *Neighbours* at precisely the point that this show became a national obsession in the UK, and on the back of this made pop records for the UK hit factory Stock Aitken and Waterman. (American PBS viewers might remember her from *The Vicar of Dibley* episode where Elton John's scheduled appearance at a community fair comes to nought, and the Vicar – Dawn French – drafts Kylie in as his replacement. She was in almost every sense bigger than Elton John.)

In the mid-90s Kylie went all serious, recording a moody single with Nick Cave and some sophisticated self-penned tracks, then circa 2000 she went back to floor-fillers. "Can't Get You Out of My Head" finally supplanted "I Should Be So Lucky" as her biggest hit. In between these, she spectacularly shed her "girl next door" image by dating INXS lead singer Michael Hutchence. Although she had a few feature film roles (*The Outsiders*, Cami in the weird Van Damme games-movie *Street Fighter* – see X1.3, "The Unquiet Dead" and 24.2, "Paradise Towers" – and the Absinthe Fairy in *Moulin Rouge*), playing Astrid was the largest role she'd had since *Neighbours*. It was part of her comeback after a two-year battle with cancer, along with a global tour and another hit single, "2 Hearts" (yes, really). More recently, you may have seen her in the already-forgotten *San Andreas*.

Despite making "Kylie" suddenly one of the most popular girls' names in Britain in 1990, she's first-name-only for most purposes. (Some American recently tried to trademark the name, despite having apparently been named after the "real" Kylie, and came badly unstuck. For people really out of the loop, the surname rhymes with "Vogue".)

• *Geoffrey Palmer* (Captain Hardaker). You'll have seen him before he was a household name in two Pertwee stories, "Doctor Who and the Silurians" (7.2) and "The Mutants" (9.4). However, after playing Uncle Jimmy in *The Fall and Rise of Reginald Perrin* (and almost the same character in *Fairly Secret Army*), he started being noted as playing Geoffrey Palmer-type characters. A long running sitcom, *Butterflies*, had him as the boring husband of a woman having an affair; another, *As Time Goes By*, paired him with Judi Dench, a team-up that springs to mind when he's playing an Admiral in the pre-credit scene of *Tomorrow Never Dies* opposite Dame Judi's M.

And to state the obvious: Charles Palmer, director of four episodes in Series 3, is his son. Whether or not this planted a seed in Davies's mind when he was writing the *Titanic* Captain is a moot point, as it's hard to imagine anyone else being anything but a stand-in – it's *that* obvious a piece of casting.

• *Debbie Chazon* (Foon Van Hoff, wife). She had worked for Davies before, as Big Claire in *Mine All Mine*, and had been offered a part as a Slitheen but wanted to be seen. Before that, she'd been in *Topsy-Turvy* and *The Lakes*, and shortly after she was in the sketch-show *Tittybangbang*. More recently, she was in *Sherlock*: "The Sign of Three". She's done all the usual soaps and whodunnits.

• *Russell Tovey* (Midshipman Alonso Frame). Nowadays best known for bittersweet sitcom *Him and Her,* and for playing a not-at-all killer werewolf George in the original BBC3 *Being Human*. He had been in *The History Boys* (see X5.11, "The Lodger"). A year from this episode, he'll be the focus of a lot of attention as Davies mentions in passing that, were he still in charge, Tovey would be the next Doctor (see **The Lore**).

• *Bernard Cribbins* (Wilfred Mott). The results of this guest appearance gave his career a serious late boost, but at the time he was best remembered from his much-beloved appearances on *Jackanory* and various other child-friendly offerings in the 60s, 70s and 80s. Before that, he had been in the

Is Kylie from Planet Zog?

continued from Page 309...

Davies said his series would never do. A bit earlier, "Planet of the Dead" landed up having more in common with *Lexx* than anything else, albeit mixed in with *Flight of the Phoenix* and a caper-movie. The Tritovores seem similarly perfunctory, as if the obligation to have an identifiable (and action-figure-worthy) humanoid alien occurred to Roberts and Davies late on in the conferences.

Another paradox: Davies was unashamedly a fan of these series, but displayed a low opinion of the attention-span and a willingness to step outside their comfort-zone among the general viewing public. Moffat, conversely, expects a lot of his viewers and expresses distaste for all of these series, but has made his version of *Doctor Who* very like them. By Series 6, it was perfectly possible to have at least two alien races that looked indistinguishable from humans. (We have no idea about Appalapachia's lost residents other than blurs, but they have two hearts – so, if that *is* the Mona Lisa, there's a story we ought to have heard; X6.10, The Girl Who Waited".) Nonetheless, to date, Sto is still the most fully-detailed non-Earth-related culture we have had since the BBC Wales series began, even counting the conflicting accounts of Gallifrey. More thought seems to have gone into evoking this unseen world than into researching the well-documented London of 1651 (X9.6, "The Woman Who Lived").

Maybe the last word on Zog as the all-purpose foreigners should go to one of those imported space-operas of the 90s. *Babylon 5*, probably the most influential of them all (see **Did Cartmel Have *Any* Plan at All?** under "Silver Nemesis") justified the preponderance of human-looking aliens by positing that all the Ancient Races evolved to a higher plane after tinkering with the next lot. Whilst seeking out one of these races, Our Heroes met a giant flaming face in space who responded to their entreaties for aid with the single word *Zog!*. The Sarcastic English One (for once, not the villain) shrugged and said "Who knew they were French?"

charts with a string of novelty records, produced by the then-unknown George Martin, notably *Right, Said Fred*. He was the more-or-less romantic lead in a couple of early *Carry On* films. He was, of course, the voice of *The Wombles*. In the 100th *Jackanory*, a reading of *The Hobbit*, he was probably the definitive Bilbo Baggins.

As you may recall from Volume 3, he was in the running to take over from Jon Pertwee as the Doctor. Oh, and he was in *Daleks-Invasion Earth: 2150 A.D.* as a slapstick policeman, making him the biggest person to appear in both one of the Cushing films and the BBC Wales series. And we've not even mentioned the Tufty Club.

• *Jimmy Vee* (Bannakaffalatta). Finally! After three series where he's always playing the little plot-critical but sidelined character, he gets more dialogue than the Moxx of Balhoon ("The End of the World") or the Pig ("Aliens of London"). He was also the Graske in the online game and several *Sarah Jane Adventures*.

• *Clive Swift* (Mr Copper). He played Jobel in 22.6, "Revelation of the Daleks". Most notably, he had been the long-suffering Richard Bucket in *Keeping Up Appearances* and had been to India making a documentary about that sitcom's adaptation for their TV network. A long and distinguished career seems to have ended shortly after this episode (see **The Lore**).

• *Gray O'Brien* (Rickston Slade, snob) had served time in *Peak Practice*, a completely different series about doctors in picturesque scenery, between *Casualty* and *Coronation Street*. Latterly he was in yet another drama about the real *Titanic*.

Things That Don't Make Sense Cute as it is, what exactly is the point of the Doctor ringing the Palace about the incoming *Titanic*? If it hits, it'll destroy London and send up a cloud of irradiated dust that will cause Adric-like effects on the world ecosystem (19.6, "Earthshock"). Except... in the Doctorless version of this event (X4.11, "Turn Left") it destroys London and, er, that's it. Either way, Her Maj is just as dead standing in The Mall as if she'd stayed in bed. We also have to ask why London can be evacuated with no problems in this instance, when it's a major logistical nightmare culminating in supposed work-camps when it happened in Donna's other timeline. In this version, most of the fugitives apparently all holed up with relatives or at hotels and booked it in advance, whilst in the "Turn Left"-iverse, the whole thing came as a complete surprise despite the much more lethal WebStar (X3.0, "The Runaway Bride") and the massacre at Royal Hope Hospital (X3.1, "Smith and Jones").

We're all meant to be amused by Mr. Copper's misunderstandings about Earth culture, but it's downright inconsistent that someone could have bits of information as detailed as Christmas turkeys and have the rest so muddled (perhaps he skimmed some Roald Dahl and mistook it for a travel manual). The people who collected genuine Earth antique dress-suits and tins of Brasso were obviously able to visit this off-limits Level Five world, so why is Mr Copper's information so off-beam? And if Earth is supposedly as dangerous as he says, isn't it a little odd that everyone's allowed to wander off by themselves? Oh, and Walterley Street apparently runs under the Thames all the way from Kennington (see X1.8, "Father's Day") to Camden. (Maybe it's a *really long* secret street full of aliens, which explains why it would take 6.5 minutes for a raven to fly along it; X9.10, "Face the Raven".)

We can count Alonzo's army salute as one of the misprisions of the Sto-based Earthonomics course, and we have so little idea of their biology that his miraculous recovery from a bullet-wound could be entirely normal. And yet, everyone else seems to act as if they get injured the way humans do, so let's just ask about it here and move on. Let's also presume that Sto isn't accustomed to the idea of terrorism – if they were, then having robots that automatically defer to whoever happens to be present when they've just seen their superior killed would be an obviously bad idea.

When the ship's hull is first breached, a few people are sucked away before the oxygen membrane stabilises. These work independently of the shields (which are switched off), but require the Doctor to fix them. With a sonic screwdriver. Once again, we'll pause for younger fans to look up the word "sonic" and apply this information to situations where the air's not there. The big point is that, rather than tripping automatically when the air gets a bit thin, there is – somehow – one small patch goes wonky and has to be rebalanced manually. So we might suppose that Max's Plan A was to let the air run out and everyone who avoided being sucked into space asphyxiating, but he's thwarted by a stranger with a gadget that ignores conventional acoustics – fair enough, but that's not said. There are shields, which Rickston notices are down, and an oxygen membrane which, even at the worst of the crisis, is holding. The Host could have killed everyone in seconds just by switching that off.

Besides, the oxygen membrane seems easy to switch off, as the Doctor opens a window to let Astrid fly around the universe. Or when he tells Astrid, "Now you can travel forever", does he mean "... around the outside of this ship they're going to scrap"? The ship is still in space when this happens, so if he's turned off the force-bubble, why are they alive when the porthole pops?

According to the Doctor, the exchange rate between Sto credits and pounds sterling is approximately 50 to one. Mr Copper therefore ends the story rich, as the computer automatically allocated him one million in the local currency (pounds), which equates to a whopping 50,000,056 credits. If the cruise line's computers allocated this windfall to a lowly cruise historian without a bit of protest, Capricorn needn't have bothered with the whole *Titanic* scheme; they're so incompetent that they'll surely be bankrupt soon. Conversely, Foon and Morvin think they're saddled for life with a five-thousand credit phone (sorry, "Vone", cos it's all spacey and kooky) bill, which comes out to approximately £100 (£99.98 if you insist) or $160 in 2007. What kind of economic setup does Sto have, if it'll take 70 years to pay that off? It only makes sense if the Doctor was using eighteenth-century prices.

After years of plot holes that you could drive a truck through, we have a *literal* hole and Kylie drives a fork-lift into it. This hole extends down into the inferno of the engines, a fall of something like 150 metres if the perspective on Astrid's slow-motion fall is accurate. Then the Doctor is hoisted by angels up and up and up and up and up to the Bridge. This ship has to be at least a mile high for a flight that fast to go on that long. And the whole preceding scene took place on Deck 31. Even if the Bridge is Deck 1 or Deck Zero, that's 30 *very* tall decks.

What's more, the whole time the Doctor was chatting with Max Capricorn, there was a gaping hole into a flaming abyss and no updraft or soot. That's possible if they have the same magic air-shields that keep the oxygen in the ship, but they don't have any such shield protecting Deck 31 from the conflagration because – as we said – Kylie can drive a fork-lift into it. Max and the Doctor can converse normally despite the ship's engines and infrastructure burning. The Doctor doesn't even take off his jacket in the heat.

Meanwhile, Alonso has sealed off the Bridge with a "maximum deadlock" to keep just about anyone and everything out, save for a pretty flimsy robotic fist from coming in through the floor. Also, if it's so easy for the Hosts to smash through the floor into the Bridge, why didn't they do that half an episode ago? (A lot of this story makes more sense if we assume that they're quite simple-minded really, and the "Kill" program gets in the way of useful independent thought. However, this makes entrusting the deaths of any survivors to them rather than letting all the air out suddenly even sillier.) For that matter, putting your super-secure crash-landing proof tank in the engine room is one thing, but putting alongside Nuclear Storm™-type engines seems a little dangerous. And why does it take Max such a long time to shut down the engines? He waits until someone shows up to explain why they haven't yet.

And there's a long and established tradition of incredibly dangerous transport methods on *Doctor Who,* but really, calling it a "Nuclear Storm Drive" is just asking for trouble. However this thing works (and the fact that Max and the Doctor mill around nearby discussing plot points might indicate a lack of actual radiation, but see below), re-igniting it with the heat from entering the Earth's atmosphere is tricky at best. (How much heat? Hard to say: the re-entry shields for shuttles and moonshots were designed for a vessel that was slowing down, not speeding up, so the temperatures generated were high because they were deliberately causing friction. *Titanic* is streamlined and not presenting the blunt end to the air to create drag. Let's say, for the sake of argument, that it's about the same temperature as the air near the Space Shuttle (around 5000 C), a re-entry period of ten minutes and the same area of hull as the prow of the real *Titanic,* around 120,000 square metres. Call it 68 gigawatts, tops. If you – somehow – saved that all up into one concentrated three-second blast, you *might* re-ignite some kind of atomic engine, but you have to duct it to the core from the shields without melting the ship.) If that heat-energy is available to be used, the ship's shields must be more porous than we thought, so everyone on board probably got cancer from solar radiation. (Unless people from Sto are utterly unlike humans, which might have been worth mentioning to get around several other apparent goofs.)

We have also to account for the Doctor's driving – if the *Titanic* had been falling, it would just as likely have reached terminal velocity, the friction making the heat partially offset by the convection of thicker air moving past the ship's hull (if it got there through the oxygen membrane), so there's no benefit from waiting until the last possible moment before using the heat (somehow) to spark up the engines. All that achieves is making the turning-arc needed to go back up again a lot tighter – which is daft, even if the ship hadn't been crashed into by flaming interplanetary objects and subjected to at least 1g acceleration for a long distance. (Even 12.5, "Revenge of the Cybermen" got this right.) Making the *Titanic* act like the Red Arrows doing a flypast on the Queen's official birthday is just as likely to shatter the hull as anything else.

One thing is especially grating because it's obviously the result of a lot of work... a few people fall to their fiery demises in slo-mo, looking up plaintively at the camera as they gracefully approach the engulfing flame. It's a cliché of films where people get burned in huge factory-like spaces (you can see Eccles do it in *Gone in 60 Seconds*). When Morvin does it, however, he's in the same shot as the Doctor, Astrid and company – all moving in normal speed.

###

For the rest of this section, Dr Science will consider the issue of geosynchronous orbits and why people who make a living creating CG planets don't know much about the planet they're on...

So, it's yet-another episode set on Christmas Eve and with lots of shots of the Earth from space, but this one finds whole new ways to make the timeline not quite work. There's the perennial difficulty anyone at The Mill has with the Moon and the Earth showing the same phase from the same viewpoint, and the way Northern Europe is almost completely illuminated by sunlight when seen from space when it's night at ground-level. There's someone selling newspapers well into the night on Christmas Eve; even if Wilf is there to show support for Her Majesty, other shops seem to be open despite the late hour and the evacuation. (Then, in a later scene, we see Earth from the *Titanic* as the meteoroids – it's Christmas, so we'll just assume they have brandy-butter and a tank of oxygen each – approach and the sun won't be seen in London for at least an hour. A few scenes later, it's even earlier – the Terminator line's over Berlin when the TARDIS falls to Earth.)

There's also the way Christmas Day dawns at

Buckingham Palace (which would be at almost 8.30am), so soon after the Doctor tells Astrid that it's midnight and a very long time after the ship starts crashing. That's "dawn" as in "a couple of scenes after the view of Earth had Great Britain fully illuminated", of course, and Camden – within walking distance of the Palace – is still pitch-dark when Wilf shakes his fist at the receding liner.

What "midnight" means in orbit is unclear, but as the *Titanic* seems to be in geosynchronous orbit over London (well, that bit of the Equator on the Greenwich Meridian), Mr Copper's group go to Camden to do shopping and the TARDIS lands in Cardiff (the same patch as an often-used location in *Torchwood* that's all "hey-look-we're-in-Cardiff"), we have to assume he means GMT. But the ship's orbit starts to decay. This isn't quite the same as simply falling as, to remain in orbit, the forward momentum has to counterbalance the Earth's gravitational pull. That's what "orbit" means. Geostationary orbits, presuming that's what this *is*, are ones where the height and speed of the satellite/ spaceship means one orbit takes exactly as long as one rotation of the Earth (one day, as we call them hereabouts). That works at 35,000 km or so, and can hold steady for decades. If losing power makes the orbit decay, then it's *not* one of those, and the ship is in a lower orbit but still hovering. That is difficult to get to work, as Earth's mass and radius are fixed. A geostationary orbit just requires the ship to have been at the right point over the Equator and travelling about 11,000 km per hour – no air, so no friction and you only have to worry about the Moon's pull, or solar winds after the first quarter century.

Nevertheless, let's go with what happens on screen. The ship starts getting closer to Earth, which means it has to have lost forward momentum. That only happens if you fire retros, because there's no air to slow it down. Right, fine, Max ordered the Host or Captain Haddock (well, he's called "Hardaker" in the script but not on screen, and with everyone else on Sto having silly names it makes just as much sense) to fire retros in a scene we missed. The ship goes into a tighter orbit. Not, however, a geosynchronous/ geostationary one. So why is the ship still over the Meridian? How come it moves 5700 km north to plummet boldly towards Buckingham Palace rather that Burkino Faso? Logically, an orbital decay would still be moving it across places on the Equator, just more of them in an hour than before.

All right, so it wasn't a geostationary orbit, just an amazing coincidence that every time we got an exterior shot of the *Titanic* it was over London, albeit in a really weird sequence of snapshots where it got dark and light and dark and light and dark. That means there was a gigantic object in close orbit around Earth when the planet was on high alert for such things (London evacuated, America lacking a President because of alien assassins) and nobody, not even UNIT, saw it. It should have been visible to the naked eye, as we can clearly see city lights on the planet's surface, so there are no clouds. Nobody even saw the mysteriously flaming-in-vacuum meteoroids.

And there's still no reason why the TARDIS should drift down to Cardiff rather than Quito or Kampala. Or, if it's because of the Time Rift, why not land on top of Torchwood? (If it's slowly levitating rather than falling at 9.81 metres-per-second faster than the second before, there's no need to imagine how big a crater it would leave, but instead we have to wonder about eye-witnesses. Unless, of course, Cardiff's track-record for alien malarkey means that it, too, has been evacuated.) That the Doctor's faithful vessel didn't land in the same street where he had recently teleported – a street he and the TARDIS keep landing up in (see, for instance, X4.12, "The Stolen Earth") is another puzzle, as it requires the Doctor and Mr Copper to over-ride the co-ordinates on an already damaged teleport mechanism. Either way, someone needs to look up the term "centre of gravity".

Critique It's all down to context. If you were Joe Public watching when sated and content on Christmas Night 2007, it would seem like chill-out yuletide viewing. If you knew the set-pieces of 70s Disaster Movies, it looked like an affectionate pastiche. If you had only a mild interest in *Doctor Who* but were a big Kylie fan, it looked like a star vehicle with a spaceship and killer robots. If you were a hardcore devotee of the series and had been disappointed by the resolution of "Last of the Time Lords" (X3.13), this just seemed to add insult to injury. If, by contrast, you were a hardcore devotee and had *liked* that, you'd probably love this.

Watched now, it looks as magical as the first part of *Fanny and Alexander* (the single most Christmasssy television episode *ever*) and a remarkably tidy piece of scripting and directing.

Better yet, the BBC America edit cuts to the chase and gets it all into one hour, with 12 minutes of that given to commercials and trailers. Paradoxically, that makes it *more* cinematic. However, this isn't what you'd call a vintage script, and the directing – with many flourishes and a lavish look – can't cover the cracks.

What we're looking at is an hour and a quarter of set-pieces rather than a story. There are reasons each section happens, set up at least perfunctorily in the earlier ones and significant in how later ones play out, but it's more bitty than any previous story, even those conceived of as bits (1.5, "The Keys of Marinus", for example, or more pertinently 20.7, "The Five Doctors"). The individual components are as good as they can be, but it's strangely disjointed. Dip into any scene (except one, which we'll discuss in a mo) and it all works, yes, but watching the whole thing *from start to finish* is difficult. No one performance is bad or outstandingly good; it's an ensemble piece with Tennant taking less of a lead than usual. Kylie has been doing television since her early teens, so it was less of a surprise to observant viewers than to TV critics that she could hold her own against scene-stealers such as Clive Swift (Mr Copper) and Jimmy Vee (Bannakaffalatta). Likeable girl-next-door was her calling-card as an actor and a pop-star; she dips back into it for effect when on a stadium tour, usually after a spectacular set-piece. If there's one performance that stands out, it's Russell Tovey as Midshipman Frame, simply because so much of his screen-time is the thankless job of looking at screens and talking to people on intercoms.

That's this episode in a nutshell, though: well-made scenes not really connecting. The more it becomes cinematic, the more *Doctor Who* loses touch with its strength as drama – the way people react to each other as much as to explosions and huge things matted in later. The episode's best scenes involve the small band of survivors bickering but working together. Davies will take this lesson on board, and soon afterwards give us X4.10, "Midnight". There are few of these, but insufficient pace or tension to justify not making this the bulk of the episode. It's like looking at illustrations from a book about a disaster-movie, but it works as long as we're all singing along to the plot we expect/ remember from 70s blockbusters. Putting in a more conventional antagonist on top of the characters fighting a situation makes it more *Doctor Who*-ish, but less interesting.

George Costigan does what he can with the part of Max, but even at Christmas, we need more than a disembodied head on a clunky robot as a Doctor-sized threat. (And, yes, we know that we'll get exactly that again in 2015, but realistically River Song is the villain of that tale.) Astrid plunges to her death almost out of contractual obligation: it's exactly what that kind of character does in that kind of story and, besides, we know it's unrealistic to expect Kylie flipping Minogue to spend the next year in Cardiff when she's got a global comeback tour planned. The moment the Doctor agrees to accept her aboard the TARDIS serves to doubly confirm that she's doomed.

The scene where it all falls down, really, is the Doctor solemnly summoning robot angels to lift him bodily to the Bridge. Apart from the ludicrous religiose imagery, it's a shocking lapse in tone and an episode that's been limping along. Thereafter we get the dismal joke about Buckingham Palace, which seems to have been grafted in from a less-good episode ("Silver Nemesis", perhaps) and the cheesy sequence of Kylie turning into the Blue Fairy. This arrests the downwards spiral and we get the ominous exchange with Mr Copper about choosing who gets to live, which is where the first seed of this Doctor's departure is sown. But lurching back onto the previous mood doesn't forgive the previous lurch away.

There are gestures towards world-building and motivating the minor characters by a set of customs unlike anything on Earth, but these are flattened out and, with a few exceptions, Sto is a crude analogue of Edwardian England, messed-up currency conversions and all. Even though it's all a huge joke to the author, this is as close as they get to emulating Robert Holmes, supposedly the guiding light of the current generation of producer-writers on the series.

So, after only two years, the "traditional" bonus-length Christmas Special was seeming like an obligation and is a textbook example of the programme's lapses into being "event" television and little more. Back in the day, when *Doctor Who* episodes were one-off transmissions for BBC1 viewers, never to be repeated, you could better make allowances when watching (for example) episode six of 5.7, "The Wheel in Space", and its peculiar ending leading into a repeat of an earlier story. Now, with the episodes in constant rerun somewhere, and the DVD and streaming sales a key part of the promotional and financial plan, making an episode that will pass muster for an audience that is sated, sozzled and sleepy (or excitable kids sugared up to the eyeballs) isn't enough.

Full disclosure: we waited until just after Christmas to write this review in the hope that some of the mince-pie-and-pudding magic would rub off, but to no avail. Once seen, no amount of yuletide cheer makes revisiting this episode less than disappointing.

The Lore

Written by Russell T Davies. Directed by James Strong. Viewing figures: (BBC1) 13.3 million and 2.4 million, (BBC3 repeat) 0.5 million. It being a Christmas episode, it got a BBC1 repeat. First-night AIs were 86%. For the first time, the BBC's iPlayer was counted towards the ratings; 12.2 million is the overnight figure, those actually in front of television sets during the whole broadcast, but many people watched bits of it on the day and this is counted towards the final figure.

But 13.3 million... that's half the people who were watching any of the five available terrestrial channels or the subscription Sky 1 or any digital channel *at all* in that hour-and-a-bit. You'd be hard-pressed to accuse the new series of ever having been a "cult" show, but it's manifestly not one now.

Repeats and Overseas Promotion *Une Croisière Autour de la Terre* (literally, a cruise around the Earth/ World), *Reise der Verdammten*.

Alternate Versions To squeeze it in the routine hour-long-with-adverts format, BBC America whittles half an hour from the running-time, so the meteoroids hit just after the first ad break (i.e. in 12 minutes of screen-time). Almost all the best lines are removed, but the plot makes about as much sense as it ever did.

As usual, the BBC and many overseas broadcasters use this and other specials as holiday fare (the first time, on BBC1, got 0.6 million viewers at Easter).

Production

In spring 2007, Russell T Davies was asked to draw up a plan of Series 4, starting with the Christmas Special (which was now inevitably a part of the format). At around the same time, he started the process of archiving his email correspondence with *Doctor Who Magazine*'s Benjamin Cook, which resulted in a bestselling book, *The Writer's Tale* (in two editions, as more was added once the run of Specials was over and production begun on Series 5). From these, we get a very partisan but illuminating idea of the sequence of events and what influenced the decisions for Series 4, possibly more reliable than Eric Saward's interview in *Starburst* (see Volume 6).

The ideas for the forthcoming year were loosely in place when Davies proposed the series to the BBC heads, with more details for the "Starship *Titanic*" Christmas episode than the one after it, the one after the Sontarans came back or the one before the big Davros finale. The big romp in history to come after the Ood story would be either Mark Gatiss's pet project about World War II or the long-delayed Pompeii jaunt, and half of the double-banked pair would be Tom McRae's *GhostWatch* parody (see X2.12, "Army of Ghosts" and "Midnight"). The Christmas episode was outlined as a pastiche of a 70s Disaster Movie, and specifics such as the little red spiky-headed alien and the golden angelic robots were there from the start. One thing specified was that it *wasn't* a strictly accurate recreation of the *Titanic*.

• Davies was toying with having the details of Earth's history amusingly mangled and passed off as accurate by a nice old man (possibly David Jason, if he was keen), but at this stage was more exercised by two other possible casting coups. Director James Strong had, on the flight back from America (doing ADR for Ryan Carnes as Lazlo, see X3.4, "Daleks in Manhattan" et seq.), met Dennis Hopper's agent and the idea of a cameo by the veteran Hollywood fireball was floated. It turned out that Hopper could make a few days in summer to go to Cardiff. Then, during the press launch for Series 3, Will Baker, the *Who*-obsessed Creative Director (that's his title, "Creative Director") responsible for Kylie Minogue's extravagant stage-shows and videos, suggested that the pop goddess ought to be in the show.

As if! A few days and some phone calls later, it emerged that he was entirely serious and asked for a more detailed breakdown of the Christmas Special. Davies and Julie Gardner started negotiating the tangle of agents and Sony executives and timetables, but found that it could be done. Davies went to London to meet Kylie (by this stage, the number of people who could command him to do anything was vanishingly small, so this gives you an idea of the star's firepower, if you were unclear). This was kept quiet while all eyes were supposed to be on Freema Agyeman.

• After a two-year absence while dealing with breast cancer, Minogue was about to embark on a carefully-paced build up to her return at the end of 2007, with an album and a tour (it included dancers with Lumic-model Cybermen heads and a TARDIS take-off sound). Once she had agreed, the next problem was security – first in the sense of secrecy, and also in terms of paparazzi and the public once the word was out. So extraordinary were the measures that Louise Page had to source the costume for "Peth", as the character was originally called, from different manufacturers and have boots made from measurements given to her without a proper fitting. (Two for Minogue and others for the stunt-double and lighting stand-in.)

• The story consolidated around an insurance fraud, partly because a traditional Disaster Movie has people against a situation rather than an antagonist, and partly because, even with the chances of Dennis Hopper coming were red-shifting away, it needed a tangible, talkative villain. (If we're to believe the emails, they were thinking of Hopper for Mr Copper, despite there only being four days available for the star.) The original notion that Peth would be a close-but-no-cigar potential companion who disappoints the Doctor by doing something bad was replaced by that of an almost-perfect potential companion who dies saving Earth. Once a busy global star was cast, there had to be a damned good reason why this character wasn't permanently aboard the TARDIS. We'd seen the failed companion idea before, of course, in "Dalek" (X1.6), and it stayed around after this (X4.15, "Planet of the Dead").

• Pre-production began in early June and was complicated by Davies having two other series to oversee and, in some cases, rewrite while handling the press coverage of the third year of *Doctor Who*. He was already contemplating a year of semi-retirement with just a few Specials between Series 4 and 5. As we will see in the next episode, the character of Penny was secretly being transmogrified into a slightly more experienced Donna Noble. This needed to be conveyed to the writers and directors indirectly, without names being named until the official announcement after Martha had been seen to leave the TARDIS.

The press were trying to pierce the veil of secrecy and, in amongst the Dennis Hopper story getting out long after it had proven impractical, plus a report that Woody Allen would be playing Einstein, *The Sun* had the Kylie story. Davies deployed this as a means to damp down the "Freema sacked" stories doing the rounds. Then came the announcement that Catherine Tate had agreed to return full time and that Martha was joining *Torchwood*. One story they *didn't* get was the serious suggestion that Prince Charles should make a cameo explaining why the Royals were staying in London. It didn't go very far. Meanwhile, David Tennant was planning to take a break after Series 4 to play Hamlet at the Royal Shakespeare Company and, as news of this emerged later in the year, speculation would grow about him quitting the series.

• Just before the read-through, Davies was asked by Brian Minchin, the new script editor, whether the teleport bracelets were included because Astrid (as she had been renamed) was to have been rescued thereby. Davies considered this, but went for the ending where even the Doctor can't save everyone (the farewell kiss to the "ghost" was Tennant's suggestion). Smaller changes were made, including the news-vendor becoming "Wilf" rather than "Stan" and Mr Maxitane becoming Max Callisto and then Max Capricorn.

• The estimates of how much this episode would cost came back, making everyone involved blanch. Savings were found in the number of corridors needed and not destroying Buckingham Palace.

• A practical problem to start with was that the "walk across the canyon" sequences needed a studio set, as nothing quite right could be found. The only places that looked even vaguely right were massively unsafe. With time running out, Phil Collinson reluctantly agreed to a built set. The read-through was a week before the first day of shooting, which was to be spent on the canyon strut. (This read-through was in London, and only one unauthorised person – from *The Sun*, predictably – was around. Many people were a bit star-struck by Kylie, but this went after a few days on set. Tennant had already been to the theatre with her and she'd watched "Last of the Time Lords" with him.)

Thus 9th July and the two days after were spent at the Upper Boat, on a set with a big translucent photo flame effect like replica coal fires. The drop was only six feet, which was potentially dangerous, but not high enough to unnerve the cast. The robot mask for this scene was articulated for the dialogue scenes but didn't look quite right, so later ones had a better Host face less like Popeye. They also spent studio time on green-screen work in the same stage as the TARDIS set. The main green-screen sequences were of people falling to fiery oblivion. The planned Morvin and Hoon's Wild West get-up was almost entirely because someone had to be carrying a lasso.

As it happens, this week at Upper Boat became known as "Magic Week", as for the first time all three series were shooting in the complex. (*Torchwood* was making several episodes at once, and both James Marsters and Minogue's former co-star from *Neighbours*, Alan Dale, were around, as was Freema Agyeman. *The Sarah Jane Adventures* was mainly making "Warriors of Kudlak".)

• The 13th saw thirty-mile drive to Swansea, as the reception scenes were to be shot at the Exchange Building. Small changes were made to the shooting schedule to allow Tennant to go to Scotland. His mother had been in a cancer hospice for a while, but her condition had suddenly deteriorated. The non-Doctor sequences got priority.

• After a weekend off, an eventful one as it turned out, Tennant and the crew were back in Cardiff for three days at the Coal Exchange in Cardiff Bay, which had been turned into the Entertainment Lounge. The oak-panelled rooms were trimmed with period chinaware, napkins embroidered with the Max Capricorn logo, Christmas decorations and monitors. Among the extras in period costumes were Ben Foster and Murray Gold as part of the house band accompanying Yamit Mamo singing Christmas songs (the version of "The Stowaway" we hear was recorded a couple of months later). Tennant had elected to stay working while dealing with the practical problems of his mother's death and funeral.

• Between 19th and 27th July, the team were based at the Johnsey Industrial Estate in Mamhilad, Pontypool for the wrecked ship's interior. Davies, meanwhile, was wrestling with Gareth Roberts's Agatha Christie script and had finally broached the subject of leaving to Steven Moffat.

They began with Deck 31. One difficulty they might have foreseen was that, in the UK, it's illegal to operate a fork-lift truck without an HGV3 licence (the same one that covers articulated lorries). Despite playing Australia's favourite automechanic, Minogue wasn't covered, and making the scene as planned would have been an insurance and legal minefield, as well as a logistical problem. The eventual scene, if you look closely, never has her in a moving vehicle – it's just close-ups of her face, tyres burning rubber, the Doctor looking aghast and so on, and very long shots of a similar-looking fork lift driver shot from behind.

The "Max Box", the buggy in which Costigan was contained, was operated by remote control and used windscreen-wiper motors for the bellows-like life-support and light aircraft wheels. The Perspex fishtank in which the head was protected was wiped between takes to remove breath-condensation. Monday the 23rd saw them do Astrid's fatal plummet, with Minogue (who'd used wires in the *Barbarella*-pastiche video for her 1994 hit "Put Yourself in My Place") suspended over 40 feet over a green cloth, and dropped as delicately as anyone can drop 40 feet. When it came time to shoot Astrid's ghost-kiss on the 28th, Tennant had to snog thin air while repeating his pose when kissing Minogue.

• July ended with the news reporting a fire at the famous Cinecessat studio complex in Rome, which nonchalantly blew the surprise that *Doctor Who* would be filming there in a few weeks (see X4.2, "The Fires of Pompeii").

• Then came a night in a street that had to be blocked off entirely. Most street-scenes or exteriors had been managed with moderate security and a few barriers, almost guerrilla-style shooting in between the normal night-life of Cardiff or Swansea. As it turned out, the beefed-up security for the location shooting on the corner of Working Street and John Street was almost surplus to requirements. ("Donovan Street W1" doesn't exist: it was a gag about Kylie's *Neighbours* co-star Jason Donovan, with whom she recorded a memorably cheesy Christmas Number 1, "Especially for You".) It was a warm night and many people might have been expected to come and gawp at Tennant and Minogue or – had they known he was there for his one day – Bernard Cribbins. In fact, they got the scenes in the can unmolested.

• Cribbins brought many of his own clothes to wear as Stan the Paper Vendor, including his badge from the Paratroop Regiment and some holly from his garden. Davies came along later in the evening, as did former Doctor Colin Baker, who was doing a play in Cardiff that week.

• Geoffrey Palmer had a military background and had shot blanks in dramas before but, by law and because the technology had moved on a bit, the in-house armourer trained him before the scene of his firing on Midshipman Frame (and at the camera). With his son Charles directing much of Series 3, and Palmer himself watching "Doctor Who and the Silurians" shortly before, in order to do the DVD commentary a week after recording his scenes as Hardaker, he was back in the swing of *Doctor Who*, watching with his grandchildren. (According to the DVD commentary for *this* story, Palmer's subdued performance looked flat on set but, miraculously, seemed a lot more animated in the rushes.)

• About mid-August, news of Tennant's bereavement had broken, and online fandom rallied to raise funds for the cancer hospice where his mother had spent her last weeks.

• The Mill took six months to make the digital model of the *Titanic*. Davies was aware that meteoroids can't burn in the vacuum of space, but requested that these ones should for added effect. They also prevented the late Captain Hardaker from blinking posthumously. By the time of the final edit, Strong was off making the first episode of *Bonekickers* (see the essay with "Midnight"). The first edit was – oh dear – nearly 90 minutes long. It was trimmed to 75 minutes to placate the BBC executives but, as it turned out, they could have adjusted the schedule on Christmas Day to fit around it. (It went out at ten to seven, and was followed by the usual grim *EastEnders* episode and a special *Strictly Come Dancing* in which the four previous winners competed against each other.)

As broadcast approached, the cross-promotion for Kylie's comeback album *X* and the episode got complicated and intense. The BBC's new iPlayer service was being launched, and *Doctor Who* was part of the sales-pitch, while the series's website was overhauled and given an "Adventure Calendar". The press had confected some outrage over the use of the *Titanic* and how Kylie was dressed, but were still interested in whether she would be back full-time as Tate had been. The BBC One schedule for Christmas Day usually sweeps the boards for ratings and audience-share, so there was a great deal of prestige attached to a place in the line-up, and the seasonal promotion. (That year it was penguins skating around a tree in the clockwise circle that became the network ident after the World was deemed too white and middle class – there was also one of two penguins under mistletoe.) A few days later, it was re-screened on BBC1, and this was projected onto giant screens around the country. Kylie's guest-spot guaranteed press interest in countries that hadn't got much interest in *Doctor Who* but were showing *Torchwood* at prime time on main networks.

• We've alluded to it before, but Clive Swift gave a remarkably churlish interview to *Doctor Who Magazine* which, despite their hints that it was to be taken as tongue-in-cheek, annoyed many fans and BBC executives for its dismissive tone. (Sample excoriation from him: "I know that you all think that this is a big world, this *Who* business. But it isn't. There are much bigger things than this.") Strangely, he has barely worked since and his planned cameo in the Series 4 finale was replaced by Harriet Jones redeeming herself.

A5: "The Infinite Quest"

(2nd April to 29th June, 2007, in episodes) 30th June, 2007, as one story)

Which One is This? Martha Jones has a rollicking adventure and learns several valuable kid-friendly morals along the way. The Doctor has a spoon.

Where Does It Go? The climax hinges on Martha getting over her long-unresolved crush on the Doctor, so this is more likely to take place in the first half of Series 3. A lot of the events could have been circumvented by Martha having a magic phone with which to contact him (or someone), so we're inclined to put it between X3.6, "The Lazarus Experiment" and X3.7, "42". He is acting as if she's a proper companion instead of being given a one-off trip, so it's unlikely to be much before that. On the other hand, she's got that red leather jacket.

Firsts and Lasts Animated *Doctor Who* was an old idea by this point, but for the first time an incumbent TV production team turned their attention to creating an animated adventure and getting it broadcast on BBC1. It works better than you might expect.

It's also a trial run for a green light on the Doctor's screwdriver and – as we discuss in a couple of paragraphs from now – early versions of ideas used in live-action episodes abound here.

Watch Out For...

• The opening sequence is in all ways exactly like the usual one, except that the TARDIS is a rather nice cel-animated reconstruction.

• As this was originally shown in five minute episodes as part of *Totally Doctor Who*, there are a lot of twists and turns but – being serialised over the same weeks as Series 3 – a diligent attempt to avoid rubbing up against Martha's character-development (such as it was) meant that the plot hinges on her unrequited crush.

• Both the infinite-wishes trap and the Great Old Ones are hackneyed even by *Doctor Who* standards, but the way they're combined here is rather pleasingly deft, and a good deal more subtle than any earlier Lovecraft rewrites. What's especially impressive is that, in serial form, the individual segments can also work as an introduction to *Doctor Who* in general. For a serial commissioned as part of a series entirely devoted to *Who*, and with a target audience who already knew about it – by definition – this is possibly redundant, but a welcome change from more recent trends.

• There's a sequence where we get a skeleton in a space-suit, a good year before Steven Moffat does it (X4.8, "Silence in the Library"). We also have spoon-based shenanigans seven years before "Robot of Sherwood" (X8.3). Plus dung-piracy two years before "Planet of the Dead" (X4.15) and an ice-planet well ahead of "Planet of the Ood" (X4.3). The Doctor surrenders on behalf of a different species (X8.8, "Mummy on the Orient Express") and we've got a giant insect-queen hatching an army (A7, "Dreamland") and an insect race living in a Conglomeration (X3.11, "Utopia"). Baltazar and Mergrave use breathing equipment that looks like a trial-run for the Hath (X4.6, "The Doctor's Daughter") and the spaceship designs, especially for Baltazar's ship, prefigure the *Hesperus* from "The End of Time Part Two" (X4.18, and not necessarily a coincidence, as we'll see).

What's more, none of these not-entirely-original motifs looks like a rough draft for a more proficient later iteration; if anything, they work better here than in the "proper" episodes.

The Continuity

The Doctor There's a definite sense he knows more than he's telling Martha all through this story. [For one, if he really did take three years to sort out the prison and take a joyride through space, to arrive at more or less the exact moment he's needed, he must have accounted for the TARDIS' arrival down to the minute. He certainly seems to have noticed the similarities of the quests they're going on, and isn't half as shocked as Martha by the revelation that her brooch is a tracking device.]

Whatever his hearts' desire is, he doesn't have much trouble batting it aside when the *Infinite* tries to supply it. Martha isn't allowed to find out what it is.

• *Background.* Some of the greatest chefs in history have used the Doctor's fungal spoon: Fanny [Cradock], Delia [Smith], Madame Cholet [Womble]. [Your choice how seriously you choose to take this. If the Wombles are real, do they all sound like Wilfred Mott? Logically, the *Doctor Who* universe can't have a Bernard Cribbins in it, or people would comment on both Wilf and PC Tom Campbell from the second Peter Cushing film looking and sounding like him.]

Mind probes and the Doctor are never reliable bedfellows, but the one conducted on the Doctor here registers charges including at least 1400 counts of traffic violations [so much for his fondness for parking anyway he likes], 250 charges of library fine evasions and 18 counts of planetary demolition [either separately, all at once, or somewhere in-between] – all 3000 years before this story, so after 1000(ish) AD. [Nothing we *know* about the Doctor's history seems to warrant this sort of claim. He does blow up Skaro, at least, in 25.1, "Remembrance of the Daleks". So presuming this is true – and not a deception he's running to deliberately get thrown in jail, or to distract from his *real* crimes and misdemeanours – we can only imagine that this happened during the Time War. He might, of course, be counting Gallifrey in that total before learning the truth in X7.15, "The Day of the Doctor", and it's not even to say that the 18 worlds (save Skaro, maybe, and Gallifrey, perhaps) were inhabited, however.] The charges amount to a sentence of two billion years' worth of time.

He refers to Boudicca as 'Boadicea' [oddly old-school for this incarnation]. He discounts the *Infinite* at first as an old legend, but it's strongly hinted that he makes light of it so that people don't take it seriously and get into trouble.

• *Ethics.* He feels responsible for dangerous

Is Animation the Way Forward?

This is a less silly question than some people thought when we announced the essay-titles. Between submitting the first draft in early 2016 and publication in late 2017, something remarkable happened. Well, *several* unforeseen events happened but the one fewest people predicted was that, by the end of the year, it would be thought possible to fill cinemas across America by showing an animated reconstruction of 4.3, "The Power of the Daleks".

BBC America serialised it, in monochrome, in the 9.00pm Saturday slot. (Until they moved it to later, apparently because their more expensive – and frankly misguided – remake of *Dirk Gently* was underperforming, but also, possibly, because the sort of people who watch BBC America were underwhelmed by something so slow, character-led and clunkily-animated. The network's been unusually cagy about releasing the ratings for either serial.) A

ll right, BBC Wales had failed to deliver a new series for them to show that year but, even so, this was an extraordinary move, not least because it was so quick off the blocks. The motion-modelling of actors for Troughton's walk and the fight sequences was shot in August, three months before the first episode aired. People have mumbled about whether something like this would ever happen for decades – suddenly it was on Amazon. It's now possible to have the conversation this essay was intended to start.

What follows is almost exactly what we wrote when David Bowie was still alive, Brangelina was still a thing and there were 16 Republican presidential candidates. If anything, we don't have to try so hard to make the case now, but we'll leave it as it was.

#####

Next volume, in **How Does This Play in Pyonyang?** under "Partners in Crime" (X4.1), we'll explore how odd it is that the BBC never really tried exporting the format of *Doctor Who* while the episodes themselves were selling well overseas. There is, however, a persistent rumour that an apocalyptically awful Hanna-Barbera show of the early 80s, *The Fonz & the Happy Days Gang*, was the detritus after a bid to franchise the series' basic concept to the kings of American Saturday Morning cartoons. Those of you who missed it (which is pretty much everyone) may need a refresher. A flying saucer lands in Milwaukee's most alien-afflicted diner (because, as you recall, Mork from Ork landed there before getting his own series). It travels in time and space, but the pilot, a twee space-fairy called "Cupcake" (and back then, nobody in Britain knew the word) can't control it properly. So Fonzie, Ritchie and the other one have Adventures in Space and Time, narrated by Wolfman Jack. The smoking gun that they were thinking more scarves and jelly-babies than manga-eyes and a tutu is that Cupcake has a talking dog. He's called "Mr Cool".

Honestly, we're making it sound heaps better than it was.

This isn't necessarily a clone of *Doctor Who*. Animators with back then often came up with a weird and cynical Pablum that took characters from defunct sitcoms, added spaceships and terrible songs, and churned out episodes by the mile. The key difference between this one and, say, *Gilligan's Planet* (1982-83) or *The Partridge Family 2200 AD* (1974-75) is that the BBC bought it. That was because, in contrast to *Gilligan's Island*, the target audience in the UK had at least heard of the Fonz. The timing, just as *Happy Days* was spinning off into *four* separate series in live-action and *Doctor Who* was catching on in the US, makes it a strangely retro version of *Who*. Just as John Nathan-Turner was making the series more soap-like, with long-running storylines playing out in different times and places, the US cartoon found new ways to do the Hartnell-era formula of Adventures in History, as per *Time Tunnel*, but not much else.

Did the BBC hope to use this as a replacement? The US broadcast dates and lead-in time for animation in those days make it seem improbable. (Don't forget, the vague awareness of *Doctor Who* back then was enough to cause all sorts of odd details in US pop culture, such as Bill and Ted's phone booth and the *Super Globetrotters* episode where Meadowlark, Curly and the boys met "The Time Lord", a naff supervillain who inflicted the plot of 9.5, "The Time Monster" on our slam-dunking superheroes.) Nonetheless, that rumour has legs because we know how much the BBC hierarchy loved the income from *Doctor Who*, whilst being profoundly embarrassed by the actual episodes and the uneven viewing-figures. (Besides, with the BBC's shenanigans and misinformation about the future of *Doctor Who* around then, so many other apparently paranoid conspiracy theo-

continued on Page 323...

leftover artefacts and legends from the Dawn of Time, describing himself as the 'last guardian'. Announcing himself to the entire galaxy as a pirate is a task he'll take on with some gusto, if it'll stop a war.

• *Inventory: Sonic Screwdriver.* The Doctor uses it to start disintegrating an entire pirate ship, and then a craft from the Dark Times. [So it's really functioning as a magic wand, even if the latter ship was a bit crumbly to start with.] Also it's green rather than blue [we might as well presume that he's experimenting with the colour a bit after the last one's destruction in the Royal Hope].

• *Inventory: Psychic Paper.* An apparently normal fortieth-century criminal can see that the psychic paper is blank. However, after he's touched it, the Doctor uses it to read off his true identity. [Perhaps the former is a function of the latter.]

• *Inventory: Other.* His old cooking spoon, which looks oddly as though it was made of gold itself, held a fungus capable of rusting away a custom-built spaceship in seconds. The Doctor admits he might have heightened its corrosive effect.

The TARDIS When the Doctor fancies going to some random coordinates, he asks Martha to pick some numbers between zero and 99.

The Supporting Cast

• *Martha.* For some reason, she thinks that the Doctor taking her to see 'the most famous despot that ever, ever lived' is simply fantastic. [There's a theatrical flair to the first scene as if the two of them had rehearsed part of the scene earlier, accentuating the general impression that the Doctor has a pretty good idea what he's doing right from the start.] She identifies the technical term for fungus ('rubicola') without too much bother [just as well, she'd've sat a test on that]. She's – understandably – surprised to hear that people in the future still use oil.

By this point, she's acquired the Doctor's trick of rambling on length when necessary to distract the villain at a strategic moment.

It turns out that her heart's desire is simply the Doctor willing to love her back [although given the lack of a way out of her situation, it could be the prospect of the TARDIS and escape]. She works out the usual "it's not real, go away" defence against the *Infinite*'s influence by herself, and repudiates it.

The Supporting Cast (Evil)

• *Baltazar* has 'Scourge of the Galaxy' as part of his official title. He is human-shaped, but talks of Earth's residents as 'carbonites', and we never see his face. He has a bandage-mask and goggles [like the original Cybermen] with two glowing green phials on his breath-mask [like the Hath] and a blue two-hoop claw [like a Thighmaster] for his right hand [like the Morbius monster]. He's a space pirate and tyrant, one with sufficient gusto and resources to attempt the destruction of the Earth single-handed – and have a go at turning all carbon-based life into diamonds. He personally forged the bird-shaped ship.

For all his hype about being the baddest dude in the Seven Galaxies, he's out and about because the warder of Volag-Noc decided that he'd repaid his debt to society and reformed. It was during his stretch in clink that he learned of the *Infinite* and the components of the flight-recorder. Knowing of the TARDIS's abilities allows him to combine his fetch-quest with revenge on the Doctor for stopping his attack on Earth before the titles.

His heart's desire is, disappointingly, a lot of gold and diamonds. And revenge.

Planet Notes

• *Bouken.* A desert planet with lots of petroleum, and run by... Oil Corp! At least three artificial suns keep it warm. [Either for the benefit of the living employees or so the petrol flows easily – our bet's on the latter. One of the suns is noticeably smaller than the other, so the original might be a dwarf star – or just closer at that particular time of "day".] The sand is soft enough for a U-Boat-style pirate vessel, the *Black Gold*, to navigate below the surface and prey on the giant, spider-like walking oil-rigs. Bouken is one of the last oil-bearing planets in 'the Solar System'.

• *Myarr.* The new home of the insectoid Mantasphids, and the part we see is mostly jungle. They require nutrient from manure. Before this, it was a human colony and populated [on the one-person sample we get] by Welsh settlers whose army has the three-feather Fleur de Lys emblem of the Prince of Wales, and regiments associated with Wales [and the rugby team]. It's coveted as the last fertile world in human space, to the extent of a [planned] controlled incineration of the Mantasphid agglomeration for a mile radius.

• *Volag-Noc.* Yer bog-standard icy prison. The cells are banked up about a hundred tiers high,

Is Animation the Way Forward?

continued from Page 321...

ries proved to be true that nobody could put anything past them.) It would make sense if the bosses enabled someone else to take on the effort and expense of making it, in a way that allowed full rein to its potential (and revenue) without clogging up valuable studio-space at Television Centre that could be used to make more Paul Daniels game-shows. Indeed, something very like that almost happened in the late 80s.

Nelvana is a Canadian animation house, then-best known for doing franchise-related works such as *The Care Bears, Beetlejuice* and the *Star Wars* spin-offs *Droids* and *Ewoks.* (They had an early champion in George Lucas. Most people agree that the one salvageable part of *The Star Wars Holiday Special* is the animated section, i.e. the one part Lucas himself commissioned.) They had made a splash with the half-hour special *Cosmic Christmas* – perhaps the most 1977 thing imaginable – which cost less than it looked like (albeit it looks fairly cheap).

However, by 1990, they were becoming known for re-doing old children's works that had been badly served by earlier animators. They started with *Babar* and *Rupert Bear*, then embarked on more faithful and cinematic-looking adaptations of the *Tintin* books than the late 50s Télé-Hachette-Belvision serials. One of the founders had worked on *Yellow Submarine*, and all of the management tried to respect the originals when adapting works. If we are to believe the most-cited source, Jean-Marc L'Officier, one of the heads of CBS approached Nelvana in 1986, the same time that all the various film projects started circling the TV series like vultures. We know that by 1990, there were talks going on. Of all the bids to make *Doctor Who* once the BBC had washed their hands of it (a story we told in Volume 6), Nelvana's early 90s proposal came closest to fruition. There were character designs and briefing documents. Some sources say that four scripts were written.

The conception of the series that this project seems to have been working towards is everything Russell T Davies junked when he successfully brought it back: a self-consciously "wacky" Doctor with a long scarf, a hat, a long coat with question-marks and big glasses (plus a mullet); K9 in a foldaway form to be carried in a Gladstone Bag (which may or may not have walked behind the Doctor on mechanical legs); screaming girls; Time Lords; a cyborg Master (with a robot eagle – very like "The Infinite Quest" and its villains, Baltazar and Caw); epic space-battles and massive continuity.

Strangely, none of this is the official reason the project was abruptly shelved. The stated reason is that a UK animation house (un-named in the most-cited account by Nelvana's Ted Bastien) had made a lower bid. (This could plausibly have been the dying embers of the Coast-to-Coast/ Greenlight/ Daltenreys "Last of the Time Lords" project.) It has also been said, by Philip Segal (of 27.0, "The TV Movie" notoriety), that the Nelvana series had a gun-toting Doctor, which alarmed the BBC (although if they were that precious about it, his conception of the series would have set off alarms as well). None of the scripts remain, so we have no way of knowing how exhilarating or excruciating it might have been. What's clear is that there wasn't any notion that just because it was animated, it would be exclusively for children. Nelvana had attempted adult animation before all this and would collaborate with Channel 4 on a sitcom, *Bob and Margaret*. As it turned out, animation for grown-ups (or at least not-for-children) was what the 1990s wanted.

The odd thing is that people still think of animation as primarily for children. Despite the rise of Pixar (and the way Disney came back from the 80s swamp with *The Little Mermaid, Aladdin* and *The Lion King* before amalgamating with John Lasseter's company and putting him in charge of production); and the runaway success of *The Simpsons, King of the Hill* and all the Mike Judge series, *Family Guy* (and Seth McFarlane's empire) and ultimately *South Park*; there remains some inertia on this. What's also interesting is that "realistic" animation – supposedly the gold-standard for audiences and professionals – is less popular than obviously hand-drawn or "crude" material with child-audiences. Apart from *The Penguins of Madagascar*, the sophisticated CGI films that are so common, and often so spectacularly successful, at the cinema never really cross over into TV spin-off shows for kids. (You can list your own "can't-fail" duds.)

So far, television animation with the film-like imaging that cinema demands has only worked if the raw material is improbable-looking. *Star Wars Rebels* is close to being a toy advert, and the source films were almost cartoons themselves, but

continued on Page 325...

and in a cylindrical pattern maybe a hundred per tier; each cell has a circular door like a submarine's hatches and houses two humanoids [or one and a robot]. The complex is under the ice, so anyone arriving is encased in a cylindrical force-cage and sent down in a literal sense [or maybe it's just that the TARDIS landed right next to a hidden reception area and the whole planet is different]. Robots service the prisoners, equipped with one big eye, a second one over the left shoulder, two articulated arms [one with a blaster built in] and hover motors [they are more-or-less egg-shaped, with the spherical eye on a stalk at the top]. Locke, the real warder, is alarmingly zealous and his reprogramming by a former inmate, Gurney, probably saved thousands of lives, but was itself a problem. The Doctor reprogrammes Locke while raising Squawk on molten gold.

• *Pheros.* It's a planet composed of living metal [cf. 12.1, "Robot"], which is how metallic birds like Caw might have evolved there. Baltazar apparently mined the planet for his spaceship [which gives us some idea how he managed to overcome all of Earth's opposition]. The sky is a livid spring-green, but the Doctor and Martha seem able to breathe unaided and have exposed skin. [So it may not be a chlorine atmosphere as would be probable with air and seas that colour. Then again, Baltazar seems to be dressed for that.]

• *Asteroid 7574b* is in the Cerys system within the Hesperus Galaxy. The *Infinite* seems to have been reefed on it. Flotsam from it has spread across known space.

The Non-Humans

• *Mantasphids.* An ordinary enough alien insect species, they look like very large green phosphorescent flies about the size of a cat, complete with a Queen the size of a church. They entered into a fight with a human colony planet over what appears to be a misunderstanding over the availability of dung. When the Doctor offers them a face-saving way out of the conflict, they accept it.

• *Caw's species.* As living metal birds, they're powered by fusion chambers ['gold fusion' sounds like a bad pun, but the specific metal seems to be fused to provide fuel and growth]. Both Caw and Squawk find gold a very appealing foodstuff. There are suggestions they're capable of handling vacuum without much trouble, and they definitely can traverse space faster than light. Caw disgorges Squawk from his gullet, which is an odd form of reproduction, and Squawk acts as a tracking beacon for Baltazar to follow the TARDIS. [It flaps its wings in vacuum, so there must be some link between that motion and space-travel. Ordinarily this flight is slower-than-light, but nonetheless fast enough for space.]

History

• *Dating.* The whole story takes place in the fortieth century, but there's a good deal of time between the Doctor and Martha's first brush with Baltazar and their later encounters [for the villains, at least]. The final segment is apparently set three years after the penultimate one. [This is debatable, as the 'three years' figure is how long it seemed to the Doctor, who started by travelling at relativistic speeds on the back of a metal parakeet, then accelerated to FTL so may have warped time. Martha and Baltazar went by TARDIS, but for the Doctor to catch them up with just a non-ferrous bio-ornithopter, it's most likely after whatever date they left Volag Noc.]

The fortieth century is as oil-hungry as the current era; giant semi-intelligent oil rigs have defence systems capable of fending off whole pirate ships, which they often do. They walk across a sand-planet, like enormous spiders, and may or may not be manned. Oil Corp runs the drilling. Other systems are being exploited now that Earth is out of oil, but the entire galaxy is running low. There is a paucity of fertile planets too [which ties with the galactic famine in 22.6, "Revelation of the Daleks", set close to this date by most estimates]. Earth's defences are vulnerable to attack from a well-armed vessel, but their army can sterilise war-zones by bombing them into another dimension. The galaxy's worst criminals are sent to Volag Noc. [Although Earth's hard-cases were under-represented among the diverse alien population and robots, so Desperus (3.4, "The Daleks' Master Plan") might still be the preferred dumping-ground for human crooks.]

Despite the fearsome firepower available to the troops at Myarr, Earth's entire defences were destroyed by Baltazar, who is claimed to be from Triton. [This may be why the duties of the Guardian of the Solar System involved making secret treaties with the heads of other galaxies in 4000 AD (again, "The Daleks' Master Plan"). Triton orbits Neptune, so mining Taranium might have been supervised from there. If you want to do fan-fic combining these facts with Snot

Is Animation the Way Forward?

continued from Page 323...

the target market for this isn't really the usual cartoon audience so much as the *Star Wars* completists. Reworking computer-game characters is often more successful than taking a hit CG movie to the small screen. While *Avatar* was considered suitable for adults (however infantile the script), and *Archer* seeks to make its drawn characters as much like dime-novel covers from the 60s as possible, kids appear to find either look unappealing and unengaging.

In seeking to figure out why this should be, some people have returned to the theories of Marshall McLuhan (arguably the most influential media analyst of the twentieth century), and argue that slick, "realistic" animation is less "hot" (in McLuhan's terminology), and leaves fewer toeholds for a viewer to work with. More recent theorists invoke advances in neurology, but have less useable shorthand. *Avatar* was presented as a visual *fait accompli* and left nothing to the imagination (as far as visual information went). A drawn face is a few gestural marks and we do the rest, inferring emotion and personality (as we do to things that look face-like, such as emoticons or craters on Mars lit a particular way). Children especially respond to this game. The stories take place in a world reduced to essentials (individual directors or animation houses differ on what's "essential", while mood-creating can involve very complex backdrops). As with comic strips and graphic novels, an animated image can guide the audience's attention more overtly than television or cinema, and does the novelist's work of singling out specifics more immediately. This is a function of animation that appeals to satirists: that nothing of the known outside world is allowed in unless the writers and animators want it there. Everything needed has to be put there deliberately, which makes animation an ideal medium for world-building – and control-freakery.

The Simpsons (before the Ricky Gervais episode widely agreed to have been where it should have ended) and moreso *Futurama*, as well as later Disney series such as *Phineas and Ferb* and *Gravity Falls*, stuffed the scripts with allusions, in-jokes, sophisticated concepts, conceptual gags and unannounced cameos (if that's the right word for voices). The look of each series not only said "suitable for children" but gave the small viewers who thought it was just for them enough to play with, while the hip adults found fresh details in every re-watch. If you're not closely monitoring the characters' faces for nuance (as you would with a visible actor or meticulous mo-cap or CG imaging of physiognomy), you can glance at the jokes in the set-design. One side-effect of the cost-per-second of traditional cel animation is that comedy has to happen *faster*. The speed of sight-gags or cutaways to other characters had to be costed in 24ths of a second. This has had a knock-on effect on the density of live-action drama and comedy over the last quarter-century. Storyboarders on early episodes of *The Simpsons* may have hoped that audiences were nimble enough to keep up, but directors of sitcoms and action shows now assume it. These days, all television (other than news or soap) aspires to the condition of *Looney Tunes*.

To be blunt, the new series of *Doctor Who* is already more like an animated programme than it is like the Hartnell-era episodes. Every episode is storyboarded, and many of the components are designed from scratch (and sometimes almost half only exist as elaborate drawings or models on a computer). A sizeable percentage of the dialogue is post-synched in ADR. The grading and image-processing that we now accept as routine (see **What Difference Did Field-Removed Video Make?** under X4.15, "Planet of the Dead") allows control over the real-world elements of the picture comparable to making it all from scratch. Indeed, many of the lapses and disappointments (and our **Things That Don't Make Sense** entries) arise from trying to make entire historical epochs and alien worlds within 30 miles of Cardiff, as well as create species out of bipedal actors with radio-controlled heads. Why not follow through? "The Infinite Quest" and, to a lesser extent, A7, "Dreamland" showed that it was at least possible to make something that exploited the full potential of *Doctor Who* more than any one 45-minute conventional episode could manage.

An animated series of *Doctor Who*, though? Forty years ago, *Star Trek* did something similar but with, to put it politely, mixed results. On the plus side, a couple of episodes used animation to tell stories the TV series couldn't have but might have wanted to. There were some tight and interesting scripts (including a cross-over episode with Larry Niven's "Known Space" books – when Paramount brought back the series in films and

continued on Page 327...

Monsters (X9.9, "Sleep No More"), keep it to yourself.]

Some time way back, a ship called the *Infinite* was stranded in deep space after a voyage that began as our universe formed. In it is ancient power from the Dark Times. [That handy catch-all term for pre-Rassilon that is the *Doctor Who* excuse for magic – 18.4, "State of Decay"; 25.3, "Silver Nemesis"; X2.9, "The Satan Pit"; X3.0, "The Runaway Bride"; X3.2, "The Shakespeare Code" and umpteen episodes of *The Sarah Jane Adventures*. The Doctor here cites entities from the Dark Times that include the Racnoss ("The Runaway Bride"), the Nestene (X7.1, "Spearhead from Space"), and the Great Vampires ("State of Decay").]

The *Infinite*'s flight recorder spilt into segments, and these have been scattered across the galaxy and collected by various nefarious types. Anyone with the right equipment and knowledge can locate the other segments and work out the location of the wreck.

The Analysis

The Big Picture As this episode's essay will explain in more detail, there were occasional reports of pitches from outside parties expressing interest in making an animated *Doctor Who* for the BBC. At least one of these, reported in *Doctor Who Magazine* in 1997, turned out to be a complete fabrication and forced editor Gary Gillat to go on record insisting that the BBC had absolutely no plans for animated *Doctor Who* whatsoever. Curiously, there was a post on the BBC's *Doctor Who* website two years after that, decrying the idea of an animated version of the show for reasons of cost (it seems to have been taken down by 2001). At this point, there seems to have been some thought that someone involved in the Amblin/ Fox/ Universal McGann movie might still want to pursue a television option, but this wasn't followed up.

By this time, the BBC was relaunching its digital and online services almost monthly, with the Drama Department's Fiction Lab unit getting into gear for interactive online content. If you were watching analogue television in Britain back when tracks by Royksopp or Air were used on adverts and the stuff the BBC puts on between programmes, you'd have seen a lot of promotions for the new facilities available free from the Corporation for people who'd paid for the programmes. (Well, *most* of them were free: if you'd bought a digital service by getting a satellite dish for BskyB or a cable subscription, you could be getting charged twice for BBC Choice, which became BBC3 shortly thereafter. As we outlined in **Why is Trinity Wells on Jackie's Telly?** under X1.4, "Aliens of London", this situation changed a little later, and now anyone who wants to watch anything broadcast in the UK needs at least a digital decoder, but gets a minimum of 40 channels – some of them watchable.)

The period from 1998 to 2003 was a transitional phase when local libraries started providing slow and limited services for anyone wanting to dip a toe into the strange waters of chatrooms and search engines. The BBC's sites were designed to not scare little old ladies, and provide something for anyone who might want to use it. They were smart enough to pay more than lip-service to the two buzzwords of the era ("interactivity" and "accessibility"), and offered a service called FictionLab to recruit/ exploit (delete according to personal experience) budding writers and provide resources including hints and old scripts. (Davies and Moffat have both posted the earlier drafts of broadcast *Doctor Who* episodes.)

The BBC Cult website was a peculiar omnium gatherum of anything that had nostalgic affection or a vaguely fantasy tinge, from the evergreen children's shows of the 60s and 70s to Test Card F. Many of the entries were researched and run by practicing *Doctor Who* fans, so it had a sincere love for things then considered kitsch and, as we explored in Volumes 5 and 6, a more detailed knowledge of how the BBC works and what was broadcast and kept. Even though it was the least fashionable programme to admit to liking (see **What's All This Stuff About Anoraks?** under 24.1, "Time and the Rani"), the Cult site had a *Doctor Who* sub-site in pride of place. James Goss, ambitious and a keen fan of the programme, had been hired for the purpose of creating animated *Doctor Who* episode for streaming, presumably on the Cult website. This apparently fell through almost immediately for budgetary reasons, and he was shifted to running the entire Cult site instead. Goss immediately set about creating a steady supply of content for his new domain with particular attention for the *Doctor Who* site. (We'll follow up on this in **What were the Best Online Extras?** under X3.4, "Daleks in Manhattan".)

Is Animation the Way Forward?

continued from Page 325...

then *The Next Generation*, the Klingons had morphed into Niven's Kzinti). However, in those days, animation meant kid's TV (or Ralph Bakshi), and so the episodes were often crudely-plotted and repetitive. For the cast of what was then a failed and cancelled series from their past, it was paid work. Animation may take a while, but the voice cast can do several in as long as it took to make one episode, with no make-up or costume-changes. They don't even all have to be on hand at the same time. The pay can be almost as good (nobody seems to want to go on-record about how much Filmation paid the stars of *Trek*). That was then. Today, animation voice-overs have more kudos and the audiences are more varied.

An objection often thrown up when such conversations happen is the cost-per-minute of live-action drama and animation. *Doctor Who* is currently in a very tasty position on this front. On the one hand, although the BBC are very tight-lipped about how much an episode of the series costs these days, we can make educated guesses based on the tariff bands the BBC set for independent producers. The 2010 categories are the best guide we've found, and they split drama into seven ranges. Drama 6 is suggested as follows: "Heavy combination of multi-location; period; high cast and short runs in serials and event singles. CGI and effects may be significant here". That sounds like a good fit. This band, back when Series 5 was about to air, was costed at £800k-£900K per hour. Admittedly, with successive governments trying to punish the Corporation for not acting as their personal mouthpiece (and with the last five Prime Ministers at Rupert Murdoch's beck and call), there has been political pressure to curtail the BBC's income and swingeing savings have been imposed. Steven Moffat was given far less money to spend than Russell T Davies, but the reasons for putting a writer in charge of production include the ability to take one for the team and find ways to make things work if they can't afford Plan A.

Let's be generous for a moment and say that the BBC Wales team made Series 9 for an average of half a million pounds per 45-minute episode (it looks like they were cost-cutting on the ones Moffat didn't write, but that's nothing new). As an average, this is about as cheap as it can be with the overheads involved. (Look at the credits and see how many carpenters, electricians and so on are involved even on something with a piss-takingly tiny cast such as X9.11, "Heaven Sent".) Half a million divided by 45 is, as you all knew, 11,111.1 recurring. Let's call the absolute minimum cost eleven grand a minute (because up to three minutes could be credits, trailers and "previously" stuff, even though the actors and Murray Gold have to be paid for even those, as does the estate of Ron Grainer).

So... how much does *animation* cost per minute? Well, how long is a piece of string? The figures for Pixar are terrifyingly huge. *Toy Story 3* came out at about $2,000,000 per minute, but with an all-star cast. (Voice actors are a significant factor in the promotion and are often paid commensurately. The backstage kerfuffle over *The Last Dinosaur* replacing its entire cast once a new storyline was imposed late on is reflected in that film's costs.) A less starry film of similar length and complexity, *Cloudy with a Chance of Meatballs*, was $1.65 million per minute, and as we get less inflated voice costs and European technical staff, we dip under half a million per minute for *Gnomeo and Juliet* and – adjusting for the 2011 exchange-rate with the Dollar and the Euro – something like a quarter-million dollars per minute for *Monster of Paris*. That's the top-of-the-line 3D CG stuff. The lowest-grade advertising 2D work could be £6000 a minute, but is only 20 seconds. (In traditional animation, that would be a day's work for two grand, but there's the design and so on.) How about the normal TV animation, either the traditional cel frame work or digital malarkey (Flash until fairly recently, or PhotoShop such as was used for "The Infinite Quest")?

We spent a few days lurking on websites of professional bodies, and came to two interesting conclusions. One is that for most half-hour series, the guideline cost is about £20,000 per minute (call it $30,000). Once basic staples such as characters and locations that are in every segment (the "assets", in gaming terms) have been designed and the walk-cycles or characteristics established and timed, the cost comes down. For computer-generated characters and places, the modelling is the most costly part other than paying actors or writers. They are essentially making one-off digital puppets rather than photographing 15 drawings per second.

The other conclusion, a bone of contention for the US Animation Guild, is that it's a lot less in the

continued on Page 329...

Goss's team realised that Real Player (and half the people reading this will get a semi-ironic rush of nostalgia with those words), technology they planned to use for the BBC's first-ever streamed audio drama, could send pictures along with the sound. Lee Sullivan, occasional lead artist for *Doctor Who Magazine*, was hired for illustrations. These were made to move (sort of) in rough-and-ready *Jackanory*-ish animation, essentially still drawings with a rostrum camera moving across them. Fiction Lab put their stamp of approval on it, and the first *Doctor Who* webcast began 13th July, 2001, took a hiatus and continued sporadically from the following February. "Death Comes to Time" had been commissioned for BBC Radio Four (the main speech channel), who rejected it outright. It seems to have been far enough along that someone wanted to salvage the project just because they'd spent so much on it. The project appears to have been intended as a springboard for producer-writer Dan Freedman's plans for his own character, the Minister of Chance.[62] It's a sub-*Silmarillion* story of how the ancient powers, including the Time Lords, retire from the universe to let mankind and other such beings develop unhindered (yes, exactly like that episode of *Babylon 5* with "Get the hell out of our galaxy!") and thus has Sylvester McCoy's Doctor voluntarily dying, only five years since his last death in the TV Movie.

Two further similar productions were made. "Real Time," a sixth Doctor/ Cybermen adventure (starring Evelyn Smythe from Big Finish) in August/ September 2002, and a remake/ completion/ "re-imagining" of 17.6, "Shada" (the script edited to feature Paul McGann instead of Tom Baker, but still with Lalla Ward as Romana) in May/ June 2003. These also had the same moving-illustration rendering as before, albeit more sophisticated each time. ("Real Time" had a clever use of a distorted, poorly-rendering video screen; "Shada" featured actual real-life imagery of Tom and Lalla for flashback purposes.) "Real Time" was written and directed by Gary Russell (with some help from Jason Haigh-Ellery), and therefore so much a Big Finish production, Russell says he thinks of it as a radio drama. (It's still for sale on the Big Finish website, which suggests some convoluted licensing deal. Big Finish dramas would show up on BBC radio in future, after the TV series had come back.)

We'll consider more of Russell's contributions to unconventional *Doctor Who*-related products in a later essay (**Are All the Comic-Strip Adventures Fair Game?** under X4.7, "The Unicorn and the Wasp"), but at this stage he was in a more ambiguous position with the BBC. Much the same situation applied to "Shada", directed by Nicholas Pegg this time. The script was identifiably the one we got as a freebie with the VHS release, but with a few new clever touches and some excruciatingly fannish Gallifrey-lore.

The next webcast, however, had to be completely under BBC control. "Scream of the Shalka", written by Paul Cornell, and produced by Goss, went out for the fortieth anniversary in November 2003. Officially, Cosgrove Hall was reported as having done the animation (but it seems to have been a semi-autonomous group of their animators working independently of the main company, and who later formed Firestep). Cosgrove Hall were a very reputable company with a string of successful series behind them. They were equally proficient in stop-motion and cel-animation. The making of this webcast was a new departure, using computer graphics but in a format that could be sent down the low-baud-rate dial-up internet of yesteryear. (They'd had a test-run with "Ghosts of Albion", a curious webcast project that culminated in a real-life treasure hunt. Written and directed by Amber Benson – Tara off *Buffy the Vampire Slayer* – it has an extraordinarily odd cast including Rory Kinnear, Paterson Joseph, Anthony Daniels, Leslie Phillips, Roy Skelton and Big Finish stalwart India Fisher.)

The "Shalka" animation is about as good as a skilled Powerpoint presentation, but it was good enough to tell a story and make it more than an illustrated radio play. As we've mentioned, the cast was newsworthy, and the three main players have all been in episodes of the TV series. (Richard E Grant, later Dr Simeon and the Great Intelligence in Series 7, was the officially-sanctioned BBC-approved ninth Doctor a few months before Christopher Eccleston got the nod; Sir Derek Jacobi was the Master four years ahead of X3.11, "Utopia"; and Sophie Okenedo was Alison, the new companion, seven years before being the bloody Queen in X5.2, "The Beast Below". Tennant blagged his way into the cast for a two-line role.)

The Cult team expected this to be the way forward for *Doctor Who*, and said so publicly. However embarrassing the BBC management of

Is Animation the Way Forward?

continued from Page 327...

UK partly because of the 2013 Budget granting an Animation Tax Credit. If you've been wondering why there have been recent reboots of *The Clangers*, *Danger Mouse*, *Thunderbirds*, *Morph* and *Teletubbies*, plus feature films of *Paddington* and *Shaun the Sheep*, this is part of the reason. The Treasury has issued a report on how much money this sector earns the UK per annum.[64] The British Film Institute's website breaks down the criteria and this links to the Inland Revenue's definition of "British-made" and different categories.

There's a small detail that might complicate things: it's almost entirely for independent producers. As the BBC doesn't have an in-house animation department any more (even *OOglies* is a loose consortium of freelancers supervised by BBC Scotland), the bulk of the animated material made and distributed under its aegis comes from indies. BBC Wales could commission animators to make *Doctor Who*-related programming and take advantage of these tax-breaks, but not make anything like it entirely themselves. This is no different from the situation for the computer-games or the animated episodes we've had, nor from the arrangements with The Mill or Milk for digital effects. So we're almost at the point where the costs are comparable, even if the half-million quid per episode figure we posited as a minimum is accurate.

This is, remember, for an *entire episode*. If we had animated sections within live-action drama consisting of two people in a room discussing it, the episode could be cheaper than usual and still have impressive aliens and planets, for example. A significant advantage of animation is that you can have a cast of thousands with a few versatile actors. In that regard, it's closer to radio (in theory, the optimum medium for fantasy, but in practice never exploited to its full potential since that incident in 1938 with Orson Welles). Once again, *Doctor Who* is already closer to animation in this regard than most television – see "Doomsday" (X2.13) for a long scene of Nick Briggs arguing with himself when playing an army of Cybermen and an army of Daleks. If we sneak a peek ahead to Steven Moffat's term as executive producer, the cast he and Andy Prior assembled for voice-overs from Series 6 onwards has considerably more firepower than the on-screen talent (although see also X1.12, "Bad Wolf"), partly because it's just an afternoon's work, partly because there's no need to get on a train to Cardiff and partly – to be frank – because it's less conspicuous than doing a full-blown part with publicity photos and make-up.

The other aspect to remember is that these days, the model has moved from cel-animation – laboriously infilled and moved slightly with up to 24 new drawings for a second of film (done on the cheap in Korea or India from storyboards devised in LA or Soho) – to something more like puppetry, with a digital simulacrum of a character or machine manipulated with a mouse. Once these have been constructed and their limits and possibilities set, they can be made to move as desired. This speeds things up, and saves a fortune in both celluloid sheeting and rough-draft versions for the voice-artists and directors to tweak. Over the course of an entire series, this amounts to a huge acceleration and reduction in cost-per-episode. Although it looks like it's made with construction-paper (as the pilot and first few episodes were), *South Park* is now made on computers and is thus able to turn around an episode in days; a great many of the best recent episodes have been topical satires on events of the previous week. "The Infinite Quest" wasn't as rapid as that, but the first episode aired 63 days after the vocal tracks had been edited. Compare this to the frantic efforts to get "The Satan Pit" (X2.9) ready before transmission, and there is a good case for animation being a less stressful and labour-intensive production-method for fantasy television these days. Even with all the effort of remaking clips that exist on film and keeping faith with the original broadcast, "Power of the Daleks" was about as fast for six 25-minute episodes. This comes with the obvious caveat that it gets cheaper and easier the more episodes you make – a one-off would still have huge overheads.

There are many other reasons for doing animated episodes or half-episodes, however. The graphic style adopted by any animator is in itself a form of information that sets expectations. Looking like a particular old style or idiom can hint at what's going on, and how we should interpret the events on screen. As we saw in **How Messed-Up is Narrative Going to Get?** under X3.10, "Blink", *Doctor Who* is already using the different picture-quality available with digital cameras and post-production grading to tell the story non-

continued on Page 331...

the day found *Doctor Who*, the record-breaking numbers for "Death Comes to Time" and the Cult website had got their attention. Pre-publicity for "Scream of the Shalka" was piquing public interest, but it was already outdated by the time it was released.

... because, funnily enough, televised *Doctor Who* was coming back. The Cult team had sorted out the tangled ownership of *Doctor Who* rights once and for all, then concluded that there were no issues with broadcasting *Doctor Who*, only that BBC Worldwide were still working on a movie. (As we have seen and will explore in later volumes, the commercial and semi-privatised BBC Worldwide are often at loggerheads with the BBC proper, who make the programmes that Worldwide sells and exploits.) A month passed between this announcement and the Controller of BBC1 Lorraine Heggessey announcing that Russell T Davies was bringing the show back. (Davies had been steadily lobbying for this for years, so negotiations could go quickly at this point.) The Grant Doctor was wiped from the slate before the webcast was even aired.

By this point, however, developments were in the works. The Blair government was increasingly irritated with the BBC (we discussed this in Volume 7); one of the side-effects of the license renewal negotiations was an agreement that the BBC sharply cut down on their website content, following tabloid and Tory accusations of interfering with private industry. (Exactly how the mere existence of a website stops others from coming into existence is left as an exercise for the reader.) As a result of this, everything from the Cult website was mothballed... with the exception of the *Doctor Who* website, which Goss and his crew started working on full-time. Some ideas for an animated work were kicked around, but the ending of X1.13, "The Parting of the Ways" seem to have knocked this out of the running. (So, we assume, it was an Eccleston-model Doctor involved. Therefore, if you haven't already, see **Did He Fall or Was He Pushed?** under X1.12, "Bad Wolf" and we'll return to this in **What were the Worst Merchandising Disasters of the 21st Century?** under X5.3, "Victory of the Daleks").

That wasn't the end of the animation story, though: as the Firestep team had been commissioned for a follow-up to "Shalka", now surplus to requirements, they were given the job of providing visual coverage for the audio-recordings of episodes one and four of "The Invasion" (6.3). This opened up a small but interesting trend within the DVD releases as various animation houses had a crack at different missing episodes, but the headline-grabbing combination of the first UNIT story and Cosgrove Hall (whose logo is on the animated replacement episodes, along with credits for Big Finish) was the necessary impetus for BBC Wales to give "The Infinite Quest" the green light. Goss had tried to interest them in an animated story a couple of years earlier, so had the test drawings and contacts to hand.

BBC Worldwide, through the agency of first 2|Entertain (the distribution company set up by BBC Worldwide and Woolworths) and Pup (formed by 2|Entertain head Dan Hall when Woolworths went into receivership), took on the task of commissioning other companies, in order that the other near-complete stories they wanted to release on DVD could be more marketably "whole". The different animators, Qurious (sic), Theta-Sigma and Littleloud, took different approaches, but it seems that the BBC's costs were kept low by these companies effectively auditioning for a full contract rather than any one getting the gig properly.

Goss was employed at the BBC until 2007. His swan-song was "The Infinite Quest" – proper animated *Doctor Who*, on BBC1, made by the same firm of animators who did "Shalka". As we explored in **Has All the Puff *Totally* Changed Things?** under X2.1, "New Earth", there was a two-year phase when the behind-the-scenes material for BBC Wales's most complicated production spawned *two* separate shows. *Doctor Who Confidential* was on the digital-only BBC3, but BBC1 made *Totally Doctor Who* for children watching on Wednesday afternoons, in the same weeks as the Series 2 episodes on Saturdays. (One of the many changes to befall the BBC was the imposition of the analogue switch-off, so that all television in the UK is now digitally encrypted. The BBC had eight channels, two explicitly for children, so BBC1 was denuded of all officially infantile television to make way for more game-shows by 2012.) The first series of *Totally* hadn't gone down as well as hoped, but the second and final run, shown in the same weeks as Series 3, had been tweaked and one of the presenters replaced. It was still clearly in the *Blue Peter* mould and, as with *Bleep and Booster* in the 1960s (which was the *Blue Peter* serial with *Doctor Who*

Is Animation the Way Forward?

continued from Page 329...

verbally before the dialogue catches up. Just as graphic novels can alert readers to shifts in authenticity by pastiching earlier styles or specific individual artists, so an animated account can adopt a visual style (or imitate an earlier animator of film genre) to accelerate storytelling or have fun. A *Rashomon*-style story told from different perspectives is only the most obvious possible use of this.

It doesn't even have to be either-or. If you've seen Richard Linklater's films *Waking Life* and *A Scanner Darkly*, the use of animation techniques over video footage established different levels of "reality" and states of consciousness (something done crudely in 19.3,"Kinda", but in a way that was at odds with the script in that case). It could be a good way to make non-human humanoids in bulk without endless prostheses or contact lenses, and capture a performance rather than just a physical presence. Then there's motion-capture. Peter Jackson and Robert Zemeckis are really enthusiastic about this technique. Andy Serkis has been in many of the highest-grossing films of all time, but can walk down the street unrecognised. Actors with dots on their faces and leotards do their stuff in front of green screens, and the dots are used as a guide to how a CG creature ought to move, thus preserving a degree of the performance (as per the wizened tiny Doctor in X3.13,"Last of the Time Lords"). You may recall that, until the Spielberg/ Jackson *Tintin* film, this was the future of cinema.[65]

As costs come down and the software gets faster and more responsive, this might allow actors to engage with CG animated characters in real-time, perhaps finally ridding us of the radio-controlled animal-heads on boiler-suited actors or – if we're really lucky – the whole business of actors staring at a tennis-ball on a stick and guessing what the finished product will look like. Or they could talk to an actor with stuck-on dots and let post-production take its course after they've ad-libbed and engaged for the camera (which isn't so different from how K9 won over audiences where Twikki failed). The main advantage for a low-budget TV series is that it cuts out three intermediate stages in the animation process and thus, ultimately, saves money once the proprietary software and equipment has been paid for. If BBC Wales got it into their heads to do this, it would be a significant investment so would have to be used a lot. (Such as for a non-humanoid regular character. Most people have forgotten Kamelion – see Volume 5 – so let's not give up on that idea.)

So far, nobody has plotted a full 45-minute animated adventure that wasn't a string of short episodes with cliffhangers and resolutions moving the plot around hairpin bends. It would require more than just "hey, look – we're animated" to keep a story going in a different direction from how a live-action one might. One frequent problem with animators is that the attention to detail often leads them to lose sight of the main plot. (This is also true of ex-animators: Terry Gilliam, Tim Burton and Joe Dante all took a while to learn storytelling all over again when dealing with actors.)

We could argue that plot is almost irrelevant to audiences who want to "bathe" in a specific type of televisual experience, but there's another way of looking at it. If we're being cynical, the main use for mo-cap at the moment is games, and this is an element of *Doctor Who*'s commercial exploitation that needs an overhaul. If they wanted to make a worthwhile game, it might be worth integrating the elements needed into the series as broadcast. It's hard not to see "Dreamland" as a trial run for the games released in 2010-11. (See **What Were the Best Online Extras?** under X3.4, "Daleks in Manhattan".)

There are sequences that have all the elements anyone might need to road-test for a game; space dogfights, car-chases, helicopters and a runaway mine-cart. The character-design is inadequate to long exposition or dialogue. (As the TV Movie Master would say: it took them a while with the walking and the talking. Some scenes have the Doctor apparently moonwalking.) Similarly, the whole misadventure with the New Paradigm Daleks (X5.3, "Victory of the Daleks") looks suspiciously like inserting a more game-friendly design for the Top Baddies into the broadcast episodes prior to launching a game with them. The games were free to BBC Licence-Fee paying households, but the attempt to sell them in other territories fell afoul of the problem that any animated series would also meet. Outside Britain, only people who have already committed to *Doctor Who* in its present form were prepared to take a punt on the games. The mainstream gaming community either didn't know anything about it, or thought it had ended some time in the 80s.

continued on Page 333...

personnel and vibe), the animated serial was made as part of it.

By this stage in the story, BBC Radio had developed a slew of radio channels that were digital-only, including a rerun channel originally called Radio 7 – then rebranded, slightly inaccurately, as Radio 4Extra (only about half their material is repeated Radio 4 stuff). In their cheesy fantasy spot, The 7th Dimension (the title indicates how long they've been running it), they occasionally put on Big Finish audio plays, making Paul McGann plausibly the Radio Doctor[63]. Big Finish have been making *Doctor Who* tie-in dramas since the late 1990s, occasionally indulging their original fan-only audience but – more seriously – providing work for actors who still sound like their characters, regardless of what time had done to their looks. Following his tenure as *Doctor Who Magazine* editor, Gary Russell had helped to build this empire with his colleagues Jason Haigh-Ellery and Nicholas Briggs. (Briggs, in between this and doing alien voices for BBC Wales, was an occasional continuity announcer on The Seventh Dimension.)

By now you'll have got the idea that the roots of "The Infinite Quest" are all in commercial fan activities between the end of Season Twenty-Six and the start of Series 1, so the fact that the script was by another former *DWM* editor, Alan Barnes (then working as editor of *2000 AD*, mysteriously still going in 2006), won't be too alarming. Many items in "The Infinite Quest" are similar to rejected submissions to BBC Books and the earlier Virgin Books *New Adventures* (dung-smuggling, turning people into diamonds with a gravity weapon, oil-pirates), but these were hardly original anyway. (For a submarine on a sand-planet, with a pirate-like crew, try *Involution Ocean* by Bruce Sterling, but that was riffing on *Dune* and *A Fall of Moondust* by way of *Moby Dick*.) Mergrass's design looks like a composite of Dogbolter from the mid-80s *DWM* strip and the now-traditional animal-head-on-a-boiler-suit BBC Wales aliens. Pilot Kelvin's inability to control an Exo-suit is like Adric's panic in the TSS in 19.3, "Kinda" done properly.

Towards the end of the story, the Doctor refers to "the Great Old Ones". Barnes, as writer of a *DWM* strip about Silurians, was familiar with the *New Adventures*' wholesale borrowing from HP Lovecraft's overblown Goth-friendly "mythos". (Short version: the Time Lords from the previous universe skived off the Big Crunch and snuck into ours, where they found themselves to be horribly mutated beings with a grudge against ordinary life. The Sea Devils worshipped them and the Animus – 2.5, "The Web Planet" – was one. We dealt with this in Volume 6, when it looked like it was cross-pollinating with broadcast *Doctor Who* – **Are All These "Gods" Related?"** under 26.3, "The Curse of Fenric" – but then elements of it also emerged in *The Sarah Jane Adventures*.) The *Infinite* seems too sophisticated and mechanical to sit very comfortably with this, but see "Terminus" (20.4).

The pre-credits sequence begins as a pastiche of the one from *Flash Gordon* (1980), of Ming looking at Earth and contemplating how many ways to destroy it he can use at once. Almost immediately, it turns into *Titanic* (1997), with Baltazar proclaiming himself "King of the World". Then he falls very slowwwwwwwly through the floor, in one of the prolonged death-plummets we mentioned in "Voyage of the Damned" (X4.0). Caw might look like a retread of the Polyphase Avatron from "The Pirate Planet" (16.2), but UK readers of certain vintage (or anyone with Anglophile tendencies) will recognise a close relative of the Iron Chicken from *The Clangers*. (Or they might have seen the recent, rather luridly-coloured reboot.) The name "Volag Noc" sounds a bit *Deep Space Nine*, but "Volag" is halfway between "Stalag" (the PoW camps run by the Nazis that form part of any prison-break story's collective mythology) and "Gulag", as in *The Gulag Archipelago*, which forms the basis for most Western thinking on Stalin-era internal exile/ work camps for dissidents. Martha tells Baltazar "He'll. Be. Back" as per *Terminator*.

Most obviously, though, this is the fetch-quest for a buried treasure that owes most to *Treasure Island*. It's a shipwreck (and, as we'll see in "The End of Time Part Two", a ship and the name "Hesperus", as in the galaxy the *Infinite* is in, is a legacy of school English lessons). The treasure-map is in pieces (rather like the Key to Time in Season Sixteen) and they can only be read by the TARDIS (see 17.6, "Shada"). There's a parrot and a ship of pirates with photonic cutlasses, headscarves and earrings (one is a ship's cook, like Long John Silver) and the story of the treasure is spread inside a jail.

Is Animation the Way Forward?

continued from Page 331...

Britain has a more savvy set of gamers (and game designers: nearly 2000 companies added £1.72 billion gross to the UK economy in 2014, mainly from phone games, but let's not forget *Grand Theft Auto*), but not such a big market as most games would want. A more precisely-targeted audience for animated *Doctor Who* is the section of the public who bought the DVDs of older episodes. Every complete story in the archives has been released, as have some with one or two episodes missing (and the cornucopia set *Lost in Time* collecting the "orphan" episodes). With the possibility of real ones returning one day, it seems unwise to invest too heavily in something so labour-intensive without a guaranteed market. The producers of the DVD "added-value" content ("extras" to the rest of us) cannily made each story's replacement visuals a try-out for a different animation team. The results were varied. "The Invasion" (6.3) got a *film noir*-ish rendition of episodes one and four from within the Cosgrove Hall company (still best known for the original *Danger Mouse*), but "The Reign of Terror" (1.8) had a frantically-edited, Spaghetti-Western-like mess when an Australian animation house (then called Theta-Sigma) replaced episodes four and five.

However, between these two poles was some solid and acceptable visual coverage for the soundtracks of the Hartnell and Troughton episodes required to make a complete story releasable. Now that this process has been extended to other series with gaps, such as the *Dad's Army* episode made available online for a fee, there might be a case for returning to this interrupted scheme. Compounding the problem of selecting one company to do all of it, some of the ones who worked on the DVDs went bust before the 2013 Budget because Worldwide was unwilling to commit to a full contract. At present, there's still a vague hope that the originals of these episodes will show up, so even if the BBC Wales team *wanted* to take over from Pup, this isn't likely to continue at length until there's more clarity on the matter.

With Dalek stories there's less chance of the episodes returning than any other, so "Power" getting a fiftieth birthday remount had less risk of being a costly white elephant than, say, "Fury from the Deep" (5.6). BBC Enterprises, as was, got their fingers burned with the unexpected reappearance of "The Tomb of the Cybermen" in 1992, just after they'd paid Jon Pertwee to narrate an audio reconstruction. "Power" was made by a team pulled together from various fan-activities: the art was by the illustrators of the *DWM* comic strip, Martin Geraghty and Adrian Salmon; the body-model for the Doctor was Nick Scovell, whose theatrical remakes of wiped stories were a hit in the early 2000s (see **Can They Do It Live?** under A6, "The Music of the Spheres"); Jonathan Wood and Mark Ayres, from the Reconstruction Crew who fixed old episodes for DVD release, handled picture-quality and the soundtrack curation respectively.

Making any serious animated *Doctor Who* from scratch would require a concerted effort, simply to benefit from economies of scale when spending development time on character-design and so on. A year-long series would amortise these costs better than half of one episode. However, the innate resistance to any animation that isn't A) expressly for children or B) filled with luridly adult humour would make this a tough sell for the overseas audiences who take their media skiffy so lip-bitingly seriously. There is, as we've established, a sizeable market for merchandising in America, enough for the content of the broadcast episodes to nod in their direction more often than the casual BBC1 viewer's, and this is a market who also follow strange cartoons and web-comics more readily than *Luther* or *Downton Abbey*. It's no less sensible than the notion of launching *Class* on BBC3 just as BBC3 stopped transmitting. (BBC America had more success with it than the real BBC. Perhaps cold-bloodedly targeting the US market – to the point that "Coal Hill Academy" resembles no school in Britain and got the show laughed off the screen in the UK – wasn't so dumb.)

However, to be cost-effective, any animated *Who* needs to win over the broad BBC1 audience who are simply in front of the telly before *Strictly* or *Casualty* – and they aren't as likely to sit still for a cartoon show. Despite Peter Capaldi's dampened overnight ratings, the intent is, as it always was, to have a hefty chunk of the people watching television as broadcast enjoying this series. It's not *so* long ago that *Doctor Who* was the most-watched thing on all week (X7.1, "Asylum of the Daleks"), and was getting half the people watching anything on television on the biggest view-

continued on Page 335...

Oh, Isn't That...?

• *Anthony Head* (Baltazar). You might remember him from last volume. If not, *Buffy the Vampire Slayer*, voice-overs of *Doctor Who Confidential*, the Prime Minister in *Little Britain*, *Manchild*, the adverts for Nescafé Gold Blend...

• *Stephen Greif* (Gurney) was the original Travis from *Blakes 7* and Harry Fenner in *Citizen Smith*. He has a long track-record of playing villains, either East End or East European.

• *Toby Longworth* (Caw). A couple of *Star Wars* and *Hitchhiker's Guide* incidental characters. More to the point, like Head, he's a long-term Big Finish alumnus.

• *Lisa Tarbuck* (Captain Kaliko). Apart from being the eponymous *Linda Green* (see last volume for heaps about that show), she's best known for being wittier than anyone has a right to be at that time in the morning on *The Big Breakfast*, and for being the daughter of the archetypal Liverpool stand-up Jimmy Tarbuck.

• *Steven Meo* (Pilot Kelvin). The Swansea-accented Kelvin sounds noticeably like Owain from *Gavin and Stacey* (see X5.11, "The Lodger"; X7.15, "The Day of the Doctor"). At time of broadcast, Meo was also in *Grown-Ups* on BBC3 and *Belonging* on BBC Wales. He'd been the dodgy video-shop worker in *TW*: "Random Shoes".

• *Barney Harwood* (Control Voice) was all over children's television at the time. As co-host of *Totally Doctor Who*, it was incumbent upon him to cover the making of this story, and thus demonstrate how voicing a character led to a fully-fledged "appearance" (two whole lines). Until recently he's been a *Blue Peter* presenter, with all the *Doctor Who* promotion that entailed, and was on the brief Elisabeth Sladen CBBC tribute.

English Lessons

• Madame Cholet: The cook in the Womble burrow, famed for dandelion pie, buttercup scones and conkers and chips. All the Wombles were named from Great Uncle Bulgaria's atlas (Cholet is a town in France best-known for the suppression of a counter-revolutionary insurgence). As you all know, she sounds like Bernard Cribbins impersonating Catherine Deneuve.

• *Fanny Cradock*: Notorious termagant TV cook from the dawn of time who looked like a Panto Dame. In the 1950s, post-rationing housewives were uncertain about all this foreign food (spaghetti, barbecues, soufflés) and bullied into treating hostessing as a competitive sport. Cradock was chief among the bullies and better at insults than recipes.

• *Delia Smith*: In the 1970s, she was the fresh new face of TV cooking (she baked the cake on the cover of the Rolling Stones's *Let It Bleed* album). Later she became the most relied-on source of recipes (and ridiculed by others).

• *Bill Oddie*: One-third of *The Goodies* (op cit) and later Britain's most famous ornithologist after Sir Peter Scott died (see 10.1, "The Three Doctors" for more on Slimbridge). He regularly presents live programmes about wild birds (and other fauna), notably the annual *SpringWatch*, in which he leads a team who make live feeds of birds' nests at least as exciting as live golf. As a near-chart-topping songwriter ("Funky Gibbon", also a minor hit in the US), he was the obvious casting for the Big Finish story *Doctor Who and the Pirates* (the answer to the seldom-asked question *why don't they do a musical episode?*).

• *Boy racer* (n.): The annoying teenagers who've just passed their driving tests and try to act like they're in *American Graffiti*, even though it's suburban England and it looks stupid over-revving a VW Polo.

• *Bendy Bus* (n.): The Mercedes-Benz Citaro bus, used successfully in most European cities and across Canada and South America that proved singularly inappropriate for the London routes to which it was assigned in the early 2000s. Instead of a double-decker, as nature intended, this has one bus then another attached with a rubber-covered hinge. The accident-rate was five times higher than proper buses, with cyclists especially prone to injury. These buses also tended to catch fire, as did their much-heralded replacements.

• *Kills all known bugs... Dead!*: Based on the slogan for Domestos, a toilet cleaner that killed all known germs (dead). The last word had a bottle of the stuff thumped on a table for emphasis.

• *Thermals* (n.): Long underwear.

• *Skill* (adj.): As an exclamation, or an adjective, as the Doctor uses it when cancelling the Governor's execution of all prisoners, "skill" had a vogue in school playgrounds c.1978 (sometimes, as "Skillamundo" – see X2.3, "School Reunion").

Things That Don't Make Sense Really, the level of coincidence in this story is worse even than Series 4. All four owners of the scattered parts of the

Is Animation the Way Forward?

continued from Page 333...

ing day of the year, Christmas Day, watching Kylie go down with Tennant (X4.0, "Voyage of the Damned"). The decision to show Series 8 and Nine too late for the family audience, and its effect on the viewing-figures for Series 10, might make a more child-friendly sister-series an attractive add-on, but that would never be accepted as a replacement for the live-action episodes.

Now that there has been another spin-off series on an online-only BBC3, this might be a viable option – even though *Class* was almost universally considered a mistake. CBBC, the 8-12s channel, was the natural home of *The Sarah Jane Adventures,* and while Russell T. Davies has tried to keep the standards off their pre-teen-friendly fantasy up, it could do with another *Who*-related show. BBC4, on the other hand, is the grown-ups channel and has shown the older episodes on occasion. (This often tied to some themed season they are running: 8.5, "The Daemons" with archaeology on television; episode one of 5.5, "The Web of Fear" with London on screen; 1.2, "The Daleks" as part of their Verity Lambert season and so on. Most recently, they offered 14.4, "Face of Evil" for no readily apparent reason.)

The non-mainstream BBC channels love having some form of *Doctor Who* to offer (well, maybe BBC Parliament has other ideas). This was part of the reason *Torchwood* happened: to link the under-performing BBC3 to a hit BBC1 series that was popular with the 16-25 audience, ostensibly the target of this channel. Similarly, *The Sarah Jane Adventures* was part of the process of moving all children's television from BBC1 to CBBC, so that they could stock the mainstream channel with game-shows from 3.30 to 6.00pm. These cleared the decks for *Doctor Who* to only do a few Yeti-in-the-Loo stories per year, because there was a child-friendly series doing six of these in a season, and an adult-targeted one doing 13 a year. An animated ancillary series expressly for children would allow the main series to continue in the grim and largely Earthbound direction it has been moving towards of late. It would also have helped plug the ever-longer gaps between seasons, when budgetary and logistical problems got in the way of a smooth production.

It's more likely that this would happen than that the main series would abruptly go into a different format. Then again, that's what people thought about making it in colour, moving it from Saturdays, doing an American co-produced TV Movie, making 45-minute one-episode stories, launching spin-offs and showing 3D episodes at cinemas. As we've been saying throughout this volume, assuming that what's been done lately is the only way *Doctor Who* can be done (or has ever been doable) is a big mistake.

Infinite's flight-log were in the same prison (possible, if only the galaxy's worst criminals could get hold of it) and, apparently, shared a cell. The TARDIS is intercepted in normal space, travelling at 685,000 mph, but in the same century and galaxy they've just left en route to Copacabana Beach (which was, allegedly, co-ordinates picked at random). It's intercepted by someone they've only just left, who warns them about someone else they'd been speaking to two minutes before in their subjective time. Out of at least 4800 cells, the Doctor is accidentally imprisoned in the same one as the governor, even though Gurney expressly ordered that this cell shouldn't be used. (His henchmen heard the opposite?) And above all, the villain searching for the *Infinite*'s data-chips is someone who's just vowed revenge on the Doctor, and found out that he has a time machine from the Old Times with the one device that can read them. (Or, all right, we might perhaps allow *all* of these as part of the weirdness surrounding Dark Times technology, and the TARDIS's sense of responsibility to arrange these for the Doctor.)

Also, the scale of this story alters alarmingly between scenes. Humanity has spread across seven galaxies, then one. Then we're told that Earth has run out of oil, so they're scouring the rest of the Solar System (with the definite article, so they mean our neighbourhood). One option is that Bouken is the moon of a gas giant (Jupiter, Saturn, Uranus or Neptune), and the three suns are there for the same reason that six were set up around Pluto (15.4, "The Sun Makers"). Baltazar's base of operations is stated as Triton, a moon of Neptune. The thing is, the only place in the Solar System that had significant amounts of life, and created the sort of oil they're drilling for, is Earth. There are other oil-like liquids that can be used as fuel that way, of course, but if they did think to mine these, then the three suns are a bit odd, as we've got a perfectly good one. Titan (a moon of Saturn) was thought, at the time of broadcast, to have oceans of butane, so the Doctor's going to have a big effect on the cosmic economy in a thousand years when he sets fire to the methane atmosphere (15.2, "The Invisible Enemy"). Or, if Bouken is in a totally different solar system (seems plausible), how is it the *only other one* to have ever produced oil? So maybe it isn't, but the it's last one undrained. In that case, is it beyond the capacity of a company running a monopoly on it to pay for better security, or at least depth-charges and mines?

The dialogue, however, makes it seem as if we're still very close to home. But, no: we're crossing seven galaxies, even though faster-than-light flight is still considered miraculous. Seven galaxies the size of ours = one trillion stars, a thousand billion, twelve zeroes after a one. And in all these seven galaxies, there is precisely *one* planet with oil and *one* worthy of being farmed. So, once again, topsoil is more valuable than gold (see our comments on X4.6, "The Doctor's Daughter" and 12.5, "Revenge of the Cybermen"), which makes Baltazar's heart's desire even stupider.

Moreover, the Doctor says *the galaxy* is "oil-starved", but what do their spaceships run on? Diesel? As compared to hydrogen for fusion reactors, which is universally abundant and the commonest substance imaginable? Besides, how conventional mineral oil was created on a planet unable to sustain life without three artificial suns is a problem – the only way this works is if the fake stars were there 140 million years ago, when it was covered in oceans and had foraminifera. Long-term planning such as that would logically have been carried out on more than one planet. And this one planet isn't guarded and doesn't even have giant sandworms or space-Tuaregs like *Dune*, or even a Magma-Beast like Androzani Minor (21.6, "The Caves of Androzani").

The other power-source mentioned is "gold fusion", in which a metal famed for its non-reactive properties (e.g. "Revenge of the Cybermen") is treated as a suitable replacement for hydrogen becoming helium, and releasing the leftover mass as energy the way stars do. Now, hydrogen becoming helium is easy(ish), because it's the simplest atom possible (a proton with an electron around it somewhere) becoming the second-simplest (a couple of protons, sometimes a couple of neutrons, then a couple of electrons around there somewhere). But gold is rather more massive, being a transition metal at number 79 in the Periodic Hit Parade, just next to Mercury. It's almost the densest naturally-occurring element. In fact, making anything denser than Magnesium (number 25) takes a lot of energy, rather than releasing any. Making iron or cobalt by conventional solar fusion is a bit of a trick (the best-guess for how the heavier elements occurred is that it's when two neutron stars collide). Of course, fusion of transuranic elements might be different (as we explored in **Why are Elements so Weird in Space?** under 22.2, "Vengeance on Varos") if it ever happened. On present available evidence, it wouldn't produce any power, just take more than humanity has ever used. To fuse an atom of gold into something four times as busy (if such a material exists even hypothetically) would just as likely take rather a lot of energy to get it started as it is to ever produce any. More, certainly, than the supernova used by Gallifrey to power time travel (10.1, "The Three Doctors").

That was our long-winded way of asking: If they've got the ability to skip this stage and fuse gold for energy-release semi-naturally (as Caw's species are implied to be a life-form rather than constructs), why are they faffing about with petrol?

In fact, if Baltazar has a handy supply of these metal birds, and they can generate energy simply by ingesting a relatively common metal, why is he piddling about with battleships and threats when he can hold the galaxy to ransom with a much more valuable and scarce power-source than hydrocarbons (which can be brewed using compost anyway)? They reproduce (which has all sorts of Second Law of Thermodynamics implications), but the customers don't need to know that. He's potentially got a stranglehold on the galactic economy, but uses it as a comic-relief sidekick and fashion statement.

Captain Kaliko has a literal skeleton crew. Let's go with this (especially in the light of the self-propelled skulls in X6.13, "The Wedding of River Song" and the Headless Monks of X6.7, "A Good Man Goes to War" and X9.13, "The Husbands of River Song"). What happened to stop them? One minute Swabb has a gang of translucent-green-sword-wielding mutineers, the next he's on his own. If they fell off when the rigs started shooting (under Swabb's orders, so that's especially inept of him), they're in the same sand that enabled him to insult people after what would have been a fatal fall under usual circumstances. They can't have been killed by the lasers because, er, they're dead. And there are no body-parts or smouldering space-suits on the deck.

The TARDIS dematerialises and reveals Baltazar standing ten feet away from where the Doctor and Martha were stood talking to Caw – so, he was in plain sight throughout the conversation. Volag-Noc, the Doctor says, is the "coldest place" in the galaxy. And yet the Doctor walks around in plimsolls (but he usually does), and – more to the point – Martha doesn't die. Perhaps this is a visitor's atrium zone, heated to allow air to remain gaseous, but the Doctor and Gurney can run across it and Martha is lugged from the prison exit to the TARDIS. If it's like that all over, it's hardly living up to its reputation. The moons of Jupiter and Saturn alone are colder, and have exotic chemistry to prove it. Indeed, most of space is three degrees above Absolute Zero.

The toughest prison in the galaxy has less strict security than an average old folks' home – the Doctor's psychic paper isn't confiscated, neither is Martha's obviously useful brooch which has a pin so could be used as a weapon or to escape. And that brooch is both alive and a homing-beacon. Do the prison authorities have any idea of how people escape from prisons?

The Mantasphids declare war on the fleshy bipeds and their cattle, and buy weapons capable of turning their settlements to ash. Do they really not know where dung comes from?

Critique Not that there's anything wrong with Celebrity Historicals once in a while, or the *occasional* Yeti-in-the-Loo present-day invasion, or the odd time-paradox or a base-under-siege adventure, but there is more to *Doctor Who* than these. There are lots of other programmes set on Earth, and the TARDIS is theoretically capable to taking us anywhere. The main way it can outfox other space-adventure shows is by putting people from our world (i.e. Britain, usually London, around the time of broadcast) into these places and find out what they're like. That was what got 13.6 million people to watch 2.5, "The Web Planet" and kept the ratings for Season Seventeen higher than any subsequent twentieth-century run (even without the ITV strike, 17.3, "The Creature From the Pit" got better viewing figures than any conventional episode in this book and "The Runaway Bride").

And in "The Infinite Quest", we get to see that approach done better than almost any BBC Wales story before or since.

Sure, it's got flaws. The three-minute episodes lead to cliffhangers that make the plot take wild chicanes; every segment has "new-viewers-start-here" dialogue that gets wearing when watched it all in one go; animated *Doctor Who* can't get enough of giant insects even if audiences can, and there are the plot-holes, daft coincidences and goofs we've just mentioned.

Nevertheless, this is almost as good a one-story sample of what *Doctor Who* can do, and how well it does it, as any single story of any era. It's witty, using slightly-amended turns of phrase to make alien worlds and over-familiar generic conventions collide (Kaliko refers to her opponents as "sand-lubbers" and has a literal skeleton crew, Volag Noc is "the cooler" writ large, Caw runs on "gold fusion" ...), and everyone makes the kind of joke that character would make in that situation.

The danger in discussing this story is the same as Dr Johnson's description of women preachers or talking bears: not discussing *how well* it did the job, so much as the fact that it does it at all. As "The Infinite Quest" wasn't quite a one-off, it's close to meaningless to say this is the best animated story to date. As a script, it's about as deft as anything made on Davies's watch. As a spectacle it takes a bit of getting used to, but makes the best possible use of the format and the series's potential. Above all, it's *excitement* at the possibilities of world-building that propels this story out of the rut of Earthbound new-series stories. It's all done in broad strokes, but by and large it avoids all the rookie-errors of Series 4's attempts at alien worlds. And we get *four* in one story. That sounds like a trivial matter, but for children – the ostensible target audience for *Totally Doctor Who* – it was long overdue.

This is an important aspect that's come back to haunt us. Although *Doctor Who* was devised in great detail as a series that all family members would watch, together, *as* a family, there has been a tension between that portion of the viewership who think it's *explicitly* for kids, and those who resent anyone not a paid-up fan with the secret handshake and cosplay gear daring to watch "their" show. But if *Doctor Who* isn't child-*friendly*, why bother? This isn't the same as being infantile; the main link between mature SF and childhood is the effort of figuring out how a world works and being surprised by what comes around each corner. "Surprise" comes in many forms, of which being scared is only the least interesting and hardest to keep doing. Although there is the Davies-era imperative to keep bringing Earth and Humans into the story, as if we won't comprehend or feel for any other kind of menace (and with the ludicrous "oil running out" running theme we mentioned in **Things That Don't Make Sense**), this is more like the sort of story that got people interested in *Doctor Who* back in the 60s, and got the ratings into the stratosphere when Tom Baker Ruled the World.

Because it's all down to voices. The performances here are noteworthy mainly for everyone sounding as if they're having *fun*. Freema Agyeman, in particular, is making her audio-drama debut here, but makes Martha a lot more winning than in, say, "Daleks in Manhattan" (X3.4). Tennant is always voice-conscious when playing a Doctor who doesn't sound especially Scottish, so there's less of a gulf here, but despite all we hear about his reluctance to do ADR he's comfortable. Not to take anything away from John Simm, but Anthony Head ought really to have been the Master in Downing Street, and he's more entertainingly villainous here than in "School Reunion" (X2.3).

Although we're almost used to the consistent quality of Edward Thomas's designs for the live-action series, the animators – not having to adapt a pre-existing derelict factory or school into an alien world or spaceship – were freed from the purely material and the look of the ships and buildings is less hidebound. In particular, the floating U-Boat and walking oil-rigs are what *Doctor Who* should be doing: smashing two radically unrelated genres and visual grammars together to make a new, but instantly-comprehensible, world. The design and script also allow use to be fooled by the flying, insect-like exo-suits of the human troops. Animated *Doctor Who* adventures seem unable to resist giant insects (such as the Shalka or the Viperox from A7, "Dreamland"), but this is as good as any and better, visually, than Huath, the Great One (11.5, "Planet of the Spiders") or Mestor (21.7, "The Twin Dilemma"). It's even a step up from the Racnoss Queen X3.0, "The Runaway Bride").

We mentioned right at the start how many ideas making their debut here were re-used in live-action episodes, and that's part of what makes this such a refreshing and enjoyable story. Without the pressure of making a hit series in which the BBC has invested a lot of money and hopes, and where nothing can be tried without consulting the hierarchy, everyone seems to have relaxed and had fun with the concepts. They've made the sort of *Doctor Who* they always wanted to make – a bit like a comic-strip, a bit like an audio drama, a lot like what they watched as kids and as unlike "Human Nature" (X3.8) or "The Lazarus Experiment" (X3.6) as any television programme with two of the same actors playing the same characters could possibly be.

The Lore

Written by Alan Barnes. Directed by Gary Russell. The complete showing on BBC1 at 10.30am got 0.6 million and most of the three-minute episodes (ensconced within *Totally Doctor Who* at 5.00pm on Wednesdays) got similar figures. Episodes five, ten and eleven rose to 0.9 million, almost unheard-of for children's television at that time.

Repeats and Overseas Promotion The DVD was the only way viewers in North America, Australia, New Zealand or any other Anglophone country that took *Doctor Who* saw it. We can't find any evidence of a dubbed rendition for export.

Alternate Versions The story was broadcast in tandem with Series 3, as part of *Totally Doctor Who*. It had been shown over 12 weeks in 3:30 minute segments, then BBC1 ran an omnibus version repeating all the previous segments and the thirteenth in the morning the final part aired. This is the version that's on DVD. Unlike the original, it has a title-sequence based on the complete Eccleston/ Tennant titles and a set of end-credits (which continue for 15 seconds after the music ends in a rather Zen way). The serial simply had the caption for "The Infinite Quest by Alan Barnes" and the relevant section of time-tunnel and music.

Production

Not really a lot to say here; a drama section was one of Russell T Davies's suggestions for how to fix *Totally Doctor Who,* and we outlined the background earlier. James Goss had some images from an abortive project with the Firestep team who had worked on "The Scream of the Shalka", which caught the eye of *Totally Doctor Who* producer

Gillane Seaborne. Firestep (essentially Steve Maher and Jon Doyle and a few mates) had budded off from Cosgrove Hall – although the more famous animation house's name was used in a lot of the BBC's promotional material – and provided animation for *Doctor Who* in both the restricted format for early online material, and a more cinematic style for replacing the wiped pictures from "The Invasion".

With the proviso that the episodes had to be sufficiently self-contained for anyone coming in half-way to pick up the basics, the project was given the nod and treated as a combined comic-strip and audio adventure. Alan Barnes was asked for a script, and Gary Russell was the slam-dunk choice to direct the actors in the recording sessions. Barnes's first go wasn't much like the finished product, but the story coalesced around Baltazar. In the script, but cut before broadcast, the villain's realisation that the TARDIS was the key to his ambitious scheme is described in flash-back to the cell on Volag Noc: Martha criticises the Doctor's decision to let Baltazar live (quoting fan-friendly comedians Lee and Herring when she says "You want the Moon on a stick") and the abrupt resolution to the Mantasphid stalemate is given a bit more breathing-space. Mergrass, originally Morgass, was a business-suited amphibian more akin to Baron Greenback from *Danger Mouse*. (Doctor Vile was originally "Doctor Oo-ar", if the "making of" with Barney Harwood is to be believed.)

• The recording sessions were two days in a studio with bits of the cast and Gary Russell (who directed and/ or wrote many of the early Big Finish audio plays) kept the mood light, but efficiently got through the scripts. As this was Agyeman's first go at recording voice-overs, she experimented with different techniques for keeping the script-page-turning quiet, settling on Tennant's preferred method of "poppadomming" (i.e. scrunching the paper so that only a small percentage of the page touches the one beneath, undulating like a poppadum). Tennant, Toby Longworth and Anthony Head had all worked with Russell on Big Finish projects before this, and Head was narrating *Doctor Who Confidential,* so was in the loop with Seaborne and the Cardiff crew. This session was from 11.00am to mid-afternoon at the Soundworks studio in Cardiff.

• The remainder of the dialogue was recorded on 3rd February in London, the frequent Big Finish venue of Moat Studios (in the Buspace complex in Ladbroke Grove). The studio they used was larger, with individual wooden booths for each actor rather than an acoustically dead office-like space as in Wales. Tennant and Agyeman were in the middle of making "Utopia" (X3.11), and by now BBC Wales had formally announced the project. As well as the guest-cast, many of them also Big Finish veterans, the session had a reporter from *Doctor Who Magazine* and – perhaps obviously – Barney Harwood, making a feature for *Totally* episode eight and doing a quick cameo as the Control Voice to show how it all works. (You may recall he did something similar the previous year, when a feature on a day in the life of an extra led to him being in the background in X2.10, "Love & Monsters".) As with the first session, Russell was in a separate control-room monitoring the recording through speakers.

• The Firestep team primarily used a souped-up version of PhotoShop for the animation, with another Adobe software package called After Effects for, well, after-effects such as blizzards, sand-storms, fake lens-flare and smoke. However, as Baltazar's head was going to be seen from so many angles, they made a 3D model. Most of the designs followed the script, but Baltazar's ship became less piratical and less like the *Infinite*. The storyboards were worked up into animatics to match the soundtrack, and these were reworked with the detailed colour images. Early test-runs of the Doctor's face were more cartoonish, with the eyebrow action potentially distracting from the dialogue, and the brief test clip of the oil-rigs looks more like the new version of *Danger Mouse*, oddly enough.

• As we mentioned, the original broadcast lacked the full credit sequence and was shown in three-and-a-half minute sections. The first two were shown in the same episode of *Doctor Who Confidential,* and the last after a round-up of the story to date. The omnibus was shown at 10.30am on the same day as "Last of the Time Lords" (X3.13). Later transmissions of this have been on BBC's designated children's channel, the digital-only CBBC.

1. Such is the ubiquity of this record in December that the BBC pays full royalties to the writers, Neville "Noddy" Holder and Jimmy Lea, despite the number of times they use it as audio shorthand for Christmas in dramas. Holder and Lea aren't listed on the PRS-MCPS database as being subject to the blanket rights arrangement negotiated by the BBC for most recordings. Holder refers to the song, which was also a No. 1 hit in France the following Easter, as his "pension" – it's certainly earned him enough to keep him in Cup-a-Soups for life. American band Train have recently released an insipid cover version which is to the original what Pat Boone's "Tutti Frutti" is to Little Richard's.

2. The title of the Monkees song came from this show, but the BBC, who were happy to use the phrase in a hit show, insisted that the title be changed for daytime radio release, so it's listed as "Alternate Title". The Randy Scouse Git was Alf's son-in-law, played by Anthony Booth. Apart from marrying a soap-diva later on, and a number of other roles before or since, the main point for non-local readers is that his fee for making this show went towards paying his kids through Cambridge, which is where his daughter Cherie met fellow law-student and wannabe rock-star Tony Blair. Thus, when Booth spearheaded a march on Downing Street demanding a better deal for pensioners, his own son-in-law was the Prime Minister against whom he was protesting.

3. This makes a bit of sense, as a lot of big companies are happy to pay more per day for temporary staff because it's cheaper than retaining someone on lower salary, but paying their National Insurance and declaring these people as staff for tax purposes. Full-time workers have better employment rights and have to be paid redundancy money if released from their contracts. If Donna had been full-time, a lot of her workload would have been handling the paperwork associated with employing her and any others like her, as well as more senior staff.

4. The odd thing to note is that – despite the impression fans of *both* series tend to have about the radical difference – original, Shatner-flavoured *Star Trek* is more like Graham Williams-produced *Doctor Who* than either is like *Deep Space Nine* or *Enterprise*. Consider Harry Mudd showing up with fembots-for-hire and then, two weeks later, a long debate on whether anyone can build an android. (The existence of machines as complex and reflexive as Lt Cmdr Data 87 years before he was proclaimed as unique is as unmentionable as the crew of USS *Voyager* showing up in 1993, unconcerned about the impending Eugenics War and nuclear holocaust.) Generically, the first *Star Trek* is all over the place – outright fantasy one week, thinly-disguised U-Boat drama the next, and generally a peculiar amalgam of 50s MGM musicals (all that purple lighting and velour) and *Hell in the Pacific* (hence the bell-bottoms and bosun's whistle communicator signal). As with *Doctor Who*, the shift from humour to intensity was more fluid than in later versions of *Trek*, although it is more likely to be from scene to scene rather than within a scene, simply because it's made of film and edited rather than done as a continuous take with multiple cameras.

5. Well, all right, maybe not *Vertigo* or *Rope*, but *Rear Window* has most of the hallmarks.

6. This purported to be the delayed screening, after being banned by Channel 4 for being "too extreme", of an 80s horror anthology set in a hospital. The parody was note-perfect. It was presented by the writer, Garth Merenghi (who combined the arrogance of Stephen King with the talent of Geoffrey Orme), who also starred in the alleged episodes. (Richard Holness, who plays him and co-wrote the series, is the only regular cast-member not to be a lot more famous now) It's very quotable, especially the author's maxims on writing – *I know writers who use subtext and they're all cowards!* – but still a bit of a secret. If it helps you get a bead on the show, a lot of UK *Doctor Who* fans referred to Series One of *Torchwood* as "Chris Chibnall's Darkplace".

7. Another had Lauren as an intern at 10 Downing Street and had Tony Blair using her catchphrases at her, and there's one with a less-famous character of hers on a dull date with Daniel Craig and a tandem, and one of the foul-mouthed Gran outwitting Noel Edmunds on *Deal or No Deal* – see "Dimension in Time" and 23.3, "Terror of the Vervoids". However, the real treat of that event was a tie-in copy of *The Beano* in which the Bash Street Kids took on a Dalek whilst the Doctor handled a more deadly threat – a school

dinner had escaped and was menacing passers-by.

14. The one inadvertently funny line that cracks up students reading the first scene is an easily-misunderstood reference to "Cormorant Devouring Time", which seems like a Dadaist 70s gameshow, and Kenneth Branagh's almost-watchable film version from – oh look! – 1999 cut even this source of potential amusement. After the main clown-actor, Will Kemp, had quit Burbage's company, Shakespeare tried different types of humour and eventually got to work with a new comic actor, Robert Armin, shortly before writing *As You Like It*. Theoretically, if they put on *Love's Labour's Lost* again in the Globe that summer, someone might have found a way to make all that baffling gibberish about Hobby Horses amusing – just as maybe Kemp had for the original audience, but we have no idea how any actor managed to get laughs from Costard or Moth.

8. Cheesy Radio One DJ Simon Bates used the main theme as the underscore for a hilariously mawkish section called "Our Tune", in which he read the supposedly-poignant true-life tales of heartbreak by supposedly real listeners, then usually played a Tina Turner record.

9. Davies's big break was with a children's series, running since 1973, entitled *Why Don't You Just Switch Off Your Television Set and Go and Do Something Less Boring Instead*? It had been a child-led DIY/ Hobbies/ Crafts series, but he remodelled it into a pre-teen soap, whereupon it was cancelled after decades of success. The idea of a TV show to make people stop watching TV was reinforced in its 70s peak by the BBC following it with black-and-white redubbed French 1960s series *Belle and Sebastian*. An estimated 15 people stayed tuned in to watch this. A couple of years later, Punk happened. Yet, in one of those attempts to rewrite our memories we mention in the essay, the root cause of Punk was attributed, by a famous historian given a BBC2 documentary series, to the lack of garden sheds. *Why Don't You...?* is at least as plausible a starting-point as this.

10. When we consider this in more detail, in **How Much of This Actually Happened?** under X5.6, "The Vampires in Venice", we will examine the human brain's routine self-editing of memories. It may disturb you to discover that you've just done it while reading this, the "saccade" effect of removing the blurry bits of what your eyes saw when they moved across the page reading this from what you thought you saw, but everyone who hears this gets on with their lives unaffected. See also **How Does Hypnosis Work?** under 8.2, "The Mind of Evil".

11. Our screens often had locally-made "International" TV shows where actors from the Caribbean put on American accents – see, for example, 6.7, "The War Games", where Rudolph Walker plays a Union soldier in the American Civil War Zone. ITC shows, made primarily for export to the States, often used a similar ploy – along with the more usual character-actor-in-make-up-and-funny-voice that kept Patrick Troughton, Philip Madoc and countless others in constant work. The real advance was in pop music, where visiting performers from racially-segregated America came to the UK and were treated like royalty. Being able to use the same washrooms was enough of a culture-shock, without getting the Beatles sending them Rolls Royces to pick them up from Heathrow. The food was a different kind of shock. American stars who launched in the US on the back of their British fan-base include many of the Stax and Motown artists and Jimi Hendrix. They all did our shows first. Black English kids thought being a rock star was a viable career-path, especially once Reggae moved from being novelty-music to the mainstream. Visibility began in youth-orientated TV which, in Britain, was mainly broadcast nationally.

12. For BBC viewers in the 70s, he was a familiar face though a couple of series. For adults, he was one of the Indian characters in the notorious sitcom *It Ain't Half Hot, Mum*. But for anyone who'd been learning to read aloud, he was instantly recognisable from the BBC Schools serial *Cloudburst*. He had played twins: one was the amiable, Troughtonish scientist Ram Pandit and the other Delgado-esque suave villain Ravi Pandit. The unimaginative names didn't bother most people then. Indeed, when the BBC floated the idea they were anxious that it might be stereotyping, they consulted the Commission for Racial Equality, who were delighted to have more than one type of character on the menu in a single drama. However, most Indian or Pakistani actors in the UK landed up playing doctors at some point. For many of us growing up in the country then, a trip to the doctor's was the first encounter

with a Sikh, Hindu or Muslim. It may complicate our argument to point out that Satna had previously played a doctor in *I, Claudius*.

13. *Lagaan* is weird if you've not seen any Hindi musicals before – it's classic Bollywood, but with cricket and evil English characters. It portrays every English character except the hero's love-interest as being Dick Dastardly. She's played by the woman from those annoying 90s ads for Brita water-filters and it's a measure of the film's fidelity to lived experience that she learns Hindi and Gujarati in three days, most of that time spent on long, dull dream-sequences of the kind endemic in these films. As it's the British versus the Indians, all the usual Hindu-Muslim enmity is abandoned in favour of production-numbers and inventing the off-break. It won the Oscar in 2002, mainly for being the first Bollywood musical to get a mainstream US release because it had a lot of dialogue in English – it had novelty-value as much as any intrinsic merit. As an introduction to cricket, it's downright bizarre.

(Not as bizarre as Disney's *Million Dollar Arm*, which isn't even excused by being based on a true story. Five seconds' thought could have prevented the whole misguided project – the scouting for baseball pitchers in a country where everyone is a spin-bowler, as well as the mawkish and patronising film.

(If you want to see good films with cricket in, apart from those mentioned in the essay, try Sanjay Talreja's Canadian-Indian film *Cricket and the Meaning of Life* (2005), in which one white face, an umpire right at the end, appears; *Trobriand Cricket: an Ingenious Response to Colonialism* (1976); Regardt van den Berg's *Hansie* (2008), in which the tragedy of Hansie Kronje is done as a feature film although it's a subject Verdi could have handled; *From the Ashes* (2011), about the 1981 Test series between England and Australia, in context with the riots and national mood; and a 50s oddity, *The Final Test*, directed by Anthony Asquith from a script by Terence Rattigan and with real players and familiar character-actors. You may also find Hitchcock's *The Lady Vanishes* more amusing with this essay under your belt.)

14. 1958 was the first major turning-point, after racists, partly inspired by a last-ditch attempt at a comeback by Oswald Mosley – see 25.1, "Remembrance of the Daleks" and 24.3, "Delta and the Bannermen" – ignited race-riots in Nottingham and London. One of the ways the new generation of black Londoners made themselves present was by organising a Caribbean-style three-day carnival in one of the flash-points, Notting Hill, in West London. This has run every year since, and is now Europe's biggest carnival, eclipsing Venice. Funnily enough, despite this being the single biggest thing anyone in Britain knows about Notting Hill, it was curiously absent from the ethnically-cleansed version of the region where Hugh Grant met Julia Roberts. One of the Carnival's mainstays was Frank Crichlow – see X3.3, "Gridlock".

15. Indeed, as part of the whole "Mummer" thing, there was a tradition to disguise the performers' faces with a mix of soot and ham-fat. In the Cromwell era, when performing Christmas plays was an offence, this was a smart move and – as it was unlikely that anybody in rural England had seen anyone who didn't look like them – not intended to be about race (the origin of "Morris" was only retrieved by Victorian scholars). Then came another peak in non-white British residence, which may be why the Mummers receded. This practice is at the root of "guising", a Scottish Hallowe'en tradition which became the US "Trick or Treat" thing. However, it's also at the root of a lot of American theatrical practices and the perpetrators of Minstrel shows cannot plead ignorance. Britain had a similar fad in the late Victorian era, after slavery had been over for two generations and most of the grandchildren of ex-slaves looked almost like everyone else.

It gets worse when American minstrel things get shown in the UK, before significant Afro-Caribbean immigration, and this inspires the wannabes from Wales from the stupefyingly popular *Black and White Minstrel Show*. That these guys didn't realise how wrong it all was is exemplified by the fact that in the 1968 Royal Variety Performance, they shared the bill with Diana Ross and the Supremes and – as big fans – came for autographs *forgetting that they were still in make-up*. From that point on, everyone knew that their days were numbered.

16. As it turns out, Elizabethan London's attitude towards black skin was complicated. For most people, it was just alien and something you read about, or heard in travellers' tales. There were a few – you could tell them at a glance, so they

were more trusted than Catholics – but numerically not more than 300, mostly servants so equally unlikely to be just walking the streets. Elizabeth I ordered that they all be deported in 1596, but evidently it didn't work, as she did it again in 1601. A century earlier, her grandfather had employed John Blanke or Blanche (yes, really), a trumpeter who has the earliest authenticated likeness of any black Briton. His career seems to have ended when Henry VIII succeeded his father, but nobody knows why – any Hilary Mantel wannabes reading now have a topic for a novel.

Those white Elizabethans who saw anyone with such skin outside domestic service might have done so at ambassadorial or trade functions, so maybe the Queen saw a higher-than-average percentage. But for a Tudor/ Jacobean theatre audience, it's the opposite of untrustworthy white skin, which was often lead-based make-up on the faces of prostitutes (covering pox) or boy-actors playing women. Just as whitewash had been used to efface all trace of Catholicism in churches, but sometimes let it show through after a few decades, so paper-white skin allowed the truth to show accidentally. Black skin was, conversely, honest. It didn't wash off, so it was held as an emblem of integrity, for good or ill. Aaron, in *Titus Andronicus*, justifies his villainy with an appeal to being that way by nature, unswayed by fancy arguments. Othello is so inflexible that he cannot adjust to evidence that contradicts his world-view, so he snaps. That's a massively simplified summary of another book-sized topic.

17. *Monty Python* fans may have heard the name, but for anyone who grew up in Britain before 1980, the books were a staple. Captain W.E. Johns wrote a string of books about a WWI air-ace and his friends in their inter-war colonial adventures and crimebusting. People who only know the books by repute imagine it's all stiff-upper-lip derring-do, but the early books had him coping with a drink problem once the war was over. Such non-readers also had fun with the idea that Biggles, Ginger, Algy and/ or Bertie might not be interested in girls. The 1960 Granada Television series left out the nuances and is the source for most of these jokes. In 1986, there was a spectacularly misguided film – Peter Cushing's last – which sought to make the character "relevant" to modern (i.e. American) youth by having a naff contemporary fake New York setting (shot in Canary Wharf), a stupid time-paradox plot and a bland American protagonist caught up in some tosh about sonic weapons, Sopwith Camels and Tower Bridge. Imagine a mash-up of *The Blue Max* and *Dempsey and Makepiece* and make the music as mid-80s as possible, and you're halfway there. The surprise is that Steven Moffat wasn't involved at all. Anyway, the point is that the sheepskin jacket, leather flying helmet, jodhpurs and goggles look is one we all know.

18. The pre-publicity hesitated between Bill being legally adopted and being fostered – a very big difference. Eventually it's stated that Moira is a foster-parent, apparently single, and oblivious to Bill's sexuality and educational aspirations. Some professionals have commented on how weird it is that Bill moves back with Moira after the abortive house-share – apparently only 3% of UK teens in care do this. Even fewer are encouraged to attempt tertiary education or supported when they do. It remains to be seen how the resolution of her story will fix these strange omissions, if at all, but it's unlikely to dwell on the legal aspects of fostering, nor the degree to which what we saw of her domestic life differs from normality for such people.

19. If you're looking for something like Banks "Culture" books with *Doctor Who* crossover potential, look no further than Ben Aaronovitch's *The Also People* and the related Doctorless Benny Summerfield *New Adventures*. However, to see where that sort of thing leads, look at any number of 70s SF novels set in cities a bit like Diaspar from Arthur C Clarke's *The City and the Stars* (also the source for the idea of the Doctor's past life in *Lungbarrow*). You could start with Tanith Lee's *Drinking Sapphire Wine* and Ed Bryant's *Cinnabar*, but the motherlode is Michael Moorcock's *Dancers at the End of Time*. More recently, you could do worse than Walter Jon Williams's *Aristoi*. Banks-inflected British SF has tended to go for post-humans, and that's a whole different ball-game, but some of Ken McLeod's early books or Charles Stross's *Singularity Sky* will be the logical next step for anyone wanting to progress from Kate Orman. This sort of thing is almost as well-worn a path as time wars where both sides alter history, or futuristic cities that are just like 30s New York.

20. He'd done a few about the series by this time, the best being his first two. The day before X1.1, "Rose", he did a song where his usual nice-

ness was on hold for 45 minutes if anyone rang him up during the first episode for 16 years, then the week after he pitched himself as Eccleston's replacement. You can also hear him in the Big Finish audio *Fanfare for the Common Men*.

21. Those of us who grew up on *Vision On* – see 24.1, "Time and the Rani" – will recall that there are precedents for the choreographed Daleks outside the odd clips we have of 4.3, "The Power of the Daleks". The DVD of 12.4, "Genesis of the Daleks" has one as an extra.

22. Yes, "Flidor Gold-Diggers" works better if you're a hard-core fan, but we'd then be obliged to explain all about the *Dalek Pocket-Book and Space Travellers' Guide* all over again, and last time we did *that*, someone dared us to watch every single Dalek story to check whether they ever use the letter "J" in dialogue. The fact that one of the Cult of Skaro is called "Jast" is pretty firm evidence that nobody making the episodes really cares about that sort of thing, so we didn't bother. We have jobs and lives, you know. Anyway, the essay with "Evolution of the Daleks" will prove that we've thought about this way too much.

23. The nearest Berkeley comes to having an Astaire-style routine, with top hats, Expressionist lighting and penthouse apartments, is the nightmarish "Lullaby of Broadway" scene at the climax of *Gold-Diggers of 1935*. This seems like a deliberate rebuke to Astaire's choreographer, Hermes Pan, and looks like an all-singing, all-dancing *Cabinet of Doctor Caligari* with a tiny hint of *Triumph of the Will* thrown in.

24. Our source for the breakdown of unemployment figures is *Or Does It Explode? Black Harlem in Depression* by Cheryl Lynn Greenberg (New York 1991), and the other facts and figures come from a long day squinting at facsimile editions of *The New York Times*.

25. Assorted has-beens and wannabes are carted off to the Australian outback and the public votes them off depending on how game they were to undergo humiliation, usually involving being smothered in insects or made to eat marsupial offal. Baker's go at this coincided with the augmented reissue of 22.2, "Vengeance on Varos", in which a corrupt society votes to torture people through interactive television. The irony did not go un-noticed.

26. Officially these entities are called the "Boneless", but that makes it seem as though the Doctor could have defeated them with breadcrumbs and a secret mix of spices rather than just saying, in effect, "I'm Doctor Who and this is my series, so clear off". Anyway, there have been many literally boneless aliens in the series – not least the Daleks themselves – so this is pointless.

27. In between all his other activities, he found time to write a fairly scholarly biography of the director James Whale, whose camp sensibility made the first two Karloff *Frankensteins* and other Universal horrors of the time more potent than if they'd been made simply to scare.

28. Erina is a new recruit from Torajii Alpha, brought onboard because of the alarming crew turnover. How seriously we want to take any of this, given that the inhabitants of Torajii presumably don't know they live under a sentient star, is an open question.

29. Translated versions ignore this and often use titles that translate as "Burn With Me", e.g. the French *Brûle Avec Moi*.

30. Johnny Ball spent most of the 70s and 80s explaining the mathematics of everyday life to kids. He'd been a *Play School* presenter, and wrote and performed in a few kids' sketch-shows and the like, but *Think of a Number* and *Think Again* were his big hits, followed by a move from BBC1 to ITV with *Johnny Ball Reveals All*, a title that could only disappoint in the execution. Most of you will have seen his daughter Zoe present the lurid special that unveiled Peter Capaldi as the twelfth Doctor – she did a fair few youth-orientated TV shows in the late 90s and was married to Fatboy Slim, so Johnny got a whole new career as the archetypal embarrassing dad in adverts for phone companies. He also became one of Britain's leading advocates for nuclear power, which has cut down on the number of times he pops up doing songs about trigonometry, dressed in a toga or a periwig.

31. This in turn requires the ability to conceptualise what a fictional, or indeed real, other per-

son thinks is happening – more like a novel or a poker game – so has been traditionally relegated to the same dump-bin of critical reception as gossip or fanfic. Neurologically speaking, these are the uniquely human traits that got us where we are now, but have until recently been dismissed as "female" and therefore "trivial". You might want to investigate Robin Dunbar's book *Grooming, Gossip and the Evolution of Language*, and cross-reference it with Ien Ang's *Watching Dallas*. The same gender-skew that has soaps ignored or sneered at while "proper" drama (i.e. about men doing "important" things) gets reviewed by serious critics and Mark Lawson is the reason novels by women had to be more than half a century old for anyone like FR Leavis or Harold Bloom to give them the seal of approval. Compare the reviews of Jonathan Frantzen's and Donna Tartt's most recent works. Or consider the Sad Puppies' reaction to *Chicks Dig Time Lords*, and anything else by people not like them, and compare it to the sexist, racist and homophobic "Disco Sucks" spasm of the late 70s.

32. The use of the word is deliberate. As you may recall from Volume 5, the source-text for 19.3, "Kinda" is Ursula Le Guin's *The Word for World is Forest*. This is also the unacknowledged source for James Cameron's 30s-style Western-with-flying-horses-and-Comanches-with-blue-skins-so-the-kids-won't-notice pulp *Avatar*. In this, the equivalent character to Nerys Hughes as Todd is played by Sigourney Weaver. It's as if they were trying to repay the compliment for making Beryl Reid play Ripley in "Earthshock".

33. A googly? It's in the wrist-action: a right-handed bowler send a balls that spins clockwise (as he sees it) to bounce on the side of the wicket-crease opposite the batsman, so that it doubles back and hits the stump – unless the batsman's good – after seeming to go the other way. It was this sort of chicanery that led to the invention of the Bouncing Bomb, as mythologised in the film *The Dambusters* (see 19.3, "Kinda"). A left-handed bowler doing the mirror-image used to be called a "Chinaman" – see 19.2, "Four to Doomsday" – and neither of these is anything like a leg-break or an off-break, because the ball leaves his hand with the seam at right-angles to how it would normally be. An off-break behaves a bit like a googly, but is done with the seam providing the spin and is thus noticeably different; a leg-break bounces on the leg-side of the batsman's crease, rather than the off-side. It is rare for a batsman's leg to be actually broken.

(The physics of cricket balls is immensely complex and recent investigations have led to confirmation of old wives' tales about how low cloud-cover makes a ball spin more. If you've ever wondered why it was a New Zealander based in Manchester who was first to split the atom, this is your first clue.)

34. The timing for this is almost the same. Shackleton's Imperial Trans-Antarctic Expedition left on the cusp of World War I, to the point that he asked the Royal Navy whether they ought to remain and fight Germans instead of exploring the polar wastes. He got back a one-word telegram from the Admirality saying "Proceed". Which isn't even getting into Captain Scott's expedition...

35. The novel *Netherlands* is partly about someone having this as a childhood memory of his homeland but mainly about an Indian entrepreneur trying to launch cricket in New York – or, as he would see it, re-launch after a two century hiatus. It was President Obama's summer reading one year, which probably confused a few people, including him.

36. Samuel Beckett is one of three people to have played international cricket and been awarded the Nobel Prize for Literature. He was a wicket-keeper, which explains a lot about *Endgame* and *Waiting for Godot*. When he lived in Grenoble, in the French Alps, the only other person who knew anything about the game was a local schoolboy whose acromegaly made him have to ride in Beckett's wagon rather than take the school bus. That lad became famous as Andre the Giant.

(Ireland, along with Afghanistan, was admitted to the ICC as a full test side in June 2017, but neither has yet played a pre-existing test nation.)

37. Will Brooker's contribution to *New Dimensions of Doctor Who* (2013). He didn't actu ally use that terminology.

38. Gaiman seems to have loved the episode so much, he rooted for it over X3.10, "Blink" in the Hugo Awards the following summer.

39. The Marylebone Cricket Club: a local,

North London side to begin with, but later both the England team *and* the de facto arbiters of the rules and ethos of the game. You'd think this would give England all the advantages, wouldn't you? It's also a very exclusive club, the members of which get special seats at Lord's, the main cricket ground; rock stars and former cabinet ministers meet on equal terms and all act like fanboys when their childhood heroes come to watch..

40. You will have seen Dr Grace even if you didn't know it: a photo of him was used as the animated image of Jehovah in *Monty Python and the Holy Grail*, as Terry Gilliam was making a pun about "the Grace of God". If you've not seen this sequence, you may have thought there was an original idea in X9.5, "The Girl Who Died".

41. While the overt allusions to *Doctor Who* have been plentiful – a line in the Marvel cross-over special has Ferb slyly acknowledge how their shed is so much larger than it ought to be, because that's how we do things in Britain – the episode-titles "Are You My Mummy?" and "Don't Even Blink" also seem suggestive (the latter even has Ferb use the same Copenhagen Interpretation doubletalk invoked by the Doctor in X3.10, "Blink"). Moreover, one episode, guest-starring David Mitchell (X7.2, "Dinosaurs on a Spaceship") apparently owes a lot to both the *DWM* strip "The Star Beast" and 18.1, "The Leisure Hive" (it's "Chronicles of Meep", if you want a look). The feature film is Series Two's arc done rather more entertainingly, but with a cyborg platypus instead of Lumic's Cybermen. The last orthodox episode riffs on Series Five's arc (and has a suspiciously familiar spiral clock face motif for when the Do-Over-Inator operates and something else falls into a crack in spacetime to be forgotten) and manages to make tigers roaming a deserted city seem plausible (X8.10, "In the Forest of the Night").

The not-as-good spin-off, *Milo Murphy's Law*, makes it impossible that the creators are unaware of the *Doctor Who* – the details of the in-show series *The Doctor Zone Files*, shown on Saturday teatimes and celebrating its fiftieth anniversary, are too exact. Conversely, Steven Moffat seems to have borrowed a scene in a time-paradox episode where a young girl is thirsty because someone from her near-future borrowed her drink to give to her later self when she said she was thirsty. The downside is that many older *Doctor Who* stories are harder to take seriously – notably 17.4, "Nightmare of Eden", in which a scientist who talks, dresses and acts exactly like the hapless Dr Heinz Doofenshmirtz is beset by giant platypus-monsters, and Season Twenty-Three, "The Trial of a Time Lord", which makes a big thing of the Doctor asking "Where's Peri?" and ends with the Valeyard and the Master comparing the size of their -Inators. You can bet your bottom dollar that YouTube has lots of clips, including the "He Burns..." spiel dubbed onto clips of Perry the Platypus in action.

42. Moffat has semi-facetiously confirmed that this is the idea. Connecting it to his Big Idea for Series Nine, of "the Doctor" being a role that the person we call that plays, with varying success and enthusiasm, Moffat suggests that the Doctor only lives up to his own standards when he has someone to impress and that when Clara/ Amy/ Rose/ Martha/ Osgood (etc etc) aren't around, he needs the BBC1 viewers to keep him from just leaving and slobbing around the TARDIS in his pyjamas. This idea first surfaced, like many of Moffat's *idées fixes*, in a Paul Cornell novel – this time *Love and War*, the one named after a *Press Gang* episode. Mind you, this was in the same *Doctor Who Magazine* Q&A column where he proposed two months earlier that the Cushing movies are the one true *Doctor Who*.

43. We spent an afternoon trying to make this work by having the Beatles' Apple Boutique decide that Martha had the right image, but that was closing. There are a few places she could have waltzed into a couple of years earlier – the Indica Gallery, Granny Takes a Trip, Deram Records – but in any normal greengrocer's or supermarket, she'd've had old ladies refusing to be served by her and thinking anything she touched was contaminated.

44. We've spent many afternoons road-testing a theory that every feature film in English links to *Doctor Who* in a maximum of four degrees of separation. It gets harder when you deliberately exclude the 1967 film *Casino Royale* or choose to exclude either the original series or the BBC Wales one – but not *much* harder.

45. It appears that, in addition to fuelling fan lore by suggesting unscreened stories such as how Mike Yates met Sara Kingdom, the scenes in "The Day of the Doctor" concerning UNIT's Black Archive was to include evidence that the two feature films were scripted and funded by UNIT as a means to distract the public from weird events.

46. Only Sir Michael Gambon has followed, to date. Sir Ian McKellen did a voice-over in X7.6, "The Snowmen", Dame Diana Rigg was in X7.12, "The Crimson Horror" and John Hurt got knighted shortly *after* X7.15, "The Day of the Doctor". As for Peers of the Realm, we had Tim Bentinck as the voice of the Monks in Series Ten – taking time out from *The Archers* – but *The Sarah Jane Adventures* had a rare return to acting for Baroness Benjamin of Beckenham, AKA former *Play School* presenter Floella Benjamin. She got her peerage just before the last series. It may astonish you to learn that one of the cast of 19.7, "Time-Flight" is also in the House of Lords – Michael Cashman was elevated for his political work and gay rights activism rather than for playing Bilton.

47. Yes, the same Brian May who's lead guitarist for Queen and the same Patrick Moore who's Rose's first guess as to who the government would call in when aliens land – and who was in X5.1, "The Eleventh Hour". Chris Lintott was, latterly, Sir Patrick's leg-man on *The Sky at Night*. The book's most recent edition isn't ambivalent on Dark Energy, but still suggests that we don't discard earlier theories just because new observations fit so exactly with what that model predicted.

48. Well, all right, many people prefer the Rani. And there's always the Valeyard. And Borusa, although he wasn't *always* evil. Neither was Omega, really, but he's more of a threat than the Master ever was. And there's mad, spitty Rassilon to come (X4.17-4.18, "The End of Time") and his reincarnation as an East End gangster (X9.12, "Hell Bent"). Oh, and Mr Meaker... er, the War Chief.

49. Extensive research into this vexed issue reveals that the eastern US franchise Five Guys has fries that approximate more closely with the UK chips, made with Idaho potatoes. Apply salt and vinegar to taste. However, they attempted to launch in the UK and suffered by the comparison with the real thing. Other places, especially the New England fish and chip shops, almost manage the same effect but with disappointing fish or chips cut too thin to be of any use. French attempts at *les chips anglais* tend to use Bintje, the classic Belgian potato variety with which the whole pommes frites thing started 200 years ago. This results in a chip that is like deep-fried parsnip. Nice, but not Maris Pipers. One did make a good stab at it using Adriana, a French spud close enough for most purposes. We have seen – and indeed eaten – chip butties made using unbuttered baguettes, which is almost too perfect a self-parody. And almost inedible.

50. The keyboards on that single were played by Professor Brian Cox, who pops up in X7.4, "The Power of Three" and did a slightly odd documentary, *The Science of Doctor Who*. He's as annoyed by the song as most other people were after 1997.

51. Those of you who have only come across *The Thick of It* since about, say, August 2013 will have to accept that Blair's spin-doctor was less inventively foul-mouthed and considerably less gifted than Malcolm Tucker – but, as only Campbell himself fails to acknowledge, was the template.

52. In fact, we have seen a *We're With Harry* poster, but only for a Mayoral election in Newport, Rhode Island. Long-standing independent Mayor Harry Winthrop had fluorescent green lawn-signs with the slogan and his face, looking like either Rassilon from 20.7, "The Five Doctors" or the Mayor in 60s kid's animation *Trumpton*. If you want to see what Trumpton run by the Master would look like, see 19.1, "Castrovalva".

53. We still think of the BBC adaptation of *House of Cards* – the first series of which was broadcast just as Thatcher was hounded from office by her own party – as the "proper" one, but have to admit that the US remake was fun. Michael Dobbs's original novel was all right, but Iain Richardson owns the part of Urquhart outright.

54. Actually, the Parliamentary Committee on the Monitoring of Sugar Standards in Exported Confectionary is potentially a very important role. Hershey's recent buy-out of Cadbury's has resulted

in changes to the recipes of Fruit and Nut bars and Creme Eggs, plus inferior US-style mixes used on American-made versions of Cadbury bars and an embargo on imports of the real thing on the spurious grounds that they would cause "brand confusion". Wars have been fought for less. Come to think of it, the US declared independence last time such a heinous blockade was imposed. American candy uses high fructose corn syrup in place of sugar, so genetically modified maize is being fed to children rather than trying to persuade them to eat fewer sweets. UK sugar products use beet sugar as much, or more, than cane sugar, so many farmers in East Anglia stand to lose their livelihoods. This issue cuts across party lines and affects the Treasury, the Department of Health, the Inland Revenue, the Foreign Office and the Department of Food and Rural Affairs. How dare Andrew Marr sneer at Joseph Green's right to intervene in a constitutional crisis!

(P.S. The first signs the general public had that Brexit wasn't going as well as advertised was the change in the amount of chocolate in a Toblerone and the steep increase in the cost and availability of Maltesers in Tesco at exactly the point when the latter sweets were finally launched in the US after 80 years. It's not quite cost-effective to post them to London yet and the mix is slightly different.)

55. In fact, we got almost exactly that in the last properly *Who*-like thing Davies wrote, *The Sarah Jane Adventures* story "Death of the Doctor", in which we find out after 37 years that Jo Grant's life after marrying Cliff and leaving the Doctor and UNIT got considerably more hectic. See next volume.

56. Armchair detectives within fandom have struggled to fill this gap, a consensus being that this was the gap made by X2.11, "Fear Her" being rushed into production to fill a Stephen Fry-shaped hole. However, with *Torchwood* Series One having so many of Davies's protégées blooded, it's tempting to ask if two-time feature-film director/ writer Noel Clarke might not have been in the loop. Obviously, he was working flat out on his films as soon as he was relieved of Mickey duties, but he'd delivered a television script on time with relatively few worries in the previous year. *Kidulthood* and *Adulthood* were produced by BBC Films, so they can't not have known about them.

57. And, due to a common but unforgiveable error, *Doctor Who Magazine* was finally able to run the front page banner "Peter Davison is the Doctor", having spelled it "Davidson" in 1980.

58. Originally, the word "conker" referred to a snail8shell. The game works with either, but using these nuts is more interesting. The nut is bored through and a string, possibly a shoelace, is inserted and knotted on the other side, securing the nut as the weight of a pendulum. One player holds this out in front of him/ her, the other uses one fist to hold the string, but keeps the nut between the first two fingers of the other hand, taut, in order to swing at the first player's hanging nut and – if possible – smash into it. If the second player missed, then the roles are reversed, and so on until one player's nut is utterly demolished. The scoring system is cumulative so, if both conkers are new, the winner scores one – but if the losing one had already a victory to its name, that nut's tally is added, plus one, to the new champion (so if yours was a fiver and you beat a three-er, your score would be nine).

Baking the conker, soaking it in vinegar or adding cement, are frowned upon. In the new compensation-culture, some schools banned the game and blamed the Health and Safety Executive (see X4.1, "Partners in Crime"; X7.9, "Hide"). This body – by now fed up with being blamed for every craven decision by a risk-averse jobsworth or misrepresentation in tabloids – now sponsors the annual international championship, held in September, the traditional month for this game.

59. This being a BBC drama, all trademarks were effaced to avoid accidental advertising on the publicly-funded channel. So the domestic realism of the early scene of Bert Lynch getting to eat PC Steele's supper in the first episode is sabotaged by a close-up of a bottle of HP Sauce with black gaffer-tape over the logo and name. Everyone "vacuums" their houses instead of "Hoovering". Then again, "Newtown" is obviously Liverpool.

60. This ran from 1965 to the late 90s, but its heyday was the 70s. Just before *Top of the Pops* and, to the kind of people who watched *Doctor Who*, just as exciting, we had reports on forthcoming technological advances and occasionally what they'd mean to society. James Burke started off

there, but the main host in its glory days was old-school BBC pro Raymond Baxter. Somehow, having someone who'd flown Spitfires in World War II and commentated on Churchill's funeral explaining black holes and microprocessors made them more enticingly real. The biggest scoops were the first interview – by a satellite phone-link – with Christian Barnaard the day after the first heart transplant and behind-the-scenes details of the making and testing of Concorde, culminating in a broadcast from the first commercial flight.

61. Officially, under English law, this originally meant any time before July 6th, 1189. That date was the coronation of Richard I (2.6, "The Crusade"; 20.6, "The King's Demons") and the Lords who drafted the Statute of Westminster in 1275 agreed that nobody could remember anything before that.

62. Thanks to the miracles of crowdfunding, he's now succeeded in this task; McCoy, Paul McGann, and Sophie Aldred were recruited for a series of Internet radio plays in which they play characters utterly unrelated to their *Doctor Who* counterparts. Oh, and Paul Darrow's in it. The cast and crew lists are only going to get more incestuous from here; "Death Comes to Time" had Jacqueline Pearce, Stephen Fry, and Nicholas Courtney starring in it (to say nothing of Head), and Nev Fountain did some script editing, a couple of years ahead of his Big Finish work.

63. To date, McGann's tally of digitally-broadcast Big Finish productions on 4Extra is in the mid-thirties, or about as many Tom Baker stories with the tunnel titles. It's worth noting that before regenerating in the mini-episode "Night of the Doctor", the eighth Doctor only mentions his companions from the audios: Lucie, played by Sheridan Smith, made her debut in the episodes being repeated that month as part of the 50th Anniversary celebrations for the series. There have been a few Peter Davison ones, some Sylvester McCoy and the odd Tom Baker – although he is more represented by talking book versions of Target novelisations of his stories. Colin Baker, the Doctor whose audio adventures are far more popular with the Big Finish customers than his on-screen ones, has yet to be broadcast in this slot. One day, we may find the recordings of the brief Peter Cushing radio serial, partly written by Malcolm Hulke before he made TV episodes and with Bernard Cribbins as Tom. These are currently more scarce than the Season Three telerecordings rumoured to be possibly out there, somewhere.

The *original* Radio Doctor, by the way, was a wartime series where Charles Hill, a GP, anonymously advised listeners on healthy eating during rationing. As head of the British Medical Authority, he was instrumental in persuading doctors to join the fledgling NHS and the government not to treat them as mere employees. He entered Parliament, but Dr Hill's interest in broadcasting continued. By 1967, he was Lord Hill of Luton and was in charge of the Independent Television Authority during the (botched) ITV Franchise Auction, and then the BBC's board of governors throughout the bids by the Prime Minister, the paranoid Harold Wilson, to stifle the BBC.

64. *Economic Contribution of the UK's Film and High-End TV, Video-Games and Animation Programme Sectors*. As we said, the 2010 prices are the most recent available to the public, which gives us a reasonable idea of the budget for Davies-era *Who*, even allowing for economies of scale and being an in-house BBC production outside London.

65. *Tintin* was about as good as it got for this process. It still had the familiar "uncanny valley" problem of not-quite-readable humanoid faces, but didn't freak people out to the extent that the Zemeckis *Polar Express* had and was less laughable than *Beowulf*. It was blighted by the 3D fad, but it didn't look as wrong as it could have. At times, it even looked like *Tintin*. However, hardly anybody's gone near this technique since, except for monster-making, so the most successful use of the technology in film therefore remain the various characters Andy Serkis has played for Peter Jackson, such as *King Kong* and Gollum/ Smeagal in his various Tolkien adaptations, plus his small but significant role in *The Force Awakens*, and Mark Ruffalo's portrayal of Hulk *and* Bruce Banner in the Marvel films. *Avatar* already looks creaky and the sequels are a long time coming. It's odd that such a lucrative film had so feeble a toe-hold on the popular imagination.

* Not final cover.

Ahistory

An Unauthorized History of the Doctor Who Universe (Fourth Edition)

Coming in 2018...

Lance Parkin and **Lars Pearson**'s seminal *Doctor Who* text reaches truly epic proportions (i.e. nearly one million words), as it continues to incorporate the whole of *Doctor Who* (nearly 2000 stories!) into a single timeline stretching from the Dawn of Time to the end of everything.

Specifically, this Fourth Edition covers all *Doctor Who*-related works released through the end of 2017... the TV series through the end of the twelfth Doctor era (*Twice Upon a Time*); *Torchwood*, *The Sarah Jane Adventures*, *K9* and *Class* stories in all formats; the Big Finish audio range and its myriad of spin-offs (*Jago & Litefoot*, *The Diary of River Song*, *UNIT*, etc.); the New Series Adventures; the Titan, IDW and *Doctor Who Magazine* comics; independent spin-offs such as the *Lethbridge-Stewart* novels and *Faction Paradox*; and so much more.

Bonus features in this new edition include a timeline to Big Finish's *The Confessions of Dorian Gray* audios.

Ahistory **Fourth Edition Vol. 1:**
Pre-History and History
ISBN: 9781935234227

Ahistory **Fourth Edition Vol. 2:**
UNIT, the Present Day and Gallifrey
ISBN: 9781935234234

Ahistory **Fourth Edition Vol. 3:**
The Future
ISBN: 9781935234241

www.madnorwegian.com

1150 46th Street
Des Moines, Iowa 50311
madnorwegian@gmail.com

who made all this ?

Since the halcyon days of Volume 7, when most people were reasonably sure what number came immediately before 9, **Tat Wood** has been working this book, the next in the series, e-book rewrites of earlier ones and other, totally non-*Doctor Who*-related ones (one of which, *World History in Minutes,* is available through Quercus Books and all good remaindered book shops) all while jet-setting. Volumes 8 and 9 were begun in hip, happening Leytonstone before he spent 2014 in southern France, then hunkered down in coastal New England for rather longer than expected. If you've not met Tat, the image you now have of an amalgam of Jason King and Jessica Fletcher is more or less right, although maybe not quite the way you think.

The past (even 2007, as this book proves) is a foreign country: the converse is also true. Tat is finding that being in America, a nation only slowly getting used to chip-and-pin payments, peshwari naan, Ikea and raves, is like paying a visit to 1991. The retro theme is compounded by his habit of watching rerun stations to find out who the guest stars on *The Muppet Show* were. Favourite story in this volume: "Gridlock"; least favourite: "Voyage of the Damned".

Dorothy Ail has been showing up all over the place: a story for Obverse Press's *Liberating Earth* that was like *Carol* with Space-Vikings (it came out before the film though); one of the more recondite entries in *Chicks Dig Gaming*; and pieces for the ATB *Outside In* collections. (If only Amazon could spell her name right.) On top of all of this, she's been coding text-adventures, teaching Americans about Cumberland Sausage and holding down a government job. In between this lot, she's learning the rudiments of British Character Actor Semiology, and trying to find anyone at work prepared to listen to her talk about cricket. Plus, since Volume 7, she's read the entire works of Anthony Trollope. Even *Ralph the Heir*. Favourite story in this volume: "The Infinite Quest"; least favourite: "Daleks in Manhattan/ Evolution of the Daleks".

Mad Norwegian Press

Publisher / Editor-in-Chief / About Time Content Editor
Lars Pearson

Senior Editor / Design Manager
Christa Dickson

Associate Editors
Joshua Wilson, Carrie Herndon

Cover
Jim Calafiore (art), Richard Martinez (colors)

The publisher wishes to thank... Tat and Dorothy, for always taking their Doctor Who analysis in unexpected and exciting directions; Lawrence Miles; Christa Dickson; Carrie Herndon; Jim Calafiore; Richard Martinez; Josh Wilson; Lance Parkin; Paul Kirkley; Robert Smith?; Gary Russell; Shawne Kleckner; Jim Boyd; Braxton Pulley; Jack Bruner; Heather Reisenberg and that nice lady who sends me newspaper articles.

The authors wish to thank... Simon Black, Anthony Brown and the Man of the Match Daniel O'Mahony, plus Unpaid Scientific Advisor Giles Sparrow.

1150 46th Street
Des Moines, Iowa 50311
madnorwegian@gmail.com
www.madnorwegian.com